Robert Browning

SELECTED POETRY

Edited by George M. Ridenour

The Signet Classic Poetry Series
GENERAL EDITOR: JOHN HOLLANDER

A SIGNET CLASSIC
NEW AMERICAN LIBRARY
TIMES MIRROR
NEW YORK AND SCARBOROUGH, ONTARIO
THE NEW ENGLISH LIBRARY LIMITED, LONDON

SIGNET CLASSIC TRADEMARK REG. U.S. PAT. OFF. AND FOREIGN COUNTRIES
REGISTERED TRADEMARK—MARCA REGISTRADA
HECHO EN WINNIPEG, CANADA

SIGNET, SIGNET CLASSICS, MENTOR, PLUME, MERIDIAN AND NAL
BOOKS are published *in the United States* by
The New American Library, Inc.,
1633 Broadway, New York, New York 10019,
in Canada by The New American Library of Canada Limited,
81 Mack Avenue, Scarborough, Ontario M1L 1M8

First Printing, July, 1966

  6   7   8   9   10   11   12   13   14

Printed in Canada

Table of Contents

INTRODUCTION

> I will tell
> My state as though 'twere none of mine.
> > Browning, *Pauline*, lines 585–86.
> I build on contrasts to discover, above those
> contrasts, the harmony of the whole.
> > Hugo von Hofmannsthal to Richard
> > Strauss, June 15, 1911.[1]

Robert Browning was born in 1812 of modestly well-to-do parents in a pleasant suburb of London. The only other child was a younger sister, and Robert was easily the main object of attention in the family. He was a spoiled child, who never learned to take opposition with much grace. His father was a mild and bookish man, a clerk in the Bank of England. His mother was Scottish by birth and had been brought up in the Church of Scotland, as her husband had been in the Church of England. Both, however, left the established churches to become Dissenters, and Browning was baptized in an independent chapel, where he was also taken to service. Under the strong influence of his mother, who was very pious, Browning acquired that part of the "Dissenting conscience" that stresses the value of individual moral decision and of a personal and immediate relationship with God. The social aspects of this conscience were less highly developed in

1 *A Working Friendship: The Correspondence between Richard Strauss and Hugo von Hofmannsthal*, Trans. Hanns Hammelmann and Ewald Osers (New York: William Collins Sons & Co., Ltd., 1961), p. 90.

him. But Browning was always fiercely Protestant, even when he was not especially Christian.

Browning grew up largely by himself, finding companions in his family, in pets, and in the great number of books he read from his father's large library. His contacts with school were brief and not very satisfactory, and his formal education came largely from private tutors and, perhaps, his father. A try at university life, in the newly established University of London, was soon abandoned, and Browning continued to live with his parents, supported by his father, until his marriage in 1846.

The circumstances of his bringing up were certainly instrumental in developing that "clear consciousness/Of self, distinct from all its qualities" that the young man— with perplexity, pride, and dismay—recognized as central to his character. His problem was what to make of so energetic an ego.

In his poem *Pauline* (published 1833), where he first defined the problem as he understood it, Browning goes on to consider two further "elements" of his character that served as checks on his consuming selfhood. The first is his power of imagination and the second his yearning after God. His imagination is an "angel" to him that sustains "a soul with such desire/Confined to clay." ("Clay" is an obsessive word with Byron, and its use here reminds us that Browning's early poems—destroyed by their author—were supposed to be in the manner of Byron, whom Browning is recalling, along with Shelley, in *Pauline*. There is strong influence of Byron's "Dream.") It enables him to master his "dark past." But the imagination itself poses problems of direction and control which are solved by the premise of a divine Love which presents itself to him as goal and as surrounding presence. The forces united for the boy in the myths of ancient Greece, which enabled his ego to exercise itself healthfully in imaginings of godlike life, and these early experiences of integration remain to some extent normative for him. It is experience of this sort he wants to regain as he addresses himself in *Pauline* to more radical representatives of imagination and religion—Shelley and Christ. It is this he seeks also from

ie woman Pauline, with her all-encompassing love, who
; also the muse of the poem. (It was something very like
iis that he found in his love for his wife, a woman of
eep piety and a poet.)

A similar view is presented sequentially in the speech
f the dying Paracelsus, in Browning's drama of that name,
efining a progression from the most primitive form of
eing to man, and from man to God. Two traditions have
een traced by scholars here. There is that of man as the
ulmination of all lower forms, moving steadily toward
3od, and taking the whole creation with him into the di-
ine life, which Browning might have been more likely to
now in an occult version, though it is found in orthodoxy.
And there is the more narrowly eighteenth-century tradi-
ion of plenitude and the chain of being that may, I sug-
est, have some obligation to James Thomson, author of
`he Seasons.

> By swift degrees the love of nature works,
> And warms the bosom; till at last, sublimed
> To rapture and enthusiastic heat,
> We feel the present Deity, and take
> The joy of God to see a happy world.
>
> *(Spring,* lines 899–903)
>
> God is ever present, ever felt,
> In the void waste as in the city full,
> And where he vital spreads there must be joy.
>
> ("Hymn to the Seasons," lines 105–7)[2]

`he two traditions unite in *Paracelsus* V, 641–47, where
he hero claims to have known

> what God is, what we are,
> What life is—how God tastes an infinite joy
> In infinite ways—one everlasting bliss,
> From whom all being emanates, all power
> Proceeds; in whom is life for evermore,
> Yet whom existence in its lowest form
> Includes; where dwells enjoyment there is he.

[2] Browning remembers the last line of the "Hymn" in a letter to Kegan
`aul, July 15, 1881.

Browning's combination of the two traditions presen'
a view that is in effect anticipatory of Teilhard de Cha
din's vision of an unbroken progression from the geolog
cal to the biological to the mental, and on to the divin
each stage once manifest revealing its implicit presence i
all preceding stages.

The vision of Paracelsus does not in itself, howeve
provide means for its implementation in other kinds of poen
It was only after years of attempts at writing a successfu
play for the stage that Browning fully developed the for
of the dramatic monologue, brought to its maturity in th
two volumes of *Men and Women* of 1855. Through th
succession of self-preoccupied egoists, engaged in exister
tial defense of the being each has made for himsel'
Browning, as J. Hillis Miller has pointed out, is able bot
to exercise his own ego and "get out of himself" by ob
jectifying his drive to egoistic self-assertion in the creatio
of fictional characters. When we have noticed that in th
course of their self-revelation they further reveal in thei
personal situation, directly or indirectly, the intensel
Protestant version of the Incarnation that was Browning'
governing myth, we can see how the monologues meet th
demands of the earlier poems.

Browning's speakers in the monologues are apt to b
persons of extremes in extreme situations. Even so win
ning a character as Lippo Lippi has something grotesqu
about him and displays an element of the pathologicall
self-dramatizing, in excess of what might be ascribed t
the demands of the form. But like Dostoyevsky or th
early Wordsworth, Browning uses his strange or abnorma
types to dramatize what he regards as centrally human
which can be seen in these cases with especial clarity. I
the following lines, for example, in which Fra Lippo list
the subjects of his first attempts as painter, he reveals no
only his own personal situation but that of all men a
Browning sees it:

First, every sort of monk, the black and white,
I drew them, fat and lean; then, folk at church,
From good old gossips waiting to confess

Their cribs of barrel-droppings, candle-ends—
To the breathless fellow at the altar-foot,
Fresh from his murder, safe and sitting there
With the little children round him in a row
Of admiration, half for his beard and half
For that white anger of his victim's son
Shaking a fist at him with one fierce arm,
Signing himself with the other because of Christ
(Whose sad face on the cross sees only this
After the passion of a thousand years)
Till some poor girl, her apron o'er her head,
(Which the intense eyes looked through) came at eve
On tiptoe, said a word, dropped in a loaf,
Her pair of earrings and a bunch of flowers
(The brute took growling), prayed, and so was gone.

(lines 145–62)

Here he elaborates the pictorial qualities implicit in the scene of the breathless murderer, the admiring children, the frustrated vindictiveness of the victim's son, and the girl's thankless devotion to the criminal—passions that arrange themselves by their inherent forces of attraction and repulsion into a satisfying composition. The picture is "placed" against another genre, that of the Man of Sorrows on the Cross. It is the world of the painting that Lippo is presented as gaining for art, but he himself sees it as under the judgment of the second, more traditional and more static mode. The exhibition of nonmoral human energies, however fine, asks the complement of the image of the dying God. The assimilation of the world of the painting into art has the effect of censuring it as life, but also, since the censor gains much of his authority by his presence to us in art, of encouraging us to enjoy the beauty produced by intense experience of any kind.

It must be confessed, however, that our main impression from the passage is less one of harmony than of competing claims that are hard to choose between, and the feeling grows that Browning's aim as a poet in the Romantic tradition is to devise forms in which the elements of reality as he experiences it may be contemplated as unified. (There seems to be at least a shift in emphasis in the development of Browning's poetry from problems of internal integration to those of perceiving reality itself as an integrated whole.) The list of attempted unions is imposing: power and love, love and knowledge, knowledge and power, imagination and reason, self and not-self, conscious and unconscious, spirit and matter, natural and supernatural, lyric and discursive, verse and prose. His attempts may usefully be broken down into at least four major types: the personal, the typical, the mythic, and the analytic. We may take "Fra Lippo Lippi" as representing the first, the vision of the dramatic monologues, where divisions are overcome in living, or which point toward harmony ironically through the dissonances of the speaker's life. The typical, mythic, and analytic modes, while not inherently more valuable, are in some ways harder to grasp, and it may be helpful to pay special attention to them. The modes will be examined by means of comment on poems drawn, like "Fra Lippo Lippi," from the great work of Browning's middle period, the *Men and Women* of 1855.

What I have called the typical mode may be seen most clearly in "Childe Roland to the Dark Tower Came." It is this typicality that causes our uneasiness in either calling the poem an allegory or in refraining from doing so. The knightly quest lends itself easily to allegorical treatment, because we are all of us looking for something all the time, in all our acts. The formality of the poem also encourages us to think of it as allegorical, even though it is not clear at once what it is allegorical of. This is especially striking since the allegorical mode invites simple and mechanical equation between the contents of the work and the world of values outside it. (This is true of even so refined a work as *The Faerie Queene,* as in the head-verses to the separate cantos. Though the poem is not limited to these crude equations, they influence our understanding of the dense and irreducible materials of the poem proper.) The allegory of "Childe Roland," in other words, is strangely self-contained, turning back on itself, so that the "allegoricalness" of the poem calls attention to itself as part of the meaning.

To shift the terms, allegory is apt to be strikingly rational and subrational, presenting a moral and conceptual organizing of the materials of fantasy; the moral will enters into close union with fierce unconscious drives. In Browning's poem the relations between the two elements are uncommonly problematic. This also tends to turn our attention into the poem in a manner unexpected in allegory, while we are still expecting the poem to fulfil its implied promise to be allegorical of something. One might be tempted to say, then, that the poem is an allegory of allegorizing (with Hawthorne's *Scarlet Letter* as partial analogy). But this would be too narrow, since the allegorical element is a metaphor of our attempts at directing our acts and at understanding them as purposive. It serves to represent the element of moral will in our acts and our understanding of those acts as directed by the moral will. It corresponds to our attempts, that is, at acting humanly for human goals—as "knights." The poem understood in this way becomes an allegory of what is involved in apparently purposeful human acts. It is "typical" of them.

Since the *geste* of Browning's knight is largely a trial by landscape, it may be useful to examine the handling of landscape in another poem, published in the same volume but apparently written later. In "Two in the Campagna" a woman speaks of her inability to love completely and constantly the man she addresses. She loves him only so much and for only so long. Her confession is placed against the reaches of the Roman Campagna, on a May morning.

> The champaign with its endless fleece
>   Of feathery grasses everywhere!
> Silence and passion, joy and peace,
>   An everlasting wash of air—
> Rome's ghost since her decease.
>
> Such life here, through such lengths of hours,
>   Such miracles performed in play,
> Such primal naked forms of flowers,
>   Such letting nature have her way
> While heaven looks from its towers.
>
>   (lines 21–30)

The setting suggests, through its vast extent, vast ranges of possibility, and the impression is reinforced by the burgeoning life of early spring. At the same time, however, it suggests immedicable solitude and a tendency in the nature of things for life to squander itself, dispersedly, to no effect:

> Must I go
> Still like the thistle-ball, no bar,
>   Onward, whenever light winds blow,
> Fixed by no friendly star?
>
> (lines 52–55)

Man's state and nature's correspond in their interplay of possibility and restriction, freedom and slavery: "Nor yours nor mine, nor slave nor free!" But the emphasis is on defeat.

These passages should recall the landscape of "Childe Roland":

> For mark! no sooner was I fairly found
>   Pledged to the plain, after a pace or two,
>   Than, pausing to throw backward a last view
> O'er the safe road, 'twas gone; gray plain all round;
> Nothing but plain to the horizon's bound.
>   I might go on; naught else remained to do.
>
> (lines 49–54)

Here the extent of plain works similarly, with important differences. The possibilities are as great, the limitations more oppressive, and we get a feeling of stuffiness in a wide expanse. This reflects the mingled purposefulness and purposelessness, will and compulsion in the mind of the knight. But the effect is different from that of the landscape in "Two in the Campagna." The vast and monotonous spaces, as well as their painful contents, diminish, to be sure, the single human being who acts in them, but also "enlarge" him, extend his range, ennoble him. The impression is rather that of Burke's "sublime," with its vision of infinite possibility rising from experience of pain and monotony.³ "Childe Roland" would seem, then, to celebrate the value of man's acts as he blunders doggedly toward goals which are both commonplace and unique:

> The round squat turret, blind as the fool's heart,
> Built of brown stone, without a counterpart
> In the whole world.
>
> (lines 182–84)

The mythic mode is in some ways similar to what I have called the typical, but the differences are important enough to make distinction worthwhile. The main difference is that the mythic mode attaches its action not merely to a central and recurring form of human experience, but to such a form as shaped and celebrated by the imagination of the race. A version of this is found in "The Heretic's Tragedy," which is presented as "a glimpse from the burning of Jacques du Bourg-Molay, at Paris, A.D. 1314; as distorted by the refraction from Flemish brain to brain, during the course of a couple of centuries." Jacques du Bourg-Molay had been grand master of the Order of the Knights Templar and was burned at the stake for reasons apparently more secular than religious. But he had been formally convicted of crimes against the faith, and was burned as a heretic.

The first thing to be noticed is Browning's emphasis on the fact that the event dealt with in the poem has been *distorted* as the account of it has passed down orally over a long period of time. It has been distorted by the un-Christian hatred of the pious Christians who cherished the tradition and handed it on, constantly sharpening in their account the hateful elements in it. By the time represented by the composition of the poem, the impiety of the victim has been made so grotesque as to be incredible. We re-

---

³ The use of landscape in these poems looks back to Shelley's in "Julian and Maddalo" and forward to Swinburne's in "On the Downs." (Geoffrey Hartman, in his *Wordsworth's Poetry 1787–1814* [New Haven: Yale University Press, 1964], pp. 118–25, discusses the landscape of *Salisbury Plain* in similar terms. The influence of Burke—or of the tradition he represents—is surely present in Wordsworth's poem.)

spect Jacques du Bourg-Molay because he is hated so
violently by persons of so little moral perception.

But the effect of this malice is not merely to discredit
the speakers and to honor the victim. The distortion is also
clarifying. The corrosive hatred of the generations of faith-
ful has burned away the accidents of the situation, leaving
only an archetype which condemns them still more radi-
cally. What one sees in the situation of the master of the
Temple, as simplified by hate, suggests typically the state
of charity, burning in the flames of love (cf. John of the
Cross's *Burning Flame of Love*), and mythically the suf-
fering Master on the cross, exalted by the hatred of his
executioners. The imagination will tell the truth, it seems,
whatever the intent of the imaginer, even as the imagina-
tions of Lippo Lippi, Childe Roland, and the singers of
"The Heretic's Tragedy" reveal not merely themselves but
permanent forms of truth as the imagination knows them.

The analytic mode, as its name suggests, breaks down
experience into its separate elements and examines possi-
bilities of interrelationship. All of the poems so far exam-
ined have done this to some extent, but there are poems
that set about doing just this. The classical analytic work,
in this sense, would be Cervantes' *Don Quixote*, read from
a perspectivist viewpoint (i.e., as acting out relationships
between the opposed but complementary world views ex-
pressed in the figures of Don Quixote and Sancho Panza).
Closer to Browning in some ways would be Euripides, his
favorite Greek dramatist, who gives many examples of
"scenes where a situation is realized first in its lyric, then
in its iambic aspect—that is to say, first emotionally, then
in its reasoned form."[4] There is a good example in the
Alcestis, which Browning himself translated, in which
Alcestis, dying, celebrates her death and its meaning in
song, and then argues it out argumentatively. Euripides
"has simply juxtaposed these two aspects of Alcestis'
parting from life, rather than leave either incomplete."[5]
And though Browning, as A. M. Dale points out, tries to

---

[4] A. M. Dale, in the commentary to her edition of Euripides' *Alcestis*
(N.Y.: Oxford University Press, 1954), p. 74.
[5] Dale, pp. 74–75.

ground the argument psychologically in his rendering of the scene, the comparison is still useful.

There is a still closer resemblance, however, to works by the modern German poet and dramatist Hugo von Hofmannsthal, especially in texts for operas by Richard Strauss. This is especially striking in *Ariadne auf Naxos,* in which the oppositions of kinds of love and views of life —generally, tragic (in Ariadne) and comic (in Zerbinetta)—are united both ironically (as Hofmannsthal partly understood) and actually (as he apparently did not grasp) through qualities inherent in all love, and through the "harmony" of Strauss's score. The two points of view expose their weaknesses and strengths, their kinds of opposition and union, within the reconciling medium of music.[6]

It is this last, the use of music to define oppositions which are at the same time harmonized, that reminds one most vividly of Browning, whose poems on music attempt something very similar. If you are worried, as Browning often was, about the relation between fact and value, mind and heart, reason and imagination—summed up generally as an opposition between fact and fancy—music can be very helpful. A musical statement can be more abstract than anything in language and still more sensuous than language can ever be. This may give it a unique closeness to reality and at the same time a quality of remoteness, spirituality, fancifulness. Furthermore, it helps us see the two terms as interchangeable: the abstract pole may suggest both reason and unreality, the sensuous both concrete fact and imaginative sentiment. In more formal terms, either pole may suggest comedy or tragedy, poetry or prose.

Browning's finest achievement in this mode is probably "A Toccata of Galuppi's." Among the oppositions to

---

[6] Browning's drama *Colombe's Birthday* suggests a Hofmannsthal libretto in the manner of *Rosenkavalier,* anticipating some of Hofmannsthal's favorite themes. The opposition of moods or types of personality is found also in the Eusebius-Florestan contrast in Schumann, e.g., the "Papillons" (as also in Handel's setting of Milton's "L'Allegro-Il Penseroso"). It appears in another form, based on Jean Paul's *Flegeljahre,* in Schumann's "Carnival," which Browning cites in *Fifine at the Fair,* one of his virtuoso works in the analytic mode.

be worked with here is that between eighteenth-century Italy and nineteenth-century England, as well as that between the "scientist" who speaks and the composer who answers. But it is the scientist who is inclined to put stress on value and the composer whose view is cold and analytic, chilling to the inhabitant of a century that is more humane and less elegant. The scientist's union of fancy and fact is unstable, and Galuppi has denied fancy in the name of fact, though his analysis is carried on in a mode that is itself an expression of fancy—i.e., through art. The main agent of union is the composer's clavichord piece, which both includes and is included by the speech of the scientist.

Within the culture that produced the musical form there are grave differences of caste and point of view, brought out by the relations between Galuppi and his audience. They are aristocrats and he a superior servant; their preoccupation with sexual conquest is the object of his rationalistic contempt. But both rationalism and sensuality are part of the period style, as formalized in its music, and the aristocratic audience is not wholly deceived in enjoying it. Furthermore, they find in Galuppi's art a compassion and solace the composer surely did not intend, but which is built into the formal qualities of the music, since it is in support of human purposes that all art inherently subsists.[7] The music, accordingly, in its expression of the central qualities of its period, is not limited by the points of view of artist or audience. The style at the same time separates and unites within its own period as well as between periods. It is in doing the first that it is able to do the second.

The identification of mode is largely on the basis of relative emphasis. It is useful to notice that a particular poem is engaged in a certain kind of activity with special concentration, but that does not mean that it is not doing other things too. "Fra Lippo Lippi" is primarily an expression of a personal state; both problems and ways of

[7] See my account of "Flute Music: with an Accompaniment" in "Browning's Music Poems: Fancy and Fact," *PMLA*, LXXVIII (1963), 369–377, pp. 372–73.

handling them are developed in terms of a vividly realized individual personality. But there are strong elements of other modes. The poem is analytic in its reduction of the problem to a competition between opposed areas of value, typical in that the state is seen as that of all men. In the same way, "Childe Roland" has a strong mythic side, as well as displaying analytic and personal aspects, and "The Heretic's Tragedy" reveals an important typical strain, as was noted in the analysis of the poem. "Galuppi" alone of the poems examined seems to be overwhelmingly in one mode, though even here there are elements of the personal and perhaps the typical.

None of this lessens the value of noticing, however, that all of these strains are united with especial force and clarity in Browning's longest and most ambitious work. *The Ring and the Book* is in this as in other ways the climax of Browning's career. *The Ring and the Book* makes a great point of the claim that it is true, and it is largely in terms of the modes I have defined that this claim is substantiated. (From the point of view of literary history, there are two main traditions of works that claim to be true and build this claim into themselves as part of their meaning.[8] There is the analytic tradition of which *Don Quixote* is exemplary, as we have seen. Works in this tradition often claim to be "true to nature." The other tradition is the mythic, represented by *Paradise Lost*, which claims to be true because the myth it enacts is true. These traditions meet in *The Ring and the Book*.)

In exploring possible relationships between the antitheses it includes, a work in the analytic mode might discover that the opposed elements fit without reduction into mythic form. This is what happens in *The Ring and the Book*, which attempts a sweeping transformation of brutal fact into ideal fancy. In terms of the four modes, *The Ring and the Book* is typical both ironically and unironi-

---

[8] This is to leave out of account such relatively simple forms as the philosophic-didactic and satiric modes, the usually less problematic modes of reportorial realism and of "sincerity," as well as the complex but more limited "epistemological" mode, in which an act of knowing is enacted in such a way as to be, presumably, self-verifying (e.g., Shelley's "Mont Blanc").

cally. Ironically, it is a typical story of intrigue, adultery, revenge, enacting a recurrent pattern in human affairs. But the irony stems from the fact that it is unironically typical in very different terms, as a type of the action of divine love. Mythically, it reenacts the scandal of a manifestation of the divine in the sordid story of a Jewish wife who bore a child not conceived by her husband, as told by Luke. Analytically, it sees in the unlikely materials of the murder story both a clear opposition between the competing claims of fancy and fact and possibilities of overcoming the division. And both oppositions and possibilities of union are developed in terms of real human beings we are made to care about.

The general outlines of the story are clear enough, and I give it in Browning's own normative account, in the first book, since all of the other accounts given in the course of the poem are to be understood as modulations of this:

> Count Guido Franceschini the Aretine,
> Descended of an ancient house, though poor,
> A beak-nosed bushy-bearded black-haired lord,
> Lean, pallid, low of stature yet robust,
> Fifty years old—having four years ago
> Married Pompilia Comparini, young,
> Good, beautiful, at Rome, where she was born,
> And brought her to Arezzo, where they lived
> Unhappy lives, whatever curse the cause—
> This husband, taking four accomplices,
> Followed this wife to Rome, where she was fled
> From their Arezzo to find peace again,
> In convoy, eight months earlier, of a priest,
> Aretine also, of still nobler birth,
> Giuseppe Caponsacchi—caught her there
> Quiet in a villa on a Christmas night,
> With only Pietro and Violante by,
> Both her putative parents;[9] killed the three,
> Aged, they, seventy each, and she, seventeen
> And, two weeks since, the mother of his babe

[9] The parents are described as "putative" because Violante claimed that she had bought the child from a prostitute, unknown to Paolo.

Firstborn and heir to what the style was worth
O' the Guido who determined, dared and did
This deed just as he purposed point by point.

In this first account, Browning is careful to label Pompilia explicitly as good and to make it pretty clear that for reasons as yet not understood, she was right in what she did and that Guido was wrong. He points up the pathos of the ages of the victims and of the fact that Pompilia was a mother of two weeks. It is less that he is unsure of the self-validating nature of truth or of his own ability to present it adequately than that he does not trust us to read correctly without help. He is conscious of the experimental nature of his poem, and he is not sure that we will be able to keep our bearings. The story of the murder will be told again and again, from different points of view. Some of these, such as the speeches of the "three halves" of Rome, of the lawyers, and of Guido, are exercises in dramatic irony, in which the speaker betrays himself and his own weaknesses, and in doing so makes clear the sense in which, in his version, the truth is being distorted. This is to help us see what then the truth is. In the case of Caponsacchi and, especially, Pompilia, deductions for personal limitations are minimal. What distortion there is tends to be a reflection of their own goodness. And the Pope, it is clear, is presented as entirely authoritative. It is in his vision, Browning would have it, that the truth revealed in the other accounts is contemplated as such, is defined and judged. For "the joke" is that the perplexed circumstances and multiple accounts do not, as we might expect, lead to relativism and an inability to make clear moral judgments, but to a polarizing of the issues into choices between radical good and radical evil, clearly recognizable as such.

It is in the speech of the Pope that all of the modes defined in this introduction manifest themselves with special clarity: typical in the enactment of the archetype of moral judgment; analytic in the understanding of the relation between unlikely fact and fanciful actuality; mythic in its integration of the life and death of Pompilia into that of Christ; personal in its depiction of a rich human being to whom we respond, and in whose personality, as we experience it, the problems raised by the work are persuasively resolved. And it is finally on the personal level, no doubt, that the poem justifies itself, in the vitality of the human beings whose lives raise the issues and offer ways of dealing with them.

It may also be at this level that it is most vulnerable. There is a cold-blooded ferocity in the handling of Guido, for example, by both Caponsacchi and the Pope that has some of the effect of the hatred of the singers of "The Heretic's Tragedy," without, in this case, the excuse of intentional irony. We are to take it all at the speaker's evaluation, and admire the speaker all the more for it. For many readers this may be hard to do. The tone is that of Browning himself at his most viciously self-righteous. It reflects a failing rather common in Browning, who had great faith in the poetic value of his own sentiments.

This weakness is increasingly evident in the volumes that follow *The Ring and the Book,* which tend to impress one as exercises in perversity or as lazy thinking in casual verse. There is nothing comparable to the rich harmonies attained by works of the middle period. Only rarely, as in "La Saisiaz," is he able to integrate argument into an imagined whole, and his success here is precarious. There are brilliant individual pieces in these later books, such as the stunning "Thamuris Marching," or some lyrics of surprising sharpness, but they must be sought out. This makes the success of his final volume, *Asolando,* all the more remarkable and gratifying. While it does not suggest the mellow old age of a Titian or Verdi—it is too thin for that —it is charming and in its way impressive. Browning takes up again his lifetime's preoccupation with "Fancies and Facts" (the subtitle of the volume), and announces his choice in the Prologue of "The naked very thing." But a world so seen is more magical, and not less, in that it points to a transcendent reality beyond itself (in the last lines of the Prologue) and that as our vision of fact becomes clearer, the more clearly we see it encompass the values of fancy (in "Flute Music," or "Development").

The tone of the book is one of delighted acceptance, the manner engagingly playful. It is a fitting *vivace*-finale to Browning's life's work.

The contents of the anthology reflect the belief that while Browning was at his best in works of some length, the sheer mass of his production can blunt the impact of his finest poems. I have chosen therefore to present fewer poems than might be expected in a collection of this length, and to give preference to longer poems of high quality. The old favorites are well represented, but the emphasis is on the Browning that seems to be taking shape for us at present.

GEORGE M. RIDENOUR
University of New Mexico

A GENERAL NOTE
ON THE TEXT

The overall textual policy for the Signet Classic Poetry Series attempts to strike a balance between the convenience and dependability of total modernization, on the one hand, and the authenticity of an established text on the other. Starting with the Restoration and Augustan poets, the General Editor has set up the following guidelines for the individual editors:

Modern American spelling will be used, although punctuation may be adjusted by the editor of each volume when he finds it advisable. In any case, syllabic final "ed" will be rendered with grave accent to distinguish it from the silent one, which is written out without apostrophe (e.g., "to gild refinèd gold," but "asked" rather than "ask'd"). Archaic words and forms are to be kept, naturally, whenever the meter or the sense may require it.

In the case of poets from earlier periods, the text is more clearly a matter of the individual editor's choice, and the type and degree of modernization has been left to his decision. But, in any event, archaic typographical conventions ("i," "j," "u," "v," etc.) have all been normalized in the modern way.

JOHN HOLLANDER

A NOTE ON THIS EDITION

The poems are arranged in the order of their appearance in the volume in which they were first collected. The text is that prepared by the poet shortly before his death which appeared in seventeen volumes in 1888–89. The spelling has been made to conform generally to modern American practice. Little attempt has been made to correct the pointing of Browning's text, which is often rhetorically effective, though the careful reader may suspect that a few passages are incorrectly punctuated.

GEORGE M. RIDENOUR

CHRONOLOGY

1812	May 7. Robert Browning born in Camberwell, a London suburb.
ca. 1820–1826	At boarding school near his home, where he spent weekends.
ca. 1824	His parents try unsuccessfully to find a publisher for his first collection of poems, called *Incondita* (i.e., irregular or confused pieces), presumably imitations, especially of Byron. The volume was destroyed by its author, and only two poems have been preserved.
ca. 1826	First reading of Shelley.
1828	Enrolls in newly opened University of London, but does not complete the first year.
1833	March. *Pauline,* paid for by his aunt. No copies sold.
1835	August. *Paracelsus,* paid for by his father.
1836	May. William Macready, the actor, asks Browning to write him a tragedy, stimulating Browning's attempt of ten years at writing a successful drama for the stage.
1837	May. *Strafford,* an historical drama. Four performances.
1838	Short visit to Italy.
1840	March. *Sordello.*
1841	April. *Pippa Passes.* This is the first of eight pamphlets that make up the series Browning called *Bells and Pomegranates.* They were paid for by his father. (Browning published

six other dramas in this series which will not be taken note of here.)

1842   November. *Dramatic Lyrics,* in which he develops the form of the dramatic monologue. (*Bells and Pomegranates,* No. III.)

1844   Fall. Leisurely tour of Italy.

Publication of *Poems* by Elizabeth Barrett.

1845   January 10. "I love your verses with all my heart," he writes to Miss Barrett, adding later, "and I love you too." But Miss Barrett was an invalid watched over by a father who had determined that none of his children should marry.

November. *Dramatic Romances and Lyrics* (*Bells and Pomegranates,* No. VII).

1846   September 12. Marries Elizabeth Barrett without her father's knowledge. The next week they elope to the continent, stopping in Pisa.

1847   April. Settle in Florence, in Casa Guidi, their home during the rest of their life together.

1849   March. Birth of son, Robert Wiedemann Barrett Browning, followed shortly afterwards by the death of Browning's mother.

1850   April. *Christmas Eve and Easter Day.*

1855   November. *Men and Women.*

1860   June. Discovers the "Old Yellow Book," from which *The Ring and the Book* is to develop, in a bookstall in Florence.

1861   June 29. Death of Mrs. Browning.

October. With his son in London, where he takes a house.

1864   May. *Dramatis Personae.*

1868–
1869   *The Ring and the Book.* Published in four separate volumes in separate months.

1871–
1876   *Balaustion's Adventure, Prince Hohenstiel-Schwangau, Fifine at the Fair, Red Cotton Nightcap Country, Aristophanes' Apology, The Inn Album, Pacchiarotto and How he Worked in Distemper.*

1878   First visit to Italy after his wife's death.
        May. *La Saisiaz: The Two Poets of Croisic*
        (one volume).
1879   April. First series of *Dramatic Idyls*.
1880   June. Second series of *Dramatic Idyls*.
1883–   *Jocoseria, Ferishtah's Fancies, Parleyings*
  1887 *with Certain People of Importance in their*
        Day.
1889   December 12. *Asolando* published. Brown-
        ing dies in Venice the evening of the same
        day, after hearing news of its success.
        December 31. Burial in Poet's Corner, West-
        minster Abbey.

SELECTED BIBLIOGRAPHY

Editions of the Works:

The Complete Works of Robert Browning ("Florentine Edition"), 12 vols., eds. Charlotte Porter and Helen A. Clarke (New York: 1898).

The Works of Robert Browning ("Centenary Edition"), 10 vols., ed. F. G. Kenyon (London: Smith, Elder & Co., 1912).

Letters:

The Letters of Robert Browning and Elizabeth Barrett Browning, 1845–46. 2 vols. (London: 1899).

Letters of Robert Browning, collected by Thomas J. Wise; ed. Thurman L. Hood (New Haven, Conn.: Yale University Press, 1933).

New Letters of Robert Browning, eds. William Clyde DeVane and Kenneth Leslie Knickerbocker (New Haven: Yale University Press, 1950).

Dearest Isa: Robert Browning's Letters to Isabella Blagden, ed. Edward C. McAleer (Austin: University of Texas Press, 1951).

Biographies:

Griffin, W. H. and Minchin, H. C., *The Life of Robert Browning,* third (revised) edition (London: Methuen & Co., Ltd., 1938).

Spiro, Betty Bergson (Mrs. Emanuel Miller), *Robert Browning: A Portrait* (New York: Charles Scribner's Sons, 1953).

Books of Reference:

Cook, A. K., *A Commentary Upon Browning's "The Ring and the Book"* (New York: Oxford University Press, 1920).

DeVane, William C., *A Browning Handbook,* revised ed. (New York: Appleton-Century-Crofts, Inc., 1955).

Criticism:

Cadbury, William, "Lyric and Anti-Lyric Forms: A Method for Judging Browning," *University of Toronto Quarterly,* XXXIV (1964), 49–67.

Charlton, H. B., series of essays in the *Bulletin of the John Rylands Library,* vols. XXII (1938), XXIII (1939), XXVII (1942–43), XXVIII (1944), XXXV (1952–53).

Crowell, Norton B., *The Triple Soul: Browning's Theory of Knowledge* (Albuquerque: University of New Mexico, 1963).

DeVane, William C., "The Virgin and the Dragon," *Yale Review,* XXXVII (1947), 33–46.

Duncan, Joseph E., "The Intellectual Kinship of John Donne and Robert Browning," *Studies in Philology,* L (1953), 81–100.

Hartle, Robert W., "Gide's Interpretation of Browning," *University of Texas Studies in English,* XXVIII (1949), 244–56.

Honan, Park, *Browning's Characters: A Study in Poetic Technique* (New Haven, Conn.: Yale University Press, 1961).

Johnson, E. D. H., *The Alien Vision of Victorian Poetry* (Princeton, New Jersey: Princeton University Press, 1952), pp. 71–143.

—————, "The Pluralistic Universe of Robert Browning," *University of Toronto Quarterly*, XXXI (1961), 20–41.

King, Roma A., *The Bow and the Lyre: The Art of Robert Browning* (Ann Arbor, Mich.: University of Michigan, 1957).

Langbaum, Robert, *The Poetry of Experience: The Dramatic Monologue in Modern Literary Tradition* (London: Chatto & Windus, Ltd., 1957).

Miller, J. Hillis, *The Disappearance of God: Five Nineteenth-Century Writers* (Cambridge, Mass.: Harvard University Press, 1963), pp. 81–156.

Preyer, Robert, "Robert Browning: A Reading of the Early Narratives," *Journal of English Literary History*, XXVI (1959), 531–48.

Raymond, William O., *The Infinite Moment and Other Essays on Robert Browning*, 2nd enlarged ed. (Toronto: University of Toronto Press, 1965).

Ridenour, George M., "Browning's Music Poems: Fancy and Fact," *PMLA*, LXXVIII (1963), 369–77.

Sypher, Wylie, Introduction to edition of *The Ring and the Book* (New York: W. W. Norton & Co., Inc., 1961).

Tracy, C. R., "Browning's Heresies," *Studies in Philology*, XXXIII (1936), 610–25.

Whitla, William, *The Central Truth: The Incarnation in Robert Browning's Poetry* (Toronto: University of Toronto Press, 1963).

Johnson, E. D. H. *The Alien Vision of Victorian Poetry.* Princeton, New Jersey: Princeton University Press, 1952. *rpt. Hamden*.

———. "The Unfulfilled Intention of Robert Browning." *University of Toronto Quarterly*, XXXI (1961), 20–41.

King, Roma A. *The Bow and the Lyre: The Art of Robert Browning.* Ann Arbor: University of Michigan Press, 1957.

Langbaum, Robert. *The Poetry of Experience: The Dramatic Monologue in Modern Literary Tradition.* New York: Random House, 1957.

Miller, J. Hillis. *The Disappearance of God: Five Nineteenth-Century Writers.* Cambridge, Mass.: Harvard University Press, 1963. *rpt. New York*.

Pearsall, Robert. *Robert Browning.* New York: Twayne Publishers, Inc., 1974.

Raymond, William O. *The Infinite Moment and Other Essays in Robert Browning.* Toronto: University of Toronto Press, 1950.

Ridenour, George M. "Browning's Music Poems: Fancy and Fact." *PMLA*, LXXVIII (1963), 369–377.

Slinn, E. Warwick. *Browning and the Fictions of Identity.* London: Macmillan, 1982.

Smith, C. Willard. *Browning's Star-Imagery.* Princeton, New Jersey: Princeton University Press, 1941.

Tracy, C. R., ed. *Browning's Mind and Art.* Edinburgh: Oliver & Boyd, 1968.

Whitla, William. *The Central Truth: The Incarnation in Robert Browning's Poetry.* Toronto: University of Toronto Press, 1963.

PAULINE°

(1883)

PAULINE, mine own, bend o'er me—thy soft breast
Shall pant to mine—bend o'er me—thy sweet eyes,
And loosened hair and breathing lips, and arms
Drawing me to thee—these build up a screen
To shut me in with thee, and from all fear;   5
So that I might unlock the sleepless brood
Of fancies from my soul, their lurking-place,
Nor doubt that each would pass, ne'er to return
To one so watched, so loved and so secured.
But what can guard thee but thy naked love?   10
Ah dearest, whoso sucks a poisoned wound
Envenoms his own veins! Thou art so good,
So calm—if thou shouldst wear a brow less light
For some wild thought which, but for me, were kept
From out thy soul as from a sacred star!   15
Yet till I have unlocked them it were vain
To hope to sing; some woe would light on me;
Nature would point at one whose quivering lip
Was bathed in her enchantments, whose brow burned
Beneath the crown to which her secrets knelt,   20
Who learned the spell which can call up the dead,
And then departed smiling like a fiend

Pauline prefatory mottoes have been omitted.

1 The degree sign (°) indicates a footnote, which is keyed to the text by line number. Text references are printed in **bold** type; the annotation follows in roman type.

Who has deceived God—if such one should seek
Again her altars and stand robed and crowned
25 Amid the faithful! Sad confession first,
Remorse and pardon and old claims renewed,
Ere I can be—as I shall be no more.

I had been spared this shame if I had sat
By thee forever from the first, in place
30 Of my wild dreams of beauty and of good,
Or with them, as an earnest of their truth:
No thought nor hope having been shut from thee,
No vague wish unexplained, no wandering aim
Sent back to bind on fancy's wings and seek
35 Some strange fair world where it might be a law;
But, doubting nothing, had been led by thee,
Through youth, and saved, as one at length awaked
Who has slept through a peril. Ah vain, vain!

Thou lovest me; the past is in its grave
40 Though its ghost haunts us; still this much is ours,
To cast away restraint, lest a worse thing
Wait for us in the dark. Thou lovest me;
And thou art to receive not love but faith,
For which thou wilt be mine, and smile and take
45 All shapes and shames, and veil without a fear
That form which music follows like a slave:
And I look to thee and I trust in thee,
As in a Northern night one looks alway
Unto the East for morn and spring and joy.
50 Thou seest then my aimless, hopeless state,
And, resting on some few old feelings won
Back by thy beauty, wouldst that I essay
The task which was to me what now thou art:
And why should I conceal one weakness more?

55 Thou wilt remember one warm morn when winter
Crept aged from the earth, and spring's first breath
Blew soft from the moist hills; the blackthorn boughs,
So dark in the bare wood, when glistening
In the sunshine were white with coming buds,

Like the bright side of a sorrow, and the banks 60
Had violets opening from sleep like eyes.
I walked with thee who knew'st not a deep shame
Lurked beneath smiles and careless words which
    sought
To hide it till they wandered and were mute,
As we stood listening on a sunny mound 65
To the wind murmuring in the damp copse,
Like heavy breathings of some hidden thing
Betrayed by sleep; until the feeling rushed
That I was low indeed, yet not so low
As to endure the calmness of thine eyes. 70
And so I told thee all, while the cool breast
I leaned on altered not its quiet beating:
And long ere words like a hurt bird's complaint
Bade me look up and be what I had been,
I felt despair could never live by thee: 75
Thou wilt remember. Thou art not more dear
Than song was once to me; and I ne'er sung
But as one entering bright halls where all
Will rise and shout for him: sure I must own
That I am fallen, having chosen gifts 80
Distinct from theirs—that I am sad and fain
Would give up all to be but where I was,
Not high as I had been if faithful found,
But low and weak yet full of hope, and sure
Of goodness as of life—that I would lose 85
All this gay mastery of mind, to sit
Once more with them, trusting in truth and love
And with an aim—not being what I am.

Oh Pauline, I am ruined who believed
That though my soul had floated from its sphere 90
Of wild dominion into the dim orb
Of self—that it was strong and free as ever!
It has conformed itself to that dim orb,
Reflecting all its shades and shapes, and now
Must stay where it alone can be adored. 95
I have felt this in dreams—in dreams in which
I seemed the fate from which I fled; I felt

A strange delight in causing my decay.
I was a fiend in darkness chained forever
100 Within some ocean-cave; and ages rolled,
Till through the cleft rock, like a moonbeam, came
A white swan to remain with me; and ages
Rolled, yet I tired not of my first free joy
In gazing on the peace of its pure wings:
105 And then I said "It is most fair to me,
Yet its soft wings must sure have suffered change
From the thick darkness, sure its eyes are dim,
Its silver pinions must be cramped and numbed
With sleeping ages here; it cannot leave me,
110 For it would seem, in light beside its kind,
Withered, though here to me most beautiful."
And then I was a young witch whose blue eyes,
As she stood naked by the river springs,
Drew down a god: I watched his radiant form
115 Growing less radiant, and it gladdened me;
Till one morn, as he sat in the sunshine
Upon my knees, singing to me of Heaven,
He turned to look at me, ere I could lose
The grin with which I viewed his perishing:
120 And he shrieked and departed and sat long
By his deserted throne, but sunk at last
Murmuring, as I kissed his lips and curled
Around him, "I am still a god—to thee."

Still I can lay my soul bare in its fall,
125 Since all the wandering and all the weakness
Will be a saddest comment on the song:
And if, that done, I can be young again,
I will give up all gained, as willingly
As one gives up a charm which shuts him out
130 From hope or part or care in human kind.
As life wanes, all its care and strife and toil
Seem strangely valueless, while the old trees
Which grew by our youth's home, the waving mass
Of climbing plants heavy with bloom and dew,
135 The morning swallows with their songs like words,
All these seem clear and only worth our thoughts:

So, aught connected with my early life,
My rude songs or my wild imaginings,
How I look on them—most distinct amid
The fever and the stir of after years!   140

I ne'er had ventured e'en to hope for this,
Had not the glow I felt at His award,°
Assured me all was not extinct within:
His whom all honor, whose renown springs up
Like sunlight which will visit all the world,   145
So that e'en they who sneered at him at first,
Come out to it, as some dark spider crawls
From his foul nets which some lit torch invades,
Yet spinning still new films for his retreat.
Thou didst smile, poet, but can we forgive?   150

Sun-treader, life and light be thine forever!
Thou art gone from us; years go by and spring
Gladdens and the young earth is beautiful,
Yet thy songs come not, other bards arise,
But none like thee: they stand, thy majesties,   155
Like mighty works which tell some spirit there
Hath sat regardless of neglect and scorn,
Till, its long task completed, it hath risen
And left us, never to return, and all
Rush in to peer and praise when all in vain.   160
The air seems bright with thy past presence yet,
But thou art still for me as thou hast been
When I have stood with thee as on a throne
With all thy dim creations gathered round
Like mountains, and I felt of mold like them,   165
And with them creatures of my own were mixed,
Like things half-lived, catching and giving life.
But thou art still for me who have adored
Though single, panting but to hear thy name
Which I believed a spell to me alone,   170
Scarce deeming thou wast as a star to men!
As one should worship long a sacred spring

142 **His award** Shelley's (**Sun-treader** of 151).

Scarce worth a moth's flitting, which long grasses cross,
And one small tree embowers droopingly—
175 Joying to see some wandering insect won
To live in its few rushes, or some locust
To pasture on its boughs, or some wild bird
Stoop for its freshness from the trackless air:
And then should find it but the fountainhead,
180 Long lost, of some great river washing towns
And towers, and seeing old woods which will live
But by its banks untrod of human foot,
Which, when the great sun sinks, lie quivering
In light as some thing lieth half of life
185 Before God's foot, waiting a wondrous change;
Then girt with rocks which seek to turn or stay
Its course in vain, for it does ever spread
Like a sea's arm as it goes rolling on,
Being the pulse of some great country—so
190 Wast thou to me, and art thou to the world!
And I, perchance, half feel a strange regret
That I am not what I have been to thee:
Like a girl one has silently loved long
In her first loneliness in some retreat,
195 When, late emerged, all gaze and glow to view
Her fresh eyes and soft hair and lips which bloom
Like a mountain berry: doubtless it is sweet
To see her thus adored, but there have been
Moments when all the world was in our praise,
200 Sweeter than any pride of after hours.
Yet, sun-treader, all hail! From my heart's heart
I bid thee hail! E'en in my wildest dreams,
I proudly feel I would have thrown to dust
The wreaths of fame which seemed o'erhanging me,
205 To see thee for a moment as thou art.

And if thou livest, if thou lovest, spirit!
Remember me who set this final seal
To wandering thought—that one so pure as thou
Could never die. Remember me who flung
210 All honor from my soul, yet paused and said
"There is one spark of love remaining yet,

or I have nought in common with him, shapes
Which followed him avoid me, and foul forms
seek me, which ne'er could fasten on his mind;
And though I feel how low I am to him,   215
Yet I aim not even to catch a tone
Of harmonies he called profusely up;
So, one gleam still remains, although the last."
Remember me who praise thee e'en with tears,
For never more shall I walk calm with thee;   220
Thy sweet imaginings are as an air,
A melody some wondrous singer sings,
Which, though it haunt men oft in the still eve,
They dream not to essay; yet it no less
But more is honored. I was thine in shame,   225
And now when all thy proud renown is out,
I am a watcher whose eyes have grown dim
With looking for some star which breaks on him
Altered and worn and weak and full of tears.

Autumn has come like spring returned to us,   230
Won from her girlishness; like one returned
A friend that was a lover, nor forgets
The first warm love, but full of sober thoughts
Of fading years; whose soft mouth quivers yet
With the old smile, but yet so changed and still! 235
And here am I the scoffer, who have probed
Life's vanity, won by a word again
Into my own life—by one little word
Of this sweet friend who lives in loving me,
Lives strangely on my thoughts and looks and words, 240
As fathoms down some nameless ocean thing
Its silent course of quietness and joy.
O dearest, if indeed I tell the past,
May'st thou forget it as a sad sick dream!
Or if it linger—my lost soul too soon   245
Sinks to itself and whispers we shall be
But closer linked, two creatures whom the earth
Bears singly, with strange feelings unrevealed
Save to each other; or two lonely things
Created by some power whose reign is done,   250

Having no part in God or his bright world.
I am to sing whilst ebbing day dies soft,
As a lean scholar dies worn o'er his book,
And in the heaven stars steal out one by one
255 As hunted men steal to their mountain watch.
I must not think, lest this new impulse die
In which I trust; I have no confidence:
So, I will sing on fast as fancies come;
Rudely, the verse being as the mood it paints.

260 I strip my mind bare, whose first elements
I shall unveil—not as they struggled forth
In infancy, nor as they now exist,
When I am grown above them and can rule
But in that middle stage when they were full
265 Yet ere I had disposed them to my will;
And then I shall show how these elements
Produced my present state, and what it is.
I am made up of an intensest life,
Of a most clear idea of consciousness
270 Of self, distinct from all its qualities,
From all affections, passions, feelings, powers;
And thus far it exists, if tracked, in all:
But linked, in me, to self-supremacy,
Existing as a center to all things,
275 Most potent to create and rule and call
Upon all things to minister to it;
And to a principle of restlessness
Which would be all, have, see, know, taste, feel, all—
This is myself; and I should thus have been
280 Though gifted lower than the meanest soul.

And of my powers, one springs up to save
From utter death a soul with such desire
Confined to clay—of powers the only one
Which marks me—an imagination which
285 Has been a very angel, coming not
In fitful visions but beside me ever
And never failing me; so, though my mind
Forgets not, not a shred of life forgets,

Yet I can take a secret pride in calling
The dark past up to quell it regally.   290

A mind like this must dissipate itself.
But I have always had one lodestar; now,
As I look back, I see that I have halted
Or hastened as I looked towards that star—
A need, a trust, a yearning after God: 295
A feeling I have analyzed but late,
But it existed, and was reconciled
With a neglect of all I deemed his laws,
Which yet, when seen in others, I abhorred.
I felt as one beloved, and so shut in   300
From fear: and thence I date my trust in signs
And omens, for I saw God everywhere;
And I can only lay it to the fruit
Of a sad after-time that I could doubt
Even his being—e'en the while I felt   305
His presence, never acted from myself,
Still trusted in a hand to lead me through
All danger; and this feeling ever fought
Against my weakest reason and resolve.

And I can love nothing—and this dull truth   310
Has come the last: but sense supplies a love
Encircling me and mingling with my life.

These make myself: I have long sought in vain
To trace how they were formed by circumstance,
Yet ever found them mold my wildest youth   315
Where they alone displayed themselves, converted
All objects to their use: now see their course!

They came to me in my first dawn of life
Which passed alone with wisest ancient books
All halo-girt with fancies of my own;   320
And I myself went with the tale—a god
Wandering after beauty, or a giant
Standing vast in the sunset—an old hunter
Talking with gods, or a high-crested chief

325 Sailing with troops of friends to Tenedos.°
     I tell you, nought has ever been so clear
     As the place, the time, the fashion of those lives:
     I had not seen a work of lofty art,
     Nor woman's beauty nor sweet nature's face,
330 Yet, I say, never morn broke clear as those
     On the dim clustered isles in the blue sea,
     The deep groves and white temples and wet caves:
     And nothing ever will surprise me now—
     Who stood beside the naked Swift-footed,
335 Who bound my forehead with Proserpine's hair.°

     And strange it is that I who could so dream
     Should e'er have stooped to aim at aught beneath—
     Aught low or painful; but I never doubted:
     So, as I grew, I rudely shaped my life
340 To my immediate wants; yet strong beneath
     Was a vague sense of power though folded up—
     A sense that, though those shades and times were past,
     Their spirit dwelt in me, with them should rule.

     Then came a pause, and long restraint chained down
345 My soul till it was changed. I lost myself,
     And were it not that I so loathe that loss,
     I could recall how first I learned to turn
     My mind against itself; and the effects
     In deeds for which remorse were vain as for
350 The wanderings of delirious dream; yet thence
     Came cunning, envy, falsehood, all world's wrong
     That spotted me: at length I cleansed my soul.
     Yet long world's influence remained; and nought
     But the still life I led, apart once more,
355 Which left me free to seek soul's old delights,
     Could e'er have brought me thus far back to peace.

321–25 **a god . . . Tenedos** rather general allusions to Greek myth.
The *god* is perhaps Apollo. The *giant* is Atlas. Some of the Greek
chiefs stopped at *Tenedos* on their return from Troy.   334–35 **the
naked Swift-footed . . . Proserpine's hair** the god Hermes had winged
feet. He led the souls of the dead to *Proserpine,* queen of the dead.

As peace returned, I sought out some pursuit;
And song rose, no new impulse but the one
With which all others best could be combined.
My life has not been that of those whose heaven   360
Was lampless save where poesy shone out;
But as a clime where glittering mountain-tops
And glancing sea and forests steeped in light
Give back reflected the far-flashing sun;
For music (which is earnest of a heaven,   365
Seeing we know emotions strange by it,
Not else to be revealed), is like a voice,
A low voice calling fancy, as a friend,
To the green woods in the gay summer time:
And she fills all the way with dancing shapes   370
Which have made painters pale, and they go on
Till stars look at them and winds call to them
As they leave life's path for the twilight world
Where the dead gather. This was not at first,
For I scarce knew what I would do. I had   375
An impulse but no yearning—only sang.

And first I sang as I in dream have seen
Music wait on a lyrist for some thought,
Yet singing to herself until it came.
I turned to those old times and scenes where all   380
That's beautiful had birth for me, and made
Rude verses on them all; and then I paused—
I had done nothing, so I sought to know
What other minds achieved. No fear outbroke
As on the works of mighty bards I gazed,   385
In the first joy at finding my own thoughts
Recorded, my own fancies justified,
And their aspirings but my very own.
With them I first explored passion and mind—
All to begin afresh! I rather sought   390
To rival what I wondered at than form
Creations of my own; if much was light
Lent by the others, much was yet my own.

I paused again: a change was coming—came:

395 I was no more a boy, the past was breaking
    Before the future and like fever worked.
    I thought on my new self, and all my powers
    Burst out. I dreamed not of restraint, but gazed
    On all things: schemes and systems went and came,
400 And I was proud (being vainest of the weak)
    In wandering o'er thought's world to seek some one
    To be my prize, as if you wandered o'er
    The White Way for a star.

                              And my choice fell
    Not so much on a system as a man—°
405 On one, whom praise of mine shall not offend,
    Who was as calm as beauty, being such
    Unto mankind as thou to me, Pauline—
    Believing in them and devoting all
    His soul's strength to their winning back to peace;
410 Who sent forth hopes and longings for their sake,
    Clothed in all passion's melodies: such first
    Caught me and set me, slave of a sweet task,
    To disentangle, gather sense from song:
    Since, song-inwoven, lurked there words which seemed
415 A key to a new world, the muttering
    Of angels, something yet unguessed by man.
    How my heart leapt as still I sought and found
    Much there, I felt my own soul had conceived,
    But there living and burning! Soon the orb
420 Of his conceptions dawned on me; its praise
    Lives in the tongues of men, men's brows are high
    When his name means a triumph and a pride,
    So, my weak voice may well forbear to shame
    What seemed decreed my fate: I threw myself
425 To meet it, I was vowed to liberty,
    Men were to be as gods and earth as heaven,
    And I—ah, what a life was mine to prove!
    My whole soul rose to meet it. Now, Pauline,
    I shall go mad, if I recall that time!

404 **a man** no doubt Shelley.

Oh let me look back ere I leave forever   430
The time which was an hour one fondly waits
For a fair girl that comes a withered hag!
And I was lonely, far from woods and fields,
And amid dullest sights, who should be loose
As a stag; yet I was full of bliss, who lived   435
With Plato and who had the key to life;
And I had dimly shaped my first attempt,
And many a thought did I build up on thought,
As the wild bee hangs cell to cell; in vain,
For I must still advance, no rest for mind.   440

Twas in my plan to look on real life,
The life all new to me; my theories
Were firm, so them I left, to look and learn
Mankind, its cares, hopes, fears, its woes and joys;
And, as I pondered on their ways, I sought   445
How best life's end might be attained—an end
Comprising every joy. I deeply mused.

And suddenly without heart-wreck I awoke
As from a dream: I said " 'Twas beautiful,
Yet but a dream, and so adieu to it!"   450
As some world-wanderer sees in a far meadow
Strange towers and high-walled gardens thick with
    trees,
Where song takes shelter and delicious mirth
From laughing fairy creatures peeping over,
And on the morrow when he comes to lie   455
Forever 'neath those garden-trees fruit-flushed
Sung round by fairies, all his search is vain.
First went my hopes of perfecting mankind,
Next—faith in them, and then in freedom's self
And virtue's self, then my own motives, ends   460
And aims and loves, and human love went last.
I felt this no decay, because new powers
Rose as old feelings left—wit, mockery,
Light-heartedness; for I had oft been sad,
Mistrusting my resolves, but now I cast   465

Hope joyously away: I laughed and said
"No more of this!" I must not think: at length
I looked again to see if all went well.

My powers were greater: as some temple seemed
470 My soul, where nought is changed and incense rolls
Around the altar, only God is gone
And some dark spirit sitteth in his seat.
So, I passed through the temple and to me
Knelt troops of shadows, and they cried "Hail, king
475 We serve thee now and thou shalt serve no more!
Call on us, prove us, let us worship thee!"
And I said "Are ye strong? Let fancy bear me
Far from the past!" And I was borne away,
As Arab birds float sleeping in the wind,
480 O'er deserts, towers and forests, I being calm.
And I said "I have nursed up energies,
They will prey on me." And a band knelt low
And cried "Lord, we are here and we will make
Safe way for thee in thine appointed life!
485 But look on us!" And I said "Ye will worship
Me; should my heart not worship too?" They shouted
"Thyself, thou art our king!" So, I stood there
Smiling—oh, vanity of vanities!
For buoyant and rejoicing was the spirit
490 With which I looked out how to end my course;
I felt once more myself, my powers—all mine;
I knew while youth and health so lifted me
That, spite of all life's nothingness, no grief
Came nigh me, I must ever be light-hearted;
495 And that this knowledge was the only veil
Betwixt joy and despair: so, if age came,
I should be left—a wreck linked to a soul
Yet fluttering, or mind-broken and aware
Of my decay. So a long summer morn
500 Found me; and ere noon came, I had resolved
No age should come on me ere youth was spent,
For I would wear myself out, like that morn
Which wasted not a sunbeam; every hour
I would make mine, and die.

And thus I sought
To chain my spirit down which erst I freed   505
For flights to fame: I said "The troubled life
Of genius, seen so gay when working forth
Some trusted end, grows sad when all proves vain—
How sad when men have parted with truth's peace
For falsest fancy's sake, which waited first   510
As an obedient spirit when delight
Came without fancy's call: but alters soon,
Comes darkened, seldom, hastens to depart,
Leaving a heavy darkness and warm tears.
But I shall never lose her; she will live   515
Dearer for such seclusion. I but catch
A hue, a glance of what I sing: so, pain
Is linked with pleasure, for I ne'er may tell
Half the bright sights which dazzle me; but now
Mine shall be all the radiance: let them fade   520
Untold—others shall rise as fair, as fast!
And when all's done, the few dim gleams trans-
    ferred,"—
(For a new thought sprang up how well it were,
Discarding shadowy hope, to weave such lays
As straight encircle men with praise and love,   525
So, I should not die utterly—should bring
One branch from the gold forest, like the knight
Of old tales, witnessing I had been there)—
"And when all's done, how vain seems e'en success—
The vaunted influence poets have o'er men!   530
'Tis a fine thing that one weak as myself
Should sit in his lone room, knowing the words
He utters in his solitude shall move
Men like a swift wind—that though dead and gone,
New eyes shall glisten when his beauteous dreams   535
Of love come true in happier frames than his.
Ay, the still night brings thoughts like these, but morn
Comes and the mockery again laughs out
At hollow praises, smiles allied to sneers;
And my soul's idol ever whispers me   540
To dwell with him and his unhonored song:
And I foreknow my spirit, that would press

First in the struggle, fail again to make
All bow enslaved, and I again should sink."

545 "And then know that this curse will come on us,
To see our idols perish; we may wither,
No marvel, we are clay, but our low fate
Should not extend to those whom trustingly
We sent before into time's yawning gulf
550 To face what dread may lurk in darkness there.
To find the painter's glory pass, and feel
Music can move us not as once, or, worst,
To weep decaying wits ere the frail body
Decays! Nought makes me trust some love is true,
555 But the delight of the contented lowness
With which I gaze on him I keep forever
Above me; I to rise and rival him?
Feed his fame rather from my heart's best blood,
Wither unseen that he may flourish still."

560 Pauline, my soul's friend, thou dost pity yet
How this mood swayed me when that soul found thine,
When I had set myself to live this life,
Defying all past glory. Ere thou camest
I seemed defiant, sweet, for old delights
565 Had flocked like birds again; music, my life,
Nourished me more than ever; then the lore
Loved for itself and all it shows—that king°
Treading the purple calmly to his death,
While round him, like the clouds of eve, all dusk,
570 The giant shades of fate, silently flitting,
Pile the dim outline of the coming doom;
And him° sitting alone in blood while friends
Are hunting far in the sunshine; and the boy°
With his white breast and brow and clustering curls
575 Streaked with his mother's blood, but striving hard

567 **that king** Agamemnon, who on his return from Troy walked on
a purple carpet as he entered his palace, where he was killed by his
queen, Clytemnestra.   572 **him** perhaps Actaeon. While hunting he
came on the goddess Artemis at her bath. The goddess had him
torn apart by his dogs.   573 **the boy** Orestes, son of Agamemnon
and Clytemnestra, who killed his mother to avenge his father's
death and was driven mad by the furies.

To tell his story ere his reason goes.
And when I loved thee as love seemed so oft,
Thou lovedst me indeed: I wondering searched
My heart to find some feeling like such love,
Believing I was still much I had been.   580
Too soon I found all faith had gone from me,
And the late glow of life, like change on clouds,
Proved not the morn-blush widening into day,
But eve faint-colored by the dying sun
While darkness hastens quickly. I will tell   585
My state as though 'twere none of mine—despair
Cannot come near us—this it is, my state.

Souls alter not, and mine must still advance;
Strange that I knew not, when I flung away
My youth's chief aims, their loss might lead to loss   590
Of what few I retained, and no resource
Be left me: for behold how changed is all!
I cannot chain my soul: it will not rest
In its clay prison, this most narrow sphere:
It has strange impulse, tendency, desire,   595
Which nowise I account for nor explain,
But cannot stifle, being bound to trust
All feelings equally, to hear all sides:
How can my life indulge them? yet they live,
Referring to some state of life unknown.   600

My selfishness is satiated not,
It wears me like a flame; my hunger for
All pleasure, howsoe'er minute, grows pain;
I envy—how I envy him whose soul
Turns its whole energies to some one end,   605
To elevate an aim, pursue success
However mean! So, my still baffled hope
Seeks out abstractions; I would have one joy,
But one in life, so it were wholly mine,
One rapture all my soul could fill: and this   610
Wild feeling places me in dream afar
In some vast country where the eye can see
No end to the far hills and dales bestrewn

With shining towers and towns, till I grow mad
615 Well-nigh, to know not one abode but holds
Some pleasure, while my soul could grasp the world,
But must remain this vile form's slave. I look
With hope to age at last, which quenching much,
May let me concentrate what sparks it spares.

620 This restlessness of passion meets in me
A craving after knowledge: the sole proof
Of yet commanding will is in that power
Repressed; for I beheld it in its dawn,
The sleepless harpy with just-budding wings,
625 And I considered whether to forego
All happy ignorant hopes and fears, to live,
Finding a recompense in its wild eyes.
And when I found that I should perish so,
I bade its wild eyes close from me forever,
630 And I am left alone with old delights;
See! it lies in me a chained thing, still prompt
To serve me if I loose its slightest bond:
I cannot but be proud of my bright slave.

How should this earth's life prove my only sphere?
635 Can I so narrow sense but that in life
Soul still exceeds it? In their elements
My love outsoars my reason; but since love
Perforce receives its object from this earth
While reason wanders chainless, the few truths
640 Caught from its wanderings have sufficed to quell
Love chained below; then what were love, set free,
Which, with the object it demands, would pass
Reason companioning the seraphim?
No, what I feel may pass all human love
645 Yet fall far short of what my love should be.
And yet I seem more warped in this than aught,
Myself stands out more hideously: of old
I could forget myself in friendship, fame,
Liberty, nay, in love of mightier souls;
650 But I begin to know what thing hate is—
To sicken and to quiver and grow white—

And I myself have furnished its first prey.
Hate of the weak and ever-wavering will,
The selfishness, the still-decaying frame . . .
But I must never grieve whom wing can waft 655
Far from such thoughts—as now. Andromeda!°
And she is with me: years roll, I shall change,
But change can touch her not—so beautiful
With her fixed eyes, earnest and still, and hair
Lifted and spread by the salt-sweeping breeze, 660
And one red beam, all the storm leaves in heaven,
Resting upon her eyes and hair, such hair,
As she awaits the snake on the wet beach
By the dark rock and the white wave just breaking
At her feet; quite naked and alone; a thing 665
I doubt not, nor fear for, secure some god
To save will come in thunder from the stars.
Let it pass! Soul requires another change.
I will be gifted with a wondrous mind,
Yet sunk by error to men's sympathy, 670
And in the wane of life, yet only so
As to call up their fears; and there shall come
A time requiring youth's best energies;
And lo, I fling age, sorrow, sickness off,
And rise triumphant, triumph through decay. 675

And thus it is that I supply the chasm
'Twixt what I am and all I fain would be:
But then to know nothing, to hope for nothing,
To seize on life's dull joys from a strange fear
Lest, losing them, all's lost and nought remains! 680

There's some vile juggle with my reason here;
I feel I but explain to my own loss
These impulses: they live no less the same.
Liberty! what though I despair? my blood
Rose never at a slave's name proud as now. 685
Oh sympathies, obscured by sophistries!—

656 **Andromeda** tied naked to a rock to be sacrificed to a sea mon-
ster, she was rescued by the hero Perseus. Browning is recalling a
print he owned of a painting on the subject.

Why else have I sought refuge in myself,
But from the woes I saw and could not stay?
Love! is not this to love thee, my Pauline?
690 I cherish prejudice, lest I be left
Utterly loveless? witness my belief
In poets, though sad change has come there too;
No more I leave myself to follow them—
Unconsciously I measure me by them—
695 Let me forget it: and I cherish most
My love of England—how her name, a word
Of hers in a strange tongue makes my heart beat!

Pauline, could I but break the spell! Not now—
All's fever—but when calm shall come again,
700 I am prepared: I have made life my own.
I would not be content with all the change
One frame should feel, but I have gone in thought
Through all conjuncture, I have lived all life
When it is most alive, where strangest fate
705 New-shapes it past surmise—the throes of men
Bit by some curse or in the grasps of doom
Half-visible and still-increasing round,
Or crowning their wide being's general aim.
These are wild fancies, but I feel, sweet friend,
710 As one breathing his weakness to the ear
Of pitying angel—dear as a winter flower,
A slight flower growing alone, and offering
Its frail cup of three leaves to the cold sun,
Yet joyous and confiding like the triumph
715 Of a child: and why am I not worthy thee?
I can live all the life of plants, and gaze
Drowsily on the bees that flit and play,
Or bare my breast for sunbeams which will kill,
Or open in the night of sounds, to look
720 For the dim stars; I can mount with the bird
Leaping airily his pyramid of leaves
And twisted boughs of some tall mountain tree,
Or rise cheerfully springing to the heavens;
Or like a fish breathe deep the morning air
725 In the misty sun-warm water; or with flower

And tree can smile in light at the sinking sun
Just as the storm comes, as a girl would look
On a departing lover—most serene.

Pauline, come with me, see how I could build
A home for us, out of the world, in thought!   730
I am uplifted: fly with me, Pauline!

Night, and one single ridge of narrow path
Between the sullen river and the woods
Waving and muttering, for the moonless night
Has shaped them into images of life,   735
Like the uprising of the giant-ghosts,
Looking on earth to know how their sons fare:
Thou art so close by me, the roughest swell
Of wind in the treetops hides not the panting
Of thy soft breasts. No, we will pass to morning—   740
Morning, the rocks and valleys and old woods.
How the sun brightens in the mist, and here,
Half in the air, like creatures of the place,
Trusting the element, living on high boughs
That swing in the wind—look at the silver spray   745
Flung from the foam-sheet of the cataract
Amid the broken rocks! Shall we stay here
With the wild hawks? No, ere the hot noon come,
Dive we down—safe! See this our new retreat
Walled in with a sloped mound of matted shrubs,   750
Dark, tangled, old and green, still sloping down
To a small pool whose waters lie asleep
Amid the trailing boughs turned water-plants:
And tall trees overarch to keep us in,
Breaking the sunbeams into emerald shafts,   755
And in the dreamy water one small group
Of two or three strange trees are got together
Wondering at all around, as strange beasts herd
Together far from their own land: all wildness,
No turf nor moss, for boughs and plants pave all,   760
And tongues of bank go shelving in the lymph,°

761 **lymph** water.

Where the pale-throated snake reclines his head,
And old gray stones lie making eddies there,
765   The wild-mice cross them dry-shod. Deeper in!
Shut thy soft eyes—now look—still deeper in!
This is the very heart of the woods all round
Mountain-like heaped above us; yet even here
One pond of water gleams; far off the river
Sweeps like a sea, barred out from land; but one—
770   One thin clear sheet has overleaped and wound
Into this silent depth, which gained, it lies
Still, as but let by sufferance; the trees bend
O'er it as wild men watch a sleeping girl,
And through their roots long creeping plants outstretch
775   Their twined hair, steeped and sparkling; farther on,
Tall rushes and thick flag-knots have combined
To narrow it; so, at length, a silver thread,
It winds, all noiselessly through the deep wood
Till through a cleft-way, through the moss and stone,
780   It joins its parent-river with a shout.

Up for the glowing day, leave the old woods!
See, they part, like a ruined arch: the sky!
Nothing but sky appears, so close the roots
And grass of the hilltop level with the air—
785   Blue sunny air, where a great cloud floats laden
With light, like a dead whale that white birds pick,
Floating away in the sun in some north sea.
Air, air, fresh life-blood, thin and searching air,
The clear, dear breath of God that loveth us,
790   Where small birds reel and winds take their delight!
Water is beautiful, but not like air:
See, where the solid azure waters lie
Made as of thickened air, and down below,
The fern-ranks like a forest spread themselves
795   As though each pore could feel the element;
Where the quick glancing serpent winds his way,
Float with me there, Pauline!—but not like air.

Down the hill! Stop—a clump of trees, see, set
On a heap of rock, which look o'er the far plain:

So, envious climbing shrubs would mount to rest   800
And peer from their spread boughs; wide they wave,
      looking
At the muleteers who whistle on their way,
To the merry chime of morning bells, past all
The little smoking cots, mid fields and banks
And copses bright in the sun. My spirit wanders: 805
Hedgerows for me—those living hedgerows where
The bushes close and clasp above and keep
Thought in—I am concentrated—I feel;
But my soul saddens when it looks beyond:
I cannot be immortal, taste all joy.   810

O God, where do they tend—these struggling aims?°
What would I have? What is this "sleep" which seems
To bound all? can there be a "waking" point
Of crowning life? The soul would never rule;
It would be first in all things, it would have   815
Its utmost pleasure filled, but, that complete,
Commanding, for commanding, sickens it.
The last point I can trace is—rest beneath
Some better essence than itself, in weakness;
This is "myself," not what I think should be: 820
And what is that I hunger for but God?

My God, my God, let me for once look on thee
As though nought else existed, we alone!
And as creation crumbles, my soul's spark
Expands till I can say—Even from myself   825
I need thee and I feel thee and I love thee.
I do not plead my rapture in thy works
For love of thee, nor that I feel as one
Who cannot die: but there is that in me
Which turns to thee, which loves or which should love.   830

Why have I girt myself with this hell-dress?
Why have I labored to put out my life?
Is it not in my nature to adore,

811 **O God . . . aims?** a long note in French by "Pauline" has been
omitted.

And e'en for all my reason do I not
835   Feel him, and thank him, and pray to him—now?
Can I forego the trust that he loves me?
Do I not feel a love which only ONE . . .
O thou pale form, so dimly seen, deep-eyed!
I have denied thee calmly—do I not
840   Pant when I read of thy consummate power,
And burn to see thy calm pure truths outflash
The brightest gleams of earth's philosophy?
Do I not shake to hear aught question thee?
If I am erring save me, madden me,
845   Take from me powers and pleasures, let me die
Ages, so I see thee! I am knit round
As with a charm by sin and lust and pride,
Yet though my wandering dreams have seen all shape
Of strange delight, oft have I stood by thee—
850   Have I been keeping lonely watch with thee
In the damp night by weeping Olivet,°
Or leaning on thy bosom, proudly less,
Or dying with thee on the lonely cross,
Or witnessing thine outburst from the tomb.

855   A mortal, sin's familiar friend, doth here
Avow that he will give all earth's reward,
But to believe and humbly teach the faith,
In suffering and poverty and shame,
Only believing he is not unloved.

860   And now, my Pauline, I am thine forever!
I feel the spirit which has buoyed me up
Desert me, and old shades are gathering fast;
Yet while the last light waits, I would say much,
This chiefly, it is gain that I have said
865   Somewhat of love I ever felt for thee
But seldom told; our hearts so beat together
That speech seemed mockery; but when dark hour
      come,
And joy departs, and thou, sweet, deem'st it strange

851 **Olivet** the Mount of Olives, called "weeping" because of Jesu
agony there before his betrayal by Judas. Luke 22:39 ff.

A sorrow moves me, thou canst not remove,
Look on this lay I dedicate to thee,   870
Which through thee I began, which thus I end,
Collecting the last gleams to strive to tell
How I am thine, and more than ever now
That I sink fast: yet though I deeplier sink,
No less song proves one word has brought me bliss,   875
Another still may win bliss surely back.
Thou knowest, dear, I could not think all calm,
For fancies followed thought and bore me off,
And left all indistinct; ere one was caught
Another glanced; so, dazzled by my wealth,   880
I knew not which to leave nor which to choose,
For all so floated, nought was fixed and firm.
And then thou said'st a perfect bard was one
Who chronicled the stages of all life,
And so thou bad'st me shadow this first stage.   885
'Tis done, and even now I recognize
The shift, the change from last to past—discern
Faintly how life is truth and truth is good.
And why thou must be mine is, that e'en now
In the dim hush of night, that I have done,   890
Despite the sad forebodings, love looks through—
Whispers—E'en at the last I have her still,
With her delicious eyes as clear as heaven
When rain in a quick shower has beat down mist,
And clouds float white above like broods of swans.   895
How the blood lies upon her cheek, outspread
As thinned by kisses! only in her lips
It wells and pulses like a living thing,
And her neck looks like marble misted o'er
With love-breath—a Pauline from heights above,   900
Stooping beneath me, looking up—one look
As I might kill her and be loved the more.

So, love me—me, Pauline, and nought but me,
Never leave loving! Words are wild and weak,
Believe them not, Pauline! I stained myself   905
But to behold thee purer by my side,
To show thou art my breath, my life, a last

Resource, an extreme want: never believe
Aught better could so look on thee; nor seek
910 Again the world of good thoughts left for mine!
There were bright troops of undiscovered suns,
Each equal in their radiant course; there were
Clusters of far fair isles which ocean kept
For his own joy, and his waves broke on them
915 Without a choice; and there was a dim crowd
Of visions, each a part of some grand whole:
And one star left his peers and came with peace
Upon a storm, and all eyes pined for him;
And one isle harbored a sea-beaten ship,
920 And the crew wandered in its bowers and plucked
Its fruits and gave up all their hopes of home;
And one dream came to a pale poet's sleep,
And he said, "I am singled out by God,
No sin must touch me." Words are wild and weak,
925 But what they would express is—Leave me not,
Still sit by me with beating breast and hair
Loosened, be watching earnest by my side,
Turning my books or kissing me when I
Look up—like summer wind! Be still to me
930 A help to music's mystery which mind fails
To fathom, its solution, no mere clue!
O reason's pedantry, life's rule prescribed!
I hopeless, I the loveless, hope and love.
Wiser and better, know me now, not when
935 You loved me as I was. Smile not! I have
Much yet to dawn on you, to gladden you.
No more of the past! I'll look within no more.
I have too trusted my own lawless wants,
Too trusted my vain self, vague intuition—
940 Draining soul's wine alone in the still night,
And seeing how, as gathering films arose,
As by an inspiration life seemed bare
And grinning in its vanity, while ends
Foul to be dreamed of, smiled at me as fixed
945 And fair, while others changed from fair to foul
As a young witch turns an old hag at night.
No more of this! We will go hand in hand,

I with thee, even as a child—love's slave,
Looking no farther than his liege commands.

And thou hast chosen where this life shall be: 950
The land which gave me thee shall be our home,
Where nature lies all wild amid her lakes
And snow-swathed mountains and vast pines begirt
With ropes of snow—where nature lies all bare,
Suffering none to view her but a race 955
Or stinted or deformed,° like the mute dwarfs
Which wait upon a naked Indian queen.
And there (the time being when the heavens are thick
With storm) I'll sit with thee while thou dost sing
Thy native songs, gay as a desert bird 960
Which crieth as it flies for perfect joy,
Or telling me old stories of dead knights;
Or I will read great lays to thee—how she,
The fair pale sister,° went to her chill grave
With power to love and to be loved and live: 965
Or we will go together, like twin gods
Of the infernal world, with scented lamp
Over the dead, to call and to awake,
Over the unshaped images which lie
Within my mind's cave: only leaving all, 970
That tells of the past doubt. So, when spring comes
With sunshine back again like an old smile,
And the fresh waters and awakened birds
And budding woods await us, I shall be
Prepared, and we will question life once more, 975
Till its old sense shall come renewed by change,
Like some clear thought which harsh words veiled
    before;
Feeling God loves us, and that all which errs
Is but a dream which death will dissipate.
And then what need of longer exile? Seek 980
My England, and, again there, calm approach
All I once fled from, calmly look on those

951–56 **The land . . . deformed** Switzerland. 964 **fair pale sister**
presumably Antigone. In Sophocles' tragedy she rejoices at joining
her family in the community of death.

The works of my past weakness, as one views
Some scene where danger met him long before.
985 Ah that such pleasant life should be but dreamed!

But whate'er come of it, and though it fade,
And though ere the cold morning all be gone,
As it may be—though music wait to wile,
And strange eyes and bright wine lure, laugh like sin
990 Which steals back softly on a soul half saved,
And I the first deny, decry, despise,
With this avowal, these intents so fair—
Still be it all my own, this moment's pride!
No less I make an end in perfect joy.

995 E'en in my brightest time, a lurking fear
Possessed me: I well knew my weak resolves,
I felt the witchery that makes mind sleep
Over its treasure, as one half afraid
To make his riches definite: but now
1000 These feelings shall not utterly be lost,
I shall not know again that nameless care
Lest, leaving all undone in youth, some new
And undreamed end reveal itself too late:
For this song shall remain to tell forever
1005 That when I lost all hope of such a change,
Suddenly beauty rose on me again.
No less I make an end in perfect joy,
For I, who thus again was visited,
Shall doubt not many another bliss awaits,
1010 And, though this weak soul sink and darkness whelm,
Some little word shall light it, raise aloft,
To where I clearlier see and better love,
As I again go o'er the tracts of thought
Like one who has a right, and I shall live
1015 With poets, calmer, purer still each time,
And beauteous shapes will come for me to seize,
And unknown secrets will be trusted me
Which were denied the waverer once; but now
I shall be priest and prophet as of old.

1020 Sun-treader, I believe in God and truth

And love; and as one just escaped from death
Would bind himself in bands of friends to feel
He lives indeed, so, I would lean on thee!
Thou must be ever with me, most in gloom
If such must come, but chiefly when I die,　　　1025
For I seem, dying, as one going in the dark
To fight a giant: but live thou forever,
And be to all what thou hast been to me!
All in whom this wakes pleasant thoughts of me
Know my last state is happy, free from doubt　　1030
Or touch of fear. Love me and wish me well.

from PARACELSUS

(1835)

SONG

HEAP cassia, sandal-buds and stripes
   Of labdanum, and aloe-balls,
Smeared with dull nard° an Indian wipes
   From out her hair: such balsam falls
5   Down seaside mountain pedestals,
From treetops where tired winds are fain,
Spent with the vast and howling main,
To treasure half their island-gain.

And strew faint sweetness from some old
10   Egyptian's fine worm-eaten shroud
Which breaks to dust when once unrolled;
   Or shredded perfume, like a cloud
   From closet long to quiet vowed,
With mothed and dropping arras hung,
15 Moldering her lute and books among,
As when a queen, long dead, was young.

1–3 **cassia . . . nard** fragrant spices and ointments.

THE CHAIN OF BEING°

I knew, I felt (perception unexpressed,
Uncomprehended by our narrow thought,
But somehow felt and known in every shift
And change in the spirit—nay, in every pore
Of the body, even)—what God is, what we are,   5
What life is—how God tastes an infinite joy
In infinite ways—one everlasting bliss,
From whom all being emanates, all power
Proceeds; in whom is life for evermore,
Yet whom existence in its lowest form   10
Includes; where dwells enjoyment there is he:
With still a flying point of bliss remote,
A happiness in store afar, a sphere
Of distant glory in full view; thus climbs
Pleasure its heights forever and forever.   15
The center-fire heaves underneath the earth,
And the earth changes like a human face;
The molten ore bursts up among the rocks,
Winds into the stone's heart, outbranches bright
In hidden mines, spots barren river-beds,   20
Crumbles into fine sand where sunbeams bask—
God joys therein. The wroth sea's waves are edged
With foam, white as the bitten lip of hate,
When, in the solitary waste, strange groups
Of young volcanoes come up, cyclops-like,°   25
Staring together with their eyes on flame—
God tastes a pleasure in their uncouth pride.
Then all is still; earth is a wintry clod:

The Chain of being editor's title. From *Paracelsus* V. 637–782, re-
numbered here. The historical Paracelsus (1493–1541) was a
magician and healer. Browning presents him as a kind of Faust,
seeking universal mastery. His error lies in attempting to achieve
good ends directly without going through the necessary preliminary
stages.   25 **cyclops-like** like the fierce semidivine beings with one eye,
who were often associated with volcanoes.

But spring-wind, like a dancing psaltress,° passes
30 Over its breast to waken it, rare verdure
Buds tenderly upon rough banks, between
The withered tree-roots and the cracks of frost,
Like a smile striving with a wrinkled face;
The grass grows bright, the boughs are swol'n with
        blooms
35 Like chrysalids impatient for the air,
The shining dorrs are busy, beetles run
Along the furrows, ants make their ado;
Above, birds fly in merry flocks, the lark
Soars up and up, shivering for very joy;
40 Afar the ocean sleeps; white fishing-gulls
Flit where the strand is purple with its tribe
Of nested limpets; savage creatures seek
Their loves in wood and plain—and God renews
His ancient rapture. Thus he dwells in all,
45 From life's minute beginnings, up at last
To man—the consummation of this scheme
Of being, the completion of this sphere
Of life: whose attributes had here and there
Been scattered o'er the visible world before,
50 Asking to be combined, dim fragments meant
To be united in some wondrous whole,
Imperfect qualities throughout creation,
Suggesting some one creature yet to make,
Some point where all those scattered rays should meet
55 Convergent in the faculties of man.
Power—neither put forth blindly, nor controlled
Calmly by perfect knowledge; to be used
At risk, inspired or checked by hope and fear:
Knowledge—not intuition, but the slow
60 Uncertain fruit of an enhancing toil,
Strengthened by love: love—not serenely pure,
But strong from weakness, like a chance-sown plant
Which, cast on stubborn soil, puts forth changed buds
And softer stains, unknown in happier climes;
65 Love which endures and doubts and is oppressed
And cherished, suffering much and much sustained,

29 **psaltress** woman who plays a psaltery, an ancient stringed instru-
ment.

And blind, oft-failing, yet believing love,
A half-enlightened, often-checkered trust—
Hints and previsions of which faculties,
Are strewn confusedly everywhere about 70
The inferior natures, and all lead up higher,
All shape out dimly the superior race,
The heir of hopes too fair to turn out false,
And man appears at last. So far the seal
Is put on life; one stage of being complete, 75
One scheme wound up: and from the grand result
A supplementary reflux of light,
Illustrates all the inferior grades, explains
Each back step in the circle. Not alone
For their possessor dawn those qualities, 80
But the new glory mixes with the heaven
And earth; man, once descried, imprints for ever
His presence on all lifeless things: the winds
Are henceforth voices, wailing or a shout,
A querulous mutter or a quick gay laugh, 85
Never a senseless gust now man is born.
The herded pines commune and have deep thoughts,
A secret they assemble to discuss
When the sun drops behind their trunks which glare
Like grates of hell: the peerless cup afloat 90
Of the lake-lily is an urn, some nymph
Swims bearing high above her head: no bird
Whistles unseen, but through the gaps above
That let light in upon the gloomy woods,
A shape peeps from the breezy forest-top, 95
Arch with small puckered mouth and mocking eye.
The morn has enterprise, deep quiet droops
With evening, triumph takes the sunset hour,
Voluptuous transport ripens with the corn
Beneath a warm moon like a happy face: 100
—And this to fill us with regard for man.
With apprehension of his passing worth,
Desire to work his proper nature out,
And ascertain his rank and final place,
For these things tend still upward, progress is 105
The law of life, man is not Man as yet.
Nor shall I deem his object served, his end

Attained, his genuine strength put fairly forth,
While only here and there a star dispels
110 The darkness, here and there a towering mind
O'erlooks its prostrate fellows: when the host
Is out at once to the despair of night,
When all mankind alike is perfected,
Equal in full-blown powers—then, not till then,
115 I say, begins man's general infancy.
For wherefore make account of feverish starts
Of restless members of a dormant whole,
Impatient nerves which quiver while the body
Slumbers as in a grave? Oh long ago
120 The brow was twitched, the tremulous lids astir,
The peaceful mouth disturbed; half-uttered speech
Ruffled the lip, and then the teeth were set,
The breath drawn sharp, the strong right-hand clenched
         stronger,
As it would pluck a lion by the jaw;
125 The glorious creature laughed out even in sleep!
But when full roused, each giant-limb awake,
Each sinew strung, the great heart pulsing fast,
He shall start up and stand on his own earth,
Then shall his long triumphant march begin,
130 Thence shall his being date—thus wholly roused,
What he achieves shall be set down to him.
When all the race is perfected alike
As man, that is; all tended to mankind,
And, man produced, all has its end thus far:
135 But in completed man begins anew
A tendency to God. Prognostics told
Man's near approach; so in man's self arise
August anticipations, symbols, types
Of a dim splendor ever on before
140 In that eternal circle life pursues.
For men begin to pass their nature's bound,
And find new hopes and cares which fast supplant
Their proper joys and griefs; they grow too great
For narrow creeds of right and wrong, which fade
145 Before the unmeasured thirst for good: while peace
Rises within them ever more and more.

from DRAMATIC LYRICS

(1842)

MY LAST DUCHESS

FERRARA°

THAT'S my last Duchess painted on the wall,
Looking as if she were alive. I call
That piece a wonder, now: Frà Pandolf's° hands
Worked busily a day, and there she stands.
Will't please you sit and look at her? I said   5
"Frà Pandolf" by design, for never read
Strangers like you that pictured countenance,
The depth and passion of its earnest glance,
But to myself they turned (since none puts by
The curtain I have drawn for you, but I)   10
And seemed as they would ask me, if they durst,
How such a glance came there; so, not the first
Are you to turn and ask thus. Sir, 'twas not
Her husband's presence only, called that spot
Of joy into the Duchess' cheek: perhaps   15
Frà Pandolf chanced to say "Her mantle laps
Over my lady's wrist too much," or "Paint
Must never hope to reproduce the faint
Half-flush that dies along her throat": such stuff

°Ferrara a city in Italy important during the Renaissance   3 Frà
Pandolf imaginary painter.

20 Was courtesy, she thought, and cause enough
    For calling up that spot of joy. She had
    A heart—how shall I say?—too soon made glad,
    Too easily impressed; she liked whate'er
    She looked on, and her looks went everywhere.
25 Sir, 'twas all one! My favor at her breast,
    The dropping of the daylight in the West,
    The bough of cherries some officious fool
    Broke in the orchard for her, the white mule
    She rode with round the terrace—all and each
30 Would draw from her alike the approving speech,
    Or blush, at least. She thanked men—good! but
        thanked
    Somehow—I know not how—as if she ranked
    My gift of a nine hundred-years-old name
    With anybody's gift. Who'd stoop to blame
35 This sort of trifling? Even had you skill
    In speech—(which I have not)—to make your will
    Quite clear to such an one, and say, "Just this
    Or that in you disgusts me; here you miss,
    Or there exceed the mark"—and if she let
40 Herself be lessoned so, nor plainly set
    Her wits to yours, forsooth, and made excuse,
    —E'en then would be some stooping; and I choose
    Never to stoop. Oh sir, she smiled, no doubt,
    Whene'er I passed her; but who passed without
45 Much the same smile? This grew; I gave commands;
    Then all smiles stopped together. There she stands
    As if alive. Will't please you rise? We'll meet
    The company below, then. I repeat,
    The Count your master's known munificence
50 Is ample warrant that no just pretense
    Of mine for dowry will be disallowed;
    Though his fair daughter's self, as I avowed
    At starting, is my object. Nay, we'll go
    Together down, sir. Notice Neptune, though,
55 Taming a sea-horse, thought a rarity,
    Which Claus of Innsbruck° cast in bronze for me!

56 **Claus of Innsbruck** imaginary artist.

SOLILOQUY OF THE SPANISH CLOISTER

I

GR-R-R—there go, my heart's abhorrence!
    Water your damned flower-pots, do!
If hate killed men, Brother Lawrence,
    God's blood, would not mine kill you!
What? your myrtle-bush wants trimming?   5
    Oh, that rose has prior claims—
Needs its leaden vase filled brimming?
    Hell dry you up with its flames!

II

At the meal we sit together:
    Salve tibi!° I must hear   10
Wise talk of the kind of weather,
    Sort of season, time of year:
Not a plenteous cork-crop: scarcely
    Dare we hope oak-galls, I doubt:
What's the Latin name for "parsley"?   15
    What's the Greek name for Swine's Snout?

III

Whew! We'll have our platter burnished,
    Laid with care on our own shelf!
With a fire-new spoon we're furnished,
    And a goblet for ourself,   20
Rinsed like something sacrificial
    Ere 'tis fit to touch our chaps—

10 **Salve tibi!** hail to thee!

Marked with L. for our initial!
   (He-he! There his lily snaps!)

IV

25 *Saint*, forsooth! While brown Dolores
   Squats outside the Convent bank
With Sanchicha, telling stories,
   Steeping tresses in the tank,
Blue-black, lustrous, thick like horsehairs,
30   —Can't I see his dead eye glow,
Bright as 'twere a Barbary corsair's?°
   (That is, if he'd let it show!)

V

When he finishes refection,
   Knife and fork he never lays
35 Crosswise, to my recollection,
   As do I, in Jesu's praise.
I the Trinity illustrate,
   Drinking watered orange-pulp—
In three sips the Arian° frustrate;
40   While he drains his at one gulp.

VI

Oh, those melons? If he's able
   We're to have a feast! so nice!
One goes to the Abbot's table,
   All of us get each a slice.
45 How go on your flowers? None double?
   Not one fruit-sort can you spy?
Strange!—And I, too, at such trouble,
   Keep them close-nipped on the sly!

---

31 **Barbary corsair** pirate from North Africa.   39 **Arian** the Arian
heresy denied the divinity of Christ, and hence the orthodox doctrine
of the Trinity.

VII

ere's a great text in Galatians,°

One you trip on it, entails   50

wenty-nine distinct damnations,

Once you trip on it, entails

I trip him just a-dying,

Sure of Heaven as sure can be,

in him round and send him flying   55

Off to hell, a Manichee?°

VIII

r, my scrofulous French novel

On gray paper with blunt type!

mply glance at it, you grovel

Hand and foot in Belial's gripe: 60

I double down its pages

At the woeful sixteenth print,

hen he gathers his greengages,

Ope a sieve and slip it in't?

IX

r, there's Satan!—one might venture   65

Pledge one's soul to him, yet leave

ch a flaw in the indenture

As he'd miss till, past retrieve,

asted lay that rose-acacia

We're so proud of! *Hy, Zy, Hine*° . . .   70

t, there's Vespers! *Plena gratiâ*

Ave, Virgo!° Gr-r-r—you swine!

a great text in Galatians Galatians 5:19–21. The brother is re-
embering hazily. (We may be expected to think of Galatians 6:7:
hatsoever a man soweth, that shall he also reap." The irony
uld anticipate that of "The Heretic's Tragedy.") **56 Manichee**
re used generally for heretic. **70 Hy, Zy, Hine** apparently begin-
ag of a curse. **71-72 Plena . . . Virgo!** hail Virgin, full of grace.
rsion of the prayer "Hail Mary" (Ave Maria).

RUDEL TO THE LADY OF TRIPOLI°

I

I KNOW a Mount, the gracious Sun perceives
First, when he visits, last, too, when he leaves
The world; and, vainly favored, it repays
The day-long glory of his steadfast gaze
5 By no change of its large calm front of snow.
And underneath the Mount, a Flower I know,
He cannot have perceived, that changes ever
At his approach; and, in the lost endeavor
To live his life, has parted, one by one,
10 With all a flower's true graces, for the grace
Of being but a foolish mimic sun,
With ray-like florets round a disk-like face.
Men nobly call by many a name the Mount
As over many a land of theirs its large
15 Calm front of snow like a triumphal targe°
Is reared, and still with old names, fresh names vie,
Each to its proper praise and own account:
Men call the Flower the Sunflower, sportively.

II

Oh, Angel of the East, one, one gold look
20 Across the waters to this twilight nook,
—The far sad waters, Angel, to this nook!

III

Dear Pilgrim, art thou for the East indeed?

Rudel . . . Tripoli Geoffrey Rudel was a troubadour of the twelft
century. He fell in love with a Countess of Tripoli, whom he kne
only by report. There is a legend that he went to Tripoli and died
his lady's arms.   **15 targe** shield.

Go!—saying ever as thou dost proceed,
That I, French Rudel, choose for my device
A sunflower outspread like a sacrifice   25
Before its idol. See! These inexpert
And hurried fingers could not fail to hurt
The woven picture; 'tis a woman's skill
Indeed; but nothing baffled me, so, ill
Or well, the work is finished. Say, men feed   30
On songs I sing, and therefore bask the bees
On my flower's breast as on a platform broad:
But, as the flower's concern is not for these
But solely for the sun, so men applaud
In vain this Rudel, he not looking here   35
But to the East—the East! Go, say this, Pilgrim dear!

JOHANNES AGRICOLA° IN MEDITATION

THERE's heaven above, and night by night
    I look right through its gorgeous roof;
No suns and moons though e'er so bright
    Avail to stop me; splendor-proof
    I keep the broods of stars aloof: 5
For I intend to get to God,
    For 'tis to God I speed so fast,
For in God's breast, my own abode,
    Those shoals of dazzling glory, passed,
    I lay my spirit down at last.   10
I lie where I have always lain,

Johannes Agricola taught that the moral law did not apply to persons saved by God's grace. This and the following poem were first published together under the title of "Madhouse Cells."

God smiles as he has always smiled;
Ere suns and moons could wax and wane,
   Ere stars were thundergirt, or piled
15   The heavens, God thought on me his child;
Ordained a life for me, arrayed
   Its circumstances every one
To the minutest; ay, God said
   This head this hand should rest upon
20   Thus, ere he fashioned star or sun.
And having thus created me,
   Thus rooted me, he bade me grow,
Guiltless forever, like a tree
   That buds and blooms, nor seeks to know
25   The law by which it prospers so:
But sure that thought and word and deed
   All go to swell his love for me,
Me, made because that love had need
   Of something irreversibly
30   Pledged solely its content to be.
Yes, yes, a tree which must ascend,
   No poison-gourd foredoomed to stoop.
I have God's warrant, could I blend
   All hideous sins, as in a cup,
35   To drink the mingled venoms up;
Secure my nature will convert
   The draught to blossoming gladness fast:
While sweet dews turn to the gourd's hurt,
   And bloat, and while they bloat it, blast,
40   As from the first its lot was cast.
For as I lie, smiled on, full-fed
   By unexhausted power to bless,
I gaze below on hell's fierce bed,
   And those its waves of flame oppress,
45   Swarming in ghastly wretchedness;
Whose life on earth aspired to be
   One altar-smoke, so pure!—to win
If not love like God's love for me,
   At least to keep his anger in;
50   And all their striving turned to sin.
Priest, doctor, hermit, monk grown white

With prayer, the broken-hearted nun,
The martyr, the wan acolyte,
  The incense-swinging child—undone
Before God fashioned star or sun!   *55*
God, whom I praise; how could I praise,
  If such as I might understand,
Make out and reckon on his ways,
  And bargain for his love, and stand,
  Paying a price, at his right hand?   *60*

PORPHYRIA'S LOVER

THE rain set early in tonight,
  The sullen wind was soon awake,
It tore the elm-tops down for spite,
  And did its worst to vex the lake:
  I listened with heart fit to break.   *5*
When glided in Porphyria; straight
  She shut the cold out and the storm,
And kneeled and made the cheerless grate
  Blaze up, and all the cottage warm;
  Which done, she rose, and from her form   *10*
Withdrew the dripping cloak and shawl,
  And laid her soiled gloves by, untied
Her hat and let the damp hair fall,
  And, last, she sat down by my side
  And called me. When no voice replied,   *15*
She put my arm about her waist,
  And made her smooth white shoulder bare,
And all her yellow hair displaced,
  And, stooping, made my cheek lie there,
  And spread, o'er all, her yellow hair,   *20*

Murmuring how she loved me—she
  Too weak, for all her heart's endeavor,
To set its struggling passion free
  From pride, and vainer ties dissever,
25   And give herself to me forever.
But passion sometimes would prevail,
  Nor could tonight's gay feast restrain
A sudden thought of one so pale
  For love of her, and all in vain:
30   So, she was come through wind and rain.
Be sure I looked up at her eyes
  Happy and proud; at last I knew
Porphyria worshipped me; surprise
  Made my heart swell, and still it grew
35   While I debated what to do.
That moment she was mine, mine, fair,
  Perfectly pure and good: I found
A thing to do, and all her hair
  In one long yellow string I wound
40   Three times her little throat around,
And strangled her. No pain felt she;
  I am quite sure she felt no pain.
As a shut bud that holds a bee,
  I warily oped her lids: again
45   Laughed the blue eyes without a stain.
And I untightened next the tress
  About her neck; her cheek once more
Blushed bright beneath my burning kiss:
  I propped her head up as before,
50   Only, this time my shoulder bore
Her head, which droops upon it still:
  The smiling rosy little head,
So glad it has its utmost will,
  That all it scorned at once is fled,
55   And I, its love, am gained instead!
Porphyria's love: she guessed not how
  Her darling one wish would be heard.
And thus we sit together now,
  And all night long we have not stirred,
60   And yet God has not said a word!

COLOMBE'S BIRTHDAY

A PLAY
(1844)

IVY and violet, what do ye here
With blossom and shoot in the warm spring-weather,
Hiding the arms of Monchenci and Vere?—HANMER.

PERSONS

COLOMBE OF RAVESTEIN, Duchess of Juliers and
    Cleves°
SABYNE, ADOLF, *her attendants*
GUIBERT, GAUCELME, MAUFROY, CLUGNET, *courtiers*
VALENCE, *advocate of Cleves*
PRINCE BERTHOLD, *claimant of the Duchy*
MELCHIOR, *his confidant*

PLACE—*The Palace at Juliers*
TIME, 16—

° Juliers and Cleves on the northern Rhine.

ACT I

MORNING

SCENE—*A corridor leading to the Audience-chamber*

GAUCELME, CLUGNET, MAUFROY *and other* Courtiers,
round GUIBERT, *who is silently reading a paper:
as he drops it at the end—*

Guibert. That this should be her birthday; and the day
We all invested her, twelve months ago,
As the late Duke's true heiress and our liege;
And that this also must become the day . . .
Oh, miserable lady!

5 *1st Courtier.*   Ay, indeed?

2nd Courtier. Well, Guibert?

3rd Courtier. But your news, my friend, your news!
The sooner, friend, one learns Prince Berthold's
      pleasure,
The better for us all: how writes the Prince?
Give me! I'll read it for the common good.

10 *Guibert.* In time, sir—but till time comes, pardon me!
Our old Duke just disclosed his child's retreat,
Declared her true succession to his rule,
And died: this birthday was the day, last year,
We convoyed her from Castle Ravestein—
15 That sleeps out trustfully its extreme age
On the Meuse' quiet bank, where she lived queen
Over the water-buds—to Juliers' court
With joy and bustle. Here again we stand;
Sir Gaucelme's buckle's constant to his cap:
20 Today's much such another sunny day!

Gaucelme. Come, Guibert, this outgrows a jest, I
      think!

You're hardly such a novice as to need
The lesson, you pretend.

Guibert.   What lesson, sir?
That everybody, if he'd thrive at court,
Should, first and last of all, look to himself?   25
Why, no: and therefore with your good example,
(—Ho, Master Adolf!)—to myself I'll look.

Enter ADOLF.

Guibert. The Prince's letter; why, of all men else,
Comes it to me?

Adolf.   By virtue of your place,
Sir Guibert! 'Twas the Prince's express charge,   30
His envoy told us, that the missive there
Should only reach our lady by the hand
Of whosoever held your place.

Guibert.   Enough: [ADOLF *retires.*]
Then, gentles, who'll accept a certain poor
Indifferently honorable place,   35
My friends, I make no doubt, have gnashed their
    teeth
At leisure minutes these half-dozen years,
To find me never in the mood to quit?
Who asks may have it, with my blessing, and—
This to present our lady. Who'll accept?   40
You—you—you? There it lies, and may, for me!

Maufroy [*a youth, picking up the paper, reads aloud*].
"Prince Berthold, proved by titles following
Undoubted Lord of Juliers, comes this day
To claim his own, with license from the Pope,
The Emperor, the Kings of Spain and France" . . .   45

Gaucelme. Sufficient "titles following," I judge!
Don't read another! Well—"to claim his own"?

Maufroy. "—And take possession of the Duchy held
Since twelve months, to the true heir's prejudice,
By" . . . Colombe, Juliers' mistress, so she thinks,   50
And Ravestein's mere lady, as we find.

Who wants the place and paper? Guibert's right.
I hope to climb a little in the world—
I'd push my fortunes—but, no more than he,
55   Could tell her on this happy day of days,
That, save the nosegay in her hand, perhaps,
There's nothing left to call her own. Sir Clugnet,
You famish for promotion; what say you?

Clugnet [*an old man*]. To give this letter were a sort,
     I take it,
60   Of service: services ask recompense:
What kind of corner may be Ravestein?

Guibert. The castle? Oh, you'd share her fortunes?
     Good!
Three walls stand upright, full as good as four,
With no such bad remainder of a roof.

Clugnet. Oh—but the town?

65   *Guibert*.   Five houses, fifteen huts;
A church whereto was once a spire, 'tis judged;
And half a dike, except in time of thaw.

Clugnet. Still, there's some revenue?

Guibert.   Else Heaven forfend!
You hang a beacon out, should fogs increase;
70   So, when the autumn floats of pinewood steer
Safe 'mid the white confusion, thanks to you,
Their grateful raftsman flings a guilder° in;
—That's if he mean to pass your way next time.

Clugnet. If not?

Guibert.   Hang guilders, then! He blesses you.

Clugnet. What man do you suppose me? Keep your
75   paper!
And, let me say, it shows no handsome spirit
To dally with misfortune: keep your place!

Gaucelme. Someone must tell her.

---

72 **guilder** Dutch coin.

Guibert.   Someone may: you may!

Gaucelme. Sir Guibert, 'tis no trifle turns me sick
  Of court-hypocrisy at years like mine,   80
  But this goes near it. Where's there news at all?
  Who'll have the face, for instance, to affirm
  He never heard, e'en while we crowned the girl,
  That Juliers' tenure was by Salic law;°
  That one, confessed her father's cousin's child,   85
  And, she away, indisputable heir,
  Against our choice protesting and the Duke's,
  Claimed Juliers?—nor, as he preferred his claim,
  That first this, then another potentate,
  Inclined to its allowance?—I or you,   90
  Or any one except the lady's self?
  Oh, it had been the direst cruelty
  To break the business to her! Things might change:
  At all events, we'd see next masque at end,
  Next mummery over first: and so the edge   95
  Was taken off sharp tidings as they came,
  Till here's the Prince upon us, and there's she
  —Wreathing her hair, a song between her lips,
  With just the faintest notion possible
  That some such claimant earns a livelihood   100
  About the world, by feigning grievances—
  Few pay the story of, but grudge its price,
  And fewer listen to, a second time.
  Your method proves a failure; now try mine!
  And, since this must be carried . . .

Guibert [*snatching the paper from him*]. By your
    leave!   105
  Your zeal transports you! 'Twill not serve the Prince
  So much as you expect, this course you'd take.
  If she leaves quietly her palace—well;
  But if she died upon its threshold—no:
  He'd have the trouble of removing her.   110
  Come, gentles, we're all—what the devil knows!
  You, Gaucelme, won't lose character, beside:

---

84 **Salic law** forbidding inheritance by women.

You broke your father's heart superiorly
To gather his succession—never blush!
115 You're from my province, and, be comforted,
They tell of it with wonder to this day.
You can afford to let your talent sleep.
We'll take the very worst supposed, as true:
There, the old Duke knew, when he hid his child
120 Among the river-flowers at Ravestein,
With whom the right lay! Call the Prince our Duke!
There, she's no Duchess, she's no anything
More than a young maid with the bluest eyes:
And now, sirs, we'll not break this young maid's
    heart
125 Coolly as Gaucelme could and would! No haste!
His talent's full-blown, ours but in the bud:
We'll not advance to his perfection yet—
Will we, Sir Maufroy? See, I've ruined Maufroy
Forever as a courtier!

Gaucelme.   Here's a coil!°
130 And, count us, will you? Count its residue,
This boasted convoy, this day last year's crowd!
A birthday, too, a·gratulation day!
I'm dumb: bid that keep silence!

Maufroy and others.   Eh, Sir Guibert?
He's right: that does say something: that's bare
    truth.
135 Ten—twelve, I make: a perilous dropping off!

Guibert. Pooh—is it audience hour? The vestibule
Swarms too, I wager, with the common sort
That want our privilege of entry here.

Gaucelme. Adolf! [*Reenter* ADOLF.] Who's outside?

Guibert.   Oh, your looks suffice!
Nobody waiting?

Maufroy [*looking through the door-folds*]. Scarce our
    number!

129 **coil** disturbance.

Guibert.   'Sdeath!   *140*
Nothing to beg for, to complain about?
It can't be! Ill news spreads, but not so fast
As thus to frighten all the world!

Gaucelme.   The world
Lives out of doors, sir—not with you and me
By presence-chamber porches, stateroom stairs,   *145*
Wherever warmth's perpetual: outside's free
To every wind from every compass point,
And who may get nipped needs be weather-wise.
The Prince comes and the lady's People go;
The snow-goose settles down, the swallows flee—   *150*
Why should they wait for winter-time? 'Tis instinct.
Don't you feel somewhat chilly?

Guibert.   That's their craft?
And last year's crowders-round and criers-forth
That strewed the garlands, overarched the roads,
Lighted the bonfires, sang the loyal songs!   *155*
Well 'tis my comfort, you could never call me
The People's Friend! The People keep their word—
I keep my place: don't doubt I'll entertain
The People when the Prince comes, and the People
Are talked of! Then, their speeches—no one tongue   *160*
Found respite, not a pen had holiday
—For they wrote, too, as well as spoke, these
   knaves!
Now see: we tax and tithe them, pill and poll,°
They wince and fret enough, but pay they must
—We manage that—so, pay with a good grace   *165*
They might as well, it costs so little more.
But when we've done with taxes, meet folk next
Outside the tollbooth and the rating-place,
In public—there they have us if they will,
We're at their mercy after that, you see!   *170*
For one tax not ten devils could extort—
Over and above necessity, a grace;
This prompt disbosoming of love, to wit—

Their vine-leaf wrappage of our tribute penny,
175 And crowning attestation, all works well.
Yet this precisely do they thrust on us!
These cappings quick, these crook-and-cringings
        low,
Hand to the heart, and forehead to the knee,
With grin that shuts the eyes and opes the mouth—
180 So tender they their love; and, tender made,
Go home to curse us, the first doit we ask.
As if their souls were any longer theirs!
As if they had not given ample warrant
To who should clap a collar on their neck,
185 Rings in their nose, a goad to either flank,
And take them for the brute they boast themselves!
Stay—there's a bustle at the outer door—
And somebody entreating . . . that's my name!
Adolf—I heard my name!

Adolf.   'Twas probably
The suitor.

Guibert. Oh, there is one?

190 *Adolf.*   With a suit
He'd fain enforce in person.

Guibert.   The good heart
—And the great fool! Just ope the mid-door's fold!
Is that a lappet of his cloak, I see?

Adolf. If it bear plenteous sign of travel . . . ay,
The very cloak my comrades tore!

195 *Guibert.*   Why tore?

Adolf. He seeks the Duchess' presence in that trim:
Since daybreak, was he posted hereabouts
Lest he should miss the moment.

Guibert.   Where's he now?

Adolf. Gone for a minute possibly, not more:
200 They have ado enough to thrust him back.

Guibert. Ay—but my name, I caught?

Adolf.   Oh, sir—he said
—What was it?—You had known him formerly,
And, he believed, would help him did you guess
He waited now; you promised him as much:
The old plea! 'Faith, he's back—renews the charge! *205*

[*Speaking at the door.*] So long as the man parleys,
    peace outside—
  Nor be too ready with your halberts,° there!

Gaucelme. My horse bespattered, as he blocked the
    path
  A thin sour man, not unlike somebody.

Adolf. He holds a paper in his breast, whereon   *210*
  He glances when his cheeks flush and his brow
  At each repulse—

Gaucelme.   I noticed he'd a brow.

Adolf. So glancing, he grows calmer, leans awhile
  Over the balustrade, adjusts his dress,
  And presently turns round, quiet again,   *215*
  With some new pretext for admittance.— Back!
  [*To* GUIBERT.]—Sir, he has seen you! Now cross
    halberts! Ha—
  Pascal is prostrate—there lies Fabian too!
  No passage! Whither would the madman press?
  Close the doors quick on me!

Guibert.   Too late! He's here.   *220*

Enter, hastily and with discomposed dress, VALENCE.

Valence. Sir Guibert, will you help me?—me, that
    come
  Charged by your townsmen, all who starve at
    Cleves,
  To represent their heights and depths of woe
  Before our Duchess and obtain relief!
  Such errands barricade such doors, it seems: *225*
  But not a common hindrance drives me back
  On all the sad yet hopeful faces, lit

207 **halberts** weapons.

With hope for the first time, which sent me forth.
Cleves, speak for me! Cleves' men and women,
        speak!
230 Who followed me—your strongest—many a mile
That I might go the fresher from their ranks,
—Who sit—your weakest—by the city gates,
To take me fuller of what news I bring
As I return—for I must needs return!
235 —Can I? 'Twere hard, no listener for their wrongs,
To turn them back upon the old despair—
Harder, Sir Guibert, than imploring thus—
So, I do—any way you please—implore!
If you . . . but how should you remember Cleves?
240 Yet they of Cleves remember you so well!
Ay, comment on each trait of you they keep,
Your words and deeds caught up at second hand,—
Proud, I believe, at bottom of their hearts,
O' the very levity and recklessness
245 Which only prove that you forget their wrongs.
Cleves, the grand town, whose men and women
        starve,
Is Cleves forgotten? Then, remember me!
You promised me that you would help me once,
For other purpose: will you keep your word?

Guibert. And who may you be, friend?

250 *Valence.*   Valence of Cleves.

Guibert. Valence of . . . not the advocate of Cleves,
I owed my whole estate to, three years back?
Ay, well may you keep silence! Why, my lords,
You've heard, I'm sure, how, Pentecost three years,
255 I was so nearly ousted of my land
By some knave's pretext—(eh? when you refused
        me
Your ugly daughter, Clugnet!)—and you've heard
How I recovered it by miracle
—(When I refused her!) Here's the very friend,
260 —Valence of Cleves, all parties have to thank!
Nay, Valence, this procedure's vile in you!
I'm no more grateful than a courtier should,

But politic am I—I bear a brain,
Can cast about a little, might require
Your services a second time. I tried   265
To tempt you with advancement here to court
—"No!"—well, for curiosity at least
To view our life here—"No!"—our Duchess, then—
A pretty woman's worth some pains to see,
Nor is she spoiled, I take it, if a crown   270
Complete the forehead pale and tresses pure . . .

Valence. Our city trusted me its miseries,
And I am come.

Guibert.   So much for taste! But "come,"—
So may you be, for anything I know,
To beg the Pope's cross, or Sir Clugnet's daughter,   275
And with an equal chance you get all three.
If it was ever worth your while to come,
Was not the proper way worth finding too?

Valence. Straight to the palace-portal, sir, I came—

Guibert. —And said?—

Valence.   —That I had brought the miseries   280
Of a whole city to relieve.

Guibert.   —Which saying
Won your admittance? You saw me, indeed,
And here, no doubt, you stand: as certainly,
My intervention, I shall not dispute,
Procures you audience; which, if I procure—   285
That paper's closely written—by Saint Paul,
Here flock the Wrongs, follow the Remedies,
Chapter and verse, One, Two, A, B and C!
Perhaps you'd enter, make a reverence,
And launch these "miseries" from first to last?   290

Valence. How should they let me pause or turn aside?

Gaucelme [*to* VALENCE]. My worthy sir, one question!
     You've come straight
From Cleves, you tell us: heard you any talk
At Cleves about our lady?

Valence.   Much.

Gaucelme.   And what?

295 *Valence.* Her wish was to redress all wrongs she knew.

Gaucelme. That, you believed?

Valence.   You see me, sir!

Gaucelme.   —Nor stopped
  Upon the road from Cleves to Juliers here,
  For any—rumors you might find afloat?

Valence. I had my townsmen's wrongs to busy me.

300 *Gaucelme.* This is the lady's birthday, do you know?
  —Her day of pleasure?

Valence.   —That the great, I know,
  For pleasure born, should still be on the watch
  To exclude pleasure when a duty offers:
  Even as, for duty born, the lowly too
305 May ever snatch a pleasure if in reach:
  Both will have plenty of their birthright, sir!

Gaucelme [*aside to* GUIBERT]. Sir Guibert, here's your
    man! No scruples now—
  You'll never find his like! Time presses hard.
  I've seen your drift and Adolf's too, this while,
310 But you can't keep the hour of audience back
  Much longer, and at noon the Prince arrives.
  [*Pointing to* VALENCE.] Entrust him with it—fool
    no chance away!

Guibert. Him?

Gaucelme.   —With the missive! What's the man to
    her?

Guibert. No bad thought! Yet, 'tis yours, who ever
    played
315 The tempting serpent: else 'twere no bad thought!
  I should—and do—mistrust it for your sake,
  Or else . . .

Enter an Official *who communicates with* ADOLF.

Adolf. The Duchess will receive the court.

Guibert. Give us a moment, Adolf! Valence, friend,
  I'll help you. We of the service, you're to mark,
  Have special entry, while the herd . . . the folk   320
  Outside, get access through our help alone;
  —Well, it is so, was so, and I suppose
  So ever will be: your natural lot is, therefore,
  To wait your turn and opportunity,
  And probably miss both. Now, I engage   325
  To set you, here and in a minute's space,
  Before the lady, with full leave to plead
  Chapter and verse, and A, and B, and C,
  To heart's content.

Valence.   I grieve that I must ask—
  This being, yourself admit, the custom here—   330
  To what the price of such a favor mounts?

Guibert. Just so! You're not without a courtier's tact.
  Little at court, as your quick instinct prompts,
  Do such as we without a recompense.

Valence. Yours is?—

Guibert.   A trifle: here's a document   335
  'Tis someone's duty to present her Grace—
  I say, not mine—these say, not theirs—such points
  Have weight at court. Will you relieve us all
  And take it? Just say, "I am bidden lay
  This paper at the Duchess' feet!"

Valence.   No more?   340
  I thank you, sir!

Adolf.   Her Grace receives the court,

Guibert [*aside*]. Now, *sursum corda*,° quoth the mass
    priest! Do—

342 **sursum corda** lift up your hearts (beginning of the most solemn
part of the Mass).

Whoever's my kind saint, do let alone
These pushings to and fro, and pullings back;
345 Peaceably let me hang o' the devil's arm
The downward path, if you can't pluck me off
Completely! Let me live quite his, or yours!
    [*The* Courtiers *begin to range themselves, and*
       move toward the door.]
After me, Valence! So, our famous Cleves
Lacks bread? Yet don't we gallants buy their lace?
350 And dear enough—it beggars me, I know,
To keep my very gloves fringed properly.
This, Valence, is our Great State Hall you cross;
Yon gray urn's veritable marcasite,
The Pope's gift: and those salvers testify
355 The Emperor. Presently you'll set your foot
. . . But you don't speak, friend Valence!

Valence.   I shall speak.

Gaucelme [*aside to* GUIBERT]. Guibert—it were no
    such ungraceful thing
If you and I, at first, seemed horror-struck
With the bad news. Look here, what you shall do.
360 Suppose you, first, clap hand to sword and cry
"Yield strangers our allegiance? First I'll perish
Beside your Grace!"—and so give me the cue
To . . .

Guibert. —Clap your hand to notebook and jot down
That to regale the Prince with? I conceive.
    [*To* VALENCE.] Do, Valence, speak, or I shall half
365 suspect
You're plotting to supplant us, me the first,
I' the lady's favor! Is't the grand harangue
You mean to make, that thus engrosses you?
—Which of her virtues you'll apostrophize?
370 Or is 't the fashion you aspire to start,
Of that close-curled, not unbecoming hair?
Or what else ponder you?

Valence.   My townsmen's wrongs.

ACT II

NOON

SCENE—*The Presence-chamber*

The DUCHESS *and* SABYNE.

The Duchess. Announce that I am ready for the court!

Sabyne. 'Tis scarcely audience-hour, I think; your Grace
May best consult your own relief, no doubt,
And shun the crowd: but few can have arrived.

The Duchess. Let those not yet arrived, then, keep away!   *5*
'Twas me, this day last year at Ravestein,
You hurried. It has been full time, beside,
This half-hour. Do you hesitate?

Sabyne.   Forgive me!

The Duchess. Stay, Sabyne; let me hasten to make sure
Of one true thanker: here with you begins   *10*
My audience, claim you first its privilege!
It is my birth's event they celebrate:
You need not wish me more such happy days,
But—ask some favor! Have you none to ask?
Has Adolf none, then? this was far from least   *15*
Of much I waited for impatiently,
Assure yourself! It seemed so natural
Your gift, beside this bunch of river-bells,
Should be the power and leave of doing good
To you, and greater pleasure to myself.   *20*
You ask my leave today to marry Adolf?
The rest is my concern.

Sabyne.   Your Grace is ever
Our lady of dear Ravestein,—but, for Adolf . . .

The Duchess. "But"? You have not, sure, changed in
    your regard
And purpose towards him?

Sabyne.   We change?

25 *The Duchess.*   Well then? Well?

Sabyne. How could we two be happy, and, most like,
    Leave Juliers, when—when . . . but 'tis audience-
    time!

The Duchess. "When, if you left me, I were left in-
    deed!"
Would you subjoin that?—Bid the court approach!
—Why should we play thus with each other,
30   Sabyne?
Do I not know, if courtiers prove remiss,
If friends detain me, and get blame for it,
There is a cause? Of last year's fervid throng
Scarce one half comes now.

Sabyne [*aside*].   One half? No, alas!

35 *The Duchess.* So can the mere suspicion of a cloud
Over my fortunes, strike each loyal heart.
They've heard of this Prince Berthold; and, forsooth,
Some foolish arrogant pretense he makes,
May grow more foolish and more arrogant,
40   They please to apprehend! I thank their love.
Admit them!

Sabyne [*aside*]. How much has she really learned?

The Duchess. Surely, whoever's absent, Tristan waits?
—Or at least Romuald, whom my father raised
From nothing—come, he's faithful to me, come!
45   (Sabyne, I should but be the prouder—yes,
The fitter to comport myself aright)
Not Romuald? Xavier—what said he to that?
For Xavier hates a parasite, I know!
                              [SABYNE *goes out.*]

The Duchess. Well, sunshine's everywhere, and summer too.

  Next year 'tis the old place again, perhaps—   *50*
  The water-breeze again, the birds again.
  —It cannot be! It is too late to be!
  What part had I, or choice in all of it?
  Hither they brought me; I had not to think
  Nor care, concern myself with doing good   *55*
  Or ill, my task was just—to live—to live,
  And, answering ends there was no need explain,
  To render Juliers happy—so they said.
  All could not have been falsehood: some was love,
  And wonder and obedience. I did all   *60*
  They looked for: why then cease to do it now?
  Yet this is to be calmly set aside,
  And—ere next birthday's dawn, for aught I know,
  Things change, a claimant may arrive, and I . . .
  It cannot nor it shall not be! His right?   *65*
  Well then, he has the right, and I have not,
  —But who bade all of you surround my life
  And close its growth up with your ducal crown
  Which, plucked off rudely, leaves me perishing?
  I could have been like one of you—loved, hoped,   *70*
  Feared, lived and died like one of you—but you
  Would take that life away and give me this,
  And I will keep this! I will face you! Come!

      Enter the Courtiers *and* VALENCE.

The Courtiers. Many such happy mornings to your Grace!

The Duchess [*aside, as they pay their devoir°*]. The
  same words, the same faces—the same love!   *75*
  I have been overfearful. These are few;
  But these, at least, stand firmly: these are mine.
  As many come as may; and if no more,
  'Tis that these few suffice—they do suffice!
  What succor may not next year bring me? Plainly,   *80*

75 devoir homage.

I feared too soon. [*To the* Courtiers.] I thank you,
   sirs: all thanks!

Valence [*aside, as the* DUCHESS *passes from one group
             to another, conversing*].

'Tis she—the vision this day last year brought,
When, for a golden moment at our Cleves,
She tarried in her progress hither. Cleves
85   Chose me to speak its welcome, and I spoke
    —Not that she could have noted the recluse
    —Ungainly, old before his time—who gazed.
Well, Heaven's gifts are not wasted, and that gaze
Kept, and shall keep me to the end, her own!
90   She was above it—but so would not sink
My gaze to earth! The People caught it, hers—
Thenceforward, mine; but thus entirely mine,
Who shall affirm, had she not raised my soul
Ere she retired and left me—them? She turns—
95   There's all her wondrous face at once! The ground
Reels and . . . [*suddenly occupying himself with
       his paper*]
            These wrongs of theirs I have to plead!

The Duchess [*to the* Courtiers]. Nay, compliment
   enough! and kindness' self
Should pause before it wish me more such years.
'Twas fortunate that thus, ere youth escaped,
100 I tasted life's pure pleasure—one such, pure,
Is worth a thousand, mixed—and youth's for pleas-
    ure:
Mine is received; let my age pay for it.

Gaucelme. So, pay, and pleasure paid for, thinks your
   Grace,
Should never go together?

Guibert.   How, Sir Gaucelme?
105 Hurry one's feast down unenjoyingly
At the snatched breathing-intervals of work?
As good you saved it till the dull day's end

When, stiff and sleepy, appetite is gone.
Eat first, then work upon the strength of food!

The Duchess. True: you enable me to risk my future,   *110*
By giving me a past beyond recall.
I lived, a girl, one happy leisure year:
Let me endeavor to be the Duchess now!
And so—what news, Sir Guibert, spoke you of?
    [*As they advance a little, and* GUIBERT *speaks—*]
—That gentleman?

Valence [*aside*].   I feel her eyes on me.   *113*

Guibert [*to* VALENCE]. The Duchess, sir, inclines to
    hear your suit.
Advance! He is from Cleves.

Valence [*coming forward. Aside*]. Their wrongs—their
    wrongs!

The Duchess. And you, sir, are from Cleves? How
    fresh in mind,
The hour or two I passed at queenly Cleves!
She entertained me bravely, but the best   *120*
Of her good pageant seemed its standers-by
With insuppressive joy on every face!
What says my ancient famous happy Cleves?

Valence. Take the truth, lady—you are made for
    truth!
So think my friends: nor do they less deserve   *125*
The having you to take it, you shall think,
When you know all—nay, when you only know
How, on that day you recollect at Cleves,
When the poor acquiescing multitude
Who thrust themselves with all their woes apart   *130*
Into unnoticed corners, that the few,
Their means sufficed to muster trappings for,
Might fill the foreground, occupy your sight
With joyous faces fit to bear away
And boast of as a sample of all Cleves   *135*
—How, when to daylight these crept out once more,

Clutching, unconscious, each his empty rags
Whence the scant coin, which had not half bought
   bread,
That morn he shook forth, counted piece by piece,
140 And, well-advisedly, on perfumes spent them
To burn, or flowers to strew, before your path
—How, when the golden flood of music and bliss
Ebbed, as their moon retreated, and again
Left the sharp black-point rocks of misery bare
145 —Then I, their friend, had only to suggest
"Saw she the horror as she saw the pomp!"
And as one man they cried "He speaks the truth:
Show her the horror! Take from our own mouths
Our wrongs and show them, she will see them too!"
150 This they cried, lady! I have brought the wrongs.

The Duchess. Wrongs? Cleves has wrongs—apparent
   now and thus?
I thank you! In that paper? Give it me!

Valence. (There, Cleves!) In this! (What did I prom-
   ise, Cleves?)
Our weavers, clothiers, spinners are reduced
155 Since . . . Oh, I crave your pardon! I forget
I buy the privilege of this approach,
And promptly would discharge my debt. I lay
This paper humbly at the Duchess' feet.
                  [*Presenting* GUIBERT'S *paper.*]

Guibert. Stay! for the present . . .

The Duchess.   Stay, sir? I take aught
160 That teaches me their wrongs with greater pride
Than this your ducal circlet. Thank you, sir!

        [*The* DUCHESS *reads hastily; then, turning
                 to the* Courtiers—]

What have I done to you? Your deed or mine
Was it, this crowning me? I gave myself
No more a title to your homage, no,
Than church-flowers, born this season, wrote the
165 words

In the saint's-book that sanctified them first.
For such a flower, you plucked me; well, you erred—
Well, 'twas a weed; remove the eyesore quick!
But should you not remember it has lain
Steeped in the candles' glory, palely shrined,   170
Nearer God's Mother than most earthly things?
—That if't be faded 'tis with prayer's sole breath—
That the one day it boasted was God's day?
Still, I do thank you! Had you used respect,
Here might I dwindle to my last white leaf,   175
Here lose life's latest freshness, which even yet
May yield some wandering insect rest and food:
So, fling me forth, and—all is best for all!
[*After a pause.*] Prince Berthold, who art Juliers'
    Duke it seems—
The King's choice, and the Emperor's, and the
    Pope's—   180
Be mine, too! Take this People! Tell not me
Of rescripts, precedents, authorities,
—But take them, from a heart that yearns to give!
Find out their love—I could not; find their fear—
I would not; find their like—I never shall,   185
Among the flowers!   [*Taking off her coronet.*]
            Colombe of Ravestein
Thanks God she is no longer Duchess here!

Valence [*advancing to* GUIBERT]. Sir Guibert, knight,
    they call you—this of mine
Is the first step I ever set at court.
You dared make me your instrument, I find;   190
For that, so sure as you and I are men,
We reckon to the utmost presently:
But as you are a courtier and I none,
Your knowledge may instruct me. I, already,
Have too far outraged, by my ignorance   195
Of courtier-ways, this lady, to proceed
A second step and risk addressing her:
—I am degraded—you let me address!
Out of her presence, all is plain enough
What I shall do—but in her presence, too,   200

Surely there's something proper to be done.
[*To the others.*] You, gentles, tell me if I guess
    aright—
May I not strike this man to earth?

The Courtiers [*as* GUIBERT *springs forward, withhold-
        ing him*].   Let go!
—The clothiers' spokesman, Guibert? Grace a
    churl?

The Duchess [*to* VALENCE]. Oh, be acquainted with
203   your party, sir!
He's of the oldest lineage Juliers boasts;
A lion crests him for a cognizance;
"Scorning to waver"—that's his 'scutcheon's word;°
His office with the new Duke—probably
210 The same in honor as with me; or more,
By so much as this gallant turn deserves.
He's now, I dare say, of a thousand times
The rank and influence that remain with her
Whose part you take! So, lest for taking it
You suffer . . .

213 *Valence.*   I may strike him then to earth?

Guibert [*falling on his knee*]. Great and dear lady, par-
        don me! Hear once!
Believe me and be merciful—be just!
I could not bring myself to give that paper
Without a keener pang than I dared meet
220 —And so felt Clugnet here, and Maufroy here
—No one dared meet it. Protestation's cheap,—
But, if to die for you did any good,
[*To* GAUCELME.] Would not I die, sir? Say your
        worst of me!
But it does no good, that's the mournful truth.
223 And since the hint of a resistance, even,
Would just precipitate, on you the first,
A speedier ruin—I shall not deny,
Saving myself indubitable pain,

207-8 **lion . . . word** his "device" (heraldic insignia) bore a lion as
its crest; his coat of arms bore the motto given.

I thought to give you pleasure (who might say?)
By showing that your only subject found   230
To carry the sad notice, was the man
Precisely ignorant of its contents;
A nameless, mere provincial advocate;
One whom 'twas like you never saw before,
Never would see again. All has gone wrong;   235
But I meant right, God knows, and you, I trust!

The Duchess. A nameless advocate, this gentleman?
—(I pardon you, Sir Guibert!)

Guibert [*rising, to* VALENCE]. Sir, and you?

Valence. —Rejoice that you are lightened of a load.
Now, you have only me to reckon with.   240

The Duchess. One I have never seen, much less
     obliged?

Valence. Dare I speak, lady?

The Duchess.   Dare you! Heard you not
I rule no longer?

Valence.   Lady, if your rule
Were based alone on such a ground as these
               [*Pointing to the* Courtiers.]
Could furnish you,—abjure it! They have hidden   245
A source of true dominion from your sight.

The Duchess. You hear them—no such source is
     left . . .

Valence.   Hear Cleves!
Whose haggard craftsmen rose to starve this day,
Starve now, and will lie down at night to starve,
Sure of a like tomorrow—but as sure   250
Of a most unlike morrow-after-that,
Since end things must, end howsoe'er things may.
What curbs the brute-force instinct in its hour?
What makes—instead of rising, all as one,
And teaching fingers, so expert to wield   255
Their tool, the broadsword's play or carbine's trick,

—What makes that there's an easier help, they
    think,
For you, whose name so few of them can spell,
Whose face scarce one in every hundred saw—
260 You simply have to understand their wrongs,
And wrongs will vanish—so, still trades are plied,
And swords lie rusting, and myself stand here?
There is a vision in the heart of each
Of justice, mercy, wisdom, tenderness
265 To wrong and pain, and knowledge of its cure:
And these embodied in a woman's form
That best transmits them, pure as first received,
From God above her, to mankind below.
Will you derive your rule from such a ground,
270 Or rather hold it by the suffrage, say,
Of this man—this—and this?

The Duchess [*after a pause*]. You come from Cleves
How many are at Cleves of such a mind?

Valence [*from his paper*]. "We, all the manufacturer
of Cleves—"

The Duchess. Or stay, sir—lest I seem too covetous—
275 Are you my subject? such as you describe,
Am I to you, though to no other man?

Valence [*from his paper*]. —"Valence, ordained you
Advocate at Cleves"—

The Duchess [*replacing the coronet*]. Then I remain
Cleves' Duchess! Take you note,
While Cleves but yields one subject of this stamp,
280 I stand her lady till she waves me off!
For her sake, all the Prince claims I withhold;
Laugh at each menace; and, his power defying,
Return his missive with its due contempt!
                     [*Casting it away*.

Guibert [*picking it up*].—Which to the Prince I will
deliver, lady,
285 (Note it down, Gaucelme)—with your message too

The Duchess. I think the office is a subject's, sir!
  —Either . . . how style you him?—my special
    guarder
  The Marshal's—for who knows but violence
  May follow the delivery?—Or, perhaps,
  My Chancellor's—for law may be to urge   *290*
  On its receipt!—Or, even my Chamberlain's—
  For I may violate established form!
  [*To* VALENCE.] Sir—for the half-hour till this service
    ends,
  Will you become all these to me?

Valence [*falling on his knee*].   My liege!

The Duchess. Give me! [*The* Courtiers *present their
    badges of office.*] [*Putting them by.*] Whatever
    was their virtue once,   *295*
  They need new consecration. [*Raising* VALENCE.]
    Are you mine?
  I will be Duchess yet!   [*She retires.*]

The Courtiers.   Our Duchess yet!
  A glorious lady! Worthy love and dread!
  I'll stand by her—And I, whate'er betide!

Guibert [*to* VALENCE]. Well done, well done, sir! I
    care not who knows,   *300*
  You have done nobly and I envy you—
  Though I am but unfairly used, I think:
  For when one gets a place like this I hold,
  One gets too the remark that its mere wages,
  The pay and the preferment, make our prize.   *305*
  Talk about zeal and faith apart from these,
  We're laughed at—much would zeal and faith sub-
    sist
  Without these also! Yet, let these be stopped,
  Our wages discontinue—then, indeed,
  Our zeal and faith (we hear on every side),   *310*
  Are not released—having been pledged away
  I wonder, for what zeal and faith in turn?
  Hard money purchased me my place! No, no—

I'm right, sir—but your wrong is better still,
315 If I had time and skill to argue it.
Therefore, I say, I'll serve you, how you please—
If you like—fight you, as you seem to wish—
(The kinder of me that, in sober truth,
I never dreamed I did you any harm) . . .

Gaucelme. —Or, kinder still, you'll introduce, no
320   doubt,
His merits to the Prince who's just at hand,
And let no hint drop he's made Chancellor
And Chamberlain and Heaven knows what beside!

Clugnet [*to* VALENCE]. You stare, young sir, and
    threaten! Let me say,
325 That at your age, when first I came to court,
I was not much above a gentleman;
While now . . .

Valence.   —You are Head-Lackey? With your
    office
I have not yet been graced, sir!

Other Courtiers [*to* CLUGNET]. Let him talk!
    Fidelity, disinterestedness,
330 Excuse so much! Men claim my worship ever
Who staunchly and steadfastly . . .

                 Enter ADOLF.

Adolf.   The Prince arrives.

Courtiers. Ha? How?

Adolf.   He leaves his guard a stage behind
At Aix, and enters almost by himself.

1st Courtier. The Prince! This foolish business puts all
    out.

2nd Courtier. Let Gaucelme speak first!

335 *3rd Courtier.*   Better I began
About the state of Juliers: should one say
All's prosperous and inviting him?

4th Courtier.   —Or rather,
  All's prostrate and imploring him?

5th Courtier.   That's best.
  Where's the Cleves' paper, by the way?

4th Courtier [*to* VALENCE].   Sir—sir—
  If you'll but lend that paper—trust it me,   340
  I'll warrant . . .

5th Courtier.   Softly, sir—the Marshal's duty!

Clugnet. Has not the Chamberlain a hearing first
  By virtue of his patent?

Gaucelme.   Patents?—Duties?
  All that, my masters, must begin again!
  One word composes the whole controversy: 345
  We're simply now—the Prince's!

The Others.   Ay—the Prince's!

                Enter SABYNE.

Sabyne. Adolf! Bid . . . Oh, no time for ceremony!
  Where's whom our lady calls her only subject?
  She needs him. Who is here the Duchess'?

Valence [*starting from his reverie*]. Most gratefully I
  follow to her feet.   350

ACT III

AFTERNOON

SCENE—*The Vestibule*

Enter PRINCE BERTHOLD *and* MELCHIOR.

Berthold. A thriving little burgh this Juliers looks.
  [*Half apart.*] Keep Juliers, and as good you kept
    Cologne:
  Better try Aix, though!—

Melchior.   Please't your Highness speak?

Berthold [*as before*]. Aix, Cologne, Frankfort—Milan;
    —Rome!—

Melchior.   The Grave.
5 More weary seems your Highness, I remark,
  Than sundry conquerors whose path I've watched
  Through fire and blood to any prize they gain.
  I could well wish you, for your proper sake,
  Had met some shade of opposition here
10 —Found a blunt seneschal° refuse unlock,
  Or a scared usher lead your steps astray.
  You must not look for next achievement's palm
  So easily: this will hurt your conquering.

Berthold. My next? Ay, as you say, my next and next!
15 Well, I am tired, that's truth, and moody too,
  This quiet entrance-morning: listen why!
  Our little burgh, now, Juliers—'tis indeed
  One link, however insignificant,
  Of the great chain by which I reach my hope,
20 —A link I must secure; but otherwise,

10 **seneschal** steward.

106

You'd wonder I esteem it worth my grasp.
Just see what life is, with its shifts and turns!
It happens now—this very nook—to be
A place that once . . . not a long while since,
    neither—
When I lived an ambiguous hanger-on   25
Of foreign courts, and bore my claims about,
Discarded by one kinsman, and the other
A poor priest merely—then, I say, this place
Shone my ambition's object; to be Duke—
Seemed then, what to be Emperor seems now.   30
My rights were far from judged as plain and sure
In those days as of late, I promise you:
And 'twas my daydream, Lady Colombe here
Might e'en compound the matter, pity me,
Be struck, say, with my chivalry and grace   35
(I was a boy!)—bestow her hand at length,
And make me Duke, in her right if not mine.
Here am I, Duke confessed, at Juliers now.
Hearken: if ever I be Emperor,
Remind me what I felt and said today!   40

Melchior. All this consoles a bookish man like me.
    —And so will weariness cling to you. Wrong,
Wrong! Had you sought the lady's court yourself—
Faced the redoubtables composing it,
Flattered this, threatened that man, bribed the
    other—   45
Pleaded by writ and word and deed, your cause—
Conquered a footing inch by painful inch—
And, after long years' struggle, pounced at last
On her for prize—the right life had been lived,
And justice done to divers faculties   50
Shut in that brow. Yourself were visible
As you stood victor, then; whom now—(your par-
    don!)
I am forced narrowly to search and see,
So are you hid by helps—this Pope, your uncle—
Your cousin, the other King! You are a mind—   55
They, body: too much of mere legs-and-arms

Obstructs the mind so! Match these with their like:
Match mind with mind!

Berthold.   And where's your mind to match?
They show me legs-and-arms to cope withal!
60   I'd subjugate this city—where's its mind?

[*The* Courtiers *enter slowly.*]

Melchior. Got out of sight when you came troops and
        all!
And in its stead, here greets you flesh-and-blood:
A smug economy of both, this first!

[*As* CLUGNET *bows obsequiously.*]

Well done, gout, all considered!—I may go?

Berthold. Help me receive them!

65   *Melchior.*   Oh, they just will say
What yesterday at Aix their fellows said—
At Treves, the day before! Sir Prince, my friend,
Why do you let your life slip thus?—Meantime,
I have my little Juliers to achieve—
70   The understanding this tough Platonist,
Your holy uncle disinterred, Amelius:
Lend me a company of horse and foot,
To help me through his tractate—gain my Duchy!

Berthold. And Empire, after that is gained, will be—?

Melchior. To help me through your uncle's comment,
75   Prince!   [*Goes.*]

Berthold. Ah? Well: he o'er-refines—the scholar's
        fault!
How do I let my life slip? Say, this life,
I lead now, differs from the common life
Of other men in mere degree, not kind,
80   Of joys and griefs—still there is such degree
Mere largeness in a life is something, sure—
Enough to care about and struggle for,
In this world: for this world, the size of things;
The sort of things, for that to come, no doubt.
85   A great is better than a little aim:

And when I wooed Priscilla's rosy mouth
And failed so, under that gray convent-wall,
Was I more happy than I should be now
[*By this time, the* Courtiers *are ranged before him.*]
If failing of my Empire? Not a whit.
—Here comes the mind, it once had tasked me sore   90
To baffle, but for my advantages!
All's best as 'tis: these scholars talk and talk.
                              [*Seats himself.*]

The Courtiers. Welcome our Prince to Juliers!—to his
    heritage!
  Our dutifullest service proffer we!

Jugnet. I, please your Highness, having exercised   95
  The function of Grand Chamberlain at court,
  With much acceptance, as men testify . . .

Berthold. I cannot greatly thank you, gentlemen!
  The Pope declares my claim to the Duchy founded
  On strictest justice—you concede it, therefore,   100
  I do not wonder: and the kings my friends
  Protest they mean to see such claim enforced—
  You easily may offer to assist.
  But there's a slight discretionary power
  To serve me in the matter, you've had long,
  Though late you use it. This is well to say—   105
  But could you not have said it months ago?
  I'm not denied my own Duke's truncheon, true—
  'Tis flung me—I stoop down, and from the ground
  Pick it, with all you placid standers-by:
  And now I have it, gems and mire at once,   110
  Grace go with it to my soiled hands, you say!

Guibert. (By Paul, the advocate our doughty friend
  Cuts the best figure!)

Gaucelme.   If our ignorance
  May have offended, sure our loyalty . . .   115

Berthold. Loyalty? Yours? Oh—of yourselves you
    speak!
  I mean the Duchess all this time, I hope!

And since I have been forced repeat my claims
As if they never had been urged before,
120   As I began, so must I end, it seems.
The formal answer to the grave demand!
What says the lady?

Courtiers [*one to another*]. 1*st Courtier.* Marshal!
    2*nd Courtier.* Orator!

Guibert. A variation of our mistress' way!
Wipe off his boots' dust, Clugnet!—that, he waits!

1*st Courtier.* Your place!

2*nd Courtier.* Just now it was your own!

125 *Guibert.*   The devil's!

Berthold [*to* GUIBERT]. Come forward, friend—you
    with the paper, there!
Is Juliers the first city I've obtained?
By this time, I may boast proficiency
In each decorum of the circumstance.
130   Give it me as she gave it—the petition,
Demand, you style it! What's required, in brief?
What title's reservation, appanage's
Allowance? I heard all at Treves, last week.

Gaucelme [*to* GUIBERT]. "Give it him as she gave it!"

Guibert.   And why not?
    [*To* BERTHOLD.] The lady crushed your summons
135   thus together,
And bade me, with the very greatest scorn
So fair a frame could hold, inform you . . .

Courtiers.   Stop—
    Idiot!

Guibert. —Inform you she denied your claim,
Defied yourself! (I tread upon his heel,
The blustering advocate!)

140 *Berthold.*   By heaven and earth!
    Dare you jest, sir?

uibert.   Did they at Treves, last week?

erthold [*starting up*]. Why then, I look much bolder
     than I knew,
And you prove better actors than I thought:
Since, as I live, I took you as you entered
For just so many dearest friends of mine,   145
Fled from the sinking to the rising power
—The sneaking'st crew, in short, I e'er despised!
Whereas, I am alone here for the moment,
With every soldier left behind at Aix!
Silence? That means the worst? I thought as much!   150
What follows next then?

Courtiers.   Gracious Prince, he raves!

Guibert. He asked the truth and why not get the
     truth?

Berthold. Am I a prisoner? Speak, will somebody?
—But why stand paltering with imbeciles?
Let me see her, or . . .

Guibert.   Her, without her leave,   155
Shall no one see: she's Duchess yet!

Courtiers [*footsteps without, as they are disputing*].
     Good chance!
She's here—the Lady Colombe's self!

Berthold.   'Tis well!
[*Aside.*] Array a handful thus against my world?
Not ill done, truly! Were not this a mind
To match one's mind with? Colombe! Let us wait!   160
I failed so, under that gray convent wall!
She comes.

Guibert. The Duchess! Strangers, range yourselves!

[*As the* DUCHESS *enters in conversation with*
VALENCE, BERTHOLD *and the* Courtiers
fall back a little.]

The Duchess. Presagefully it beats, presagefully,
My heart: the right is Berthold's and not mine.

165 *Valence.* Grant that he has the right, dare I mistrust
       Your power to acquiesce so patiently
       As you believe, in such a dream-like change
       Of fortune—change abrupt, profound, complete?

The Duchess. Ah, the first bitterness is over now!
170   Bitter I may have felt it to confront
       The truth, and ascertain those natures' value
       I had so counted on; that was a pang:
       But I did bear it, and the worst is over.
       Let the Prince take them!

Valence.   And take Juliers too?
175   —Your people without crosses, wands and chains—
       Only with hearts?

The Duchess.   There I feel guilty, sir!
       I cannot give up what I never had:
       For I ruled these, not them—these stood between.
       Shall I confess, sir? I have heard by stealth
180   Of Berthold from the first; more news and more:
       Closer and closer swam the thundercloud,
       But I was safely housed with these, I knew.
       At times when to the casement I would turn,
       At a bird's passage or a flower-trail's play,
185   I caught the storm's red glimpses on its edge—
       Yet I was sure some one of all these friends
       Would interpose: I followed the bird's flight
       Or plucked the flower: someone would interpose!

Valence. Not one thought on the People—and Cleves
       there!

The Duchess. Now, sadly conscious my real sway was
190   missed,
       Its shadow goes without so much regret:
       Else could I not again thus calmly bid you,
       Answer Prince Berthold!

Valence.   Then you acquiesce?

The Duchess. Remember over whom it was I ruled!

Guibert [*stepping forward*]. Prince Berthold, yonder,
 craves an audience, lady!   *195*

The Duchess [*to* VALENCE]. I only have to turn, and I
 shall face
 Prince Berthold! Oh, my very heart is sick!
 It is the daughter of a line of dukes
 This scornful insolent adventurer
 Will bid depart from my dead father's halls! *200*
 I shall not answer him—dispute with him—
 But, as he bids, depart! Prevent it, sir!
 Sir—but a mere day's respite! Urge for me
 —What I shall call to mind I should have urged
 When time's gone by: 'twill all be mine, you urge! *205*
 A day—an hour—that I myself may lay
 My rule down! 'Tis too sudden—must not be!
 The world's to hear of it! Once done—forever!
 How will it read, sir? How be sung about?
 Prevent it!

Berthold [*approaching*]. Your frank indignation, lady, *210*
 Cannot escape me. Overbold I seem;
 But somewhat should be pardoned my surprise
 At this reception—this defiance, rather.
 And if, for their and your sake, I rejoice
 Your virtues could inspire a trusty few   *215*
 To make such gallant stand in your behalf,
 I cannot but be sorry, for my own,
 Your friends should force me to retrace my steps:
 Since I no longer am permitted speak
 After the pleasant peaceful course prescribed *220*
 No less by courtesy than relationship—
 Which I remember, if you once forgot.
 But never must attack pass unrepelled.
 Suffer that, through you, I demand of these,
 Who controverts my claim to Juliers?

The Duchess.   —Me *225*
 You say, you do not speak to—

Berthold.   Of your subjects

I ask, then: whom do you accredit? Where
Stand those should answer?

Valence [*advancing*].   The lady is alone.

Berthold. Alone, and thus? So weak and yet so bold?

Valence. I said she was alone—

230 *Berthold.*   And weak, I said.

Valence. When is man strong until he feels alone?
It was some lonely strength at first, be sure,
Created organs, such as those you seek,
By which to give its varied purpose shape:
235 And, naming the selected ministrants,
Took sword, and shield, and scepter—each, a man!
That strength performed its work and passed its
          way:
You see our lady: there, the old shapes stand!
—A Marshal, Chamberlain, and Chancellor—
240 "Be helped their way, into their death put life
And find advantage!"—so you counsel us.
But let strength feel alone, seek help itself—
And, as the inland-hatched sea-creature hunts
The sea's breast out—as, littered 'mid the waves
245 The desert-brute makes for the desert's joy—
So turns our lady to her true resource,
Passing o'er hollow fictions, worn-out types,
—And I am first her instinct fastens on.
And prompt I say, as clear as heart can speak,
250 The People will not have you; nor shall have!
It is not merely I shall go bring Cleves
And fight you to the last—though that does much,
And men and children—ay, and women too,
Fighting for home, are rather to be feared
255 Than mercenaries fighting for their pay—
But, say you beat us, since such things have been,
And, where this Juliers laughed, you set your foot
Upon a steaming bloody plash—what then?
Stand you the more our lord that there you stand?
260 Lord it o'er troops whose force you concentrate,

A pillared flame whereto all ardors tend—
Lord it 'mid priests whose schemes you amplify,
A cloud of smoke 'neath which all shadows brood—
But never, in this gentle spot of earth,
Can you become our Colombe, our play-queen,   265
For whom, to furnish lilies for her hair,
We'd pour our veins forth to enrich the soil.
—Our conqueror? Yes!—Our despot? Yes!—Our
    Duke?
Know yourself, know us!

Berthold [*who has been in thought*]. Know your lady,
    also!
[*Very deferentially.*]—To whom I needs must excul-
    pate myself   270
For having made a rash demand, at least.
Wherefore to you, sir, who appear to be
Her chief adviser, I submit my claims,
                                    [*Giving papers.*]
But, this step taken, take no further step,
Until the Duchess shall pronounce their worth.   275
Here be our meeting-place; at night, its time:
Till when I humbly take the lady's leave!

        [*He withdraws. As the* DUCHESS *turns to*
          VALENCE, *the* Courtiers *interchange
          glances and come forward a little.*]

1st Courtier. So, this was their device!

2nd Courtier. No bad device!

3rd Courtier. You'd say they love each other, Gui-
    bert's friend
From Cleves, and she, the Duchess!

4th Courtier.   —And moreover,   280
That all Prince Berthold comes for, is to help
Their loves!

5th Courtier. Pray, Guibert, what is next to do?

Guibert [*advancing*]. I laid my office at the Duchess'
    foot—

Others. And I—and I—and I!

The Duchess.   I took them, sirs.

Guibert [*apart to* VALENCE]. And now, sir, I am sim-
285   ple knight again—
Guibert, of the great ancient house, as yet
That never bore affront; whate'er your birth—
As things stand now, I recognize yourself
(If you'll accept experience of some date)
290   As like to be the leading man o' the time,
Therefore as much above me now, as I
Seemed above you this morning. Then, I offered
To fight you: will you be as generous
And now fight me?

Valence.   Ask when my life is mine!

Guibert. ('Tis hers now!)

Clugnet [*apart to* VALENCE, *as* GUIBERT *turns from*
295   *him*].   You, sir, have insulted me
Grossly—will grant me, too, the selfsame favor
You've granted him, just now, I make no question?

Valence. I promise you, as him, sir.

Clugnet.   Do you so?
Handsomely said! I hold you to it, sir.
300   You'll get me reinstated in my office
As you will Guibert!

The Duchess.   I would be alone!

[*They begin to retire slowly; as* VALENCE
is about to follow—]

Alone, sir—only with my heart: you stay!

Gaucelme. You hear that? Ah, light breaks upon me!
Cleves—
It was at Cleves some man harangued us all—
305   With great effect—so those who listened said,
My thoughts being busy elsewhere: was this he?
Guibert—your strange, disinterested man!

Your uncorrupted, if uncourtly friend!
The modest worth you mean to patronize!
He cares about no Duchesses, not he—   510
His sole concern is with the wrongs of Cleves!
What, Guibert? What, it breaks on you at last?

Guibert. Would this hall's floor were a mine's roof! I'd back
    And in her very face . . .

Gaucelme.   Apply the match
That fired the train—and where would you be,
    pray?   515

Guibert. With him!

Gaucelme.   Stand, rather, safe outside with me!
The mine's charged: shall I furnish you the match
And place you properly? To the antechamber!

Guibert. Can you?

Gaucelme.   Try me! Your friend's in fortune!

Guibert.   Quick—   520
To the antechamber! He is pale with bliss!

Gaucelme. No wonder! Mark her eyes!

Guibert.   To the antechamber!
                                    [*The* Courtiers *retire.*]

The Duchess. Sir, could you know all you have done
    for me
You were content! You spoke, and I am saved.

Valence. Be not too sanguine, lady! Ere you dream,   525
That transient flush of generosity
Fades off, perchance. The man, beside, is gone—
Him we might bend; but see, the papers here—
Inalterably his requirement stays,
And cold hard words have we to deal with now.   530
In that large eye there seemed a latent pride,
To self-denial not incompetent,
But very like to hold itself dispensed

From such a grace: however, let us hope!
335   He is a noble spirit in noble form.
I wish he less had bent that brow to smile
As with the fancy how he could subject
Himself upon occasion to—himself!
From rudeness, violence, you rest secure;
340   But do not think your Duchy rescued yet!

The Duchess. You—who have opened a new world
     to me,
Will never take the faded language up
Of that I leave? My Duchy—keeping it,
Or losing it—is that my sole world now?

345 *Valence.* Ill have I spoken if you thence despise
Juliers; although the lowest, on true grounds,
Be worth more than the highest rule, on false:
Aspire to rule, on the true grounds!

The Duchess.   Nay, hear—
False, I will never—rash, I would not be!
350   This is indeed my birthday—soul and body,
Its hours have done on me the work of years.
You hold the requisition: ponder it!
If I have right, my duty's plain: if he—
Say so, nor ever change a tone of voice!
355   At night you meet the Prince; meet me at eve!
Till when, farewell! This discomposes you?
Believe in your own nature, and its force
Of renovating mine! I take my stand
Only as under me the earth is firm:
360   So, prove the first step stable, all will prove.
That first, I choose: [*Laying her hand on his.*]—the
     next to take, choose you!   [*She withdraws.*]

Valence [*after a pause*]. What drew down this on me?
     —on me, dead once,
She thus bids live—since all I hitherto
Thought dead in me, youth's ardors and emprise,
365   Burst into life before her, as she bids
Who needs them. Whither will this reach, where
     end?

Her hand's print burns on mine. . . . Yet she's
    above—
So very far above me! All's too plain:
I served her when the others sank away,
And she rewards me as such souls reward—   570
The changed voice, the suffusion of the cheek,
The eye's acceptance, the expressive hand,
—Reward, that's little, in her generous thought,
Though all to me . . .
                  I cannot so disclaim
Heaven's gift, nor call it other than it is!   575
She loves me!
[*Looking at the* Prince's *papers.*]—Which love,
    these, perchance, forbid.
Can I decide against myself—pronounce
She is the Duchess and no mate for me?
—Cleves, help me! Teach me—every haggard
    face—
To sorrow and endure! I will do right   580
Whatever be the issue. Help me, Cleves!

ACT IV

EVENING

Scene—*An Antechamber*
Enter the Courtiers.

Maufroy. Now, then, that we may speak—how spring
    this mine?

Gaucelme. Is Guibert ready for its match? He cools!
Not so friend Valence with the Duchess there!
"Stay, Valence! Are not you my better self?"
And her cheek mantled—

5   *Guibert.*   Well, she loves him, sir:
    And more—since you will have it I grow cool—
    She's right: he's worth it.

    Gaucelme.   For his deeds today?
    Say so!

    Guibert. What should I say beside?

    Gaucelme.   Not this—
    For friendship's sake leave this for me to say—
10 That we're the dupes of an egregious cheat!
    This plain unpracticed suitor, who found way
    To the Duchess through the merest die's turn-up
    A year ago, had seen her and been seen,
    Loved and been loved.

    Guibert.   Impossible!

    Gaucelme.   —Nor say,
15 How sly and exquisite a trick, moreover,
    Was this which—taking not their stand on facts
    Boldly, for that had been endurable,
    But worming on their way by craft, they choose
    Resort to, rather—and which you and we,
20 Sheep-like, assist them in the playing-off!
    The Duchess thus parades him as preferred,
    Not on the honest ground of preference,
    Seeing first, liking more, and there an end—
    But as we all had started equally,
25 And at the close of a fair race he proved
    The only valiant, sage and loyal man.
    Herself, too, with the pretty fits and starts—
    The careless, winning, candid ignorance
    Of what the Prince might challenge or forego—
30 She had a hero in reserve! What risk
    Ran she? This deferential easy Prince
    Who brings his claims for her to ratify
    —He's just her puppet for the nonce! You'll see—
    Valence pronounces, as is equitable,
35 Against him: off goes the confederate:
    As equitably, Valence takes her hand!

The Chancellor. You run too fast: her hand, no sub-
　　ject takes.
　Do not our archives hold her father's will?
　That will provides against such accident,
　And gives next heir, Prince Berthold, the reversion　*40*
　Of Juliers, which she forfeits, wedding so.

Gaucelme. I know that, well as you—but does the
　　Prince?
　Knows Berthold, think you, that this plan, he helps,
　For Valence's ennoblement—would end,
　If crowned with the success which seems its due,　*45*
　In making him the very thing he plays,
　The actual Duke of Juliers? All agree
　That Colombe's title waived or set aside,
　He is next heir.

The Chancellor. Incontrovertibly.

Gaucelme. Guibert, your match, now, to the train!

Guibert.　　　　　　　　　　　　　　Enough!　*50*
　I'm with you: selfishness is best again.
　I thought of turning honest—what a dream!
　Let's wake now!

Gaucelme.　　　　Selfish, friend, you never were:
　'Twas but a series of revenges taken
　On your unselfishness for prospering ill.　*55*
　But now that you're grown wiser, what's our course?

Guibert. —Wait, I suppose, till Valence weds our
　　lady,
　And then, if we must needs revenge ourselves,
　Apprise the Prince.

Gaucelme.　　　　　　　—The Prince, ere then dismissed　*60*
　With thanks for playing his mock part so well?
　Tell the Prince now, sir! Ay, this very night,
　Ere he accepts his dole and goes his way,
　Explain how such a marriage makes him Duke,
　Then trust his gratitude for the surprise!

Guibert. —Our lady wedding Valence all the same　*65*

As if the penalty were undisclosed?
Good! If she loves, she'll not disown her love,
Throw Valence up. I wonder you see that.

Gaucelme. The shame of it—the suddenness and
shame!
70   Within her, the inclining heart—without,
A terrible array of witnesses—
And Valence by, to keep her to her word,
With Berthold's indignation or disgust!
We'll try it!—Not that we can venture much.
75   Her confidence we've lost forever: Berthold's
Is all to gain.

Guibert.   Tonight, then, venture we!
Yet—if lost confidence might be renewed?

Gaucelme. Never in noble natures! With the base
ones—
Twist off the crab's claw, wait a smarting-while,
80   And something grows and grows and gets to be
A mimic of the lost joint, just so like
As keeps in mind it never, never will
Replace its predecessor! Crabs do that:
But lop the lion's foot—and . . .

Guibert.   To the Prince!

Gaucelme [*aside*]. And come what will to the lion's
85   foot, I pay you,
My cat's-paw, as I long have yearned to pay.
[*Aloud.*] Footsteps! Himself! 'Tis Valence breaks
on us,
Exulting that their scheme succeeds. We'll hence—
And perfect ours! Consult the archives, first—
90   Then, fortified with knowledge, seek the Hall!

Clugnet [*to* GAUCELME *as they retire*]. You have not
smiled so since your father died!

As they retire, enter VALENCE *with papers.*

Valence. So must it be! I have examined these
With scarce a palpitating heart—so calm,

Keeping her image almost wholly off,
Setting upon myself determined watch,   95
Repelling to the uttermost his claims:
And the result is—all men would pronounce
And not I, only, the result to be—
Berthold is heir; she has no shade of right
To the distinction which divided us,   100
But, suffered to rule first, I know not why,
Her rule connived at by those Kings and Popes,
To serve some devil's purpose—now 'tis gained,
Whate'er it was, the rule expires as well.
—Valence, this rapture . . . selfish can it be?   105
Eject it from your heart, her home!—It stays!
Ah, the brave world that opens on us both!
—Do my poor townsmen so esteem it? Cleves—
I need not your pale faces! This, reward
For service done to you? Too horrible!   110
I never served you: 'twas myself I served—
Nay, served not—rather saved from punishment
Which, had I failed you then, would plague me now.
My life continues yours, and your life, mine.
But if, to take God's gift, I swerve no step—   115
Cleves! If I breathe no prayer for it—if she,
                                        [*Footsteps without.*]
Colombe, that comes now, freely gives herself—
Will Cleves require, that, turning thus to her,
I . . .

Enter Prince BERTHOLD.

                    Pardon, sir! I did not look for you
Till night, i' the Hall; nor have as yet declared   120
My judgment to the lady.

Berthold.   So I hoped.

Valence. And yet I scarcely know why that should
    check
The frank disclosure of it first to you—
What her right seems, and what, in consequence,
She will decide on.

125 *Berthold.*   That I need not ask.

Valence. You need not: I have proved the lady's
      mind:
   And, justice being to do, dare act for her.

Berthold. Doubtless she has a very noble mind.

Valence. Oh, never fear but she'll in each conjuncture
130   Bear herself bravely! She no whit depends
   On circumstance; as she adorns a throne,
   She had adorned . . .

Berthold.   A cottage—in what book
   Have I read that, of every queen that lived?
   A throne! You have not been instructed, sure,
   To forestall my request?

135 *Valence.*   'Tis granted, sir!
   My heart instructs me. I have scrutinized
   Your claims . . .

Berthold.   Ah—claims, you mean, at first pre-
      ferred?
   I come, before the hour appointed me,
   To pray you let those claims at present rest,
140   In favor of a new and stronger one.

Valence. You shall not need a stronger: on the part
   O' the lady, all you offer I accept,
   Since one clear right suffices: yours is clear.
   Propose!

Berthold. I offer her my hand.

Valence.   Your hand?

145 *Berthold.* A Duke's, yourself say; and, at no far time,
   Something here whispers me—an Emperor's.
   The lady's mind is noble: which induced
   This seizure of occasion ere my claims
   Were—settled, let us amicably say!

Valence. Your hand!

150 *Berthold.*   (He will fall down and kiss it next!)

Sir, this astonishment's too flattering,
Nor must you hold your mistress' worth so cheap.
Enhance it, rather—urge that blood is blood—
The daughter of the Burgraves, Landgraves, Mark-
    graves,
Remains their daughter! I shall scarce gainsay.   *155*
Elsewhere or here, the lady needs must rule:
Like the imperial crown's great chrysoprase,
They talk of—somewhat out of keeping there,
And yet no jewel for a meaner cap.

Valence. You wed the Duchess?

Berthold.   Cry you mercy, friend! *160*
Will the match also influence fortunes here?
A natural solicitude enough.
Be certain, no bad chance it proves for you!
However high you take your present stand,
There's prospect of a higher still remove—   *165*
For Juliers will not be my resting-place,
And, when I have to choose a substitute
To rule the little burgh, I'll think of you
Who need not give your mates a character.
And yet I doubt your fitness to supplant   *170*
The gray smooth Chamberlain: he'd hesitate
A doubt his lady could demean herself
So low as to accept me. Courage, sir!
I like your method better: feeling's play
Is franker much, and flatters me beside.   *175*

Valence. I am to say, you love her?

Berthold.   Say that too!
Love has no great concernment, thinks the world,
With a duke's marriage. How go precedents
In Juliers' story—how use Juliers' dukes?
I see you have them here in goodly row;   *180*
Yon must be Luitpold—ay, a stalwart sire!
Say, I have been arrested suddenly
In my ambition's course, its rocky course,
By this sweet flower: I fain would gather it
And then proceed: so say and speedily   *185*

—(Nor stand there like Duke Luitpold's brazen
 self!)
Enough, sir: you possess my mind, I think.
This is my claim, the others being withdrawn,
And to this be it that, i' the Hall tonight,
190 Your lady's answer comes; till when, farewell!
            [*He retires.*]

Valence [*after a pause*]. The heavens and earth stay
 as they were; my heart
Beats as it beat: the truth remains the truth.
What falls away, then, if not faith in her?
Was it my faith, that she could estimate
195 Love's value, and, such faith still guiding me,
Dare I now test her? Or grew faith so strong
Solely because no power of test was mine?

Enter the DUCHESS.

The Duchess. My fate, sir! Ah, you turn away. All's
 over.
But you are sorry for me? Be not so!
200 What I might have become, and never was,
Regret with me! What I have merely been,
Rejoice I am no longer! What I seem
Beginning now, in my new state, to be,
Hope that I am!—for, once my rights proved void,
205 This heavy roof seems easy to exchange
For the blue sky outside—my lot henceforth.

Valence. And what a lot is Berthold's!

The Duchess.   How of him?

Valence. He gathers earth's whole good into his arms;
Standing, as man now, stately, strong and wise,
210 Marching to fortune, not surprised by her.
One great aim, like a guiding-star, above—
Which tasks strength, wisdom, stateliness, to lift
His manhood to the height that takes the prize;
A prize not near—lest overlooking earth
215 He rashly spring to seize it—nor remote,
So that he rest upon his path content:

But day by day, while shimmering grows shine,
And the faint circlet prophesies the orb,
He sees so much as, just evolving these,
The stateliness, the wisdom and the strength,   220
To due completion, will suffice this life,
And lead him at his grandest to the grave.
After this star, out of a night he springs;
A beggar's cradle for the throne of thrones
He quits; so, mounting, feels each step he mounts,   225
Nor, as from each to each exultingly
He passes, overleaps one grade of joy.
This, for his own good:—with the world, each gift
Of God and man—reality, tradition,
Fancy and fact—so well environ him,   230
That as a mystic panoply they serve—
Of force, untenanted, to awe mankind,
And work his purpose out with half the world,
While he, their master, dexterously slipped
From such encumbrance, is meantime employed   235
With his own prowess on the other half.
Thus shall he prosper, every day's success
Adding, to what is he, a solid strength—
An aery might to what encircles him,
Till at the last, so life's routine lends help,   240
That as the Emperor only breathes and moves,
His shadow shall be watched, his step or stalk
Become a comfort or a portent, how
He trails his ermine take significance—
Till even his power shall cease to be most power,   245
And men shall dread his weakness more, nor dare
Peril their earth its bravest, first and best,
Its typified invincibility.
Thus shall he go on, greatening, till he ends—
The man of men, the spirit of all flesh,   250
The fiery center of an earthly world!

The Duchess. Some such a fortune I had dreamed
        should rise
    Out of my own—that is, above my power
    Seemed other, greater potencies to stretch—

Valence. For you?

255 *The Duchess.*   It was not I moved there, I think:
   But one I could—though constantly beside,
   And aye approaching—still keep distant from,
   And so adore. 'Twas a man moved there.

Valence.   Who?

The Duchess. I felt the spirit, never saw the face.

260 *Valence.* See it! 'Tis Berthold's! He enables you
   To realize your vision.

The Duchess.   Berthold?

Valence.   Duke—
   Emperor to be: he proffers you his hand.

The Duchess. Generous and princely!

Valence.   He is all of this.

The Duchess. Thanks, Berthold, for my father's sake!
   No hand
   Degrades me.

265 *Valence.*   You accept the proffered hand?

The Duchess. That he should love me!

Valence.   "Loved" I did not say.
   Had that been—love might so incline the Prince
   To the world's good, the world that's at his foot—
   I do not know, this moment, I should dare
270 Desire that you refused the world—and Cleves—
   The sacrifice he asks.

The Duchess.   Not love me, sir?

Valence. He scarce affirmed it.

The Duchess.   May not deeds affirm?

Valence. What does he? . . . Yes, yes, very much he
   does!
   All the shame saved, he thinks, and sorrow saved—

Immitigable sorrow, so he thinks— 275
Sorrow that's deeper than we dream, perchance.

he Duchess. Is not this love?

alence.   So very much he does!
For look, you can descend now gracefully:
All doubts are banished, that the world might have,
Or worst, the doubts yourself, in after-time, 280
May call up of your heart's sincereness now.
To such, reply, "I could have kept my rule—
Increased it to the utmost of my dreams—
Yet I abjured it." This, he does for you:
It is munificently much.

he Duchess.   Still "much!" 285
But why is it not love, sir? Answer me!

alence. Because not one of Berthold's words and
     looks
Had gone with love's presentment of a flower
To the beloved: because bold confidence,
Open superiority, free pride— 290
Love owns not, yet were all that Berthold owned:
Because where reason, even, finds no flaw,
Unerringly a lover's instinct may.

he Duchess. You reason, then, and doubt?

alence.   I love, and know.

he Duchess. You love? How strange! I never cast a
     thought 295
On that. Just see our selfishness! You seemed
So much my own ... I had no ground—and yet,
I never dreamed another might divide
My power with you, much less exceed it.

alence.   Lady,
I am yours wholly.

he Duchess.   Oh, no, no, not mine! 300
'Tis not the same now, never more can be.

—Your first love, doubtless. Well, what's gone from
me?
What have I lost in you?

Valence.   My heart replies—
No loss there! So, to Berthold back again:
305 This offer of his hand, he bids me make—
Its obvious magnitude is well to weigh.

The Duchess. She's . . . yes, she must be very fair for
you!

Valence. I am a simple advocate of Cleves.

The Duchess. You! With the heart and brain that so
helped me,
310 I fancied them exclusively my own,
Yet find are subject to a stronger sway!
She must be . . . tell me, is she very fair?

Valence. Most fair, beyond conception or belief.

The Duchess. Black eyes?—no matter! Colombe, the
world leads
315 Its life without you, whom your friends professed
The only woman: see how true they spoke!
One lived this while, who never saw your face,
Nor heard your voice—unless. . . . Is she from
Cleves?

Valence. Cleves knows her well.

The Duchess.   Ah—just a fancy, now!
When you poured forth the wrongs of Cleves—I
320 said,
—Thought, that is, afterward . . .

Valence.   You thought of me?

The Duchess. Of whom else? Only such great cause,
I thought,
For such effect: see what true love can do!
Cleves is his love. I almost fear to ask
325 . . . And will not. This is idling: to our work!
Admit before the Prince, without reserve,

My claims misgrounded; then may follow better
. . . . When you poured out Cleves' wrongs im-
     petuously,
Was she in your mind?

Valence.   All done was done for her
—To humble me!

The Duchess.   She will be proud at least.   *330*

Valence. She?

The Duchess. When you tell her.

Valence.   That will never be.

The Duchess. How—are there sweeter things you
     hope to tell?
No, sir! You counseled me—I counsel you
In the one point I—any woman—can.
Your worth, the first thing; let her own come next—   *335*
Say what you did through her, and she through
     you—
The praises of her beauty afterward!
Will you?

Valence. I dare not.

The Duchess.   Dare not?

Valence.   She I love
Suspects not such a love in me.

The Duchess.   You jest.

Valence. The lady is above me and away.   *340*
Not only the brave form, and the bright mind,
And the great heart, combine to press me low—
But all the world calls rank divides us.

The Duchess.   Rank!
Now grant me patience! Here's a man declares
Oracularly in another's case—   *345*
Sees the true value and the false, for them—
Nay, bids them see it, and they straight do see.
You called my court's love worthless—so it turned:

I threw away as dross my heap of wealth,
350 And here you stickle for a piece or two!
First—has she seen you?

Valence.   Yes.

The Duchess.   She loves you, then.

Valence. One flash of hope burst; then succeeded night:
And all's at darkest now. Impossible!

The Duchess. We'll try: you are—so to speak—my subject yet?

Valence. As ever—to the death.

355 *The Duchess.*   Obey me, then!

Valence. I must.

The Duchess. Approach her, and . . . no! first of all
Get more assurance. "My instructress," say,
"Was great, descended from a line of kings,
And even fair"—(wait why I say this folly)—
360 "She said, of all men, none for eloquence,
Courage, and (what cast even these to shade)
The heart they sprung from—none deserved like him
Who saved her at her need: if she said this,
What should not one I love, say?"

Valence.   Heaven—this hope—
365 Oh, lady, you are filling me with fire!

The Duchess. Say this!—nor think I bid you cast aside
One touch of all the awe and reverence;
Nay, make her proud for once to heart's content
That all this wealth of heart and soul's her own!
370 Think you are all of this—and, thinking it,
 . . . (Obey!)

Valence. I cannot choose.

The Duchess.   Then, kneel to her!
                    [VALENCE *sinks on his knee.*]
    I dream!

Valence. Have mercy! Yours, unto the death—
    I have obeyed. Despise, and let me die!

The Duchess. Alas, sir, is it to be ever thus?
    Even with you as with the world? I know   375
    This morning's service was no vulgar deed
    Whose motive, once it dares avow itself,
    Explains all done and infinitely more,
    So, takes the shelter of a nobler cause.
    Your service named its true source—loyalty!   380
    The rest's unsaid again. The Duchess bids you,
    Rise, sir! The Prince's words were in debate.

Valence [*rising*]. Rise? Truth, as ever, lady, comes
        from you!
    I should rise—I who spoke for Cleves, can speak
    For Man—yet tremble now, who stood firm then.   385
    I laughed—for 'twas past tears—that Cleves should
        starve
    With all hearts beating loud the infamy,
    And no tongue daring trust as much to air:
    Yet here, where all hearts speak, shall I be mute?
    Oh, lady, for your own sake look on me!   390
    On all I am, and have, and do—heart, brain,
    Body and soul—this Valence and his gifts!
    I was proud once: I saw you, and they sank,
    So that each, magnified a thousand times,
    Were nothing to you—but such nothingness,   395
    Would a crown gild it, or a scepter prop,
    A treasure speed, a laurel-wreath enhance?
    What is my own desert? But should your love
    Have . . . there's no language helps here . . . singled
        me—
    Then—oh, that wild word "then!"—be just to love,   400
    In generosity its attribute!
    Love, since you pleased to love! All's cleared—a
        stage
    For trial of the question kept so long:
    Judge you—Is love or vanity the best?
    You, solve it for the world's sake—you, speak first 405
    What all will shout one day—you, vindicate
    Our earth and be its angel! All is said.

Lady, I offer nothing—I am yours:
But, for the cause' sake, look on me and him,
And speak!

410 *The Duchess.* I have received the Prince's message:
Say, I prepare my answer!

Valence.   Take me, Cleves!
                              [*He withdraws.*]

The Duchess. Mournful—that nothing's what it calls
     itself!
Devotion, zeal, faith, loyalty—mere love!
And, love in question, what may Berthold's be?
415 I did ill to mistrust the world so soon:
Already was this Berthold at my side.
The valley-level has its hawks no doubt:
May not the rock-top have its eagles, too?
Yet Valence . . . let me see his rival then!

ACT V

NIGHT

SCENE—*The Hall*

Enter BERTHOLD *and* MELCHIOR.

Melchior. And here you wait the matter's issue?

Berthold.   Here.

Melchior. I don't regret I shut Amelius, then.
But tell me, on this grand disclosure—how
Behaved our spokesman with the forehead?

Berthold.   Oh,
5   Turned out no better than the foreheadless—

Was dazzled not so very soon, that's all!
For my part, this is scarce the hasty showy
Chivalrous measure you give me credit of.
Perhaps I had a fancy—but 'tis gone.
—Let her commence the unfriended, innocent   10
And carry wrongs about from court to court?
No, truly! The least shake of fortune's sand,
—My uncle-Pope chokes in a coughing fit,
King-cousin takes a fancy to blue eyes—
And wondrously her claims would brighten up;   15
Forth comes a new gloss on the ancient law,
O'er-looked provisos, o'er-past premises,
Follow in plenty. No: 'tis the safe step.
The hour beneath the convent-wall is lost:
Juliers and she, once mine, are ever mine.   20

Melchior. Which is to say, you, losing heart already,
Elude the adventure.

Berthold.   Not so—or, if so—
Why not confess at once that I advise
None of our kingly craft and guild just now
To lay, one moment, down their privilege   25
With the notion they can any time at pleasure
Retake it: that may turn out hazardous.
We seem, in Europe, pretty well at end
O' the night, with our great masque:° those favored few
Who keep the chamber's top, and honor's chance   30
Of the early evening, may retain their place
And figure as they list till out of breath.
But it is growing late: and I observe
A dim grim kind of tipstaves° at the doorway
Not only bar newcomers entering now,   35
But caution those who left, for any cause,
And would return, that morning draws too near;
The ball must die off, shut itself up. We—
I think, may dance lights out and sunshine in,
And sleep off headache on our frippery: 40

9 **masque** elaborate court drama.   34 **tipstaves** constables.

But friend the other, who cunningly stole out,
And, after breathing the fresh air outside,
Means to reenter with a new costume,
Will be advised go back to bed, I fear.
45   I stick to privilege, on second thoughts.

Melchior. Yes—you evade the adventure: and, beside,
Give yourself out for colder than you are.
King Philip, only, notes the lady's eyes?
Don't they come in for somewhat of the motive
With you too?

50   *Berthold.*   Yes—no: I am past that now.
Gone 'tis: I cannot shut my soul to fact.
Of. course, I might by forethought and contrivance
Reason myself into a rapture. Gone:
And something better come instead, no doubt.

55   *Melchior.* So be it! Yet, all the same, proceed my way,
Though to your ends; so shall you prosper best!
The lady—to be won for selfish ends—
Will be won easier my unselfish . . . call it,
Romantic way.

    Berthold.   Won easier?

    Melchior.   Will not she?

60   *Berthold.* There I profess humility without bound:
Ill cannot speed—not I—the Emperor.

Melchior. And I should think the Emperor best
    waived,
From your description of her mood and way.
You could look, if it pleased you, into hearts;
65   But are too indolent and fond of watching
Your own—you know that, for you study it.

Berthold. Had you but seen the orator her friend,
So bold and voluble an hour before,
Abashed to earth at aspect of the change!
70   Make her an Empress? Ah, that changed the case!
Oh, I read hearts! 'Tis for my own behoof,
I court her with my true worth: wait the event!

I learned my final lesson on that head
When years ago—my first and last essay—
Before the priest my uncle could by help 75
Of his superior, raise me from the dirt—
Priscilla left me for a Brabant lord
Whose cheek was like the topaz on his thumb.
I am past illusion on that score.

Melchior.   Here comes
The lady—

Berthold. —And there you go. But do not! Give me 80
Another chance to please you! Hear me plead!

Melchior. You'll keep, then, to the lover, to the man?

Enter the DUCHESS—*followed by* ADOLF *and* SABYNE
and, after an interval, by the Courtiers.

Berthold. Good auspice to our meeting!

The Duchess   May it prove!
—And you, sir, will be Emperor one day?

Berthold. (Ay, that's the point!) I may be Emperor. 85

The Duchess. 'Tis not for my sake only, I am proud
Of this you offer: I am prouder far
That from the highest state should duly spring
The highest, since most generous, of deeds.

Berthold. (Generous—still that!) You underrate your-
self. 90
You are, what I, to be complete, must gain—
Find now, and may not find, another time.
While I career on all the world for stage,
There needs at home my representative.

The Duchess. —Such, rather, would some warrior-
woman be— 95
One dowered with lands and gold, or rich in
friends—
One like yourself.

Berthold.   Lady, I am myself,

And have all these: I want what's not myself,
Nor has all these. Why give one hand two swords?
100   Here's one already: be a friend's next gift
A silk glove, if you will—I have a sword.

The Duchess. You love me, then?

Berthold.   Your lineage I revere,
Honor your virtue, in your truth believe,
Do homage to your intellect, and bow
Before your peerless beauty.

105   *The Duchess.*   But, for love—

Berthold. A further love I do not understand.
Our best course is to say these hideous truths,
And see them, once said, grow endurable:
Like waters shuddering from their central bed,
110   Black with the midnight bowels of the earth,
That, once upspouted by an earthquake's throe,
A portent and a terror—soon subside,
Freshen apace, take gold and rainbow hues
In sunshine, sleep in shadow, and at last
115   Grow common to the earth as hills or trees—
Accepted by all things they came to scare.

The Duchess. You cannot love, then?

Berthold.   —Charlemagne,° perhaps!
Are you not over-curious in love-lore?

The Duchess. I have become so, very recently.
120   It seems, then, I shall best deserve esteem,
Respect, and all your candor promises,
By putting on a calculating mood—
Asking the terms of my becoming yours?

Berthold. Let me not do myself injustice, neither.
125   Because I will not condescend to fictions
That promise what my soul can ne'er acquit,
It does not follow that my guarded phrase
May not include far more of what you seek,

117 **Charlemagne** emperor of the Franks.

Than wide profession of less scrupulous men.
You will be Empress, once for all: with me   *130*
The Pope disputes supremacy—you stand,
And none gainsays, the earth's first woman.

The Duchess.   That—
Or simple Lady of Ravestein again?

Berthold. The matter's not in my arbitrament:
Now I have made my claims—which I regret—   *135*
Cede one, cede all.

The Duchess.   This claim then, you enforce?

Berthold. The world looks on.

The Duchess.   And when must I decide?

Berthold. When, lady? Have I said thus much so
     promptly
For nothing?—Poured out, with such pains, at once
What I might else have suffered to ooze forth   *140*
Droplet by droplet in a lifetime long—
For aught less than as prompt an answer, too?
All's fairly told now: who can teach you more?

The Duchess. I do not see him.

Berthold.   I shall ne'er deceive.
This offer should be made befittingly   *145*
Did time allow the better setting forth
The good of it, with what is not so good,
Advantage, and disparagement as well:
But as it is, the sum of both must serve.
I am already weary of this place;   *150*
My thoughts are next stage on to Rome. Decide!
The Empire—or—not even Juliers now!
Hail to the Empress—farewell to the Duchess!

[*The* Courtiers, *who have been drawing nearer
          and nearer, interpose.*]

Gaucelme. —"Farewell," Prince? when we break in
     at our risk—

155 *Clugnet.* Almost upon court-license trespassing—

Gaucelme. —To point out how your claims are valid
                yet!
        You know not, by the Duke her father's will,
        The lady, if she weds beneath her rank,
        Forfeits her Duchy in the next heir's favor—
160   So 'tis expressly stipulate. And if
        It can be shown 'tis her intent to wed
        A subject, then yourself, next heir, by right
        Succeed to Juliers.

Berthold.   What insanity?—

Guibert. Sir, there's one Valence, the pale fiery man
        You saw and heard this morning—thought, no
165   doubt,
        Was of considerable standing here:
        I put it to your penetration, Prince,
        If aught save love, the truest love for her
        Could make him serve the lady as he did!
170   He's simply a poor advocate of Cleves
        —Creeps here with difficulty, finds a place
        With danger, gets in by a miracle,
        And for the first time meets the lady's face—
        So runs the story: is that credible?
175   For, first—no sooner in, than he's apprised
        Fortunes have changed; you are all-powerful here,
        The lady as powerless: he stands fast by her!

The Duchess [*aside*]. And do such deeds spring up
        from love alone?

Guibert. But here occurs the question, does the lady
180   Love him again? I say, how else can she?
        Can she forget how he stood singly forth
        In her defense, dared outrage all of us,
        Insult yourself—for what, save love's reward?

The Duchess [*aside*]. And is love then the sole reward
        of love?

185 *Guibert.* But, love him as she may and must—you ask,

Means she to wed him? "Yes," both natures answer!
Both, in their pride, point out the sole result;
Naught less would he accept nor she propose.
For each conjecture was she great enough
—Will be, for this.

ugnet.   Though, now that this is known,   *190*
Policy, doubtless, urges she deny . . .

he Duchess. —What, sir, and wherefore?—since I
     am not sure
That all is any other than you say!
You take this Valence, hold him close to me,
Him with his actions: can I choose but look?   *195*
I am not sure, love trulier shows itself
Than in this man, you hate and would degrade,
Yet, with your worst abatement, show me thus.
Nor am I—(thus made look within myself,
Ere I had dared)—now that the look is dared—   *200*
Sure that I do not love him!

uibert.   Hear you, Prince?

erthold. And what, sirs, please you, may this prattle
     mean
Unless to prove with what alacrity
You give your lady's secrets to the world?
How much indebted, for discovering   *205*
That quality, you make me, will be found
When there's a keeper for my own to seek.

ourtiers. "Our lady?"

erthold.   —She assuredly remains.

he Duchess. Ah, Prince—and you too can be gen-
     erous?
You could renounce your power, if this were so,   *210*
And let me, as these phrase it, wed my love
Yet keep my Duchy? You perhaps exceed
Him, even, in disinterestedness!

erthold. How, lady, should all this affect my purpose?
Your will and choice are still as ever, free.   *215*

Say, you have known a worthier than myself
In mind and heart, of happier form and face—
Others must have their birthright: I have gifts.
To balance theirs, not blot them out of sight.
220 Against a hundred alien qualities,
I lay the prize I offer. I am nothing:
Wed you the Empire?

The Duchess.   And my heart away?

Berthold. When have I made pretension to your
     heart?
I give none. I shall keep your honor safe;
225 With mine I trust you, as the sculptor trusts
Yon marble woman with the marble rose,
Loose on her hand, she never will let fall,
In graceful, slight, silent security.
You will be proud of my worldwide career,
230 And I content in you the fair and good.
What were the use of planting a few seeds
The thankless climate never would mature—
Affections all repelled by circumstance?
Enough: to these no credit I attach—
235 To what you own, find nothing to object.
Write simply on my requisition's face
What shall content my friends—that you admit,
As Colombe of Ravestein, the claims therein,
Or never need admit them, as my wife—
And either way, all's ended!

240 *The Duchess.*   Let all end!

Berthold. The requisition!

Guibert.   —Valence holds, of course!

Berthold. Desire his presence!   [ADOLF *goes out.*]

Courtiers [*to each other*]. Out it all comes yet;
He'll have his word against the bargain yet;
He's not the man to tamely acquiesce.
245 One passionate appeal—upbraiding even,
May turn the tide again. Despair not yet!
          [*They retire a little.*]

Berthold [*to* MELCHIOR]. The Empire has its old suc-
　　cess, my friend!

Melchior. You've had your way: before the spokes-
　　man speaks,
　　Let me, but this once, work a problem out,
　　And ever more be dumb! The Empire wins?　　　　250
　　To better purpose have I read my books!

　　　　　　　Enter VALENCE.

Melchior [*to the* Courtiers]. Apart, my masters!
　　　　　　[*To* VALENCE.] Sir, one word with you!
　　I am a poor dependent of the Prince's—
　　Pitched on to speak, as of slight consequence.
　　You are no higher, I find: in other words,　　　　255
　　We two, as probably the wisest here,
　　Need not hold diplomatic talk like fools.
　　Suppose I speak, divesting the plain fact
　　Of all their tortuous phrases, fit for them?
　　Do you reply so, and what trouble saved!　　　　260
　　The Prince, then—an embroiled strange heap of
　　　　news
　　This moment reaches him—if true or false,
　　All dignity forbids he should inquire
　　In person, or by worthier deputy;
　　Yet somehow must inquire, lest slander come:　　265
　　And so, 'tis I am pitched on. You have heard
　　His offer to your lady?

Valence.　　　　　　　Yes.

Melchior.　　　　　　　　—Conceive
　　Her joy thereat?

Valence.　　　　I cannot.

Melchior.　　　　　　　No one can.
　　All draws to a conclusion, therefore.

Valence [*aside*].　　　　　So!
　　No after-judgment—no first thought revised—　　270
　　Her first and last decision!—me, she leaves,
　　Takes him; a simple heart is flung aside,

The ermine o'er a heartless breast embraced.
Oh Heaven, this mockery has been played too oft!
275 Once, to surprise the angels—twice, that fiends
Recording, might be proud they chose not so—
Thrice, many thousand times, to teach the world
All men should pause, misdoubt their strength, since men
Can have such chance yet fail so signally,
280 —But ever, ever this farewell to Heaven,
Welcome to earth—this taking death for life—
This spurning love and kneeling to the world—
Oh Heaven, it is too often and too old!

Melchior. Well, on this point, what but an absurd rumor
285 Arises—these, its source—its subject, you!
Your faith and loyalty misconstruing,
They say, your service claims the lady's hand!
Of course, nor Prince nor lady can respond:
Yet something must be said: for, were it true
You made such claim, the Prince would . . .

290 *Valence*.   Well, sir—would?

Melchior. —Not only probably withdraw his suit,
But, very like, the lady might be forced
Accept your own. Oh, there are reasons why!
But you'll excuse at present all save one—
295 I think so. What we want is, your own witness,
For, or against—her good, or yours: decide!

Valence [*aside*]. Be it her good if she accounts it so!
[*After a contest.*] For what am I but hers, to choose as she?
Who knows how far, beside, the light from her
300 May reach, and dwell with, what she looks upon?

Melchior [*to the* Prince]. Now to him, you!

Berthold [*to* VALENCE]. My friend acquaints you, sir,
The noise runs . . .

Valence.   —Prince, how fortunate are you,

Wedding her as you will, in spite of noise,
To show belief in love! Let her but love you,
All else you disregard! What else can be?   *305*
You know how love is incompatible
With falsehood—purifies, assimilates
All other passions to itself.

Melchior.   Ay, sir:
But softly! Where, in the object we select,
Such love is, perchance, wanting?

Valence.   Then indeed,   *310*
What is it you can take?

Melchior.   Nay, ask the world!
Youth, beauty, virtue, an illustrious name,
An influence o'er mankind.

Valence.   When man perceives . . .
—Ah, I can only speak as for myself!

The Duchess. Speak for yourself!

Valence.   May I?—no, I have spoken,   *315*
And time's gone by. Had I seen such an one,
As I loved her—weighing thoroughly that word—
So should my task be to evolve her love:
If for myself!—if for another—well.

Berthold. Heroic truly! And your sole reward—   *320*
The secret pride in yielding up love's right?

Valence. Who thought upon reward? And yet how
    much
Comes after—oh, what amplest recompense!
Is the knowledge of her, naught? the memory,
    naught?
—Lady, should such an one have looked on you,   *325*
Ne'er wrong yourself so far as quote the world
And say, love can go unrequited here!
You will have blessed him to his whole life's end—
Low passions hindered, baser cares kept back,
All goodness cherished where you dwelled—and   *330*
    dwell.

What would he have? He holds you—you, both
    form
And mind, in his—where self-love makes such
    room
For love of you, he would not serve you now
The vulgar way—repulse your enemies,
335 Win you new realms, or best, to save the old
Die blissfully—that's past so long ago!
He wishes you no need, thought, care of him—
Your good, by any means, himself unseen,
Away, forgotten!—He gives that life's task up,
340 As it were . . . but this charge which I return—
        [*Offers the requisition, which she takes.*]
Wishing your good.

The Duchess [*having subscribed it*]. And opportunely,
    sir—
Since at a birthday's close, like this of mine,
Good wishes gentle deeds reciprocate.
Most on a wedding-day, as mine is too,
Should gifts be thought of: yours comes first by
345   right.
Ask of me!

Berthold. He shall have whate'er he asks,
For your sake and his own.

Valence [*aside*].   If I should ask—
The withered bunch of flowers she wears—perhaps,
One last touch of her hand, I never more
Shall see!
    [*After a pause, presenting his paper to the* Prince.]
350   Cleves' Prince, redress the wrongs of Cleves!

Berthold. I will, sir!

The Duchess [*as* VALENCE *prepares to retire*]. —Nay,
    do out your duty, first!
You bore this paper; I have registered
My answer to it: read it and have done!
                [VALENCE *reads it.*]
I take him—give up Juliers and the world.
This is my Birthday.

Melchior.   Berthold, my one hero   355
   Of the world she gives up, one friend worth my
     books,
   Sole man I think it pays the pains to watch—
   Speak, for I know you through your Popes and
     Kings!

Berthold [*after a pause*]. Lady, well rewarded! Sir,
    as well deserved!
   I could not imitate—I hardly envy—   360
   I do admire you. All is for the best.
   Too costly a flower were this, I see it now,
   To pluck and set upon my barren helm
   To wither—any garish plume will do.
   I'll not insult you and refuse your Duchy—   365
   You can so well afford to yield it me,
   And I were left, without it, sadly lorn.
   As it is—for me—if that will flatter you,
   A somewhat wearier life seems to remain
   Than I thought possible where . . . 'faith, their life   370
   Begins already! They're too occupied
   To listen: and few words content me best.
   [*Abruptly to the* Courtiers.] I am your Duke, though!
    Who obey me here?

The Duchess. Adolf and Sabyne follow us—

Guibert [*starting from the* Courtiers]. —And I?
   Do I not follow them, if I mayn't you?
   Shall not I get some little duties up   375
   At Ravestein and emulate the rest?
   God save you, Gaucelme! 'Tis my Birthday, too!

Berthold. You happy handful that remain with me
   . . . That is, with Dietrich the black Barnabite°   380
   I shall leave over you—will earn your wages
   Or Dietrich has forgot to ply his trade!
   Meantime—go copy me the precedents
   Of every installation, proper styles
   And pedigrees of all your Juliers' dukes—   385

380 **Barnabite** monk.

While I prepare to plod on my old way,
And somewhat wearily, I must confess!

The Duchess [*with a light joyous laugh as she turns
from them*]. Come, Valence, to our friends, God's
earth . . .

Valence [*as she falls into his arms*].—And thee!

from DRAMATIC ROMANCES AND LYRICS

(1845)

GARDEN FANCIES

I. THE FLOWER'S NAME

I

HERE's the garden she walked across,
    Arm in my arm, such a short while since:
Hark, now I push its wicket, the moss
    Hinders the hinges and makes them wince!
She must have reached this shrub ere she turned,   5
    As back with that murmur the wicket swung;
For she laid the poor snail, my chance foot spurned,
    To feed and forget it the leaves among.

II

Down this side of the gravel-walk
    She went while her robe's edge brushed the box: 10
And here she paused in her gracious talk
    To point me a moth on the milk-white phlox.
Roses, ranged in valiant row,
    I will never think that she passed you by!
She loves you noble roses, I know;   15
    But yonder, see, where the rock-plants lie!

III

This flower she stopped at, finger on lip,
  Stooped over, in doubt, as settling its claim;
Till she gave me, with pride to make no slip,
20 Its soft meandering Spanish name:
What a name! Was it love or praise?
  Speech half-asleep or song half-awake?
I must learn Spanish, one of these days,
  Only for that slow sweet name's sake.

IV

25 Roses, if I live and do well,
  I may bring her, one of these days,
To fix you fast with as fine a spell,
  Fit you each with his Spanish phrase;
But do not detain me now; for she lingers
30 There, like sunshine over the ground,
And ever I see her soft white fingers
  Searching after the bud she found.

V

Flower, you Spaniard, look that you grow not,
  Stay as you are and be loved forever!
35 Bud, if I kiss you 'tis that you blow not:
  Mind, the shut pink mouth opens never!
For while it pouts, her fingers wrestle,
  Twinkling the audacious leaves between,
Till round they turn and down they nestle—
40 Is not the dear mark still to be seen?

VI

Where I find her not, beauties vanish;
  Whither I follow her, beauties flee;
Is there no method to tell her in Spanish
  June's twice June since she breathed it with me?

Come, bud, show me the least of her traces,
    Treasure my lady's lightest footfall!
—Ah, you may flout and turn up your faces—
    Roses, you are not so fair after all!   *45*

II. SIBRANDUS SCHAFNABURGENSIS°

I

Plague take all your pedants, say I!
    He who wrote what I hold in my hand,
Centuries back was so good as to die,
    Leaving this rubbish to cumber the land;
This, that was a book in its time,   *5*
    Printed on paper and bound in leather,
Last month in the white of a matin-prime
    Just when the birds sang all together.

II

Into the garden I brought it to read,
    And under the arbute and laurustine   *10*
Read it, so help me grace in my need,
    From title page to closing line.
Chapter on chapter did I count,
    As a curious traveler counts Stonehenge;
Added up the mortal amount;   *15*
    And then proceeded to my revenge.

III

Yonder's a plum-tree with a crevice
    An owl would build in, were he but sage;

Sibrandus Schafnaburgensis name of the "pedant" who wrote the
book.

For a lap of moss, like a fine pont-levis°
20   In a castle of the Middle Age,
Joins to a lip of gum, pure amber;
    When he'd be private, there might he spend
Hours alone in his lady's chamber:
    Into this crevice I dropped our friend.

IV

25 Splash, went he, as under he ducked,
    —At the bottom, I knew, rain-drippings stagnate:
Next, a handful of blossoms I plucked
    To bury him with, my bookshelf's magnate;
Then I went indoors, brought out a loaf,
30   Half a cheese, and a bottle of Chablis;
Lay on the grass and forgot the oaf
    Over a jolly chapter of Rabelais.°

V

Now, this morning, betwixt the moss
    And gum that locked our friend in limbo,
35 A spider had spun his web across,
    And sat in the midst with arms akimbo:
So, I took pity, for learning's sake,
    And, *de profundis, accentibus lætis,*
Cantate!° quoth I, as I got a rake;
40   And up I fished his delectable treatise.

VI

Here you have it, dry in the sun,
    With all the binding all of a blister,
And great blue spots where the ink has run,
    And reddish streaks that wink and glister
45 O'er the page so beautifully yellow:
    Oh, well have the droppings played their tricks!

19 **pont-levis** drawbridge. 32 **Rabelais** lusty humorist. 38–39 **de
profundis . . . Cantate!** sing joyfully from the depths!

Did he guess how toadstools grow, this fellow?
  Here's one stuck in his chapter six!

VII

How did he like it when the live creatures
  Tickled and toused and browsed him all over,   50
And worm, slug, eft, with serious features,
  Came in, each one, for his right of trover?°
—When the water-beetle with great blind deaf face
  Made of her eggs the stately deposit,
And the newt borrowed just so much of the preface   55
  As tiled in the top of his black wife's closet?

VIII

All that life and fun and romping,
  All that frisking and twisting and coupling,
While slowly our poor friend's leaves were swamping
  And clasps were cracking and covers suppling!   60
As if you had carried sour John Knox°
  To the playhouse at Paris, Vienna or Munich,
Fastened him into a front-row box,
  And danced off the ballet with trousers and tunic.

IX

Come, old martyr! What, torment enough is it?   65
  Back to my room shall you take your sweet self.
Good-bye, mother-beetle; husband-eft, *sufficit!*°
  See the snug niche I have made on my shelf!
A.'s book shall prop you up, B.'s shall cover you,
  Here's C. to be grave with, or D. to be gay,   70
And with E. on each side, and F. right over you,
  Dry-rot at ease till the Judgment Day!

52 **trover** finder.   61 **John Knox** Calvinist preacher and theologian.
67 **sufficit!** enough!

from MEN AND WOMEN
(1855)

A WOMAN'S LAST WORD

I

LET'S contend no more, Love,
    Strive nor weep:
All be as before, Love,
    —Only sleep!

II

5   What so wild as words are?
        I and thou
    In debate, as birds are,
        Hawk on bough!

III

    See the creature stalking
10   While we speak!
    Hush and hide the talking,
        Cheek on cheek!

IV

What so false as truth is,
  False to thee?
Where the serpent's tooth is   15
  Shun the tree—

V

Where the apple reddens
  Never pry—
Lest we lose our Edens,
  Eve and I.   20

VI

Be a god and hold me
  With a charm!
Be a man and fold me
  With thine arm!

VII

Teach me, only teach, Love!   25
  As I ought
I will speak thy speech, Love,
  Think thy thought—

VIII

Meet, if thou require it,
  Both demands,   30
Laying flesh and spirit
  In thy hands.

IX

That shall be tomorrow
  Not tonight:

³⁵
I must bury sorrow
Out of sight:

X

—Must a little weep, Love,
(Foolish me!)
And so fall asleep, Love,
⁴⁰   Loved by thee.

FRA LIPPO LIPPI°

I AM poor brother Lippo, by your leave!
You need not clap your torches to my face.
Zooks,° what's to blame? you think you see a monk!
What, 'tis past midnight, and you go the rounds,
⁵ And here you catch me at an alley's end
Where sportive ladies leave their doors ajar?
The Carmine's my cloister: hunt it up,
Do—harry out, if you must show your zeal,
Whatever rat, there, haps on his wrong hole,
¹⁰ And nip each softling of a wee white mouse,
Weke, weke, that's crept to keep him company!
Aha, you know your betters! Then, you'll take
Your hand away that's fiddling on my throat,
And please to know me likewise. Who am I?
¹⁵ Why, one, sir, who is lodging with a friend
Three streets off—he's a certain . . . how d'ye call?
Master—a . . . Cosimo of the Medici,°

Fra Lippo Lippi Florentine painter of the Renaissance. **3 Zooks**
mild oath. **17 Cosimo of the Medici** banker, statesman, patron of
art. A man of great wealth and power.

' the house that caps the corner. Boh! you were best!
Remember and tell me, the day you're hanged,
How you affected such a gullet's-gripe!   20
But you, sir, it concerns you that your knaves
Pick up a manner nor discredit you:
Zooks, are we pilchards,° that they sweep the streets
And count fair prize what comes into their net?
He's Judas to a tittle, that man is!   25
Just such a face! Why, sir, you make amends.
Lord, I'm not angry! Bid your hangdogs go
Drink out this quarter-florin to the health
Of the munificent House that harbors me
(And many more beside, lads! more beside!)   30
And all's come square again. I'd like his face—
His, elbowing on his comrade in the door
With the pike and lantern—for the slave that holds
John Baptist's head a-dangle by the hair
With one hand ("Look you, now," as who should say)   35
And his weapon in the other, yet unwiped!
It's not your chance to have a bit of chalk,
A wood-coal or the like? or you should see!
Yes, I'm the painter, since you style me so.
What, brother Lippo's doings, up and down,   40
You know them and they take you? like enough!
I saw the proper twinkle in your eye—
Tell you, I liked your looks at very first.
Let's sit and set things straight now, hip to haunch.
Here's spring come, and the nights one makes up
        bands   45
To roam the town and sing out carnival,
And I've been three weeks shut within my mew,
A-painting for the great man, saints and saints
And saints again. I could not paint all night—
Ouf! I leaned out of window for fresh air.   50
There came a hurry of feet and little feet,
A sweep of lute-strings, laughs, and whiffs of song—
Flower o' the broom,
Take away love, and our earth is a tomb!

23 **pilchards** sardines.

55 *Flower o' the quince,*
    I let Lisa go, and what good in life since?
    Flower o' the thyme—and so on. Round they went.
    Scarce had they turned the corner when a titter
    Like the skipping of rabbits by moonlight—three slim
        shapes,
60 And a face that looked up . . . zooks, sir, flesh and
        blood,
    That's all I'm made of! Into shreds it went,
    Curtain and counterpane and coverlet,
    All the bed-furniture—a dozen knots,
    There was a ladder! Down I let myself,
65 Hands and feet, scrambling somehow, and so dropped,
    And after them. I came up with the fun
    Hard by Saint Lawrence, hail fellow, well met—
    Flower o' the rose,
    If I've been merry, what matter who knows?
70 And so as I was stealing back again
    To get to bed and have a bit of sleep
    Ere I rise up tomorrow and go work
    On Jerome° knocking at his poor old breast
    With his great round stone to subdue the flesh,
75 You snap me of the sudden. Ah, I see!
    Though your eye twinkles still, you shake your head—
    Mine's shaved—a monk, you say—the sting's in that!
    If Master Cosimo announced himself,
    Mum's the word naturally; but a monk!
80 Come, what am I a beast for? tell us, now!
    I was a baby when my mother died
    And father died and left me in the street.
    I starved there, God knows how, a year or two
    On fig-skins, melon-parings, rinds and shucks,
85 Refuse and rubbish. One fine frosty day,
    My stomach being empty as your hat,
    The wind doubled me up and down I went.
    Old Aunt Lapaccia trussed me with one hand,
    (Its fellow was a stinger as I knew)
90 And so along the wall, over the bridge,

73 Jerome the saint.

By the straight cut to the convent. Six words there,
While I stood munching my first bread that month:
"So, boy, you're minded," quoth the good fat father
Wiping his own mouth, 'twas refection-time—
"To quit this very miserable world?   93
Will you renounce" . . . "the mouthful of bread?"
        thought I;
By no means! Brief, they made a monk of me;
I did renounce the world, its pride and greed,
Palace, farm, villa, shop and banking-house,
Trash, such as these poor devils of Medici   100
Have given their hearts to—all at eight years old.
Well, sir, I found in time, you may be sure,
'Twas not for nothing—the good bellyful,
The warm serge and the rope that goes all round,
And day-long blessed idleness beside!   105
'Let's see what the urchin's fit for"—that came next.
Not overmuch their way, I must confess.
Such a to-do! They tried me with their books:
Lord, they'd have taught me Latin in pure waste!
Flower o' the clove,   110
All the Latin I construe is, "amo" I love!
But, mind you, when a boy starves in the streets
Eight years together, as my fortune was,
Watching folk's faces to know who will fling
The bit of half-stripped grape-bunch he desires,   115
And who will curse or kick him for his pains—
Which gentleman processional and fine,
Holding a candle to the Sacrament,
Will wink and let him lift a plate and catch
The droppings of the wax to sell again,   120
Or holla for the Eight° and have him whipped—
How say I?—nay, which dog bites, which lets drop
His bone from the heap of offal in the street—
Why, soul and sense of him grow sharp alike,
He learns the look of things, and none the less   125
For admonition from the hunger-pinch.
I had a store of such remarks, be sure,

121 the Eight magistrates of Florence.

Which, after I found leisure, turned to use.
I drew men's faces on my copy-books,
130 Scrawled them within the antiphonary's° marge,
Joined legs and arms to the long music-notes,
Found eyes and nose and chin for A's and B's,
And made a string of pictures of the world
Betwixt the ins and outs of verb and noun,
On the wall, the bench, the door. The monks looked
135   black.
"Nay," quoth the Prior, "turn him out, d'ye say?
In no wise. Lose a crow and catch a lark.
What if at last we get our man of parts,
We Carmelites, like those Camaldolese
140 And Preaching Friars,° to do our church up fine
And put the front on it that ought to be!"
And hereupon he bade me daub away.
Thank you! my head being crammed, the walls a
     blank,
Never was such prompt disemburdening.
145 First, every sort of monk, the black and white,
I drew them, fat and lean: then, folk at church,
From good old gossips waiting to confess
Their cribs of barrel-droppings, candle-ends—
To the breathless fellow at the altar-foot,
150 Fresh from his murder, safe and sitting there
With the little children round him in a row
Of admiration, half for his beard and half
For that white anger of his victim's son
Shaking a fist at him with one fierce arm,
155 Signing himself with the other because of Christ
(Whose sad face on the cross sees only this
After the passion of a thousand years)
Till some poor girl, her apron o'er her head,
(Which the intense eyes look through) came at eve
160 On tiptoe, said a word, dropped in a loaf,
Her pair of earrings and a bunch of flowers
(The brute took growling), prayed, and so was gone.
I painted all, then cried " 'Tis ask and have;

130 **antiphonary** choir book.   139–140 **Carmelites . . . Friars** monastic orders.

Choose, for more's ready!"—laid the ladder flat,
And showed my covered bit of cloister-wall.   165
The monks closed in a circle and praised loud
Till checked, taught what to see and not to see,
Being simple bodies—"That's the very man!
Look at the boy who stoops to pat the dog!
That woman's like the Prior's niece who comes   170
To care about his asthma: it's the life!"
But there my triumph's straw-fire flared and funked;
Their betters took their turn to see and say:
The Prior and the learned pulled a face
And stopped all that in no time. "How? what's here?   175
Quite from the mark of painting, bless us all!
Faces, arms, legs and bodies like the true
As much as pea and pea! it's devil's-game!
Your business is not to catch men with show,
With homage to the perishable clay,   180
But lift them over it, ignore it all,
Make them forget there's such a thing as flesh.
Your business is to paint the souls of men—
Man's soul, and it's a fire, smoke . . . no, it's not . . .
It's vapor done up like a newborn babe—   185
(In that shape when you die it leaves your mouth)
It's . . . well, what matters talking, it's the soul!
Give us no more of body than shows soul!
Here's Giotto,° with his Saint a-praising God,
That sets us praising—why not stop with him?   190
Why put all thoughts of praise out of our head
With wonder at lines, colors, and what not?
Paint the soul, never mind the legs and arms!
Rub all out, try at it a second time.
Oh, that white smallish female with the breasts,   195
She's just my niece . . . Herodias,° I would say—
Who went and danced and got men's heads cut off!
Have it all out!" Now, is this sense, I ask?
A fine way to paint soul, by painting body
So ill, the eye can't stop there, must go further   200
And can't fare worse! Thus, yellow does for white

89 **Giotto** Florentine painter (1276–1337).   196 **Herodias** Matthew
4:6–11.

When what you put for yellow's simply black,
And any sort of meaning looks intense
When all beside itself means and looks naught.
205 Why can't a painter lift each foot in turn,
Left foot and right foot, go a double step,
Make his flesh liker and his soul more like,
Both in their order? Take the prettiest face,
The Prior's niece . . . patron-saint—is it so pretty
210 You can't discover if it means hope, fear,
Sorrow or joy? won't beauty go with these?
Suppose I've made her eyes all right and blue,
Can't I take breath and try to add life's flash,
And then add soul and heighten them threefold?
215 Or say there's beauty with no soul at all—
(I never saw it—put the case the same—)
If you get simple beauty and naught else,
You get about the best thing God invents:
That's somewhat: and you'll find the soul you have
       missed,
220 Within yourself, when you return him thanks.
"Rub all out!" Well, well, there's my life, in short,
And so the thing has gone on ever since.
I'm grown a man no doubt, I've broken bounds:
You should not take a fellow eight years old
225 And make him swear to never kiss the girls.
I'm my own master, paint now as I please—
Having a friend, you see, in the Corner-house!
Lord, it's fast holding by the rings in front—
Those great rings serve more purposes than just
230 To plant a flag in, or tie up a horse!
And yet the old schooling sticks, the old grave eyes
Are peeping o'er my shoulder as I work,
The heads shake still—"It's art's decline, my son!
You're not of the true painters, great and old;
235 Brother Angelico's the man, you'll find;
Brother Lorenzo° stands his single peer;
Fag on at flesh, you'll never make the third!"

235–36 **Brother Angelico . . . Brother Lorenzo** Fra Angelico and
Lorenzo Monaco, monastic painters of great piety.

*Flower o' the pine,
You keep your mistr . . . manners, and I'll stick to
    mine!*
I'm not the third, then: bless us, they must know!   240
Don't you think they're the likeliest to know,
They with their Latin? So, I swallow my rage,
Clench my teeth, suck my lips in tight, and paint
To please them—sometimes do and sometimes don't;
For, doing most, there's pretty sure to come   245
A turn, some warm eve finds me at my saints—
A laugh, a cry, the business of the world—
*(Flower o' the peach,
Death for us all, and his own life for each!)*
And my whole soul revolves, the cup runs over,   250
The world and life's too big to pass for a dream,
And I do these wild things in sheer despite,
And play the fooleries you catch me at,
In pure rage! The old mill-horse, out at grass
After hard years, throws up his stiff heels so,   255
Although the miller does not preach to him
The only good of grass is to make chaff.
What would men have? Do they like grass or no—
May they or mayn't they? all I want's the thing
Settled forever one way. As it is,   260
You tell too many lies and hurt yourself:
You don't like what you only like too much,
You do like what, if given you at your word,
You find abundantly detestable.
For me, I think I speak as I was taught;   265
I always see the garden and God there
A-making man's wife: and, my lesson learned,
The value and significance of flesh,
I can't unlearn ten minutes afterwards,

    You understand me: I'm a beast, I know.   270
But see, now—why, I see as certainly
As that the morning-star's about to shine,
What will hap some day. We've a youngster here
Comes to our convent, studies what I do,

275 Slouches and stares and lets no atom drop:
    His name is Guidi°—he'll not mind the monks—
    They call him Hulking Tom, he lets them talk—
    He picks my practice up—he'll paint apace,
    I hope so—though I never live so long,
280 I know what's sure to follow. You be judge!
    You speak no Latin more than I, belike;
    However, you're my man, you've seen the world
    —The beauty and the wonder and the power,
    The shapes of things, their colors, lights and shades,
285 Changes, surprises—and God made it all!
    —For what? Do you feel thankful, ay or no,
    For this fair town's face, yonder river's line,
    The mountain round it and the sky above,
    Much more the figures of man, woman, child,
290 These are the frame to? What's it all about?
    To be passed over, despised? or dwelled upon,
    Wondered at? oh, this last of course!—you say.
    But why not do as well as say—paint these
    Just as they are, careless what comes of it?
295 God's works—paint anyone, and count it crime
    To let a truth slip. Don't object, "His works
    Are here already; nature is complete:
    Suppose you reproduce her—(which you can't)
    There's no advantage! you must beat her, then."
300 For, don't you mark? we're made so that we love
    First when we see them painted, things we have passed
    Perhaps a hundred times nor cared to see;
    And so they are better, painted—better to us,
    Which is the same thing. Art was given for that;
305 God uses us to help each other so,
    Lending our minds out. Have you noticed, now,
    Your cullion's° hanging face? A bit of chalk,
    And trust me but you should, though! How much
        more,
    If I drew higher things with the same truth!
310 That were to take the Prior's pulpit-place,

276 **Guidi** Browning thought Tommaso Guidi (Masaccio) was
Lippo Lippi's pupil. He actually was his predecessor.   307 **cullion**
rascal (i.e. the guard who had collared him earlier).

Interpret God to all of you! Oh, oh,
It makes me mad to see what men shall do
And we in our graves! This world's no blot for us,
Nor blank; it means intensely, and means good:
To find its meaning is my meat and drink.   315
"Ay, but you don't so instigate to prayer!"
Strikes in the Prior: "when your meaning's plain
It does not say to folk—remember matins,
Or, mind you fast next Friday!" Why, for this
What need of art at all? A skull and bones,   320
Two bits of stick nailed crosswise, or, what's best,
A bell to chime the hour with, does as well.
I painted a Saint Lawrence six months since
At Prato, splashed the fresco in fine style:
"How looks my painting, now the scaffold's down?"   325
I ask a brother: "Hugely," he returns—
"Already not one phiz of your three slaves
Who turn the Deacon off his toasted side,
But's scratched and prodded to our heart's content,
The pious people have so eased their own   330
With coming to say prayers there in a rage:
We get on fast to see the bricks beneath.
Expect another job this time next year,
For pity and religion grow i' the crowd—
Your painting serves its purpose!" Hang the fools!   335

—That is—you'll not mistake an idle word
Spoke in a huff by a poor monk, Got wot,
Tasting the air this spicy night which turns
The unaccustomed head like Chianti wine!
Oh, the church knows! don't misreport me, now!   340
It's natural a poor monk out of bounds
Should have his apt word to excuse himself:
And hearken how I plot to make amends.
I have bethought me: I shall paint a piece
. . . There's for you! Give me six months, then go, see   345
Something in Sant' Ambrogio's! Bless the nuns!
They want a cast o' my office. I shall paint
God in the midst, Madonna and her babe,
Ringed by a bowery flowery angel-brood,

350 Lilies and vestments and white faces, sweet
    As puff on puff of grated orris-root°
    When ladies crowd to church at midsummer.
    And then i' the front, of course a saint or two—
    Saint John, because he saves the Florentines,
355 Saint Ambrose, who puts down in black and white
    The convent's friends and gives them a long day,
    And Job, I must have him there past mistake,
    The man of Uz (and Us without the z,
    Painters who need his patience). Well, all these
360 Secured at their devotion, up shall come
    Out of a corner when you least expect,
    As one by a dark stair into a great light,
    Music and talking, who but Lippo! I!—
    Mazed, motionless and moonstruck—I'm the man!
365 Back I shrink—what is this I see and hear?
    I, caught up with my monk's-things by mistake,
    My old serge gown and rope that goes all round,
    I, in this presence, this pure company!
    Where's a hole, where's a corner for escape?
370 Then steps a sweet angelic slip of a thing
    Forward, puts out a soft palm—"Not so fast!"
    —Addresses the celestial presence, "nay—
    He made you and devised you, after all,
    Though he's none of you! Could Saint John there
        draw—
375 His camel-hair° make up a painting-brush?
    We come to brother Lippo for all that,
    Iste perfecit opus!"° So, all smile—
    I shuffle sideways with my blushing face
    Under the cover of a hundred wings
380 Thrown like a spread of kirtles° when you're gay
    And play hot cockles, all the doors being shut,
    Till, wholly unexpected, in there pops

---

351 **grated orris-root** root of the orris plant, used pulverized as perfume.   375 **camel-hair** John the Baptist wore a garment of camel's hair.   377 **"Iste perfecit opus!"** Browning understood these words, painted in the lower right-hand corner of Lippo Lippi's "Coronation of the Virgin," to mean "This is the maker of the work," and to call attention to a portrait of the painter himself.   380 **kirtles** skirts.

The hothead husband! Thus I scuttle off
To some safe bench behind, not letting go
The palm of her, the little lily thing   385
That spoke the good word for me in the nick,
Like the Prior's niece . . . Saint Lucy, I would say.
And so all's saved for me, and for the church
A pretty picture gained. Go, six months hence!
Your hand, sir, and good-bye: no lights, no lights!   390
The street's hushed, and I know my own way back,
Don't fear me! There's the gray beginning. Zooks!

A TOCCATA OF GALUPPI'S°

I

OH Galuppi, Baldassaro, this is very sad to find!
I can hardly misconceive you; it would prove me deaf
      and blind;
But although I take your meaning, 'tis with such a
      heavy mind!

II

Here you come with your old music, and here's all the
      good it brings.
What, they lived once thus at Venice where the mer-   5
      chants were the kings,
Where Saint Mark's is, where the Doges used to wed
      the sea with rings?

A Toccata of Galuppi's a toccata is a rapid piece for keyboard in
which the instrument is "touched" only lightly, nothing dwelt upon.
Here it suggests the light and inconclusive nature of the poem.
Baldassare Galuppi was a Venetian composer of the eighteenth
century.

III

Ay, because the sea's the street there; and 'tis arched
    by . . . what you call
. . . Shylock's bridge with houses on it, where they
    kept the carnival:
I was never out of England—it's as if I saw it all.

IV

Did young people take their pleasure when the sea
    was warm in May?
Balls and masks begun at midnight, burning ever to
    midday,
When they made up fresh adventures for the morrow,
    do you say?

V

Was a lady such a lady, cheeks so round and lips so
    red—
On her neck the small face buoyant, like a bellflower
    on its bed,
O'er the breast's superb abundance where a man
    might base his head?

VI

Well, and it was graceful of them—they'd break talk
    off and afford
—She, to bite her mask's black velvet—he, to finger
    on his sword,
While you sat and played toccatas, stately at the clavi-
    chord?

VII

What? Those lesser thirds so plaintive, sixths dimin-
    ished, sigh on sigh,

'old them something? Those suspensions, those solu-
 tions—"Must we die?"   20
'hose commiserating sevenths—"Life might last! we
 can but try!"

VIII

Were you happy?"—"Yes."—"And are you still as
 happy?"—"Yes. And you?"
—"Then, more kisses!"—"Did *I* stop them, when a
 million seemed so few?"
Iark, the dominant's persistence till it must be an-
 swered to!

IX

;o, an octave struck the answer. Oh, they praised you,
 I dare say!   25
'Brave Galuppi! that was music! good alike at grave
 and gay!
 can always leave off talking when I hear a master
 play!"

X

;hen they left you for their pleasure: till in due time,
 one by one,
;ome with lives that came to nothing, some with deeds
 as well undone,
Death stepped tacitly and took them where they never
 see the sun.   30

XI

;ut when I sit down to reason, think to take my stand
 nor swerve,
Vhile I triumph o'er a secret wrung from nature's
 close reserve,
;n you come with your cold music till I creep through
 every nerve.

XII

Yes, you, like a ghostly cricket, creaking where a
    house was burned:
35 "Dust and ashes, dead and done with, Venice spent
    what Venice earned.
The soul, doubtless, is immortal—where a soul can be
    discerned.

XIII

"Yours for instance: you know physics, something of
    geology,
Mathematics are your pastime; souls shall rise in their
    degree;
Butterflies may dread extinction—you'll not die, it
    cannot be!

XIV

"As for Venice and her people, merely born to bloom
40   and drop,
Here on earth they bore their fruitage, mirth and folly
    were the crop:
What of soul was left, I wonder, when the kissing had
    to stop?

XV

"Dust and ashes!" So you creak it, and I want the
    heart to scold.
Dear dead women, with such hair, too—what's be-
    come of all the gold
Used to hang and brush their bosoms? I feel chilly
45   and grown old.

BY THE FIRESIDE

I

HOW well I know what I mean to do
    When the long dark autumn-evenings come.
And where, my soul, is thy pleasant hue?
    With the music of all thy voices, dumb
In life's November too!   5

II

I shall be found by the fire, suppose,
    O'er a great wise book as beseemeth age,
While the shutters flap as the crosswind blows
    And I turn the page, and I turn the page,
Not verse now, only prose!   10

III

Till the young ones whisper, finger on lip,
    "There he is at it, deep in Greek:
Now then, or never, out we slip
    To cut from the hazels by the creek
A mainmast for our ship!"   15

IV

I shall be at it indeed, my friends:
    Greek puts already on either side
Such a branch-work forth as soon extends
    To a vista opening far and wide,
And I pass out where it ends.   20

171

V

The outside-frame, like your hazel-trees:
    But the inside-archway widens fast,
And a rarer sort succeeds to these,
    And we slope to Italy at last
25 And youth, by green degrees.

VI

I follow wherever I am led,
    Knowing so well the leader's hand:
Oh woman-country, wooed not wed,
    Loved all the more by earth's male-lands,
30 Laid to their hearts instead!

VII

Look at the ruined chapel again
    Halfway up in the Alpine gorge!
Is that a tower, I point you plain,
    Or is it a mill, or an iron-forge
35 Breaks solitude in vain?

VIII

A turn, and we stand in the heart of things;
    The woods are round us, heaped and dim;
From slab to slab how it slips and springs,
    The thread of water single and slim,
40 Through the ravage some torrent brings!

IX

Does it feed the little lake below?
    That speck of white just on its marge
Is Pella; see, in the evening-glow,
    How sharp the silver spearheads charge
45 When Alp meets heaven in snow!

X

On our other side is the straight-up rock;
   And a path is kept 'twixt the gorge and it
By boulder-stones where lichens mock
   The marks on a moth, and small ferns fit
Their teeth to the polished block.   *50*

XI

Oh the sense of the yellow mountain-flowers,
   And thorny balls, each three in one,
The chestnuts throw on our path in showers!
   For the drop of the woodland fruit's begun,
These early November hours,   *55*

XII

That crimson the creeper's leaf across
   Like a splash of blood, intense, abrupt,
O'er a shield else gold from rim to boss,
   And lay it for show on the fairy-cupped
Elf-needled mat of moss,   *60*

XIII

By the rose-flesh mushrooms, undivulged
   Last evening—nay, in today's first dew
Yon sudden coral nipple bulged,
   Where a freaked fawn-colored flaky crew
Of toadstools peep indulged.   *65*

XIV

And yonder, at foot of the fronting ridge
   That takes the turn to a range beyond,
Is the chapel reached by the one-arched bridge
   Where the water is stopped in a stagnant pond
Danced over by the midge.   *70*

XV

The chapel and bridge are of stone alike,
　　Blackish-gray and mostly wet;
Cut hemp-stalks steep in the narrow dyke.
　　See here again, how the lichens fret
75　And the roots of the ivy strike!

XVI

Poor little place, where its one priest comes
　　On a festa-day, if he comes at all,
To the dozen folk from their scattered homes,
　　Gathered within that precinct small
80　By the dozen ways one roams—

XVII

To drop from the charcoal-burners' huts,
　　Or climb from the hemp-dressers' low shed,
Leave the grange where the woodman stores his
　　　　nuts,
　　Or the wattled cote where the fowlers spread
85　Their gear on the rock's bare juts.

XVIII

It has some pretension too, this front,
　　With its bit of fresco half-moon-wise
Set over the porch, art's early wont:
　　'Tis John in the Desert, I surmise,
90　But has borne the weather's brunt—

XIX

Not from the fault of the builder, though,
　　For a penthouse properly projects
Where three carved beams make a certain show,
　　Dating—good thought of our architect's—
95　'Five, six, nine, he lets you know.

XX

d all day long a bird sings there,
  And a stray sheep drinks at the pond at times;
ie place is silent and aware;
  It has had its scenes, its joys and crimes,
it that is its own affair.   *100*

XXI

y perfect wife, my Leonor,
  Oh heart, my own, oh eyes, mine too,
hom else could I dare look backward for,
  With whom beside should I dare pursue
ie path gray heads abhor?   *105*

XXII

or it leads to a crag's sheer edge with them;
  Youth, flowery all the way, there stops—
ot they; age threatens and they contemn,
  Till they reach the gulf wherein youth drops,
ne inch from life's safe hem!   *110*

XXIII

/ith me, youth led . . . I will speak now,
  No longer watch you as you sit
:eading by firelight, that great brow
  And the spirit-small hand propping it,
lutely, my heart knows how—   *115*

XXIV

/hen, if I think but deep enough,
  You are wont to answer, prompt as rhyme;
.nd you, too, find without rebuff
  Response your soul seeks many a time
'iercing its fine flesh-stuff.   *120*

XXV

My own, confirm me! If I tread
    This path back, is it not in pride
To think how little I dreamed it led
    To an age so blessed that, by its side,
125 Youth seems the waste instead?

XXVI

My own, see where the years conduct!
    At first, 'twas something our two souls
Should mix as mists do; each is sucked
    In each now: on, the new stream rolls,
130 Whatever rocks obstruct.

XXVII

Think, when our one soul understands
    The great Word which makes all things new,°
When earth breaks up and heaven expands,
    How will the change strike me and you
135 In the house not made with hands?

XXVIII

Oh I must feel your brain prompt mine,
    Your heart anticipate my heart,
You must be just before, in fine,
    See and make me see, for your part,
140 New depths of the divine!

XXIX

But who could have expected this
    When we two drew together first
Just for the obvious human bliss,
    To satisfy life's daily thirst
145 With a thing men seldom miss?

132 **Word** . . . new Revelation 21:5.

XXX

Come back with me to the first of all,
    Let us lean and love it over again,
Let us now forget and now recall,
    Break the rosary in a pearly rain,
And gather what we let fall!   *150*

XXXI

What did I say?—that a small bird sings
    All day long, save when a brown pair
Of hawks from the wood float with wide wings
    Strained to a bell: 'gainst noonday glare
You count the streaks and rings.   *155*

XXXII

But at afternoon or almost eve
    'Tis better; then the silence grows
To that degree, you half believe
    It must get rid of what it knows,
Its bosom does so heave.   *160*

XXXIII

Hither we walked then, side by side,
    Arm in arm and cheek to cheek,
And still I questioned or replied,
    While my heart, convulsed to really speak,
Lay choking in its pride.   *165*

XXXIV

Silent the crumbling bridge we cross,
    And pity and praise the chapel sweet,
And care about the fresco's loss,
    And wish for our souls a like retreat,
And wonder at the moss.   *170*

XXXV

Stoop and kneel on the settle under,
  Look through the window's grated square:
Nothing to see! For fear of plunder,
  The cross is down and the altar bare,
175 As if thieves don't fear thunder.

XXXVI

We stoop and look in through the grate,
  See the little porch and rustic door,
Read duly the dead builder's date;
  Then cross the bridge that we crossed before,
180 Take the path again—but wait!

XXXVII

Oh moment, one and infinite!
  The water slips o'er stock and stone;
The West is tender, hardly bright:
  How gray at once is the evening grown—
185 One star, its chrysolite!°

XXXVIII

We two stood there with never a third,
  But each by each, as each knew well:
The sights we saw and the sounds we heard,
  The lights and the shades made up a spell
190 Till the trouble grew and stirred.

XXXIX

Oh, the little more, and how much it is!
  And the little less, and what worlds away!
How a sound shall quicken content to bliss,
  Or a breath suspend the blood's best play,
195 And life be a proof of this!

185 **chrysolite** semiprecious stone. "Jewel."

XL

Had she willed it, still had stood the screen
    So slight, so sure, 'twixt my love and her:
I could fix her face with a guard between,
    And find her soul as when friends confer,
Friends—lovers that might have been.   200

XLI

For my heart had a touch of the woodland-time,
    Wanting to sleep now over its best.
Shake the whole tree in the summer-prime,
    But bring to the last leaf no such test!
"Hold the last fast!" runs the rhyme.   205

XLII

For a chance to make your little much,
    To gain a lover and lose a friend,
Venture the tree and a myriad such,
    When nothing you mar but the year can mend:
But a last leaf—fear to touch!   210

XLIII

Yet should it unfasten itself and fall
    Eddying down till it find your face
At some slight wind—best chance of all!
    Be your heart henceforth its dwelling-place
You trembled to forestall!   215

XLIV

Worth how well, those dark gray eyes,
    That hair so dark and dear, how worth
That a man should strive and agonize,
    And taste a veriest hell on earth
For the hope of such a prize!   220

XLV

You might have turned and tried a man,
  Set him a space to weary and wear,
And prove which suited more your plan,
  His best of hope or his worst despair,
225 Yet end as he began.

XLVI

But you spared me this, like the heart you are,
  And filled my empty heart at a word.
If two lives join, there is oft a scar,
  They are one and one, with a shadowy third;
230 One near one is too far.

XLVII

A moment after, and hands unseen
  Were hanging the night around us fast;
But we knew that a bar was broken between
  Life and life: we were mixed at last
235 In spite of the mortal screen.

XLVIII

The forests had done it; there they stood;
  We caught for a moment the powers at play:
They had mingled us so, for once and good,
  Their work was done—we might go or stay,
240 They relapsed to their ancient mood.

XLIX

How the world is made for each of us!
  How all we perceive and know in it
Tends to some moment's product thus,
  When a soul declares itself—to wit,
245 By its fruit, the thing it does!

L

Be hate that fruit or love that fruit,
 It forwards the general deed of man,
And each of the many helps to recruit
 The life of the race by a general plan;
Each living his own, to boot.   250

LI

I am named and known by that moment's feat;
 There took my station and degree;
So grew my own small life complete,
 As nature obtained her best of me—
One born to love you, sweet!   255

LII

And to watch you sink by the fireside now
 Back again, as you mutely sit
Musing by firelight, that great brow
 And the spirit-small hand propping it,
Yonder, my heart knows how!   260

LIII

So, earth has gained by one man the more,
 And the gain of earth must be heaven's gain too;
And the whole is well worth thinking o'er
 When autumn comes: which I mean to do
One day, as I said before.   265

"CHILDE ROLAND TO THE DARK TOWER CAME"

(See Edgar's song in *Lear*°)

I

My first thought was, he lied in every word,
  That hoary cripple, with malicious eye
  Askance to watch the working of his lie
On mine, and mouth scarce able to afford
5 Suppression of the glee, that pursed and scored
  Its edge, at one more victim gained thereby.

II

What else should he be set for, with his staff?
  What, save to waylay with his lies, ensnare
  All travelers who might find him posted there,
10 And ask the road? I guessed what skull-like laugh
  Would break, what crutch 'gin write my epitaph
  For pastime in the dusty thoroughfare,

III

If at his counsel I should turn aside
  Into that ominous tract which, all agree,
15 Hides the Dark Tower. Yet acquiescingly
I did turn as he pointed: neither pride
Nor hope rekindling at the end descried,
  So much as gladness that some end might be.

IV

For, what with my whole worldwide wandering,

Edgar's song in King Lear III.iv.

What with my search drawn out through years, my
   hope   20
  Dwindled into a ghost not fit to cope
With that obstreperous joy success would bring—
I hardly tried now to rebuke the spring
  My heart made, finding failure in its scope.

V

As when a sick man very near to death   25
  Seems dead indeed, and feels begin and end
  The tears and takes the farewell of each friend,
And hears one bid the other go, draw breath
Freelier outside ("since all is o'er," he saith,
  "And the blow fallen no grieving can amend;")   30

VI

While some discuss if near the other graves
  Be room enough for this, and when a day
  Suits best for carrying the corpse away,
With care about the banners, scarves and staves:
And still the man hears all, and only craves   35
  He may not shame such tender love and stay.

VII

Thus, I had so long suffered in this quest,
  Heard failure prophesied so oft, been writ
  So many times among "The Band"—to wit,
The knights who to the Dark Tower's search
   addressed   40
Their steps—that just to fail as they, seemed best,
  And all the doubt was now—should I be fit?

VIII

So, quiet as despair, I turned from him,
  That hateful cripple, out of his highway
  Into the path he pointed. All the day   45

Had been a dreary one at best, and dim
Was settling to its close, yet shot one grim
    Red leer to see the plain catch its estray.°

IX

For mark! no sooner was I fairly found
50   Pledged to the plain, after a pace or two,
    Than, pausing to throw backward a last view
O'er the safe road, 'twas gone; gray plain all round:
Nothing but plain to the horizon's bound.
    I might go on; naught else remained to do.

X

55 So, on I went. I think I never saw
    Such starved ignoble nature; nothing throve:
    For flowers—as well expect a cedar grove!
But cockle, spurge, according to their law
Might propagate their kind, with none to awe,
60   You'd think; a burr had been a treasure-trove.

XI

No! penury, inertness and grimace,
    In some strange sort, were the land's portion. "See
Or shut your eyes," said Nature peevishly,
    "It nothing skills: I cannot help my case:
65 'Tis is the Last Judgment's fire must cure this place,
    Calcine its clods and set my prisoners free."

XII

If there pushed any ragged thistle-stalk
    Above its mates, the head was chopped; the bents°
    Were jealous else. What made those holes and
        rents
70 In the dock's harsh swarth leaves, bruised as to balk

48 **estray** strayed animal.   68 **bents** rough grass.

All hope of greenness; 'tis a brute must walk
   Pashing their life out, with a brute's intents.

XIII

As for the grass, it grew as scant as hair
   In leprosy; thin dry blades pricked the mud
   Which underneath looked kneaded up with blood. 75
One stiff blind horse, his every bone a-stare,
Stood stupefied, however he came there:
   Thrust out past service from the devil's stud!

XIV

Alive? he might be dead for aught I know,
   With that red gaunt and colloped° neck a-strain, 80
   And shut eyes underneath the rusty mane;
Seldom went such grotesqueness with such woe;
I never saw a brute I hated so;
   He must be wicked to deserve such pain.

XV

I shut my eyes and turned them on my heart. 85
   As a man calls for wine before he fights,
   I asked one draught of earlier, happier sights,
Ere fitly I could hope to play my part.
Think first, fight afterwards—the soldier's art:
   One taste of the old time sets all to rights. 90

XVI

Not it! I fancied Cuthbert's reddening face
   Beneath its garniture of curly gold,
   Dear fellow, till I almost felt him fold
An arm in mine to fix me to the place,
That way he used. Alas, one night's disgrace! 95
   Out went my heart's new fire and left it cold.

80 **colloped** ridged.

XVII

Giles then, the soul of honor—there he stands
    Frank as ten years ago when knighted first.
    What honest man should dare (he said) he durst.
Good—but the scene shifts—faugh! what hangman-
100   hands
    Pin to his breast a parchment? His own bands
    Read it. Poor traitor, spit upon and cursed!

XVIII

Better this present than a past like that;
    Back therefore to my darkening path again!
105   No sound, no sight as far as eye could strain.
Will the night send a howlet or a bat?
    I asked: when something on the dismal flat
    Came to arrest my thoughts and change their train.

XIX

A sudden little river crossed my path
110   As unexpected as a serpent comes.
    No sluggish tide congenial to the glooms;
This, as it frothed by, might have been a bath
    For the fiend's glowing hoof—to see the wrath
    Of its black eddy bespate with flakes and spumes.

XX

115 So petty yet so spiteful! All along,
    Low scrubby alders kneeled down over it;
    Drenched willows flung them headlong in a fit
Of mute despair, a suicidal throng:
    The river which had done them all the wrong,
120   Whate'er that was, rolled by, deterred no whit.

XXI

Which, while I forded—good saints, how I feared

To set my foot upon a dead man's cheek,
   Each step, or feel the spear I thrust to seek
For hollows tangled in his hair or beard!
—It may have been a water-rat I speared,   *125*
   But, ugh! it sounded like a baby's shriek.

XXII

Glad was I when I reached the other bank.
   Now for a better country. Vain presage!
   Who were the strugglers, what war did they wage,
Whose savage trample thus could pad the dank   *130*
Soil to a plash? Toads in a poisoned tank,
   Or wild cats in a red-hot iron cage—

XXIII

The fight must so have seemed in that fell cirque.
   What penned them there, with all the plain to
      choose?
   No footprint leading to that horrid mews,°   *135*
None out of it. Mad brewage set to work
Their brains, no doubt, like galley-slaves the Turk
   Pits for his pastime, Christians against Jews.

XXIV

And more than that—a furlong on—why, there!
   What bad use was that engine for, that wheel,   *140*
   Or brake, not wheel—that harrow fit to reel
Men's bodies out like silk? with all the air
Of Tophet's° tool, on earth left unaware,
   Or brought to sharpen its rusty teeth of steel.

XXV

Then came a bit of stubbed ground, once a wood,   *145*
   Next a marsh, it would seem, and now mere earth

135 mews place of confinement. 143 Tophet hell.

Desperate and done with; (so a fool finds mirth,
Makes a thing and then mars it, till his mood
Changes and off he goes!) within a rood—
150　Bog, clay and rubble, sand and stark black dearth.

XXVI

Now blotches rankling, colored gay and grim,
　　Now patches where some leanness of the soil's
　　Broke into moss or substances like boils;
Then came some palsied oak, a cleft in him
155　Like a distorted mouth that splits its rim
　　Gaping at death, and dies while it recoils.

XXVII

And just as far as ever from the end!
　　Naught in the distance but the evening, naught
　　To point my footstep further! At the thought,
160　A great black bird, Apollyon's° bosom-friend,
Sailed past, nor beat his wide wing dragon-penned°
　　That brushed my cap—perchance the guide I
　　　　sought.

XXVIII

For, looking up, aware I somehow grew,
　　'Spite of the dusk, the plain had given place
165　All round to mountains—with such name to grace
Mere ugly heights and heaps now stolen in view.
How thus they had surprised me—solve it, you!
　　How to get from them was no clearer case.

XXIX

Yet half I seemed to recognize some trick
170　Of mischief happened to me, God knows when—
In a bad dream perhaps. Here ended, then,

160 **Apollyon** the devil.　161 **dragon-penned** with dragon feathers.

Progress this way. When, in the very nick
Of giving up, one time more, came a click
  As when a trap shuts—you're inside the den!

XXX

Burningly it came on me all at once,   173
  This was the place! those two hills on the right,
  Crouched like two bulls locked horn in horn in
    fight;
While to the left, a tall scalped mountain . . . Dunce,
Dotard, a-dozing at the very nonce,
  After a life spent training for the sight!   180

XXXI

What in the midst lay but the Tower itself?
  The round squat turret, blind as the fool's heart,
  Built of brown stone, without a counterpart
In the whole world. The tempest's mocking elf
Points to the shipman thus the unseen shelf   185
  He strikes on, only when the timbers start.

XXXII

Not see? because of night perhaps?—why, day
  Came back again for that! before it left,
  The dying sunset kindled through a cleft:
The hills, like giants at a hunting, lay,   190
Chin upon hand, to see the game at bay—
  "Now stab and end the creature—to the heft!"

XXXIII

Not hear? when noise was everywhere! it tolled
  Increasing like a bell. Names in my ears
  Of all the lost adventurers my peers—   195
How such a one was strong, and such was bold,
And such was fortunate, yet each of old
  Lost, lost! one moment knelled the woe of years.

XXXIV

There they stood, ranged along the hillsides, met
200   To view the last of me, a living frame
    For one more picture! in a sheet of flame
I saw them and I knew them all. And yet
Dauntless the slug-horn° to my lips I set,
    And blew. *"Childe Roland to the Dark Tower
      came."*

MASTER HUGUES OF SAXE-GOTHA°

I

HIST, but a word, fair and soft!
    Forth and be judged, Master Hugues!
Answer the question I've put you so oft:
    What do you mean by your mountainous fugues?°
5 See, we're alone in the loft—

II

I, the poor organist here,
    Hugues, the composer of note,
Dead though, and done with, this many a year:
    Let's have a colloquy, something to quote,
10 Make the world prick up its ear!

---

203 slug-horn (incorrect archaism).
Master Hugues of Saxe-Gotha Hugues is an imaginary composer
from the former German duchy of Saxe-Coburg-Gotha. **4 fugues**
the fugue is a musical form in which a melody is taken up by suc-
cessive voices, each entering before the previous voice has com-
pleted the melody (as in a round). After further development the
piece may end in the original key.

III

See, the church empties apace:
    Fast they extinguish the lights.
Hallo there, sacristan! Five minutes' grace!
    Here's a crank pedal wants setting to rights,
Balks one of holding the base.   15

IV

See, our huge house of the sounds,
    Hushing its hundreds at once,
Bids the last loiterer back to his bounds!
    —O you may challenge them, not a response
Get the church-saints on their rounds!   20

V

(Saints go their rounds, who shall doubt?
    —March, with the moon to admire,
Up nave, down chancel, turn transept about,
    Supervise all betwixt pavement and spire,
Put rats and mice to the rout—   25

VI

Aloys and Jurien and Just—
    Order things back to their place,
Have a sharp eye lest the candlesticks rust,
    Rub the church-plate, darn the sacrament-lace,
Clear the desk-velvet of dust.)   30

VII

Here's your book, younger folks shelve!
    Played I not offhand and runningly,
Just now, your masterpiece, hard number twelve?
    Here's what should strike, could one handle it
        cunningly:
Help the ax, give it a helve!   35

VIII

Page after page as I played,
    Every bar's rest, where one wipes
Sweat from one's brow, I looked up and surveyed,
    O'er my three claviers,° yon forest of pipes
40 Whence you still peeped in the shade.

IX

Sure you were wishful to speak?
    You, with brow ruled like a score,
Yes, and eyes buried in pits on each cheek,
    Like two great breves,° as they wrote them of yore,
45 Each side that bar, your straight beak!

X

Sure you said—"Good, the mere notes!
    Still, couldst thou take my intent,
Know what procured me our Company's votes—
    A master were lauded and sciolists shent,
50 Parted the sheep from the goats!"

XI

Well then, speak up, never flinch!
    Quick, ere my candle's a snuff
—burned, do you see? to its uttermost inch—
    I believe in you, but that's not enough:
55 Give my conviction a clinch!

XII

First you deliver your phrase
    —Nothing propound, that I see,
Fit in itself for much blame or much praise—
    Answered no less, where no answer needs be:
60 Off start the Two on their ways.

39 **claviers** keyboards. 44 **breves** marks of musical notation,
formerly square.

XIII

Straight must a Third interpose,
  Volunteer needlessly help;
In strikes a Fourth, a Fifth thrusts in his nose,
  So the cry's open, the kennel's a-yelp,
Argument's hot to the close.   65

XIV

One dissertates, he is candid;
  Two must discept°—has distinguished;
Three helps the couple, if ever yet man did;
  Four protests; Five makes a dart at the thing
      wished:
Back to One, goes the case bandied.   70

XV

One says his say with a difference;
  More of expounding, explaining!
All now is wrangle, abuse, and vociferance;
  Now there's a truce, all's subdued, self-restraining,
Five, though, stands out all the stiffer hence.   75

XVI

One is incisive, corrosive;
  Two retorts, nettled, curt, crepitant;
Three makes rejoinder, expansive, explosive;
  Four overbears them all, strident and strepitant:
Five . . . O Danaides,° O Sieve!   80

XVII

Now, they ply axes and crowbars;
  Now, they prick pins at a tissue

---

67 **discept** differ.   80 **Danaides** daughters of Danaus. Their punishment in Hades was to pour water through a seive forever.

Fine as a skein of the casuist Escobar's
  Worked on the bone of a lie. To what issue?
85 Where is our gain at the Two-bars?

XVIII

Est fuga, volvitur rota.°
  On we drift: where looms the dim port?
One, Two, Three, Four, Five, contribute their quota;
  Something is gained, if one caught but the import—
90 Show it us, Hugues of Saxe-Gotha!

XIX

What with affirming, denying,
  Holding, risposting, subjoining,
All's like ... it's like ... for an instance I'm trying ...
  There! See our roof, its gilt molding and groining
95 Under those spider webs lying!

XX

So your fugue broadens and thickens,
  Greatens and deepens and lengthens,
Till we exclaim—"But where's music, the dickens?
  Blot ye the gold, while your spider web strengthens
100 —Blacked to the stoutest of tickens?"°

XXI

I for man's effort am zealous:
  Prove me such censure unfounded!
Seems it surprising a lover grows jealous—
  Hopes 'twas for something, his organ-pipes sounded,
105 Tiring three boys at the bellows?

86 **Est fuga, volvitur rota** it is a flight [i.e. fugue], the wheel revolves.
100 **ticken** ticking is a heavy material used to cover pillows and
mattresses.

XXII

Is it your moral of Life?
　　Such a web, simple and subtle,
Weave we on earth here in impotent strife,
　　Backward and forward each throwing his shuttle,
Death ending all with a knife?   110

XXIII

Over our heads truth and nature—
　　Still our life's zigzags and dodges,
Ins and outs, weaving a new legislature—
　　God's gold just shining its last where that lodges,
Palled beneath man's usurpature.   115

XXIV

So we o'ershroud stars and roses,
　　Cherub and trophy and garland;
Nothings grow something which quietly closes
　　Heaven's earnest eye: not a glimpse of the far land
Gets through our comments and glozes.   120

XXV

Ah but traditions, inventions,
　　(Say we and make up a visage)
So many men with such various intentions,
　　Down the past ages, must know more than this age!
Leave we the web its dimensions!   125

XXVI

Who thinks Hugues wrote for the deaf,
　　Proved a mere mountain in labor?
Better submit; try again; what's the clef?
　　'Faith, 'tis no trifle for pipe and for tabor—
Four flats, the minor in F.   130

XXVII

Friend, your fugue taxes the finger:
　　Learning it once, who would lose it?
Yet all the while a misgiving will linger,
　　Truth's golden o'er us although we refuse it—
135 Nature, through cobwebs we string her.

XXVIII

Hugues! I advise *meâ poenâ*°
　　(Counterpoint glares like a Gorgon)°
Bid One, Two, Three, Four, Five, clear the arena!
　　Say the word, straight I unstop the full-organ,
140 Blare out the *mode Palestrina.*°

XXIX

While in the roof, if I'm right there,
　　. . . Lo you, the wick in the socket!
Hallo, you sacristan, show us a light there!
　　Down it dips, gone like a rocket.
145 What, you want, do you, to come unawares,
Sweeping the church up for first morning-prayers,
And find a poor devil has ended his cares
　　At the foot of your rotten-runged rat-riddled stairs?
　　　Do I carry the moon in my pocket?

---

136 meâ poenâ at my peril. **137 Gorgon** monster whose glance
turned beholders to stone. **140 mode Palestrina** he threatens to
abandon Hugues for something less pointlessly ingenious, in the
manner of the composer Palestrina.

MEMORABILIA°

I

Ah, did you once see Shelley plain,
  And did he stop and speak to you
And did you speak to him again?
  How strange it seems and new!

II

But you were living before that,   5
  And also you are living after;
And the memory I started at—
  My starting moves your laughter.

III

I crossed a moor, with a name of its own
  And a certain use in the world no doubt,   10
Yet a hand's-breadth of it shines alone
  'Mid the blank miles round about:

IV

For there I picked up on the heather
  And there I put inside my breast
A molted feather, an eagle-feather!   15
  Well, I forget the rest.

Memorabilia things worth remembering.

ANDREA DEL SARTO°

(CALLED "THE FAULTLESS PAINTER")

BUT do not let us quarrel any more,
No, my Lucrezia; bear with me for once:
Sit down and all shall happen as you wish.
You turn your face, but does it bring your heart?
5   I'll work then for your friend's friend, never fear,
Treat his own subject after his own way,
Fix his own time, accept too his own price,
And shut the money into this small hand
When next it takes mine. Will it? tenderly?
10   Oh, I'll content him—but tomorrow, Love!
I often am much wearier than you think,
This evening more than usual, and it seems
As if—forgive now—should you let me sit
Here by the window with your hand in mine
15   And look a half hour forth on Fiesole,°
Both of one mind, as married people use,
Quietly, quietly the evening through,
I might get up tomorrow to my work
Cheerful and fresh as ever. Let us try.
20   Tomorrow, how you shall be glad for this!
Your soft hand is a woman of itself,
And mine the man's bared breast she curls inside.
Don't count the time lost, neither; you must serve
For each of the five pictures we require:
25   It saves a model. So! keep looking so—
My serpentining beauty, rounds on rounds!
—How could you ever prick those perfect ears,
Even to put the pearl there! oh, so sweet—

Andrea del Sarto Florentine painter of the sixteenth century.
15 Fiesole town on the hills above Florence.

My face, my moon, my everybody's moon,
Which everybody looks on and calls his,   30
And, I suppose, is looked on by in turn,
While she looks—no one's: very dear, no less.
You smile? why, there's my picture ready made,
There's what we painters call our harmony!
A common grayness silvers everything—   35
All in a twilight, you and I alike
—You, at the point of your first pride in me
(That's gone you know)—but I, at every point;
My youth, my hope, my art, being all toned down
To yonder sober pleasant Fiesole.   40
There's the bell clinking from the chapel-top;
That length of convent-wall across the way
Holds the trees safer, huddled more inside;
The last monk leaves the garden; days decrease,
And autumn grows, autumn in everything.   45
Eh? the whole seems to fall into a shape
As if I saw alike my work and self
And all that I was born to be and do,
A twilight-piece. Love, we are in God's hand.
How strange now, looks the life he makes us lead;   50
So free we seem, so fettered fast we are!
I feel he laid the fetter: let it lie!
This chamber for example—turn your head—
All that's behind us! You don't understand
Nor care to understand about my art,   55
But you can hear at least when people speak:
And that cartoon, the second from the door
—It is the thing, Love! so such things should be—
Behold Madonna!—I am bold to say.
I can do with my pencil what I know,   60
What I see, what at bottom of my heart
I wish for, if I ever wish so deep—
Do easily, too—when I say, perfectly,
I do not boast, perhaps: yourself are judge,
Who listened to the Legate's° talk last week,   65

65 Legate the Pope's representative.

And just as much they used to say in France.
At any rate 'tis easy, all of it!
No sketches first, no studies, that's long past:
I do what many dream of, all their lives,
70   —Dream? strive to do, and agonize to do,
And fail in doing. I could count twenty such
On twice your fingers, and not leave this town,
Who strive—you don't know how the others strive
To paint a little thing like that you smeared
75   Carelessly passing with your robes afloat—
Yet do much less, so much less, Someone says,
(I know his name, no matter)—so much less!
Well, less is more, Lucrezia: I am judged.
There burns a truer light of God in them,
80   In their vexed beating stuffed and stopped-up brain
Heart, or whate'er else, than goes on to prompt
This low-pulsed forthright craftsman's hand of mine.
Their works drop groundward, but themselves, I know
Reach many a time a Heaven that's shut to me,
85   Enter and take their place there sure enough,
Though they come back and cannot tell the world.
My works are nearer Heaven, but I sit here.
The sudden blood of these men! at a word—
Praise them, it boils, or blame them, it boils too.
90   I, painting from myself and to myself,
Know what I do, am unmoved by men's blame
Or their praise either. Somebody remarks
Morello's outline there is wrongly traced,
His hue mistaken; what of that? or else,
95   Rightly traced and well ordered; what of that?
Speak as they please, what does the mountain care?
Ah, but a man's reach should exceed his grasp,
Or what's a Heaven for? All is silver-gray
Placid and perfect with my art: the worse!
100 I know both what I want and what might gain,
And yet how profitless to know, to sigh
"Had I been two, another and myself,
Our head would have o'erlooked the world!" No
     doubt.
Yonder's a work now, of that famous youth

The Urbinate° who died five years ago.   105
('Tis copied, George Vasari sent it me.)
Well, I can fancy how he did it all,
Pouring his soul, with kings and popes to see,
Reaching, that heaven might so replenish him,
Above and through his art—for it gives way;   110
That arm is wrongly put—and there again—
A fault to pardon in the drawing's lines,
Its body, so to speak: its soul is right,
He means right—that, a child may understand.
Still, what an arm! and I could alter it: 115
But all the play, the insight and the stretch—
Out of me, out of me! And wherefore out?
Had you enjoined them on me, given me soul,
We might have risen to Raphael, I and you!
Nay, Love, you did give all I asked, I think—   120
More than I merit, yes, by many times.
But had you—oh, with the same perfect brow,
And perfect eyes, and more than perfect mouth,
And the low voice my soul hears, as a bird
The fowler's pipe, and follows to the snare—   125
Had you, with these the same, but brought a mind!
Some women do so. Had the mouth there urged
"God and the glory! never care for gain.
The present by the future, what is that?
Live for fame, side by side with Agnolo!°   130
Raphael is waiting: up to God, all three!"
I might have done it for you. So it seems:
Perhaps not. All is as God overrules.
Beside, incentives come from the soul's self;
The rest avail not. Why do I need you?   135
What wife had Raphael, or has Agnolo?
In this world, who can do a thing, will not;
And who would do it, cannot, I perceive:
Yet the will's somewhat—somewhat, too, the power—
And thus we half-men struggle. At the end,   140
God, I conclude, compensates, punishes.
'Tis safer for me, if the award be strict,

105 **The Urbinate** the painter Raphael, born in Urbino. 130
Agnolo Michelangelo.

That I am something underrated here,
Poor this long while, despised, to speak the truth.
145 I dared not, do you know, leave home all day,
For fear of chancing on the Paris lords.°
The best is when they pass and look aside;
But they speak sometimes; I must bear it all.
Well may they speak! That Francis, that first time,
150 And that long festal year at Fontainebleau!
I surely then could sometimes leave the ground,
Put on the glory, Raphael's daily wear,
In that humane great monarch's golden look—
One finger in his beard or twisted curl
155 Over his mouth's good mark that made the smile,
One arm about my shoulder, round my neck,
The jingle of his gold chain in my ear,
I painting proudly with his breath on me,
All his court round him, seeing with his eyes,
160 Such frank French eyes, and such a fire of souls
Profuse, my hand kept plying by those hearts—
And, best of all, this, this, this face beyond,
This in the background, waiting on my work,
To crown the issue with a last reward!
165 A good time, was it not, my kingly days?
And had you not grown restless . . . but I know—
'Tis done and past; 'twas right, my instinct said;
Too live the life grew, golden and not gray,
And I'm the weak-eyed bat no sun should tempt
170 Out of the grange whose four walls make his world.
How could it end in any other way?
You called me, and I came home to your heart.
The triumph was—to reach and stay there; since
I reached it ere the triumph, what is lost?
175 Let my hands frame your face in your hair's gold,
You beautiful Lucrezia that are mine!
"Raphael did this, Andrea painted that;
The Roman's° is the better when you pray,

146 the Paris lords Andrea del Sarto had served Francis I of Franc
(149). He was said to have spent on his wife money Francis ha
given him to buy works of art. 178 The Roman Raphael, wh
worked in Rome.

But still the other's Virgin was his wife—"
Men will excuse me. I am glad to judge
Both pictures in your presence; clearer grows
My better fortune, I resolve to think.
For, do you know, Lucrezia, as God lives,
Said one day Agnolo, his very self,
To Raphael . . . I have known it all these years . . .   *185*
(When the young man was flaming out his thoughts
Upon a palace-wall for Rome to see,
Too lifted up in heart because of it)
"Friend, there's a certain sorry little scrub
Goes up and down our Florence, none cares how,   *190*
Who, were he set to plan and execute
As you are, pricked on by your popes and kings,
Would bring the sweat into that brow of yours!"
To Raphael's!—And indeed the arm is wrong.
I hardly dare . . . yet, only you to see,   *195*
Give the chalk here—quick, thus the line should go!
Ay, but the soul! he's Raphael! rub it out!
Still, all I care for, if he spoke the truth,
(What he? why, who but Michel Agnolo?
Do you forget already words like those?)   *200*
If really there was such a chance, so lost—
Is, whether you're—not grateful—but more pleased.
Well, let me think so. And you smile indeed!
This hour has been an hour! Another smile?
If you would sit thus by me every night   *205*
I should work better, do you comprehend?
I mean that I should earn more, give you more.
See, it is settled dusk now; there's a star;
Morello's gone, the watch-lights show the wall,
The cue-owls speak the name we call them by.   *210*
Come from the window, love—come in, at last,
Inside the melancholy little house
We built to be so gay with. God is just.
King Francis may forgive me: oft at nights
When I look up from painting, eyes tired out,   *215*
The walls become illumined, brick from brick
Distinct, instead of mortar, fierce bright gold,
That gold of his I did cement them with!

Let us but love each other. Must you go?
220 That Cousin here again? he waits outside?
Must see you—you, and not with me? Those loans?
More gaming debts to pay? you smiled for that?
Well, let smiles buy me! have you more to spend?
While hand and eye and something of a heart
225 Are left me, work's my ware, and what's it worth?
I'll pay my fancy. Only let me sit
The gray remainder of the evening out,
Idle, you call it, and muse perfectly
How I could paint, were I but back in France,
230 One picture, just one more—the Virgin's face,
Not yours this time! I want you at my side
To hear them—that is, Michel Agnolo—
Judge all I do and tell you of its worth.
Will you? Tomorrow, satisfy your friend.
235 I take the subjects for his corridor,
Finish the portrait out of hand—there, there,
And throw him in another thing or two
If he demurs; the whole should prove enough
To pay for this same Cousin's freak. Beside,
240 What's better and what's all I care about,
Get you the thirteen scudi for the ruff!
Love, does that please you? Ah, but what does he,
The Cousin! what does he to please you more?

I am grown peaceful as old age tonight.
245 I regret little, I would change still less.
Since there my past life lies, why alter it?
The very wrong to Francis!—it is true
I took his coin, was tempted and complied,
And built this house and sinned, and all is said.
250 My father and my mother died of want.
Well, had I riches of my own? you see
How one gets rich! Let each one bear his lot.
They were born poor, lived poor, and poor they died
And I have labored somewhat in my time
255 And not been paid profusely. Some good son
Paint my two hundred pictures—let him try!
No doubt, there's something strikes a balance. Yes,

You loved me quite enough, it seems tonight.
This must suffice me here. What would one have?
In Heaven, perhaps, new chances, one more chance—   260
Four great walls in the New Jerusalem,°
Meted on each side by the angel's reed,
For Leonard,° Raphael, Agnolo and me
To cover—the three first without a wife,
While I have mine! So—still they overcome   265
Because there's still Lucrezia—as I choose.

Again the cousin's whistle! Go, my Love.

WOMEN AND ROSES

I

I DREAM of a red-rose tree.
And which of its roses three
Is the dearest rose to me?

II

Round and round, like a dance of snow
In a dazzling drift, as its guardians, go   5
Floating the women faded for ages,
Sculptured in stone, on the poet's pages.
Then follow women fresh and gay,
Living and loving and loved today.
Last, in the rear, flee the multitude of maidens,   10

261 New Jerusalem Heaven.   263 Leonard Leonardo da Vinci.

Beauties yet unborn. And all, to one cadence,
They circle their rose on my rose tree.

III

Dear rose, thy term is reached,
Thy leaf hangs loose and bleached:
15　Bees pass it unimpeached.

IV

Stay then, stoop, since I cannot climb,
You, great shapes of the antique time!
How shall I fix you, fire you, freeze you,
Break my heart at your feet to please you?
20　Oh, to possess and be possessed!
Hearts that beat 'neath each pallid breast!
Once but of love, the poesy, the passion,
Drink but once and die!—In vain, the same fashion,
They circle their rose on my rose tree.

V

25　Dear rose, thy joy's undimmed,
Thy cup is ruby-rimmed,
Thy cup's heart nectar-brimmed.

VI

Deep, as drops from a statue's plinth°
The bee sucked in by the hyacinth,
30　So will I bury me while burning,
Quench like him at a plunge my yearning,
Eyes in your eyes, lips on your lips!
Fold me fast where the cincture slips,
Prison all my soul in eternities of pleasure,
35　Girdle me for once! But no—the old measure,
They circle their rose on my rose tree.

28 **plinth** base.

VII

Dear rose without a thorn,°
Thy bud's the babe unborn:
First streak of a new morn.

VIII

Wings, lend wings for the cold, the clear!   40
What is far conquers what is near.
Roses will bloom nor want beholders,
Sprung from the dust where our flesh molders.
What shall arrive with the cycle's change?
A novel grace and a beauty strange.   45
I will make an Eve, be the artist that began her,
Shaped her to his mind!—Alas! in like manner
They circle their rose on my rose tree.

37 **rose without a thorn** symbol of the Virgin Mary.

THE HERETIC'S TRAGEDY

A MIDDLE-AGE INTERLUDE°

ROSA MUNDI; SEU, FULCITE ME FLORIBUS. A CONCEIT OF
MASTER GYSBRECHT, CANON-REGULAR OF SAINT JODOCUS-
BY-THE-BAR, YPRES CITY. CANTUQUE, *Virgilius.* AND
HATH OFTEN BEEN SUNG AT HOCK-TIDE AND FESTIVALS.
GAVISUS ERAM, *Jessides.*°

(It would seem to be a glimpse from the burning of Jacques du
Bourg-Molay, at Paris, A.D. 1314; as distorted by the refraction
from Flemish brain to brain, during the course of a couple of
centuries. R. B.)

I

PREADMONISHETH THE ABBOT DEODAET

THE Lord, we look to once for all,
  Is the Lord we should look at, all at once:
He knows not to vary, saith Saint Paul,
  Nor the shadow of turning, for the nonce.
5 See him no other than as he is!
  Give both the infinitudes their due—
Infinite mercy, but, I wis,
  As infinite a justice too.

                    [*Organ: plagal-cadence.*°]

  As infinite a justice too.

Interlude a short play performed at banquets between acts of a
mystery play. **ROSA MUNDI . . . Jessides:** *Rosa mundi* rose of the
world. *Fulcite me floribus* support me with flowers (Song of Solomon
2:5). **Conceit** invention. **Cantuque, Virgilius** the music is by Virgil-
ius. **Gavisus eram, Jessides** I, a son of Jesse, rejoice in it. The author
is putting himself in the line of David, the Psalmist, who was the
son of Jesse. See "Introduction." 8 **Plagal-cadence** closing chords.
Pun.

II

ONE SINGETH

John, Master of the Temple of God,   10
    Falling to sin the Unknown Sin,
What he bought of Emperor Aldabrod,
    He sold it to Sultan Saladin:
Till, caught by Pope Clement, a-buzzing there,
    Hornet-prince of the mad wasps' hive,   15
And clipped of his wings in Paris square,
    They bring him now to be burned alive.
       [*And wanteth there grace of lute or clavicithern,*
          ye shall say to confirm him who singeth—]
We bring John now to be burned alive.

III

In the midst is a goodly gallows built;
    'Twixt fork and fork, a stake is stuck;   20
But first they set divers tumbrils° atilt,
    Make a trench all round with the city muck;
Inside they pile log upon log, good store;
    Faggots no few, blocks great and small,
Reach a man's mid-thigh, no less, no more—   25
    For they mean he should roast in the sight of all.

CHORUS

We mean he should roast in the sight of all.

IV

Good sappy bavins that kindle forthwith;
    Billets that blaze substantial and slow;
Pine-stump split deftly, dry as pith;   30
    Larch-heart that chars to a chalk-white glow:
Then up they hoist me John in a chafe,
    Sling him fast like a hog to scorch,

21 tumbril cart.

Spit in his face, then leap back safe,
35   Sing "Laudes"° and bid clap-to the torch.

CHORUS

Laus Deo°—who bids clap-to the torch.

V

John of the Temple, whose fame so bragged,
    Is burning alive in Paris square!
How can he curse, if his mouth is gagged?
40   Or wriggle his neck, with a collar there?
Or heave his chest, which a band goes round?
    Or threat with his fist, since his arms are spliced?
Or kick with his feet, now his legs are bound?
    —Thinks John, I will call upon Jesus Christ.
                    [*Here one crosseth himself.*]

VI

45 Jesus Christ—John had bought and sold,
    Jesus Christ—John had eaten and drunk;
To him, the Flesh meant silver and gold.
    (*Salvâ reverêntiâ.*)°
Now it was, "Savior, bountiful lamb,
50   "I have roasted thee Turks, though men roast me!
"See thy servant, the plight wherein I am!
    "Art thou a savior? Save thou me!"

CHORUS

'Tis John the mocker cries, "Save thou me!"

VII

Who maketh God's menace an idle word?

35 "**Laudes**" hymns of praise. 36 **Laus Deo** praise be to God.
48 **Salvâ reverêntiâ** direction to make a reverence (bow or genu-
flection) to the Body of God (the "Flesh") in the Sacrament.

—Saith, it no more means what it proclaims,   *55*
Than a damsel's threat to her wanton bird?—
    For she too prattles of ugly names.
—Saith, he knoweth but one thing—what he knows?
    That God is good and the rest is breath;
Why else is the same styled Sharon's rose?°   *60*
    Once a rose, ever a rose, he saith.

CHORUS

O, John shall yet find a rose, he saith!

VIII

Alack, there be roses and roses, John!
    Some, honied of taste like your leman's° tongue:
Some, bitter; for why? (roast gaily on!)   *65*
    Their tree struck root in devil's-dung.
When Paul once reasoned of righteousness
    And of temperance and of judgment to come,
Good Felix trembled,° he could no less:
    John, snickering, crook'd his wicked thumb.   *70*

CHORUS

What cometh to John of the wicked thumb?

IX

Ha ha, John plucketh now at his rose
    To rid himself of a sorrow at heart!
Lo—petal on petal, fierce rays unclose;
    Anther on anther, sharp spikes outstart;   *75*
And with blood for dew, the bosom boils;
    And a gust of sulphur is all its smell;
And lo, he is horribly in the toils
    Of a coal-black giant flower of hell!

60 **Sharon's rose** Song of Solomon 2:1.   64 **leman** mistress.   67–69
Paul . . . trembled Acts 24:25.

CHORUS

80   What maketh Heaven, That maketh hell.

X

So, as John called now, through the fire amain,
   On the Name, he had cursed with, all his life—
To the Person, he bought and sold again—
   For the Face, with his daily buffets rife—
85   Feature by feature It took its place:
   And his voice, like a mad dog's choking bark,
At the steady whole of the Judge's face—
   Died. Forth John's soul flared into the dark.

SUBJOINETH THE ABBOT DEODAET

God help all poor souls lost in the dark!

TWO IN THE CAMPAGNA°

I

I WONDER do you feel today
   As I have felt since, hand in hand,
We sat down on the grass, to stray
   In spirit better through the land,
5   This morn of Rome and May?

Campagna the great plain (*champaign*, 21) surrounding the City of
Rome, sprinkled with ruins.

II

For me, I touched a thought, I know,
   Has tantalized me many times,
(Like turns of thread the spiders throw
   Mocking across our path) for rhymes
To catch at and let go.   10

III

Help me to hold it! First it left
   The yellowing fennel, run to seed
There, branching from the brickwork's cleft,
   Some old tomb's ruin: yonder weed
Took up the floating weft,   15

IV

Where one small orange cup amassed
   Five beetles—blind and green they grope
Among the honey-meal: and last,
   Everywhere on the grassy slope
I traced it. Hold it fast!   20

V

The champaign with its endless fleece
   Of feathery grasses everywhere!
Silence and passion, joy and peace,
   An everlasting wash of air—
Rome's ghost since her decease.   25

VI

Such life here, through such lengths of hours,
   Such miracles performed in play,
Such primal naked forms of flowers,
   Such letting nature have her way
While heaven looks from its towers!   30

VII

How say you? Let us, O my dove,
   Let us be unashamed of soul,
As earth lies bare to heaven above!
   How is it under our control
35 To love or not to love?

VIII

I would that you were all to me,
   You that are just so much, no more.
Nor yours nor mine, nor slave nor free!
   Where does the fault lie? What the core
40 O' the wound, since wound must be?

IX

I would I could adopt your will,
   See with your eyes, and set my heart
Beating by yours, and drink my fill
   At your soul's springs—your part my part
45 In life, for good and ill.

X

No. I yearn upward, touch you close,
   Then stand away. I kiss your cheek,
Catch your soul's warmth—I pluck the rose
   And love it more than tongue can speak—
50 Then the good minute goes.

XI

Already how am I so far
   Out of that minute? Must I go
Still like the thistle-ball, no bar,
   Onward, whenever light winds blow,
55 Fixed by no friendly star?

XII

Just when I seemed about to learn!
   Where is the thread now? Off again!
The old trick! Only I discern—
   Infinite passion, and the pain
Of finite hearts that yearn.   *60*

from *DRAMATIS PERSONAE*

(1864)

ABT VOGLER°

(AFTER HE HAS BEEN EXTEMPORIZING UPON THE
MUSICAL INSTRUMENT° OF HIS INVENTION)

I

Would that the structure brave, the manifold music I
    build,
    Bidding my organ obey, calling its keys to their
      work,
Claiming each slave of the sound, at a touch, as when
    Solomon willed
    Armies of angels that soar, legions of demons that
      lurk,
Man, brute, reptile, fly—alien of end and of aim,
    Adverse, each from the other heaven-high, hell-
      deep removed—
Should rush into sight at once as he named the in-
    effable Name,°
    And pile him a palace straight, to pleasure the prin-
      cess he loved!

Abt Vogler German musician of the eighteenth and early nine-
teenth centuries. **Musical Instrument** a small organ. 7 **the in-
effable Name** the name of God, not spoken by pious Jews, used in
magic.

II

Would it might tarry like his, the beautiful building of
    mine,
    This which my keys in a crowd pressed and impor-
        tuned to raise!   10
Ah, one and all, how they helped, would dispart now
    and now combine,
    Zealous to hasten the work, heighten their master
        his praise!
And one would bury his brow with a blind plunge
    down to hell,
    Burrow awhile and build, broad on the roots of
        things,
Then up again swim into sight, having based me my
    palace well,   15
    Founded it, fearless of flame, flat on the nether
        springs.

III

And another would mount and march, like the excellent
    minion° he was,
    Ay, another and yet another, one crowd but with
        many a crest,
Raising my rampired walls of gold as transparent as
    glass,
    Eager to do and die, yield each his place to the rest: 20
For higher still and higher (as a runner tips with fire,
    When a great illumination surprises a festal night—
Outlining round and round Rome's dome from space
    to spire)
    Up, the pinnacled glory reached, and the pride of
    my soul was in sight.

IV

In sight? Not half! for it seemed, it was certain, to
    match man's birth,   25

17 **minion** servant.

Nature in turn conceived, obeying an impulse as I;

And the emulous heaven yearned down, made effort to reach the earth,

As the earth had done her best, in my passion, to scale the sky:

Novel splendors burst forth, grew familiar and dwelled with mine,

30   Not a point nor peak but found and fixed its wandering star;

Meteor-moons, balls of blaze: and they did not pale nor pine,

For earth had attained to heaven, there was no more near nor far.

V

Nay more; for there wanted not who walked in the glare and glow,

Presences plain in the place; or, fresh from the Protoplast,°

Furnished for ages to come, when a kindlier wind should blow,

35   Lured now to begin and live, in a house to their liking at last;

Or else the wonderful dead who have passed through the body and gone,

But were back once more to breathe in an old world worth their new:

What never had been, was now; what was, as it shall be anon;

40   And what is—shall I say, matched both? for I was made perfect too.

VI

All through my keys that gave their sounds to a wish of my soul,

34 **Protoplast** first fashioner or creator.

All through my soul that praised as its wish flowed
    visibly forth,
All through music and me! For think, had I painted
    the whole,
    Why, there it had stood, to see, nor the process so
      wonder-worth:
Had I written the same, made verse—still, effect pro-
    ceeds from cause,   45
    Ye know why the forms are fair, ye hear how the
      tale is told;
It is all triumphant art, but art in obedience to laws,
    Painter and poet are proud in the artist-list en-
      rolled:—

VII

But here is the finger of God, a flash of the will that
    can,
    Existent behind all laws, that made them and, lo,
      they are!   50
And I know not if, save in this, such gift be allowed
    to man,
    That out of three sounds he frame, not a fourth
      sound, but a star.
Consider it well: each tone of our scale in itself is
    naught;
    It is everywhere in the world—loud, soft, and all
      is said:
Give it to me to use! I mix it with two in my thought: 55
    And, there! Ye have heard and seen: consider and
      bow the head!

VIII

Well, it is gone at last, the palace of music I reared;
    Gone! and the good tears start, the praises that
      come too slow;
For one is assured at first, one scarce can say that he
    feared,

That he even gave it a thought, the gone thing wa
60   to go.
Never to be again! But many more of the kind
    As good, nay, better perchance: is this your com
         fort to me?
To me, who must be saved because I cling with m
     mind
    To the same, same self, same love, same God: ay
         what was, shall be.

IX

Therefore to whom turn I but to thee, the ineffabl
65   Name?
    Builder and maker, thou, of houses not made wit
         hands!
What, have fear of change from thee who art ever th
     same?
    Doubt that thy power can fill the heart that th
         power expands?
There shall never be one lost good! What was, shal
     live as before;
70   The evil is null, is naught, is silence implying sound
What was good shall be good, with, for evil, so muc
     good more;
    On the earth the broken arcs; in the Heaven, a per
         fect round.

X

All we have willed or hoped or dreamed of good shal
     exist;
    Not its semblance, but itself; no beauty, nor good
         nor power
Whose voice has gone forth, but each survives fo
75   the melodist
    When eternity affirms the conception of an hour.
The high that proved too high, the heroic for earth
     too hard,

The passion that left the ground to lose itself in
    the sky,
Are music sent up to God by the lover and the bard;
    Enough that he heard it once: we shall hear it by-
    and-by.   80

XI

And what is our failure here but a triumph's evidence
    For the fullness of the days? Have we withered or
    agonized?
Why else was the pause prolonged but that singing
    might issue thence?
    Why rushed the discords in but that harmony
    should be prized?
Sorrow is hard to bear, and doubt is slow to clear,   85
    Each sufferer says his say, his scheme of the weal
    and woe:
But God has a few of us whom he whispers in the ear;
    The rest may reason and welcome: 'tis we
    musicians know.

XII

Well, it is earth with me; silence resumes her reign:
    I will be patient and proud, and soberly acquiesce.   90
Give me the keys. I feel for the common chord again,
    Sliding by semitones, till I sink to the minor—yes,
And I blunt it into a ninth, and I stand on alien
    ground,
    Surveying awhile the heights I rolled from into the
    deep;
Which, hark, I have dared and done, for my resting-
    place is found,   95
    The C Major of this life: so, now I will try to sleep.

CALIBAN UPON SETEBOS; OR, NATURAL
THEOLOGY IN THE ISLAND°

"Thou thoughtest that I was altogether such a one as thy-
self."°

['WILL sprawl, now that the heat of day is best,
Flat on his belly in the pit's much mire,
With elbows wide, fists clenched to prop his chin.
And, while he kicks both feet in the cool slush,
5   And feels about his spine small eft-things° course,
Run in and out each arm, and make him laugh:
And while above his head a pompion-plant,
Coating the cave-top as a brow its eye,
Creeps down to touch and tickle hair and beard,
10 And now a flower drops with a bee inside,
And now a fruit to snap at, catch and crunch—
He looks out o'er yon sea which sunbeams cross
And recross till they weave a spider web
(Meshes of fire, some great fish breaks at times)
15 And talks to his own self, howe'er he please,
Touching that other, whom his dam° called God.
Because to talk about Him, vexes—ha,
Could He but know! and time to vex is now,
When talk is safer than in winter-time.
20 Moreover Prosper and Miranda° sleep
In confidence he drudges at their task,
And it is good to cheat the pair, and gibe,
Letting the rank tongue blossom into speech.]

Caliban . . . Island Caliban is the brute in Shakespeare's *The Tem-
pest.* Setebos is his God. Natural theology claims to prove the
existence of God and to define his nature apart from revelation by
arguing from the created to the creator. **"Thou thoughtest . . . thy-
self"** Psalm 50:21.   **5 eft-things** lizards, etc.   **16 his dam** Caliban's
mother worshipped Setebos.   **20 Prosper and Miranda** Caliban's
master and mistress.

Setebos, Setebos, and Setebos!
'Thinketh, He dwelleth i' the cold o' the moon.   25

'Thinketh He made it, with the sun to match,
But not the stars; the stars came otherwise;
Only made clouds, winds, meteors, such as that:
Also this isle, what lives and grows thereon,
And snaky sea which rounds and ends the same.   30

'Thinketh, it came of being ill at ease:
He hated that He cannot change His cold,
Nor cure its ache. 'Hath spied an icy fish
That longed to 'scape the rock-stream where she lived,
And thaw herself within the lukewarm brine   35
O' the lazy sea her stream thrusts far amid,
A crystal spike 'twixt two warm walls of wave;
Only, she ever sickened, found repulse
At the other kind of water, not her life,
(Green-dense and dim-delicious, bred o' the sun)   40
Flounced back from bliss she was not born to breathe,
And in her old bounds buried her despair,
Hating and loving warmth alike: so He.

'Thinketh, He made thereat the sun, this isle,
Trees and the fowls here, beast and creeping thing.   45
Yon otter, sleek-wet, black, lithe as a leech;
Yon auk, one fire-eye in a ball of foam,
That floats and feeds; a certain badger brown
He hath watched hunt with that slant white-wedge eye
By moonlight; and the pie with the long tongue   50
That pricks deep into oakwarts for a worm,
And says a plain word when she finds her prize,
But will not eat the ants; the ants themselves
That build a wall of seeds and settled stalks
About their hole—He made all these and more,   55
Made all we see, and us, in spite: how else?
He could not, Himself, make a second self
To be His mate; as well have made Himself:
He would not make what he mislikes or slights,
An eyesore to Him, or not worth His pains: 60

But did, in envy, listlessness or sport,
Make what Himself would fain, in a manner, be—
Weaker in most points, stronger in a few,
Worthy, and yet mere playthings all the while,
65 Things He admires and mocks too—that is it.
Because, so brave, so better though they be,
It nothing skills if He begin to plague.
Look now, I melt a gourd-fruit into mash,
Add honeycomb and pods, I have perceived,
70 Which bite like finches when they bill and kiss—
Then, when froth rises bladdery, drink up all,
Quick, quick, till maggots scamper through my brain;
Last, throw me on my back i' the seeded thyme,
And wanton, wishing I were born a bird.
75 Put case, unable to be what I wish,
I yet could make a live bird out of clay:
Would not I take clay, pinch my Caliban
Able to fly?—for, there, see, he hath wings,
And great comb like the hoopoe's to admire,
80 And there, a sting to do his foes offense,
There, and I will that he begin to live,
Fly to yon rock-top, nip me off the horns
Of grigs high up that make the merry din,
Saucy through their veined wings, and mind me not.
85 In which feat, if his leg snapped, brittle clay,
And he lay stupid-like—why, I should laugh;
And if he, spying me, should fall to weep,
Beseech me to be good, repair his wrong,
Bid his poor leg smart less or grow again—
90 Well, as the chance were, this might take or else
Not take my fancy: I might hear his cry,
And give the mankin three sound legs for one,
Or pluck the other off, leave him like an egg,
And lessoned he was mine and merely clay.
95 Were this no pleasure, lying in the thyme,
Drinking the mash, with brain become alive,
Making and marring clay at will? So He.

'Thinketh, such shows nor right nor wrong in Him,
Nor kind, nor cruel: He is strong and Lord.

'Am strong myself compared to yonder crabs   100
That march now from the mountain to the sea,
'Let twenty pass, and stone the twenty-first,
Loving not, hating not, just choosing so.
'Say, the first straggler that boasts purple spots
Shall join the file, one pincer twisted off;   105
'Say, this bruised fellow shall receive a worm,
And two worms he whose nippers end in red;
As it likes me each time, I do: so He.

Well then, 'supposeth He is good i' the main,
Placable if His mind and ways were guessed,   110
But rougher than His handiwork, be sure!
Oh, He hath made things worthier than Himself,
And envieth that, so helped, such things do more
Than He who made them! What consoles but this?
That they, unless through Him, do naught at all,   115
And must submit: what other use in things?
'Hath cut a pipe of pithless elder-joint
That, blown through, gives exact the scream o' the
    jay
When from her wing you twitch the feathers blue:
Sound this, and little birds that hate the jay   120
Flock within stone's throw, glad their foe is hurt:
Put case such pipe could prattle and boast forsooth
"I catch the birds, I am the crafty thing,
I make the cry my maker cannot make
With his great round mouth; he must blow through
    mine!"   125
Would not I smash it with my foot? So He.

But wherefore rough, why cold and ill at ease?
Aha, that is a question! Ask, for that,
What knows—the something over Setebos
That made Him, or He, may be, found and fought,   130
Worsted, drove off and did to nothing, perchance.
There may be something quiet o'er His head,
Out of His reach, that feels nor joy nor grief,
Since both derive from weakness in some way.
I joy because the quails come; would not joy   135

Could I bring quails here when I have a mind:
This Quiet, all it hath a mind to, doth.
'Esteemeth stars the outposts of its couch,
But never spends much thought nor care that way.
140 It may look up, work up—the worse for those
It works on! 'Careth but for Setebos
The many-handed as a cuttle-fish,
Who, making Himself feared through what He does,
Looks up, first, and perceives he cannot soar
145 To what is quiet and hath happy life;
Next looks down here, and out of very spite
Makes this a bauble-world to ape yon real,
These good things to match those as hips do grapes.
'Tis solace making baubles, ay, and sport.
150 Himself peeped late, eyed Prosper at his books
Careless and lofty, lord now of the isle:
Vexed, 'stitched a book of broad leaves, arrow-shaped,
Wrote thereon, he knows what, prodigious words;
Has peeled a wand and called it by a name;
155 Weareth at whiles for an enchanter's robe
The eyed skin of a supple oncelot;
And hath an ounce sleeker than youngling mole,
A four-legged serpent he makes cower and couch,
Now snarl, now hold its breath and mind his eye.
160 And saith she is Miranda and my wife:
'Keeps for his Ariel° a tall pouch-bill crane
He bids go wade for fish and straight disgorge;
Also a sea-beast, lumpish, which he snared,
Blinded the eyes of, and brought somewhat tame,
165 And split its toe-webs, and now pens the drudge
In a hole o' the rock and calls him Caliban;
A bitter heart that bides its time and bites.
'Plays thus at being Prosper in a way,
Taketh his mirth with make-believes: so He.

170 His dam held that the Quiet made all things
Which Setebos vexed only: 'holds not so.
Who made them weak, meant weakness He might vex.

161 **Ariel** Prospero's fairy servant.

Had He meant other, while His hand was in,
Why not make horny eyes no thorn could prick,
Or plate my scalp with bone against the snow,   175
Or overscale my flesh 'neath joint and joint,
Like an orc's armor? Ay—so spoil His sport!
He is the One now: only He doth all.

'Saith, He may like, perchance, what profits Him.
Ay, himself loves what does him good; but why?   180
'Gets good no otherwise. This blinded beast
Loves whoso places flesh-meat on his nose,
But, had he eyes, would want no help, but hate
Or love, just as it liked him: He hath eyes.
Also it pleaseth Setebos to work,   185
Use all His hands, and exercise much craft,
By no means for the love of what is worked.
'Tasteth, himself, no finer good i' the world
When all goes right, in this safe summertime,
And he wants little, hungers, aches not much,   190
Than trying what to do with wit and strength.
'Falls to make something: 'piled yon pile of turfs,
And squared and stuck there squares of soft white
      chalk,
And, with a fish-tooth, scratched a moon on each,
And set up endwise certain spikes of tree,   195
And crowned the whole with a sloth's skull atop,
Found dead i' the woods, too hard for one to kill.
No use at all i' the work, for work's sole sake;
'Shall some day knock it down again: so He.

'Saith He is terrible: watch His feats in proof!   200
One hurricane will spoil six good months' hope.
He hath a spite against me, that I know,
Just as He favors Prosper, who knows why?
So it is, all the same, as well I find.
'Wove wattles° half the winter, fenced them firm   205
With stone and stake to stop she-tortoises
Crawling to lay their eggs here: well, one wave,

205 **wattles** wattling is the interlacing of rods with twigs or the like
for making enclosures.

Feeling the foot of Him upon its neck,
Gaped as a snake does, lolled out its large tongue,
210 And licked the whole labor flat: so much for spite.
'Saw a ball flame down late (yonder it lies)
Where, half an hour before, I slept i' the shade:
Often they scatter sparkles: there is force!
'Dug up a newt He may have envied once
215 And turned to stone, shut up inside a stone.
Please Him and hinder this?—What Prosper does?
Aha, if He would tell me how! Not He!
There is the sport: discover how or die!
All need not die, for of the things o' the isle
220 Some flee afar, some dive, some run up trees;
Those at His mercy—why, they please Him most
When .. when .. well, never try the same way twice!
Repeat what act has pleased, He may grow wroth.
You must not know His ways, and play Him off,
225 Sure of the issue. 'Doth the like himself:
'Spareth a squirrel that it nothing fears
But steals the nut from underneath my thumb,
And when I threat, bites stoutly in defense:
'Spareth an urchin that contrariwise,
230 Curls up into a ball, pretending death
For fright at my approach: the two ways please.
But what would move my choler more than this,
That either creature counted on its life
Tomorrow and next day and all days to come,
235 Saying, forsooth, in the inmost of its heart,
"Because he did so yesterday with me,
And otherwise with such another brute,
So must he do henceforth and always."—Ay?
Would teach the reasoning couple what "must" means
240 'Doth as he likes, or wherefore Lord? So He.

'Conceiveth all things will continue thus,
And we shall have to live in fear of Him
So long as He lives, keeps His strength: no change,
If He have done His best, make no new world
245 To please Him more, so leave off watching this—
If He surprise not even the Quiet's self

Some strange day—or, suppose, grow into it
As grubs grow butterflies: else, here are we,
And there is He, and nowhere help at all.

'Believeth with the life, the pain shall stop.   250
His dam held different, that after death
He both plagued enemies and feasted friends:
Idly! He doth His worst in this our life,
Giving just respite lest we die through pain,
Saving last pain for worst—with which, an end.   255
Meanwhile, the best way to escape His ire
Is, not to seem too happy. 'Sees, himself,
Yonder two flies, with purple films and pink,
Bask on the pompion-bell above: kills both.
'Sees two black painful beetles roll their ball   260
On head and tail as if to save their lives:
Moves them the stick away they strive to clear.

Even so, 'would have Him misconceive, suppose
This Caliban strives hard and ails no less,
And always, above all else, envies Him;   265
Wherefore he mainly dances on dark nights,
Moans in the sun, gets under holes to laugh,
And never speaks his mind save housed as now:
Outside, 'groans, curses. If He caught me here,
O'erheard this speech, and asked "What chucklest at?"   270
'Would, to appease Him, cut a finger off,
Or of my three kid yearlings burn the best,
Or let the toothsome apples rot on tree,
Or push my tame beast for the orc to taste:
While myself lit a fire, and made a song   275
And sung it, *"What I hate, be consecrate
To celebrate Thee and Thy state, no mate
For Thee; what see for envy in poor me?"*
Hoping the while, since evils sometimes mend,
Warts rub away and sores are cured with slime,   280
That some strange day, will either the Quiet catch
And conquer Setebos, or likelier He
Decrepit may doze, doze, as good as die.
[What, what? A curtain o'er the world at once!

285 Crickets stop hissing; not a bird—or, yes,
   There scuds His raven that has told Him all!
   It was fool's play, this prattling! Ha! The wind
   Shoulders the pillared dust, death's house o' the move,
   And fast invading fires begin! White blaze—
   A tree's head snaps—and there, there, there, there,
290   there,
   His thunder follows! Fool to gibe at Him!
   Lo! 'Lieth flat and loveth Setebos!
   'Maketh his teeth meet through his upper lip,
   Will let those quails fly, will not eat this month
295 One little mess of whelks, so he may 'scape!]

EPILOGUE

FIRST SPEAKER, *as David*

I

On the first of the Feast of Feasts,
   The Dedication Day,°
When the Levites joined the Priests
   At the Altar in robed array,
5 Gave signal to sound and say—

II

When the thousands, rear and van,
   Swarming with one accord
Became as a single man
   (Look, gesture, thought and word)
10 In praising and thanking the Lord—

2 **Dedication Day** ceremonial dedication of the Temple in Jerusalem.

III

When the singers lift up their voice,
   And the trumpets made endeavor,
Sounding, "In God rejoice!"
    Saying, "In Him rejoice
Whose mercy endureth forever!"—   15

IV

Then the Temple filled with a cloud,
   Even the House of the Lord;
Porch bent and pillar bowed:
    For the presence of the Lord,
In the glory of His cloud,
    Had filled the House of the Lord.   20

SECOND SPEAKER, as Renan°

Gone now! All gone across the dark so far,
   Sharpening fast, shuddering ever, shutting still,
Dwindling into the distance, dies that star
    Which came, stood, opened once! We gazed our
       fill   25
With upturned faces on as real a Face
   That, stooping from grave music and mild fire,
Took in our homage, made a visible place
    Through many a depth of glory, gyre on gyre,°
For the dim human tribute. Was this true?   30
   Could man indeed avail, mere praise of his,
To help by rapture God's own rapture too,
    Thrill with a heart's red tinge that pure pale bliss?
Why did it end? Who failed to beat the breast,
   And shriek, and throw the arms protesting wide,   35
When a first shadow showed the star addressed
    Itself to motion, and on either side
The rims contracted as the rays retired;
    The music, like a fountain's sickening pulse,

Renan Ernest Renan, author of a *Life of Jesus* (1863) that ex-
plained away the mysteries. 29 **gyre** spiral.

40   Subsided on itself; awhile transpired
        Some vestige of a Face no pangs convulse,
     No prayers retard; then even this was gone,
        Lost in the night at last. We, lone and left
     Silent through centuries, ever and anon
45   Venture to probe again the vault bereft
     Of all now save the lesser lights, a mist
        Of multitudinous points, yet suns, men say—
     And this leaps ruby, this lurks amethyst,
        But where may hide what came and loved our clay?
50   How shall the sage detect in yon expanse
        The star which chose to stoop and stay for us?
     Unroll the records! Hailed ye such advance
        Indeed, and did your hope evanish thus?
     Watchers of twilight, is the worst averred?
55   We shall not look up, know ourselves are seen,
     Speak, and be sure that we again are heard,
        Acting or suffering, have the disk's serene
     Reflect our life, absorb an earthly flame,
        Nor doubt that, were mankind inert and numb,
60   Its core had never crimsoned all the same,
        Nor, missing ours, its music fallen dumb?
     Oh, dread succession to a dizzy post,
        Sad sway of scepter whose mere touch appalls,
     Ghastly dethronement, cursed by those the most
65   On whose repugnant brow the crown next falls!

THIRD SPEAKER

I

Witless alike of will and way divine,
How heaven's high with earth's low should intertwine!
Friends, I have seen through your eyes: now use mine!

II

Take the least man of all mankind, as I;

Look at his head and heart, find how and why   70
He differs from his fellows utterly:

III

Then, like me, watch when nature by degrees
Grows alive round him, as in Arctic seas
(They said of old) the instinctive water flees

IV

Toward some elected point of central rock,   75
As though, for its sake only, roamed the flock
Of waves about the waste: awhile they mock

V

With radiance caught for the occasion—hues
Of blackest hell now, now such reds and blues
As only heaven could fitly interfuse—   80

VI

The mimic monarch of the whirlpool, king
O' the current for a minute: then they wring
Up by the roots and oversweep the thing,

VII

And hasten off, to play again elsewhere
The same part, choose another peak as bare,   85
They find and flatter, feast and finish there.

VIII

When you see what I tell you—nature dance
About each man of us, retire, advance,
As though the pageant's end were to enhance

IX

90   His worth, and——once the life, his product, gained—
Roll away elsewhere, keep the strife sustained,
And show thus real, a thing the North but feigned—

X

When you acknowledge that one world could do
All the diverse work, old yet ever new,
95   Divide us, each from other, me from you—

XI

Why, where's the need of Temple, when the walls
O' the world are that? What use of swells and falls
From Levites' choir, Priests' cries, and trumpet-calls?

XII

That one Face, far from vanish, rather grows,
100   Or decomposes but to recompose,
Become my universe that feels and knows.

from THE RING AND THE BOOK

(1868–69)

O LYRIC LOVE°

O LYRIC Love, half angel and half bird
And all a wonder and a wild desire—
Boldest of hearts that ever braved the sun,
Took sanctuary within the holier blue,
And sang a kindred soul out to his face—   5
Yet human at the red-ripe of the heart—
When the first summons from the darkling earth
Reached thee amid thy chambers, blanched their blue,
And bared them of the glory—to drop down,
To toil for man, to suffer or to die—   10
This is the same voice: can thy soul know change?
Hail then, and hearken from the realms of help!
Never may I commence my song, my due
To God who best taught song by gift of thee,

O lyric Love conclusion of the first book of *The Ring and the Book*,
here renumbered. It is addressed to the poet's wife, now dead,
thought of as the muse of the poem. A ring given him by his wife
suggested the ring of the title, the circle of truth created by the
imagination out of the square of fact (literally the Old Yellow Book
Browning had found in a bookstall in Florence, a collection of
documents dealing with a seventeenth century Roman murder case;
See "Introduction").

13 Except with bent head and beseeching hand—
That still, despite the distance and the dark,
What was, again may be; some interchange
Of grace, some splendor once thy very thought,
Some benediction anciently thy smile:
20 —Never conclude, but raising hand and head
Thither where eyes, that cannot reach, yet yearn
For all hope, all sustainment, all reward,
Their utmost up and on—so blessing back
In those thy realms of help, that heaven thy home,
25 Some whiteness which, I judge, thy face makes proud,
Some wanness where, I think, thy foot may fall!

GIUSEPPE CAPONSACCHI°

ANSWER you, Sirs? Do I understand aright?
Have patience! In this sudden smoke from hell—
So things disguise themselves—I cannot see
My own hand held thus broad before my face
5 And know it again. Answer you? Then that means
Tell over twice what I, the first time, told
Six months ago: 'twas here, I do believe,
Fronting you same three in this very room,
I stood and told you: yet now no one laughs,
10 Who then . . . nay, dear my lords, but laugh you did,
As good as laugh, what in a judge we style
Laughter—no levity, nothing indecorous, lords!
Only—I think I apprehend the mood:

Giuseppe Caponsacchi the priest who accompanied Pompilia in her
flight from her husband, Guido. (Selections from *The Ring and the
Book* have been renumbered in accordance with usual practice.)

There was the blameless shrug, permissible smirk,
The pen's pretense at play with the pursed mouth,   15
The titter stifled in the hollow palm
Which rubbed the eyebrow and caressed the nose,
When I first told my tale: they meant, you know,
"The sly one, all this we are bound believe!
Well, he can say no other than what he says.   20
We have been young, too—come, there's greater
          guilt!
Let him but decently disembroil himself,
Scramble from out the scrape nor move the mud—
We solid ones may risk a finger-stretch!
And now you sit as grave, stare as aghast   25
As if I were a phantom: now 'tis—"Friend,
Collect yourself!"—no laughing matter more—
"Counsel the Court in this extremity,
Tell us again!"—tell that, for telling which,
I got the jocular piece of punishment,   30
Was sent to lounge a little in the place
Whence now of a sudden here you summon me
To take the intelligence from just—your lips!
You, Judge Tommati, who then tittered most—
That she I helped eight months since to escape   35
Her husband, was retaken by the same,
Three days ago, if I have seized your sense—
(I being disallowed to interfere,
Meddle or make in a matter none of mine,
For you and law were guardians quite enough   40
O' the innocent, without a pert priest's help)—
And that he has butchered her accordingly,
As she foretold and as myself believed—
And, so foretelling and believing so,
We were punished, both of us, the merry way: 45
Therefore, tell once again the tale! For what?
Pompilia is only dying while I speak!
Why does the mirth hang fire and miss the smile?
My masters, there's an old book, you should con
For strange adventures, applicable yet,   50
'Tis stuffed with. Do you know that there was once
This thing: a multitude of worthy folk

Took recreation, watched a certain group
Of soldiery intent upon a game—
55 How first they wrangled, but soon fell to play,
Threw dice—the best diversion in the world.
A word in your ear—they are now casting lots,
Ay, with that gesture quaint and cry uncouth,
For the coat of One murdered an hour ago!
60 I am a priest—talk of what I have learned.
Pompilia is bleeding out her life belike,
Gasping away the latest breath of all,
This minute, while I talk—not while you laugh?

Yet, being sobered now, what is it you ask
65 By way of explanation? There's the fact!
It seems to fill the universe with sight
And sound—from the four corners of this earth
Tells itself over, to my sense at least.
But you may want it lower set i' the scale—
70 Too vast, too close it clangs in the ear, perhaps;
You'd stand back just to comprehend it more.
Well then, let me, the hollow rock, condense
The voice o' the sea and wind, interpret you
The mystery of this murder. God above!
75 It is too paltry, such a transference
O' the storm's roar to the cranny of the stone!

This deed, you saw begin—why does its end
Surprise you? Why should the event enforce
The lesson, we ourselves learned, she and I,
80 From the first o' the fact, and taught you, all in vain?
This Guido from whose throat you took my grasp,
Was this man to be favored, now, or feared,
Let do his will, or have his will restrained,
In the relation with Pompilia? Say!
85 Did any other man need interpose
—Oh, though first comer, though as strange at the
    work
As fribble must be, coxcomb, fool that's near
To knave as, say, a priest who fears the world—
Was he bound brave the peril, save the doomed,

Or go on, sing his snatch and pluck his flower,   90
Keep the straight path and let the victim die?
I held so; you decided otherwise,
Saw no such peril, therefore no such need
To stop song, loosen flower, and leave path. Law,
Law was aware and watching, would suffice,   95
Wanted no priest's intrusion, palpably
Pretense, too manifest a subterfuge!
Whereupon I, priest, coxcomb, fribble and fool,
Ensconced me in my corner, thus rebuked,
A kind of culprit, overzealous hound   100
Kicked for his pains to kennel; I gave place
To you, and let the law reign paramount:
I left Pompilia to your watch and ward,
And now you point me—there and thus she lies!

Men, for the last time, what do you want with me?   105
Is it—you acknowledge, as it were, a use,
A profit in employing me?—at length
I may conceivably help the august law?
I am free to break the blow, next hawk that swoops
On next dove, nor miss much of good repute?   110
Or what if this your summons, after all,
Be but the form of mere release, no more,
Which turns the key and lets the captive go?
I have paid enough in person at Civita,
Am free—what more need I concern me with?   115
Thank you! I am rehabilitated then,
A very reputable priest. But she—
The glory of life, the beauty of the world,
The splendor of heaven . . . well, Sirs, does no one
        move?
Do I speak ambiguously? The glory, I say,   120
And the beauty, I say, and splendor, still say I,
Who, priest and trained to live my whole life long
On beauty and splendor, solely at their source,
God—have thus recognized my food in her,
You tell me, that's fast dying while we talk,   125
Pompilia! How does lenity to me,
Remit one deathbed pang to her? Come smile!

The proper wink at the hot-headed youth
Who lets his soul show, through transparent words,
130 The mundane love that's sin and scandal too!
You are all struck acquiescent now, it seems:
It seems the oldest, gravest signor here,
Even the redoubtable Tommati, sits
Chop-fallen—understands how law might take
135 Service like mine, of brain and heart and hand,
In good part. Better late than never, law
You understand of a sudden, gospel too
Has a claim here, may possibly pronounce
Consistent with my priesthood, worthy Christ,
That I endeavored to save Pompilia?

140   Then,
You were wrong, you see: that's well to see, though
    late:
That's all we may expect of man, this side
The grave: his good is—knowing he is bad:
Thus will it be with us when the books ope
145 And we stand at the bar on Judgment Day.
Well then, I have a mind to speak, see cause
To relume the quenched flax° by this dreadful light,
Burn my soul out in showing you the truth.
I heard, last time I stood here to be judged,
150 What is priest's-duty—labor to pluck tares
And weed the corn of Molinism;° let me
Make you hear, this time, how, in such a case,
Man, be he in the priesthood or at plough,
Mindful of Christ or marching step by step
155 With . . . what's his style, the other potentate
Who bids have courage and keep honor safe,
Nor let minuter admonition tease?—
How he is bound, better or worse, to act.
Earth will not end through this misjudgment, no!

---

147 **quenched flax** Isaiah 42:3.   151 **Molinism** Miguel de Molinos
was a Spanish writer on the spiritual life who minimized the im-
portance of the externals of religion. Browning thinks of him as a
kind of Protestant.

For you and the others like you sure to come, 160
Fresh work is sure to follow—wickedness
That wants withstanding. Many a man of blood,
Many a man of guile will clamor yet,
Bid you redress his grievance—as he clutched
The prey, forsooth a stranger stepped between, 165
And there's the good gripe in pure waste! My part
Is done; i' the doing it, I pass away
Out of the world. I want no more with earth.
Let me, in Heaven's name, use the very snuff
O' the taper in one last spark shall show truth 170
For a moment, show Pompilia who was true!
Not for her sake, but yours: if she is dead,
Oh, Sirs, she can be loved by none of you
Most or least priestly! Saints, to do us good,
Must be in Heaven, I seem to understand: 175
We never find them saints before, at least.
Be her first prayer then presently for you—
She has done the good to me . . .

                What is all this?
There, I was born, have lived, shall die, a fool!
This is a foolish outset:—might with cause 180
Give color to the very lie o' the man,
The murderer—make as if I loved his wife,
In the way he called love. He is the fool there!
Why, had there been in me the touch of taint,
I had picked up so much of knaves'-policy 185
As hide it, keep one hand pressed on the place
Suspected of a spot would damn us both.
Or no, not her!—not even if any of you
Dares think that I, i' the face of death, her death
That's in my eyes and ears and brain and heart, 190
Lie—if he does, let him! I mean to say,
So he stop there, stay thought from smirching her
The snow-white soul that angels fear to take
Untenderly. But, all the same, I know
I too am taintless, and I bare my breast. 195
You can't think, men as you are, all of you,
But that, to hear thus suddenly such an end
Of such a wonderful white soul, that comes

Of a man and murderer calling the white black,
200 Must shake me, trouble and disadvantage. Sirs,
Only seventeen!

                    Why, good and wise you are!
You might at the beginning stop my mouth:
Só, none would be to speak for her, that knew.
I talk impertinently, and you bear,
205 All the same. This it is to have to do
With honest hearts: they easily may err,
But in the main they wish well to the truth.
You are Christians; somehow, no one ever plucked
A rag, even, from the body of the Lord,
210 To wear and mock with, but, despite himself,
He looked the greater and was the better. Yes,
I shall go on now. Does she need or not
I keep calm? Calm I'll keep as monk that croons
Transcribing battle, earthquake, famine, plague,
215 From parchment to his cloister's chronicle.
Not one word more from the point now!

                              I begin.
Yes, I am one of your body and a priest.
Also I am a younger son o' the House
Oldest now, greatest once, in my birth-town
220 Arezzo, I recognize no equal there—
(I want all arguments, all sorts of arms
That seem to serve—use this for a reason, wait!)
Not therefore thrust into the Church, because
O' the piece of bread one gets there. We were first
225 Of Fiesole, that rings still with the fame
Of Capo-in-Sacco our progenitor:
When Florence ruined Fiesole, our folk
Migrated to the victor-city, and there
Flourished—our palace and our tower attest,
230 In the Old Mercato—this was years ago,
Four hundred, full—no, it wants fourteen just.
Our arms are those of Fiesole itself,
The shield quartered with white and red: a branch
Are the Salviati of us, nothing more.

That were good help to the Church? But better still— 235
Not simply for the advantage of my birth
I' the way of the world, was I proposed for priest;
But because there's an illustration, late
I' the day, that's loved and looked to as a saint
Still in Arezzo, he was bishop of,   240
Sixty years since: he spent to the last doit
His bishop's-revenue among the poor,
And used to tend the needy and the sick,
Barefoot, because of his humility.
He it was—when the Granduke Ferdinand   245
Swore he would raze our city, plough the place
And sow it with salt, because we Aretines
Had tied a rope about the neck, to hale
The statue of his father from its base
For hate's sake—he availed by prayers and tears   250
To pacify the Duke and save the town.
This was my father's father's brother. You see,
For his sake, how it was I had a right
To the selfsame office, bishop in the egg,
So, grew i' the garb and prattled in the school,   255
Was made expect, from infancy almost,
The proper mood o' the priest; till time ran by
And brought the day when I must read the vows,
Declare the world renounced and undertake
To become priest and leave probation—leap   260
Over the ledge into the other life,
Having gone trippingly hitherto up to the height
O'er the wan water. Just a vow to read!

I stopped short awestruck. "How shall holiest flesh
Engage to keep such vow inviolate,   265
How much less mine? I know myself too weak,
Unworthy! Choose a worthier stronger man!"
And the very Bishop smiled and stopped my mouth
In its mid-protestation. "Incapable?
Qualmish of conscience? Thou ingenuous boy!   270
Clear up the clouds and cast thy scruples far!
I satisfy thee there's an easier sense
Wherein to take such vow than suits the first

Rough rigid reading. Mark what makes all smooth,
275 Nay, has been even a solace to myself!
The Jews who needs must, in their synagogue,
Utter sometimes the holy name of God,
A thing their superstition boggles at,
Pronounce aloud the ineffable sacrosanct—
280 How does their shrewdness help them? In this wise;
Another set of sounds they substitute,
Jumble so consonants and vowels—how
Should I know?—that there grows from out the old
Quite a new word that means the very same—
285 And o'er the hard place slide they with a smile.
Giuseppe Maria Caponsacchi mine,
Nobody wants you in these latter days
To prop the Church by breaking your backbone—
As the necessary way was once, we know,
290 When Diocletian flourished and his like.
That building of the buttress-work was done
By martyrs and confessors: let it bide,
Add not a brick, but, where you see a chink,
Stick in a sprig of ivy or root a rose
295 Shall make amends and beautify the pile!
We profit as you were the painfullest
O' the martyrs, and you prove yourself a match
For the cruelest confessor ever was,
If you march boldly up and take your stand
300 Where their blood soaks, their bones yet strew the soil,
And cry 'Take notice, I the young and free
And well-to-do i' the world, thus leave the world,
Cast in my lot thus with no gay young world
But the grand old Church: she tempts me of the two!'
305 Renounce the world? Nay, keep and give it us!
Let us have you, and boast of what you bring.
We want the pick o' the earth to practice with,
Not its offscouring, halt and deaf and blind
In soul and body. There's a rubble-stone
310 Unfit for the front o' the building, stuff to stow
In a gap behind and keep us weather-tight;
There's porphyry for the prominent place. Good lack!
Saint Paul has had enough and to spare, I trow,

Of ragged runaway Onesimus:°
He wants the right-hand with the signet-ring   315
Of King Agrippa,° now, to shake and use.
I have a heavy scholar cloistered up,
Close under lock and key, kept at his task
Of letting Fénelon° know the fool he is,
In a book I promise Christendom next spring.   320
Why, if he covets so much meat, the clown,
As a lark's wing next Friday, or, any day,
Diversion beyond catching his own fleas,
He shall be properly swinged, I promise him.
But you, who are so quite another paste   325
Of a man—do you obey me? Cultivate
Assiduous that superior gift you have
Of making madrigals—(who told me? Ah!)
Get done a Marinesque Adoniad° straight
With a pulse o' the blood a-pricking, here and there,   330
That I may tell the lady 'And he's ours!' "

   So I became a priest: those terms changed all,
I was good enough for that, nor cheated so;
I could live thus and still hold head erect.
Now you see why I may have been before   335
A fribble and coxcomb, yet, as priest, break word
Nowise, to make you disbelieve me now.
I need that you should know my truth. Well, then,
According to prescription did I live,
—Conformed myself, both read the breviary   340
And wrote the rhymes, was punctual to my place
I' the Pieve,° and as diligent at my post
Where beauty and fashion rule. I throve apace,
Subdeacon, canon, the authority
For delicate play at tarocs,° and arbiter   345
O' the magnitude of fan-mounts: all the while

314 **Onesimus** Philemon 10-18.   316 **Agrippa** Acts 25-26.   319
Fénelon French churchman and man of letters who taught Molinist
doctrines.   329 **Marinesque Adoniad** i.e. in the manner of the
Adone of Marino, a fashionable poet whose work is elaborately
artificial.   342 **Pieve** Caponsacchi was attached to the Church of
Santa Maria della Pieve.   345 **tarocs** card game.

Wanting no whit the advantage of a hint
Benignant to the promising pupil—thus:
"Enough attention to the Countess now,
350 The young one; 'tis her mother rules the roast,
We know where, and puts in a word: go pay
Devoir tomorrow morning after mass!
Break that rash promise to preach, Passion-week!
Has it escaped you the Archbishop grunts
355 And snuffles when one grieves to tell his Grace
No soul dares treat the subject of the day
Since his own masterly handling it (ha, ha!)
Five years ago—when somebody could help
And touch up an odd phrase in time of need,
360 (He, he!)—and somebody helps you, my son!
Therefore, don't prove so indispensable
At the Pieve, sit more loose i' the seat, nor grow
A fixture by attendance morn and eve!
Arezzo's just a haven midway Rome—
365 Rome's the eventual harbor—make for port,
Crowd sail, crack cordage! And your cargo be
A polished presence, a genteel manner, wit
At will, and tact at every pore of you!
I sent our lump of learning, Brother Clout,
370 And Father Slouch, our piece of piety,
To see Rome and try suit the Cardinal.
Thither they clump-clumped, beads and book in hand
And ever since 'tis meat for man and maid
How both flopped down, prayed blessing on bent pate
375 Bald many an inch beyond the tonsure's need,
Never once dreaming, the two moony dolts,
There's nothing moves his Eminence so much
As—far from all this awe at sanctitude—
Heads that wag, eyes that twinkle, modified mirth
380 At the closet-lectures on the Latin tongue
A lady learns so much by, we know where.
Why, body o' Bacchus, you should crave his rule
For pauses in the elegiac couplet, chasms
Permissible only to Catullus! There!
385 Now go to duty: brisk, break Priscian's head
By reading the day's office—there's no help.

You've Ovid° in your poke to plaster that;
Amen's at the end of all: then sup with me!"

   Well, after three or four years of this life,
In prosecution of my calling, I
Found myself at the theater one night   390
With a brother canon, in a mood and mind
Proper enough for the place, amused or no:
When I saw enter, stand, and seat herself
A lady, young, tall, beautiful, strange and sad.   395
It was as when, in our cathedral once,
As I got yawningly through matin-song,
I saw *facchini*° bear a burden up,
Base it on the high-altar, break away
A board or two, and leave the thing inside   400
Lofty and lone: and lo, when next I looked,
There was the Raphael! I was still one stare,
When—"Nay, I'll make her give you back your gaze"—
Said Canon Conti; and at the word he tossed
A paper-twist of comfits to her lap,   405
And dodged and in a trice was at my back
Nodding from over my shoulder. Then she turned,
Looked our way, smiled the beautiful sad strange smile.
"Is not she fair? 'Tis my new cousin," said he:
"The fellow lurking there i' the black o' the box   410
Is Guido, the old scapegrace: she's his wife,
Married three years since: how his Countship sulks!
He has brought little back from Rome beside,
After the bragging, bullying. A fair face,
And—they do say—a pocketful of gold   415
When he can worry both her parents dead.
I don't go much there, for the chamber's cold
And the coffee pale. I got a turn at first
Paying my duty: I observed they crouched
—The two old frightened family specters—close   420

384–87 **Catullus . . . Ovid** the poet *Catullus* takes liberties with the
usual rules for elision in Latin verse. *Priscian* was a grammarian.
To "break his head" meant to use ungrammatical or impure forms
such as are common in the unclassical Latin of the Church. **Ovid** is
a Latin poet of high elegance.   398 **facchini** porters.

In a corner, each on each like mouse on mouse
I' the cat's cage: ever since, I stay at home.
Hallo, there's Guido, the black, mean and small,
Bends his brows on us—please to bend your own
425 On the shapely nether limbs of Light-skirts there
By way of a diversion! I was a fool
To fling the sweetmeats. Prudence, for God's love!
Tomorrow I'll make my peace, e'en tell some fib,
Try if I can't find means to take you there."

430 That night and next day did the gaze endure,
Burnt to my brain, as sunbeam through shut eyes,
And not once changed the beautiful sad strange smile.
At vespers Conti leaned beside my seat
I' the choir—part said, part sung—*"In ex-cel-sis*—
435 All's to no purpose; I have louted low,
But he saw you staring—*quia sub*—don't incline
To know you nearer: him we would not hold
For Hercules—the man would lick your shoe
If you and certain efficacious friends
440 Managed him warily—but there's the wife:
Spare her, because he beats her, as it is,
She's breaking her heart quite fast enough—*jam tu*—
So, be you rational and make amends
With little Light-skirts yonder—*in secula*
445 *Secu-lo-o-o-o-rum*.° Ah, you rogue! Everyone knows
What great dame she makes jealous: one against one,
Play, and win both!"

                        Sirs, ere the week was out,
I saw and said to myself "Light-skirts hides teeth
Would make a dog sick—the great dame shows spite
450 Should drive a cat mad: 'tis but poor work this—
Counting one's fingers till the sonnet's crowned.
I doubt much if Marino really be
A better bard than Dante after all.
'Tis more amusing to go pace at eve
455 I' the Duomo°—watch the day's last gleam outside

434–45 **In ex-cel-sis . . . Secu-lo-o-o-o-rum** bits of Latin from the
service.   455 **Duomo** cathedral.

Turn, as into a skirt of God's own robe,
Those lancet-windows' jeweled miracle—
Than go eat the Archbishop's ortolans,°
Digest his jokes. Luckily Lent is near:
Who cares to look will find me in my stall   460
At the Pieve, constant to this faith at least—
Never to write a canzonet any more."

So, next week, 'twas my patron spoke abrupt,
In altered guise. "Young man, can it be true
That after all your promise of sound fruit,   465
You have kept away from Countess young or old
And gone play truant in church all day long?
Are you turning Molinist?" I answered quick:
"Sir, what if I turned Christian? It might be.
The fact is, I am troubled in my mind,   470
Beset and pressed hard by some novel thoughts.
This your Arezzo is a limited world;
There's a strange Pope—'tis said, a priest who thinks.
Rome is the port, you say: to Rome I go.
I will live alone, one does so in a crowd,   475
And look into my heart a little." "Lent
Ended"—I told friends—"I shall go to Rome."

One evening I was sitting in a muse
Over the opened "Summa,"° darkened round
By the mid-March twilight, thinking how my life   480
Had shaken under me—broke short indeed
And showed the gap 'twixt what is, what should be—
And into what abysm the soul may slip,
Leave aspiration here, achievement there,
Lacking omnipotence to connect extremes—   485
Thinking moreover . . . oh, thinking, if you like,
How utterly dissociated was I
A priest and celibate, from the sad strange wife
Of Guido—just as an instance to the point,
Naught more—how I had a whole store of strengths   490

---

458 **ortolans** small birds. Table delicacies.   479 **"Summa"** compendium of Christian doctrine.

Eating into my heart, which craved employ,
And she, perhaps, need of a finger's help—
And yet there was no way in the wide world
To stretch out mine and so relieve myself—
495 How when the page o' the "Summa" preached its best,
Her smile kept glowing out of it, as to mock
The silence we could break by no one word—
There came a tap without the chamber-door,
And a whisper; when I bade who tapped speak out.
500 And, in obedience to my summons, last
In glided a masked muffled mystery,
Laid lightly a letter on the opened book,
Then stood with folded arms and foot demure,
Pointing as if to mark the minutes' flight.

505 I took the letter, read to the effect
That she, I lately flung the comfits to,
Had a warm heart to give me in exchange,
And gave it—loved me and confessed it thus,
And bade me render thanks by word of mouth,
510 Going that night to such a side o' the house
Where the small terrace overhangs a street
Blind and deserted, not the street in front:
Her husband being away, the surly patch,
At his villa of Vittiano.

                              "And you?"—I asked:
515 "What may you be?" "Count Guido's kind of maid—
Most of us have two functions in his house.
We all hate him, the lady suffers much,
'Tis just we show compassion, furnish help,
Specially since her choice is fixed so well.
520 What answer may I bring to cheer the sweet
Pompilia?"

                    Then I took a pen and wrote
"No more of this! That you are fair, I know:
But other thoughts now occupy my mind.
I should not thus have played the insensible
525 Once on a time. What made you—may one ask—

Marry your hideous husband? 'Twas a fault,
And now you taste the fruit of it. Farewell."

"There!" smiled I as she snatched it and was gone—
"There, let the jealous miscreant—Guido's self,
Whose mean soul grins through this transparent trick—   530
Be baulked so far, defrauded of his aim!
What fund of satisfaction to the knave,
Had I kicked this his messenger downstairs,
Trussed to the middle of her impudence,
And set his heart at ease so! No, indeed!   535
There's the reply which he shall turn and twist
At pleasure, snuff at till his brain grow drunk,
As the bear does when he finds a scented glov
That puzzles him—a hand and yet no hand,
Of other perfume than his own foul paw!   540
Last month, I had doubtless chosen to play the dupe,
Accepted the mock-invitation, kept
The sham appointment, cudgel beneath cloak,
Prepared myself to pull the appointer's self
Out of the window from his hiding-place   545
Behind the gown of this part-messenger
Part-mistress who would personate the wife.
Such had seemed once a jest permissible:
Now I am not i' the mood."

                        Back next morn brought
The messenger, a second letter in hand.   550
"You are cruel, Thyrsis, and Myrtilla° moans
Neglected but adores you, makes request
For mercy: why is it you dare not come?
Such virtue is scarce natural to your age.
You must love someone else; I hear you do,   555
The Baron's daughter or the Advocate's wife,
Or both—all's one, would you make me the third—
I take the crumbs from table gratefully
Nor grudge who feasts there. 'Faith, I blush and blaze!
Yet if I break all bounds, there's reason sure.   560

551 **Thyrsis . . . Myrtilla** conventional names in pastoral literature.

Are you determinedly bent on Rome?
I am wretched here, a monster tortures me:
Carry me with you! Come and say you will!
Concert this very evening! Do not write!
565 I am ever at the window of my room
Over the terrace, at the *Ave.*° Come!"

I questioned—lifting half the woman's mask
To let her smile loose. "So, you gave my line
To the merry lady?" "She kissed off the wax,
570 And put what paper was not kissed away,
In her bosom to go burn: but merry, no!
She wept all night when evening brought no friend,
Alone, the unkind missive at her breast;
Thus Philomel,° the thorn at her breast too,
575 Sings" . . . "Writes this second letter?" "Even so!
Then she may peep at vespers forth?"—"What risk
Do we run o' the husband?"—"Ah—no risk at all!
He is more stupid even than jealous. Ah—
That was the reason? Why, the man's away!
580 Beside, his bugbear is that friend of yours,
Fat little Canon Conti. He fears him,
How should he dream of you? I told you truth:
He goes to the villa at Vittiano—'tis
The time when Spring-sap rises in the vine—
585 Spends the night there. And then his wife's a child:
Does he think a child outwits him? A mere child:
Yet so full grown, a dish for any duke.
Don't quarrel longer with such cates,° but come!"
I wrote "In vain do you solicit me.
590 I am a priest: and you are wedded wife,
Whatever kind of brute your husband prove.
I have scruples, in short. Yet should you really show
Sign at the window . . . but nay, best be good!
My thoughts are elsewhere," "Take her that!"

"Again
595 Let the incarnate meanness, cheat and spy,

566 **Ave** Evidently vespers (see 1.576). 574 **Philomel** poetic name
for nightingale. 588 **cates** delicacies.

Mean to the marrow of him, make his heart
His food, anticipate hell's worm once more!
Let him watch shivering at the window—ay,
And let this hybrid, this his light-of-love
And lackey-of-lies—a sage economy   600
Paid with embracings for the rank brass coin—
Let her report and make him chuckle o'er
The breakdown of my resolution now,
And lour at disappointment in good time!
—So tantalize and so enrage by turns,   605
Until the two fall each on the other like
Two famished spiders, as the coveted fly
That toys long, leaves their net and them at last!"
And so the missives followed thick and fast
For a month, say—I still came at every turn   610
On the soft sly adder, endlong 'neath my tread.
I was met i' the street, made sign to in the church,
A slip was found i' the doorsill, scribbled word
'Twixt page and page o' the prayer book in my place.
A crumpled thing dropped even before my feet,   615
Pushed through the blind, above the terrace-rail,
As I passed, by day, the very window once.
And ever from corners would be peering up
The messenger, with the self-same demand
"Obdurate still, no flesh but adamant?   620
Nothing to cure the wound, assuage the throe
O' the sweetest lamb that ever loved a bear?"
And ever my one answer in one tone—
"Go your ways, temptress! Let a priest read, pray,
Unplagued of vain talk, visions not for him!   625
In the end, you'll have your will and ruin me!"

One day, a variation: thus I read:
"You have gained little by timidity.
My husband has found out my love at length,
Sees cousin Conti was the stalking-horse,   630
And you the game he covered, poor fat soul!
My husband is a formidable foe,
Will stick at nothing to destroy you. Stand
Prepared, or better, run till you reach Rome!

635 I bade you visit me, when the last place
　　　My tyrant would have turned suspicious at,
　　　Or cared to seek you in, was . . . why say, where?
　　　But now all's changed: beside, the season's past
640 At the villa—wants the master's eye no more.
　　　Anyhow, I beseech you, stay away
　　　From the window! He might well be posted there."

　　　I wrote—"You raise my courage, or call up
　　　My curiosity, who am but man.
　　　Tell him he owns the palace, not the street
645 Under—that's his and yours and mine alike.
　　　If it should please me pad the path this eve,
　　　Guido will have two troubles, first to get
　　　Into a rage and then get out again.
　　　Be cautious, though: at the *Ave!*"

　　　　　　　　　　　　　　You of the Court!
650 When I stood question here and reached this point
　　　O' the narrative—search notes and see and say
　　　If someone did not interpose with smile
　　　And sneer, "And prithee why so confident
　　　That the husband must, of all needs, not the wife,
655 Fabricate thus—what if the lady loved?
　　　What if she wrote the letters?"

　　　　　　　　　　　　　　　Learned Sir,
　　　I told you there's a picture in our church.
　　　Well, if a low-browed verger sidled up
　　　Bringing me, like a blotch, on his prod's point,
660 A transfixed scorpion, let the reptile writhe,
　　　And then said "See a thing that Raphael made—
　　　This venom issued from Madonna's mouth!"
　　　I should reply, "Rather, the soul of you
　　　Has issued from your body, like from like,
　　　By way of the ordure-corner!"

665
　　　　　　　　　　　　　　But no less,
　　　I tired of the same long black teasing lie
　　　Obtruded thus at every turn; the pest
　　　Was far too near the picture, anyhow:

One does Madonna service, making clowns
Remove their dung-heap from the sacristy.   670
"I will to the window, as he tempts," said I:
"Yes, whom the easy love has failed allure,
This new bait of adventure tempts—thinks he.
Though the imprisoned lady keeps afar,
There will they lie in ambush, heads alert,   675
Kith, kin, and Count mustered to bite my heel.
No mother nor brother viper of the brood
Shall scuttle off without the instructive bruise!"

So I went: crossed street and street: "The next street's
    turn,
I stand beneath the terrace, see, above,   680
The black of the ambush-window. Then, in place
Of hand's throw of soft prelude over lute,
And cough that clears way for the ditty last"—
I began to laugh already—"he will have
'Out of the hole you hide in, on to the front,   685
Count Guido Franceschini, show yourself!
Hear what a man thinks of a thing like you,
And after, take this foulness in your face!' "

The words lay living on my lip, I made
The one-turn more—and there at the window stood,   690
Framed in its black square length, with lamp in hand,
Pompilia; the same great, grave, griefful air
As stands i' the dusk, on altar that I know,
Left alone with one moonbeam in her cell,
Our Lady of all the Sorrows. Ere I knelt—   695
Assured myself that she was flesh and blood—
She had looked one look and vanished.

                              I thought—"Just so:
It was herself, they have set her there to watch—
Stationed to see some wedding-band go by,
On fair pretense that she must bless the bride,   700
Or wait some funeral with friends wind past,
And crave peace for the corpse that claims its due.
She never dreams they used her for a snare,

And now withdraw the bait has served its turn.
705 Well done, the husband, who shall fare the worse!"
And on my lip again was—"Out with thee,
Guido!" When all at once she reappeared;
But, this time, on the terrace overhead,
So close above me, she could almost touch
710 My head if she bent down; and she did bend,
While I stood still as stone, all eye, all ear.

She began—"You have sent me letters, Sir:
I have read none, I can neither read nor write;
But she you gave them to, a woman here,
715 One of the people in whose power I am,
Partly explained their sense, I think, to me
Obliged to listen while she inculcates
That you, a priest, can dare love me, a wife,
Desire to live or die as I shall bid,
720 (She makes me listen if I will or no)
Because you saw my face a single time.
It cannot be she says the thing you mean;
Such wickedness were deadly to us both:
But good true love would help me now so much—
725 I tell myself, you may mean good and true.
You offer me, I seem to understand,
Because I am in poverty and starve,
Much money, where one piece would save my life.
The silver cup upon the altar-cloth
730 Is neither yours to give nor mine to take;
But I might take one bit of bread therefrom,
Since I am starving, and return the rest,
Yet do no harm: this is my very case.
I am in that strait, I may not dare abstain
735 From so much of assistance as would bring
The guilt of theft on neither you nor me;
But no superfluous particle of aid.
I think, if you will let me state my case,
Even had you been so fancy-fevered here,
740 Not your sound self, you must grow healthy now—
Care only to bestow what I can take.
That it is only you in the wide world,

Knowing me nor in thought nor word nor deed,
Who, all unprompted save by your own heart,
Come proffering assistance now—were strange 745
But that my whole life is so strange: as strange
It is, my husband whom I have not wronged
Should hate and harm me. For his own soul's sake,
Hinder the harm! But there is something more,
And that the strangest: it has got to be 750
Somehow for my sake too, and yet not mine,
—This is a riddle—for some kind of sake
Not any clearer to myself than you,
And yet as certain as that I draw breath—
I would fain live, not die—oh no, not die! 755
My case is, I was dwelling happily
At Rome with those dear Comparini, called
Father and mother to me; when at once
I found I had become Count Guido's wife:
Who then, not waiting for a moment, changed 760
Into a fury of fire, if once he was
Merely a man: his face threw fire at mine,
He laid a hand on me that burned all peace,
All joy, all hope, and last all fear away,
Dipping the bough of life, so pleasant once, 765
In fire which shriveled leaf and bud alike,
Burning not only present life but past,
Which you might think was safe beyond his reach.
He reached it, though, since that beloved pair,
My father once, my mother all those years, 770
That loved me so, now say I dreamed a dream
And bid me wake, henceforth no child of theirs,
Never in all the time their child at all.°
Do you understand? I cannot: yet so it is.
Just so I say of you that proffer help: 775
I cannot understand what prompts your soul,
I simply needs must see that it is so,
Only one strange and wonderful thing more.

772–73 **no child . . . at all** Violante claimed to have bought Pompilia
from a prostitute in order to secure for herself and her husband an
inheritance that was contingent on their having a child.

They came here with me, those two dear ones, kept
780 All the old love up, till my husband, till
His people here so tortured them, they fled.
And now, is it because I grow in flesh
And spirit one with him their torturer,
That they, renouncing him, must cast off me?
785 If I were graced by God to have a child,
Could I one day deny God graced me so?
Then, since my husband hates me, I shall break
No law that reigns in this fell house of hate,
By using—letting have effect so much
790 Of hate as hides me from that whole of hate
Would take my life which I want and must have—
Just as I take from your excess of love
Enough to save my life with, all I need.
The Archbishop said to murder me were sin:
795 My leaving Guido were a kind of death
With no sin—more death, he must answer for.
Hear now what death to him and life to you
I wish to pay and owe. Take me to Rome!
You go to Rome, the servant makes me hear.
800 Take me as you would take a dog, I think,
Masterless left for strangers to maltreat:
Take me home like that—leave me in the house
Where the father and the mother are; and soon
They'll come to know and call me by my name,
805 Their child once more, since child I am, for all
They now forget me, which is the worst o' the dream—
And the way to end dreams is to break them, stand,
Walk, go: then help me to stand, walk and go!
The Governor said the strong should help the weak:
810 You know how weak the strongest women are.
How could I find my way there by myself?
I cannot even call out, make them hear—
Just as in dreams: I have tried and proved the fact.
I have told this story and more to good great men,
815 The Archbishop and the Governor: they smiled.
'Stop your mouth, fair one!'—presently they frowned,
'Get you gone, disengage you from our feet!'
I went in my despair to an old priest,

Only a friar, no great man like these two,
But good, the Augustinian, people name   820
Romano—he confessed me two months since:
He fears God, why then needs he fear the world?
And when he questioned how it came about
That I was found in danger of a sin—
Despair of any help from providence—   825
'Since, though your husband outrage you,' said he,
'That is a case too common, the wives die
Or live, but do not sin so deep as this'—
Then I told—what I never will tell you—
How, worse than husband's hate, I had to bear   830
The love—soliciting to shame called love—
Of his brother—the young idle priest i' the house
With only the devil to meet there. 'This is grave—
Yes, we must interfere: I counsel—write
To those who used to be your parents once,   835
Of dangers here, bid them convey you hence!'
'But,' said I, 'when I neither read nor write?'
Then he took pity and promised 'I will write.'
If he did so—why, they are dumb or dead:
Either they give no credit to the tale,   840
Or else, wrapped wholly up in their own joy
Of such escape, they care not who cries, still
I' the clutches. Anyhow, no word arrives.
All such extravagance and dreadfulness
Seems incident to dreaming, cured one way—   845
Wake me! The letter I received this morn,
Said—if the woman spoke your very sense—
'You would die for me:' I can believe it now:
For now the dream gets to involve yourself.
First of all, you seemed wicked and not good,   850
In writing me those letters: you came in
Like a thief upon me. I this morning said
In my extremity, entreat the thief!
Try if he have in him no honest touch!
A thief might save me from a murderer.   855
'Twas a thief said the last kind word to Christ:
Christ took the kindness and forgave the theft:
And so did I prepare what I now say.

But now, that you stand and I see your face,
860 Though you have never uttered word yet—well, I know,
Here too has been dream-work, delusion too,
And that at no time, you with the eyes here,
Ever intended to do wrong by me,
Nor wrote such letters therefore. It is false,
865 And you are true, have been true, will be true.
To Rome then—when is it you take me there?
Each minute lost is mortal. When?—I ask."

I answered "It shall be when it can be.
I will go hence and do your pleasure, find
870 The sure and speedy means of travel, then
Come back and take you to your friends in Rome.
There wants a carriage, money and the rest—
A day's work by tomorrow at this time.
How shall I see you and assure escape?"

875 She replied, "Pass, tomorrow at this hour.
If I am at the open window, well:
If I am absent, drop a handkerchief
And walk by! I shall see from where I watch,
And know that all is done. Return next eve,
880 And next, and so till we can meet and speak!"
"Tomorrow at this hour I pass," said I.
She was withdrawn.

                    Here is another point
I bid you pause at. When I told thus far,
Someone said, subtly, "Here at least was found
885 Your confidence in error—you perceived
The spirit of the letters, in a sort,
Had been the lady's, if the body should be
Supplied by Guido: say, he forged them all!
Here was the unforged fact—she sent for you,
890 Spontaneously elected you to help,
—What men call, loved you: Guido read her mind,
Gave it expression to assure the world
The case was just as he foresaw: he wrote,
She spoke."

Sirs, that first simile serves still—
That falsehood of a scorpion hatched, I say,   895
Nowhere i' the world but in Madonna's mouth.
Go on! Suppose, that falsehood foiled, next eve
Pictured Madonna raised her painted hand,
Fixed the face Raphael bent above the Babe,
On my face as I flung me at her feet: 900
Such miracle vouchsafed and manifest,
Would that prove the first lying tale was true?
Pompilia spoke, and I at once received,
Accepted my own fact, my miracle
Self-authorized and self-explained—she chose   905
To summon me and signify her choice.
Afterward—oh! I gave a passing glance
To a certain ugly cloud-shape, goblin-shred
Of hell-smoke hurrying past the splendid moon
But now to tolerate no darkness more,   910
And saw right through the thing that tried to pass
For truth and solid, not an empty lie:
So, he not only forged the words for her
But words for me, made letters he called mine:
What I sent, he retained, gave these in place,   915
All by the mistress-messenger! As I
Recognized her, at potency of truth,
So she, by the crystalline soul, knew me,
Never mistook the signs. Enough of this—
Let the wraith go to nothingness again,   920
Here is the orb, have only thought for her!"

Thought?" nay, Sirs, what shall follow was not
        thought:
I have thought sometimes, and thought long and hard.
I have stood before, gone round a serious thing,
Tasked my whole mind to touch and clasp it close,   925
As I stretch forth my arm to touch this bar.
God and man, and what duty I owe both—
I dare to say I have confronted these
A thought: but no such faculty helped here.
I put forth no thought—powerless, all that night   930
I paced the city: it was the first spring.

By the invasion I lay passive to,
In rushed new things, the old were rapt away;
Alike abolished—the imprisonment
935 Of the outside air, the inside weight o' the world
That pulled me down. Death meant, to spurn the ground,
Soar to the sky—die well and you do that.
The very immolation made the bliss;
Death was the heart of life, and all the harm
940 My folly had crouched to avoid, now proved a veil
Hiding all gain my wisdom strove to grasp:
As if the intense center of the flame
Should turn a heaven to that devoted fly
Which hitherto, sophist alike and sage,
945 Saint Thomas with his sober gray goose-quill,
And sinner Plato by Cephisian reed,°
Would fain, pretending just the insect's good,
Whisk off, drive back, consign to shade again.
Into another state, under new rule
950 I knew myself was passing swift and sure;
Whereof the initiatory pang approached,
Felicitous annoy, as bitter-sweet
As when the virgin-band, the victors chaste,
Feel at the end the earthly garments drop,
955 And rise with something of a rosy shame
Into immortal nakedness: so I
Lay, and let come the proper throe would thrill
Into the ecstasy and outthrob pain.

I' the gray of dawn it was I found myself
960 Facing the pillared front o' the Pieve—mine,
My church: it seemed to say for the first time,
"But am not I the Bride, the mystic love
O' the Lamb, who took thy plighted troth, my priest,
To fold thy warm heart on my heart of stone
965 And freeze thee nor unfasten any more?
This is a fleshly woman—let the free
Bestow their life-blood, thou art pulseless now!"

946 **Cephisian reed** pen made from a reed of the river Cephisus at Athens.

See! Day by day I had risen and left this church
At the signal waved me by some foolish fan,
With half a curse and half a pitying smile   970
For the monk I stumbled over in my haste,
Prostrate and corpse-like at the altar-foot
Intent on his *corona*:° then the church
Was ready with her quip, if word conduced,
To quicken my pace nor stop for prating—"There!   975
Be thankful you are no such ninny, go
Rather to teach a black-eyed novice cards
Than gabble Latin and protrude that nose
Smoothed to a sheep's through no brains and much
      faith!"
That sort of incentive! Now the church changed tone— 980
Now, when I found out first that life and death
Are means to an end, that passion uses both,
Indisputably mistress of the man
Whose form of worship is self-sacrifice:
Now, from the stone lungs sighed the scrannel voice   985
"Leave that live passion, come be dead with me!"
As if, i' the fabled garden,° I had gone
On great adventure, plucked in ignorance
Hedge-fruit, and feasted to satiety,
Laughing at such high fame for hips and haws,°   990
And scorned the achievement: then come all at once
O' the prize o' the place, the thing of perfect gold,
The apple's self: and, scarce my eye on that,
Was 'ware as well o' the sevenfold dragon's watch.

Sirs, I obeyed. Obedience was too strange—   995
This new thing that had been struck into me
By the look o' the lady—to dare disobey
The first authoritative word. 'Twas God's.
I had been lifted to the level of her,
Could take such sounds into my sense. I said   1000
"We two are cognizant o' the Master now;

973 **corona** rosary. 987 **fabled garden** in the Garden of the Hes-
perides there was a tree bearing a golden apple, guarded by a
dragon. Hercules killed the dragon and took the fruit. 990 **hips
and haws** fruits of rose and hawthorn.

She it is bids me bow the head: how true,
I am a priest! I see the function here;
I thought the other way self-sacrifice:
1005 This is the true, seals up the perfect sum.
I pay it, sit down, silently obey."

So, I went home. Dawn broke, noon broadened, I—
I sat stone-still, let time run over me.
The sun slanted into my room, had reached
1010 The west. I opened book—Aquinas° blazed
With one black name only on the white page.
I looked up, saw the sunset: vespers rang:
"She counts the minutes till I keep my word
And come say all is ready. I am a priest.
1015 Duty to God is duty to her: I think
God, who created her, will save her too
Some new way, by one miracle the more,
Without me. Then, prayer may avail perhaps."
I went to my own place i' the Pieve, read
1020 The office: I was back at home again
Sitting i' the dark. "Could she but know—but know
That, were there good in this distinct from God's,
Really good as it reached her, though procured
By a sin of mine—I should sin: God forgives.
1025 She knows it is no fear withholds me: fear?
Of what? Suspense here is the terrible thing.
If she should, as she counts the minutes, come
On the fantastic notion that I fear
The world now, fear the Archbishop, fear perhaps
1030 Count Guido, he who, having forged the lies,
May wait the work, attend the effect—I fear
The sword of Guido! Let God see to that—
Hating lies, let not her believe a lie!"

Again the morning found me. "I will work,
1035 Tie down my foolish thoughts. Thank God so far!
I have saved her from a scandal, stopped the tongues
Had broken else into a cackle and hiss

1010 **Aquinas** St. Thomas Aquinas, whose *Summa* he had been
reading.

Around the noble name. Duty is still
Wisdom: I have been wise." So the day wore.

At evening—"But, achieving victory,   1040
I must not blink the priest's peculiar part,
Nor shrink to counsel, comfort: priest and friend—
How do we discontinue to be friends?
I will go minister, advise her seek
Help at the source—above all, not despair: 1045
There may be other happier help at hand.
I hope it—wherefore then neglect to say?"

There she stood—leaned there, for the second time,
Over the terrace, looked at me, then spoke:
"Why is it you have suffered me to stay   1050
Breaking my heart two days more than was need?
Why delay help, your own heart yearns to give?
You are again here, in the selfsame mind,
I see here, steadfast in the face of you—
You grudge to do no one thing that I ask.   1055
Why then is nothing done? You know my need.
Still, through God's pity on me, there is time
And one day more: shall I be saved or no?"
I answered—"Lady, waste no thought, no word
Even to forgive me! Care for what I care—   1060
Only! Now follow me as I were fate!
Leave this house in the dark tomorrow night,
Just before daybreak:—there's new moon this eve—
It sets, and then begins the solid black.
Descend, proceed to the Torrione, step   1065
Over the low dilapidated wall,
Take San Clemente, there's no other gate
Unguarded at the hour: some paces thence
An inn stands; cross to it; I shall be there."

She answered, "If I can but find the way.   1070
But I shall find it. Go now!"

                    I did go,
Took rapidly the route myself prescribed,

Stopped at Torrione, climbed the ruined place,
Proved that the gate was practicable, reached
1075 The inn, no eye, despite the dark, could miss,
Knocked there and entered, made the host secure:
"With Caponsacchi it is ask and have;
I know my betters. Are you bound for Rome?
I get swift horse and trusty man," said he.

1080 Then I retraced my steps, was found once more
In my own house for the last time: there lay
The broad pale opened *Summa*. "Shut his book,
There's other showing! 'Twas a Thomas too
Obtained—more favored than his namesake here—
1085 A gift, tied faith fast, foiled the tug of doubt—
Our Lady's girdle; down he saw it drop
As she ascended into Heaven, they say:
He kept that safe and bade all doubt adieu.°
I too have seen a lady and hold a grace."

1090 I know not how the night passed: morning broke;
Presently came my servant. "Sir, this eve—
Do you forget?" I started. "How forget?
What is it you know?" "With due submission, Sir,
This being last Monday in the month but one
1095 And a vigil, since tomorrow is Saint George,°
And feast day, and moreover day for copes,
And Canon Conti now away a month,
And Canon Crispi sour because, forsooth,
You let him sulk in stall and bear the brunt
Of the octave . . . Well, Sir, 'tis important!"

                                           "True!
1100
Hearken, I have to start for Rome this night.
No word, lest Crispi overboil and burst!

1083-88 **a Thomas . . . doubt adieu** Thomas the Apostle, who had
doubted Christ's Resurrection, was said also to have doubted that
the Virgin Mary had been taken up into Heaven. In order to con-
vince him of the fact she threw down the belt of her garment.
1095 **Saint George** Browning altered the date of the flight (April 29)
so it could take place on the Feast of St. George (April 23).

Provide me with a laic dress! Throw dust
I' the Canon's eye, stop his tongue's scandal so!
See there's a sword in case of accident."   1105
I knew the knave, the knave knew me.

                And thus
Through each familiar hindrance of the day
Did I make steadily for its hour and end—
Felt time's old barrier-growth of right and fit
Give way through all its twines, and let me go.   1110
Use and wont recognized the excepted man,
Let speed the special service—and I sped
Till, at the dead between midnight and morn,
There was I at the goal, before the gate,
With a tune in the ears, low leading up to loud,   1115
A light in the eyes, faint that would soon be flare,
Ever some spiritual witness new and new
In faster frequence, crowding solitude
To watch the way o' the warfare—till, at last,
When the ecstatic minute must bring birth,   1120
Began a whiteness in the distance, waxed
Whiter and whiter, near grew and more near,
Till it was she: there did Pompilia come:
The white I saw shine through her was her soul's,
Certainly, for the body was one black,   1125
Black from head down to foot. She did not speak,
Glided into the carriage—so a cloud
Gathers the moon up. "By San Spirito,
To Rome, as if the road burned underneath!
Reach Rome, then hold my head in pledge, I pay   1130
The run and the risk to heart's content!" Just that
I said—then, in another tick of time,
Sprang, was beside her, she and I alone.

So it began, our flight thro' dusk to clear,
Through day and night and day again to night   1135
Once more, and to last dreadful dawn of all.
Sirs, how should I lie quiet in my grave
Unless you suffer me wring, drop by drop,
My brain dry, make a riddance of the drench
Of minutes with a memory in each,   1140

Recorded motion, breath or look of hers,
Which poured forth would present you one pure glass,
Mirror you plain—as God's sea,° glassed in gold,
His saints—the perfect soul Pompilia? Men,
1145 You must know that a man gets drunk with truth
Stagnant inside him! Oh, they've killed her, Sirs!
Can I be calm?

            Calmly! Each incident
Proves, I maintain, that action of the flight
For the true thing it was. The first faint scratch
1150 O' the stone will test its nature, teach its worth
To idiots who name Parian—coprolite.°
After all, I shall give no glare—at best
Only display you certain scattered lights
Lamping the rush and roll of the abyss:
1155 Nothing but here and there a fire-point pricks
Wavelet from wavelet: well!

                        For the first hour
We both were silent in the night, I know:
Sometimes I did not see nor understand.
Blackness engulfed me—partial stupor, say—
1160 Then I would break way, breathe through the surprise,
And be aware again, and see who sat
In the dark vest with the white face and hands.
I said to myself—"I have caught it, I conceive
The mind o' the mystery: 'tis the way they wake
1165 And wait, two martyrs somewhere in a tomb
Each by each as their blessing was to die;
Some signal they are promised and expect—
When to arise before the trumpet scares:
So, through the whole course of the world they wait
1170 The last day, but so fearless and so safe!
No otherwise, in safety and not fear,
I lie, because she lies too by my side."
You know this is not love, Sirs—it is faith,

1143 **God's sea** Revelation 4:6–7.   1151 **Parian—coprolite** Parian
marble is of high quality; coprolite is petrified excrement of ancient
reptiles.

The feeling that there's God, he reigns and rules
Out of this low world: that is all; no harm!   *1175*
At times she drew a soft sigh—music seemed
Always to hover just above her lips,
Not settle—break a silence music too.

In the determined morning, I first found
Her head erect, her face turned full to me,   *1180*
Her soul intent on mine through two wide eyes.
I answered them. "You are saved hitherto.
We have passed Perugia—gone round by the wood,
Not through, I seem to think—and opposite
I know Assisi; this is holy ground."°   *1185*
Then she resumed. "How long since we both left
Arezzo?" "Years—and certain hours beside."

It was at . . . ah, but I forget the names!
'Tis a mere post-house and a hovel or two;
I left the carriage and got bread and wine   *1190*
And brought it her. "Does it detain to eat?"
"They stay perforce, change horses—therefore eat!
We lose no minute: we arrive, be sure!"
This was—I know not where—there's a great hill
Close over, and the stream has lost its bridge,   *1195*
One fords it. She began—"I have heard say
Of some sick body that my mother knew,
'Twas no good sign when in a limb diseased
All the pain suddenly departs—as if
The guardian angel discontinued pain   *1200*
Because the hope of cure was gone at last:
The limb will not again exert itself,
It needs be pained no longer: so with me,
—My soul whence all the pain is past at once:
All pain must be to work some good in the end.   *1205*
True, this I feel now, this may be that good,
Pain was because of—otherwise, I fear!"

She said—a long while later in the day,

1185 Assisi . . . holy ground birthplace of St. Francis.

When I had let the silence be—abrupt—
1210 "Have you a mother?" "She died, I was born."
"A sister then?" "No sister." "Who was it—
What woman were you used to serve this way,
Be kind to, till I called you and you came?"
I did not like that word. Soon afterward—
1215 "Tell me, are men unhappy, in some kind
Of mere unhappiness at being men,
As women suffer, being womanish?
Have you, now, some unhappiness, I mean,
Born of what may be man's strength overmuch,
1220 To match the undue susceptibility,
The sense at every pore when hate is close?
It hurts us if a baby hides its face
Or child strikes at us punily, calls names
Or makes a mouth—much more if stranger men
1225 Laugh or frown—just as that were much to bear!
Yet rocks split—and the blow-ball does no more,
Quivers to feathery nothing at a touch;
And strength may have its drawback weakness 'scapes."
Once she asked "What is it that made you smile,
1230 At the great gate with the eagles and the snakes,
Where the company entered, 'tis a long time since?"
"—Forgive—I think you would not understand:
Ah, but you ask me—therefore, it was this.
That was a certain bishop's villa-gate,
1235 I knew it by the eagles—and at once
Remembered this same bishop was just he
People of old were wont to bid me please
If I would catch preferment: so, I smiled
Because an impulse came to me, a whim—
1240 What if I prayed the prelate leave to speak,
Began upon him in his presence-hall
—'What, still at work so gray and obsolete?
Still rocheted and mitered more or less?
Don't you feel all that out of fashion now?
1245 I find out when the day of things is done!' "

At eve we heard the *angelus*: she turned—

"I told you I can neither read nor write.
My life stopped with the playtime; I will learn,
If I begin to live again: but you—
Who are a priest—wherefore do you not read   1250
The service at this hour? Read Gabriel's song,
The lesson, and then read the little prayer
To Raphael, proper for us travelers!"
I did not like that, neither, but I read.

When we stopped at Foligno it was dark.   1255
The people of the post came out with lights:
The driver said, "This time tomorrow, may
Saints only help, relays continue good,
Nor robbers hinder, we arrive at Rome."
I urged, "Why tax your strength a second night?   1260
Trust me, alight here and take brief repose!
We are out of harm's reach, past pursuit: go sleep
If but an hour! I keep watch, guard the while
Here in the doorway." But her whole face changed,
The misery grew again about her mouth,   1265
The eyes burned up from faintness, like the fawn's
Tired to death in the thicket, when she feels
The probing spear o' the huntsman. "Oh, no stay!"
She cried, in the fawn's cry, "On to Rome, on, on—
Unless 'tis you who fear—which cannot be!"   1270

We did go on all night; but at its close
She was troubled, restless, moaned low, talked at
    whiles
To herself, her brow on quiver with the dream:
Once, wide awake, she menaced, at arms' length
Waved away something—"Never again with you!   1275
My soul is mine, my body is my soul's:
You and I are divided ever more
In soul and body: get you gone!" Then I—
"Why, in my whole life I have never prayed!
Oh, if the God, that only can, would help!   1280
Am I his priest with power to cast out fiends?
Let God arise and all his enemies

Be scattered!"° By morn, there was peace, no sigh
Out of the deep sleep.

                        When she woke at last,
1285 I answered the first look—"Scarce twelve hours more,
Then, Rome! There probably was no pursuit,
There cannot now be peril: bear up brave!
Just some twelve hours to press through to the prize:
Then, no more of the terrible journey!" "Then,
1290 No more o' the journey: if it might but last!
Always, my life-long, thus to journey still!
It is the interruption that I dread—
With no dread, ever to be here and thus!
Never to see a face nor hear a voice!
1295 Yours is no voice; you speak when you are dumb;
Nor face, I see it in the dark. I want
No face nor voice that change and grow unkind."
That I liked, that was the best thing she said.

In the broad day, I dared entreat, "Descend!"
1300 I told a woman, at the garden-gate
By the post-house, white and pleasant in the sun,
"It is my sister—talk with her apart!
She is married and unhappy, you perceive;
I take her home because her head is hurt;
1305 Comfort her as you women understand!"
So, there I left them by the garden-wall,
Paced the road, then bade put the horses to,
Came back, and there she sat: close to her knee,
A black-eyed child still held the bowl of milk,
1310 Wondered to see how little she could drink,
And in her arms the woman's infant lay.
She smiled at me "How much good this has done!
This is a whole night's rest and how much more!
I can proceed now, though I wish to stay.
1315 How do you call that tree with the thick top
That holds in all its leafy green and gold
The sun now like an immense egg of fire?"

1282–83 **Let God arise ... scattered!** Psalm 68:1.

(It was a million-leaved mimosa.) "Take
The babe away from me and let me go!"
And in the carriage "Still a day, my friend!   1320
And perhaps half a night, the woman fears.
I pray it finish since it cannot last:
There may be more misfortune at the close,
And where will you be? God suffice me then!"
And presently—for there was a roadside-shrine—   1325
"When I was taken first to my own church
Lorenzo in Lucina, being a girl,
And bid confess my faults, I interposed
'But teach me what fault to confess and know!'
So, the priest said—'You should bethink yourself: 1330
Each human being needs must have done wrong!'
Now, be you candid and no priest but friend—
Were I surprised and killed here on the spot,
A runaway from husband and his home,
Do you account it were in sin I died?   1335
My husband used to seem to harm me, not . . .
Not on pretense he punished sin of mine,
Nor for sin's sake and lust of cruelty,
But as I heard him bid a farming-man
At the villa take a lamb once to the wood   1340
And there ill-treat it, meaning that the wolf
Should hear its cries, and so come, quick be caught,
Enticed to the trap: he practiced thus with me
That so, whatever were his gain thereby,
Others than I might become prey and spoil.   1345
Had it been only between our two selves—
His pleasure and my pain—why, pleasure him
By dying, nor such need to make a coil!
But this was worth an effort, that my pain
Should not become a snare, prove pain threefold   1350
To other people—strangers—or unborn—
How should I know? I sought release from that—
I think, or else from—dare I say, some cause
Such as is put into a tree, which turns
Away from the north wind with what nest it holds—   1355
The woman said that trees so turn: now, friend,
Tell me, because I cannot trust myself!

You are a man: what have I done amiss?"
You must conceive my answer—I forget—
1360 Taken up wholly with the thought, perhaps,
This time she might have said—might, did not say—
"You are a priest." She said, "my friend."

                                        Day wore,
We passed the places, somehow the calm went,
Again the restless eyes began to rove
1365 In new fear of the foe mine could not see.
She wandered in her mind—addressed me once
"Gaetano!"°—that is not my name: whose name?
I grew alarmed, my head seemed turning too.
I quickened pace with promise now, now threat:
1370 Bade drive and drive, nor any stopping more.
"Too deep i' the thick of the struggle, struggle through!
Then drench her in repose though death's self pour
The plenitude of quiet—help us, God,
Whom the winds carry!"

                                        Suddenly I saw
1375 The old tower, and the little white-walled clump
Of buildings and the cypress-tree or two—
"Already Castelnuovo—Rome!" I cried,
"As good as Rome—Rome is the next stage, think!
This is where travelers' hearts are wont to beat.
1380 Say you are saved, sweet lady!" Up she woke.
The sky was fierce with color from the sun
Setting. She screamed out "No, I must not die!
Take me no farther, I should die: stay here!
I have more life to save than mine!"

                                        She swooned.
1385 We seemed safe: what was it foreboded so?
Out of the coach into the inn I bore
The motionless and breathless pure and pale
Pompilia—bore her through a pitying group
And laid her on a couch, still calm and cured

1367 **Gaetano** the name Pompilia is to give her son.

By deep sleep of all woes at once. The host   *1390*
Was urgent "Let her stay an hour or two!
Leave her to us, all will be right by morn!"
Oh, my foreboding! But I could not choose.

I paced the passage, kept watch all night long.
I listened—not one movement, not one sigh.   *1395*
"Fear not: she sleeps so sound!" they said: but I
Feared, all the same, kept fearing more and more,
Found myself throb with fear from head to foot,
Filled with a sense of such impending woe,
That, at first pause of night, pretense of gray,   *1400*
I made my mind up it was morn.—"Reach Rome,
Lest hell reach her! A dozen miles to make,
Another long breath, and we emerge!" I stood
I' the courtyard, roused the sleepy grooms. "Have out
Carriage and horse, give haste, take gold!" said I.   *1405*
While they made ready in the doubtful morn—
'Twas the last minute—needs must I ascend
And break her sleep; I turned to go.

                                        And there
Faced me Count Guido, there posed the mean man
As master—took the field, encamped his rights,   *1410*
Challenged the world: there leered new triumph, there
Scowled the old malice in the visage bad
And black o' the scamp. Soon triumph suppled the
        tongue
A little, malice glued to his dry throat,
And he part howled, part hissed . . . oh, how he kept *1415*
Well out o' the way, at arm's length and to spare!—
"My salutation to your priestship! What?
Matutinal, busy with book so soon
Of an April day that's damp as tears that now
Deluge Arezzo at its darling's flight?—   *1420*
'Tis unfair, wrongs feminity at large,
To let a single dame monopolize
A heart the whole sex claims, should share alike:
Therefore I overtake you, Canon! Come!
The lady—could you leave her side so soon?   *1425*

You have not yet experienced at her hands
My treatment, you lay down undrugged, I see!
Hence this alertness—hence no death-in-life
Like what held arms fast when she stole from mine.
1430 To be sure, you took the solace and repose
That first night at Foligno!—news abound
O' the road by this time—men regaled me much,
As past them I came halting after you,
Vulcan pursuing Mars,° as poets sing—
1435 Still at the last here pant I, but arrive,
Vulcan—and not without my Cyclops° too,
The Commissary and the unpoisoned arm
O' the Civil Force, should Mars turn mutineer.
Enough of fooling: capture the culprits, friend!
1440 Here is the lover in the smart disguise
With the sword—he is a priest, so mine lies still.
There upstairs hides my wife the runaway,
His leman: the two plotted, poisoned first,
Plundered me after, and eloped thus far
1445 Where now you find them. Do your duty quick!
Arrest and hold him! That's done: now catch her!"
During this speech of that man—well, I stood
Away, as he managed—still, I stood as near
The throat of him—with these two hands, my own—
1450 As now I stand near yours, Sir—one quick spring,
One great good satisfying gripe, and lo!
There had he lain abolished with his lie,
Creation purged o' the miscreate, man redeemed,
A spittle wiped off from the face of God!
1455 I, in some measure, seek a poor excuse
For what I left undone, in just this fact
That my first feeling at the speech I quote
Was—not of what a blasphemy was dared,
Not what a bag of venomed purulence
1460 Was split and noisome—but how splendidly

1434 **Vulcan pursuing Mars** ugly Vulcan was the husband of Venus, goddess of love and beauty, the dashing Mars her lover. 1436 **Cyclops** the one-eyed monsters of the *Odyssey* were sometimes thought of as workmen of Vulcan.

Mirthful, how ludicrous a lie was launched!
Would Molière's self° wish more than hear such man
Call, claim such woman for his own, his wife,
Even though, in due amazement at the boast,
He had stammered, she moreover was divine?   1465
She to be his—were hardly less absurd
Than that he took her name into his mouth,
Licked, and then let it go again, the beast,
Signed with his slaver. Oh, she poisoned him,
Plundered him, and the rest! Well, what I wished   1470
Was, that he would but go on, say once more
So to the world, and get his meed of men,
The fist's reply to the filth. And while I mused,
The minute, oh the misery, was gone!
On either idle hand of me there stood   1475
Really an officer, nor laughed i' the least:
Nay, rendered justice to his reason, laid
Logic to heart, as 'twere submitted them
"Twice two makes four."

                "And now, catch her!" he cried.
That sobered me. "Let myself lead the way—   1480
Ere you arrest me, who am somebody,
Being, as you hear, a priest and privileged—
To the lady's chamber! I presume you—men
Expert, instructed how to find out truth,
Familiar with the guise of guilt. Detect   1485
Guilt on her face when it meets mine, then judge
Between us and the mad dog howling there!"
Up we all went together, in they broke
O' the chamber late my chapel. There she lay,
Composed as when I laid her, that last eve,   1490
O' the couch, still breathless, motionless, sleep's self,
Wax-white, seraphic, saturate with the sun
O' the morning that now flooded from the front
And filled the window with a light like blood.
"Behold the poisoner, the adulteress,   1495
—And feigning sleep too! Seize, bind!" Guido hissed.

1462 **Molière's self** in Molière's *Don Juan* the libertine claims a nun
as his wife.

She started up, stood erect, face to face
With the husband: back he fell, was buttressed there
By the window all a flame with morning-red,
1500 He the black figure, the opprobrious blur
Against all peace and joy and light and life.
"Away from between me and hell!" she cried:
"Hell for me, no embracing any more!
I am God's, I love God, God—whose knees I clasp,
1505 Whose utterly most just award I take,
But bear no more love-making devils: hence!"
I may have made an effort to reach her side
From where I stood i' the doorway—anyhow
I found the arms, I wanted, pinioned fast,
1510 Was powerless in the clutch to left and right
O' the rabble pouring in, rascality
Enlisted, rampant on the side of hearth,
Home and the husband—pay in prospect too!
They heaped themselves upon me. "Ha!—and him
1515 Also you outrage? Him, too, my sole friend,
Guardian and savior? That I balk you of,
Since—see how God can help at last and worst!"
She sprang at the sword that hung beside him, seized,
Drew, brandished it, the sunrise burned for joy
1520 O' the blade, "Die," cried she, "devil, in God's name!"
Ah, but they all closed round her, twelve to one
—The unmanly men, no woman-mother made,
Spawned somehow! Dead-white and disarmed she lay.
No matter for the sword, her word sufficed
1525 To spike the coward through and through: he shook,
Could only spit between the teeth—"You see?
You hear? Bear witness, then! Write down . . but no—
Carry these criminals to the prison-house,
For first thing! I begin my search meanwhile
1530 After the stolen effects, gold, jewels, plate,
Money and clothes, they robbed me of and fled,
With no few amorous pieces, verse and prose,
I have much reason to expect to find."

When I saw that—no more than the first mad speech,
1535 Made out the speaker mad and a laughing-stock,

So neither did this next device explode
One listener's indignation—that a scribe
Did sit down, set himself to write indeed,
While sundry knaves began to peer and pry
In corner and hole—that Guido, wiping brow   1540
And getting him a countenance, was fast
Losing his fear, beginning to strut free
O' the stage of his exploit, snuff here, sniff there—
Then I took truth in, guessed sufficiently
The service for the moment. "What I say,   1545
Slight at your peril! We are aliens here,
My adversary and I, called noble both;
I am the nobler, and a name men know.
I could refer our cause to our own Court
In our own country, but prefer appeal   1550
To the nearer jurisdiction. Being a priest,
Though in a secular garb—for reasons good
I shall adduce in due time to my peers—
I demand that the Church I serve, decide
Between us, right the slandered lady there.   1555
A Tuscan noble, I might claim the Duke:
A priest, I rather choose the Church—bid Rome
Cover the wronged with her inviolate shield."

There was no refusing this: they bore me off,
They bore her off, to separate cells o' the same   1560
Ignoble prison, and, separate, thence to Rome.
Pompilia's face, then and thus, looked on me
The last time in this life: not one sight since,
Never another sight to be! And yet
I thought I had saved her. I appealed to Rome: 1565
It seems I simply sent her to her death.
You tell me she is dying now, or dead;
I cannot bring myself to quite believe
This is a place you torture people in:
What if this your intelligence were just   1570
A subtlety, an honest wile to work
On a man at unawares? 'Twere worthy you.
No, Sirs, I cannot have the lady dead!
That erect form, flashing brow, fulgurant eye,

1575 That voice immortal (oh, that voice of hers!)
That vision in the blood-red daybreak—that
Leap to life of the pale electric sword
Angels go armed with—that was not the last
O' the lady! Come, I see through it, you find—
1580 Know the maneuver! Also herself said
I had saved her: do you dare say she spoke false?
Let me see for myself if it be so!
Though she were dying, a priest might be of use,
The more when he's a friend too—she called me
1585 Far beyond "friend." Come, let me see her—indeed
It is my duty, being a priest: I hope
I stand confessed, established, proved a priest?
My punishment had motive that, a priest
I, in a laic garb, a mundane mode,
1590 Did what were harmlessly done otherwise.
I never touched her with my fingertip
Except to carry her to the couch, that eve,
Against my heart, beneath my head, bowed low,
As we priests carry the paten:° that is why
1595 —To get leave and go see her of your grace—
I have told you this whole story over again.
Do I deserve grace? For I might lock lips,
Laugh at your jurisdiction: what have you
To do with me in the matter? I suppose
1600 You hardly think I donned a bravo's dress
To have a hand in the new crime; on the old,
Judgment's delivered, penalty imposed,
I was chained fast at Civita hand and foot—
She had only you to trust to, you and Rome,
1605 Rome and the Church, and no pert meddling priest
Two days ago, when Guido, with the right,
Hacked her to pieces. One might well be wroth;
I have been patient, done my best to help:
I come from Civita and punishment
1610 As friend of the Court—and for pure friendship's sake
Have told my tale to the end—nay, not the end—
For, wait—I'll end—not leave you that excuse!

1594 **paten** plate used in the celebration of the Eucharist. It is
carried in this manner by the subdeacon at High Mass.

When we were parted—shall I go on there?
I was presently brought to Rome—yes, here I stood
Opposite yonder very crucifix— 1615
And there sat you and you, Sirs, quite the same.
I heard charge, and bore question, and told tale
Noted down in the book there—turn and see
If, by one jot or tittle, I vary now!
I' the color the tale takes, there's change perhaps; 1620
'Tis natural, since the sky is different,
Eclipse in the air now; still, the outline stays.
I showed you how it came to be my part
To save the lady. Then your clerk produced
Papers, a pack of stupid and impure 1625
Banalities called letters about love—
Love, indeed—I could teach who styled them so,
Better, I think, though priest and loveless both!
"—How was it that a wife, young, innocent,
And stranger to your person, wrote this page?"— 1630
"—She wrote it when the Holy Father wrote
The bestiality that posts through Rome,
Put in his mouth by Pasquin."° "Nor perhaps
Did you return these answers, verse and prose,
Signed, sealed and sent the lady? There's your hand!" 1635
"—This precious piece of verse, I really judge,
Is meant to copy my own character,
A clumsy mimic; and this other prose,
Not so much even; both rank forgery:
Verse, quotha? Bembo's verse! When Saint John
  wrote 1640
The tract *De Tribus*,° I wrote this to match."
"—How came it, then, the documents were found
At the inn on your departure?"—"I opine,
Because there were no documents to find
In my presence—you must hide before you find. 1645
Who forged them hardly practiced in my view;

1633 **Pasquin** a statue in Rome to which satiric verses, often scur-
rilous or obscene, were fastened. 1640-41 **Bembo's verse . . . De
Tribus** Cardinal Bembo was a celebrated humanist and elegant man
of letters. The "tract *De Tribus*" was referred to as a piece of es-
pecially terrible blasphemy.

Who found them waited till I turned my back."
"—And what of the clandestine visits paid,
Nocturnal passage in and out the house
1650 With its lord absent? 'Tis alleged you climbed . . ."
"—Flew on a broomstick to the man i' the moon!
Who witnessed or will testify this trash?"
"—The trusty servant, Margherita's self,
Even she who brought you letters, you confess,
1655 And, you confess, took letters in reply:
Forget not we have knowledge of the facts!"
"—Sirs, who have knowledge of the facts, defray
The expenditure of wit I waste in vain,
Trying to find out just one fact of all!
1660 She who brought letters from who could not write,
And took back letters to who could not read—
Who was that messenger, of your charity?"
"—Well, so far favors you the circumstance
That this same messenger . . . how shall we say? . . .
1665 *Sub imputatione meretricis*
Laborat°—which makes accusation null:
We waive this woman's: naught makes void the next.
Borsi, called Venerino, he who drove,
O' the first night when you fled away, at length
1670 Deposes to your kissings in the coach,
—Frequent, frenetic . . ." "When deposed he so?"
"After some weeks of sharp imprisonment . . ."
"—Granted by friend the Governor, I engage—"
"—For his participation in your flight!
1675 At length his obduracy melting made
The avowal mentioned . . ." "Was dismissed forthwith
To liberty, poor knave, for recompense.
Sirs, give what credit to the lie you can!
For me, no word in my defense I speak,
And God shall argue for the lady!"

1680   So
Did I stand question, and make answer, still
With the same result of smiling disbelief,

1665–66 Sub . . . laborat labors under the imputation of being a
prostitute.

Polite impossibility of faith
In such affected virtue in a priest;
But a showing fair play, an indulgence, even,   1685
To one no worse than others after all—
Who had not brought disgrace to the order, played
Discreetly, ruffled gown nor ripped the cloth
In a bungling game at romps: I have told you, Sirs—
If I pretended simply to be pure   1690
Honest and Christian in the case—absurd!
As well go boast myself above the needs
O' the human nature, careless how meat smells,
Wine tastes—a saint above the smack! But once
Abate my crest, own flaws i' the flesh, agree   1695
To go with the herd, be hog no more nor less,
Why, hogs in common herd have common rights:
I must not be unduly borne upon,
Who just romanced a little, sowed wild oats,
But 'scaped without a scandal, flagrant fault.   1700
My name helped to a mirthful circumstance:
"Joseph would do well to amend his plea:
Undoubtedly—some toying with the wife,
But as for ruffian violence and rape,
Potiphar pressed too much on the other side!°   1705
The intrigue, the elopement, the disguise—well
      charged!
The letters and verse looked hardly like the truth.
Your apprehension was—of guilt enough
To be compatible with innocence,
So, punished best a little and not too much.   1710
Had I struck Guido Franceschini's face,
You had counseled me withdraw for my own sake,
Balk him of bravo-hiring. Friends came round,
Congratulated, "Nobody mistakes!
The pettiness o' the forfeiture defines   1715
The peccadillo: Guido gets his share:
His wife is free of husband and hook-nose,

1702–5 **"Joseph"** . . . **other side** the story of Joseph and Potiphar's
wife is found in Genesis 39. From Browning's point of view, Capon-
sacchi has more in common with St. Joseph, husband of the Virgin
Mary.

The moldy viands and the mother-in-law.
To Civita with you and amuse the time,
1720 Travesty us *De Raptu Helenae!*°
A funny figure must the husband cut
When the wife makes him skip—too ticklish, eh?
Do it in Latin, not the Vulgar, then!
Scazons°—we'll copy and send his Eminence.
1725 Mind—one iambus in the final foot!
He'll rectify it, be your friend for life!"
Oh, Sirs, depend on me for much new light
Thrown on the justice and religion here
By this proceeding, much fresh food for thought!

1730 And I was just set down to study these
In relegation, two short days ago,
Admiring how you read the rules, when, clap,
A thunder comes into my solitude—
I am caught up in a whirlwind and cast here,
1735 Told of a sudden, in this room where so late
You dealt out law adroitly, that those scales,
I meekly bowed to, took my allotment from,
Guido has snatched at, broken in your hands,
Metes to himself the murder of his wife,
1740 Full measure, pressed down, running over now!
Can I assist to an explanation?—Yes,
I rise in your esteem, sagacious Sirs,
Stand up a renderer of reasons, not
The officious priest would personate Saint George
1745 For a mock Princess in undragoned days.
What, the blood startles you? What, after all
The priest who needs must carry sword on thigh
May find imperative use for it? Then, there was
A Princess, was a dragon belching flame,
1750 And should have been a Saint George also? Then,
There might be worse schemes than to break the bonds
At Arezzo, lead her by the little hand,
Till she reached Rome, and let her try to live?
But you were law and gospel—would one please

1720 'De Raptu Helenae' a late Greek poem on the rape of Helen
of Troy.   1724 Scazons classical verse form.

Stand back, allow your faculty elbow-room? 1755
You blind guides who must needs lead eyes that see!
Fools, alike ignorant of man and God!
What was there here should have perplexed your wit
For a wink of the owl-eyes of you? How miss, then,
What's now forced on you by this flare of fact— 1760
As if Saint Peter failed to recognize
Nero as no apostle, John or James,
Till someone burned a martyr, made a torch
O' the blood and fat to show his features by!
Could you fail read this cartulary aright 1765
On head and front of Franceschini there,
Large-lettered like hell's masterpiece of print—
That he, from the beginning pricked at heart
By some lust, letch of hate against his wife,
Plotted to plague her into overt sin 1770
And shame, would slay Pompilia body and soul,
And save his mean self—miserably caught
I' the quagmire of his own tricks, cheats and lies?
—That himself wrote those papers—from himself
To himself—which, i' the name of me and her, 1775
His mistress-messenger gave her and me,
Touching us with such pustules of the soul
That she and I might take the taint, be shown
To the world and shuddered over, speckled so?
—That the agent put her sense into my words, 1780
Made substitution of the thing she hoped,
For the thing she had and held, its opposite,
While the husband in the background bit his lips
At each fresh failure of his precious plot?
—That when at the last we did rush each on each, 1785
By no chance but because God willed it so—
The spark of truth was struck from out our souls—
Made all of me, descried in the first glance,
Seem fair and honest and permissible love
O' the good and true—as the first glance told me 1790
There was no duty patent in the world
Like daring try be good and true myself,
Leaving the shows of things to the Lord of Show
And Prince o' the Power of the Air. Our very flight,

1795 Even to its most ambiguous circumstance,
Irrefragably proved how futile, false . . .
Why, men—men and not boys—boys and not babes—
Babes and not beasts—beasts and not stocks and
    stones!—
Had the liar's lie been true one pinpoint speck,
1800 Were I the accepted suitor, free o' the place,
Disposer of the time, to come at a call
And go at a wink as who should say me nay—
What need of flight, what were the gain therefrom
But just damnation, failure or success?
1805 Damnation pure and simple to her the wife
And me the priest—who bartered private bliss
For public reprobation, the safe shade
For the sunshine which men see to pelt me by:
What other advantage—we who led the days
1810 And nights alone i' the house—was flight to find?
In our whole journey did we stop an hour,
Diverge a foot from straight road till we reached
Or would have reached—but for that fate of ours—
The father and mother, in the eye of Rome,
1815 The eye of yourselves we made aware of us
At the first fall of misfortune? And indeed
You did so far give sanction to our flight,
Confirm its purpose, as lend helping hand,
Deliver up Pompilia not to him
1820 She fled, but those the flight was ventured for.
Why then could you, who stopped short, not go on
One poor step more, and justify the means,
Having allowed the end?—not see and say
"Here's the exceptional conduct that should claim
1825 To be exceptionally judged on rules
Which, understood, make no exception here"—
Why play instead into the devil's hands
By dealing so ambiguously as gave
Guido the power to intervene like me,
1830 Prove one exception more? I saved his wife
Against law: against law he slays her now:
Deal with him!

I have done with being judged.
I stand here guiltless in thought, word and deed,
To the point that I apprise you—in contempt
For all misapprehending ignorance   1835
O' the human heart, much more the mind of Christ—
That I assuredly did bow, was blessed
By the revelation of Pompilia. There!
Such is the final fact I fling you, Sirs,
To mouth and mumble and misinterpret: there!   1840
"The priest's in love," have it the vulgar way!
Unpriest me, rend the rags o' the vestment, do—
Degrade deep, disenfranchise all you dare—
Remove me from the midst, no longer priest
And fit companion for the like of you—   1845
Your gay Abati with the well-turned leg
And rose i' the hat-rim, Canons, cross at neck
And silk mask in the pocket of the gown,
Brisk Bishops with the world's musk still unbrushed
From the rochet; I'll no more of these good things: 1850
There's a crack somewhere, something that's unsound
I' the rattle!

For Pompilia—be advised,
Build churches, go pray! You will find me there,
I know, if you come—and you will come, I know.
Why, there's a Judge weeping! Did not I say   1855
You were good and true at bottom? You see the
    truth—
I am glad I helped you: she helped me just so.

But for Count Guido—you must counsel there!
I bow my head, bend to the very dust,
Break myself up in shame of faultiness.   1860
I had him one whole moment, as I said—
As I remember, as will never out
O' the thoughts of me—I had him in arm's reach
There—as you stand, Sir, now you cease to sit—
I could have killed him ere he killed his wife,   1865
And did not: he went off alive and well

And then effected this last feat—through me!
Me—not through you—dismiss that fear! 'Twas you
Hindered me staying here to save her—not
1870 From leaving you and going back to him
And doing service in Arezzo. Come,
Instruct me in procedure! I conceive—
In all due self-abasement might I speak—
How you will deal with Guido: oh, not death!
1875 Death, if it let her life be: otherwise
Not death—your lights will teach you clearer! I
Certainly have an instinct of my own
I' the matter: bear with me and weigh its worth!
Let us go away—leave Guido all alone
1880 Back on the world again that knows him now!
I think he will be found (indulge so far!)
Not to die so much as slide out of life,
Pushed by the general horror and common hate
Low, lower—left o' the very ledge of things,
1885 I seem to see him catch convulsively
One by one at all honest forms of life,
At reason, order, decency and use—
To cramp him and get foothold by at least;
And still they disengage them from his clutch.
1890 "What, you are he, then, had Pompilia once
And so forwent her? Take not up with us!"
And thus I see him slowly and surely edged
Off all the tableland whence life upsprings
Aspiring to be immortality,
1895 As the snake, hatched on hilltop by mischance,
Despite his wriggling, slips, slides, slidders down
Hillside, lies low and prostrate on the smooth
Level of the outer place, lapsed in the vale:
So I lose Guido in the loneliness,
1900 Silence and dusk, till at the doleful end,
At the horizontal line, creation's verge,
From what just is to absolute nothingness—
Whom is it, straining onward still, he meets?
What other man deep further in the fate,
1905 Who, turning at the prize of a footfall
To flatter him and promise fellowship,

Discovers in the act a frightful face—
Judas, made monstrous by much solitude!
The two are at one now! Let them love their love
That bites and claws like hate, or hate their hate   1910
That mops and mows and makes as it were love!
There, let them each tear each in devil's-fun,
Or fondle this the other while malice aches—
Both teach, both learn detestability!
Kiss him the kiss, Iscariot! Pay that back,   1915
That smatch o' the slaver blistering on your lip,
By the better trick, the insult he spared Christ—
Lure him the lure o' the letters, Aretine!
Lick him o'er slimy-smooth with jelly-filth
O' the verse-and-prose pollution in love's guise!   1920
The cockatrice is with the basilisk!°
There let them grapple, denizens o' the dark,
Foes or friends, but indissolubly bound,
In their one spot out of the ken of God
Or care of man, forever and ever more!   1925

Why, Sirs, what's this? Why, this is sorry and strange!
Futility, divagation: this from me
Bound to be rational, justify an act
Of sober man!—whereas, being moved so much,
I give you cause to doubt the lady's mind: 1930
A pretty sarcasm for the world! I fear
You do her wit injustice—all through me!
Like my fate all through—ineffective help!
A poor rash advocate I prove myself.
You might be angry with good cause: but sure   1935
At the advocate—only at the undue zeal
That spoils the force of his own plea, I think?
My part was just to tell you how things stand,
State facts and not be flustered at their fume.
But then 'tis a priest speaks: as for love—no!   1940
If you let buzz a vulgar fly like that
About your brains, as if I loved, forsooth,
Indeed, Sirs, you do wrong! We had no thought

1921 **cockatrice . . . basilisk!** mythological monsters supposed to
kill beholders with their glance.

Of such infatuation, she and I:
1945 There are many points that prove it: do be just!
I told you—at one little roadside-place
I spent a good half-hour, paced to and fro
The garden; just to leave her free awhile,
I plucked a handful of spring herb and bloom:
1950 I might have sat beside her on the bench
Where the children were: I wish the thing had been
Indeed: the event could not be worse, you know:
One more half-hour of her saved! She's dead now,
    Sirs!
While I was running on at such a rate,
1955 Friends should have plucked me by the sleeve: I went
Too much o' the trivial outside of her face
And the purity that shone there—plain to me,
Not to you, what more natural? Nor am I
Infatuated—oh, I saw, be sure!
1960 Her brow had not the right line, leaned too much,
Painters would say; they like the straight-up Greek:
This seemed bent somewhat with an invisible crown
Of martyr and saint, not such as art approves.
And how the dark orbs dwelt deep underneath,
1965 Looked out of such a sad sweet heaven on me!
The lips, compressed a little, came forward too,
Careful for a whole world of sin and pain.
That was the face, her husband makes his plea,
He sought just to disfigure—no offense
1970 Beyond that! Sirs, let us be rational!
He needs must vindicate his honor—ay,
Yet shirks, the coward, in a clown's disguise,
Away from the scene, endeavors to escape.
Now, had he done so, slain and left no trace
1975 O' the slayer—what were vindicated, pray?
You had found his wife disfigured or a corpse,
For what and by whom? It is too palpable!
Then, here's another point involving law:
I use this argument to show you meant
1980 No calumny against us by that title
O' the sentence—liars try to twist it so:
What penalty it bore, I had to pay

Till further proof should follow of innocence—
Probationis ob defectum°—proof?
How could you get proof without trying us? 1985
You went through the preliminary form,
Stopped there, contrived this sentence to amuse
The adversary. If the title ran
For more than fault imputed and not proved,
That was a simple penman's error, else 1990
A slip i' the phrase—as when we say of you
"Charged with injustice"—which may either be
Or not be—'tis a name that sticks meanwhile.
Another relevant matter: fool that I am!
Not what I wish true, yet a point friends urge: 1995
It is not true—yet, since friends think it helps—
She only tried me when some others failed—
Began with Conti, whom I told you of,
And Guillichini, Guido's kinsfolk both,
And when abandoned by them, not before, 2000
Turned to me. That's conclusive why she turned.
Much good they got by the happy cowardice!
Conti is dead, poisoned a month ago:
Does that much strike you as a sin? Not much,
After the present murder—one mark more 2005
On the Moor's skin—what is black by blacker still?
Conti had come here and told truth. And so
With Guillichini; he's condemned of course
To the galleys, as a friend in this affair,
Tried and condemned for no one thing i' the world, 2010
A fortnight since by who but the Governor?—
The just judge, who refused Pompilia help
At first blush, being her husband's friend, you know.
There are two tales to suit the separate courts,
Arezzo and Rome: he tells you here, we fled 2015
Alone, unhelped—lays stress on the main fault,
The spiritual sin, Rome looks to: but elsewhere
He likes best we should break in, steal, bear off,
Be fit to brand and pillory and flog—
That's the charge goes to the heart of the Governor: 2020

1984 **Probationis ob defectum** through lack of sufficient proof.

If these unpriest me, you and I may yet
Converse, Vincenzo Marzi-Medici!
Oh, Sirs, there are worse men than you, I say!
More easily duped, I mean; this stupid lie,
2025 Its liar never dared propound in Rome,
He gets Arezzo to receive—nay more,
Gets Florence and the Duke to authorize!
This is their Rota's° sentence, their Granduke
Signs and seals! Rome for me henceforward—Rome,
2030 Where better men are—most of all, that man
The Augustinian of the Hospital,
Who writes the letter—he confessed, he says,
Many a dying person, never one
So sweet and true and pure and beautiful.
2035 A good man! Will you make him Pope one day?
Not that he is not good too, this we have—
But old—else he would have his word to speak,
His truth to teach the world: I thirst for truth,
But shall not drink it till I reach the source.

2040 Sirs, I am quiet again. You see, we are
So very pitiable, she and I,
Who had conceivably been otherwise.
Forget distemperature and idle heat!
Apart from truth's sake, what's to move so much?
2045 Pompilia will be presently with God;
I am, on earth, as good as out of it,
A relegated priest; when exile ends,
I mean to do my duty and live long.
She and I are mere strangers now: but priests
2050 Should study passion; how else cure mankind,
Who come for help in passionate extremes?
I do but play with an imagined life
Of who, unfettered by a vow, unblessed
By the higher call—since you will have it so—
2055 Leads it companioned by the woman there.
To live, and see her learn, and learn by her,
Out of the low obscure and petty world—

2028 **Rota** court.

Or only see one purpose and one will
Evolve themselves i' the world, change wrong to right:
To have to do with nothing but the true,   *2060*
The good, the eternal—and these, not alone
In the main current of the general life,
But small experiences of every day,
Concerns of the particular hearth and home:
To learn not only by a comet's rush   *2065*
But a rose's birth—not by the grandeur, God—
But the comfort, Christ. All this, how far away!
Mere delectation, meet for a minute's dream!—
Just as a drudging student trims his lamp,
Opens his Plutarch,° puts him in the place   *2070*
Of Roman, Grecian; draws the patched gown close,
Dreams, "Thus should I fight, save or rule the
    world!"—
Then smilingly, contentedly, awakes
To the old solitary nothingness.
So I, from such communion, pass content . . .   *2075*

O great, just, good God! Miserable me!

THE POPE

LIKE to Ahasuerus,° that shrewd prince,
I will begin—as is, these seven years now,
My daily wont—and read a History
(Written by one whose deft right hand was dust
To the last digit, ages ere my birth)   *5*
Of all my predecessors, Popes of Rome:

2070 **Plutarch** ancient biographer.
1 **Ahasuerus** Esther 6:1.

For though mine ancient early dropped the pen,
Yet others picked it up and wrote it dry,
Since of the making books there is no end.
10 And so I have the papacy complete
From Peter first to Alexander last;
Can question each and take instruction so.
Have I to dare?—I ask, how dared this Pope?
To suffer?—Suchanone, how suffered he?
15 Being about to judge, as now, I seek
How judged once, well or ill, some other Pope;
Study some signal judgment that subsists
To blaze on, or else blot, the page which seals
The sum up of what gain or loss to God
20 Came of His one more Vicar in the world.
So, do I find example, rule of life;
So, square and set in order the next page,
Shall be stretched smooth o'er my own funeral cyst.°

Eight hundred years exact before the year
25 I was made Pope, men made Formosus Pope,
Say Sigebert and other chroniclers.
Ere I confirm or quash the trial here
Of Guido Franceschini and his friends,
Read—How there was a ghastly trial once
30 Of a dead man by a live man, and both, Popes:
Thus—in the antique penman's very phrase.

"Then Stephen, Pope and seventh of the name,
Cried out, in synod as he sat in state,
While choler quivered on his brow and beard,
35 'Come into court, Formosus, thou lost wretch,
That claimedst to be late Pope as even I!'

"And at the word the great door of the church
Flew wide, and in they brought Formosus' self,
The body of him, dead, even as embalmed
40 And buried duly in the Vatican
Eight months before, exhumed thus for the nonce.

23 funeral cyst coffin.

They set it, that dead body of a Pope,
Clothed in pontific vesture now again,
Upright on Peter's chair as if alive.

"And Stephen, springing up, cried furiously   45
'Bishop of Porto, wherefore didst presume
'To leave that see and take this Roman see,
Exchange the lesser for the greater see,
—A thing against the canons of the Church?'

"Then one—(a Deacon who, observing forms,   50
Was placed by Stephen to repel the charge,
Be advocate and mouthpiece of the corpse)—
Spoke as he dared, set stammeringly forth
With white lips and dry tongue—as but a youth,
For frightful was the corpse-face to behold—   55
How nowise lacked there precedent for this.

"But when, for his last precedent of all,
Emboldened by the Spirit, out he blurts
'And, Holy Father, didst not thou thyself
Vacate the lesser for the greater see,   60
Half a year since change Arago for Rome?'
'—Ye have the sin's defense now, Synod mine!'
Shrieks Stephen in a beastly froth of rage:
'Judge now betwixt him dead and me alive!
Hath he intruded, or do I pretend?   65
Judge, judge!'—breaks wavelike one whole foam of
          wrath.

"Whereupon they, being friends and followers,
Said 'Ay, thou art Christ's Vicar, and not he!
Away with what is frightful to behold!
This act was uncanonic and a fault.'   70

"Then, swallowed up in rage, Stephen exclaimed
'So, guilty! So, remains I punish guilt!
He is unpoped, and all he did I damn:
The Bishop, that ordained him, I degrade:
Depose to laics those he raised to priests: 75

What they have wrought is mischief nor shall stand
It is confusion, let it vex no more!
Since I revoke, annul and abrogate
All his decrees in all kinds: they are void!
80 In token whereof and warning to the world,
Strip me yon miscreant of those robes usurped,
And clothe him with vile serge befitting such!
Then hale the carrion to the marketplace:
Let the town-hangman chop from his right hand
85 Those same three fingers which he blessed withal;
Next cut the head off once was crowned forsooth:
And last go fling them, fingers, head and trunk,
To Tiber that my Christian fish may sup!'
—Either because of IXθYΣ which means Fish
90 And very aptly symbolizes Christ,
Or else because the Pope is Fisherman,
And seals with Fisher's-signet.°

                                "Anyway,
So said, so done: himself, to see it done,
Followed the corpse they trailed from street to street
95 Till into Tiber wave they threw the thing.
The people, crowded on the banks to see,
Were loud or mute, wept or laughed, cursed or jeered,
According as the deed addressed their sense;
A scandal verily: and out spake a Jew
100 'Wot ye your Christ had vexed our Herod thus?'

"Now when, Formosus being dead a year,
His judge Pope Stephen tasted death in turn,
Made captive by the mob and strangled straight,
Romanus, his successor for a month,
105 Did make protest Formosus was with God,
Holy, just, true in thought and word and deed.
Next Theodore, who reigned but twenty days,

89–92 IXθYΣ ... Fisher's signet the Greek word for fish is a com-
mon symbol of Christ, the letters standing for the first letters, in
Greek, of "Jesus Christ, Son of God, Savior." The Pope is a Fisher-
man because of Jesus' promise to make Peter (considered the first
Pope) a "fisher of men" (Matthew 4:19). The Pope's ring is called
the Ring of the Fisherman.

Therein convoked a synod, whose decree
Did reinstate, repope the late unpoped,
And do away with Stephen as accursed.   *110*
So that when presently certain fisher-folk
(As if the queasy river could not hold
Its swallowed Jonas, but discharged the meal)
Produced the timely product of their nets,
The mutilated man, Formosus—saved   *115*
From putrefaction by the embalmer's spice,
Or, as some said, by sanctity of flesh—
'Why, lay the body again,' bade Theodore,
'Among his predecessors, in the church
And burial-place of Peter!' which was done.   *120*
'And,' addeth Luitprand, 'many of repute,
Pious and still alive, avouch to me
That, as they bore the body up the aisle,
The saints in imaged row bowed each his head
For welcome to a brother-saint come back.'   *125*
As for Romanus and this Theodore,
These two Popes, through the brief reign granted
        each,
Could but initiate what John came to close
And give the final stamp to: he it was
Ninth of the name (I follow the best guides)   *130*
Who—in full synod at Ravenna held
With Bishops seventy-four, and present too
Eude King of France with his Archbishopry—
Did condemn Stephen, anathematize
The disinterment, and make all blots blank,   *135*
'For,' argueth here Auxilius in a place
De Ordinationibus,° 'precedents
Had been, no lack, before Formosus long,
Of Bishops so transferred from see to see—
Marinus, for example:' read the tract.   *140*

"But, after John, came Sergius, reaffirmed
The right of Stephen, cursed Formosus, nay
Cast out, some say, his corpse a second time.

137 *De Ordinationibus* concerning ordinations.

And here—because the matter went to ground,
145 Fretted by new griefs, other cares of the age—
Here is the last pronouncing of the Church,
Her sentence that subsists unto this day.
Yet constantly opinion hath prevailed
I' the Church, Formosus was a holy man."

150 Which of the judgments was infallible?
Which of my predecessors spoke for God?
And what availed Formosus that this cursed,
That blessed, and then this other cursed again?
"Fear ye not those whose power can kill the body
155 And not the soul," saith Christ, "but rather those
Can cast both soul and body into hell!"

John judged thus in Eight Hundred Ninety-Eight,
Exact eight hundred years ago today
When, sitting in his stead, Vice-gerent here,
160 I must give judgment on my own behoof.
So worked the predecessor: now, my turn!

In God's name! Once more on this earth of God's,
While twilight lasts and time wherein to work,
I take His staff with my uncertain hand,
165 And stay my six and fourscore years, my due
Labor and sorrow, on His judgment-seat,
And forthwith think, speak, act, in place of Him—
The Pope for Christ. Once more appeal is made
From man's assize to mine: I sit and see
170 Another poor weak trembling human wretch
Pushed by his fellows, who pretend the right,
Up to the gulf which, where I gaze, begins
From this world to the next—gives way and way,
Just on the edge over the awful dark:
175 With nothing to arrest him but my feet.
He catches at me with convulsive face,
Cries "Leave to live the natural minute more!"
While hollowly the avengers echo "Leave?
None! So has he exceeded man's due share
180 In man's fit license, wrung by Adam's fall,

To sin and yet not surely die—that we,
All of us sinful, all with need of grace,
All chary of our life—the minute more
Or minute less of grace which saves a soul—
Bound to make common cause with who craves time, 185
—We yet protest against the exorbitance
Of sin in this one sinner, and demand
That his poor sole remaining piece of time
Be plucked from out his clutch: put him to death!
Punish him now! As for the weal or woe 190
Hereafter, God grant mercy! Man be just,
Nor let the felon boast he went scot-free!"
And I am bound, the solitary judge,
To weigh the worth, decide upon the plea,
And either hold a hand out, or withdraw 195
A foot and let the wretch drift to the fall.
Ay, and while thus I dally, dare perchance
Put fancies for a comfort 'twixt this calm
And yonder passion that I have to bear—
As if reprieve were possible for both 200
Prisoner and Pope—how easy were reprieve!
A touch o' the hand-bell here, a hasty word
To those who wait, and wonder they wait long,
I' the passage there, and I should gain the life!—
Yea, though I flatter me with fancy thus, 205
I know it is but nature's craven-trick.
The case is over, judgment at an end,
And all things done now and irrevocable:
A mere dead man is Franceschini here,
Even as Formosus centuries ago. 210
I have worn through this somber wintry day,
With winter in my soul beyond the world's,
Over these dismalest of documents
Which drew night down on me ere eve befell—
Pleadings and counter-pleadings, figure of fact 215
Beside fact's self, these summaries to wit—
How certain three were slain by certain five:
I read here why it was, and how it went,
And how the chief o' the five preferred excuse,
And how law rather chose defense should lie— 220

What argument he urged by wary word
When free to play off wile, start subterfuge,
And what the unguarded groan told, torture's feat
When law grew brutal, outbroke, overbore
225 And glutted hunger on the truth, at last—
No matter for the flesh and blood between.
All's a clear rede° and no more riddle now.
Truth, nowhere, lies yet everywhere in these—
Not absolutely in a portion, yet
230 Evolvible from the whole: evolved at last
Painfully, held tenaciously by me.
Therefore there is not any doubt to clear
When I shall write the brief word presently
And chink the hand-bell, which I pause to do.
235 Irresolute? Not I, more than the mound
With the pine-trees on it yonder! Some surmise,
Perchance, that since man's wit is fallible,
Mine may fail here? Suppose it so—what then?
Say—Guido, I count guilty, there's no babe
240 So guiltless, for I misconceive the man!
What's in the chance should move me from my mind
If, as I walk in a rough countryside,
Peasants of mine cry "Thou art he can help,
Lord of the land and counted wise to boot:
245 Look at our brother, strangling in his foam,
He fell so where we find him—prove thy worth!"
I may presume, pronounce, "A frenzy-fit,
A falling-sickness or a fever-stroke!
Breathe a vein, copiously let blood at once!"
250 So perishes the patient, and anon
I hear my peasants—"All was error, lord!
Our story, thy prescription: for there crawled
In due time from our hapless brother's breast
The serpent which had stung him: bleeding slew
255 Whom a prompt cordial had restored to health."
What other should I say than "God so willed:
Mankind is ignorant, a man am I:
Call ignorance my sorrow, not my sin!"

227 rede story.

So and not otherwise, in after-time,
If some acuter wit, fresh probing, sound   260
This multifarious mass of words and deeds
Deeper, and reach through guilt to innocence,
I shall face Guido's ghost nor blench a jot.
"God who set me to judge thee, meted out
So much of judging faculty, no more: 265
Ask Him if I was slack in use thereof!"
I hold a heavier fault imputable
Inasmuch as I changed a chaplain once,
For no cause—no, if I must bare my heart—
Save that he snuffled somewhat saying mass.   270
For I am ware it is the seed of act,
God holds appraising in His hollow palm,
Not act grown great thence on the world below,
Leafage and branchage, vulgar eyes admire.
Therefore I stand on my integrity,   275
Nor fear at all: and if I hesitate,
It is because I need to breathe awhile,
Rest, as the human right allows, review
Intent the little seeds of act, my tree—
The thought, which, clothed in deed, I give the world   280
At chink of bell and push of arrased door.

O pale departure, dim disgrace of day!
Winter's in wane, his vengeful worst art thou,
To dash the boldness of advancing March!
Thy chill persistent rain has purged our streets   285
Of gossipry; pert tongue and idle ear
By this, consort 'neath archway, portico.
But wheresoe'er Rome gathers in the gray,
Two names now snap and flash from mouth to
        mouth—
(Sparks, flint and steel strike) Guido and the Pope.   290
By this same hour tomorrow eve—aha,
How do they call him?—the sagacious Swede°
Who finds by figures how the chances prove,
Why one comes rather than another thing,

292 sagacious Swede authority on probability theory, not identified.

295 As, say, such dots turn up by throw of dice,
     Or, if we dip in Virgil here and there
     And prick for such a verse, when such shall point.°
     Take this Swede, tell him, hiding name and rank,
     Two men are in our city this dull eve;
300 One doomed to death—but hundreds in such plight
     Slip aside, clean escape by leave of law
     Which leans to mercy in this latter time;
     Moreover in the plenitude of life
     Is he, with strength of limb and brain adroit,
305 Presumably of service here: beside,
     The man is noble, backed by nobler friends:
     Nay, they so wish him well, the city's self
     Makes common cause with who—house-magistrate,
     Patron of hearth and home, domestic lord—
310 But ruled his own, let aliens cavil. Die?
     He'll bribe a gaoler or break prison first!
     Nay, a sedition may be helpful, give
     Hint to the mob to batter wall, burn gate,
     And bid the favorite malefactor march.
315 Calculate now these chances of escape!
     "It is not probable, but well may be."
     Again, there is another man, weighed now
     By twice eight years beyond the seven-times-ten,
     Appointed overweight to break our branch.
320 And this man's loaded branch lifts, more than snow
     All the world's cark and care, though a bird's nest
     Were a superfluous burden: notably
     Hath he been pressed, as if his age were youth,
     From today's dawn till now that day departs,
325 Trying one question with true sweat of soul
     "Shall the said doomed man fitlier die or live?"
     When a straw swallowed in his posset, stool
     Stumbled on where his path lies, any puff
     That's incident to such a smoking flax,
330 Hurries the natural end and quenches him!
     Now calculate, thou sage, the chances here,

296–97 Virgil . . . point the practice of opening a volume of Virgil at
random and taking counsel from the passage on which one's finger
lights.

Say, which shall die the sooner, this or that?
"That, possibly, this in all likelihood."
I thought so: yet thou tripp'st, my foreign friend!
No, it will be quite otherwise—today   *335*
Is Guido's last: my term is yet to run.

But say the Swede were right, and I forthwith
Acknowledge a prompt summons and lie dead:
Why, then I stand already in God's face
And hear "Since by its fruit a tree is judged,   *340*
Show me thy fruit, the latest act of thine!
For in the last is summed the first and all—
What thy life last put heart and soul into,
There shall I taste thy product." I must plead
This condemnation of a man today.   *345*

Not so! Expect nor question nor reply
At what we figure as God's judgment-bar!
None of this vile way by the barren words
Which, more than any deed, characterize
Man as made subject to a curse: no speech—   *350*
That still bursts o'er some lie which lurks inside,
As the split skin across the coppery snake,
And most denotes man! since, in all beside,
In hate or lust or guile or unbelief,
Out of some core of truth the excrescence comes,   *355*
And, in the last resort, the man may urge
"So was I made, a weak thing that gave way
To truth, to impulse only strong since true,
And hated, lusted, used guile, forwent faith."
But when man walks the garden of this world   *360*
For his own solace, and, unchecked by law,
Speaks or keeps silence as himself sees fit,
Without the least incumbency to lie,
—Why, can he tell you what a rose is like,
Or how the birds fly, and not slip to false   *365*
Though truth serve better? Man must tell his mate
Of you, me and himself, knowing he lies,
Knowing his fellow knows the same—will think
"He lies, it is the method of a man!"

370 And yet will speak for answer "It is truth"
To him who shall rejoin "Again a lie!"
Therefore these filthy rags of speech, this coil
Of statement, comment, query and response,
Tatters all too contaminate for use,
375 Have no renewing: He, the Truth, is, too,
The Word. We men, in our degree, may know
There, simply, instantaneously, as here
After long time and amid many lies,
Whatever we dare think we know indeed
380 —That I am I, as He is He—what else?
But be man's method for man's life at least!
Wherefore, Antonio Pignatelli, thou
My ancient self, who wast no Pope so long
But studiedst God and man, the many years
385 I' the school, i' the cloister, in the diocese
Domestic, legate-rule in foreign lands—
Thou other force in those old busy days
Than this gray ultimate decrepitude—
Yet sensible of fires that more and more
390 Visit a soul, in passage to the sky,
Left nakeder than when flesh-robe was new—
Thou, not Pope but the mere old man o' the world,
Supposed inquisitive and dispassionate,
Wilt thou, the one whose speech I somewhat trust,
395 Question the after-me, this self now Pope,
Hear his procedure, criticize his work?
Wise in its generation is the world.

This is why Guido is found reprobate.
I see him furnished forth for his career,
400 On starting for the life-chance in our world,
With nearly all we count sufficient help:
Body and mind in balance, a sound frame,
A solid intellect: the wit to seek,
Wisdom to choose, and courage wherewithal
405 To deal in whatsoever circumstance
Should minister to man, make life succeed.
Oh, and much drawback! what were earth without?
Is this our ultimate stage, or starting-place

To try man's foot, if it will creep or climb,
'Mid obstacles in seeming, points that prove   410
Advantage for who vaults from low to high
And makes the stumbling block a stepping-stone?
So, Guido, born with appetite, lacks food:
Is poor, who yet could deftly play-off wealth:
Straitened, whose limbs are restless till at large,   415
He, as he eyes each outlet of the cirque°
And narrow penfold for probation, pines
After the good things just outside its grate,
With less monition, fainter conscience-twitch,
Rarer instinctive qualm at the first feel   420
Of greed unseemly, prompting grasp undue,
Than nature furnishes her main mankind—
Making it harder to do wrong than right
The first time, careful lest the common ear
Break measure, miss the outstep of life's march.   425
Wherein I see a trial fair and fit
For one else too unfairly fenced about,
Set above sin, beyond his fellows here:
Guarded from the arch-tempter all must fight,
By a great birth, traditional name,   430
Diligent culture, choice companionship,
Above all, conversancy with the faith
Which puts forth for its base of doctrine just
"Man is born nowise to content himself,
But please God." He accepted such a rule,   435
Recognized man's obedience; and the Church,
Which simply is such rule's embodiment,
He clave to, he held on by—nay, indeed,
Near pushed inside of, deep as layman durst,
Professed so much of priesthood as might sue   440
For priest's-exemption where the layman sinned—
Got his arm frocked which, bare, the law would
        bruise.
Hence, at this moment, what's his last resource,
His extreme stay and utmost stretch of hope
But that—convicted of such crime as law   445

416 cirque arena.

Wipes not away save with a worldling's blood—
Guido, the three-parts consecrate, may 'scape?
Nay, the portentous brothers of the man
Are veritably priests, protected each
450 May do his murder in the Church's pale,
Abate Paul, Canon Girolamo!
This is the man proves irreligiousest
Of all mankind, religion's parasite!
This may forsooth plead dinned ear, jaded sense,
455 The vice o' the watcher who bides near the bell,
Sleeps sound because the clock is vigilant,
And cares not whether it be shade or shine,
Doling out day and night to all men else!
Why was the choice o' the man to niche himself
460 Perversely 'neath the tower where Time's own tongue
Thus undertakes to sermonize the world?
Why, but because the solemn is safe too,
The belfry proves a fortress of a sort,
Has other uses than to teach the hour:
465 Turns sunscreen, paravent and ombrifuge°
To whoso seeks a shelter in its pale,
—Ay, and attractive to unwary folk
Who gaze at storied portal, statued spire,
And go home with full head but empty purse,
470 Nor dare suspect the sacristan the thief!
Shall Judas—hard upon the donor's heel,
To filch the fragments of the basket—plead
He was too near the preacher's mouth, nor sat
Attent with fifties in a company?°
475 No—closer to promulgated decree,
Clearer the censure of default. Proceed!

I find him bound, then, to begin life well;
Fortified by propitious circumstance,
Great birth, good breeding, with the Church for guide,
480 How lives he? Cased thus in a coat of proof,
Mailed like a man-at-arms, though all the while
A puny starveling—does the breast pant big,

465 paravent and ombrifuge shelters from wind and rain. 471–74
donor's heel . . . company Mark 6:34–44.

The limb swell to the limit, emptiness
Strive to become solidity indeed?
Rather, he shrinks up like the ambiguous fish,°   485
Detaches flesh from shell and outside show,
And steals by moonlight (I have seen the thing)
In and out, now to prey and now to skulk.
Armor he boasts when a wave breaks on beach,
Or bird stoops for the prize: with peril nigh—   490
The man of rank, the much-befriended-man,
The man almost affiliate to the Church,
Such is to deal with, let the world beware!
Does the world recognize, pass prudently?
Do tides abate and seafowl hunt i' the deep?   495
Already is the slug from out its mew,
Ignobly faring with all loose and free,
Sand fly and slush-worm at their garbage-feast,
A naked blotch no better than they all:
Guido has dropped nobility, slipped the Church,   500
Plays trickster if not cutpurse, body and soul
Prostrate among the filthy feeders—faugh!
And when Law takes him by surprise at last,
Catches the foul thing on its carrion-prey,
Behold, he points to shell left high and dry,   505
Pleads "But the case out yonder is myself!"
Nay, it is thou, Law prongs amid thy peers,
Congenial vermin; that was none of thee,
Thine outside—give it to the soldier-crab!

For I find this black mark impinge the man,   510
That he believes in just the vile of life.
Low instinct, base pretension, are these truth?
Then, that aforesaid armor, probity
He figures in, is falsehood scale on scale;
Honor and faith—a lie and a disguise,   515
Probably for all livers in this world,
Certainly for himself! All say good words
To who will hear, all do thereby bad deeds
To who must undergo; so thrive mankind!

485 ambiguous fish hermit (or soldier) crab. It lives in abandoned
shells.

520 See this habitual creed exemplified
Most in the last deliberate act; as last,
So, very sum and substance of the soul
Of him that planned and leaves one perfect piece,
The sin brought under jurisdiction now,
525 Even the marriage of the man: this act
I sever from his life as sample, show
For Guido's self, intend to test him by,
As, from a cup filled fairly at the fount,
By the components we decide enough
530 Or to let flow as late, or staunch the source.

He purposes this marriage, I remark,
On no one motive that should prompt thereto—
Farthest, by consequence, from ends alleged
Appropriate to the action; so they were:
535 The best, he knew and feigned, the worst he took.
Not one permissible impulse moves the man,
From the mere liking of the eye and ear,
To the true longing of the heart that loves,
No trace of these: but all to instigate,
540 Is what sinks man past level of the brute
Whose appetite if brutish is a truth.
All is the lust for money: to get gold—
Why, lie, rob, if it must be, murder! Make
Body and soul wring gold out, lured within
545 The clutch of hate by love, the trap's pretense!
What good else get from bodies and from souls?
This got, there were some life to lead thereby,
—What, where or how, appreciate those who tell
How the toad lives: it lives—enough for me!
550 To get this good—with but a groan or so,
Then, silence of the victims—were the feat.
He foresaw, made a picture in his mind—
Of father and mother stunned and echoless
To the blow, as they lie staring at fate's jaws
555 Their folly danced into, till the woe fell;
Edged in a month by strenuous cruelty
From even the poor nook whence they watched the
        wolf

Feast on their heart, the lamb-like child his prey;
Plundered to the last remnant of their wealth,
(What daily pittance pleased the plunderer dole)   560
Hunted forth to go hide head, starve and die,
And leave the pale awestricken wife, past hope
Of help i' the world now, mute and motionless,
His slave, his chattel, to first use, then destroy.
All this, he bent mind how to bring about,   565
Put plain in act and life, as painted plain,
So have success, reach crown of earthly good,
In this particular enterprise of man,
By marriage—undertaken in God's face
With all these lies so opposite God's truth,   570
For end so other than man's end.

                              Thus schemes
Guido, and thus would carry out his scheme:
But when an obstacle first blocks the path,
When he finds none may boast monopoly
Of lies and trick i' the tricking lying world—   575
That sorry timid natures, even this sort
O' the Comparini, want nor trick nor lie
Proper to the kind—that as the gorcrow treats
The bramble-finch so treats the finch the moth,
And the great Guido is minutely matched   580
By this same couple—whether true or false
The revelation of Pompilia's birth,
Which in a moment brings his scheme to naught—
Then, he is piqued, advances yet a stage,
Leaves the low region to the finch and fly,   585
Soars to the zenith whence the fiercer fowl
May dare the inimitable swoop. I see.
He draws now on the curious crime, the fine
Felicity and flower of wickedness;
Determines, by the utmost exercise   590
Of violence, made safe and sure by craft,
To satiate malice, pluck one last arch-pang
From the parents, else would triumph out of reach,
By punishing their child, within reach yet,
Who, by thought, word or deed, could nowise wrong   595

I' the matter that now moves him. So plans he,
Always subordinating (note the point!)
Revenge, the manlier sin, to interest
The meaner—would pluck pang forth, but unclench
600 No gripe in the act, let fall no money-piece.
Hence a plan for so plaguing, body and soul,
His wife, so putting, day by day, hour by hour,
The untried torture to the untouched place,
As must precipitate an end foreseen,
605 Goad her into some plain revolt, most like
Plunge upon patent suicidal shame,
Death to herself, damnation by rebound
To those whose hearts he, holding hers, holds still:
Such plan as, in its bad completeness, shall
610 Ruin the three together and alike,
Yet leave himself in luck and liberty,
No claim renounced, no right a forfeiture,
His person unendangered, his good fame
Without a flaw, his pristine worth intact—
615 While they, with all their claims and rights that cling
Shall forthwith crumble off him every side,
Scorched into dust, a plaything for the winds.
As when, in our Campagna, there is fired
The nest-like work that overruns a hut;
620 And, as the thatch burns here, there, everywhere,
Even to the ivy and wild vine, that bound
And blessed the home where men were happy once,
There rises gradual, black amid the blaze,
Some grim and unscathed nucleus of the nest—
625 Some old malicious tower, some obscene tomb
They thought a temple in their ignorance,
And clung about and thought to lean upon—
There laughs it o'er their ravage—where are they?
So did his cruelty burn life about,
630 And lay the ruin bare in dreadfulness,
Try the persistency of torment so
Upon the wife, that, at extremity,
Some crisis brought about by fire and flame,
The patient frenzy-stung must needs break loose,
635 Fly anyhow, find refuge anywhere,

Even in the arms of who should front her first,
No monster but a man—while nature shrieked
"Or thus escape, or die!" The spasm arrived,
Not the escape by way of sin—O God,
Who shall pluck sheep Thou holdest, from Thy hand?   640
Therefore she lay resigned to die—so far
The simple cruelty was foiled. Why then,
Craft to the rescue, let craft supplement
Cruelty and show hell a masterpiece!
Hence this consummate lie, this love-intrigue,   645
Unmanly simulation of a sin,
With place and time and circumstance to suit—
These letters false beyond all forgery—
Not just handwriting and mere authorship,
But false to body and soul they figure forth—   650
As though the man had cut out shape and shape
From fancies of that other Aretine,°
To paste below—incorporate the filth
With cherub faces on a missal-page!

Whereby the man so far attains his end   655
That strange temptation is permitted—see!
Pompilia wife, and Caponsacchi priest,
Are brought together as nor priest nor wife
Should stand, and there is passion in the place,
Power in the air for evil as for good,   660
Promptings from heaven and hell, as if the stars
Fought in their courses for a fate to be.
Thus stand the wife and priest, a spectacle,
I doubt not, to unseen assemblage there.
No lamp will mark that window for a shrine,   665
No tablet signalize the terrace, teach
New generations which succeed the old
The pavement of the street is holy ground;
No bard describe in verse how Christ prevailed
And Satan fell like lightning! Why repine?   670
What does the world, told truth, but lie the more?

652 that other Aretine Pietro Aretino, author of ribald and scur-
rilous works.

A second time the plot is foiled; nor, now,
By corresponding sin for countercheck,
No wile and trick that baffle trick and wile—
675 The play o' the parents! Here the blot is blanched
By God's gift of a purity of soul
That will not take pollution, ermine-like
Armed from dishonor by its own soft snow.
Such was this gift of God who showed for once
680 How He would have the world go white: it seems
As a new attribute were born of each
Champion of truth, the priest and wife I praise—
As a new safeguard sprang up in defense
Of their new noble nature: so a thorn
685 Comes to the aid of and completes the rose—
Courage to wit, no woman's gift nor priest's,
I' the crisis; might leaps vindicating right.
See how the strong aggressor, bad and bold,
With every vantage, preconcerts surprise,
690 Leaps of a sudden at his victim's throat
In a byway—how fares he when face to face
With Caponsacchi? Who fights, who fears now?
There quails Count Guido armed to the chattering
        teeth,
Cowers at the steadfast eye and quiet word
695 O' the Canon of the Pieve! There skulks crime
Behind law called in to back cowardice:
While out of the poor trampled worm the wife,
Springs up a serpent!

                        But anon of these.
Him I judge now—of him proceed to note,
700 Failing the first, a second chance befriends
Guido, gives pause ere punishment arrive.
The law he called, comes, hears, adjudicates,
Nor does amiss i' the main—secludes the wife
From the husband, respites the oppressed one, grants
705 Probation to the oppressor, could he know
The mercy of a minute's fiery purge!
The furnace-coals alike of public scorn,

Private remorse, heaped glowing on his head,
What if—the force and guile, the ore's alloy,
Eliminate, his baser soul refined— 710
The lost be saved even yet, so as by fire?
Let him, rebuked, go softly all his days
And, when no graver musings claim their due,
Meditate on a man's immense mistake
Who, fashioned to use feet and walk, deigns crawl— 715
Takes the unmanly means—ay, though to ends
Man scarce should make for, would but reach through
wrong—
May sin, but nowise needs shame manhood so:
Since fowlers hawk, shoot, nay and snare the game,
And yet eschew vile practice, nor find sport 720
In torchlight treachery or the luring owl.

But how hunts Guido? Why, the fraudful trap—
Late spurned to ruin by the indignant feet
Of fellows in the chase who loved fair play—
Here he picks up its fragments to the least, 725
Lades him and hies to the old lurking-place
Where haply he may patch again, refit
The mischief, file its blunted teeth anew,
Make sure, next time, first snap shall break the bone.
Craft, greed and violence complot revenge: 730
Craft, for its quota, schemes to bring about
And seize occasion and be safe withal:
Greed craves its act may work both far and near,
Crush the tree, branch and trunk and root, beside.
Whichever twig or leaf arrests a streak 735
Of possible sunshine else would coin itself,
And drop down one more gold piece in the path:
Violence stipulates "Advantage proved
And safety sure, be pain the overplus!
Murder with jagged knife! Cut but tear too! 740
Foiled oft, starved long, glut malice for amends!"
And what, craft's scheme? scheme sorrowful and
strange
As though the elements, whom mercy checked,

Had mustered hate for one eruption more,
745 One final deluge to surprise the Ark
Cradled and sleeping on its mountaintop:
Their outbreak-signal—what but the dove's coo,
Back with the olive in her bill for news
Sorrow was over?° 'Tis an infant's birth,
750 Guido's first born, his son and heir, that gives
The occasion: other men cut free their souls
From care in such a case, fly up in thanks
To God, reach, recognize His love for once:
Guido cries "Soul, at last the mire is thine!
755 Lie there in likeness of a money-bag
My babe's birth so pins down past moving now,
That I dare cut adrift the lives I late
Scrupled to touch lest thou escape with them!
These parents and their child my wife—touch one,
760 Lose all! Their rights determined on a head
I could but hate, not harm, since from each hair
Dangled a hope for me: now—chance and change!
No right was in their child but passes plain
To that child's child and through such child to me.
765 I am a father now—come what, come will,
I represent my child; he comes between—
Cuts sudden off the sunshine of this life
From those three: why, the gold is in his curls!
Not with old Pietro's, Violante's head,
770 Not his gray horror, her more hideous black—
Go these, devoted to the knife!"

                                        'Tis done:
Wherefore should mind misgive, heart hesitate?
He calls to counsel, fashions certain four
Colorless natures counted clean till now,
775 —Rustic simplicity, uncorrupted youth,
Ignorant virtue! Here's the gold o' the prime
When Saturn° ruled, shall shock our leaden day—
The clown abash the courtier! Mark it, bards!
The courtier tries his hand on clownship here,

745-49 deluge . . . over Genesis 8.   777 Saturn supreme god during
the Golden Age, when men lived in happy simplicity.

Speaks a word, names a crime, appoints a price—   780
Just breathes on what, suffused with all himself,
Is red-hot henceforth past distinction now
I' the common glow of hell. And thus they break
And blaze on us at Rome, Christ's birthnight-eve!
Oh angels that sang erst "On the earth, peace!   785
To man, good will!"—such peace finds earth today!
After the seventeen hundred years, so man
Wills good to man, so Guido makes complete
His murder! what is it I said?—cuts loose
Three lives that hitherto he suffered cling,   790
Simply because each served to nail secure,
By a corner of the money-bag, his soul—
Therefore, lives sacred till the babe's first breath
O'erweights them in the balance—off they fly!

So is the murder managed, sin conceived   795
To the full: and why not crowned with triumph too?
Why must the sin, conceived thus, bring forth death?
I note how, within hair'sbreadth of escape,
Impunity and the thing supposed success,
Guido is found when the check comes, the change,   800
The monitory touch o' the tether—felt
By few, not marked by many, named by none
At the moment, only recognized aright
I' the fullness of the days, for God's, lest sin
Exceed the service, leap the line: such check—   805
A secret which this life finds hard to keep,
And, often guessed, is never quite revealed—
Needs must trip Guido on a stumbling block
Too vulgar, too absurdly plain i' the path!
Study this single oversight of care,   810
This hebetude° that marred sagacity,
Forgetfulness of all the man best knew—
How any stranger having need to fly,
Needs but to ask and have the means of flight.
Why, the first urchin tells you, to leave Rome,   815
Get horses, you must show the warrant, just
The banal scrap, clerk's scribble, a fair word buys,

811 **hebetude** dullness.

Or foul one, if a ducat sweeten word—
And straight authority will back demand,
820 Give you the pick o' the post-house!—how should he,
Then, resident at Rome for thirty years,
Guido, instruct a stranger! And himself
Forgets just this poor paper scrap, wherewith
Armed, every door he knocks at opens wide
825 To save him: horsed and manned, with such advance
O' the hunt behind, why, 'twere the easy task
Of hours told on the fingers of one hand,
To reach the Tuscan frontier, laugh at-home,
Lighthearted with his fellows of the place—
830 Prepared by that strange shameful judgment, that
Satire upon a sentence just pronounced
By the Rota and confirmed by the Granduke—
Ready in a circle to receive their peer,
Appreciate his good story how, when Rome,
835 The Pope-King and the populace of priests
Made common cause with their confederate
The other priestling who seduced his wife,
He, all unaided, wiped out the affront
With decent bloodshed and could face his friends,
840 Frolic it in the world's eye. Ay, such tale
Missed such applause, and by such oversight!
So, tired and footsore, those blood-flustered five
Went reeling on the road through dark and cold,
The few permissible miles, to sink at length,
845 Wallow and sleep in the first wayside straw,
As the other herd quenched, i' the wash o' the wave,
—Each swine, the devil inside him:° so slept they,
And so were caught and caged—all through one trip,
One touch of fool in Guido the astute!
850 He curses the omission, I surmise,
More than the murder. Why, thou fool and blind,
It is the mercy-stroke that stops thy fate,
Hamstrings and holds thee to thy hurt—but how?
On the edge o' the precipice! One minute more,
855 Thou hadst gone farther and fared worse, my son,

846–47 other herd ... inside him Matthew 8:30–32.

Fathoms down on the flint and fire beneath!
Thy comrades each and all were of one mind,
Thy murder done, to straightway murder thee
In turn, because of promised pay withheld.
So, to the last, greed found itself at odds   860
With craft in thee, and, proving conqueror,
Had sent thee, the same night that crowned thy hope,
Thither where, this same day, I see thee not,
Nor, through God's mercy, need, tomorrow, see.

Such I find Guido, midmost blotch of black   865
Discernible in this group of clustered crimes
Huddling together in the cave they call
Their palace outraged day thus penetrates.
Around him ranged, now close and now remote,
Prominent or obscure to meet the needs   870
O' the mage and master, I detect each shape
Subsidiary i' the scene nor loathed the less,
All alike colored, all descried akin
By one and the same pitchy furnace stirred
At the center: see, they lick the master's hand—   875
This fox-faced horrible priest, this brother-brute
The Abate—why, mere wolfishness looks well,
Guido stands honest in the red o' the flame,
Beside this yellow that would pass for white,
Twice Guido, all craft but no violence,   880
This copier of the mien and gait and garb
Of Peter and Paul, that he may go disguised,
Rob halt and lame, sick folk i' the temple-porch!
Armed with religion, fortified by law,
A man of peace, who trims the midnight lamp   885
And turns the classic page—and all for craft,
All to work harm with, yet incur no scratch!
While Guido brings the struggle to a close,
Paul steps back the due distance, clear o' the trap
He builds and baits. Guido I catch and judge;   890
Paul is past reach in this world and my time:
That is a case reserved. Pass to the next,
The boy of the brood, the young Girolamo
Priest, Canon, and what more? nor wolf nor fox,

895　But hybrid, neither craft nor violence
　　　Wholly, part violence part craft: such cross
　　　Tempts speculation—will both blend one day,
　　　And prove hell's better product? Or subside
　　　And let the simple quality emerge,
900　Go on with Satan's service the old way?
　　　Meanwhile, what promise—what performance too!
　　　For there's a new distinctive touch, I see,
　　　Lust—lacking in the two—hell's own blue tint
　　　That gives a character and marks the man
905　More than a match for yellow and red. Once more,
　　　A case reserved: why should I doubt? Then comes
　　　The gaunt gray nightmare in the furthest smoke,
　　　The hag that gave these three abortions birth,
　　　Unmotherly mother and unwomanly
910　Woman, that near turns motherhood to shame,
　　　Womanliness to loathing: no one word,
　　　No gesture to curb cruelty a whit
　　　More than the she-pard thwarts her playsome whelps
　　　Trying their milk-teeth on the soft o' the throat
915　O' the first fawn, flung, with those beseeching eyes,
　　　Flat in the covert! How should she but couch,
　　　Lick the dry lips, unsheath the blunted claw,
　　　Catch 'twixt her placid eyewinks at what chance
　　　Old bloody half-forgotten dream may flit,
920　Born when herself was novice to the taste,
　　　The while she lets youth take its pleasure. Last,
　　　These God-abandoned wretched lumps of life,
　　　These four companions—countryfolk this time,
　　　Not tainted by the unwholesome civic breath,
925　Much less the curse o' the Court! Mere striplings too,
　　　Fit to do human nature justice still!
　　　Surely when impudence in Guido's shape
　　　Shall propose crime and proffer money's-worth
　　　To these stout tall rough bright-eyed black-haired
　　　　　　boys,
930　The blood shall bound in answer to each cheek
　　　Before the indignant outcry break from lip!
　　　Are these i' the mood to murder, hardly loosed
　　　From healthy autumn-finish of ploughed glebe,

Grapes in the barrel, work at happy end,
And winter near with rest and Christmas play?   935
How greet they Guido with his final task—
(As if he but proposed "One vineyard more
To dig, ere frost come, then relax indeed!")
"Anywhere, anyhow and anywhy,
Murder me some three people, old and young,   940
Ye never heard the names of—and be paid
So much!" And the whole four accede at once.
Demur? Do cattle bidden march or halt?
Is it some lingering habit, old fond faith
I' the lord o' the land, instructs them—birthright
        badge   945
Of feudal tenure claims its slaves again?
Not so at all, thou noble human heart!
All is done purely for the pay—which, earned,
And not forthcoming at the instant, makes
Religion heresy, and the lord o' the land   950
Fit subject for a murder in his turn.
The patron with cut throat and rifled purse,
Deposited i' the roadside-ditch, his due,
Naught hinders each good fellow trudging home,
The heavier by a piece or two in poke,   955
And so with new zest to the common life,
Mattock and spade, plow-tail and wagon-shaft,
Till some such other piece of luck betide,
Who knows? Since this is a mere start in life,
And none of them exceeds the twentieth year.   960
Nay, more i' the background yet? Unnoticed forms
Claim to be classed, subordinately vile?
Complacent lookers-on that laugh—perchance
Shake head as their friend's horseplay grows too rough
With the mere child he manages amiss—   965
But would not interfere and make bad worse
For twice the fractious tears and prayers: thou
        know'st
Civility better, Marzi-Medici,
Governor for thy kinsman the Granduke!
Fit representative of law, man's lamp   970
I' the magistrate's grasp full-flare, no rushlight-end

Sputtering 'twixt thumb and finger of the priest!
Whose answer to the couple's cry for help
Is a threat—whose remedy of Pompilia's wrong,
975 A shrug o' the shoulder, and facetious word
Or wink, traditional with Tuscan wits,
To Guido in the doorway. Laud to law!
The wife is pushed back to the husband, he
Who knows how these home-squabblings persecute
980 People who have the public good to mind,
And work best with a silence in the court!

Ah, but I save my word at least for thee,
Archbishop, who art under, i' the Church,
As I am under God—thou, chosen by both
985 To do the shepherd's office, feed the sheep—
How of this lamb that panted at thy foot
While the wolf pressed on her within crook's reach?
Wast thou the hireling that did turn and flee?
With thee at least anon the little word!

990 Such denizens o' the cave now cluster round
And heat the furnace sevenfold: time indeed
A bolt from heaven should cleave roof and clear
        place,
Transfix and show the world, suspiring flame,
The main offender, scar and brand the rest
995 Hurrying, each miscreant to his hole: then flood
And purify the scene with outside day—
Which yet, in the absolutest drench of dark,
Ne'er wants a witness, some stray beauty-beam
To the despair of hell.

                    First of the first,
1000 Such I pronounce Pompilia, then as now
Perfect in whiteness: stoop thou down, my child,
Give one good moment to the poor old Pope
Heartsick at having all his world to blame—
Let me look at thee in the flesh as erst,
1005 Let me enjoy the old clean linen garb,
Not the new splendid vesture! Armed and crowned,

Would Michael, yonder, be, nor crowned nor armed,
The less pre-eminent angel? Everywhere
I see in the world the intellect of man,
That sword, the energy his subtle spear,   1010
The knowledge which defends him like a shield—
Everywhere; but they make not up, I think,
The marvel of a soul like thine, earth's flower
She holds up to the softened gaze of God!
It was not given Pompilia to know much,   1015
Speak much, to write a book, to move mankind,
Be memorized by who records my time.
Yet if in purity and patience, if
In faith held fast despite the plucking fiend,
Safe like the signet stone with the new name   1020
That saints are known by—if in right returned
For wrong, most pardon for worst injury,
If there be any virtue, any praise—
Then will this woman-child have proved—who
     knows?—
Just the one prize vouchsafed unworthy me,   1025
Seven years a gardener of the untoward ground,
I till—this earth, my sweat and blood manure
All the long day that barrenly grows dusk:
At least one blossom makes me proud at eve
Born 'mid the briers of my enclosure! Still   1030
(Oh, here as elsewhere, nothingness of man!)
Those be the plants, imbedded yonder South
To mellow in the morning, those made fat
By the master's eye, that yield such timid leaf,
Uncertain bud, as product of his pains!   1035
While—see how this mere chance-sown cleft-nursed
     seed
That sprang up by the wayside 'neath the foot
Of the enemy, this breaks all into blaze,
Spreads itself, one wide glory of desire
To incorporate the whole great sun it loves   1040
From the inch-height whence it looks and longs! My
     flower,
My rose, I gather for the breast of God,
This I praise most in thee, where all I praise,

That having been obedient to the end
1045 According to the light allotted, law
Prescribed thy life, still tried, still standing test—
Dutiful to the foolish parents first,
Submissive next to the bad husband—nay,
Tolerant of those meaner miserable
1050 That did his hests, eked out the dole of pain—
Thou, patient thus, couldst rise from law to law,
The old to the new, promoted at one cry
O' the trump of God to the new service, not
To longer bear, but henceforth fight, be found
1055 Sublime in new impatience with the foe!
Endure man and obey God: plant firm foot
On neck of man, tread man into the hell
Meet for him, and obey God all the more!
Oh child that didst despise thy life so much
1060 When it seemed only thine° to keep or lose,
How the fine ear felt fall the first low word
"Value life, and preserve life for My sake!"
Thou didst . . . how shall I say? . . . receive so long
The standing ordinance of God on earth,
1065 What wonder if the novel claim had clashed
With old requirement, seemed to supersede
Too much the customary law? But, brave,
Thou at first prompting of what I call God,
And fools call Nature, didst hear, comprehend,
1070 Accept the obligation laid on thee,
Mother elect, to save the unborn child,
As brute and bird do, reptile and the fly,
Ay and, I nothing doubt, even tree, shrub, plant
And flower o' the field, all in a common pact
1075 To worthily defend the trust of trusts,
Life from the Ever Living:—didst resist—
Anticipate the office that is mine—
And with his own sword stay the upraised arm,
The endeavor of the wicked, and defend
1080 Him who—again in my default—was there
For visible providence: one less true than thou

1060 **only thine** before she knew she was to have a child.

To touch, i' the past, less practiced in the right,
Approved less far in all docility
To all instruction—how had such an one
Made scruple "Is this motion a decree?"   1085
It was authentic to the experienced ear
O' the good and faithful servant. Go past me
And get thy praise—and be not far to seek
Presently when I follow if I may!

And surely not so very much apart   1090
Need I place thee, my warrior-priest—in whom
What if I gain the other rose, the gold,°
We grave to imitate God's miracle,
Greet monarchs with, good rose in its degree?
Irregular noble scapegrace—son the same!   1095
Faulty—and peradventure ours the fault
Who still misteach, mislead, throw hook and line,
Thinking to land leviathan forsooth,
Tame the scaled neck, play with him as a bird,
And bind him for our maidens! Better bear   1100
The King of Pride° go wantoning awhile,
Unplagued by cord in nose and thorn in jaw,
Through deep to deep, followed by all that shine,
Churning the blackness hoary: He who made
The comely terror, He shall make the sword   1105
To match that piece of netherstone his heart,
Ay, nor miss praise thereby; who else shut fire
I' the stone, to leap from mouth at sword's first stroke,
In lamps of love and faith, the chivalry
That dares the right and disregards alike   1110
The yea and nay o' the world? Self-sacrifice—
What if an idol took it? Ask the Church
Why she was wont to turn each Venus here—
Poor Rome perversely lingered round, despite
Instruction, for the sake of purblind love—   1115
Into Madonna's shape, and waste no whit

1092 **the other rose, the gold** golden rose given by the Pope as mark
of distinction. 1098–1101 **leviathan . . . King of Pride** Job 41.

Of aught so rare on earth as gratitude!
All this sweet savor was not ours but thine,
Nard of the rock, a natural wealth we name
1120 Incense, and treasure up as food for saints,
When flung to us—whose function was to give
Not find the costly perfume. Do I smile?
Nay, Caponsacchi, much I find amiss,
Blameworthy, punishable in this freak
1125 Of thine, this youth prolonged, though age was ripe,
This masquerade in sober day, with change
Of motley too—now hypocrite's disguise,
Now fool's-costume: which lie was least like truth,
Which the ungainlier, more discordant garb
1130 With that symmetric soul inside my son,
The churchman's or the worldling's—let him judge,
Our adversary° who enjoys the task!
I rather chronicle the healthy rage—
When the first moan broke from the martyr-maid
1135 At that uncaging of the beasts—made bare
My athlete on the instant, gave such good
Great undisguised leap over post and pale
Right into the mid-cirque, free fighting-place.
There may have been rash stripping—every rag
1140 Went to the winds—infringement manifold
Of laws prescribed pudicity,° I fear,
In this impulsive and prompt self-display!
Ever such tax comes of the foolish youth;
Men mulct the wiser manhood, and suspect
1145 No veritable star swims out of cloud.
Bear thou such imputation, undergo
The penalty I nowise dare relax—
Conventional chastisement and rebuke.
But for the outcome, the brave starry birth
1150 Conciliating earth with all that cloud,
Thank heaven as I do! Ay, such championship
Of God at first blush, such prompt cheery thud
Of glove on ground that answers ringingly
The challenge of the false knight—watch we long

1132 Our adversary the devil.   1141 pudicity modesty.

And wait we vainly for its gallant like   1155
From those appointed to the service, sworn
His bodyguard with pay and privilege—
White-cinct, because in white walks sanctity,
Red-socked, how else proclaim fine scorn of flesh,
Unchariness of blood when blood faith begs!   1160
Where are the men-at-arms with cross on coat?
Aloof, bewraying their attire: whilst thou
In mask and motley, pledged to dance not fight,
Sprang'st forth the hero! In thought, word and deed,
How throughout all thy warfare thou wast pure,   1165
I find it easy to believe: and if
At any fateful moment of the strange
Adventure, the strong passion of that strait,
Fear and surprise, may have revealed too much—
As when a thundrous midnight, with black air   1170
That burns, raindrops that blister, breaks a spell,
Draws out the excessive virtue of some sheathed
Shut unsuspected flower that hoards and hides
Immensity of sweetness—so, perchance,
Might the surprise and fear release too much   1175
The perfect beauty of the body and soul
Thou savedst in thy passion for God's sake,
He who is Pity. Was the trial sore?
Temptation sharp? Thank God a second time!
Why comes temptation but for man to meet   1180
And master and make crouch beneath his foot,
And so be pedestaled in triumph? Pray
"Lead us into no such temptations, Lord!"
Yea, but, O Thou whose servants are the bold,
Lead such temptations by the head and hair,   1185
Reluctant dragons, up to who dares fight,
That so he may do battle and have praise!
Do I not see the praise?—that while thy mates
Bound to deserve i' the matter, prove at need
Unprofitable through the very pains   1190
We gave to train them well and start them fair—
Are found too stiff, with standing ranked and ranged,
For onset in good earnest, too obtuse
Of ear, through iteration of command,

1195 For catching quick the sense of the real cry—
Thou, whose sword-hand was used to strike the lute,
Whose sentry-station graced some wanton's gate,
Thou didst push forward and show mettle, shame
The laggards, and retrieve the day. Well done!
1200 Be glad thou hast let light into the world
Through that irregular breach o' the boundary—see
The same upon thy path and march assured,
Learning anew the use of soldiership,
Self-abnegation, freedom from all fear,
1205 Loyalty to the life's end! Ruminate,
Deserve the initiatory spasm—once more
Work, be unhappy but bear life, my son!

And troop you, somewhere 'twixt the best and worst,
Where crowd the indifferent product, all too poor
1210 Makeshift, starved samples of humanity!
Father and mother, huddle there and hide!
A gracious eye may find you! Foul and fair,
Sadly mixed natures: self-indulgent—yet
Self-sacrificing too: how the love soars,
1215 How the craft, avarice, vanity and spite
Sink again! So they keep the middle course,
Slide into silly crime at unaware,
Slip back upon the stupid virtue, stay
Nowhere enough for being classed, I hope
1220 And fear. Accept the swift and rueful death,
Taught, somewhat sternlier than is wont, what waits
The ambiguous creature—how the one black tuft
Steadies the aim of the arrow just as well
As the wide faultless white on the bird's breast!
1225 Nay, you were punished in the very part
That looked most pure of speck—'twas honest love
Betrayed you—did love seem most worthy pains,
Challenge such purging, since ordained survive
When all the rest of you was done with? Go!
1230 Never again elude the choice of tints!
White shall not neutralize the black, nor good
Compensate bad in man, absolve him so:
Life's business being just the terrible choice.

So do I see, pronounce on all and some
Grouped for my judgment now—profess no doubt   1235
While I pronounce: dark, difficult enough
The human sphere, yet eyes grow sharp by use,
I find the truth, dispart the shine from shade,
As a mere man may, with no special touch
O' the lynx-gift in each ordinary orb: 1240
Nay, if the popular notion class me right,
One of well-nigh decayed intelligence—
What of that? Through hard labor and good will,
And habitude that gives a blind man sight
At the practiced finger-ends of him, I do   1245
Discern, and dare decree in consequence,
Whatever prove the peril of mistake.
Whence, then, this quite new quick cold thrill—
     cloudlike,
This keen dread creeping from a quarter scarce
Suspected in the skies I nightly scan?   1250
What slacks the tense nerve, saps the wound-up
     spring
Of the act that should and shall be, sends the mount
And mass o' the whole man's-strength—conglobed so
     late—
Shudderingly into dust, a moment's work?
While I stand firm, go fearless, in this world,   1255
For this life recognize and arbitrate,
Touch and let stay, or else remove a thing,
Judge "This is right, this object out of place,"
Candle in hand that helps me and to spare—
What if a voice deride me, "Perk and pry!   1260
Brighten each nook with thine intelligence!
Play the good householder, ply man and maid
With tasks prolonged into the midnight, test
Their work and nowise stint of the due wage
Each worthy worker: but with gyves and whip   1265
Pay thou misprision° of a single point
Plain to thy happy self who lift'st the light,
Lament'st the darkling—bold to all beneath!

1266 **misprision** mistake.

What if thyself adventure, now the place
1270 Is purged so well? Leave pavement and mount roof,
Look round thee for the light of the upper sky,
The fire which lit thy fire which finds default
In Guido Franceschini to his cost!
What if, above in the domain of light,
1275 Thou miss the accustomed signs, remark eclipse?
Shalt thou still gaze on ground nor lift a lid—
Steady in thy superb prerogative,
Thy inch of inkling—nor once face the doubt
I' the sphere above thee, darkness to be felt?"

1280 Yet my poor spark had for its source, the sun;
Thither I sent the great looks which compel
Light from its fount: all that I do and am
Comes from the truth, or seen or else surmised,
Remembered or divined, as mere man may:
1285 I know just so, nor otherwise. As I know,
I speak—what should I know, then, and how speak
Were there a wild mistake of eye or brain
As to recorded governance above?
If my own breath, only, blew coal alight
1290 I styled celestial and the morning-star?
I, who in this world act resolvedly,
Dispose of men, their bodies and their souls,
As they acknowledge or gainsay the light
I show them—shall I too lack courage?—leave
1295 I, too, the post of me, like those I blame?
Refuse, with kindred inconsistency,
To grapple danger whereby souls grow strong?
I am near the end; but still not at the end;
All to the very end is trial in life:
1300 At this stage is the trial of my soul
Danger to face, or danger to refuse?
Shall I dare try the doubt now, or not dare?

O Thou—as represented here to me
In such conception as my soul allows—
1305 Under Thy measureless, my atom width!—
Man's mind, what is it but a convex glass

Wherein are gathered all the scattered points
Picked out of the immensity of sky,
To reunite there, be our heaven for earth,
Our known unknown,° our God revealed to man?   *1310*
Existent somewhere, somehow, as a whole;
Here, as a whole proportioned to our sense—
There (which is nowhere, speech must babble thus!)
In the absolute immensity, the whole
Appreciable solely by Thyself—   *1315*
Here, by the little mind of man, reduced
To littleness that suits his faculty,
In the degree appreciable too;
Between Thee and ourselves—nay even, again,
Below us, to the extreme of the minute,   *1320*
Appreciable by how many and what diverse
Modes of the life Thou madest be! (why live
Except for love—how love unless they know?)
Each of them, only filling to the edge,
Insect or angel, his just length and breadth,   *1325*
Due facet of reflection—full, no less,
Angel or insect, as Thou framedst things.
I it is who have been appointed here
To represent Thee, in my turn, on earth,
Just as, if new philosophy° know aught,   *1330*
This one earth, out of all the multitude
Of peopled worlds, as stars are now supposed—
Was chosen, and no sun-star of the swarm,
For stage and scene of Thy transcendent act°
Beside which even the creation fades   *1335*
Into a puny exercise of power.
Choice of the world, choice of the thing I am,
Both emanate alike from Thy dread play
Of operation outside this our sphere
Where things are classed and counted small or great— *1340*
Incomprehensibly the choice is Thine!
I therefore bow my head and take Thy place.
There is, beside the works, a tale of Thee

1310 **Our known unknown** cf. Keats's *Endymion*, Bk. II, l. 739.
1330 **new philosophy** "modern science."   1334 **Thy transcendent act**
the Incarnation.

In the world's mouth, which I find credible:
1345 I love it with my heart: unsatisfied,
I try it with my reason, nor discept°
From any point I probe and pronounce sound.
Mind is not matter nor from matter, but
Above—leave matter then, proceed with mind!
1350 Man's be the mind recognized at the height—
Leave the inferior minds and look at man!
Is he the strong, intelligent and good
Up to his own conceivable height? Nowise.
Enough o' the low—soar the conceivable height,
1355 Find cause to match the effect in evidence,
The work i' the world, not man's but God's; leave
man!
Conjecture of the worker by the work:
Is there strength there?—enough: intelligence?
Ample: but goodness in a like degree?
1360 Not to the human eye in the present state,
An isoscele deficient in the base.
What lacks, then, of perfection fit for God
But just the instance which this tale supplies
Of love without a limit? So is strength,
1365 So is intelligence; let love be so,
Unlimited in its self-sacrifice,
Then is the tale true and God shows complete.
Beyond the tale, I reach into the dark,
Feel what I cannot see, and still faith stands:
1370 I can believe this dread machinery
Of sin and sorrow, would confound me else,
Devised—all pain, at most expenditure
Of pain by Who devised pain—to evolve,
By new machinery in counterpart,
1375 The moral qualities of man—how else?—
To make him love in turn and be beloved,
Creative and self-sacrificing too,
And thus eventually God-like, (ay,
"I have said ye are Gods,"°—shall it be said for
naught?)

1346 **discept** dissent.   1379 **"I . . . Gods"** John 10:34.

Enable man to wring, from out all pain,   1380
All pleasure for a common heritage
To all eternity: this may be surmised,
The other is revealed—whether a fact,
Absolute, abstract, independent truth,
Historic, not reduced to suit man's mind—   1385
Or only truth reverberate, changed, made pass
A spectrum into mind, the narrow eye—
The same and not the same, else unconceived—
Though quite conceivable to the next grade
Above it in intelligence—as truth   1390
Easy to man were blindness to the beast
By parity of procedure—the same truth
In a new form, but changed in either case:
What matter so intelligence be filled?
To a child, the sea is angry, for it roars: 1395
Frost bites, else why the tooth-like fret on face?
Man makes acoustics deal with the sea's wrath,
Explains the choppy cheek by chymic law°—
To man and child remains the same effect
On drum of ear and root of nose, change cause   1400
Never so thoroughly: so my heart be struck,
What care I—by God's gloved hand or the bare?
Nor do I much perplex me with aught hard,
Dubious in the transmitting of the tale—
No, nor with certain riddles set to solve.   1405
This life is training and a passage; pass—
Still, we march over some flat obstacle
We made give way before us; solid truth
In front of it, what motion for the world?
The moral sense grows but by exercise.   1410
'Tis even as man grew probatively
Initiated in Godship, set to make
A fairer moral world than this he finds,
Guess now what shall be known hereafter. Deal
Thus with the present problem: as we see,   1415
A faultless creature is destroyed, and sin
Has had its way i' the world where God should rule.

1398 **Explains . . . law** man explains how cheeks become chapped by
appealing to chemical laws.

Ay, but for this irrelevant circumstance
Of inquisition after blood, we see
1420 Pompilia lost and Guido saved: how long?
For his whole life: how much is that whole life?
We are not babes, but know the minute's worth,
And feel that life is large and the world small,
So, wait till life have passed from out the world.
1425 Neither does this astonish at the end,
That whereas I can so receive and trust,
Other men, made with hearts and souls the same,
Reject and disbelieve—subordinate
The future to the present—sin, nor fear.
1430 This I refer still to the foremost fact,
Life is probation and the earth no goal
But starting-point of man: compel him strive,
Which means, in man, as good as reach the goal—
Why institute that race, his life, at all?
1435 But this does overwhelm me with surprise,
Touch me to terror—not that faith, the pearl,
Should be let lie by fishers wanting food—
Nor, seen and handled by a certain few
Critical and contemptuous, straight consigned
1440 To shore and shingle for the pebble it proves—
But that, when haply found and known and named
By the residue made rich for evermore,
These—that these favored ones, should in a trice
Turn, and with double zest go dredge for whelks,
1445 Mud-worms that make the savory soup! Enough
O' the disbelievers, see the faithful few!
How do the Christians here deport them, keep
Their robes of white unspotted by the world?
What is this Aretine Archbishop, this
1450 Man under me as I am under God,
This champion of the faith, I armed and decked,
Pushed forward, put upon a pinnacle,
To show the enemy his victor—see!
What's the best fighting when the couple close?
1455 Pompilia cries, "Protect me from the wolf!"
He—"No, thy Guido is rough, heady, strong,
Dangerous to disquiet: let him bide!

He needs some bone to mumble, help amuse
The darkness of his den with: so, the fawn
Which limps up bleeding to my foot and lies,   1460
—Come to me, daughter!—thus I throw him back!"
Have we misjudged here, overarmed our knight,
Given gold and silk where plain hard steel serves best,
Enfeebled whom we sought to fortify,
Made an archbishop and undone a saint?   1465
Well, then, descend these heights, this pride of life,
Sit in the ashes with a barefoot monk
Who long ago stamped out the worldly sparks,
By fasting, watching, stone cell and wire scourge,
—No such indulgence as unknits the strength—   1470
These breed the tight nerve and tough cuticle,
And the world's praise or blame runs rillet-wise
Off the broad back and brawny breast, we know!
He meets the first cold sprinkle of the world,
And shudders to the marrow. "Save this child?   1475
Oh, my superiors, oh, the Archbishop's self!
Who was it dared lay hand upon the ark
His betters saw fall nor put finger forth?°
Great ones could help yet help not: why should small?
I break my promise: let her break her heart!"   1480
These are the Christians not the worldlings, not
The skeptics, who thus battle for the faith!
If foolish virgins disobey and sleep,
What wonder? But, this time, the wise that watch,
Sell lamps and buy lutes, exchange oil for wine,   1485
The mystic Spouse betrays the Bridegroom here.°
To our last resource, then! Since all flesh is weak,
Bind weaknesses together, we get strength:
The individual weighed, found wanting, try
Some institution, honest artifice   1490
Whereby the units grow compact and firm!
Each props the other, and so stand is made
By our embodied cowards that grow brave.
The Monastery called of Convertites,
Meant to help women because these helped Christ—   1495

1477–78 Who . . . forth? 2 Samuel 6:6–7.   1483–86 foolish virgins
. . . Bridegroom here Matthew 25.

A thing existent only while it acts,
Does as designed, else a nonentity—
For what is an idea unrealized?—
Pompilia is consigned to these for help.
1500 They do help: they are prompt to testify
To her pure life and saintly dying days.
She dies, and lo, who seemed so poor, proves rich.
What does the body that lives through helpfulness
To women for Christ's sake? The kiss turns bite,
1505 The dove's note changes to the crow's cry: judge!
"Seeing that this our Convent claims of right
What goods belong to those we succor, be
The same proved women of dishonest life—
And seeing that this trial made appear
1510 Pompilia was in such predicament—
The Convent hereupon pretends to said
Succession of Pompilia, issues writ,
And takes possession by the Fisc's° advice."
Such is their attestation to the cause
1515 Of Christ, who had one saint at least, they hoped:
But, is a title-deed to filch, a corpse
To slander, and an infant-heir to cheat?
Christ must give up his gains then! They unsay
All the fine speeches—who was saint is whore.
1520 Why, scripture yields no parallel for this!
The soldiers only threw dice for Christ's coat;
We want another legend of the Twelve
Disputing if it was Christ's coat at all,
Claiming as prize the woof of price—for why?
1525 The Master was a thief, purloined the same,
Or paid for it out of the common bag!
Can it be this is end and outcome, all
I take with me to show as stewardship's fruit,
The best yield of the latest time, this year
1530 The seventeen-hundredth since God died for man?
Is such effect proportionate to cause?
And still the terror keeps on the increase
When I perceive . . . how can I blink the fact?

1513 **Fisc** prosecutor.

That the fault, the obduracy to good,
Lies not with the impracticable stuff   *1535*
Whence man is made, his very nature's fault,
As if it were of ice the moon may gild
Not melt, or stone 'twas meant the sun should warm
Not make bear flowers—nor ice nor stone to blame:
But it can melt, that ice, can bloom, that stone,   *1540*
Impassible to rule of day and night!
This terrifies me, thus compelled perceive,
Whatever love and faith we looked should spring
At advent of the authoritative star,
Which yet lie sluggish, curdled at the source—   *1545*
These have leaped forth profusely in old time,
These still respond with promptitude today,
At challenge of—what unacknowledged powers
O' the air, what uncommissioned meteors, warmth
By law, and light by rule should supersede?   *1550*
For see this priest, this Caponsacchi, stung
At the first summons—"Help for honor's sake,
Play the man, pity the oppressed!"—no pause,
How does he lay about him in the midst,
Strike any foe, right wrong at any risk,   *1555*
All blindness, bravery and obedience!—blind?
Ay, as a man would be inside the sun,
Delirious with the plenitude of light
Should interfuse him to the finger-ends—
Let him rush straight, and how shall he go wrong?   *1560*
Where are the Christians in their panoply?
The loins we girt about with truth, the breasts
Righteousness plated round, the shield of faith,
The helmet of salvation, and that sword
O' the Spirit, even the word of God°—where these? *1565*
Slunk into corners! Oh, I hear at once
Hubbub of protestation! "What, we monks
We friars, of such an order, such a rule,
Have not we fought, bled, left our martyr-mark
At every point along the boundary-line   *1570*
'Twixt true and false, religion and the world,

1562–65 **The loins . . . of God** Ephesians 6:13–17.

Where this or the other dogma of our Church
Called for defense?" And I, despite myself,
How can I but speak loud what truth speaks low,
1575 "Or better than the best, or nothing serves!
What boots deed, I can cap and cover straight
With such another doughtiness to match,
Done at an instinct of the natural man?"
Immolate body, sacrifice soul too—
1580 Do not these publicans the same? Outstrip!
Or else stop race you boast runs neck and neck,
You with the wings, they with the feet—for shame!
Oh, I remark your diligence and zeal!
Five years long, now, rounds faith into my ears,
1585 "Help thou, or Christendom is done to death!"
Five years since, in the Province of To-kien,
Which is in China as some people know,
Maigrot, my Vicar Apostolic there,
Having a great qualm, issues a decree.
1590 Alack, the converts use as God's name, not
Tien-chu but plain *Tien* or else mere *Shang-ti*,
As Jesuits please to fancy politic,
While, say Dominicans, it calls down fire—
For *Tien* means Heaven, and *Shang-ti*, supreme
prince,
1595 While *Tien-chu* means the lord of Heaven: all cry,
"There is no business urgent for dispatch
As that thou send a legate, specially
Cardinal Tournon, straight to Pekin, there
To settle and compose the difference!"
1600 So have I seen a potentate all fume
For some infringement of his realm's just right,
Some menace to a mud-built straw-thatched farm
O' the frontier; while inside the mainland lie,
Quite undisputed-for in solitude,
1605 Whole cities plague may waste or famine sap:
What if the sun crumble, the sands encroach,
While he looks on sublimely at his ease?
How does their ruin touch the empire's bound?

And is this little all that was to be?

Where is the gloriously decisive change,   *1610*
Metamorphosis the immeasurable
Of human clay to divine gold, we looked
Should, in some poor sort, justify its price?
Had an adept of the mere Rosy Cross
Spent his life to consummate the Great Work,°   *1615*
Would not we start to see the stuff it touched
Yield not a grain more than the vulgar got
By the old smelting-process years ago?
If this were sad to see in just the sage
Who should profess so much, perform no more,   *1620*
What is it when suspected in that Power
Who undertook to make and made the world,
Devised and did effect man, body and soul,
Ordained salvation for them both, and yet . . .
Well, is the thing we see, salvation?

               I   *1625*

Put no such dreadful question to myself,
Within whose circle of experience burns
The central truth, Power, Wisdom, Goodness—God:
I must outlive a thing ere know it dead:
When I outlive the faith there is a sun,   *1630*
When I lie, ashes to the very soul—
Someone, not I, must wail above the heap,
"He died in dark whence never morn arose."
While I see day succeed the deepest night—
How can I speak but as I know?—my speech   *1635*
Must be, throughout the darkness, "It will end:
The light that did burn, will burn!" Clouds obscure—
But for which obscuration all were bright?
Too hastily concluded! Sun-suffused,
A cloud may soothe the eye made blind by blaze— *1640*
Better the very clarity of heaven:
The soft streaks are the beautiful and dear.
What but the weakness in a faith supplies
The incentive to humanity, no strength

1614–15 **an adept . . . Great Work** an alchemist of the Rosicrucian order, who claims to have found the secret of turning base metals into gold.

1645 Absolute, irresistible, comports?
How can man love but what he yearns to help?
And that which men think weakness within strength,
But angels know for strength and stronger yet—
What were it else but the first things made new,
1650 But repetition of the miracle,
The divine instance of self-sacrifice
That never ends and aye begins for man?
So, never I miss footing in the maze,
No—I have light nor fear the dark at all.

1655 But are mankind not real, who pace outside
My petty circle, world that's measured me?
And when they stumble even as I stand,
Have I a right to stop ear when they cry,
As they were phantoms who took clouds for crags,
Tripped and fell, where man's march might safely
1660   move?
Beside, the cry is other than a ghost's,
When out of the old time there pleads some bard,°
Philosopher, or both, and—whispers not,
But words it boldly. "The inward work and worth
1665 Of any mind, what other mind may judge
Save God who only knows the thing He made,
The veritable service He exacts?
It is the outward product men appraise.
Behold, an engine hoists a tower aloft:
1670 'I looked that it should move the mountain too!'
Or else 'Had just a turret toppled down,
Success enough!'—may say the Machinist
Who knows what less or more result might be:
But we, who see that done we cannot do,
1675 'A feat beyond man's force,' we men must say.
Regard me and that shake I gave the world!
I was born, not so long before Christ's birth
As Christ's birth haply did precede thy day—
But many a watch before the star of dawn:
1680 Therefore I lived—it is thy creed affirms,

1662 some bard Euripides.

Pope Innocent, who art to answer me!—
Under conditions, nowise to escape,
Whereby salvation was impossible.
Each impulse to achieve the good and fair,
Each aspiration to the pure and true,   *1685*
Being without a warrant or an aim,
Was just as sterile a felicity
As if the insect, born to spend his life
Soaring his circles, stopped them to describe
(Painfully motionless in the mid-air)   *1690*
Some word of weighty counsel for man's sake,
Some 'Know thyself' or 'Take the golden mean!'
—Forwent his happy dance and the glad ray,
Died half an hour the sooner and was dust.
I, born to perish like the brutes, or worse,   *1695*
Why not live brutishly, obey brutes' law?
But I, of body as of soul complete,
A gymnast at the games, philosopher
I' the schools, who painted, and made music—all
Glories that met upon the tragic stage   *1700*
When the Third Poet's tread surprised the Two°—
Whose lot fell in a land where life was great
And sense went free and beauty lay profuse,
I, untouched by one adverse circumstance,
Adopted virtue as my rule of life,   *1705*
Waived all reward, loved but for loving's sake,
And, what my heart taught me, I taught the world,
And have been teaching now two thousand years.
Witness my work—plays that should please, forsooth!
'They might please, they may displease, they shall
      teach,   *1710*
For truth's sake,' so I said, and did, and do.
Five hundred years ere Paul spoke, Felix° heard—
How much of temperance and righteousness,
Judgment to come, did I find reason for,
Corroborate with my strong style that spared   *1715*
No sin, nor swerved the more from branding brow

1701 **Third Poet . . . the Two** Euripides, the third of the great Greek
dramatists, after Aeschylus and Sophocles. 1712 **Paul . . . Felix**
Acts 24.

Because the sinner was called Zeus and God?
How nearly did I guess at that Paul knew?
How closely come, in what I represent
1720 As duty, to his doctrine yet a blank?
And as that limner not untruly limns
Who draws an object round or square, which square
Or round seems to the unassisted eye,
Though Galileo's tube° display the same
1725 Oval or oblong—so, who controverts
I rendered rightly what proves wrongly wrought
Beside Paul's picture? Mine was true for me.
I saw that there are, first and above all,
The hidden forces, blind necessities,
1730 Named Nature, but the thing's self unconceived:
Then follow—how dependent upon these,
We know not, how imposed above ourselves,
We well know—what I name the gods, a power
Various or one: for great and strong and good
1735 Is there, and little, weak and bad there too,
Wisdom and folly: say, these make no God—
What is it else that rules outside man's self?
A fact then—always, to the naked eye—
And so, the one revealment possible
1740 Of what were unimagined else by man.
Therefore, what gods do, man may criticize,
Applaud, condemn—how should he fear the truth?—
But likewise have in awe because of power,
Venerate for the main munificence,
1745 And give the doubtful deed its due excuse
From the acknowledged creature of a day
To the Eternal and Divine. Thus, bold
Yet self-mistrusting, should man bear himself,
Most assured on what now concerns him most—
1750 The law of his own life, the path he prints—
Which law is virtue and not vice, I say—
And least inquisitive where search least skills,
I' the nature we best give the clouds to keep.
What could I paint beyond a scheme like this

1724 **Galileo's tube** telescope.

Out of the fragmentary truths where light   1755
Lay fitful in a tenebrific time?
You have the sunrise now, joins truth to truth,
Shoots life and substance into death and void;
Themselves compose the whole we made before:
The forces and necessity grow God—   1760
The beings so contrarious that seemed gods,
Prove just His operation manifold
And multiform, translated, as must be,
Into intelligible shape so far
As suits our sense and sets us free to feel.   1765
What if I let a child think, childhood-long,
That lightning, I would have him spare his eye,
Is a real arrow shot at naked orb?
The man knows more, but shuts his lids the same:
Lightning's cause comprehends nor man nor child.   1770
Why then, my scheme, your better knowledge broke,
Presently readjusts itself, the small
Proportioned largelier, parts and whole named new:
So much, no more two thousand years have done!
Pope, dost thou dare pretend to punish me,   1775
For not descrying sunshine at midnight,
Me who crept all-fours, found my way so far—
While thou rewardest teachers of the truth,
Who miss the plain way in the blaze of noon—
Though just a word from that strong style of mine,   1780
Grasped honestly in hand as guiding-staff,
Had pricked them a sure path across the bog,
That mire of cowardice and slush of lies
Wherein I find them wallow in wide day!"
How should I answer this Euripides?   1785
Paul—'tis a legend—answered Seneca,°
But that was in the day-spring; noon is now:
We have got too familiar with the light.
Shall I wish back once more that thrill of dawn?
When the whole truth-touched man burned up, one
     fire?   1790
—Assured the trial, fiery, fierce, but fleet,

1786 Seneca Roman philosopher.

Would, from his little heap of ashes, lend
Wings to that conflagration of the world
Which Christ awaits ere He makes all things new:
1795 So should the frail become the perfect, rapt
From glory of pain to glory of joy; and so,
Even in the end—the act renouncing earth,
Lands, houses, husbands, wives and children here—
Begin that other act which finds all, lost,
1800 Regained, in this time even, a hundredfold,
And, in the next time, feels the finite love
Blent and embalmed with the eternal life.
So does the sun ghastlily seem to sink
In those north parts, lean all but out of life,
1805 Desist a dread mere breathing-stop, then slow
Reassert day, begin the endless rise.
Was this too easy for our after-stage?
Was such a lighting-up of faith, in life,
Only allowed initiate, set man's step
1810 In the true way by help of the great glow?
A way wherein it is ordained he walk,
Bearing to see the light from heaven still more
And more encroached on by the light of earth,
Tentatives earth puts forth to rival heaven,
1815 Earthly incitements that mankind serve God
For man's sole sake, not God's and therefore man's.
Till at last, who distinguishes the sun
From a mere Druid fire on a far mount?
More praise to him who with his subtle prism
1820 Shall decompose both beams and name the true.
In such sense, who is last proves first indeed
For how could saints and martyrs fail see truth
Streak the night's blackness? Who is faithful now?
Who untwists heaven's white from the yellow flare
O' the world's gross torch, without night's foil that
1825   helped
Produce the Christian act so possible
When in the way stood Nero's cross and stake—
So hard now when the world smiles "Right and wise!
Faith points the politic, the thrifty way,
1830 Will make who plods it in the end returns

Beyond mere fool's-sport and improvidence.
We fools dance through the cornfield of this life,
Pluck ears to left and right and swallow raw,
—Nay, tread, at pleasure, a sheaf underfoot,
To get the better at some poppy-flower—   1835
Well aware we shall have so much less wheat
In the eventual harvest: you meantime
Waste not a spike—the richlier will you reap!
What then? There will be always garnered meal
Sufficient for our comfortable loaf,   1840
While you enjoy the undiminished sack!"
Is it not this ignoble confidence,
Cowardly hardihood, that dulls and damps,
Makes the old heroism impossible?

Unless . . . what whispers me of times to come?   1845
What if it be the mission of that age
My death will usher into life, to shake
This torpor of assurance from our creed,
Reintroduce the doubt discarded, bring
That formidable danger back, we drove   1850
Long ago to the distance and the dark?
No wild beast now prowls round the infant camp:
We have built wall and sleep in city safe:
But if some earthquake try the towers that laugh
To think they once saw lions rule outside,   1855
And man stand out again, pale, resolute,
Prepared to die—which means, alive at last?
As we broke up that old faith of the world,
Have we, next age, to break up this the new—
Faith, in the thing, grown faith in the report—   1860
Whence need to bravely disbelieve report
Through increased faith i' the thing reports belie?
Must we deny—do they, these Molinists,
At peril of their body and their soul—
Recognized truths, obedient to some truth   1865
Unrecognized yet, but perceptible?—
Correct the portrait by the living face,
Man's God, by God's God in the mind of man?
Then, for the few that rise to the new height,

1870 The many that must sink to the old depth,
The multitude found fall away! A few,
E'en ere new law speak clear, may keep the old,
Preserve the Christian level, call good good
And evil evil (even though razed and blank
1875 The old titles), helped by custom, habitude,
And all else they mistake for finer sense
O' the fact that reason warrants—as before,
They hope perhaps, fear not impossibly.
At least some one Pompilia left the world
1880 Will say "I know the right place by foot's feel,
I took it and tread firm there; wherefore change?"
But what a multitude will surely fall
Quite through the crumbling truth, late subjacent,
Sink to the next discoverable base,
1885 Rest upon human nature, settle there
On what is firm, the lust and pride of life!
A mass of men, whose very souls even now
Seem to need recreating—so they slink
Worm-like into the mud, light now lays bare—
1890 Whose future we dispose of with shut eyes
And whisper—"They are grafted, barren twigs,
Into the living stock of Christ: may bear
One day, till when they lie deathlike, not dead"—
Those who with all the aid of Christ succumb,
1895 How, without Christ, shall they, unaided, sink?
Whither but to this gulf before my eyes?
Do not we end, the century and I?
The impatient antimasque treads close on kibe
O' the very masque's self it will mock°—on me,
1900 Last lingering personage, the impatient mime
Pushes already—will I block the way?
Will my slow trail of garments ne'er leave space
For pantaloon, sock,° plume and castanet?
Here comes the first experimentalist
1905 In the new order of things—he plays a priest;
Does he take inspiration from the Church,

1898-99 **antimasque** . . . **mock** grotesque interlude between acts of a masque. *Kibe* is here used loosely for heel.　1903 **sock** boot worn by comic actor.

Directly make her rule his law of life?
Not he: his own mere impulse guides the man—
Happily sometimes, since ourselves allow
He has danced, in gaiety of heart, i' the main   1910
The right step through the maze we bade him foot.
But if his heart had prompted him break loose
And mar the measure? Why, we must submit,
And thank the chance that brought him safe so far.
Will he repeat the prodigy? Perhaps.   1915
Can he teach others how to quit themselves,
Show why this step was right while that were wrong?
How should he? "Ask your hearts as I asked mine,
And get discreetly through the morrice° too;
If your hearts misdirect you—quit the stage,   1920
And make amends—be there amends to make!"
Such is, for the Augustin that was once,
This Canon Caponsacchi we see now.
"But my heart answers to another tune,"
Puts in the Abate, second in the suite,   1925
"I have my taste too, and tread no such step!
You choose the glorious life, and may, for me!
I like the lowest of life's appetites—
So you judge—but the very truth of joy
To my own apprehension which decides.   1930
Call me knave and you get yourself called fool!
I live for greed, ambition, lust, revenge;
Attain these ends by force, guile: hypocrite,
Today, perchance tomorrow recognized
The rational man, the type of common sense."   1935
There's Loyola° adapted to our time!
Under such guidance Guido plays his part,
He also influencing in the due turn
These last clods where I track intelligence
By any glimmer, these four at his beck   1940
Ready to murder any, and, at their own,
As ready to murder him—such make the world!
And, first effect of the new cause of things,
There they lie also duly—the old pair

1919 **morrice** morris dance. 1936 **Loyola** St. Ignatius **Loyola,**
founder of the Society of Jesus.

1945 Of the weak head and not so wicked heart,
With the one Christian mother, wife and girl,
—Which three gifts seem to make an angel up—
The world's first foot o' the dance is on their heads!
Still, I stand here, not off the stage though close
1950 On the exit: and my last act, as my first,
I owe the scene, and Him who armed me thus
With Paul's sword as with Peter's key. I smite
With my whole strength once more, ere end my part,
Ending, so far as man may, this offense.
1955 And when I raise my arm, who plucks my sleeve?
Who stops me in the righteous function—foe
Or friend? Oh, still as ever, friends are they
Who, in the interest of outraged truth
Deprecate such rough handling of a lie!
1960 The facts being proved and incontestable,
What is the last word I must listen to?
Perchance—"Spare yet a term this barren stock
We pray thee dig about and dung and dress
Till he repent and bring forth fruit even yet!"
1965 Perchance—"So poor and swift a punishment
Shall throw him out of life with all that sin:
Let mercy rather pile up pain on pain
Till the flesh expiate what the soul pays else!"
Nowise! Remonstrants on each side commence
1970 Instructing, there's a new tribunal now
Higher than God's—the educated man's!
Nice sense of honor in the human breast
Supersedes here the old coarse oracle—
Confirming none the less a point or so
1975 Wherein blind predecessors worked aright
By rule of thumb: as when Christ said—when, where?
Enough, I find it pleaded in a place—
"All other wrongs done, patiently I take:
But touch my honor and the case is changed!
1980 I feel the due resentment—*nemini
Honorem trado*° is my quick retort."

1980–81 **nemini . . . trado** *I will not give my honor to another.
The Pope is echoing the misuse of a biblical text by the defense
attorney.*

Right of Him, just as if pronounced today!
Still, should the old authority be mute
Or doubtful or in speaking clash with new,
The younger takes permission to decide.   1985
At last we have the instinct of the world
Ruling its household without tutelage:
And while the two laws, human and divine,
Have busied finger with this tangled case,
In pushes the brisk junior, cuts the knot,   1990
Pronounces for acquittal. How it trips
Silverly o'er the tongue! "Remit the death!
Forgive . . . well, in the old way, if thou please,
Decency and the relics of routine
Respected—let the Count go free as air!   1995
Since he may plead a priest's immunity—
The minor orders help enough for that,
With Farinacci's° license—who decides
That the mere implication of such man,
So privileged, in any cause, before   2000
Whatever Court except the Spiritual,
Straight quashes law-procedure—quash it, then!
Remains a pretty loophole of escape
Moreover, that, beside the patent fact
O' the law's allowance, there's involved the weal 2005
O' the Popedom: a son's privilege at stake,
Thou wilt pretend the Church's interest,
Ignore all finer reasons to forgive!
But herein lies the crowning cogency—
(Let thy friends teach thee while thou tellest beads) 2010
That in this case the spirit of culture speaks,
Civilization is imperative.
To her shall we remand all delicate points
Henceforth, nor take irregular advice
O' the sly, as heretofore: she used to hint   2015
Remonstrances, when law was out of sorts
Because a saucy tongue was put to rest,
An eye that roved was cured of arrogance:
But why be forced to mumble under breath

1998 **Farinacci** legal authority.

2020 What soon shall be acknowledged as plain fact,
Outspoken, say, in thy successor's time?
Methinks we see the golden age return!
Civilization and the Emperor
Succeed to Christianity and Pope.

2025 One Emperor then, as one Pope now: meanwhile,
Anticipate a little! We tell thee 'Take
Guido's life, sapped society shall crash,
Whereof the main prop was, is, and shall be
—Supremacy of husband over wife!'

2030 Does the man rule i' the house, and may his mate
Because of any plea dispute the same?
Oh, pleas of all sorts shall abound, be sure,
One but allowed validity—for, harsh
And savage, for, inept and silly-sooth,

2035 For, this and that, will the ingenious sex
Demonstrate the best master e'er graced slave:
And there's but one short way to end the coil—
Acknowledge right and reason steadily
I' the man and master: then the wife submits

2040 To plain truth broadly stated. Does the time
Advise we shift—a pillar? nay, a stake
Out of its place i' the social tenement?
One touch may send a shudder through the heap
And bring it toppling on our children's heads!

2045 Moreover, if ours breed a qualm in thee,
Give thine own better feeling play for once!
Thou, whose own life winks o'er the socket-edge,
Wouldst thou it went out in such ugly snuff
As dooming sons dead, e'en though justice prompt?

2050 Why, on a certain feast, Barabbas'° self
Was set free, not to cloud the general cheer:
Neither shalt thou pollute thy Sabbath close!
Mercy is safe and graceful. How one hears
The howl begin, scarce the three little taps

2055 O' the silver mallet silent on thy brow°—
'His last act was to sacrifice a Count
And thereby screen a scandal of the Church!'

2050 **Barabbas** Matthew 27. 2054–55 **three little taps . . . on thy brow** ceremony ascertaining that the Pope is dead.

Guido condemned, the Canon justified
Of course—delinquents of his cloth go free!'
And so the Luthers chuckle, Calvins scowl,   2060
So thy hand helps Molinos to the chair
Whence he may hold forth till doom's day on just
These *petit-maître*° priestlings—in the choir
Sanctus et Benedictus,° with a brush
Of soft guitar-strings that obey the thumb,   2065
Touched by the bedside, for accompaniment!
Does this give umbrage to a husband? Death
To the fool, and to the priest impunity!
But no impunity to any friend
So simply over-loyal as these four   2070
Who made religion of their patron's cause,
Believed in him and did his bidding straight,
Asked not one question but laid down the lives
This Pope took—all four lives together make
Just his own length of days—so, dead they lie,   2075
As these were times when loyalty's a drug,
And zeal in a subordinate too cheap
And common to be saved when we spend life!
Come, 'tis too much good breath we waste in words:
The pardon, Holy Father! Spare grimace,   2080
Shrugs and reluctance! Are not we the world,
Art not thou Priam? Let soft culture plead
Hecuba-like, '*non tali*' (Virgil serves)
'*Auxilio*'° and the rest! Enough, it works!
The Pope relaxes, and the Prince is loth,   2085
The father's bowels yearn, the man's will bends,
Reply is apt. Our tears on tremble, hearts
Big with a benediction, wait the word
Shall circulate through the city in a trice,
Set every window flaring, give each man   2090
O' the mob his torch to wave for gratitude.
Pronounce then, for our breath and patience fail!"

2063 **petit-maître** fop, dandy.   2064 **Sanctus et Benedictus** holy and
blessed. Sanctus and Benedictus are parts of the Latin Mass.
2083–84 **'non tali . . . Auxilio'** as Troy is falling, Hecuba tells her
aged husband, King Priam, who is arming himself, that the situation
does not call for such aid as his. *Aeneid* II. 521–22.

I will, Sirs: but a voice other than yours
Quickens my spirit. *"Quis pro Domino?"*
2095 "Who is upon the Lord's side?" asked the Count.
I, who write—

    "On receipt of this command,
Acquaint Count Guido and his fellows four
They die tomorrow: could it be tonight,
The better, but the work to do, takes time.
2100 Set with all diligence a scaffold up,
Not in the customary place, by Bridge
Saint Angelo, where die the common sort;
But since the man is noble, and his peers
By predilection haunt the People's Square,
2105 There let him be beheaded in the midst,
And his companions hanged on either side:
So shall the quality see, fear and learn.
All which work takes time: till tomorrow, then,
Let there be prayer incessant for the five!"

2110 For the main criminal I have no hope
Except in such a suddenness of fate.
I stood at Naples once, a night so dark
I could have scarce conjectured there was earth
Anywhere, sky or sea or world at all:
2115 But the night's black was burst through by a blaze—
Thunder struck blow on blow, earth groaned and
  bore,
Through her whole length of mountain visible:
There lay the city thick and plain with spires,
And, like a ghost disshrouded, white the sea.
2120 So may the truth be flashed out by one blow,
And Guido see, one instant, and be saved.
Else I avert my face, nor follow him
Into that sad obscure sequestered state
Where God unmakes but to remake the soul
2125 He else made first in vain; which must not be.
Enough, for I may die this very night
And how should I dare die, this man let live?

Carry this forthwith to the Governor!

GUIDO

YOU are the Cardinal Acciaiuoli, and you,
Abate Panciatichi—two good Tuscan names:
Acciaiuoli—ah, your ancestor it was
Built the huge battlemented convent-block
Over the little forky flashing Greve   5
That takes the quick turn at the foot o' the hill
Just as one first sees Florence: oh those days!
'Tis Ema, though, the other rivulet,
The one-arched brown brick bridge yawns over—yes,
Gallop and go five minutes, and you gain   10
The Roman Gate from where the Ema's bridged:
Kingfishers fly there: how I see the bend
O'erturreted by Certosa which he built,
That Seneschal (we styled him) of your House!
I do adjure you, help me, Sirs! My blood   15
Comes from as far a source: ought it to end
This way, by leakage through their scaffold-planks
Into Rome's sink where her red refuse runs?
Sirs, I beseech you by blood-sympathy,
If there be any vile experiment   20
In the air—if this your visit simply prove,
When all's done, just a well-intentioned trick
That tries for truth truer than truth itself,
By startling up a man, ere break of day,
To tell him he must die at sunset—pshaw!   25
That man's a Franceschini; feel his pulse,
Laugh at your folly, and let's all go sleep!
You have my last word—innocent am I
As Innocent my Pope and murderer,
Innocent as a babe, as Mary's own,   30
As Mary's self—I said, say and repeat—

351

And why, then, should I die twelve hours hence? I—
Whom, not twelve hours ago, the jailer bade
Turn to my straw-truss, settle and sleep sound
35 That I might wake the sooner, promptlier pay
His due of meat-and-drink-indulgence, cross
His palm with fee of the good-hand, beside,
As gallants use who go at large again!
For why? All honest Rome approved my part;
40 Whoever owned wife, sister, daughter—nay,
Mistress—had any shadow of any right
That looks like right, and, all the more resolved,
Held it with tooth and nail—these manly men
Approved! I being for Rome, Rome was for me.
45 Then, there's the point reserved, the subterfuge
My lawyers held by, kept for last resource,
Firm should all else—the impossible fancy!—fail,
And sneaking burgess-spirit° win the day.
The knaves! One plea at least would hold—they
        laughed—
50 One grappling-iron scratch the bottom-rock
Even should the middle mud let anchor go!
I hooked my cause on to the Clergy's—plea
Which, even if law tipped off my hat and plume,
Revealed my priestly tonsure, saved me so.
55 The Pope moreover, this old Innocent,
Being so meek and mild and merciful,
So fond o' the poor and so fatigued of earth,
So . . . fifty thousand devils in deepest hell!
Why must he cure us of our strange conceit
60 Of the angel in man's likeness, that we loved
And looked should help us at a pinch? He help?
He pardon? Here's his mind and message—death!
Thank the good Pope! Now, is he good in this,
Never mind, Christian—no such stuff's extant—
65 But will my death do credit to his reign,
Show he both lived and let live, so was good?
Cannot I live if he but like? "The law!"
Why, just the law gives him the very chance,

48 **burgess-spirit** middle class point of view.

he precise leave to let my life alone,
Vhich the archangelic soul of him (he says) 70
earns after! Here they drop it in his palm,
Iy lawyers, capital o' the cursed kind—
►rop life to take and hold and keep: but no!
Ie sighs, shakes head, refuses to shut hand,
Iotions away the gift they bid him grasp, 75
.nd of the coyness comes—that off I run
.nd down I go, he best knows whither! mind,
Ie knows, who sets me rolling all the same!
►isinterested Vicar of our Lord,
'his way he abrogates and disallows, 80
Iullifies and ignores—reverts in fine
'o the good and right, in detriment of me!
'alk away! Will you have the naked truth?
Ie's sick of his life's supper—swallowed lies:
.o, hobbling bedward, needs must ease his maw 85
ust where I sit o' the doorsill. Sir Abate,
Can you do nothing? Friends, we used to frisk:
Vhat of this sudden slash in a friend's face,
'his cut across our good companionship
'hat showed its front so gay when both were young? 90
Vere not we put into a beaten path,
►id pace the world, we nobles born and bred,
Ve body of friends with each his scutcheon full
►f old achievement and impunity—
'aking the laugh of morn and Sol's salute 95
.s forth we fared, pricked on to breathe our steeds
.nd take equestrian sport over the green
Jnder the blue, across the crop—what care?
f we went prancing up hill and down dale,
n and out of the level and the straight, 100
►y the bit of pleasant byway, where was harm?
.till Sol salutes me and the morning laughs:
I see my grandsire's hoof-prints—point the spot
Vhere he drew rein, slipped saddle, and stabbed
        knave
'or daring throw gibe—much less, stone—from pale: 105
'hen back, and on, and up with the cavalcade.
ust so wend we, now canter, now converse,

Till, 'mid the jauncing° pride and jaunty port,
Something of a sudden jerks at somebody—
110 A dagger is out, a flashing cut and thrust,
Because I play some prank my grandsire played,
And here I sprawl: where is the company? Gone!
A trot and a trample! only I lie trapped,
Writhe in a certain novel springe just set
By the good old Pope: I'm first prize. Warn me?
115   Why?
Apprise me that the law o' the game is changed?
Enough that I'm a warning, as I writhe,
To all and each my fellows of the file,
And make law plain henceforward past mistake,
120 "For such a prank, death is the penalty!"
Pope the Five Hundredth (what do I know or care?)
Deputes your Eminency and Abateship
To announce that, twelve hours from this time, he
     needs
I just essay upon my body and soul
125 The virtue of his brand-new engine, prove
Represser of the pranksome! I'm the first!
Thanks. Do you know what teeth you mean to try
The sharpness of, on this soft neck and throat?
I know it—I have seen and hate it—ay,
130 As you shall, while I tell you! Let me talk,
Or leave me, at your pleasure! talk I must:
What is your visit but my lure to talk?
Nay, you have something to disclose?—a smile,
At end of the forced sternness, means to mock
135 The heartbeats here? I call your two hearts stone!
Is your charge to stay with me till I die?
Be tacit as your bench, then! Use your ears,
I use my tongue: how glibly yours will run
At pleasant supper-time . . . God's curse! . . . tonight
140 When all the guests jump up, begin so brisk
"Welcome, his Eminence who shrived the wretch!
Now we shall have the Abate's story!"

108 **jauncing** prancing

Life!

How I could spill this overplus of mine
Among those hoar-haired, shrunk-shanked odds and
    ends
Of body and soul old age is chewing dry!   *145*
Those windlestraws that stare while purblind death
Mows here, mows there, makes hay of juicy me,
And misses just the bunch of withered weed
Would brighten hell and streak its smoke with flame!
How the life I could shed yet never shrink,   *150*
Would drench their stalks with sap like grass in May!
Is it not terrible, I entreat you, Sirs?—
With manifold and plenitudinous life,
Prompt at death's menace to give blow for threat,
Answer his "Be thou not!" by "Thus I am!"—   *155*
Terrible so to be alive yet die?

How I live, how I see! so—how I speak!
Lucidity of soul unlocks the lips:
I never had the words at will before.
How I see all my folly at a glance!   *160*
"A man requires a woman and a wife":
There was my folly; I believed the saw.
I knew that just myself concerned myself,
Yet needs must look for what I seemed to lack,
In a woman—why, the woman's in the man!   *165*
Fools we are, how we learn things when too late!
Overmuch life turns round my woman-side:
The male and female in me, mixed before,
Settle of a sudden: I'm my wife outright
In this unmanly appetite for truth,   *170*
This careless courage as to consequence,
This instantaneous sight through things and through,
This voluble rhetoric, if you please—'tis she!
Here you have that Pompilia whom I slew,
Also the folly for which I slew her!

Fool!   *175*

And, fool-like, what is it I wander from?
What did I say of your sharp iron tooth?

Ah—that I know the hateful thing! this way.
I chanced to stroll forth, many a good year gone,
180 One warm spring eve in Rome, and unaware
Looking, mayhap, to count what stars were out,
Came on your fine ax in a frame, that falls
And so cuts off a man's head underneath,
Mannaia°—thus we made acquaintance first:
185 Out of the way, in a by-part o' the town,
At the Mouth-of-Truth° o' the riverside, you know:
One goes by the Capitol: and wherefore coy,
Retiring out of crowded noisy Rome?
Because a very little time ago
190 It had done service, chopped off head from trunk
Belonging to a fellow whose poor house
The thing must make a point to stand before—
Felice Whatsoever-was-the-name
Who stabled buffaloes and so gained bread,
195 (Our clowns unyoke them in the ground hard by)
And, after use of much improper speech,
Had struck at Duke Some-title-or-other's face,
Because he kidnaped, carried away and kept
Felice's sister who would sit and sing
200 I' the filthy doorway while she plaited fringe
To deck the brutes with—on their gear it goes—
The good girl with the velvet in her voice.
So did the Duke, so did Felice, so
Did Justice, intervening with her ax.
205 There the man-mutilating engine stood
At ease, both gay and grim, like a Swiss guard
Off duty—purified itself as well,
Getting dry, sweet and proper for next week—
And doing incidental good, 'twas hoped,
210 To the rough lesson-lacking populace
Who now and then, forsooth, must right their wrongs!
There stood the twelve-foot-square of scaffold, railed
Considerately round to elbow-height,
For fear an officer should tumble thence

184 **Mannaia** guillotine. 186 **Mouth-of-Truth.** marble mask of a
Triton with an open mouth said to bite off the hands of perjurers.

And sprain his ankle and be lame a month   *215*
Through starting when the ax fell and head too!
Railed likewise were the steps whereby 'twas reached.
All of it painted red: red, in the midst,
Ran up two narrow tall beams barred across,
Since from the summit, some twelve feet to reach,   *220*
The iron plate with the sharp shearing edge
Had slammed, jerked, shot, slid—I shall soon find
    which!—
And so lay quiet, fast in its fit place,
The wooden half-moon collar, now eclipsed
By the blade which blocked its curvature: apart,   *225*
The other half—the under half-moon board
Which, helped by this, completes a neck's embrace—
Joined to a sort of desk that wheels aside
Out of the way when done with—down you kneel,
In you're pushed, over you the other drops,   *230*
Tight you're clipped, whiz, there's the blade cleaves
    its best,
Out trundles body, down flops head on floor,
And where's your soul gone? That, too, I shall find!
This kneeling-place was red, red, never fear!
But only slimy-like with paint, not blood,   *235*
For why? a decent pitcher stood at hand,
A broad dish to hold sawdust, and a broom
By some unnamed utensil—scraper-rake—
Each with a conscious air of duty done.
Underneath, loungers—boys and some few men—   *240*
Discoursed this platter, named the other tool,
Just as, when grooms tie up and dress a steed,
Boys lounge and look on, and elucubrate
What the round brush is used for, what the square—
So was explained—to me the skill-less then—   *245*
The manner of the grooming for next world
Undergone by Felice What's-his-name.
There's no such lovely month in Rome as May—
May's crescent is no half-moon of red plank,
And came now tilting o'er the wave i' the west,   *250*
One greenish-golden sea, right 'twixt those bars
Of the engine—I began acquaintance with,

Understood, hated, hurried from before,
To have it out of sight and cleanse my soul!
255 Here it is all again, conserved for use:
Twelve hours hence, I may know more, not hate
    worse.

That young May-moon-month! Devils of the deep!
Was not a Pope then Pope as much as now?
Used not he chirrup o'er the Merry Tales,
260 Chuckle—his nephew so exact the wag
To play a jealous cullion° such a trick
As wins the wife i' the pleasant story! Well?
Why do things change? Wherefore is Rome un-
    Romed?
I tell you, ere Felice's corpse was cold,
265 The Duke, that night, threw wide his palace-doors,
Received the compliments o' the quality
For justice done him—bowed and smirked his best,
And in return passed round a pretty thing,
A portrait of Felice's sister's self,
270 Florid old rogue Albano's masterpiece,
As—better than virginity in rags—
Bouncing Europa on the back o' the bull°:
They laughed and took their road the safelier home.
Ah, but times change, there's quite another Pope,
275 I do the Duke's deed, take Felice's place,
And, being no Felice, lout and clout,
Stomach but ill the phrase "I lose my head!"
How euphemistic! Lose what? Lose your ring.
Your snuffbox, tablets, kerchief!—but, your head?
280 I learned the process at an early age;
'Twas useful knowledge, in those same old days,
To know the way a head is set on neck.
My fencing-master urged "Would you excel?
Rest not content with mere bold give-and-guard,
285 Nor pink the antagonist somehow-anyhow!
See me dissect a little, and know your game!
Only anatomy makes a thrust the thing."

261 **cullion** rascal.   272 **Europa . . . bull** Zeus took the form of a
bull to carry off the maiden Europa.

Oh Cardinal, those lithe live necks of ours!
Here go the vertebrae, here's *Atlas,* here
Axis, and here the symphyses stop short, 290
So wisely and well—as, o'er a corpse, we cant—
And here's the silver cord which . . . what's our word?
Depends from the gold bowl,° which loosed (not
    "lost")
Lets us from Heaven to hell—one chop, we're loose!
"And not much pain i' the process," quoth a sage: 295
Who told him? Not Felice's ghost, I think!
Such "losing" is scarce Mother Nature's mode.
She fain would have cord ease itself away,
Worn to a thread by threescore years and ten,
Snap while we slumber: that seems bearable. 300
I'm told one clot of blood extravasate
Ends one as certainly as Roland's sword—
One drop of lymph suffused proves Oliver's° mace—
Intruding, either of the pleasant pair,
On the arachnoid tunic of my brain. 305
That's Nature's way of loosing cord!—but Art,
How of Art's process with the engine here,
When bowl and cord alike are crushed across,
Bored between, bruised through? Why, if Fagon's self,
The French Court's pride, that famed practitioner, 310
Would pass his cold pale lightning of a knife,
Pistoja-ware, adroit 'twixt joint and joint,
With just a "See how facile, gentlefolk!"—
The thing were not so bad to bear! Brute force
Cuts as he comes, breaks in, breaks on, breaks out 315
O' the hard and soft of you: is that the same?
A lithe snake thrids the hedge, makes throb no leaf:
A heavy ox sets chest to brier and branch,
Bursts somehow through, and leaves one hideous hole
Behind him!

              And why, why must this needs be? 320
Oh, if men were but good! They are not good,
Nowise like Peter: people called him rough,

292–93 **silver cord . . . bowl** Ecclesiastes 12:6.   302–3 **Roland . . .
Oliver** heroes of romance.

But if, as I left Rome, I spoke the Saint,
—"*Petrus, quo vadis?*"°—doubtless, I should hear,
325 "To free the prisoner and forgive his fault!
I plucked the absolute dead from God's own bar,
And raised up Dorcas°—why not rescue thee?"
What would cost one such nullifying word?
If Innocent succeeds to Peter's place,
330 Let him think Peter's thought, speak Peter's speech!
I say, he is bound to it: friends, how say you?
Concede I be all one bloodguiltiness
And mystery of murder in the flesh,
Why should that fact keep the Pope's mouth shut
      fast?
335 He execrates my crime—good!—sees hell yawn
One inch from the red plank's end which I press—
Nothing is better! What's the consequence?
How should a Pope proceed that knows his cue?
Why, leave me linger out my minute here,
Since close on death comes judgment and comes
340   doom,
Not crib at dawn its pittance from a sheep
Destined ere dewfall to be butcher's-meat!
Think, Sirs, if I have done you any harm,
And you require the natural revenge,
345 Suppose, and so intend to poison me,
—Just as you take and slip into my draft
The paperful of powder that clears scores,
You notice on my brow a certain blue:
How you both overset the wine at once!
350 How you both smile! "Our enemy has the plague!
Twelve hours hence he'll be scraping his bones bare
Of that intolerable flesh, and die,
Frenzied with pain: no need for poison here!
Step aside and enjoy the spectacle!"
355 Tender for souls are you, Pope Innocent!

324 **"Petrus, quo vadis?"** When Peter was fleeing from Rome he met
Jesus and asked him "Domine, quo vadis?" (Where are you going,
Lord?). When Jesus replied that he had come to be crucified again,
Peter returned to the city and was martyred. 327 **Dorcas** Acts
9:36–41.

Christ's maxim is—one soul outweighs the world:
Respite me, save a soul, then, curse the world!
"No," venerable sire, I hear you smirk,
"No: for Christ's gospel changes names, not things,
Renews the obsolete, does nothing more!   360
Our fire-new gospel is re-tinkered law,
Our mercy, justice—Jove's rechristened God—
Nay, whereas, in the popular conceit,
'Tis pity that old harsh Law somehow limps,
Lingers on earth, although Law's day be done,   365
Else would benignant Gospel interpose,
Not furtively as now, but bold and frank
O'erflutter us with healing in her wings,
Law being harshness, Gospel only love—
We tell the people, on the contrary,   370
Gospel takes up the rod which Law lets fall;
Mercy is vigilant when justice sleeps!
Does Law permit a taste of Gospel-grace?
The secular arm allow the spiritual power
To act for once?—no compliment so fine   375
As that our Gospel handsomely turn harsh,
Thrust victim back on Law the nice and coy!"
Yes, you do say so, else you would forgive
Me whom Law does not touch but tosses you!
Don't think to put on the professional face!   380
You know what I know: casuists as you are,
Each nerve must creep, each hair start, sting and
    stand,
At such illogical inconsequence!
Dear my friends, do but see! A murder's tried,
There are two parties to the cause: I'm one,   385
—Defend myself, as somebody must do:
I have the best o' the battle: that's a fact,
Simple fact—fancies find no place just now.
What though half Rome condemned me? Half ap-
    proved:
And, none disputes, the luck is mine at last,   390
All Rome, i' the main, acquitting me: whereon,
What has the Pope to ask but "How finds Law?"
"I find," replies Law, "I have erred this while:

Guilty or guiltless, Guido proves a priest,
395 No layman: he is therefore yours, not mine:
I bound him: loose him, you whose will is Christ's!"
And now what does this Vicar of our Lord,
Shepherd o' the flock—one of whose charge bleats
       sore
For crook's help from the quag wherein it drowns?
400 Law suffers him employ the crumpled end:
His pleasure is to turn staff, use the point,
And thrust the shuddering sheep, he calls a wolf,
Back and back, down and down to where hell gapes!
"Guiltless," cries Law—"Guilty" corrects the Pope!
"Guilty," for the whim's sake! "Guilty," he somehow
405   thinks,
And anyhow says: 'tis truth; he dares not lie!

Others should do the lying. That's the cause
Brings you both here: I ought in decency
Confess to you that I deserve my fate,
410 Am guilty, as the Pope thinks—ay, to the end,
Keep up the jest, lie on, lie ever, lie
I' the latest gasp of me! What reason, Sirs?
Because tomorrow will succeed today
For you, though not for me: and if I stick
415 Still to the truth, declare with my last breath,
I die an innocent and murdered man—
Why, there's the tongue of Rome will wag apace
This time tomorrow: don't I hear the talk!
"So, to the last he proved impenitent?
420 Pagans have said as much of martyred saints!
Law demurred, washed her hands of the whole case.
Prince Somebody said this, Duke Something, that,
Doubtless the man's dead, dead enough, don't fear!
But, hang it, what if there have been a spice,
425 A touch of . . . eh? You see, the Pope's so old,
Some of us add, obtuse: age never slips
The chance of shoving youth to face death first!"
And so on. Therefore to suppress such talk
You two come here, entreat I tell you lies,
430 And end, the edifying way. I end,

'elling the truth! Your self-styled shepherd thieves!
A thief—and how thieves hate the wolves we know:
Damage to theft, damage to thrift, all's one!
The red hand is sworn foe of the black jaw.
That's only natural, that's right enough: 435
But why the wolf should compliment the thief
With shepherd's title, bark out life in thanks,
And, spiteless, lick the prong that spits him—eh,
Cardinal? My Abate, scarcely thus!
There, let my sheepskin-garb, a curse on't, go— 440
Leave my teeth free if I must show my shag!
Repent? What good shall follow? If I pass
Twelve hours repenting, will that fact hold fast
The thirteenth at the horrid dozen's end?
If I fall forthwith at your feet, gnash, tear, 445
Foam, rave, to give your story the due grace,
Will that assist the engine halfway back
Into its hiding-house?—boards, shaking now,
Bone against bone, like some old skeleton bat
That wants, at winter's end, to wake and prey! 450
Will howling put the specter back to sleep?
Ah, but I misconceive your object, Sirs!
Since I want new life like the creature—life,
Being done with here, begins i' the world away:
I shall next have "Come, mortals, and be judged!" 455
There's but a minute betwixt this and then:
So, quick, be sorry since it saves my soul!
Sirs, truth shall save it, since no lies assist!
Hear the truth, you, whatever you style yourselves,
Civilization and society! 460
Come, one good grapple, I with all the world!
Dying in cold blood is the desperate thing;
The angry heart explodes, bears off in blaze
The indignant soul, and I'm combustion-ripe.
Why, you intend to do your worst with me! 465
That's in your eyes! You dare no more than death,
And mean no less. I must make up my mind.
So Pietro—when I chased him here and there,
Morsel by morsel cut away the life
I loathed—cried for just respite to confess 470

And save his soul: much respite did I grant!
Why grant me respite who deserve my doom?
Me—who engaged to play a prize,° fight you,
Knowing your arms, and foil you, trick for trick,
475 At rapier-fence, your match and, maybe, more.
I knew that if I chose sin certain sins,
Solace my lusts out of the regular way
Prescribed me, I should find you in the path,
Have to try skill with a redoubted foe;
480 You would lunge, I would parry, and make end.
At last, occasion of a murder comes:
We cross blades, I, for all my brag, break guard,
And in goes the cold iron at my breast,
Out at my back, and end is made of me.
485 You stand confessed the adroiter swordsman—ay,
But on your triumph you increase, it seems,
Want more of me than lying flat on face:
I ought to raise my ruined head, allege
Not simply I pushed worse blade o' the pair,
490 But my antagonist dispensed with steel!
There was no passage of arms, you looked me low,
With brow and eye abolished cut and thrust
Nor used the vulgar weapon! This chance scratch,
This incidental hurt, this sort of hole
495 I' the heart of me? I stumbled, got it so!
Fell on my own sword as a bungler may!
Yourself proscribe such heathen tools, and trust
To the naked virtue: it was virtue stood
Unarmed and awed me—on my brow there burned
500 Crime out so plainly intolerably red,
That I was fain to cry—"Down to the dust
With me, and bury there brow, brand and all!"
Law had essayed the adventure—but what's Law?
Morality exposed the Gorgon shield!°
505 Morality and Religion conquer me.
If Law sufficed would you come here, entreat
I supplement law, and confess forsooth?

473 **play a prize** play and win.   504 **Gorgon shield** Athene bore on
her shield the head of the Gorgon, whose glance turned the beholder
to stone.

Did not the trial show things plain enough?
"Ah, but a word of the man's very self
Would somehow put the keystone in its place   510
And crown the arch!" Then take the word you want!

I say that, long ago, when things began,
All the world made agreement, such and such
Were pleasure-giving profit-bearing acts,
But henceforth extralegal, nor to be: 515
You must not kill the man whose death would please
And profit you, unless his life stop yours
Plainly, and need so be put aside:
Get the thing by a public course, by law,
Only no private bloodshed as of old!   520
All of us, for the good of everyone,
Renounced such license and conformed to law:
Who breaks law, breaks pact therefore, helps himself
To pleasure and profit over and above the due,
And must pay forfeit—pain beyond his share: 525
For, pleasure being the sole good in the world,
Anyone's pleasure turns to someone's pain,
So, law must watch for everyone—say we,
Who call things wicked that give too much joy,
And nickname mere reprisal, envy makes,
Punishment: quite right! thus the world goes round. 530
I, being well aware such pact there was,
I, in my time who found advantage come
Of law's observance and crime's penalty—
Who, but for wholesome fear law bred in friends,   535
Had doubtless given example long ago,
Furnished forth some friend's pleasure with my pain,
And, by my death, pieced out his scanty life—
I could not, for that foolish life of me,
Help risking law's infringement—I broke bond,   540
And needs must pay price—wherefore, here's my
      head,
Flung with a flourish! But, repentance too?
But pure and simple sorrow for law's breach
Rather than blunderer's-ineptitude?
Cardinal, no! Abate, scarcely thus!   545

'Tis the fault, not that I dared try a fall
With Law and straightway am found undermost,
But that I failed to see, above man's law,
God's precept you, the Christians, recognize?
550 Colly my cow! Don't fidget, Cardinal!
Abate, cross your breast and count your beads
And exorcize the devil, for here he stands
And stiffens in the bristly nape of neck,
Daring you drive him hence! You, Christians both?
555 I say, if ever was such faith at all
Born in the world, by your community
Suffered to live its little tick of time,
'Tis dead of age, now, ludicrously dead;
Honor its ashes, if you be discreet,
560 In epitaph only! For, concede its death,
Allow extinction, you may boast unchecked
What feats the thing did in a crazy land
At a fabulous epoch—treat your faith, that way,
Just as you treat your relics: "Here's a shred
565 Of saintly flesh, a scrap of blessed bone,
Raised King Cophetua, who was dead, to life
In Mesopotamy twelve centuries since,
Such was its virtue!"—twangs the Sacristan,
Holding the shrine-box up, with hands like feet
570 Because of gout in every finger joint:
Does he bethink him to reduce one knob,
Allay one twinge by touching what he vaunts?
I think he half uncrooks fist to catch fee,
But, for the grace, the quality of cure—
575 Cophetua was the man put that to proof!
Not otherwise, your faith is shrined and shown
And shamed at once: you banter while you bow!
Do you dispute this? Come, a monster-laugh,
A madman's laugh, allowed his Carnival
580 Later ten days than when all Rome, but he,
Laughed at the candle-contest:° mine's alight,
'Tis just it sputter till the puff o' the Pope
End it tomorrow and the world turn ash.

581 **candle-contest** game of blowing out each others' candles on the
last night of Carnival.

Come, thus I wave a wand and bring to pass
In a moment, in the twinkle of an eye,   *585*
What but that—feigning everywhere grows fact,
Professors turn possessors, realize
The faith they play with as a fancy now,
And bid it operate, have full effect
On every circumstance of life, today,   *590*
In Rome—faith's flow set free at fountainhead!
Now, you'll own, at this present, when I speak,
Before I work the wonder, there's no man
Woman or child in Rome, faith's fountainhead,
But might, if each were minded, realize   *595*
Conversely unbelief, faith's opposite—
Set it to work on life unflinchingly,
Yet give no symptom of an outward change:
Why should things change because men disbelieve
What's incompatible, in the whited tomb,   *600*
With bones and rottenness one inch below?
What saintly act is done in Rome today
But might be prompted by the devil—"is"
I say not—"has been, and again may be—"
I do say, full i' the face o' the crucifix   *605*
You try to stop my mouth with! Off with it!
Look in your own heart, if your soul have eyes!
You shall see reason why, though faith were fled,
Unbelief still might work the wires and move
Man, the machine, to play a faithful part.   *610*
Preside your college, Cardinal, in your cape,
Or—having got above his head, grown Pope—
Abate, gird your loins and wash my feet!°
Do you suppose I am at loss at all
Why you crook, why you cringe, why fast or feast? *615*
Praise, blame, sit, stand, lie or go!—all of it,
In each of you, purest unbelief may prompt,
And wit explain to who has eyes to see.
But, lo, I wave wand, made the false the true!
Here's Rome believes in Christianity!   *620*
What an explosion, how the fragments fly

613 **gird . . . feet** John 13:4–14.

Of what was surface, mask and make-believe!
Begin now—look at this Pope's-halberdier
In wasp-like black and yellow foolery!°
625 He, doing duty at the corridor,
Wakes from a muse and stands convinced of sin!
Down he flings halbert, leaps the passage-length,
Pushes into the presence, pantingly
Submits the extreme peril of the case
630 To the Pope's self—whom in the world beside?—
And the Pope breaks talk with ambassador,
Bids aside bishop, wills the whole world wait
Till he secure that prize, outweighs the world,
A soul, relieve the sentry of his qualm!
635 His Altitude the Referendary—
Robed right, and ready for the usher's word
To pay devoir—is, of all times, just then
'Ware of a masterstroke of argument
Will cut the spinal cord . . . ugh, ugh! . . . I mean,
640 Paralyse Molinism for evermore!
Straight he leaves lobby, trundles, two and two,
Down steps to reach home, write, if but a word
Shall end the impudence: he leaves who likes
Go pacify the Pope: there's Christ to serve!
645 How otherwise would men display their zeal?
If the same sentry had the least surmise
A powder-barrel 'neath the pavement lay
In neighborhood with what might prove a match,
Meant to blow sky-high Pope and presence both—
650 Would he not break through courtiers, rank and file,
Bundle up, bear off and save body so,
The Pope, no matter for his priceless soul?
There's no fool's-freak here, naught to soundly
        swinge,
Only a man in earnest, you'll so praise
655 And pay and prate about, that earth shall ring!
Had thought possessed the Referendary
His jewel-case at home was left ajar,
What would be wrong in running, robes awry,

623–24 look . . . foolery the Swiss Guard, whose costume was de-
signed by Michelangelo.

To be beforehand with the pilferer?
What talk then of indecent haste? Which means,   660
That both these, each in his degree, would do
Just that—for a comparative nothing's sake,
And thereby gain approval and reward—
Which, done for what Christ says is worth the world,
Procures the doer curses, cuffs and kicks.   665
I call such difference 'twixt act and act,
Sheer lunacy unless your truth on lip
Be recognized a lie in heart of you!
How do you all act, promptly or in doubt,
When there's a guest poisoned at supper-time   670
And he sits chatting on with spot on cheek?
"Pluck him by the skirt, and round him in the ears,
Have at him by the beard, warn anyhow!"
Good, and this other friend that's cheat and thief
And dissolute—go stop the devil's feast,   675
Withdraw him from the imminent hellfire!
Why, for your life, you dare not tell your friend
"You lie, and I admonish you for Christ!"
Who yet dare seek that same man at the Mass
To warn him—on his knees, and tinkle° near—   680
He left a cask atilt, a tap unturned,
The Trebbian running: what a grateful jump
Out of the Church rewards your vigilance!
Perform that selfsame service just a thought
More maladroitly—since a bishop sits   685
At function!—and he budges not, bites lip—
"You see my case: how can I quit my post?
He has an eye to any such default.
See to it, neighbor, I beseech your love!"
He and you know the relative worth of things,   690
What is permissible or inopportune.
Contort your brows! You know I speak the truth:
Gold is called gold, and dross called dross, i' the
     Book:
Gold you let lie and dross pick up and prize!
—Despite your muster of some fifty monks   695

680 **tinkle** of the mass bell.

And nuns a-maundering here and mumping there,
Who could, and on occasion would, spurn dross,
Clutch gold, and prove their faith a fact so far—
I grant you! Fifty times the number squeak
700 And gibber in the madhouse—firm of faith,
This fellow, that his nose supports the moon;
The other, that his straw hat crowns him Pope:
Does that prove all the world outside insane?
Do fifty miracle-mongers match the mob
705 That acts on the frank faithless principle,
Born-baptized-and-bred Christian-atheists, each
With just as much a right to judge as you—
As many senses in his soul, and nerves
I' neck of him as I—whom, soul and sense,
710 Neck and nerve, you abolish presently—
I being the unit in creation now
Who pay the Maker, in this speech of mine,
A creature's duty, spend my last of breath
In bearing witness, even by my worst fault,
715 To the creature's obligation, absolute,
Perpetual: my worst fault protests, "The faith
Claims all of me: I would give all she claims,
But for a spice of doubt: the risk's too rash:
Double or quits, I play, but, all or naught,
720 Exceeds my courage: therefore, I descend
To the next faith with no dubiety—
Faith in the present life, made last as long
And prove as full of pleasure as may hap,
Whatever pain it cause the world." I'm wrong?
725 I've had my life, whate'er I lose: I'm right?
I've got the single good there was to gain.
Entire faith, or else complete unbelief!
Aught between has my loathing and contempt,
Mine and God's also, doubtless: ask yourself,
730 Cardinal, where and how you like a man!
Why, either with your feet upon his head,
Confessed your caudatory,° or, at large,
The stranger in the crowd who caps to you

732 caudatory train-bearer.

But keeps his distance—why should he presume?
You want no hanger-on and dropper-off,   735
Now yours, and now not yours but quite his own,
According as the sky looks black or bright.
Just so I capped to and kept off from faith—
You promised trudge behind through fair and foul,
Yet leave i' the lurch at the first spit of rain.   740
Who holds to faith whenever rain begins?
What does the father when his son lies dead,
The merchant when his money-bags take wing,
The politician whom a rival ousts?
No case but has its conduct, faith prescribes: 745
Where's the obedience that shall edify?
Why, they laugh frankly in the face of faith
And take the natural course—this rends his hair
Because his child is taken to God's breast,
That gnashes teeth and raves at loss of trash   750
Which rust corrupts and thieves break through and
        steal,
And this, enabled to inherit earth
Through meekness, curses till your blood runs cold!
Down they all drop to my low level, rest
Heart upon dungy earth that's warm and soft,   755
And let who please attempt the altitudes.
Each playing prodigal son of heavenly sire,
Turning his nose up at the fatted calf,
Fain to fill belly with the husks, we swine
Did eat by born depravity of taste!   760

Enough of the hypocrites. But you, Sirs, you—
Who never budged from litter where I lay,
And buried snout i' the draff-box while I fed,
Cried amen to my creed's one article—
"Get pleasure, 'scape pain—give your preference   765
To the immediate good, for time is brief,
And death ends good and ill and everything!
What's got is gained, what's gained soon is gained
        twice,
And—inasmuch as faith gains most—feign faith!"
So did we brother-like pass word about: 770

—You, now—like bloody drunkards but half-drunk,
Who fool men yet perceive men find them fools—
Vexed that a titter gains the gravest mouth—
O' the sudden you must needs reintroduce
775 Solemnity, straight sober undue mirth
By a blow dealt me your boon companion here
Who, using the old license, dreamed of harm
No more than snow in harvest: yet it falls!
You check the merriment effectually
780 By pushing your abrupt machine i' the midst,
Making me Rome's example: blood for wine!
The general good needs that you chop and change!
I may dislike the hocus-pocus—Rome,
The laughter-loving people, won't they stare
785 Chap-fallen!—while serious natures sermonize
"The magistrate, he beareth not the sword
In vain; who sins may taste its edge, we see!"
Why my sin, drunkards? Where have I abused
Liberty, scandalized you all so much?
790 Who called me, who crooked finger till I came,
Fool that I was, to join companionship?
I knew my own mind, meant to live my life,
Elude your envy, or else make a stand,
Take my own part and sell you my life dear.
795 But it was "Fie! No prejudice in the world
To the proper manly instinct! Cast your lot
Into our lap, one genius ruled our births,
We'll compass joy by concert; take with us
The regular irregular way i' the wood;
800 You'll miss no game through riding breast by breast,
In this preserve, the Church's park and pale,
Rather than outside where the world lies waste!"
Come, if you said not that, did you say this?
Give plain and terrible warning, "Live, enjoy?
805 Such life begins in death and ends in hell!
Dare you bid us assist your sins, us priests
Who hurry sin and sinners from the earth?
No such delight for us, why then for you?
Leave earth, seek Heaven or find its opposite!"
810 Had you so warned me, not in lying words

But veritable deeds with tongues of flame,
That had been fair, that might have struck a man,
Silenced the squabble between soul and sense,
Compelled him to make mind up, take one course
Or the other, peradventure!—wrong or right,   815
Foolish or wise, you would have been at least
Sincere, no question—forced me choose, indulge
Or else renounce my instincts, still play wolf
Or find my way submissive to your fold,
Be red-crossed on my fleece, one sheep the more.   820
But you as good as bade me wear sheep's wool
Over wolf's skin, suck blood and hide the noise
By mimicry of something like a bleat—
Whence it comes that because, despite my care,
Because I smack my tongue too loud for once,   825
Drop baaing, here's the village up in arms!
Have at the wolf's throat, you who hate the breed!
Oh, were it only open yet to choose—
One little time more—whether I'd be free
Your foe, or subsidized your friend forsooth!   830
Should not you get a growl through the white fangs
In answer to your beckoning! Cardinal,
Abate, managers o' the multitude,
I'd turn your gloved hands to account, be sure!
You should manipulate the coarse rough mob: 835
'Tis you I'd deal directly with, not them—
Using your fears: why touch the thing myself
When I could see you hunt, and then cry "Shares!
Quarter the carcase or we quarrel; come,
Here's the world ready to see justice done!"   840
Oh, it had been a desperate game, but game
Wherein the winner's chance were worth the pains!
We'd try conclusions!—at the worst, what worse
Than this Mannaia-machine, each minute's talk
Helps push an inch the nearer me? Fool, fool!   845

You understand me and forgive, sweet Sirs?
I blame you, tear my hair and tell my woe—
All's but a flourish, figure of rhetoric!
One must try each expedient to save life.

850 One makes fools look foolisher fifty-fold
By putting in their place men wise like you,
To take the full force of an argument
Would buffet their stolidity in vain.
If you should feel aggrieved by the mere wind
855 O' the blow that means to miss you and maul them,
That's my success! Is it not folly, now,
To say with folk, "A plausible defense—
We see through notwithstanding, and reject?"
Reject the plausible they do, these fools,
860 Who never even make pretense to show
One point beyond its plausibility
In favor of the best belief they hold!
"Saint Somebody-or-other raised the dead":
Did he? How do you come to know as much?
865 "Know it, what need? The story's plausible,
Avouched for by a martyrologist,
And why should good men sup on cheese and leeks
On such a saint's day, if there were no saint?"
I praise the wisdom of these fools, and straight
870 Tell them my story—"plausible, but false!"
False, to be sure! What else can story be
That runs—a young wife tired of an old spouse,
Found a priest whom she fled away with—both
Took their full pleasure in the two-days' flight,
875 Which a gray-headed grayer-hearted pair,
(Whose best boast was, their life had been a lie)
Helped for the love they bore all liars. Oh,
Here incredulity begins! Indeed?
Allow then, were no one point strictly true,
880 There's that i' the tale might seem like truth at least
To the unlucky husband—jaundiced patch—
Jealousy maddens people, why not him?
Say, he was maddened, so forgivable!
Humanity pleads that though the wife were true,
885 The priest true, and the pair of liars true,
They might seem false to one man in the world!
A thousand gnats make up a serpent's sting,
And many sly soft stimulants to wrath

Compose a formidable wrong at last
That gets called easily by some one name   *890*
Not applicable to the single parts,
And so draws down a general revenge,
Excessive if you take crime, fault by fault.
Jealousy! I have known a score of plays,
Were listened to and laughed at in my time   *895*
As like the everyday-life on all sides,
Wherein the husband, mad as a March hare,
Suspected all the world contrived his shame.
What did the wife? The wife kissed both eyes blind,
Explained away ambiguous circumstance,   *900*
And while she held him captive by the hand,
Crowned his head—you know what's the mockery—
By half her body behind the curtain. That's
Nature now! That's the subject of a piece
I saw in Vallombrosa Convent, made   *905*
Expressly to teach men what marriage was!
But say "Just so did I misapprehend,
Imagine she deceived me to my face,"
And that's pretense too easily seen through!
All those eyes of all husbands in all plays,   *910*
At stare like one expanded peacock-tail,
Are laughed at for pretending to be keen
While horn-blind: but the moment I step forth—
Oh, I must needs o' the sudden prove a lynx
And look the heart, that stone-wall, through and
    through!   *915*
Such an eye, God's may be—not yours nor mine.

Yes, presently . . . what hour is fleeting now?
When you cut earth away from under me,
I shall be left alone with, pushed beneath
Some such an apparitional dread orb   *920*
As the eye of God, since such an eye there glares:
I fancy it go filling up the void
Above my mote-self it devours, or what
Proves—wrath, immensity wreaks on nothingness.
Just how I felt once, couching through the dark, *925*

Hard by Vittiano; young I was, and gay,
And wanting to trap fieldfares:° first a spark
Tipped a bent, as a mere dew-globule might
Any stiff grass-stalk on the meadow—this
930 Grew fiercer, flamed out full, and proved the sun.
What do I want with proverbs, precepts here?
Away with man! What shall I say to God?
This, if I find the tongue and keep the mind—
"Do Thou wipe out the being of me, and smear
935 This soul from off Thy white of things, I blot!
I am one huge and sheer mistake—whose fault?
Not mine at least, who did not make myself!"
Someone declares my wife excused me so!
Perhaps she knew what argument to use.
940 Grind your teeth, Cardinal: Abate, writhe!
What else am I to cry out in my rage,
Unable to repent one particle
O' the past? Oh, how I wish some cold wise man
Would dig beneath the surface which you scrape,
945 Deal with the depths, pronounce on my desert
Groundedly! I want simple sober sense,
That asks, before it finishes with a dog,
Who taught the dog that trick you hang him for?
You both persist to call that act a crime,
950 Which sense would call . . . yes, I maintain it, Sirs, . . .
A blunder! At the worst, I stood in doubt
On crossroad, took one path of many paths:
It leads to the red thing, we all see now,
But nobody saw at first: one primrose-patch
955 In bank, one singing-bird in bush, the less,
Had warned me from such wayfare: let me prove!
Put me back to the crossroad, start afresh!
Advise me when I take the first false step!
Give me my wife: how should I use my wife,
960 Love her or hate her? Prompt my action now!
There she is, there she stands alive and pale,
The thirteen-years' old child, with milk for blood,
Pompilia Comparini, as at first,

927 fieldfares thrushes.

Which first is only four brief years ago!
I stand too in the little ground-floor room   965
O' the father's house at Via Vittoria: see!
Her so-called mother—one arm round the waist
O' the child to keep her from the toys, let fall
At wonder I can live yet look so grim—
Ushers her in, with deprecating wave   970
Of the other—and she fronts me loose at last,
Held only by the mother's fingertip.
Struck dumb—for she was white enough before!—
She eyes me with those frightened balls of black,
As heifer—the old simile comes pat—   975
Eyes tremblingly the altar and the priest.
The amazed look, all one insuppressive prayer—
Might she but breathe, set free as heretofore,
Have this cup leave her lips unblistered, bear
Any cross anywhither anyhow,   980
So but alone, so but apart from me!
You are touched? So am I, quite otherwise,
If 'tis with pity. I resent my wrong,
Being a man: I only show man's soul
Through man's flesh: she sees mine, it strikes her
    thus!   985
Is that attractive? To a youth perhaps—
Calf-creature, one-part boy to three-parts girl,
To whom it is a flattering novelty
That he, men use to motion from their path,
Can thus impose, thus terrify in turn   990
A chit whose terror shall be changed apace
To bliss unbearable when grace and glow,
Prowess and pride descend the throne and touch
Esther in all that pretty tremble,° cured
By the dove o' the scepter! But myself am old,   995
O' the wane at least, in all things: what do you say
To her who frankly thus confirms my doubt?
I am past the prime, I scare the woman-world,
Done-with that way: you like this piece of news?
A little saucy rosebud minx can strike   1000

994 Esther . . . tremble Apochryphal addition to Esther, ch. 15.

Death-damp into the breast of doughty king
Though 'twere French Louis—soul I understand—
Saying, by gesture of repugnance, just
"Sire, you are regal, puissant and so forth,
1005 But—young you have been, are not, nor will be!"
In vain the mother nods, winks, bustles up,
"Count, girls incline to mature worth like you!
As for Pompilia, what's flesh, fish, or fowl
To one who apprehends no difference,
1010 And would accept you even were you old
As you are . . . youngish by her father's side?
Trim but your beard a little, thin your bush
Of eyebrow; and for presence, portliness,
And decent gravity, you beat a boy!"
1015 Deceive yourself one minute, if you may,
In presence of the child that so loves age,
Whose neck writhes, cords itself against your kiss,
Whose hand you wring stark, rigid with despair!
Well, I resent this; I am young in soul,
1020 Nor old in body—thews and sinews here—
Though the vile surface be not smooth as once—
Far beyond that first wheelwork which went wrong
Through the untempered iron ere 'twas proof:
I am the wrought man worth ten times the crude,
1025 Would woman see what this declines to see,
Declines to say "I see"—the officious word
That makes the thing, pricks on the soul to shoot
New fire into the half-used cinder, flesh!
Therefore 'tis she begins with wronging me,
1030 Who cannot but begin with hating her.
Our marriage follows: there she stands again!
Why do I laugh? Why, in the very gripe
O' the jaws of death's gigantic skull, do I
Grin back his grin, make sport of my own pangs?
1035 Why from each clashing of his molars, ground
To make the devil bread from out my grist,
Leaps out a spark of mirth, a hellish toy?
Take notice we are lovers in a church,
Waiting the sacrament to make us one
1040 And happy! Just as bid, she bears herself,

Comes and kneels, rises, speaks, is silent—goes:
So have I brought my horse, by word and blow,
To stand stock-still and front the fire he dreads.
How can I other than remember this,
Resent the very obedience? Gain thereby? 1045
Yes, I do gain my end and have my will—
Thanks to whom? When the mother speaks the word,
She obeys it—even to enduring me!
There had been compensation in revolt—
Revolt's to quell: but martyrdom rehearsed, 1050
But predetermined saintship for the sake
O' the mother?—"Go!" thought I, "we meet again!"
Pass the next weeks of dumb contented death,
She lives—wakes up, installed in house and home,
Is mine, mine all day-long, all night-long mine. 1055
Good folk begin at me with open mouth
"Now, at least, reconcile the child to life!
Study and make her love . . . that is, endure
The . . . hem! the . . . all of you though somewhat
        old,
Till it amount to something, in her eye, 1060
As good as love, better a thousand times—
Since nature helps the woman in such strait,
Makes passiveness her pleasure: failing which,
What if you give up boy-and-girl-fools'-play
And go on to wise friendship all at once? 1065
Those boys and girls kiss themselves cold, you know,
Toy themselves tired and slink aside full soon
To friendship, as they name satiety:
Thither go you and wait their coming!" Thanks,
Considerate advisers—but, fair play! 1070
Had you and I, friends, started fair at first
We, keeping fair, might reach it, neck by neck,
This blessed goal, whenever fate so please:
But why am I to miss the daisied mile
The course begins with, why obtain the dust 1075
Of the end precisely at the starting-point?
Why quaff life's cup blown free of all the beads,
The bright red froth wherein our beard should steep
Before our mouth essay the black o' the wine?

1080 Foolish, the love-fit? Let me prove it such
Like you, before like you I puff things clear!
"The best's to come, no rapture but content!
Not love's first glory but a sober glow,
Not a spontaneous outburst in pure boon,
1085 So much as, gained by patience, care and toil,
Proper appreciation and esteem!"
Go preach that to your nephews, not to me
Who, tired i' the midway of my life, would stop
And take my first refreshment, pluck a rose:
1090 What's this coarse woolly hip, worn smooth of leaf,
You counsel I go plant in garden-plot,
Water with tears, manure with sweat and blood,
In confidence the seed shall germinate
And, for its very best, some far-off day,
1095 Grow big, and blow me out a dog-rose bell?
Why must your nephews begin breathing spice
O' the hundred-petaled Provence prodigy?°
Nay, more and worse—would such my root bear
         rose—
Prove really flower and favorite, not the kind
That's queen, but those three leaves that make one
1100   cup
And hold the hedge-bird's breakfast—then indeed
The prize though poor would pay the care and toil!
Respect we Nature that makes least as most,
Marvelous in the minim! But this bud,
1105 Bit through and burned black by the tempter's tooth,
This bloom whose best grace was the slug outside
And the wasp inside its bosom—call you "rose"?
Claim no immunity from a weed's fate
For the horrible present! What you call my wife
1110 I call a nullity in female shape,
Vapid disgust, soon to be pungent plague,
When mixed with, made confusion and a curse
By two abominable nondescripts,
That father and that mother: think you see
1115 The dreadful bronze our boast, we Aretines,

1097 hundred-petaled Provence prodigy "prize rose."

The Etruscan monster, the three-headed thing,
Bellerophon's foe! How name you the whole beast?
You choose to name the body from one head,
That of the simple kid which droops the eye,
Hangs the neck and dies tenderly enough: 1120
I rather see the grizzly lion belch
Flame out i' the midst, the serpent writhe her rings,
Grafted into the common stock for tail,
And name the brute, Chimera° which I slew!
How was there ever more to be—(concede   1125
My wife's insipid harmless nullity)—
Dissociation from that pair of plagues—
That mother with her cunning and her cant—
The eyes with first their twinkle of conceit,
Then, dropped to earth in mock-demureness—now,   1130
The smile self-satisfied from ear to ear,
Now, the prim pursed-up mouth's protruded lips,
With deferential duck, slow swing of head,
Tempting the sudden fist of man too much—
That owl-like screw of lid and rock of ruff!   1135
As for the father—Cardinal, you know,
The kind of idiot!—such are rife in Rome,
But they wear velvet commonly; good fools,
At the end of life, to furnish forth young folk
Who grin and bear with imbecility: 1140
Since the stalled ass, the joker, sheds from jaw
Corn, in the joke, for those who laugh or starve.
But what say we to the same solemn beast
Wagging his ears and wishful of our pat,
When turned, with holes in hide and bones laid bare,   1145
To forage for himself i' the waste o' the world,
Sir Dignity i' the dumps? Pat him? We drub
Self-knowledge, rather, into frowzy pate,
Teach Pietro to get trappings or go hang!
Fancy this quondam oracle in vogue   1150
At Via Vittoria, this personified

1115–24 **dreadful bronze . . . Chimera** ancient Etruscan statue of the
monster Chimera, a lion in front, kid in the middle, and serpent
behind, named incongruously for its middle part.

Authority when time was—Pantaloon°
Flaunting his tomfool tawdry just the same
As if Ash Wednesday were mid-Carnival!
1155 That's the extreme and unforgivable
Of sins, as I account such. Have you stooped
For your own ends to bestialize yourself
By flattery of a fellow of this stamp?
The ends obtained or else shown out of reach,
1160 He goes on, takes the flattery for pure truth—
"You love, and honor me, of course: what next?"
What, but the trifle of the stabbing, friend?—
Which taught you how one worships when the shrine
Has lost the relic that we bent before.
1165 Angry! And how could I be otherwise?
'Tis plain: this pair of old pretentious fools
Meant to fool me: it happens, I fooled them.
Why could not these who sought to buy and sell
Me—when they found themselves were bought and
        sold,
1170 Make up their mind to the proved rule of right,
Be chattel and not chapman° any more?
Miscalculation has its consequence;
But when the shepherd crooks a sheep-like thing
And meaning to get wool, dislodges fleece
1175 And finds the veritable wolf beneath,
(How that staunch image serves at every turn!)
Does he, by way of being politic,
Pluck the first whisker grimly visible?
Or rather grow in a trice all gratitude,
1180 Protest this sort-of-what-one-might-name sheep
Beats the old other curly-coated kind,
And shall share board and bed, if so it deign,
With its discoverer, like a royal ram?
Ay, thus, with chattering teeth and knocking knees,
1185 Would wisdom treat the adventure! these, forsooth,
Tried whisker-plucking, and so found what trap
The whisker kept perdue,° two rows of teeth—

1152 **Pantaloon** clownish old man in comedy.   1171 **Be chattel and not chapman** be goods and not merchant.   1187 **perdue** concealed.

Sharp, as too late the prying fingers felt.
What would you have? The fools transgress, the fools
Forthwith receive appropriate punishment: 1190
They first insult me, I return the blow!
There follows noise enough: four hubbub months,
Now hue and cry, now whimpering and wail—
A perfect goose-yard cackle of complaint
Because I do not gild the geese their oats—   1195
I have enough of noise, ope wicket wide,
Sweep out the couple to go whine elsewhere,
Frightened a little, hurt in no respect,
And am just taking thought to breathe again,
Taste the sweet sudden silence all about,   1200
When, there they raise it, the old noise I know,
At Rome i' the distance! "What, begun once more?
Whine on, wail ever, 'tis the loser's right!"
But eh, what sort of voice grows on the wind?
Triumph it sounds and no complaint at all!   1205
And triumph it is. My boast was premature:
The creatures, I turned forth, clapped wing and crew
Fighting-cock-fashion—they had filched a pearl
From dung-heap, and might boast with cause enough!
I was defrauded of all bargained for: 1210
You know, the Pope knows, not a soul but knows
My dowry was derision, my gain—muck,
My wife (the Church declared my flesh and blood)
The nameless bastard of a common whore:
My old name turned henceforth to . . . shall I say   1215
"He that received the ordure in his face?"
And they who planned this wrong, performed this
        wrong,
And then revealed this wrong to the wide world,
Rounded myself in the ears with my own wrong—
Why, these were (note hell's lucky malice, now!)   1220
These were just they who, they alone, could act
And publish and proclaim their infamy,
Secure that men would in a breath believe
Compassionate and pardon them—for why?
They plainly were too stupid to invent,   1225
Too simple to distinguish wrong from right—

Inconscious agents they, the silly-sooth,
Of heaven's retributive justice on the strong
Proud cunning violent oppressor—me!
1230 Follow them to their fate and help your best,
You Rome, Arezzo, foes called friends of me,
They gave the good long laugh to, at my cost!
Defray your share o' the cost, since you partook
The entertainment! Do!—assured the while,
1235 That not one stab, I dealt to right and left,
But went the deeper for a fancy—this—
That each might do me twofold service, find
A friend's face at the bottom of each wound,
And scratch its smirk a little!

                              Panciatichi!
1240 There's a report at Florence—is it true?—
That when your relative the Cardinal
Built, only the other day, that barrack-bulk,
The palace in Via Larga, someone picked
From out the street a saucy quip enough
1245 That fell there from its day's flight through the town,
About the flat front and the windows wide
And bulging heap of cornice—hitched the joke
Into a sonnet, signed his name thereto,
And forthwith pinned on post the pleasantry:
1250 For which he's at the galleys, rowing now
Up to his waist in water—just because
Panciatic and *lymphatic* rhymed so pat!
I hope, Sir, those who passed this joke on me
Were not unduly punished? What say you,
1255 Prince of the Church, my patron? Nay, indeed,
I shall not dare insult your wits so much
As think this problem difficult to solve.
This Pietro and Violante then, I say,
These two ambiguous insects, changing name
1260 And nature with the season's warmth or chill—
Now, groveled, grubbing toiling moiling ants,
A very synonym of thrift and peace—
Anon, with lusty June to prick their heart,
Soared i' the air, winged flies for more offense,

Circled me, buzzed me deaf and stung me blind,   1265
And stunk me dead with fetor° in the face
Until I stopped the nuisance: there's my crime!
Pity I did not suffer them subside
Into some further shape and final form
Of execrable life? My masters, no!   1270
I, by one blow, wisely cut short at once
Them and their transformations of disgust,
In the snug little villa out of hand.
"Grant me confession, give bare time for that!"—
Shouted the sinner till his mouth was stopped.   1275
His life confessed!—that was enough for me,
Who came to see that he did penance. 'S death!
Here's a coil raised, a pother and for what?
Because strength, being provoked by weakness, fought
And conquered—the world never heard the like!   1280
Pah, how I spend my breath on them, as if
'Twas their fate troubled me, too hard to range
Among the right and fit and proper things!

Ay, but Pompilia—I await your word—
She, unimpeached of crime, unimplicate   1285
In folly, one of alien blood to these
I punish, why extend my claim, exact
Her portion of the penalty? Yes, friends,
I go too fast: the orator's at fault:
Yes, ere I lay her, with your leave, by them   1290
As she was laid at San Lorenzo late,
I ought to step back, lead you by degrees,
Recounting at each step some fresh offense,
Up to the red bed—never fear, I will!
Gaze at her, where I place her, to begin,   1295
Confound me with her gentleness and worth!
The horrible pair have fled and left her now,
She has her husband for her sole concern:
His wife, the woman fashioned for his help,
Flesh of his flesh, bone of his bone, the bride   1300
To groom as is the Church and Spouse to Christ:

1266 fetor stench, "foulness."

There she stands in his presence: "Thy desire
Shall be to the husband, o'er thee shall he rule!"
—"Pompilia, who declare that you love God,
1305 You know who said that: then, desire my love,
Yield me contentment and be ruled aright!"
She sits up, she lies down, she comes and goes,
Kneels at the couch-side, overleans the sill
O' the window, cold and pale and mute as stone,
1310 Strong as stone also. "Well, are they not fled?
Am I not left, am I not one for all?
Speak a word, drop a tear, detach a glance,
Bless me or curse me of your own accord!
Is it the ceiling only wants your soul,
1315 Is worth your eyes?" And then the eyes descend,
And do look at me. Is it at the meal?
"Speak!" she obeys, "Be silent!" she obeys,
Counting the minutes till I cry "Depart,"
As brood-bird when you saunter past her eggs.
1320 Departs she? just the same through door and wall
I see the same stone strength of white despair.
And all this will be never otherwise!
Before, the parents' presence lent her life:
She could play off her sex's armory,
1325 Entreat, reproach, be female to my male,
Try all the shrieking doubles of the hare,
Go clamor to the Commissary,° bid
The Archbishop hold my hands and stop my tongue,
And yield fair sport so: but the tactics change,
1330 The hare stands stock-still to enrage the hound!
Since that day when she learned she was no child
Of those she thought her parents—that their trick
Had tricked me whom she thought sole trickster late—
Why, I suppose she said within herself
1335 "Then, no more struggle for my parents' sake!
And, for my own sake, why needs struggle be?"
But is there no third party to the pact?
What of her husband's relish or dislike

1327 **Commissary** "Governor" of Arezzo.

For this new game of giving up the game,
This worst offense of not offending more?   1340
I'll not believe but instinct wrought in this,
Set her on to conceive and execute
The preferable plague: how sure they probe—
These jades, the sensitivest soft of man!
The long black hair was wound now in a wisp,   1345
Crowned sorrow better than the wild web late:
No more soiled dress, 'tis trimness triumphs now,
For how should malice go with negligence?
The frayed silk looked the fresher for her spite!
There was an end to springing out of bed,   1350
Praying me, with face buried on my feet,
Be hindered of my pastime—so an end
To my rejoinder, "What, on the ground at last?
Vanquished in fight, a supplicant for life?
What if I raise you? 'Ware the casting down   1355
When next you fight me!" Then, she lay there, mine:
Now, mine she is if I please wring her neck—
A moment of disquiet, working eyes,
Protruding tongue, a long sigh, then no more—
As if one killed the horse one could not ride!   1360
Had I enjoined "Cut off the hair!"—why, snap
The scissors, and at once a yard or so
Had fluttered in black serpents to the floor:
But till I did enjoin it, how she combs,
Uncurls and draws out to the complete length,   1365
Plaits, places the insulting rope on head
To be an eyesore past dishevelment!
Is all done? Then sit still again and stare!
I advise—no one think to bear that look
Of steady wrong, endured as steadily   1370
—Through what sustainment of deluding hope?
Who is the friend i' the background that notes all?
Who may come presently and close accounts?
This self-possession to the uttermost,
How does it differ in aught, save degree,   1375
From the terrible patience of God?
                              "All which just means,
She did not love you!" Again the word is launched

And the fact fronts me! What, you try the wards°
With the true key and the dead lock flies ope?
1380 No, it sticks fast and leaves you fumbling still!
You have some fifty servants, Cardinal—
Which of them loves you? Which subordinate
But makes parade of such officiousness
That—if there's no love prompts it—love, the sham,
1385 Does twice the service done by love, the true?
God bless us liars, where's one touch of truth
In what we tell the world, or world tells us,
Of how we love each other? All the same,
We calculate on word and deed, nor err—
1390 Bid such a man do such a loving act,
Sure of effect and negligent of cause,
Just as we bid a horse, with cluck of tongue,
Stretch his legs arch-wise, crouch his saddled back
To foot-reach of the stirrup—all for love,
1395 And some for memory of the smart of switch
On the inside of the foreleg—what care we?
Yet where's the bond obliges horse to man
Like that which binds fast wife to husband? God
Laid down the law: gave man the brawny arm
1400 And ball of fist—woman the beardless cheek
And proper place to suffer in the side:
Since it is he can strike, let her obey!
Can she feel no love? Let her show the more,
Sham the worse, damn herself praiseworthily!
1405 Who's that soprano, Rome went mad about
Last week while I lay rotting in my straw?
The very jailer gossiped in his praise—
How—dressed up like Armida, though a man;
And painted to look pretty, though a fright—
1410 He still made love so that the ladies swooned,
Being a eunuch. "Ah, Rinaldo mine!
But to breathe by thee while Jove slays us both!"
All the poor bloodless creature never felt,
Si, do, re, mi, fa, squeak and squall—for what?
1415 Two gold zecchines the evening. Here's my slave,

1378 wards "fit" of a lock.

Whose body and soul depend upon my nod,
Can't falter out the first note in the scale
For her life! Why blame me if I take the life?
All women cannot give men love, forsooth!
No, nor all pullets lay the henwife eggs—   *1420*
Whereat she bids them remedy the fault,
Brood on a chalk-ball: soon the nest is stocked—
Otherwise, to the plucking and the spit!
This wife of mine was of another mood—
Would not begin the lie that ends with truth,   *1425*
Nor feign the love that brings real love about:
Wherefore I judged, sentenced and punished her.
But why particularize, defend the deed?
Say that I hated her for no one cause
Beyond my pleasure so to do—what then?   *1430*
Just on as much incitement acts the world,
All of you! Look and like! You favor one,
Browbeat another, leave alone a third—
Why should you master natural caprice?
Pure nature! Try: plant elm by ash in file;   *1435*
Both unexceptionable trees enough,
They ought to overlean each other, pair
At top, and arch across the avenue
The whole path to the pleasaunce: do they so—
Or loathe, lie off abhorrent each from each?   *1440*
Lay the fault elsewhere: since we must have faults,
Mine shall have been—seeing there's ill in the end
Come of my course—that I fare somehow worse
For the way I took: my fault . . . as God's my judge,
I see not where my fault lies, that's the truth!   *1445*
I ought . . . oh, ought in my own interest
Have let the whole adventure go untried,
This chance by marriage: or else, trying it,
Ought to have turned it to account, some one
O' the hundred otherwises? Ay, my friend,   *1450*
Easy to say, easy to do: step right
Now you've stepped left and stumbled on the thing,
—The red thing! Doubt I any more than you
That practice makes man perfect? Give again
The chance—same marriage and no other wife,   *1455*

Be sure I'll edify you! That's because
I'm practiced, grown fit guide for Guido's self.
You proffered guidance—I know, none so well—
You laid down law and rolled decorum out,
1460 From pulpit-corner on the gospel-side°—
Wanted to make your great experience mine,
Save me the personal search and pains so: thanks!
Take your word on life's use? When I take his—
The muzzled ox that treadeth out the corn,
1465 Gone blind in padding round and round one path—
As to the taste of green grass in the field!
What do you know o' the world that's trodden flat
And salted sterile with your daily dung,
Leavened into a lump of loathsomeness?
1470 Take your opinion of the modes of life,
The aims of life, life's triumph or defeat,
How to feel, how to scheme, and how to do
Or else leave undone? You preached long and loud
On high-days, "Take our doctrine upon trust!
1475 Into the mill-house with you! Grind our corn,
Relish our chaff, and let the green grass grow!"
I tried chaff, found I famished on such fare,
So made this mad rush at the mill-house-door,
Buried my head up to the ears in dew,
1480 Browsed on the best: for which you brain me, Sirs!
Be it so. I conceived of life that way,
And still declare—life, without absolute use
Of the actual sweet therein, is death, not life.
Give me—pay down—not promise, which is air—
1485 Something that's out of life and better still,
Make sure reward, make certain punishment,
Entice me, scare me—I'll forgo this life;
Otherwise, no!—the less that words, mere wind,
Would cheat me of some minutes while they plague,
1490 Balk fullness of revenge here—blame yourselves
For this eruption of the pent-up soul
You prisoned first and played with afterward!
"Deny myself" meant simply pleasure you,

1460 **gospel-side** left (where the gospel is read).

The sacred and superior, save the mark!
You—whose stupidity and insolence   *1495*
I must defer to, soothe at every turn—
Whose swine-like snuffling greed and grunting lust
I had to wink at or help gratify—
While the same passions—dared they perk in me,
Me, the immeasurably marked, by God,   *1500*
Master of the whole world of such as you—
I, boast such passions? 'Twas "Suppress them straight!
Or stay, we'll pick and choose before destroy.
Here's wrath in you, a serviceable sword—
Beat it into a ploughshare! What's this long   *1505*
Lance-like ambition? Forge a pruning hook,
May be of service when our vines grow tall!
But—sword use swordwise, spear thrust out as spear?
Anathema! Suppression is the word!"
My nature, when the outrage was too gross,   *1510*
Widened itself an outlet over-wide
By way of answer, sought its own relief
With more of fire and brimstone than you wished.
All your own doing: preachers, blame yourselves!

'Tis I preach while the hourglass runs and runs!   *1515*
God keep me patient! All I say just means—
My wife proved, whether by her fault or mine—
That's immaterial—a true stumbling block
I' the way of me her husband. I but plied
The hatchet yourselves use to clear a path,   *1520*
Was politic, played the game you warrant wins,
Plucked at law's robe a-rustle through the courts,
Bowed down to kiss divinity's buckled shoe
Cushioned i' the church: efforts all wide the aim!
Procedures to no purpose! Then flashed truth.   *1525*
The letter kills, the spirit keeps alive
In law and gospel: there be nods and winks
Instruct a wise man to assist himself
In certain matters, nor seek aid at all.
"Ask money of me"—quoth the clownish saw°—   *1530*

1530 **clownish saw** rustic saying.

"And take my purse! But—speaking with respect—
Need you a solace for the troubled nose?
Let everybody wipe his own himself!"
Sirs, tell me free and fair! Had things gone well
1535 At the wayside inn: had I surprised asleep
The runaways, as was so probable,
And pinned them each to other partridge-wise,
Through back and breast to breast and back, then
          bade
Bystanders witness if the spit, my sword,
1540 Were loaded with unlawful game for once—
Would you have interposed to damp the glow
Applauding me on every husband's cheek?
Would you have checked the cry "A judgment, see!
A warning, note! Be henceforth chaste, ye wives,
1545 Nor stray beyond your proper precinct, priests!"
If you had, then your house against itself
Divides, nor stands your kingdom any more.
Oh why, why was it not ordained just so?
Why fell not things out so nor otherwise?
1550 Ask that particular devil whose task it is
To trip the all-but-at perfection—slur
The line o' the painter just where paint leaves off
And life begins—put ice into the ode
O' the poet while he cries "Next stanza—fire!"
1555 Inscribe all human effort with one word,
Artistry's haunting curse, the Incomplete!
Being incomplete, my act escaped success.
Easy to blame now! Every fool can swear
To hole in net that held and slipped the fish.
1560 But, treat my act with fair unjaundiced eye,
What was there wanting to a masterpiece
Except the luck that lies beyond a man?
My way with the woman, now proved grossly wrong,
Just missed of being gravely grandly right
1565 And making mouths laugh on the other side.
Do, for the poor obstructed artist's sake,
Go with him over that spoiled work once more!
Take only its first flower, the ended act
Now in the dusty pod, dry and defunct!

I march to the villa, and my men with me,   1570
That evening, and we reach the door and stand.
I say . . . no, it shoots through me lightning-like
While I pause, breathe, my hand upon the latch,
"Let me forebode! Thus far, too much success:
I want the natural failure—find it where?   1575
Which thread will have to break and leave a loop
I' the meshy combination, my brain's loom
Wove this long while, and now next minute tests?
Of three that are to catch, two should go free,
One must: all three surprised—impossible!   1580
Beside, I seek three and may chance on six—
This neighbor, t'other gossip—the babe's birth
Brings such to fireside, and folks give them wine—
'Tis late: but when I break in presently
One will be found outlingering the rest   1585
For promise of a posset—one whose shout
Would raise the dead down in the catacombs,
Much more the city-watch that goes its round.
When did I ever turn adroitly up
To sun some brick embedded in the soil,   1590
And with one blow crush all three scorpions there?
Or Pietro or Violante shambles off—
It cannot be but I surprise my wife—
If only she is stopped and stamped on, good!
That shall suffice: more is improbable.   1595
Now I may knock!" And this once for my sake
The impossible was effected: I called king,
Queen and knave in a sequence, and cards came,
All three, three only! So, I had my way,
Did my deed: so, unbrokenly lay bare   1600
Each taenia° that had sucked me dry of juice,
At last outside me, not an inch of ring
Left now to writhe about and root itself
I' the heart all powerless for revenge! Henceforth
I might thrive: these were drawn and dead and
        damned.   1605
Oh Cardinal, the deep long sigh you heave

1601 **taenia** tapeworm.

When the load's off you, ringing as it runs
All the way down the serpent-stair to hell!
No doubt the fine delirium flustered me,
1610 Turned my brain with the influx of success
As if the sole need now were to wave wand
And find doors fly wide—wish and have my will—
The rest o' the scheme would care for itself: escape
Easy enough were that, and poor beside!
1615 It all but proved so—ought to quite have proved,
Since, half the chances had sufficed, set free
Anyone, with his senses at command,
From thrice the danger of my flight. But, drunk,
Redundantly triumphant—some reverse
1620 Was sure to follow! There's no other way
Accounts for such prompt perfect failure then
And there on the instant. Any day o' the week,
A ducat slid discreetly into palm
O' the mute postmaster, while you whisper him—
1625 How you the Count and certain four your knaves,
Have just been mauling who was malapert,
Suspect the kindred may prove troublesome,
Therefore, want horses in a hurry—that
And nothing more secures you any day
1630 The pick o' the stable! Yet I try the trick,
Double the bribe, call myself Duke for Count,
And say the dead man only was a Jew,
And for my pains find I am dealing just
With the one scrupulous fellow in all Rome—
1635 Just this immaculate official stares,
Sees I want hat on head and sword in sheath,
Am splashed with other sort of wet than wine,
Shrugs shoulder, puts my hand by, gold and all,
Stands on the strictness of the rule o' the road!
1640 "Where's the permission?" Where's the wretched rag
With the due seal and sign of Rome's Police,
To be had for asking, half-an-hour ago?
"Gone? Get another, or no horses hence!"
He dares not stop me, we five glare too grim,
1645 But hinders—hacks and hamstrings sure enough,
Gives me some twenty miles of miry road

More to march in the middle of that night
Whereof the rough beginning taxed the strength
O' the youngsters, much more mine, both soul and
    flesh,
Who had to think as well as act: dead beat, 1650
We gave in ere we reached the boundary
And safe spot out of this irrational Rome—
Where, on dismounting from our steeds next day,
We had snapped our fingers at you, safe and sound,
Tuscans once more in blessed Tuscany, 1655
Where laws make wise allowance, understand
Civilized life and do its champions right!
Witness the sentence of the Rota there,
Arezzo uttered, the Granduke confirmed,
One week before I acted on its hint— 1660
Giving friend Guillichini, for his love,
The galleys, and my wife your saint, Rome's saint—
Rome manufactures saints enough to know—
Seclusion at the Stinche° for her life.
All this, that all but was, might all have been, 1665
Yet was not! balked by just a scrupulous knave
Whose palm was horn through handling horses' hoofs
And could not close upon my proffered gold!
What say you to the spite of fortune? Well,
The worst's in store: thus hindered, haled this way 1670
To Rome again by hangdogs, whom find I
Here, still to fight with, but my pale frail wife?
—Riddled with wounds by one not like to waste
The blows he dealt—knowing anatomy—
I think I told you) bound to pick and choose 1675
The vital parts! 'Twas learning all in vain!
She too must shimmer through the gloom o' the grave,
Come and confront me—not at judgment-seat
Where I could twist her soul, as erst her flesh,
And turn her truth into a lie—but there, 1680
O' the deathbed, with God's hand between us both,
Striking me dumb, and helping her to speak,
Tell her own story her own way, and turn

664 **Stinche** prison.

　　　　My plausibility to nothingness!
1685　Four whole days did Pompilia keep alive,
　　　　With the best surgery of Rome agape
　　　　At the miracle—this cut, the other slash,
　　　　And yet the life refusing to dislodge,
　　　　Four whole extravagant impossible days,
1690　Till she had time to finish and persuade
　　　　Every man, every woman, every child
　　　　In Rome, of what she would: the selfsame she
　　　　Who, but a year ago, had wrung her hands,
　　　　Reddened her eyes and beat her breasts, rehearsed
1695　The whole game at Arezzo, nor availed
　　　　Thereby to move one heart or raise one hand!
　　　　When destiny intends you cards like these,
　　　　What good of skill and preconcerted play?
　　　　Had she been found dead, as I left her dead,
1700　I should have told a tale brooked no reply:
　　　　You scarcely will suppose me found at fault
　　　　With that advantage! "What brings me to Rome?
　　　　Necessity to claim and take my wife:
　　　　Better, to claim and take my new born babe—
1705　Strong in paternity a fortnight old,
　　　　When 'tis at strongest: warily I work,
　　　　Knowing the machinations of my foe;
　　　　I have companionship and use the night:
　　　　I seek my wife and child—I find—no child
1710　But wife, in the embraces of that priest
　　　　Who caused her to elope from me. These two,
　　　　Backed by the pander-pair who watch the while,
　　　　Spring on me like so many tiger-cats,
　　　　Glad of the chance to end the intruder. I—
1715　What should I do but stand on my defense,
　　　　Strike right, strike left, strike thick and threefold, slay,
　　　　Not all—because the coward priest escapes.
　　　　Last, I escape, in fear of evil tongues,
　　　　And having had my taste of Roman law."
1720　What's disputable, refutable here?—
　　　　Save by just this one ghost-thing half on earth,
　　　　Half out of it—as if she held God's hand

While she leaned back and looked her last at me,
Forgiving me (here monks begin to weep)
Oh, from her very soul, commending mine 1725
To heavenly mercies which are infinite—
While fixing fast my head beneath your knife!
'Tis fate not fortune. All is of a piece!
When was it chance informed me of my youths?
My rustic four o' the family, soft swains, 1730
What sweet surprise had they in store for me,
Those of my very household—what did Law
Twist with her rack-and-cord-contrivance late
From out their bones and marrow? What but this—
Had no one of these several stumbling blocks 1735
Stopped me, they yet were cherishing a scheme,
All of their honest country homespun wit,
To quietly next day at crow of cock
Cut my own throat too, for their own behoof,
Seeing I had forgot to clear accounts 1740
O' the instant, nowise slackened speed for that—
And somehow never might find memory,
Once safe back in Arezzo, where things change,
And a court-lord needs mind no country lout.
Well, being the arch-offender, I die last— 1745
May, ere my head falls, have my eyesight free,
Nor miss them dangling high on either hand,
Like scarecrows in a hemp-field, for their pains!

And then my trial—'tis my trial that bites
Like a corrosive, so the cards are packed, 1750
Dice loaded, and my life-stake tricked away!
Look at my lawyers, lacked they grace of law,
Latin or logic? Were not they fools to the height,
Fools to the depth, fools to the level between,
O' the foolishness set to decide the case? 1755
They feign, they flatter; nowise does it skill,
Everything goes against me: deal each judge
His dole of flattery and feigning—why,
He turns and tries and snuffs and savors it,
As some old fly the sugar-grain, your gift; 1760

Then eyes your thumb and finger, brushes clean
The absurd old head of him, and whisks away,
Leaving your thumb and finger dirty. Faugh!

And finally, after this long-drawn range
1765 Of affront and failure, failure and affront—
This path, 'twixt crosses leading to a skull,°
Paced by me barefoot, bloodied by my palms
From the entry to the end—there's light at length,
A cranny of escape: appeal may be
1770 To the old man, to the father, to the Pope,
For a little life—from one whose life is spent,
A little pity—from pity's source and seat,
A little indulgence to rank, privilege,
From one who is the thing personified,
1775 Rank, privilege, indulgence, grown beyond
Earth's bearing, even, ask Jansenius° else!
Still the same answer, still no other tune
From the cicala perched at the treetop
Than crickets noisy round the root: 'tis "Die!"
1780 Bids Law—"Be damned!" adds Gospel—nay,
No word so frank—'tis rather, "Save yourself!"
The Pope subjoins—"Confess and be absolved!
So shall my credit countervail your shame,
And the world see I have not lost the knack
1785 Of trying all the spirits: yours, my son,
Wants but a fiery washing to emerge
In clarity! Come, cleanse you, ease the ache
Of these old bones, refresh our bowels, boy!"
Do I mistake your mission from the Pope?
1790 Then, bear his Holiness the mind of me!
I do get strength from being thrust to wall,
Successively wrenched from pillar and from post
By this tenacious hate of fortune, hate
Of all things in, under, and above earth.
1795 Warfare, begun this mean unmanly mode,
Does best to end so—gives earth spectacle
Of a brave fighter who succumbs to odds

1766 **path . . . skull** ascent of Golgotha.   1776 **Jansenius** Catholic
puritan reformer, condemned by the Church.

That turn defeat to victory. Stab, I fold
My mantle round me! Rome approves my act:
Applauds the blow which costs me life but keeps   1800
My honor spotless: Rome would praise no more
Had I fallen, say, some fifteen years ago,
Helping Vienna when our Aretines
Flocked to Duke Charles and fought Turk Mustafa;
Nor would you two be trembling o'er my corpse   1805
With all this exquisite solicitude.
Why is it that I make such suit to live?
The popular sympathy that's round me now
Would break like bubble that o'er-domes a fly:
Solid enough while he lies quiet there,   1810
But let him want the air and ply the wing,
Why, it breaks and bespatters him, what else?
Cardinal, if the Pope had pardoned me,
And I walked out of prison through the crowd,
It would not be your arm I should dare press!   1815
Then, if I got safe to my place again,
How sad and sapless were the years to come!
I go my old ways and find things grown gray;
You priests leer at me, old friends look askance,
The mob's in love, I'll wager, to a man,   1820
With my poor young good beauteous murdered wife:
For hearts require instruction how to beat,
And eyes, on warrant of the story, wax
Wanton at portraiture in white and black
Of dead Pompilia gracing ballad-sheet,   1825
Which eyes, lived she unmurdered and unsung,
Would never turn though she paced street as bare
As the mad penitent ladies do in France.
My brothers quietly would edge me out
Of use and management of things called mine;   1830
Do I command? "You stretched command before!"
Show anger? "Anger little helped you once!"
Advise? "How managed you affairs of old?"
My very mother, all the while they gird,
Turns eye up, gives confirmatory groan;   1835
For unsuccess, explain it how you will,
Disqualifies you, makes you doubt yourself,

—Much more, is found decisive by your friends.
Beside, am I not fifty years of age?
1840 What new leap would a life take, checked like mine
I' the spring at outset? Where's my second chance?
Ay, but the babe ... I had forgot my son,
My heir! Now for a burst of gratitude!
There's some appropriate service to intone,
1845 Some *gaudeamus*° and thanksgiving-psalm!
Old, I renew my youth in him, and poor
Possess a treasure—is not that the phrase?
Only I must wait patient twenty years—
Nourishing all the while, as father ought,
1850 The excrescence with my daily blood of life.
Does it respond to hope, such sacrifice—
Grows the wen plump while I myself grow lean?
Why, here's my son and heir in evidence,
Who stronger, wiser, handsomer than I
1855 By fifty years, relieves me of each load—
Tames my hot horse, carries my heavy gun,
Courts my coy mistress—has his apt advice
On house-economy, expenditure,
And what not. All which good gifts and great growth
1860 Because of my decline, he brings to bear
On Guido, but half apprehensive how
He cumbers earth, crosses the brisk young Count,
Who civilly would thrust him from the scene.
Contrariwise, does the blood-offering fail?
1865 There's an ineptitude, one blank the more
Added to earth in semblance of my child?
Then, this has been a costly piece of work,
My life exchanged for his!—why he, not I,
Enjoy the world, if no more grace accrue?
1870 Dwarf me, what giant have you made of him?
I do not dread the disobedient son:
I know how to suppress rebellion there,
Being not quite the fool my father was.
But grant the medium measure of a man,
1875 The usual compromise 'twixt fool and sage,

1845 **gaudeamus** let us rejoice.

—You know—the tolerably-obstinate,
The not-so-much-perverse but you may train,
The true son-servant that, when parent bids
"Go work, son, in my vineyard!" makes reply
"I go, Sir!"—Why, what profit in your son   *1880*
Beyond the drudges you might subsidize,
Have the same work from, at a paul the head?
Look at those four young precious olive-plants
Reared at Vittiano—not on flesh and blood,
These twenty years, but black bread and sour wine! *1885*
I bade them put forth tender branch, hook, hold,
And hurt three enemies I had in Rome:
They did my hest as unreluctantly,
At promise of a dollar, as a son
Adjured by mumping memories of the past.   *1890*
No, nothing repays youth expended so—
Youth, I say, who am young still: grant but leave
To live my life out, to the last I'd live
And die conceding age no right of youth!
It is the will runs the renewing nerve   *1895*
Through flaccid flesh that faints before the time.
Therefore no sort of use for son have I—
Sick, not of life's feast but of steps to climb
To the house where life prepares her feast—of means
To the end: for make the end attainable   *1900*
Without the means—my relish were like yours.
A man may have an appetite enough
For a whole dish of robins ready cooked,
And yet lack courage to face sleet, pad snow,
And snare sufficiently for supper.

                              Thus   *1905*
The time's arrived when, ancient Roman-like,
I am bound to fall on my own sword: why not
Say—Tuscan-like, more ancient, better still?
Will you hear truth can do no harm nor good?
I think I never was at any time   *1910*
A Christian, as you nickname all the world,
Me among others: truce to nonsense now!
Name me, a primitive religionist—

As should the aboriginary be
1915 I boast myself, Etruscan, Aretine,
One sprung—your frigid Virgil's fieriest word—
From fauns and nymphs, trunks and the heart of oak,
With—for a visible divinity—
The portent of a Jove Aegiochus
1920 Descried 'mid clouds, lightning and thunder, couched
On topmost crag of your Capitoline:
'Tis in the Seventh Aeneid—wat, the Eighth?°
Right—thanks, Abate—though the Christian's dumb,
The Latinist's vivacious in you yet!
1925 I know my grandsire had our tapestry
Marked with the motto, 'neath a certain shield,
Whereto his grandson presently will give gules°
To vary azure. First we fight for faiths,
But get to shake hands at the last of all:
1930 Mine's your faith too—in Jove Aegiochus!
Nor do Greek gods, that serve as supplement,
Jar with the simpler scheme, if understood.
We want such intermediary race
To make communication possible;
1935 The real thing were too lofty, we too low,
Midway hang these: we feel their use so plain
In linking height to depth, that we doff hat
And put no question nor pry narrowly
Into the nature hid behind the names.
1940 We grudge no rite the fancy may demand;
But never, more than needs, invent, refine,
Improve upon requirement, idly wise
Beyond the letter, teaching gods their trade,
Which is to teach us: we'll obey when taught.
1945 Why should we do our duty past the need?
When the sky darkens, Jove is wroth—say prayer!
When the sun shines and Jove is glad—sing psalm!
But wherefore pass prescription and devise
Blood-offering for sweat-service, lend the rod
1950 A pungency through pickle of our own?
Learned Abate—no one teaches you

1916–22 **Virgil . . . Eighth** *Aeneid* VIII 314–15; 351–54. 1927 **gules**
red (in heraldry).

What Venus means and who's Apollo here!
I spare you, Cardinal—but, though you wince,
You know me, I know you, and both know that!
So, if Apollo bids us fast, we fast: 1955
But where does Venus order we stop sense
When Master Pietro rhymes a pleasantry?
Give alms prescribed on Friday: but, hold hand
Because your foe lies prostrate—where's the word
Explicit in the book debars revenge?   1960
The rationale of your scheme is just
"Pay toll here, there pursue your pleasure free!"
So do you turn to use the medium-powers,
Mars and Minerva, Bacchus and the rest,
And so are saved propitiating—whom?   1965
What all-good, all-wise and all-potent Jove
Vexed by the very sins in man, himself
Made life's necessity when man he made?
Irrational bunglers! So, the living truth
Revealed to strike Pan dead, ducks low at last,   1970
Prays leave to hold its own and live good days
Provided it go masque grotesquely, called
Christian not Pagan. Oh, you purged the sky
Of all gods save the One, the great and good,
Clapped hands and triumphed! But the change came
      fast: 1975
The inexorable need in man for life—
(Life, you may mulct and minish to a grain
Out of the lump, so that the grain but live)
Laughed at your substituting death for life,
And bade you do your worst: which worst was done 1980
In just that age styled primitive and pure
When Saint this, Saint that, dutifully starved,
Froze, fought with beasts, was beaten and abused
And finally ridded of his flesh by fire:
He kept life-long unspotted from the world!   1985
Next age, how goes the game, what mortal gives
His life and emulates Saint that, Saint this?
Men mutter, make excuse or mutiny,
In fine are minded all to leave the new,
Stick to the old—enjoy old liberty,   1990

No prejudice in enjoyment, if you please,
To the new profession: sin o' the sly, henceforth!
The law stands though the letter kills: what then?
The spirit saves as unmistakably.
1995 Omniscience sees, Omnipotence could stop,
Omnibenevolence pardons: it must be,
Frown law its fiercest, there's a wink somewhere!

Such was the logic in this head of mine:
I, like the rest, wrote "poison" on my bread,
2000 But broke and ate:—said "Those that use the sword
Shall perish by the same"; then stabbed my foe.
I stand on solid earth, not empty air:
Dislodge me, let your Pope's crook hale me hence!
Not he, nor you! And I so pity both,
2005 I'll make the true charge you want wit to make:
"Count Guido, who reveal our mystery,
And trace all issues to the love of life,
We having life to love and guard, like you,
Why did you put us upon self-defense?
2010 You well knew what prompt password would appease
The sentry's ire when folk infringed his bounds,
And yet kept mouth shut: do you wonder then
If, in mere decency, he shot you dead?
He can't have people play such pranks as yours
2015 Beneath his nose at noonday: you disdained
To give him an excuse before the world
By crying 'I break rule to save our camp!'
Under the old rule, such offense were death;
And you had heard the Pontifex° pronounce
2020 'Since you slay foe and violate the form,
Slaying turns murder, which were sacrifice
Had you, while, say, law-suiting foe to death,
But raised an altar to the Unknown God
Or else the Genius of the Vatican.'
2025 Why then this pother?—all because the Pope,
Doing his duty, cried 'A foreigner,
You scandalize the natives: here at Rome

2019 **Pontifex** high priest of Rome (title taken over by the pope).

Romano vivitur more:° wise men, here,
Put the Church forward and efface themselves.
The fit defense had been—you stamped on wheat,   2030
Intending all the time to trample tares—
Were fain extirpate, then, the heretic,
You now find, in your haste was slain a fool:
Nor Pietro, nor Violante, nor your wife
Meant to breed up your babe a Molinist!   2035
Whence you are duly contrite. Not one word
Of all this wisdom did you urge: which slip
Death must atone for.' "

                So, let death atone!
So ends mistake, so end mistakers!—end
Perhaps to recommence—how should I know?   2040
Only, be sure, no punishment, no pain
Childish, preposterous, impossible,
But some such fate as Ovid could foresee—
Byblis in fluvium, let the weak soul end
In water, *sed Lycaon in lupum,* but   2045
The strong become a wolf for evermore!°
Change that Pompilia to a puny stream
Fit to reflect the daisies on its bank!
Let me turn wolf, be whole, and sate, for once—
Wallow in what is now a wolfishness   2050
Coerced too much by the humanity
That's half of me as well! Grow out of man,
Glut the wolf-nature—what remains but grow
Into the man again, be man indeed
And all man? Do I ring the changes right?   2055
Deformed, transformed, reformed, informed, con-
    formed!
The honest instinct, pent and crossed through life,
Let surge by death into a visible flow
Of rapture: as the strangled thread of flame
Painfully winds, annoying and annoyed,   2060
Malignant and maligned, through stone and ore,
Till earth exclude the stranger: vented once,

2028 **Romano vivitur more** do as the Romans do.   2043–46 **Ovid
. . . evermore** stories in the *Metamorphoses*. The delicate Byblis was
turned into a fountain, the fierce Lycaon into a wolf.

It finds full play, is recognized atop
Some mountain as no such abnormal birth,
2065 Fire for the mount, not streamlet for the vale!
Ay, of the water was that wife of mine—
Be it for good, be it for ill, no run
O' the red thread through that insignificance!
Again, how she is at me with those eyes!
2070 Away with the empty stare! Be holy still,
And stupid ever! Occupy your patch
Of private snow that's somewhere in what world
May now be growing icy round your head,
And aguish at your footprint—freeze not me,
2075 Dare follow not another step I take,
Not with so much as those detested eyes,
No, though they follow but to pray me pause
On the incline, earth's edge that's next to hell!
None of your abnegation of revenge!
2080 Fly at me frank, tug while I tear again!
There's God, go tell Him, testify your worst!
Not she! There was no touch in her of hate:
And it would prove her hell, if I reached mine!
To know I suffered, would still sadden her,
2085 Do what the angels might to make amends!
Therefore there's either no such place as hell,
Or thence shall I be thrust forth, for her sake,
And thereby undergo three hells, not one—
I who, with outlet for escape to Heaven,
2090 Would tarry if such flight allowed my foe
To raise his head, relieved of that firm foot
Had pinned him to the fiery pavement else!
So am I made, "who did not make myself":
(How dared she rob my own lip of the word?)
2095 Beware me in what other world may be!—
Pompilia, who have brought me to this pass!
All I know here, will I say there, and go
Beyond the saying with the deed. Some use
There cannot but be for a mood like mine,
2100 Implacable, persistent in revenge.
She maundered "All is over and at end:
I go my own road, go you where God will!

Forgive you? I forget you!" There's the saint
That takes your taste, you other kind of men!
How you had loved her! Guido wanted skill   2105
To value such a woman at her worth!
Properly the instructed criticize
"What's here, you simpleton have tossed to take
Its chance i' the gutter? This a daub, indeed?
Why, 'tis a Raphael that you kicked to rags!"   2110
Perhaps so: some prefer the pure design:
Give me my gorge of color, glut of gold
In a glory round the Virgin made for me!
Titian's the man, not Monk Angelico
Who traces you some timid chalky ghost   2115
That turns the church into a charnel: ay,
Just such a pencil might depict my wife!
She—since she, also, would not change herself—
Why could not she come in some heart-shaped cloud,
Rainbowed about with riches, royalty   2120
Rimming her round, as round the tintless lawn°
Guardingly runs the selvage° cloth of gold?
I would have left the faint fine gauze untouched,
Needle-worked over with its lily and rose,
Let her bleach unmolested in the midst,   2125
Chill that selected solitary spot
Of quietude she pleased to think was life.
Purity, pallor grace the lawn no doubt
When there's the costly bordure to unthread
And make again an ingot: but what's grace   2130
When you want meat and drink and clothes and fire?
A tale comes to my mind that's apposite—
Possibly true, probably false, a truth
Such as all truths we live by, Cardinal!
'Tis said, a certain ancestor of mine   2135
Followed—whoever was the potentate,
To Paynimrie, and in some battle, broke
Through more than due allowance of the foe,
And, risking much his own life, saved the lord's.
Battered and bruised, the Emperor scrambles up,   2140

2121 **lawn** fine linen (used for bishop's sleeves). 2122 **selvage**
edging.

Rubs his eyes and looks round and sees my sire,
Picks a furze-sprig from out his hauberk-joint,
(Token how near the ground went majesty)
And says "Take this, and if thou get safe home,
2145 Plant the same in thy garden-ground to grow:
   Run thence an hour in a straight line, and stop:
Describe a circle round (for central point)
The furze aforesaid, reaching every way
The length of that hour's run: I give it thee—
2150 The central point, to build a castle there,
The space circumjacent, for fit demesne,
The whole to be thy children's heritage—
Whom, for thy sake, bid thou wear furze on cap!"
Those are my arms: we turned the furze a tree
2155 To show more, and the greyhound tied thereto,
Straining to start, means swift and greedy both;
He stands upon a triple mount of gold—
By Jove, then, he's escaping from true gold
And trying to arrive at empty air!
2160 Aha! the fancy never crossed my mind!
My father used to tell me, and subjoin
"As for the castle, that took wings and flew:
The broad lands—why, to traverse them today
Scarce tasks my gouty feet, and in my prime
2165 I doubt not I could stand and spit so far:
But for the furze, boy, fear no lack of that,
So long as fortune leaves one field to grub!
Wherefore, hurra for furze and loyalty!"
What may I mean, where may the lesson lurk?
2170 "Do not bestow on man, by way of gift,
Furze without land for framework—vaunt no grace
Of purity, no furze-sprig of a wife,
To me, i' the thick of battle for my bread,
Without some better dowry—gold will do!"
2175 No better gift than sordid muck? Yes, Sirs!
Many more gifts much better. Give them me!
O those Olimpias bold, those Biancas brave,
That brought a husband power worth Ormuz' wealth!
Cried "Thou being mine, why, what but thine am I?
2180 Be thou to me law, right, wrong, heaven and hell!

Let us blend souls, blent, thou in me, to bid
Two bodies work one pleasure! What are these
Called king, priest, father, mother, stranger, friend?
They fret thee or they frustrate? Give the word—
Be certain they shall frustrate nothing more!   2185
And who is this young florid foolishness
That holds thy fortune in his pigmy clutch,
—Being a prince and potency, forsooth!—
He hesitates to let the trifle go?
Let me but seal up eye, sing ear to sleep   2190
Sounder than Samson—pounce thou on the prize
Shall slip from off my breast, and down couchside,
And on to floor, and far as my lord's feet—
Where he stands in the shadow with the knife,
Waiting to see what Delilah dares do!   2195
Is the youth fair? What is a man to me
Who am thy call-bird?° Twist his neck—my dupe's—
Then take the breast shall turn a breast indeed!"
Such women are there; and they marry whom?
Why, when a man has gone and hanged himself   2200
Because of what he calls a wicked wife—
See, if the very turpitude bemoaned
Prove not mere excellence the fool ignores!
His monster is perfection—Circe,° sent
Straight from the sun, with wand the idiot blames   2205
As not an honest distaff to spin wool!
O thou Lucrezia,° is it long to wait
Yonder where all the gloom is in a glow
With thy suspected presence?—virgin yet,
Virtuous again, in face of what's to teach—   2210
Sin unimagined, unimaginable—
I come to claim my bride—thy Borgia's self
Not half the burning bridegroom I shall be!
Cardinal, take away your crucifix!
Abate, leave my lips alone—they bite!   2215
Vainly you try to change what should not change,
And shall not. I have bared, you bathe my heart—

2197 **call-bird** decoy. 2204 **Circe** daughter of the sun-god, sorceress
and temptress of the *Odyssey*. 2207 **Lucrezia** sister and, it was
said, the lover of *Cesare Borgia*.

It grows the stonier for your saving dew!
You steep the substance, you would lubricate,
2220 In waters that but touch to petrify!

You too are petrifactions of a kind:
Move not a muscle that shows mercy. Rave
Another twelve hours, every word were waste!
I thought you would not slay impenitence,
2225 But teased, from men you slew, contrition first—
I thought you had a conscience. Cardinal,
You know I am wronged!—wronged, say, and
          wronged, maintain.
Was this strict inquisition made for blood
When first you showed us scarlet on your back,
2230 Called to the College? Your straightforward way
To your legitimate end—I think it passed
Over a scantling of heads brained, hearts broke,
Lives trodden into dust! How otherwise?
Such was the way o' the world, and so you walked.
2235 Does memory haunt your pillow? Not a whit.
God wills you never pace your garden-path,
One appetizing hour ere dinner-time,
But your intrusion there treads out of life
A universe of happy innocent things:
2240 Feel you remorse about that damsel-fly
Which buzzed so near your mouth and flapped your
          face?
You blotted it from being at a blow:
It was a fly, you were a man, and more,
Lord of created things, so took your course.
2245 Manliness, mind—these are things fit to save,
Fit to brush fly from: why, because I take
My course, must needs the Pope kill me?—kill you!
You! for this instrument, he throws away,
Is strong to serve a master, and were yours
2250 To have and hold and get much good from out!
The Pope who dooms me needs must die next year;
I'll tell you how the chances are supposed
For his successor: first the Chamberlain,
Old San Cesario—Colloredo, next—

Then, one, two, three, four, I refuse to name;   2255
After these, comes Altieri; then come you—
Seventh on the list you come, unless . . . ha, ha,
How can a dead hand give a friend a lift?
Are you the person to despise the help
O' the head shall drop in pannier presently?   2260
So a child seesaws on or kicks away
The fulcrum-stone that's all the sage requires
To fit his lever to and move the world.
Cardinal, I adjure you in God's name,
Save my life, fall at the Pope's feet, set forth   2265
Things your own fashion, not in words like these
Made for a sense like yours who apprehend!
Translate into the Court-conventional
"Count Guido must not die, is innocent!
Fair, be assured! But what an he were foul,   2270
Blood-drenched and murder-crusted head to foot?
Spare one whose death insults the Emperor,
Nay, outrages the Louis you so love!
He has friends who will avenge him; enemies
Who will hate God now with impunity,   2275
Missing the old coercive: would you send
A soul straight to perdition, dying frank
An atheist?" Go and say this, for God's sake!
—Why, you don't think I hope you'll say one word?
Neither shall I persuade you from your stand   2280
Nor you persuade me from my station: take
Your crucifix away, I tell you twice!

Come, I am tired of silence! Pause enough!
You have prayed: I have gone inside my soul
And shut its door behind me: 'tis your torch   2285
Makes the place dark: the darkness let alone
Grows tolerable twilight: one may grope
And get to guess at length and breadth and depth.
What is this fact I feel persuaded of—
This something like a foothold in the sea,   2290
Although Saint Peter's bark scuds, billow-borne,
Leaves me to founder where it flung me first?
Spite of your splashing, I am high and dry!

God takes his own part in each thing He made;
2295 Made for a reason, He conserves his work,
Gives each its proper instinct of defense.
My lamblike wife could neither bark nor bite,
She bleated, bleated, till for pity pure
The village roused up, ran with pole and prong
2300 To the rescue, and behold the wolf's at bay!
Shall he try bleating?—or take turn or two,
Since the wolf owns some kinship with the fox,
And, failing to escape the foe by craft,
Give up attempt, die fighting quietly?
2305 The last bad blow that strikes fire in at eye
And on to brain, and so out, life and all,
How can it but be cheated of a pang
If, fighting quietly, the jaws enjoy
One re-embrace in mid backbone they break,
2310 After their weary work through the foe's flesh?
That's the wolf-nature. Don't mistake my trope!
A Cardinal so qualmish? Eminence,
My fight is figurative, blows i' the air,
Brain-war with powers and principalities,
2315 Spirit-bravado, no real fisticuffs!
I shall not presently, when the knock comes,
Cling to this bench nor claw the hangman's face,
No, trust me! I conceive worse lots than mine.
Whether it be, the old contagious fit
2320 And plague o' the prison have surprised me too,
The appropriate drunkenness of the death-hour
Crept on my sense, kind work o' the wine and
    myrrh°—
I know not—I begin to taste my strength,
Careless, gay even. What's the worth of life?
2325 The Pope's dead now, my murderous old man,
For Tozzi told me so: and you, forsooth—
Why, you don't think, Abate, do your best,
You'll live a year more with that hacking cough
And blotch of crimson where the cheek's a pit?
2330 Tozzi has got you also down in book!

2322 **wine and myrrh** Mark 15:23. Given to deaden pain.

Cardinal, only seventh of seventy near,
Is not one called Albano in the lot?
Go eat your heart, you'll never be a Pope!
Inform me, is it true you left your love,
A Pucci, for promotion in the church?   *2335*
She's more than in the church—in the churchyard!
Plautilla Pucci, your affianced bride,
Has dust now in the eyes that held the love—
And Martinez, suppose they make you Pope,
Stops that with *veto*°—so, enjoy yourself!   *2340*
I see you all reel to the rock, you waves—
Some forthright, some describe a sinuous track,
Some, crested brilliantly, with heads above,
Some in a strangled swirl sunk who knows how,
But all bound whither the main-current sets,   *2345*
Rockward, an end in foam for all of you!
What if I be o'ertaken, pushed to the front
By all you crowding smoother souls behind,
And reach, a minute sooner than was meant,
The boundary whereon I break to mist?   *2350*
Go to! the smoothest safest of you all,
Most perfect and compact wave in my train,
Spite of the blue tranquillity above,
Spite of the breadth before of lapsing peace
Where broods the halcyon and the fish leaps free,   *2355*
Will presently begin to feel the prick
At lazy heart, the push at torpid brain,
Will rock vertiginously in turn, and reel,
And, emulative, rush to death like me.
Later or sooner by a minute then,   *2360*
So much for the untimeliness of death!
And, as regards the manner that offends,
The rude and rough, I count the same for gain.
Be the act harsh and quick! Undoubtedly
The soul's condensed and, twice itself, expands   *2365*
To burst through life, by alternation due,
Into the other state whate'er it prove.
You never know what life means till you die:

2339–40 **Martinez . . . veto** minister of the emperor, who had veto
power over papal elections.

Even throughout life, 'tis death that makes life live,
2370 Gives it whatever the significance.
For see, on your own ground and argument,
Suppose life had no death to fear, how find
A possibility of nobleness
In man, prevented daring any more?
2375 What's love, what's faith without a worst to dread?
Lackluster jewelry! but faith and love
With death behind them bidding do or die—
Put such a foil at back, the sparkle's born!
From out myself how the strange colors come!
2380 Is there a new rule in another world?
Be sure I shall resign myself: as here
I recognized no law I could not see,
There, what I see, I shall acknowledge too:
On earth I never took the Pope for God,
2385 In Heaven I shall scarce take God for the Pope.
Unmanned, remanned: I hold it probable—
With something changeless at the heart of me
To know me by, some nucleus that's myself:
Accretions did it wrong? Away with them—
You soon shall see the use of fire!

2390   Till when,
All that was, is; and must forever be.
Nor is it in me to unhate my hates—
I use up my last strength to strike once more
Old Pietro in the wine-house-gossip-face,
2395 To trample underfoot the whine and wile
Of beast Violante—and I grow one gorge
To loathingly reject Pompilia's pale
Poison my hasty hunger took for food.
A strong tree wants no wreaths about its trunk,
2400 No cloying cups, no sickly sweet of scent,
But sustenance at root, a bucketful.
How else lived that Athenian who died so,
Drinking hot bull's blood, fit for men like me?
I lived and died a man, and take man's chance,
2405 Honest and bold: right will be done to such.

Who are these you have let descend my stair?
Ha, their accursed psalm! Lights at the sill!
Is it "Open" they dare bid you? Treachery!
Sirs, have I spoken one word all this while
Out of the world of words I had to say?   *2410*
Not one word! All was folly—I laughed and mocked!
Sirs, my first true word, all truth and no lie,
Is—save me notwithstanding! Life is all!
I was just stark mad—let the madman live
Pressed by as many chains as you please pile!   *2415*
Don't open! Hold me from them! I am yours,
I am° the Granduke's—no, I am the Pope's!
Abate—Cardinal—Christ—Maria—God, . . .
Pompilia, will you let them murder me?

2417 **am** in jurisdiction.

from *FIFINE AT THE FAIR*

(1872)

AMPHIBIAN°

I

THE fancy I had today,
    Fancy which turned a fear!
I swam far out in the bay,
    Since waves laughed warm and clear.

II

I lay and looked at the sun,   5
    The noon-sun looked at me:
Between us two, no one
    Live creature, that I could see.

III

Yes! There came floating by
    Me, who lay floating too.   10
Such a strange butterfly!
    Creature as dear as new:

Amphibian prologue to *Fifine at the Fair*.

IV

Because the membraned wings
    So wonderful, so wide,
15 So sun-suffused, were things
    Like soul and naught beside.

V

A handbreadth over head!
    All of the sea my own,
It owned the sky instead;
20   Both of us were alone.

VI

I never shall join its flight,
    For, naught buoys flesh in air.
If it touch the sea—good night!
    Death sure and swift waits there.

VII

25 Can the insect feel the better
    For watching the uncouth play
Of limbs that slip the fetter,
    Pretend as they were not clay?

VIII

Undoubtedly I rejoice
30   That the air comports so well
With a creature which had the choice
    Of the land once. Who can tell?

IX

What if a certain soul
    Which early slipped its sheath,

And has for its home the whole
   Of Heaven, thus look beneath,   35

X

Thus watch one who, in the world,
   Both lives and likes life's way,
Nor wishes the wings unfurled
   That sleep in the worm, they say?   40

XI

But sometimes when the weather
   Is blue, and warm waves tempt
To free oneself of tether,
   And try a life exempt

XII

From worldly noise and dust,   45
   In the sphere which overbrims
With passion and thought—why, just
   Unable to fly, one swims!

XIII

By passion and thought upborne,
   One smiles to oneself—"They fare   50
Scarce better, they need not scorn
   Our sea, who live in the air!"

XIV

Emancipate through passion
   And thought, with sea for sky,
We substitute, in a fashion,   55
   For Heaven—poetry:

XV

Which sea, to all intent,
    Gives flesh such noon-disport
As a finer element
    Affords the spirit-sort.

XVI

Whatever they are, we seem:
    Imagine the thing they know;
All deeds they do, we dream;
    Can Heaven be else but so?

XVII

And meantime, yonder streak
    Meets the horizon's verge;
That is the land, to seek
    If we tire or dread the surge:

XVIII

Land the solid and safe—
    To welcome again (confess!)
When, high and dry, we chafe
    The body, and don the dress.

XIX

Does she look, pity, wonder
    At one who mimics flight,
Swims—Heaven above, sea under,
    Yet always earth in sight?

from *ARISTOPHANES'*
APOLOGY

(1875)

THAMURIS MARCHING°

THAMURIS marching—lyre and song of Thrace—
(Perpend the first, the worst of woes that were
Allotted lyre and song, ye poet-race!)

Thamuris from Oichalia, feasted there
By kingly Eurutos of late, now bound   5
For Dorion at the uprise broad and bare

Of Mount Pangaios (ore with earth enwound
Glittered beneath his footstep)—marching gay
And glad, Thessalia through, came, robed and crowned,

From triumph on to triumph, mid a ray   10
Of early morn—came, saw and knew the spot
Assigned him for his worst of woes, that day.

Thamuris Marching interlude in a long poem, *Aristophanes' Apology*
(ll. 104–80 of conclusion, here renumbered). Thamyris was a mu-
sician of Thrace who challenged the muses to a song contest. When
he was defeated, the muses punished him with blindness and by de-
priving him of song.

Balura—happier while its name was not°—
Met him, but nowise menaced; slipped aside,
15   Obsequious river to pursue its lot

Of solacing the valley—say, some wide
Thick busy human cluster, house and home,
Embanked for peace, or thrift that thanks the tide.

Thamuris, marching, laughed "Each flake of foam"
20   (As sparklingly the ripple raced him by)
"Mocks slower clouds adrift in the blue dome!"

For Autumn was the season; red the sky
Held morn's conclusive signet of the sun
To break the mists up, bid them blaze and die.

25   Morn had the mastery as, one by one
All pomps produced themselves along the tract
From earth's far ending to near Heaven begun.

Was there a ravaged tree? it laughed compact
With gold, a leaf-ball crisp, high-brandished now,
30   Tempting to onset frost which late attacked.

Was there a wizened shrub, a starveling bough,
A fleecy thistle filched from by the wind,
A weed, Pan's trampling hoof would disallow?

Each, with a glory and a rapture twined
35   About it, joined the rush of air and light
And force: the world was of one joyous mind.

Say not the birds flew! they forebore their right—
Swam, reveling onward in the roll of things.
Say not the beasts' mirth bounded! that was flight—

40   How could the creatures leap, no lift of wings?

13 **Balura . . . not** according to legend the river Balyra took its
name from the fact that it was there the blinded Thamyris threw
away (*ballein* in Greek) his lyre.

uch earth's community of purpose, such
he ease of earth's fulfilled imaginings—

So did the near and far appear to touch
' the moment's transport—that an interchange
Of function, far with near, seemed scarce too much;   45

And had the rooted plant aspired to range
With the snake's license, while the insect yearned
To glow fixed as the flower, it were not strange—

No more than if the fluttery treetop turned
To actual music, sang itself aloft;   50
Or if the wind, impassioned chantress, earned

The right to soar embodied in some soft
Fine form all fit for cloud-companionship,
And, blissful, once touch beauty chased so oft.

Thamuris, marching, let no fancy slip   55
Born of the fiery transport; lyre and song
Were his, to smite with hand and launch from lip—

Peerless recorded, since the list grew long
Of poets (saith Homeros) free to stand
Pedestaled mid the Muses' temple-throng,   60

A statued service, laureled, lyre in hand,
(Ay, for we see them)—Thamuris of Thrace
Predominating foremost of the band.

Therefore the morn-ray that enriched his face,
If it gave lambent chill, took flame again   65
From flush of pride; he saw, he knew the place.

What wind arrived with all the rhythms from plain,
Hill, dale, and that rough wildwood interspersed?
Compounding these to one consummate strain,

It reached him, music; but his own outburst   70

Of victory concluded the account,
And that grew song which was mere music erst.

"Be my Parnassos, thou Pangaian mount!
And turn thee, river, nameless hitherto!
75 Famed shalt thou vie with famed Pieria's fount!°

"Here I await the end of this ado:
Which wins—Earth's poet or the Heavenly Muse." . . .

75 **Pieria's fount** haunt of the Muses.

from PACCHIAROTTO AND HOW HE WORKED IN DISTEMPER; WITH OTHER POEMS

(1876)

NATURAL MAGIC

I

ALL I can say is—I saw it!
The room was as bare as your hand.
I locked in the swarth little lady—I swear,
From the head to the foot of her—well, quite as bare!
"No Nautch° shall cheat me," said I, "taking my stand   5
At this bolt which I draw!" And this bolt—I withdraw it,
And there laughs the lady, not bare, but embowered
With—who knows what verdure, o'erfruited, o'erflowered?
    Impossible! Only—I saw it!

II

    All I can sing is—I feel it!   10
This life was as blank as that room;

5 **Nautch** here seems to mean something like gypsy.

425

I let you pass in here. Precaution, indeed?
Walls, ceiling and floor—not a chance for a weed!
Wide opens the entrance: where's cold now, where's
    gloom?
15 No May to sow seed here, no June to reveal it,
Behold you enshrined in these blooms of your bring-
    ing,
These fruits of your bearing—nay, birds of your
    winging!
    A fairy tale! Only—I feel it!

MAGICAL NATURE

I

FLOWER—I never fancied, jewel—I profess you!
    Bright I see and soft I feel the outside of a flower.
Save but glow inside and—jewel, I should guess you,
    Dim to sight and rough to touch: the glory is the
    dower.

II

5 You, forsooth, a flower? Nay, my love, a jewel—
    Jewel at no mercy of a moment in your prime!
Time may fray the flower-face: kind be time or cruel,
    Jewel, from each facet, flash your laugh at time!

NUMPHOLEPTOS°

STILL you stand, still you listen, still you smile!
Still melts your moonbeam through me, white awhile,
Softening, sweetening, till sweet and soft
Increase so round this heart of mine, that oft
I could believe your moonbeam-smile has passed   5
The pallid limit, lies, transformed at last
To sunlight and salvation—warms the soul
It sweetens, softens! Would you pass that goal,
Gain love's birth at the limit's happier verge,
And, where an iridescence lurks, but urge   10
The hesitating pallor on to prime
Of dawn!—true blood-streaked, sun-warmth, action-
time,
By heart-pulse ripened to a ruddy glow
Of gold above my clay—I scarce should know
From gold's self, thus suffused! For gold means love. 15
What means the sad slow silver smile above
My clay but pity, pardon?—at the best,
But acquiescence that I take my rest,
Contented to be clay, while in your Heaven
The sun reserves love for the Spirit-Seven   20
Companioning God's throne they lamp before,°
—Leaves earth a mute waste only wandered o'er
By that pale soft sweet disempassioned moon
Which smiles me slow forgiveness! Such the boon
I beg? Nay, dear, submit to this—just this   25
Supreme endeavor! As my lips now kiss
Your feet, my arms convulse your shrouding robe,
My eyes, acquainted with the dust, dare probe
Your eyes above for—what, if born, would blind
Mine with redundant bliss, as flash may find   30

Numpholeptos one captured by a nymph.   **20-21 Spirit-Seven . . .
before** Revelation 4:5.

427

The inert nerve, sting awake the palsied limb,
Bid with life's ecstasy sense overbrim
And suck back death in the resurging joy—
Love, the love whole and sole without alloy!

35 Vainly! The promise withers! I employ
Lips, arms, eyes, pray the prayer which finds the
    word,
Make the appeal which must be felt, not heard,
And none the more is changed your calm regard:
Rather, its sweet and soft grow harsh and hard—
40 Forbearance, then repulsion, then disdain.
Avert the rest! I rise, see!—make, again
Once more, the old departure for some track
Untried yet through a world which brings me back
Ever thus fruitlessly to find your feet,
45 To fix your eyes, to pray the soft and sweet
Which smile there—take from his new pilgrimage
Your outcast, once your inmate, and assuage
With love—not placid pardon now—his thirst
For a mere drop from out the ocean erst
50 He drank at! Well, the quest shall be renewed.
Fear nothing! Though I linger, unembued
With any drop, my lips thus close. I go!
So did I leave you, I have found you so,
And doubtlessly, if fated to return,
55 So shall my pleading persevere and earn
Pardon—not love—in that same smile, I learn,
And lose the meaning of, to learn once more,
Vainly!

What fairy track do I explore?
What magic hall return to, like the gem
60 Centuply-angled o'er a diadem?
You dwell there, hearted; from your midmost home
Rays forth—through that fantastic world I roam
Ever—from center to circumference,
Shaft upon colored shaft: this crimsons thence,
65 That purples out its precinct through the waste.
Surely I had your sanction when I faced,

Fared forth upon that untried yellow ray
Whence I retrack my steps? They end today
Where they began—before your feet, beneath
Your eyes, your smile: the blade is shut in sheath,   70
Fire quenched in flint; irradiation, late
Triumphant through the distance, finds its fate,
Merged in your blank pure soul, alike the source
And tomb of that prismatic glow: divorce
Absolute, all-conclusive! Forth I fared,   75
Treading the lambent flamelet: little cared
If now its flickering took the topaz tint,
If now my dull-caked path gave sulphury hint
Of subterranean rage—no stay nor stint
To yellow, since you sanctioned that I bathe,   80
Burnish me, soul and body, swim and swathe
In yellow license. Here I reek suffused
With crocus, saffron, orange, as I used
With scarlet, purple, every dye o' the bow
Born of the storm-cloud. As before, you show   85
Scarce recognition, no approval, some
Mistrust, more wonder at a man become
Monstrous in garb, nay—flesh disguised as well,
Through his adventure. Whatsoe'er befell,
I followed, whereso'er it wound, that vein   90
You authorized should leave your whiteness, stain
Earth's somber stretch beyond your midmost place
Of vantage—trode that tinct whereof the trace
On garb and flesh repel you! Yes, I plead
Your own permission—your command, indeed,   95
That who would worthily retain the love
Must share the knowledge shrined those eyes above,
Go boldly on adventure, break through bounds
O' the quintessential whiteness that surrounds
Your feet, obtain experience of each tinge   100
That bickers forth to broaden out, impinge
Plainer his foot its pathway all distinct
From every other. Ah, the wonder, linked
With fear, as exploration manifests
What agency it was first tipped the crests   105
Of unnamed wildflower, soon protruding grew

Portentous mid the sands, as when his hue
Betrays him and the burrowing snake gleams through;
Till, last . . . but why parade more shame and pain?
110 Are not the proofs upon me? Here again
I pass into your presence, I receive
Your smile of pity, pardon, and I leave . . .
No, not this last of times I leave you, mute,
Submitted to my penance, so my foot
115 May yet again adventure, tread, from source
To issue, one more ray of rays which course
Each other, at your bidding, from the sphere
Silver and sweet, their birthplace, down that drear
Dark of the world—you promise shall return
120 Your pilgrim jeweled as with drops o' the urn
The rainbow paints from, and no smatch° at all
Of ghastliness at edge of some cloud-pall
Heaven cowers before, as earth awaits the fall
O' the bolt and flash of doom. Who trusts your word
125 Tries the adventure: and returns—absurd
As frightful—in that sulphur-steeped disguise
Mocking the priestly cloth-of-gold, sole prize
The arch-heretic was wont to bear away
Until he reached the burning. No, I say:
130 No fresh adventure! No more seeking love
At end of toil, and finding, calm above
My passion, the old statuesque regard,
The sad petrific smile!

O you—less hard
And hateful than mistaken and obtuse
135 Unreason of a she-intelligence!
You very woman with the pert pretense
To match the male achievement! Like enough!
Ay, you were easy victors, did the rough
Straightway efface itself to smooth, the gruff
140 Grind down and grow a whisper—did man's truth
Subdue, for sake of chivalry and ruth,

---

121 **smatch** smack, touch or suggestion of something.

Its rapier-edge to suit the bulrush-spear
Womanly falsehood fights with! O that ear
All fact pricks rudely, that thrice-superfine
Feminity of sense, with right divine   145
To waive all process, take result stain-free
From out the very muck wherein . . .

                    Ah me!
The true slave's querulous outbreak! All the rest
Be resignation! Forth at your behest
I fare. Who knows but this—the crimson-quest—   150
May deepen to a sunrise, not decay
To that cold sad sweet smile?—which I obey.

ST. MARTIN'S SUMMER°

I

No protesting, dearest!
   Hardly kisses even!
      Don't we both know how it ends?
How the greenest leaf turns serest:
   Bluest outbreak—blankest heaven,   5
      Lovers—friends?

II

You would build a mansion,
   I would weave a bower

St. Martin's Summer "Indian Summer."

   —Want the heart for enterprise.
10 Walls admit of no expansion:
   Trellis-work may haply flower
    Twice the size.

III

  What makes glad Life's Winter?
   New buds, old blooms after.
15   Sad the sighing "How suspect
  Beams would ere mid-Autumn splinter,
   Rooftree scarce support a rafter,
    Walls lie wrecked?"

IV

  You are young, my princess!
20 I am hardly older:
   Yet—I steal a glance behind.
  Dare I tell you what convinces
   Timid me that you, if bolder,
    Bold—are blind?

V

25 Where we plan our dwelling
   Glooms a graveyard surely!
   Headstone, footstone moss may drape—
  Name, date, violets hide from spelling—
   But, though corpses rot obscurely,
30   Ghosts escape.

VI

  Ghosts! O breathing Beauty,
   Give my frank word pardon!
   What if I—somehow, somewhere—
  Pledged my soul to endless duty
35 Many a time and oft? Be hard on
   Love—laid there?

VII

Nay, blame grief that's fickle,
  Time that proves a traitor,
    Chance, change, all that purpose warps—
Death who spares to thrust the sickle   40
  Laid Love low, through flowers which later
    Shroud the corpse!

VIII

And you, my winsome lady,
  Whisper with like frankness!
    Lies nothing buried long ago?
Are yon—which shimmer mid the shady   45
  Where moss and violet run to rankness—
    Tombs or no?

IX

Who taxes you with murder?
  My hands are clean—or nearly!
    Love being mortal needs must pass.   50
Repentance? Nothing were absurder.
  Enough: we felt Love's loss severely;
    Though now—alas!

X

Love's corpse lies quiet therefore,   55
  Only Love's ghost plays truant,
    And warns us have in wholesome awe
Durable mansionry; that's wherefore
  I weave but trellis-work, pursuant
    —Life, to law.   60

XI

The solid, not the fragile,
  Tempts rain and hail and thunder.

If bower stand firm at Autumn's close,
    Beyond my hope—why, boughs were agile;
65   If bower fall flat, we scarce need wonder
        Wreathing—rose!

XII

So, truce to the protesting,
    So, muffled be the kisses!
        For, would we but avow the truth,
70   Sober is genuine joy. No jesting!
        Ask else Penelope, Ulysses—
            Old in youth!

XIII

For why should ghosts feel angered?
    Let all their interference
75   Be faint march-music in the air!
    "Up! Join the rear of us the vanguard!
        Up, lovers, dead to all appearance,
            Laggard pair!"

XIV

The while you clasp me closer,
80   The while I press you deeper,
        As safe we chuckle—under breath,
    Yet all the slier, the jocoser—
        "So, life can boast its day, like leap year,
            Stolen from death!"

XV

85 Ah me—the sudden terror!
        Hence quick—avaunt, avoid me,
            You cheat, the ghostly flesh-disguised!
    Nay, all the ghosts in one! Strange error!
        So, 'twas Death's self that clipped and coyed me,
90   Loved—and lied!

XVI

Ay, dead loves are the potent!
   Like any cloud they used you,
      Mere semblance you, but substance they!
Build we no mansion, weave we no tent!
   Mere flesh—their spirit interfused you!   *95*
      Hence, I say!

XVII

All theirs, none yours the glamor!
   Theirs each low word that won me,
      Soft look that found me Love's, and left
What else but you—the tears and clamor   *100*
   That's all your very own! Undone me—
      Ghost-bereft!

from JOCOSERIA

(1883)

WANTING IS—WHAT?

WANTING is—what?
Summer redundant,
Blueness abundant,
—Where is the blot?
Beamy the world, yet a blank all the same,   *5*
—Framework which waits for a picture to frame:
What of the leafage, what of the flower?
Roses embowering with naught they embower!
Come then, complete incompletion, O comer,
Pant through the blueness, perfect the summer!   *10*
Breathe but one breath
Rose-beauty above,
And all that was death
Grows life, grows love,
Grows love!   *15*

from *FERISHTAH'S FANCIES*

(1884)

NOT WITH MY SOUL, LOVE!

ot with my Soul, Love!—bid no Soul like mine
  Lap thee around nor leave the poor Sense room!
oul—travel-worn, toil-weary—would confine
  Along the Soul, Soul's gains from glow and gloom,
aptures from soarings high and divings deep.   5
poil-laden Soul, how should such memories sleep?
ake Sense, too—let me love entire and whole—
    Not with my Soul!

yes shall meet eyes and find no eyes between,
  Lips feed on lips, no other lips to fear!   10
o past, no future—so thine arms but screen
  The present from surprise! not there, 'tis here—
ot then, 'tis now:—back, memories that intrude!
ake, Love, the universe our solitude,
nd, over all the rest, oblivion roll—   15
    Sense quenching Soul!

EPILOGUE TO *FERISHTAH'S FANCIES*

OH, Love—no, Love! All the noise below, Love,
  Groanings all and moanings—none of Life I los
All of Life's a cry just of weariness and woe, Love—
  "Hear at least, thou happy one!" How can I, Lov
    but choose?

5 Only, when I do hear, sudden circle round me
  —Much as when the moon's might frees a spa
    from cloud—
Iridescent splendors: gloom—would else confou
  me—
  Barriered off and banished far—bright-edged tl
    blackest shroud!

Thronging through the cloud-rift, whose are they, tl
  faces
  Faint revealed yet sure divined, the famous ones
10   old?
"What"—they smile—"our names, our deeds so so
  erases
  Time upon his tablet where Life's glory lies e
    rolled?

"Was it for mere fool's-play, make-believe and mur
  ming,
  So we battled it like men, not boylike sulked
    whined?
Each of us heard clang God's 'Come!' and each w
15   coming?
  Soldiers all, to forward-face, not sneaks to lag b
    hind!

"How of the field's fortune? That concerned our
    Leader!
  Led, we struck our stroke nor cared for doings left
    and right:
Each as on his sole head, failer or succeeder,
  Lay the blame or lit the praise: no care for cow-
    ards: fight!"   20

Then the cloud-rift broadens, spanning earth that's
    under
  Wide our world displays its worth, man's strife and
    strife's success:
All the good and beauty, wonder crowning wonder,
  Till my heart and soul applaud perfection, nothing
    less.

Only, at heart's utmost joy and triumph, terror   25
  Sudden turns the blood to ice: a chill wind disen-
    charms
All the late enchantment! What if all be error—
  If the halo irised round my head were, Love, thine
    arms?

from PARLEYINGS WITH CERTAIN PEOPLE OF IMPORTANCE IN THEIR DAY

(1887)

APOLLO AND THE FATES°

Apollo. [*From above.*] FLAME at my footfall, Parnassus! Apollo,
    Breaking ablaze on thy topmost peak,
Burns thence, down to the depths—dread hollow—
    Haunt of the Dire Ones. Haste! They wreak
Wrath on Admetus whose respite I seek.   5

The Fates. [*Below. Darkness.*] Dragonwise couched in
    the womb of our Mother,
    Coiled at thy nourishing heart's core, Night!
Dominant Dreads, we, one by the other,
    Deal to each mortal his dole of light
On earth—the upper, the glad, the bright.   10

Clotho. Even so: thus from my loaded spindle

Apollo and the Fates prologue to the volume in which it appears.
In an introductory note Browning cites the passage in the Homeric
Hymn to Hermes that says that the Fates will speak truth when fed
honey. References (omitted here) to Aeschylus' *Eumenides* and
Euripides' *Alcestis* refer to Apollo's success in saving the life of
Admetus by getting the Fates drunk.

Plucking a pinch of the fleece, lo, "Birth"
Brays from my bronze lip: life I kindle:
Look, 'tis a man! go, measure on earth
15   The minute thy portion, whatever its worth!

Lachesis. Woe-purfled, weal-pranked°—if it speed, if
it linger—
Life's substance and show are determined by me,
Who, meting out, mixing with sure thumb and
finger,
Lead life the due length: is all smoothness and
glee,
20   All tangle and grief? Take the lot, my decree!

Atropos. —Which I make an end of: the smooth as
the tangled
My shears cut asunder: each snap shrieks "One
more
Mortal makes sport for us Moirai who dangled
The puppet grotesquely till earth's solid floor
Proved film he fell through, lost in Naught as be-
25   fore."

Clotho. I spin thee a thread. Live, Admetus! Produce
him!

Lachesis. Go—brave, wise, good, happy; Now checker
the thread!
He is slaved for, yet loved by a god. I unloose him
A goddess-sent plague. He has conquered, is
wed,°
Men crown him, he stands at the height—

Atropos.   He is . . .

30   *Apollo.* [*Entering: Light.*]   "Dead?"
Nay, swart spinsters! So I surprise you
Making and marring the fortunes of Man?
Huddling—no marvel, your enemy eyes you—

---

16 **Woe-purfled, weal-pranked** adorned with grief or prosperity.
28–29 **slaved for . . . wed** Apollo had served Admetus as herdsman
as a punishment from Zeus. Artemis plagued Admetus with serpents
when he neglected his offering to her on his wedding day.

Head by head batlike, blots under the ban
 Of daylight earth's blessing since time began! *35*

The Fates. Back to thy blessed earth, prying Apollo!
 Shaft upon shaft transpierce with thy beams
Earth to the center—spare but this hollow
 Hewn out of Night's heart, where our mystery
  seems
Mewed° from day's malice: wake earth from her
  dreams! *40*

Apollo. Crones, 'tis your dusk selves I startle from
  slumber:
 Day's god deposes you—queens Night-crowned!
—Plying your trade in a world ye encumber,
 Fashioning Man's web of life—spun, wound,
Left the length ye allot till a clip strews the ground! *45*

Behold I bid truce to your doleful amusement—
 Annulled by a sunbeam!

The Fates.   Boy, are not we peers?

Apollo. You with the spindle grant birth: whose in-
  ducement
 But yours—with the niggardly digits—endears
To mankind chance and change, good and evil?
 Your shears . . . *50*

Atropos. Ay, mine end the conflict: so much is no
  fable.
 We spin, draw to length, cut asunder: what then?
So it was, and so is, and so shall be: art able
 To alter life's law for ephemeral men?

Apollo. Nor able nor willing. To threescore and ten *55*

Extend but the years of Admetus! Disaster
 O'ertook me, and, banished by Zeus, I became
A servant to one who forbore me though master:
 True lovers were we. Discontinue your game,

---

40 **mewed** sheltered.   *3*

Let him live whom I loved, then hate on, all the
60   same!

The Fates. And what if we granted—law-flouter, use-
    trampler—
    His life at the suit of an upstart? Judge, thou—
Of joy were it fuller, of span because ampler?
    For love's sake, not hate's, end Admetus—ay,
    now—
65 Not a gray hair on head, nor a wrinkle on brow!

For, boy, 'tis illusion: from thee comes a glimmer
    Transforming to beauty life blank at the best.
Withdraw—and how looks life at worst, when to
    shimmer
    Succeeds the sure shade, and Man's lot frowns—
    confessed
Mere blackness chance-brightened? Whereof shall
70   attest

The truth this same mortal, the darling thou stylest,
    Whom love would advantage—eke out, day by
    day,
A life which 'tis solely thyself reconcilest
    Thy friend to endure—life with hope: take away
Hope's gleam from Admetus, he spurns it. For,
75   say—

What's infancy? Ignorance, idleness, mischief:
    Youth ripens to arrogance, foolishness, greed:
Age—impotence, churlishness, rancor: call *this*
    chief
    Of boons for thy loved one? Much rather bid
    speed
80 Our function, let live whom thou hatest indeed!

Persuade thee, bright boy-thing! Our eld be instruc-
    tive!

Apollo. And certes youth owns the experience of age.

Ye hold then, grave seniors, my beams are produc-
    tive
    —They solely—of good that's mere semblance,
      engage
Man's eye—gilding evil, Man's true heritage?   *85*

The Fates. So, even so! From without—at due dis-
    tance
    If viewed—set a-sparkle, reflecting thy rays—
Life mimics the sun: but withdraw such assistance,
    The counterfeit goes, the reality stays—
An ice-ball disguised as a fire-orb.

Apollo.   What craze   *90*

Possesses the fool then whose fancy conceits him
    As happy?

The Fates.   Man happy?

Apollo.   If otherwise—solve
This doubt which besets me! What friend ever
    greets him
    Except with "Live long as the seasons revolve,"
Not "Death to thee straightway"? Your doctrines
    absolve   *95*
Such hailing from hatred: yet Man should know
    best.
    He talks it, and glibly, as life were a load
Man fain would be rid off: when put to the test,
    He whines "Let it lie, leave me trudging the road
That is rugged so far, but methinks . . ."

The Fates.   Ay, 'tis owed   *100*

To that glamor of thine, he bethinks him "Once
    past
    The stony, some patch, nay, a smoothness of
      sward
Awaits my tired foot: life turns easy at last"—
    Thy largess so lures him, he looks for reward
Of the labor and sorrow.

105 *Apollo.*   It seems, then—debarred

Of illusion—(I needs must acknowledge the plea)
    Man desponds and despairs. Yet—still further to
        draw
Due profit from counsel—suppose there should be
    Some power in himself, some compensative law
By virtue of which, independently . . .

110 *The Fates.*   Faugh!

Strength hid in the weakling!
                 What bowl-shape hast there,
    Thus laughingly proffered? A gift to our shrine?
Thanks—worsted in argument! Not so? Declare
    Its purpose!

Apollo.   I proffer earth's product, not mine.
115 Taste, try, and approve Man's invention of—WINE!

The Fates. We feeding suck honeycombs.

Apollo.   Sustenance meager!
Such fare breeds the fumes that show all things
        amiss.
Quaff wine—how the spirits rise nimble and eager,
    Unscale the dim eyes! To Man's cup grant one
        kiss
120 Of your lip, then allow—no enchantment like this!

Clotho. Unhook wings, unhood brows! Dost hearken?

Lachesis.   I listen:
I see—smell the food these fond mortals prefer
    To our feast, the bee's bounty!

Atropos.   The thing leaps! But—glisten
Its best, I withstand it—unless all concur
In adventure so novel.

Apollo.   Ye drink?

125 *The Fates.*   We demur.

Apollo. Sweet Trine, be indulgent nor scout the con-
  trivance
 Of Man—Bacchus°-prompted! The juice, I up-
  hold,
Illuminates gloom without sunny connivance,
 Turns fear into hope and makes cowardice
  bold—
Touching all that is leadlike in life turns it gold! *130*

The Fates. Faith foolish as false!

Apollo.   But essay it, soft sisters!
 Then mock as ye may. Lift the chalice to lip!
 Good: thou next—and thou! Seems the web, to
  you twisters
 Of life's yarn, so worthless?

Clotho.   Who guessed that one sip
 Would impart such a lightness of limb?

Lachesis.   I could skip *135*

In a trice from the pied to the plain in my woof!
 What parts each from either? A hair's breadth,
  no inch.
Once learn the right method of stepping aloof,
 Though on black next foot falls, firm I fix it, nor
  flinch,
 —Such my trust white succeeds!

Atropos.   One could live—at a pinch! *140*

Apollo. What beldames? Earth's yield, by Man's skill,
  can effect
 Such a cure of sick sense that ye spy the relation
 Of evil to good? But drink deeper, correct
 Blear sight more convincingly still! Take your
  station
Beside me, drain dregs! Now for edification! *145*

127 **Bacchus** god of wine.

Whose gift have ye gulped? Thank not me but my
    brother,
    Blithe Bacchus, our youngest of godships. 'Twas
        he
Found all boons to all men, by one god or other
    Already conceded, so judged there must be
150 New guerdon to grace the new advent, you see!

Else how would a claim to Man's homage arise?
    The plan lay arranged of his mixed woe and
        weal,
So disposed—such Zeus' will—with design to make
        wise
    The witless—that false things were mingled with
        real,
Good with bad: such the lot whereto law set the
155   seal.

Now, human of instinct—since Semele's son,
    Yet minded divinely—since fathered by Zeus,
With naught Bacchus tampered, undid not things
        done,
    Owned wisdom anterior, would spare wont and
        use,
160 Yet change—without shock to old rule—introduce.

Regard how your cavern from crag-tip to base
    Frowns sheer, height and depth adamantine,°
        one death!
I rouse with a beam the whole rampart, displace
    No splinter—yet see how my flambeau,° beneath
And above, bids this gem wink, that crystal un-
165   sheath!

Withdraw beam—disclosure once more Night for-
        bids you
    Of spangle and sparkle—Day's chance-gift, sur-
        mised

162 **adamantine** impenetrable.   164 **flambeau** torch.

Rock's permanent birthright: my potency rids you
    No longer of darkness, yet light—recognized—
Proves darkness a mask: day lives on though dis-
    guised.   *170*

If Bacchus by wine's aid avail so to fluster
    Your sense, that life's fact grows from adverse
        and thwart
To helpful and kindly by means of a cluster—
    Mere hand-squeeze, earth's nature sublimed by
        Man's art—
Shall Bacchus claim thanks wherein Zeus has no
    part?   *175*

Zeus—wisdom anterior? No, maids, be admonished!
    If morn's touch at base worked such wonders,
        much more
Had noontide in absolute glory astonished
    Your den, filled atop to o'erflowing. I pour
No such mad confusion. 'Tis Man's to explore   *180*

Up and down, inch by inch, with the taper his rea-
    son:
    No torch, it suffices—held deftly and straight.
Eyes, purblind at first, feel their way in due season,
    Accept good with bad, till unseemly debate
Turns concord—despair, acquiescence in fate.   *185*

Who works this but Zeus? Are not instinct and im-
    pulse,
    Not concept and incept his work through Man's
        soul
On Man's sense? Just as wine ere it reach brain
    must brim pulse,
    Zeus' flash stings the mind that speeds body to
        goal,
Bids pause at no part but press on, reach the whole.   *190*

For petty and poor is the part ye envisage

When—(quaff away, cummers°!)—ye view, las
  and first,
As evil Man's earthly existence. Come! *Is* age,
  Is infancy—manhood—so uninterspersed
With good—some faint sprinkle?

195 *Clotho.*   I'd speak if I durst

Apollo. Drafts dregward loose tongue-tie.

Lachesis.   I'd see, did no web
Set eyes somehow winking.

Apollo.   Drains-deep lies their purge
  —True collyrium!°

Atropos.   Words, surging at high tide, soon ebb
From starved ears.

Apollo. Drink but down to the source, they resurge
  Join hands! Yours and yours too! A dance or a
200   dirge?

Chorus. Quashed be our quarrel! Sourly and smilingly
  Bare and gowned, bleached limbs and browned
Drive we a dance, three and one, reconcilingly,
  Thanks to the cup where dissension is drowned
205 Defeat proves triumphant and slavery crowned.

Infancy? What if the rose-streak of morning
  Pale and depart in a passion of tears?
Once to have hoped is no matter for scorning!
  Love once—e'en love's disappointment endears
210 A minute's success pays the failure of years.

Manhood—the actual? Nay, praise the potential!
  (Bound upon bound, foot it around!)
What *is*? No, what *may* be—sing! that's Man's
  essential!
  (Ramp, tramp, stamp and compound
215 Fancy with fact—the lost secret is found!)

---

192 **cummers** "gossips" (women friends). 198 **collyrium** medicine
for the eyes.

Age? Why, fear ends there: the contest concluded,
 Man *did* live his life, *did* escape from the fray:
Not scratchless but unscathed, he somehow eluded
 Each blow fortune dealt him, and conquers today:
Tomorrow—new chance and fresh strength—might
 we say?   220

Laud then Man's life—no defeat but a triumph!
   [*Explosion from the earth's center.*]

Clotho. Ha, loose hands!

Lachesis.   I reel in a swound.

Atropos. Horror yawns under me, while from on high
 —humph!
 Lightnings astound, thunders resound,
Vault-roof reverberates, groans the ground! 225
        [*Silence.*]

Apollo. I acknowledge.

The Fates. Hence, trickster! Straight sobered are we!
 The portent assures 'twas our tongue spoke the
  truth,
Not thine. While the vapor encompassed us three
 We conceived and bore knowledge—a bantling
  uncouth,
Old brains shudder back from: so—take it, rash
  youth!   230

Lick the lump into shape till a cry comes!

Apollo.   I hear.

The Fates. Dumb music, dead eloquence! Say it, or
  sing!
 What was quickened in us and thee also?

Apollo.   I fear.

The Fates. Half female, half male—go, ambiguous
  thing!
 While we speak—perchance sputter—pick up what
  we fling!   235

Known yet ignored, nor divined nor unguessed,
 Such is Man's law of life. Do we strive to declare
What is ill, what is good in our spinning? Worst
  best,
 Change hues of a sudden: now here and now
  there
240 Flits the sign which decides: all about yet nowhere.

'Tis willed so—that Man's life be lived, first to last
 Up and down, through and through—not in
  portions, forsooth,
To pick and to choose from. Our shuttles fly fast,
 Weave living, not life sole and whole: as age—
  youth,
245 So death completes living, shows life in its truth.

Man learningly lives: till death helps him—no lore
 It is doom and must be. Dost submit?

Apollo.   I assent—
 Concede but Admetus! So much if no more
  Of my prayer grant as peace-pledge! Be gracious
   though, blent,
 Good and ill, love and hate streak your life-gift!

250 *The Fates.*   Content!

Such boon we accord in due measure. Life's term
 We lengthen should any be moved for love's sake
To forego life's fulfillment, renounce in the germ
 Fruit mature—bliss or woe—either infinite. Take
255 Or leave thy friend's lot: on his head be the stake!

Apollo. On mine, grizzly gammers! Admetus, I know
  thee!
 Thou prizest the right these unwittingly give
Thy subjects to rush, pay obedience they owe thee!
 Importunate one with another they strive
260 For the glory to die that their king may survive.

Friends rush: and who first in all Pherae appears
  But thy father to serve as thy substitute?

Clotho.   **Bah!**

Apollo. Ye wince? Then his mother, well-stricken in
    years,
  Advances her claim—or his wife—

Lachesis.   **Tra-la-la!**

Apollo. But he spurns the exchange, rather dies!°

Atropos.   **Ha, ha, ha!** 265
               [Apollo ascends. Darkness.]

58–65 **Thy subjects . . . dies** but only his wife is willing and he accepts her offer.

from *ASOLANDO*

(1889)

PROLOGUE

"THE Poet's age is sad: for why?
   In youth, the natural world could show
No common object but his eye
   At once involved with alien glow—
His own soul's iris-bow.°   5

"And now a flower is just a flower:
   Man, bird, beast are but beast, bird, man—
Simply themselves, uncinct by dower
   Of dyes which, when life's day began,
Round each in glory ran."   10

Friend, did you need an optic glass,
   Which were your choice? A lens to drape
In ruby, emerald, chrysopras,
   Each object—or reveal its shape
Clear outlined, past escape,   15

The naked very thing?—so clear
   That, when you had the chance to gaze,

---

5 **iris-bow** rainbow. Cf. the "visionary gleam" of Wordsworth's Intimations Ode.

You found its inmost self appear
   Through outer seeming—truth ablaze,
20 Not falsehood's fancy-haze?

How many a year, my Asolo,°
   Since—one step just from sea to land—
I found you, loved yet feared you so—
   For natural objects seemed to stand
25 Palpably fire-clothed! No—

No mastery of mine o'er these!
   Terror with beauty, like the Bush
Burning but unconsumed.° Bend knees,
   Drop eyes to earthward! Language? Tush!
30 Silence 'tis awe decrees.

And now? The lambent flame is—where?
   Lost from the naked world: earth, sky,
Hill, vale, tree, flower—Italia's rare
   O'er-running beauty crowds the eye—
35 But flame? The Bush is bare.

Hill, vale, tree, flower—they stand distinct,
   Nature to know and name. What then?
A Voice spoke thence which straight unlinked
   Fancy from fact: see, all's in ken:
40 Has once my eyelid winked?

No, for the purged ear apprehends
   Earth's import, not the eye late dazed:
The Voice said "Call my works thy friends!
   At Nature dost thou shrink amazed?
45 God is it who transcends."

21 **Asolo** city in northern Italy   27–28 **the Bush . . . unconsumed**
Exodus 3:2.

FLUTE MUSIC, WITH AN ACCOMPANIMENT

He. AH, the bird-like fluting
    Through the ash-tops yonder—
Bullfinch-bubblings, soft sounds suiting
    What sweet thoughts, I wonder?
Fine-pearled notes that surely   5
    Gather, dewdrop-fashion,
Deep-down in some heart which purely
    Secretes globuled passion—
Passion insuppressive—
    Such is piped, for certain;   10
Love, no doubt, nay, love excessive
    'Tis, your ash-tops curtain.

Would your ash-tops open
    We might spy the player—
Seek and find some sense which no pen   15
    Yet from singer, sayer,
Ever has extracted:
    Never, to my knowledge,
Yet has pedantry enacted
    That, in Cupid's College,   20
Just this variation
    Of the old old yearning
Should by plain speech have salvation,
    Yield new men new learning.

"Love!" but what love, nicely   25
    New from old disparted,
Would the player teach precisely?
    First of all, he started
In my brain Assurance—
    Trust—entire Contentment—   30
Passion proved by much endurance;

Then came—not resentment,
No, but simply Sorrow:
What was seen had vanished:
35   Yesterday so blue! Tomorrow
Blank, all sunshine banished.

Hark! 'Tis Hope resurges,
Struggling through obstruction—
Forces a poor smile which verges
40   On Joy's introduction.
Now, perhaps, mere Musing:
"Holds earth such a wonder?
Fairy-mortal, soul-sense-fusing
Past thought's power to sunder!"
45   What? calm Acquiescence?
"Daisied turf gives room to
Trefoil, plucked once in her presence—
Growing by her tomb too!"

She. All's your fancy-spinning!
50   Here's the fact: a neighbor
Never-ending, still beginning,
Recreates his labor:
Deep o'er desk he drudges,
Adds, divides, subtracts and
55   Multiplies, until he judges
Noonday-hour's exact sand
Shows the hourglass emptied:
Then comes lawful leisure,
Minutes rare from toil exempted,
60   Fit to spend in pleasure.

Out then with—what treatise?
Youth's Complete Instructor
How to play the Flute. Quid petis?°
Follow Youth's conductor
65   On and on, through Easy,
Up to Harder, Hardest

63 Quid petis? what do you want?

Flute-piece, till thou, flautist wheezy,
    Possibly discardest
Tootlings hoarse and husky,
    Mayst expend with courage   70
Breath—on tunes once bright now dusky—
    Meant to cool thy porridge.

That's an air of Tulou's
    He maltreats persistent,
Till as lief I'd hear some Zulu's   75
    Bone-piped bag, breath-distent,
Madden native dances.
    I'm the man's familiar:
Unexpectedness enhances
    What your ear's auxiliar   80
—Fancy—finds suggestive.
    Listen! That's *legato*
Rightly played, his fingers restive
    Touch as if *staccato*.°

e. Ah, you trick-betrayer!   85
    Telling tales, unwise one?
So the secret of the player
    Was—he could surprise one
Well-nigh into trusting
    Here was a musician   90
Skilled consummately, yet lusting
    Through no vile ambition
After making captive
    All the world—rewarded
Amply by one stranger's rapture,   95
    Common praise discarded.

So, without assistance
    Such as music rightly
Needs and claims—defying distance,
    Overleaping lightly   100

83–84 **legato . . . staccato** musical terms referring to pasages played,
respectively, without a break between notes and with a pronounced
break.

Obstacles which hinder—
    He, for my approval,
All the same and all the kinder
    Made mine what might move all
105 Earth to kneel adoring:
    Took—while he piped Gounod's
Bit of passionate imploring—
    Me for Juliet:° who knows?

No! as you explain things,
110   All's mere repetition,
Practice-pother: of all vain things
    Why waste pooh or pish on
Toilsome effort—never
    Ending, still beginning—
115 After what should pay endeavor
    —Right-performance? winning
Weariness from you who,
    Ready to admire some
Owl's fresh hooting—Tu-whit, tu-who—
120   Find stale thrush-songs tiresome.

She. Songs, Spring thought perfection,
    Summer criticizes:
What in May escaped detection,
    August, past surprises,
125 Notes, and names each blunder.
    You, the just-initiate,
Praise to heart's content (what wonder?)
    Tootings I hear vitiate
Romeo's serenading—
130   I who, times full twenty,
Turned to ice—no ash-tops aiding—
    At his *caldamente.*°

So, 'twas distance altered
    Sharps to flats? The missing
135 Bar when syncopation faltered

106–8 **Gounod's . . . Juliet** Charles Gounod's opera based on Shake-
speare's play. 132 **caldamente** with warmth (musical term).

THE AUTOBIOGRAPHY

OF MALCOLM X

With the assistance of Alex Haley
Foreword by Attallah Shabazz
Introduction by M. S. Handler
Epilogue by Alex Haley
Afterword by Ossie Davis

BALLANTINE BOOKS • NEW YORK

2015 Ballantine Books Mass Market Edition

Copyright © 1964 by Alex Haley and Malcolm X
Copyright © 1965 by Alex Haley and Betty Shabazz
Copyright renewed 1993 by Betty Shabazz, Myran Haley, Cynthia Haley, William Haley, and Lydia Haley
Introduction copyright © 1965 by M. S. Handler
Foreword copyright © 1999 by Attaliah Shabazz

Published in the United States by Ballantine Books, an imprint of Random House, a division of Penguin Random House LLC, New York.

BALLANTINE and the HOUSE colophon are registered trademarks of Penguin Random House LLC.

Originally published in the United States in hardcover by Grove Press, Inc., in 1965.

"On Malcolm X" by Ossie Davis originally appeared in *Group* magazine and is reprinted by permission.

ISBN 978-0-345-35068-8

Cover photograph: © Michael Ochs Archives/Corbis

Printed in the United States of America

www.ballantinebooks.com

100 99 98 97

Ballantine Books mass market edition: February 2015

This book, I dedicate to my beloved wife, Betty, and to our children, whose understanding and whose sacrifices made it possible for me to do my work.

CONTENTS

ATTALLAH SHABAZZ

FOREWORD

Behold, America. Just when our country's cultural evolution appears to have stagnated and we've grown insensitive to justice, the U.S. Postal Service has issued a commemorative stamp to honor one of our country's most outspoken revolutionaries—my father, Malcolm X Shabazz. This national commemoration, three decades after his lifetime, pays tribute to his immeasurable contributions on behalf of one's innate right to self-preservation and human dignity.

Although Malcolm X is no longer with us physically, tens of millions have gotten to know him through this timeless volume that you now hold in your hands. *The Autobiography of Malcolm X* has served as an everlasting testament to my father's life and legacy. In light of the cultural and political climate of the 1960s, when the book was first published, both my father and my godfather, Alex Haley, would feel great peace in knowing that *Time* magazine's "Best of the Century" issue named *The Autobiography of Malcolm X* one of the top ten works of nonfiction of this century. My father's life story stands alongside such monumental works as *The Diary of Anne Frank* and others. A lover of language, my father believed very much in the power of words to influence and transform lives.

His own life stands as an affirmation of that power. Our literature and our history are filled with stories of men and women whose will and inner strength nourished their rise from impoverishment to wealth, whether material, spiritual, or educational. My father's life and its stages of personal metamorphosis and enlightenment documented in this text stand as a confirmation of how one can, through witness and transformation, ultimately claim one's own divine path. At this point in my life, and significantly as his daughter, it is quite meaningful for me to contribute my prose to this living record.

My godfather, Alex Haley, bequeathed me the opportunity to write this foreword to my father's autobiography. He had set the process in motion almost a year before the offer was formally brought to my attention in the fall of 1992. It was, indeed, a spiritual gift of timing. Eight months earlier, in February 1992, the man who was the author of the internationally acclaimed *Roots* passed away suddenly in the middle of the night. Alex Haley and I had discussed the possibility of my writing his autobiography to acknowledge our literary circle, our family of writers—my father to him and him to me.

Six years have passed since I received this initial request to prepare a new foreword for my father's life story. My godfather's wish was that I commemorate my father's life by writing about some of the significant events that have served as a postscript for his extraordinary life story, but to do this it is essential to begin with the legacy that my father himself was heir to from the beginning.

In 1919, my paternal grandparents, Earl and Louisa Little, married and began their large family of eight children. At the same time they both worked steadfastly as crusaders for Marcus Garvey's Universal Negro Improvement Association, acting as chapter president and writer/translator for more than a decade. Their children were deeply involved and inspired by their parents' mission to encourage self-reliance and uphold a sense of empowerment for people of the African Diaspora.

Given the turbulence, fear, and despair of the depression era, with its economic droughts and racial and social inequities, my grandparents could never have imagined that one of their own children would have his likeness on a United States postal stamp before the century's end.

Eighty years later, on January 20, 1999, pride filled Harlem's historic Apollo Theatre as six of Earl and Louisa Little's granddaughters sat encircled by a body of fifteen hundred, as family, friends, esteemed guests, and well-wishers gathered to celebrate a momentous occasion—the unveiling of the United States Postal Service's newest release in its Black Heritage Stamp Series.

The issuance of the stamp with the image of El-Hajj Malik El-Shabazz—known to the world as Malcolm X and fondly loved by myself and my five sisters as Daddy—will provide a source of eternal pride to his children. While this was indeed a glorious moment, it does not cancel the pain of the loss of both our parents, or even kiss away the ache of their absence. What it certainly does is add to the blessings of our dowry.

The stamp also serves as a reminder of the stock from which we were born and confirms significantly that how one lives his or her life today stands as a testament to one's forever after.

In his genuine humility and pure dedication to service, my father had no idea of the potency of his deeds, of the impact his life would have on others, or of the legacy that was to unfold. As he and my godfather, Alex Haley, worked diligently to complete this classic work—in person, from airport telephones, via ship to shore, or over foreign wire services—he could never have imagined by America's tone in his final days that his words, philosophy, and wisdom would be so appreciated and honored around the world, or that it would still offer inspiration and guidance to so many.

In my father's absence, my mother nurtured and protected the significance and value of her husband's endless devotion to human rights. She was thrilled by the opening discussions about her husband's image appearing on a U.S. postal stamp. From her perspective, it was not as inconceivable as others have found it. To my mother, it was his due.

As the house lights dimmed in the Apollo Theatre, the flickering images of black-and-white photographs and film clips on the screen chronicled my father's life. Bittersweet, his youthful face and broad smile caressed my heart. As the documentary film moved forward, the voice-over of our dear family friend and loving "uncle" actor Ossie Davis delivered the eulogy from my father's funeral in 1965. This became the backdrop for the montage of nostalgic childhood memories that played in my mind. Life with both parents and my little sisters. Life joyous and uninterrupted.

When people ask how my mother managed to keep my father's memory alive, all I can say is—for my mother, he never left. He never left her. He never left us. My father's spiritual presence is what sustained my mother. And we, their children, were the beneficiaries of their timeless love for one another.

Born and raised in a family that was culturally varied, I innately gravitated to the rhythms of the world. Mommie was our constant, as many mothers are. Daddy was the jubilant energy in our world. He was not at all like the descriptions I grew up hearing. In addition to being determined, focused, honest, he was also greatly humorous, delightful, and boy-like, while at the same time a strong, firm male presence in a house filled with little women. His women. My sisters, me, and our mother. A collaboration of qualities that enchants me even now.

". . . If you knew him you would know why we must honor him," Uncle Ossie's voice continued. "Malcolm was our manhood, our living, black manhood. . . . and, in honoring him, we honor the best in ourselves. . . ."

A spotlight on the Apollo podium brought me back to the present as the announcer introduced Ruby Dee and Ossie Davis, the first of an intimate selection of my father's esteemed comrades and appreciators from the "front line" to speak and share their remembrances.

Aunt Ruby opened, "What a privilege to witness the radical gone respectable in our times. . . ." Uncle Ossie continued, "We in this community look upon this commemorative stamp finally as America's stamp of approval. . . ."

When I had mentioned the issuance of the stamp to others, the news simply stopped folks in their tracks. Touched. Teary-eyed. They could hardly believe it. They had to catch their breath, or ask me to repeat myself. "How can this be?" they wondered. "A stamp with Brother Malcolm's face on it?" "What does it mean?" "Is America really ready for a Malcolm X stamp, even if it is thirty-four years after his assassination?"

I reflected on the message of Congressman Chaka Fattah, the ranking Democrat on the Postal subcommittee, who commented, "There is no more appropriate honor than this stamp because Malcolm X sent all of us a message through his life and his life's work.

"Stamps are affixed to envelopes that contain messages, and when we receive an envelope with this particular stamp on it hopefully it is a message that will speak again to the conscience of this nation. Hopefully not just to those of African descent in America but to those who want to speak and be heard on the question of human rights throughout the world. To this day Malcolm X stands as a leader. His thoughts, his ideas, his conviction, and his courage provide an inspiration even now to new generations that come."

I've asked myself, What change in our society today permits the reevaluation of my father's convictions or his stance on the human injustices that plagued the international landscape? For years, he's been the subject of a patchwork of commentaries, numerous judgments, and endless character assessments from a spectrum of self-appointed experts. But, in spite of the psychoanalysis, Malcolm will always be exactly who he is, whether or not we as a society ever succeed in figuring him out. Truth does not change, only our awareness of it.

Not everyone agreed with my father's philosophy or methodology; he was considered complicated, intricate, and complex. Nevertheless, he was always a focused man with a commitment and a program. His plan of action, regardless of the stages of his life, his agenda, and his perspective were always poignantly clear.

Malcolm X never advocated violence. He was an advocate of cultural and social reconstruction—until a balance of equality was shared, "by any means necessary." Generally, this phrase of his was misused, even by those who were his supporters. But the statement was intended to encourage a paralyzed constituent of American culture to consider the range of options to which they were entitled—the "means." "By any means necessary" meant examine the obstacles, determine the vision, find the resolve, and explore the alternatives toward dissolving the obstacles. Anyone truly familiar with my father's ideology, autobiography, and speeches sincerely understands the significance of the now-famous phrase.

My father affected Americans—black and white—in untold measure and not always in ways as definitive as census charts and polls have dictated. We've misrepresented the silent majority on both sides. There were black folks who carried as much disdain for my father as some white folks did, and then there were some white folks for whom his life's lessons were as valuable a blueprint for personal and spiritual development as they have been for many black folks. Nevertheless, within the range of the boisterous and the silent there are still folks brown, red, and yellow on this continent and elsewhere who honor and respect the true message of Malcolm X Shabazz.

Fortunately, as a child, my surroundings were filled with my father's partners for social change. This warm, devoted circle of people was always on the front lines of the struggle, working to ensure the rightful equilibrium of human rights—not just domestically, but globally—"by any means necessary." Whether they were persons of note or simply hardworking citizens, these individuals in my early life were missionaries of justice, each committed to doing his or her part.

As the dedication ceremony continued at the Apollo, the master of ceremonies, activist-entertainer Harry Belafonte—yet another childhood "uncle"—framed the importance of this historic moment for the audience assembled.

"Each year the Postal Service receives more than forty thousand requests recommending subjects for U.S. stamps. Only thirty or so are chosen. Short of a national monument in Washington—and that's not a bad idea—a stamp is among the highest honors that our country can pay to any of its citizens."

The El-Hajj Malik El-Shabazz/Malcolm X stamp is the twenty-second in the Black Heritage Series, which was inaugurated in 1978. It joins such luminaries as Harriet Tubman, Frederick Douglass, A. Philip Randolph, Mary McLeod Bethune, Martin Luther King, Jr., and others. I am hopeful that the initial printing of 100 million stamps will be some inspiration to those who collect them or pass them on as gifts to represent or encourage one's personal enlightenment and triumph.

What my father aspired to be and what Allah had destined for him was nurtured chiefly by the fertile tutelage of his parents while his family was still together and thriving as a unit. This was before his father's murder by the Klan, his mother's emotional breakdown, and the subsequent scattering of his siblings and himself into an inadequate and inattentive foster care system.

My grandmother had a direct hand in the cultural, social, and intellectual education of her children. The attitude of people of color during the '20s and '30s festered with racial tension that produced varying degrees of misguided social and personal paralysis. Knowing this and being globally educated members of the Garvey movement cognizant of the true origins of the African in the Western Hemisphere, both my grandmother and her husband were intent on equipping their children with a clear awareness of the seed of their origins and its ancestral power. They knew that this would provide a base of strength for their children. My grandmother knew that in spite of America's social climate, her children would be able to discern for themselves when an act was generated by pure racism, or simply by ignorance.

For example, there are many who know the story about when my father, while on the honor roll and the eighth-grade class president, was told by his white teacher that his dream to be a lawyer was unrealistic for a "colored boy." Maybe he should consider carpentry. . . . He shared this story with us directly. The teacher actually admired my father greatly and didn't want to encourage him to enter a field of study that he believed wouldn't allow my father to excel. Misguided, yet well intended. A teacher crippled by a country that offered little promise or future for its indigenous and colored inhabitants.

Without the strong support of life with his parents and siblings under one roof and chafing under foster parents and teachers imposing limited state policies, Malcolm simply dropped out.

This is usually where the recounting of my father's life begins. In the street. Hustling, numbers running, stealing . . . Indeed these accounts were factual and he was always the first to tell them. But if his first fourteen years hadn't been rooted in a healthy diet of education and the richness of his heritage, Malcolm wouldn't have found himself gravitating to the prison libraries after he was incarcerated. The movie *Malcolm X*, which was originally contracted as *X: The Movie*, shows him learning how to read the dictionary as if he didn't already know how. The truth is, it had been a while since he'd read anything. But after being reacquainted with books, he proceeded to out-read the library stock. I've seen letters that my father wrote from prison in his early twenties, eagerly looking for the third volume of a text, or wanting help to track down out-of-print books, or even suggesting books to his friends and family on the outside.

The honor roll student reappeared as the layers of street life faded. He read so much that he had to begin to wear glasses.

With the encouragement of his brothers, he began studying the tenets of the Nation of Islam. While the Little brothers didn't adhere to all of the teachings personally, they did believe it was the only current American-based ideology that had the potential to unify black people and teach self-pride the way their childhood affiliation with the Garvey movement had done. Also, the brothers believed that through the Nation of Islam they could finally become part of a larger family that could reunite them once again.

It was as a result of the documentary he was producing on the Nation of Islam that Mike Wallace, an uncompromising, truth-seeking pioneer of broadcast journalism and now the senior correspondent of *60 Minutes*, first met my father on an assignment. He recalled those early meetings in his remarks at the stamp's unveiling:

"It was forty years ago, back in 1959, that I first heard about a man who called himself Malcolm X. We at Channel 13 had set out to produce a documentary that we had intended to call 'The Hate That Hate Produced.' It was a report about a group and a man just beginning to get some attention in the white world. The group was the Black Muslims and their leader was Elijah Muhammad. [When] we finally broadcast the documentary, America at large finally learned about the Nation and their desire to separate from the white man. Their hatred of the white man for that effectively was their credo back then: The white man hates us, so we should hate the white man back. Not long after the broadcast, which caused a considerable stir, Louis Lomax invited me to sit down for breakfast for my first meeting with Malcolm, and strangely and rather swiftly after that morning a curious friendship began to develop, and slowly a trust. And on my part a growing understanding and eventually an admiration for a man with a daring mind and heart. And gradually it became apparent to me that here was a genuine, compassionate, and far-seeing leader in the making. A man utterly devoted to his people, but at the same time he was bent on reconciliation between the races in America.

"And that, of course, that was heresy to the Nation of Islam at the time.

"Malcolm was still evolving, still finding his way, still finding his constituency back then when he was struck down—to him not unexpectedly—struck down by forces who feared that his way, his leadership, might be a serious threat to their power. I have treasured the memory of the Malcolm that I knew. I know he trusted me as a reporter, but in the few years that I had the chance to know him, he sent me on my own voyage of reportorial discovery and understanding.

"[The] stamp that honors him today is the kind of recognition he deserves as a courageous American hero."

In time my father's growth and independence would be his undoing. The Nation reprimanded him, stripped him of all powers of attorney, silenced him, and then exiled him. At first his expulsion left him feeling like a man without a home, much the way it had been in his childhood. Ultimately, however, it gave him the freedom he needed.

He finally began accepting long-standing invitations he'd received to travel abroad. There were many foreign heads of state and prime ministers who had long taken note of this charismatic champion of the people.

With my mother's blessings for his journey, my father set out to visit Kwame Nkrumah of Ghana, Nasser of Egypt, Prince Faisal of Saudi Arabia, and more. The warm welcomes and instant paternal relationships became an essential component of his cleansing and rebirth as he traveled throughout Europe, Africa, and the Middle East, culminating in his great pilgrimage to Mecca.

As my father's philosophy expanded, he began to empower, enlighten, and embrace an untold populace extending far beyond the limits of governmental control. However, as long as Dr. Martin Luther King, Jr., remained in the South, and my father in the North, neither was too difficult to monitor. But when my father and Dr. King became colleagues and decided to bridge their two philosophies and unite the American commonwealth toward a greater goal, they both became tremendous threats to the status quo. Sadly, this fear was shared by some of their own constituents and supporters who believed that the union of both would weaken or detract from the strength of each movement.

One man whose brethrenship never wavered was the Honorable Percy Sutton, my father's attorney and a perpetual drum for our family, who approached the podium at the Apollo. He paused reflectively and warmly paid tribute to my father, while placing my father's life in its proper perspective:

"It is a miracle, really, if you think about it!" The audience burst into applause. ". . . The journey of Malcolm X was long and hard. . . . I can remember a Minister Malcolm that nobody wanted to be near; lawyers, accountants, persons of consequence to the black community . . . were afraid to be identified with him, afraid to be seen with him. . . .

"We would invite them to come because we needed lawyers, we needed doctors, we needed persons of ability, but they were frightened, they were frightened by other people's attitudes toward Minister Malcolm. . . .

"Let me for a moment tell you who Malcolm X was. Malcolm was not a spiteful man. Malcolm X was a revolutionary. But he was not a mean-spirited revolutionary, he was a gentle man. A kind man, a concerned man.

"It was so bad, ladies and gentleman, that even at Malcolm's death there were people who were afraid to come to the funeral. . . . There was not a major black church in the entire city of New York that was willing to let us bury him from their edifices. It was a small church up on Amsterdam Avenue [the Faith Temple Church of God] that permitted us to come."

Looking into Mr. Sutton's face and seeing him diplomatically balance all that he knew of my parents' challenges brought back an old sadness, one that had not healed since the loss of his "little sister," my mother, Betty. Feeling Mr. Sutton's steadfast devotion, I found myself massaging the ache from my own heart as I reflected on America's treatment of my parents during my childhood. Despite my youthful joys and sense of safety, the trials my parents faced were unrelenting. As well, the way my father was regarded during his lifetime robbed him of any peace in knowing that his life and contributions mattered, and that his family would live without jeopardy or repercussion.

Now, perhaps sanctioned by a karmic wave of "in due time," America is acknowledging Malcolm yet again.

The Honorable S. David Fineman, member of the Board of Governors of the U.S. Postal Service, commented on the appropriateness of this acknowledgment during his introduction to the stamp's official unveiling, "Today we honor not only a great African American but a great American. Malcolm X was one of the most charismatic and pivotal figures of our time. He was a passionate and persuasive voice for change, and his controversial ideas helped bring race relations to a national stage.

"[Malcolm] X poured his energy and anger into speaking the truth about the plight of African Americans. He spoke with a rare passion and eloquence. He became a worldwide hero. A symbol of strength and defiance. He wasn't shy about telling us where society was going wrong.

"['Although] it has been thirty-four years since we lost Malcolm X, his words, his voice, his vision, his story of transformation lives on. They have become part of us in a journey to wholeness.

"We must never forget the challenge Malcolm X issued to us. 'Let us learn to live together in justice and love.'"

I had long known of the individual and cultural values that others placed on my father's life. But I would learn of another measurement and display of that value in the marketplace.

On October 2, 1992, I was on location in southern Africa producing a segment for a documentary film. During a break in the day, I returned to my hotel room for my afternoon siesta.

This particular afternoon, I turned on my television and searched until I found a CNN broadcast. Global news commentaries now became the backdrop in my room. I then pulled down the top sheet and blanket on my bed so I could rest. No sooner had my head touched the pillow, I began to fade, exchanging conscious sounds of the television for those of my inner thoughts. But in a matter of moments I was interrupted by the broadcaster stating, "Earlier today the Alex Haley estate auctioned off his items. . . ." I instantly sat up and listened in disbelief. The newscast continued, "Among the items sold was the original manuscript of *The Autobiography of Malcolm X*, with actual handwritten notes by Malcolm X himself."

I cannot possibly recapture in words how I felt at that instant. It seemed inconceivable that such a personal and historic document could be bartered away so carelessly.

It was yet another loss to contend with. I was still brokenhearted about my godfather being gone, and greatly disappointed by the decision to diminish the value of his life's contributions by way of the auction block, a symbol that he fought so hard to dismantle in the telling of *Roots*. Doubly painful was the fact that this bidding war included a part of me and my family with neither our permission nor participation. Had anyone thought to offer my father's wife and children first right of refusal?

I jotted down as much data as possible during the news coverage and then called the legal firm handling my godfather's estate auction in Tennessee. Although I did reach a representative, little information was given over the telephone so I scheduled a subsequent call following my return to the States.

During my long hours of travel across the Atlantic, I worried about how this gross display may have been tugging at my mother. How was she feeling about it all? As it was, she'd become increasingly busy due to the explosion of interest about her husband, and the preparations for the release of *X: The Movie*.

Malcolm X had been reborn during this period. It was approximately six weeks prior to the world premiere and my mother and I were about to embark on a press junket that was to exceed a hundred interviews—print, electronic, video—to promote the film and discuss the resurgence of Malcolm.

The vibrant, pop-culture marketing of the film gave people permission to claim and learn about Malcolm in a forum that was not threatening. For people who didn't know anything about his life, America now provided a healthier, safer atmosphere to do so. It also gave the public the freedom and opportunity to talk about Malcolm out loud, as opposed to in the murmured huddles that reflected the climate of the previous generation.

So much of the public and the media were under the impression that the making of *X: The Movie* was a new venture. That its director had to battle alone, tooth and nail, on behalf of 35 million black Americans. Things aren't always as they seem. The components in the making of this film were very significant and intertwined like the main branches on a family tree. They were not to be forgotten.

Shortly after my father's assassination in 1965 and the publication of *The Autobiography of Malcolm X*, Marvin Worth, a friend of my father's from their teenage years, approached Alex and my mother about making a film about my father's life. Once both agreed, Marvin brought James Baldwin on board to write the script and Arnold Perl to modify the screenplay. During what was to take twenty-five years to realization, Marvin Worth produced the Warner Bros. documentary *El-Hajj Malik El-Shabazz*. This was the first definitive film stock collection of the life of Malcolm X and it traveled extensively throughout the nation's university circuit as well as to civil rights and Afro-American nationalist events. In the meantime, this fraternity of men worked diligently against all setbacks and odds to create a film respectfully representative of their brother, now gone—the man who, in their eyes, America had betrayed.

But old attitudes and distorted stubborn impressions of my father outlived Arnold Perl and James Baldwin. Marvin Worth was the lone torchbearer, a thorn in Hollywood's side, holding true to the initial dream for almost twenty-five years, despite the taboo image of my father. Single-handedly, while keeping my mother abreast of all updates, he continued to commission writers again and again.

Marvin's tenacity was astonishing, to the dismay of many. His dedication and faithfulness were due to his own personal loyalty to my parents and his passion for displaying onscreen the integrity and power of my father's message.

In the late '70s, Marvin began to include me informally in the process of the film development. This became very cathartic for me. I accompanied him to meetings with prospective directors and writers. Shortly thereafter, I began reading through different drafts submitted, and I recall him telling me, "Some of them are overwriting. They are trying to 'create' Malcolm as the hero. I just told them to start from scratch; if you write honestly, the hero will emerge."

Those who knew Malcolm X Shabazz personally wanted to be sure that the negative myth around his memory would be erased by portraying the truths of his mission, and the depth of his heart.

Finally, it was the right time. In 1991, without any further delays, the deal to make the film of my father's life came through. A long-awaited dream was to be realized. But before it made it to the screen, we lost Alex.

My father, James Baldwin, Arnold Perl, and my godfather, Alex Haley, were all with us in spirit as my mother, her daughters, and Marvin Worth journeyed forth toward the final realization of this history-making film, which not only made it come to life, it ignited a cultural phenomenon.

During this period, total sales of *The Autobiography of Malcolm X* reached record numbers. Nearly 3 million copies have been sold worldwide. At least twenty new literary works that used my father's life as a subject appeared on bookshelves. Young males, newly born, were being named Malcolm, Malik, and Omowale after my father. His philosophy, speeches, and life transitions were now being adopted by a whole new generation of youngsters, internationally.

Adult appreciators were coming out of the closet, waving their Malcolm banners boldly. Both American and foreign students utilized him as their prototype for human development, spiritual dedication, and equality.

Parents of the '90s were not as apprehensive as the parents of the '60s, '70s, and '80s. Instead, as their many letters and comments informed me, they were relieved that at a stage when their children's discipline and social mores were being challenged, their son or daughter had claimed characteristics and habits associated with Malcolm's.

Psychologists, professors, journalists, and critics rediscovered Malcolm X for review and general analysis. New documentaries unfolded, revealing film footage long existing yet previously edited from cultural consumption.

The sensations, passions, and sincerities of this black American crusader, plus his new crossover and international marketability, now challenged all the preceding assessments of twentieth-century historians, social experts, the media, and most pointedly our government.

The resurrection of Malcolm X also precipitated a new wave of unauthorized exploitation of his image. In the early days—the '60s, '70s, and '80s, before my father's likeness had become a licensed commodity—my mother didn't mind the bootlegged T-shirts, cassette tapes, and framed photos being sold at various events around the country during his birthday, Black History Month, and the like. In those years she felt it was one of the pulses that kept Malcolm alive on campuses, in community centers, and on cultural occasions. As a mother and educator, she was comforted by the thought that such remembrances would enable young people to have an opportunity to be exposed to her husband, ask questions, learn, and achieve. Pass it on!

When people commented on the exploitation, she'd generously reply, "It's love that's making them do this for my husband."

On the other hand, if the intentions of the merchant were not honorable, you'd better believe that she'd be heading in their direction to inform them of their malfeasance and impropriety. It was imperative to my mother that the memory of her husband be respected with the honor she knew he deserved. It was not okay to mistreat her husband. *Not okay*. In his absence, for more than thirty years, she tirelessly guarded his legacy and fought to ensure that his ideology was clear. For her, it was essential that if she was going to lose her lifemate to the struggle, then those for whom he had struggled must be educated. They must be made aware of the conviction, dedication, and sacrifices he made on behalf of his faith in humanity and his mission to unite us as one community, certain of our inherent right to our own destiny. My mother took note of anyone who maligned any characteristic of her husband or anything associated with him.

To my mother, Malcolm X Shabazz was reserved for herself, her children, and the many persons, young and mature, who have been fortified, caressed, and inspired to employ aspects of my father's life lessons and personal discoveries as a bridge to their own inner strength and as a foundation for their "personhood."

"Personhood" is a word I first heard as I listened to the eloquence of Brother Randall Robinson, president of the TransAfrica Forum, during his remarks at the Apollo commemoration. While he is a generation younger than my father, both he and his elder brother Max always symbolized a genuine and authentic continuity throughout the struggle. They are men of their word, like Haki Madhubuti, Kweisi Mfume, and Danny Glover—the few in their generation who say it, mean it, and live it. Thank God for them as they continue to make certain that my father's beat goes on.

"I grew up in the Old South in Richmond, Virginia," said Brother Randall Robinson.

"I am one of the unfortunate millions who never knew or met Malcolm X.

"So perhaps I can presume to speak for those millions like me, then and now, when I say that Malcolm X was a shining model for a new, whole, and proud black personhood.

"*Before* we in the South could see through the mean veil of Southern segregation—there was Malcolm X.

"*Before* we could function beyond the humiliation of Southern bigotry—there was Malcolm X.

"*Before* we could come to know Africa's glorious past—there was Malcolm X.

"*Before* we could find our self-esteem and self-respect—there was Malcolm X.

"And we owe him so dearly in ways our young must never be allowed to forget.

"Where we have now the very possibility of courage—we *owe* Malcolm X.

"Where we have the wisdom to search for our history before the Atlantic slave trade—we *owe* Malcolm X.

"Where we have the political integrity to simply stand for something because it is right—we *owe* Malcolm X.

"It is not often that an American government institution honors those who embody a whole and uncompromised truth. But today is one such rare occasion. And I will keep it in my heart for the rest of my life."

At that moment, Brother Robinson spoke for all of us, and I will forever carry in my heart the sincerities of that ceremony. In particular, I will remember that as my five younger sisters and I gathered onstage for Harry Belafonte's closing remarks, I remained full. As I listened to the final notes sung by the Boys Choir of Harlem their song's message still lingered in my heart: "All black boys are born of heroes."

I thought of my father and his parents, my mother and her parents, each family's respective lineage and history of participation in social movements—Garvey on one side and Booker T. Washington on the other. I thought of my sisters and I standing there, parentless, yet in constant celebration of our parents' lives. We are blessed every day by the union and the victorious sojourns that Malcolm X Shabazz and his beloved Betty Saunders Shabazz shared on this earth.

When I first realized that my mother wouldn't be here to witness her husband's likeness being unveiled on a United States postal stamp, after participating in the initial discussions, a lonely tear began to slip down my cheek. But then it dawned on me that she wasn't missing the occasion. In fact, she had the best seat in the house. She is now where she longed to be. Beside her husband. And together they are toasting our healthy continuance and productive lives.

As their eldest, I have pledged time and again to care for their daughters, my younger sisters, in their memory, in their honor, and with their celestial guidance.

When the curtain descends on this current wave of attention and the thematic celebrations cool down, my sisters and I will remain proud. Proud of a man and his wife, proud of a cause and a heartbeat that was a metronome for us long before the crossover audience considered them worthy of praise. We, the Shabazz daughters and our children, will forever be nurtured by our legacy.

My inherent idealism yearns for the issuance of the commemorative stamp and the living document of *The Autobiography of Malcolm X* to continue to bridge ignorance with insight, and despondency with hope. It is essential for people to trust—even through long periods when dreams may appear to have been deferred, delayed, and overshadowed—that there comes a time when an unwavering will, a strong belief, and endless prayers bring great visions to realization.

The Autobiography of Malcolm X is evidence of one man's will and belief in prayer and purpose. As you read my father's autobiography, whether for the first time or after a long absence, it is my hope that you will come to know him foremost as a man. A man who lived to serve—initially a specific people, then a nation, and eventually all people of the world. Some have said that my father was ahead of his time, but the truth is he was on time and perhaps we were late. I trust that through his words we may come to honor and respect all members of the human family as he did. In closing, I offer you my father's own words: "One day, may we all meet together in the light of understanding."

M. S. HANDLER

INTRODUCTION

The Sunday before he was to officially announce his rupture with Elijah Muhammad, Malcolm X came to my home to discuss his plans and give me some necessary documentation.

Mrs. Handler had never met Malcolm before this fateful visit. She served us coffee and cakes while Malcolm spoke in the courteous, gentle manner that was his in private. It was obvious to me that Mrs. Handler was impressed by Malcolm. His personality filled our living room.

Malcolm's attitude was that of a man who had reached a crossroads in his life and was making a choice under an inner compulsion. A wistful smile illuminated his countenance from time to time—a smile that said many things. I felt uneasy because Malcolm was evidently trying to say something which his pride and dignity prevented him from expressing. I sensed that Malcolm was not confident he would succeed in escaping from the shadowy world which had held him in thrall.

Mrs. Handler was quiet and thoughtful after Malcolm's departure. Looking up suddenly, she said:

"You know, it was like having tea with a black panther."

The description startled me. The black panther is an aristocrat in the animal kingdom. He is beautiful. He is dangerous. As a man, Malcolm X had the physical bearing and the inner self-confidence of a born aristocrat. And he was potentially dangerous. No man in our time aroused fear and hatred in the white man as did Malcolm, because in him the white man sensed an implacable foe who could not be had for any price—a man unreservedly committed to the cause of liberating the black man in American society rather than integrating the black man into that society.

My first meeting with Malcolm X took place in March 1963 in the Muslim restaurant of Temple Number Seven on Lenox Avenue. I had been assigned by *The New York Times* to investigate the growing pressures within the Negro community. Thirty years of experience as a reporter in Western and Eastern Europe had taught me that the forces in a developing social struggle are frequently buried beneath the visible surface and make themselves felt in many ways long before they burst out into the open. These generative forces make themselves felt through the power of an idea long before their organizational forms can openly challenge the establishment. It is the merit of European political scientists and sociologists to give a high priority to the power of ideas in a social struggle. In the United States, it is our weakness to confuse the numerical strength of an organization and the publicity attached to leaders with the germinating forces that sow the seeds of social upheaval in our community.

In studying the growing pressures within the Negro community, I had not only to seek the opinions of the established leaders of the civil rights organizations but the opinions of those working in the penumbra of the movement—"underground," so to speak. This is why I sought out Malcolm X, whose ideas had reached me through the medium of Negro integrationists. Their thinking was already reflecting a high degree of nascent Negro nationalism.

I did not know what to expect as I waited for Malcolm. I was the only white person in the restaurant, an immaculate establishment tended by somber, handsome, uncommunicative Negroes. Signs reading "Smoking Forbidden" were pasted on the highly polished mirrors. I was served coffee but became uneasy in this aseptic, silent atmosphere as time passed. Malcolm finally arrived. He was very tall, handsome, of impressive bearing. His skin had a bronze hue.

I rose to greet him and extended my hand. Malcolm's hand came up slowly. I had the impression it was difficult for him to take my hand, but, *noblesse oblige,* he did. Malcolm then did a curious thing which he always repeated whenever we met in public in a restaurant in New York or Washington. He asked whether I would mind if he took a seat facing the door. I had

had similar requests put to me in Eastern European capitals. Malcolm was on the alert; he wished to see every person who entered the restaurant. I quickly realized that Malcolm constantly walked in danger.

We spoke for more than three hours at this first encounter. His views about the white man were devastating, but at no time did he transgress against my own personality and make me feel that I, as an individual, shared in the guilt. He attributed the degradation of the Negro people to the white man. He denounced integration as a fraud. He contended that if the leaders of the established civil rights organizations persisted, the social struggle would end in bloodshed because he was certain the white man would never concede full integration. He argued the Muslim case for separation as the only solution in which the Negro could achieve his own identity, develop his own culture, and lay the foundations for a self-respecting productive community. He was vague about where the Negro state could be established.

Malcolm refused to see the impossibility of the white man conceding secession from the United States; at this stage in his career he contended it was the only solution. He defended Islam as a religion that did not recognize color bars. He denounced Christianity as a religion designed for slaves and the Negro clergy as the curse of the black man, exploiting him for their own purposes instead of seeking to liberate him, and acting as handmaidens of the white community in its determination to keep the Negroes in a subservient position.

During this first encounter Malcolm also sought to enlighten me about the Negro mentality. He repeatedly cautioned me to beware of Negro affirmations of good will toward the white man. He said that the Negro had been trained to dissemble and conceal his real thoughts, as a matter of survival. He argued that the Negro only tells the white man what he believes the white man wishes to hear, and that the art of dissembling reached a point where even Negroes cannot truthfully say they understand what their fellow Negroes believe. The art of deception practiced by the Negro was based on a thorough understanding of the white man's mores, he said; at the same time the Negro has remained a closed book to the white man, who has never displayed any interest in understanding the Negro.

Malcolm's exposition of his social ideas was clear and thoughtful, if somewhat shocking to the white initiate, but most disconcerting in our talk was Malcolm's belief in Elijah Muhammad's history of the origins of man, and in a genetic theory devised to prove the superiority of black over white—a theory stunning to me in its sheer absurdity.

After this first encounter, I realized that there were two Malcolms—the private and the public person. His public performances on television and at meeting halls produced an almost terrifying effect. His implacable marshaling of facts and his logic had something of a new dialectic, diabolic in its force. He frightened white television audiences, demolished his Negro opponents, but elicited a remarkable response from Negro audiences. Many Negro opponents in the end refused to make any public appearances on the same platform with him. The troubled white audiences were confused, disturbed, felt themselves threatened. Some began to consider Malcolm evil incarnate.

Malcolm appealed to the two most disparate elements in the Negro community—the depressed mass, and the galaxy of Negro writers and artists who have burst on the American scene in the past decade. The Negro middle class—the Negro "establishment"—abhorred and feared Malcolm as much as he despised it.

The impoverished Negroes respected Malcolm in the way that wayward children respect the grandfather image. It was always a strange and moving experience to walk with Malcolm in Harlem. He was known to all. People glanced at him shyly. Sometimes Negro youngsters would ask for his autograph. It always seemed to me that their affection for Malcolm was inspired by the fact that although he had become a national figure, he was still a man of the people who, they felt, would never betray them. The Negroes have suffered too long from betrayals and in Malcolm they sensed a man of mission. They knew his origins, with which they could identify. They knew his criminal and prison record, which he had never concealed. They looked upon Malcolm with a certain wonderment. Here was a man who had come from the lower depths which they still inhabited, who had triumphed over his own criminality and his own ignorance to become a forceful leader and spokesman, an uncompromising champion of his people.

Although many could not share his Muslim religious beliefs, they found in Malcolm's puritanism a standing reproach to their own lives. Malcolm had purged himself of all the ills that afflict the depressed Negro mass: drugs, alcohol, tobacco, not to speak of criminal pursuits. His personal life was impeccable—of a puritanism unattainable for the mass. Human redemption—Malcolm had achieved it in his own lifetime, and this was known to the Negro community.

In his television appearances and at public meetings Malcolm articulated the woes and the aspirations of the depressed Negro mass in a way it was unable to do for itself. When he attacked the white man, Malcolm did for the Negroes what they couldn't do for themselves—he attacked with a violence and anger that spoke for the ages of misery. It was not an academic exercise of just giving hell to "Mr. Charlie."

Many of the Negro writers and artists who are national figures today revered Malcolm for what they considered his ruthless honesty in stating the Negro case, his refusal to compromise, and his search for a group identity that had been destroyed by the white man when he brought the Negroes in chains from Africa. The Negro writers and artists regarded Malcolm as the great catalyst, the man who inspired self-respect and devotion in the downtrodden millions.

A group of these artists gathered one Sunday in my home, and we talked about Malcolm. Their devotion to him as a man was moving. One said: "Malcolm will never betray us. We have suffered too much from betrayals in the past."

Malcolm's attitude toward the white man underwent a marked change in 1964—a change that contributed to his break with Elijah Muhammad and his racist doctrines. Malcolm's meteoric eruption on the national scene brought him into wider contact with white men who were not the "devils" he had thought they were. He was much in demand as a speaker at student forums in Eastern universities and had appeared at many by the end of his short career as a national figure. He always spoke respectfully and with a certain surprise of the positive response of white students to his lectures.

A second factor that contributed to his conversion to wider horizons was a growing doubt about the authenticity of Elijah Muhammad's version of the Muslim religion—a doubt that grew into a certainty with more knowledge and more experience. Certain secular practices at the Chicago headquarters of Elijah Muhammad had come to Malcolm's notice and he was profoundly shocked.

Finally, he embarked on a number of prolonged trips to Mecca and the newly independent African states through the good offices of the representatives of the Arab League in the United States. It was on his first trip to Mecca that he came to the conclusion that he had yet to discover Islam.

Assassins' bullets ended Malcolm's career before he was able to develop this new approach, which in essence recognized the Negroes as an integral part of the American community—a far cry from Elijah Muhammad's doctrine of separation. Malcolm had reached the midpoint in redefining his attitude to this country and the white-black relationship. He no longer inveighed against the United States but against a segment of the United States represented by overt white supremacists in the South and covert white supremacists in the North.

It was Malcolm's intention to raise Negro militancy to a new high point with the main thrust aimed at both the Southern and Northern white supremacists. The Negro problem, which he had always said should be renamed "the white man's problem," was beginning to assume new dimensions for him in the last months of his life.

To the very end, Malcolm sought to refashion the broken strands between the American Negroes and African culture. He saw in this the road to a new sense of group identity, a self-conscious role in history, and above all a sense of man's own worth which he claimed the white man had destroyed in the Negro.

American autobiographical literature is filled with numerous accounts of remarkable men who pulled themselves to the summit by their bootstraps. Few are as poignant as Malcolm's memoirs. As testimony to the power of redemption and the force of human personality, the autobiography of Malcolm X is a revelation.

New York, June 1965

CHAPTER ONE

NIGHTMARE

When my mother was pregnant with me, she told me later, a party of hooded Ku Klux Klan riders galloped up to our home in Omaha, Nebraska, one night. Surrounding the house, brandishing their shotguns and rifles, they shouted for my father to come out. My mother went to the front door and opened it. Standing where they could see her pregnant condition, she told them that she was alone with her three small children, and that my father was away, preaching, in Milwaukee. The Klansmen shouted threats and warnings at her that we had better get out of town because "the good Christian white people" were not going to stand for my father's "spreading trouble" among the "good" Negroes of Omaha with the "back to Africa" preachings of Marcus Garvey.

My father, the Reverend Earl Little, was a Baptist minister, a dedicated organizer for Marcus Aurelius Garvey's U.N.I.A. (Universal Negro Improvement Association). With the help of such disciples as my father, Garvey, from his headquarters in New York City's Harlem, was raising the banner of black-race purity and exhorting the Negro masses to return to their ancestral African homeland—a cause which had made Garvey the most controversial black man on earth.

Still shouting threats, the Klansmen finally spurred their horses and galloped around the house, shattering every window pane with their gun butts. Then they rode off into the night, their torches flaring, as suddenly as they had come.

My father was enraged when he returned. He decided to wait until I was born—which would be soon—and then the family

1

would move. I am not sure why he made this decision, for he was not a frightened Negro, as most then were, and many still are today. My father was a big, six-foot-four, very black man. He had only one eye. How he had lost the other one I have never known. He was from Reynolds, Georgia, where he had left school after the third or maybe fourth grade. He believed, as did Marcus Garvey, that freedom, independence and self-respect could never be achieved by the Negro in America, and that therefore the Negro should leave America to the white man and return to his African land of origin. Among the reasons my father had decided to risk and dedicate his life to help disseminate this philosophy among his people was that he had seen four of his six brothers die by violence, three of them killed by white men, including one by lynching. What my father could not know then was that of the remaining three, including himself, only one, my Uncle Jim, would die in bed, of natural causes. Northern white police were later to shoot my Uncle Oscar. And my father was finally himself to die by the white man's hands.

It has always been my belief that I, too, will die by violence. I have done all that I can to be prepared.

I was my father's seventh child. He had three children by a previous marriage—Ella, Earl, and Mary, who lived in Boston. He had met and married my mother in Philadelphia, where their first child, my oldest full brother, Wilfred, was born. They moved from Philadelphia to Omaha, where Hilda and then Philbert were born.

I was next in line. My mother was twenty-eight when I was born on May 19, 1925, in an Omaha hospital. Then we moved to Milwaukee, where Reginald was born. From infancy, he had some kind of hernia condition which was to handicap him physically for the rest of his life.

Louise Little, my mother, who was born in Grenada, in the British West Indies, looked like a white woman. Her father *was* white. She had straight black hair, and her accent did not sound like a Negro's. Of this white father of hers, I know nothing except her shame about it. I remember hearing her say she was glad that she had never seen him. It was, of course, because of him that I got my reddish-brown "mariny" color of skin, and my hair of the same color. I was the lightest child in our family. (Out in the world later on, in Boston and New York, I was among the millions of Negroes who were insane enough to feel that it was some kind of status symbol to be light-complexioned—that one was actually fortunate to be born thus. But, still later, I learned to hate every drop of that white rapist's blood that is in me.)

Our family stayed only briefly in Milwaukee, for my father wanted to find a place where he could raise our own food and perhaps build a business. The teaching of Marcus Garvey stressed becoming independent of the white man. We went next, for some reason, to Lansing, Michigan. My father bought a house and soon, as had been his pattern, he was doing free-lance Christian preaching in local Negro Baptist churches, and during the week he was roaming about spreading word of Marcus Garvey.

He had begun to lay away savings for the store he had always wanted to own when, as always, some stupid local Uncle Tom Negroes began to funnel stories about his revolutionary beliefs to the local white people. This time, the get-out-of-town threats came from a local hate society called The Black Legion. They wore black robes instead of white. Soon, nearly everywhere my father went, Black Legionnaires were reviling him as an "uppity nigger" for wanting to own a store, for living outside the Lansing Negro district, for spreading unrest and dissention among "the good niggers."

As in Omaha, my mother was pregnant again, this time with my youngest sister. Shortly after Yvonne was born came the nightmare night in 1929, my earliest vivid memory. I remember being suddenly snatched awake into a frightening confusion of pistol shots and shouting and smoke and flames. My father had shouted and shot at the two white men who had set the fire and were running away. Our home was burning down around us. We were lunging and bumping and tumbling all over each other trying to escape. My mother, with the baby in her arms, just made it into the yard before the house crashed in, showering sparks. I remember we were outside in the night in our underwear, crying and yelling our heads off. The white police and firemen came and stood around watching as the house burned down to the ground.

My father prevailed on some friends to clothe and house us temporarily; then he moved us into another house on the outskirts of East Lansing. In those days Negroes weren't allowed after dark in East Lansing proper. There's where Michigan State University is located; I related all of this to an audience of students when I spoke there in January, 1963 (and had the first reunion in a long while with my younger brother, Robert, who was there doing postgraduate studies in psychology). I told them how East Lansing harassed us so much that we had to move again, this time two miles out of town, into the country. This was where my father built for us with his own hands a four-room house. This is where I really begin to remember things—this home where I started to grow up.

After the fire, I remember that my father was called in and questioned about a permit for the pistol with which he had shot at the white men who set the fire. I remember that the police were always dropping by our house, shoving things around, "just checking" or "looking for a gun." The pistol they were looking for—which they never found, and for which they wouldn't issue a permit—was sewed up inside a pillow. My father's .22 rifle and his shotgun, though, were right out in the open; everyone had them for hunting birds and rabbits and other game.

After that, my memories are of the friction between my father and mother. They seemed to be nearly always at odds. Sometimes my father would beat her. It might have had something to do with the fact that my mother had a pretty good education. Where she got it I don't know. But an educated woman, I suppose, can't resist the temptation to correct an uneducated man. Every now and then, when she put those smooth words on him, he would grab her.

My father was also belligerent toward all of the children, except me. The older ones he would beat almost savagely if they broke any of his rules—and he had so many rules it was hard to know them all. Nearly all my whippings came from my mother. I've thought a lot about why. I actually believe that as anti-white as my father was, he was subconsciously so afflicted with the white man's brainwashing of Negroes that he inclined to favor the light ones, and I was his lightest child. Most Negro parents in those days would almost instinctively treat any lighter children better than they did the darker ones. It came directly from the slavery tradition that the "mulatto," because he was visibly nearer to white, was therefore "better."

My two other images of my father are both outside the home. One was his role as a Baptist preacher. He never pastored in any regular church of his own; he was always a "visiting preacher." I remember especially his favorite sermon: "That little *black* train is a-comin' . . . an' you better get all your business right!" I guess this also fit his association with the back-to-Africa movement, with Marcus Garvey's "Black Train Homeward." My brother Philbert, the one just older than me, loved church, but it confused and amazed me. I would sit goggle-eyed at my father jumping and shouting as he preached, with the congregation jumping and shouting behind him, their souls and bodies devoted to singing and praying. Even at that young age, I just couldn't believe in the Christian concept of Jesus as someone divine. And no religious person, until I was a man in my twenties—and then in prison—could tell me anything. I had very little respect for most people who represented religion.

It was in his role as a preacher that my father had most contact with the Negroes of Lansing. Believe me when I tell you that those Negroes were in bad shape then. They are still in bad shape—though in a different way. By that I mean that I don't know a town with a higher percentage of complacent and misguided so-called "middle-class" Negroes—the typical status-symbol-oriented, integration-seeking type of Negroes. Just recently, I was standing in a lobby at the United Nations talking with an African ambassador and his wife, when a Negro came up to me and said, "You know me?" I was a little embarrassed because I thought he was someone I should remember. It turned out that he was one of those bragging, self-satisfied, "middle-class" Lansing Negroes. I wasn't ingratiated. He was the type who would never have been associated with Africa, until the fad of having African friends became a status-symbol for "middle-class" Negroes.

Back when I was growing up, the "successful" Lansing Negroes were such as waiters and bootblacks. To be a janitor at some downtown store was to be highly respected. The real "elite," the "big shots," the "voices of the race," were the waiters at the Lansing Country Club and the shoeshine boys at the state capitol. The only Negroes who really had any money were the ones in the numbers racket, or who ran the gambling houses, or who in some other way lived parasitically off the poorest ones, who were the masses. No Negroes were hired then by Lansing's big Oldsmobile plant, or the Reo plant. (Do you remember the Reo? It was manufactured in Lansing, and R. E. Olds, the man after whom it was named, also lived in Lansing. When the war came along, they hired some Negro janitors.) The bulk of the Negroes were either on Welfare, or W.P.A., or they starved.

The day was to come when our family was so poor that we would eat the hole out of a doughnut; but at that time we were much better off than most town Negroes. The reason was that we raised much of our own food out there in the country where we were. We were much better off than the town Negroes who would shout, as my father preached, for the pie-in-the-sky and their heaven in the hereafter while the white man had his here on earth.

I knew that the collections my father got for his preaching were mainly what fed and clothed us, and he also did other odd jobs, but still the image of him that made me proudest was his crusading and militant campaigning with the words of Marcus Garvey. As young as I was then, I knew from what I overheard that my father was saying something that made him a "tough" man. I remember an old lady, grinning and saying to my father, "You're scaring these white folks to death!"

One of the reasons I've always felt that my father favored me was that to the best of my remembrance, it was only me that he sometimes took with him to the Garvey U.N.I.A. meetings which he held quietly in different people's homes. There were never more than a few people at any one time—twenty at most. But that was a lot, packed into someone's living room. I noticed how differently they all acted, although sometimes they were the same people who jumped and shouted in church. But in these meetings both they and my father were more intense, more intelligent and down to earth. It made me feel the same way.

I can remember hearing of "Adam driven out of the garden into the caves of Europe," "Africa for the Africans," "Ethiopians, Awake!" And my father would talk about how it would not be much longer before Africa would be completely run by Negroes—"by black men," was the phrase he always used.

"No one knows when the hour of Africa's redemption cometh. It is in the wind. It is coming. One day, like a storm, it will be here."

I remember seeing the big, shiny photographs of Marcus Garvey that were passed from hand to hand. My father had a big envelope of them that he always took to these meetings. The pictures showed what seemed to me millions of Negroes thronged in parade behind Garvey riding in a fine car, a big black man dressed in a dazzling uniform with gold braid on it, and he was wearing a thrilling hat with tall plumes. I remember hearing that he had black followers not only in the United States but all around the world, and I remember how the meetings always closed with my father saying, several times, and the people chanting after him, "Up, you mighty race, you can accomplish what you will!"

I have never understood why, after hearing as much as I did of these kinds of things, I somehow never thought, then, of the black people in Africa. My image of Africa, at that time, was of naked savages, cannibals, monkeys and tigers and steaming jungles.

My father would drive in his old black touring car, sometimes taking me, to meeting places all around the Lansing area. I remember one daytime meeting (most were at night) in the town of Owosso, forty miles from Lansing, which the Negroes called "White City." (Owosso's greatest claim to fame is that it is the home town of Thomas E. Dewey.) As in East Lansing, no Negroes were allowed on the streets there after dark—hence the daytime meeting. In point of fact, in those days lots of Michigan towns were like that. Every town had a few "home" Negroes who lived there. Sometimes it would be just one family, as in the nearby county seat, Mason, which had a single Negro family named Lyons. Mr. Lyons had been a famous football star at Mason High School, was highly thought of in Mason, and consequently he now worked around that town in menial jobs.

My mother at this time seemed to be always working—cooking, washing, ironing, cleaning, and fussing over us eight children. And she was usually either arguing with or not speaking to my father. One cause of friction was that she had strong ideas about what she wouldn't eat—and didn't want *us* to eat—including pork and rabbit, both of which my father loved dearly.

He was a real Georgia Negro, and he believed in eating plenty of what we in Harlem today call "soul food."

I've said that my mother was the one who whipped me—at least she did whenever she wasn't ashamed to let the neighbors think she was killing me. For if she even acted as though she was about to raise her hand to me, I would open my mouth and let the world know about it. If anybody was passing by out on the road, she would either change her mind or just give me a few licks.

Thinking about it now, I feel definitely that just as my father favored me for being lighter than the other children, my mother gave me more hell for the same reason. She was very light herself but she favored the ones who were darker. Wilfred, I know, was particularly her angel. I remember that she would tell me to get out of the house and "Let the sun shine on you so you can get some color." She went out of her way never to let me become afflicted with a sense of color-superiority. I am sure that she treated me this way partly because of how she came to be light herself.

I learned early that crying out in protest could accomplish things. My older brothers and sister had started to school when, sometimes, they would come in and ask for a buttered biscuit or something and my mother, impatiently, would tell them no. But I would cry out and make a fuss until I got what I wanted. I remember well how my mother asked me why I couldn't be a nice boy like Wilfred; but I would think to myself that Wilfred, for being so nice and quiet, often stayed hungry. So early in life, I had learned that if you want something, you had better make some noise.

Not only did we have our big garden, but we raised chickens. My father would buy some baby chicks and my mother would raise them. We all loved chicken. That was one dish there was no argument with my father about. One thing in particular that I remember made me feel grateful toward my mother was that one day I went and asked her for my own garden, and she did let me have my own little plot. I loved it and took care of it well. I loved especially to grow peas. I was proud when we had them on our table. I would pull out the grass in my garden by hand when the first little blades came up. I would patrol the rows on my hands and knees for any worms and bugs, and I would kill and bury them. And sometimes when I had every-thing straight and clean for my things to grow, I would lie down on my back between two rows, and I would gaze up in the blue sky at the clouds moving and think all kinds of things.

At five, I, too, began to go to school, leaving home in the morning along with Wilfred, Hilda, and Philbert. It was the Pleasant Grove School that went from kindergarten through the eighth grade. It was two miles outside the city limits, and I guess there was no problem about our attending because we were the only Negroes in the area. In those days white people in the North usually would "adopt" just a few Negroes; they didn't see them as any threat. The white kids didn't make any great thing about us, either. They called us "nigger" and "dar-kie" and "Rastus" so much that we thought those were our natural names. But they didn't think of it as an insult; it was just the way they thought about us.

One afternoon in 1931 when Wilfred, Hilda, Philbert, and I came home, my mother and father were having one of their arguments. There had lately been a lot of tension around the house because of Black Legion threats. Anyway, my father had taken one of the rabbits which we were raising, and ordered my mother to cook it. We raised rabbits, but sold them to whites. My father had taken a rabbit from the rabbit pen. He had pulled off the rabbit's head. He was so strong, he needed no knife to behead chickens or rabbits. With one twist of his big black hands he simply twisted off the head and threw the bleeding-necked thing back at my mother's feet.

My mother was crying. She started to skin the rabbit, prepa-ratory to cooking it. But my father was so angry he slammed on out of the front door and started walking up the road toward town.

It was then that my mother had this vision. She had always been a strange woman in this sense, and had always had a strong intuition of things about to happen. And most of her children are the same way, I think. When something is about to happen, I can feel something, sense something. I never have known something to happen that has caught me completely off guard— except once. And that was when, years later, I discovered facts

I couldn't believe about a man who, up until that discovery, I would gladly have given my life for.

My father was well up the road when my mother ran screaming out onto the porch. *"Early! Early!"* She screamed his name. She clutched up her apron in one hand, and ran down across the yard and into the road. My father turned around. He saw her. For some reason, considering how angry he had been when he left, he waved at her. But he kept on going.

She told me later, my mother did, that she had a vision of my father's end. All the rest of the afternoon, she was not herself, crying and nervous and upset. She finished cooking the rabbit and put the whole thing in the warmer part of the black stove. When my father was not back home by our bedtime, my mother hugged and clutched us, and we felt strange, not knowing what to do, because she had never acted like that.

I remember waking up to the sound of my mother's screaming again. When I scrambled out, I saw the police in the living room; they were trying to calm her down. She had snatched on her clothes to go with them. And all of us children who were staring knew without anyone having to say it that something terrible had happened to our father.

My mother was taken by the police to the hospital, and to a room where a sheet was over my father in a bed, and she wouldn't look, she was afraid to look. Probably it was wise that she didn't. My father's skull, on one side, was crushed in, I was told later. Negroes in Lansing have always whispered that he was attacked, and then laid across some tracks for a streetcar to run over him. His body was cut almost in half.

He lived two and a half hours in that condition. Negroes then were stronger than they are now, especially Georgia Negroes. Negroes born in Georgia had to be strong simply to survive.

It was morning when we children at home got the word that he was dead. I was six. I can remember a vague commotion, the house filled up with people crying, saying bitterly that the white Black Legion had finally gotten him. My mother was hysterical. In the bedroom, women were holding smelling salts under her nose. She was still hysterical at the funeral.

I don't have a very clear memory of the funeral, either. Oddly, the main thing I remember is that it wasn't in a church, and that surprised me, since my father was a preacher, and I had been where he preached people's funerals in churches. But his was in a funeral home.

And I remember that during the service a big black fly came down and landed on my father's face, and Wilfred sprang up from his chair and he shooed the fly away, and he came groping back to his chair—there were folding chairs for us to sit on—and the tears were streaming down his face. When we went by the casket, I remember that I thought that it looked as if my father's strong black face had been dusted with flour, and I wished they hadn't put on such a lot of it.

Back in the big four-room house, there were many visitors for another week or so. They were good friends of the family, such as the Lyons from Mason, twelve miles away, and the Walkers, McGuires, Liscoes, the Greens, Randolphs, and the Turners, and others from Lansing, and a lot of people from other towns, whom I had seen at the Garvey meetings.

We children adjusted more easily than our mother did. We couldn't see, as clearly as she did, the trials that lay ahead. As the visitors tapered off, she became very concerned about collecting the two insurance policies that my father had always been proud he carried. He had always said that families should be protected in case of death. One policy apparently paid off without any problem—the smaller one. I don't know the amount of it. I would imagine it was not more than a thousand dollars, and maybe half of that.

But after that money came, and my mother had paid out a lot of it for the funeral and expenses, she began going into town and returning very upset. The company that had issued the bigger policy was balking at paying off. They were claiming that my father had committed suicide. Visitors came again, and there was bitter talk about white people: how could my father bash himself in the head, then get down across the streetcar tracks to be run over?

So there we were. My mother was thirty-four years old now, with no husband, no provider or protector to take care of her eight children. But some kind of a family routine got going again. And for as long as the first insurance money lasted, we did all right.

Wilfred, who was a pretty stable fellow, began to act older than his age. I think he had the sense to see, when the rest of us didn't, what was in the wind for us. He quietly quit school and went to town in search of work. He took any kind of job he could find and he would come home, dog-tired, in the evenings, and give whatever he had made to my mother.

Hilda, who always had been quiet, too, attended to the babies. Philbert and I didn't contribute anything. We just fought all the time—each other at home, and then at school we would team up and fight white kids. Sometimes the fights would be racial in nature, but they might be about anything.

Reginald came under my wing. Since he had grown out of the toddling stage, he and I had become very close. I suppose I enjoyed the fact that he was the little one, under me, who looked up to me.

My mother began to buy on credit. My father had always been very strongly against credit. "Credit is the first step into debt and back into slavery," he had always said. And then she went to work herself. She would go into Lansing and find different jobs—in housework, or sewing—for white people. They didn't realize, usually, that she was a Negro. A lot of white people around there didn't want Negroes in their houses.

She would do fine until in some way or other it got to people who she was, whose widow she was. And then she would be let go. I remember how she used to come home crying, but trying to hide it, because she had lost a job that she needed so much.

Once when one of us—I cannot remember which—had to go for something to where she was working, and the people saw us, and realized she was actually a Negro, she was fired on the spot, and she came home crying, this time not hiding it.

When the state Welfare people began coming to our house, we would come from school sometimes and find them talking with our mother, asking a thousand questions. They acted and looked at her, and at us, and around in our house, in a way that had about it the feeling—at least for me—that we were not people. In their eyesight we were just *things*, that was all.

My mother began to receive two checks—a Welfare check and, I believe, widow's pension. The checks helped. But they weren't enough, as many of us as there were. When they came, about the first of the month, one always was already owed in full, if not more, to the man at the grocery store. And, after that, the other one didn't last long.

We began to go swiftly downhill. The physical downhill wasn't as quick as the psychological. My mother was, above everything else, a proud woman, and it took its toll on her that she was accepting charity. And her feelings were communicated to us.

She would speak sharply to the man at the grocery store for padding the bill, telling him that she wasn't ignorant, and he didn't like that. She would talk back sharply to the state Welfare people, telling them that she was a grown woman, able to raise her children, that it wasn't necessary for them to keep coming around so much, meddling in our lives. And they didn't like that.

But the monthly Welfare check was their pass. They acted as if they owned us, as if we were their private property. As much as my mother would have liked to, she couldn't keep them out. She would get particularly incensed when they began insisting upon drawing us older children aside, one at a time, out on the porch or somewhere, and asking us questions, or telling us things—against our mother and against each other.

We couldn't understand why, if the state was willing to give us packages of meat, sacks of potatoes and fruit, and cans of all kinds of things, our mother obviously hated to accept. We really couldn't understand. What I later understood was that my mother was making a desperate effort to preserve her pride—and ours.

Pride was just about all we had to preserve, for by 1934, we really began to suffer. This was about the worst depression year, and no one we knew had enough to eat or live on. Some old family friends visited us now and then. At first they brought food. Though it was charity, my mother took it.

Wilfred was working to help. My mother was working, when she could find any kind of job. In Lansing, there was a bakery where, for a nickel, a couple of us children would buy a tall flour sack of day-old bread and cookies, and then walk the two miles back out into the country to our house. Our mother knew, I guess, dozens of ways to cook things with bread and out of bread. Stewed tomatoes with bread, maybe that would be a meal. Something like French toast, if we had any eggs. Bread pudding, sometimes with raisins in it. If we got hold of some hamburger, it came to the table more bread than meat. The cookies that were always in the sack with the bread, we just gobbled down straight.

But there were times when there wasn't even a nickel and we would be so hungry we were dizzy. My mother would boil a big pot of dandelion greens, and we would eat that. I remember that some small-minded neighbor put it out, and children would tease us, that we ate "fried grass." Sometimes, if we were lucky, we would have oatmeal or cornmeal mush three times a day. Or mush in the morning and cornbread at night.

Philbert and I were grown up enough to quit fighting long enough to take the .22 caliber rifle that had been our father's, and shoot rabbits that some white neighbors up or down the road would buy. I know now that they just did it to help us, because they, like everyone, shot their own rabbits. Sometimes, I remember, Philbert and I would take little Reginald along with us. He wasn't very strong, but he was always so proud to be along. We would trap muskrats out in the little creek in back of our house. And we would lie quiet until unsuspecting bullfrogs appeared, and we would spear them, cut off their legs, and sell them for a nickel a pair to people who lived up and down the road. The whites seemed less restricted in their dietary tastes.

Then, about in late 1934, I would guess, something began to happen. Some kind of psychological deterioration hit our family circle and began to eat away our pride. Perhaps it was the constant tangible evidence that we were destitute. We had known other families who had gone on relief. We had known without anyone in our home ever expressing it that we had felt prouder not to be at the depot where the free food was passed out. And, now, we were among them. At school, the "on relief" finger suddenly was pointed at us, too, and sometimes it was said aloud.

It seemed that everything to eat in our house was stamped Not To Be Sold. All Welfare food bore this stamp to keep the recipients from selling it. It's a wonder we didn't come to think of Not To Be Sold as a brand name.

Sometimes, instead of going home from school, I walked the two miles up the road into Lansing. I began drifting from store to store, hanging around outside where things like apples were displayed in boxes and barrels and baskets, and I would watch my chance and steal me a treat. You know what a treat was to me? Anything!

Or I began to drop in about dinnertime at the home of some family that we knew. I knew that they knew exactly why I was there, but they never embarrassed me by letting on. They would invite me to stay for supper, and I would stuff myself.

Especially, I liked to drop in and visit at the Gohannases' home. They were nice, older people, and great churchgoers. I had watched them lead the jumping and shouting when my father preached. They had, living with them—they were raising him—a nephew whom everyone called "Big Boy," and he and I got along fine. Also living with the Gohannases was old Mrs. Adcock, who went with them to church. She was always trying to help anybody she could, visiting anyone she heard was sick, carrying them something. She was the one who, years later, would tell me something that I remembered a long time: "Malcolm, there's one thing I like about you. You're no good, but you don't try to hide it. You are not a hypocrite."

The more I began to stay away from home and visit people and steal from the stores, the more aggressive I became in my inclinations. I never wanted to wait for anything.

I was growing up fast, physically more so than mentally. As I began to be recognized more around the town, I started to become aware of the peculiar attitude of white people toward me. I sensed that it had to do with my father. It was an adult version of what several white children had said at school, in hints, or sometimes in the open, which really expressed what their parents had said—that the Black Legion or the Klan had killed my father, and the insurance company had pulled a fast one in refusing to pay my mother the policy money.

When I began to get caught stealing now and then, the state Welfare people began to focus on me when they came to our house. I can't remember how I first became aware that they were talking of taking me away. What I first remember along that line was my mother raising a storm about being able to bring up her own children. She would whip me for stealing, and I would try to alarm the neighborhood with my yelling. One thing I have always been proud of is that I never raised my hand against my mother.

In the summertime, at night, in addition to all the other things we did, some of us boys would slip out down the road, or across the pastures, and go "cooning" watermelons. White people always associated watermelons with Negroes, and they sometimes called Negroes "coons" among all the other names, and so stealing watermelons became "cooning" them. If white boys were doing it, it implied that they were only acting like Negroes. Whites have always hidden or justified all of the guilts they could by ridiculing or blaming Negroes.

One Halloween night, I remember that a bunch of us were out tipping over those old country outhouses, and one old farmer—I guess he had tipped over enough in his day—had set a trap for us. Always, you sneak up from behind the outhouse, then you gang together and push it, to tip it over. This farmer had taken his outhouse off the hole, and set it just in *front* of the hole. Well, we came sneaking up in single file, in the darkness, and the two white boys in the lead fell down into the outhouse hole neck deep. They smelled so bad it was all we could stand to get them out, and that finished us all for that Halloween. I had just missed falling in myself. The whites were so used to taking the lead, this time it had really gotten them in the hole.

Thus, in various ways, I learned various things. I picked strawberries, and though I can't recall what I got per crate for picking, I remember that after working hard all one day, I wound up with about a dollar, which was a whole lot of money in those times. I was so hungry, I didn't know what to do. I was walking away toward town with visions of buying something good to eat, and this older white boy I knew, Richard Dixon, came up and asked me if I wanted to match nickels. He had plenty of change for my dollar. In about a half hour, he had all the change back, including my dollar, and instead of going to town to buy something, I went home with nothing, and I was bitter. But that was nothing compared to what I felt when I found out later that he had cheated. There is a way that you can catch and hold the nickel and make it come up the way you want. This was my first lesson about gambling: if you see somebody winning all the time, he isn't gambling, he's cheating. Later on in life, if I were continuously losing in any gambling situation, I would watch very closely. It's like the Negro in America seeing the white man win all the time. He's a professional gambler; he has all the cards and the odds stacked on his side, and he has always dealt to our people from the bottom of the deck.

About this time, my mother began to be visited by some Seventh Day Adventists who had moved into a house not too far down the road from us. They would talk to her for hours at a time, and leave booklets and leaflets and magazines for her to read. She read them, and Wilfred, who had started back to school after we had begun to get the relief food supplies, also read a lot. His head was forever in some book.

Before long, my mother spent much time with the Adventists. It's my belief that what mostly influenced her was that they had even more diet restrictions than she always had taught and practiced with us. Like us, they were against eating rabbit and pork; they followed the Mosaic dietary laws. They ate nothing of the flesh without a split hoof, or that didn't chew a cud. We began to go with my mother to the Adventist meetings that were held further out in the country. For us children, I know that the major attraction was the good food they served. But we listened, too. There were a handful of Negroes, from small towns in the area, but I would say that it was ninety-nine percent white people. The Adventists felt that we were living at the end of time, that the world soon was coming to an end. But they were the friendliest white people I had ever seen. In some ways, though, we children noticed, and, when we were back at home, discussed, that they were different from us—such as the lack of enough seasoning in their food, and the different way that white people smelled.

Meanwhile, the state Welfare people kept after my mother. By now, she didn't make it any secret that she hated them, and didn't want them in her house. But they exerted their right to come, and I have many, many times reflected upon how, talking to us children, they began to plant the seeds of division in our minds. They would ask such things as who was smarter than the other. And they would ask me why I was "so different."

I think they felt that getting children into foster homes was a legitimate part of their function, and the result would be less troublesome, however they went about it.

And when my mother fought them, they went after her—first,

through me. I was the first target. I stole; that implied that I wasn't being taken care of by my mother.

All of us were mischievous at some time or another, I more so than any of the rest. Philbert and I kept a battle going. And this was just one of a dozen things that kept building up the pressure on my mother.

I'm not sure just how or when the idea was first dropped by the Welfare workers that our mother was losing her mind.

But I can distinctly remember hearing "crazy" applied to her by them when they learned that the Negro farmer who was in the next house down the road from us had offered to give us some butchered pork—a whole pig, maybe even two of them— and she had refused. We all heard them call my mother "crazy" to her face for refusing good meat. It meant nothing to them even when she explained that we had never eaten pork, that it was against her religion as a Seventh Day Adventist.

They were as vicious as vultures. They had no feelings, understanding, compassion, or respect for my mother. They told us, "She's crazy for refusing food." Right then was when our home, our unity, began to disintegrate. We were having a hard time, and I wasn't helping. But we could have made it, we could have stayed together. As bad as I was, as much trouble and worry as I caused my mother, I loved her.

The state people, we found out, had interviewed the Gohannas family, and the Gohannases had said that they would take me into their home. My mother threw a fit, though, when she heard that—and the home wreckers took cover for a while.

It was about this time that the large, dark man from Lansing began visiting. I don't remember how or where he and my mother met. It may have been through some mutual friends. I don't remember what the man's profession was. In 1935, in Lansing, Negroes didn't have anything you could call a profession. But the man, big and black, looked something like my father. I can remember his name, but there's no need to mention it. He was a single man, and my mother was a widow only thirty-six years old. The man was independent; naturally she admired that. She was having a hard time disciplining us, and a big man's presence alone would help. And if she had a man to provide, it would send the state people away forever.

We all understood without ever saying much about it. Or at

least we had no objection. We took it in stride, even with some amusement among us, that when the man came, our mother would be all dressed up in the best that she had—she still was a good-looking woman—and she would act differently, light-hearted and laughing, as we hadn't seen her act in years.

It went on for about a year, I guess. And then, about 1936, or 1937, the man from Lansing jilted my mother suddenly. He just stopped coming to see her. From what I later understood, he finally backed away from taking on the responsibility of those eight mouths to feed. He was afraid of so many of us. To this day, I can see the trap that Mother was in, saddled with all of us. And I can also understand why he would shun taking on such a tremendous responsibility.

But it was a terrible shock to her. It was the beginning of the end of reality for my mother. When she began to sit around and walk around talking to herself—almost as though she was un-aware that we were there—it became increasingly terrifying.

The state people saw her weakening. That was when they began the definite steps to take me away from home. They began to tell me how nice it was going to be at the Gohannases' home, where the Gohannases and Big Boy and Mrs. Adcock had all said how much they liked me, and would like to have me live with them.

I liked all of them, too. But I didn't want to leave Wilfred. I looked up to and admired my big brother. I didn't want to leave Hilda, who was like my second mother. Or Philbert; even in our fighting, there was a feeling of brotherly union. Or Regi-nald, especially, who was weak with his hernia condition, and who looked up to me as his big brother who looked out for him, as I looked up to Wilfred. And I had nothing, either, against the babies, Yvonne, Wesley, and Robert.

As my mother talked to herself more and more, she gradually became less responsive to us. And less responsible. The house became less tidy. We began to be more unkempt. And usually, now, Hilda cooked.

We children watched our anchor giving way. It was some-thing terrible that you couldn't get your hands on, yet you couldn't get away from. It was a sensing that something bad was going to happen. We younger ones leaned more and more heavily on the relative strength of Wilfred and Hilda, who were the oldest.

When finally I was sent to the Gohannases' home, at least in a surface way I was glad. I remember that when I left home with the state man, my mother said one thing: "Don't let them feed him any pig."

It was better, in a lot of ways, at the Gohannases'. Big Boy and I shared his room together, and we hit it off nicely. He just wasn't the same as my blood brothers. The Gohannases were very religious people. Big Boy and I attended church with them. They were sanctified Holy Rollers now. The preachers and congregations jumped even higher and shouted even louder than the Baptists I had known. They sang at the top of their lungs, and swayed back and forth and cried and moaned and beat on tambourines and chanted. It was spooky, with ghosts and spirituals and "ha'nts" seeming to be in the very atmosphere when finally we all came out of the church, going back home.

The Gohannases and Mrs. Adcock loved to go fishing, and some Saturdays Big Boy and I would go along. I had changed schools now, to Lansing's West Junior High School. It was right in the heart of the Negro community, and a few white kids were there, but Big Boy didn't mix much with any of our schoolmates, and I didn't either. And when we went fishing, neither he nor I liked the idea of just sitting and waiting for the fish to jerk the cork under the water—or make the tight line quiver, when we fished that way. I figured there should be some smarter way to get the fish—though we never discovered what it might be.

Mr. Gohannas was close cronies with some other men who, some Saturdays, would take me and Big Boy with them hunting rabbits. I had my father's .22 caliber rifle; my mother had said it was all right for me to take it with me. The old men had a set rabbit-hunting strategy that they had always used. Usually when a dog jumps a rabbit, and the rabbit gets away, that rabbit will always somehow instinctively run in a circle and return sooner or later past the very spot where he originally was jumped. Well, the old men would just sit and wait in hiding somewhere for the rabbit to come back, then get their shots at him. I got to thinking about it, and finally I thought of a plan. I would separate from them and Big Boy and I would go to a point where I figured that the rabbit, returning, would have to pass me first.

It worked like magic. I began to get three and four rabbits before they got one. The astonishing thing was that none of the old men ever figured out why. They outdid themselves exclaiming what a sure shot I was. I was about twelve, then. All I had done was to improve on their strategy, and it was the beginning of a very important lesson in life—that anytime you find someone more successful than you are, especially when you're both engaged in the same business—you know they're doing something that you aren't.

I would return home to visit fairly often. Sometimes Big Boy and one or another, or both, of the Gohannases would go with me—sometimes not. I would be glad when some of them did go, because it made the ordeal easier.

Soon the state people were making plans to take over all of my mother's children. She talked to herself nearly all of the time now, and there was a crowd of new white people entering the picture—always asking questions. They would even visit me at the Gohannases'. They would ask me questions out on the porch, or sitting out in their cars.

Eventually my mother suffered a complete breakdown, and the court orders were finally signed. They took her to the State Mental Hospital at Kalamazoo.

It was seventy-some miles from Lansing, about an hour and a half on the bus. A Judge McClellan in Lansing had authority over me and all of my brothers and sisters. We were "state children," court wards; he had the full say-so over us. A white man in charge of a black man's children! Nothing but legal, modern slavery—however kindly intentioned.

My mother remained in the same hospital at Kalamazoo for about twenty-six years. Later, when I was still growing up in Michigan, I would go to visit her every so often. Nothing that I can imagine could have moved me as deeply as seeing her pitiful state. In 1963, we got my mother out of the hospital, and she now lives there in Lansing with Philbert and his family.

It was so much worse than if it had been a physical sickness, for which a cause might be known, medicine given, a cure effected. Every time I visited her, when finally they led her—a case, a number—back inside from where we had been sitting together, I felt worse.

My last visit, when I knew I would never come to see her again—there—was in 1952. I was twenty-seven. My brother Philbert had told me that on his last visit, she had recognized him somewhat. "In spots," he said.

But she didn't recognize me at all.

She stared at me. She didn't know who I was.

Her mind, when I tried to talk, to reach her, was somewhere else. I asked, "Mama, do you know what day it is?"

She said, staring, "All the people have gone."

I can't describe how I felt. The woman who had brought me into the world, and nursed me, and advised me, and chastised me, and loved me, didn't know me. It was as if I was trying to walk up the side of a hill of feathers. I looked at her. I listened to her "talk." But there was nothing I could do.

I truly believe that if ever a state social agency destroyed a family, it destroyed ours. We wanted and tried to stay together. Our home didn't have to be destroyed. But the Welfare, the courts, and their doctor, gave us the one-two-three punch. And ours was not the only case of this kind.

I knew I wouldn't be back to see my mother again because it could make me a very vicious and dangerous person—knowing how they had looked at us as numbers and as a case in their book, not as human beings. And knowing that my mother in there was a statistic that didn't have to be, that existed because of a society's failure, hypocrisy, greed, and lack of mercy and compassion. Hence I have no mercy or compassion in me for a society that will crush people, and then penalize them for not being able to stand up under the weight.

I have rarely talked to anyone about my mother, for I believe that I am capable of killing a person, without hesitation, who happened to make the wrong kind of remark about my mother. So I purposely don't make any opening for some fool to step into.

Back then when our family was destroyed, in 1937, Wilfred and Hilda were old enough so that the state let them stay on their own in the big four-room house that my father had built. Philbert was placed with another family in Lansing, a Mrs. Hackett, while Reginald and Wesley went to live with a family called Williams, who were friends of my mother's. And Yvonne and Robert went to live with a West Indian family named McGuire.

Separated though we were, all of us maintained fairly close touch around Lansing—in school and out—whenever we could get together. Despite the artificially created separation and distance between us, we still remained very close in our feelings toward each other.

CHAPTER TWO

MASCOT

On June twenty-seventh of that year, nineteen thirty-seven, Joe Louis knocked out James J. Braddock to become the heavyweight champion of the world. And all the Negroes in Lansing, like Negroes everywhere, went wildly happy with the greatest celebration of race pride our generation had ever known. Every Negro boy old enough to walk wanted to be the next Brown Bomber. My brother Philbert, who had already become a pretty good boxer in school, was no exception. (I was trying to play basketball. I was gangling and tall, but I wasn't very good at it—too awkward.) In the fall of that year, Philbert entered the amateur bouts that were held in Lansing's Prudden Auditorium.

He did well, surviving the increasingly tough eliminations. I would go down to the gym and watch him train. It was very exciting. Perhaps without realizing it I became secretly envious; for one thing, I know I could not help seeing some of my younger brother Reginald's lifelong admiration for me getting siphoned off to Philbert.

People praised Philbert as a natural boxer. I figured that since we belonged to the same family, maybe I would become one, too. So I put myself in the ring. I think I was thirteen when I signed up for my first bout, but my height and rawboned frame let me get away with claiming that I was sixteen, the minimum age—and my weight of about 128 pounds got me classified as a bantamweight.

They matched me with a white boy, a novice like myself, named Bill Peterson. I'll never forget him. When our turn in the next amateur bouts came up, all of my brothers and sisters were

24

there watching, along with just about everyone else I knew in town. They were there not so much because of me but because of Philbert, who had begun to build up a pretty good following, and they wanted to see how his brother would do.

I walked down the aisle between the people thronging the rows of seats, and climbed in the ring. Bill Peterson and I were introduced, and then the referee called us together and mumbled all of that stuff about fighting fair and breaking clean. Then the bell rang and we came out of our corners. I knew I was scared, but I didn't know, as Bill Peterson told me later on, that he was scared of me, too. He was so scared I was going to hurt him that he knocked me down fifty times if he did once.

He did such a job on my reputation in the Negro neighborhood that I practically went into hiding. A Negro just can't be whipped by somebody white and return with his head up to the neighborhood, especially in those days, when sports and, to a lesser extent show business, were the only fields open to Negroes, and when the ring was the only place a Negro could whip a white man and not be lynched. When I did show my face again, the Negroes I knew rode me so badly I knew I had to do something.

But the worst of my humiliations was my younger brother Reginald's attitude: he simply never mentioned the fight. It was the way he looked at me—and avoided looking at me. So I went back to the gym, and I trained—hard. I beat bags and skipped rope and grunted and sweated all over the place. And finally I signed up to fight Bill Peterson again. This time, the bouts were held in his hometown of Alma, Michigan.

The only thing better about the rematch was that hardly anyone I knew was there to see it; I was particularly grateful for Reginald's absence. The moment the bell rang, I saw a fist, then the canvas coming up, and ten seconds later the referee was saying *"Ten!"* over me. It was probably the shortest "fight" in history. I lay there listening to the full count, but I couldn't move. To tell the truth, I'm not sure I wanted to move.

That white boy was the beginning and the end of my fight career. A lot of times in these later years since I became a Muslim, I've thought back to that fight and reflected that it was Allah's work to stop me: I might have wound up punchy.

Not long after this, I came into a classroom with my hat on. I did it deliberately. The teacher, who was white, ordered me to keep the hat on, and to walk around and around the room until he told me to stop. "That way," he said, "everyone can see you. Meanwhile, we'll go on with class for those who are here to learn something."

I was still walking around when he got up from his desk and turned to the blackboard to write something on it. Everyone in the classroom was looking when, at this moment, I passed behind his desk, snatched up a thumbtack and deposited it in his chair. When he turned to sit back down, I was far from the scene of the crime, circling around the rear of the room. Then he hit the tack, and I heard him holler and caught a glimpse of him spraddling up as I disappeared through the door.

With my deportment record, I wasn't really shocked when the decision came that I had been expelled.

I guess I must have had some vague idea that if I didn't have to go to school, I'd be allowed to stay on with the Gohannases and wander around town, or maybe get a job if I wanted one for pocket money. But I got rocked on my heels when a state man whom I hadn't seen before came and got me at the Gohannases' and took me down to court.

They told me I was going to go to a reform school. I was still thirteen years old.

But first I was going to the detention home. It was in Mason, Michigan, about twelve miles from Lansing. The detention home was where all the "bad" boys and girls from Ingham County were held, on their way to reform school—waiting for their hearings.

The white state man was a Mr. Maynard Allen. He was nicer to me than most of the state Welfare people had been. He even had consoling words for the Gohannases and Mrs. Adcock and Big Boy; all of them were crying. But I wasn't. With the few clothes I owned stuffed into a box, we rode in his car to Mason. He talked as he drove along, saying that my school marks showed that if I would just straighten up, I could make something of myself. He said that reform school had the wrong reputation; he talked about what the word "reform" meant—to change and become better. He said the school was really a place where boys like me could have time to see their mistakes and start a new life and become somebody everyone would be proud of. And he told me that the lady in charge of the detention home, a Mrs. Swerlin, and her husband were very good people.

They were good people. Mrs. Swerlin was bigger than her husband, I remember, a big, buxom, robust, laughing woman, and Mr. Swerlin was thin, with black hair, and a black mustache and a red face, quiet and polite, even to me.

They liked me right away, too. Mrs. Swerlin showed me to my room, my own room—the first in my life. It was in one of those huge dormitory-like buildings where kids in detention were kept in those days—and still are in most places. I discovered next, with surprise, that I was allowed to eat with the Swerlins. It was the first time I'd eaten with white people—at least with grown white people—since the Seventh Day Adventist country meetings. It wasn't my own exclusive privilege, of course. Except for the very troublesome boys and girls at the detention home, who were kept locked up—those who had run away and been caught and brought back, or something like that—all of us ate with the Swerlins sitting at the head of the long tables.

They had a white cook-helper, I recall—Lucille Lathrop. (It amazes me how these names come back, from a time I haven't thought about for more than twenty years.) Lucille treated me well, too. Her husband's name was Duane Lathrop. He worked somewhere else, but he stayed there at the detention home on the weekends with Lucille.

I noticed again how white people smelled different from us, and how their food tasted different, not seasoned like Negro cooking. I began to sweep and mop and dust around in the Swerlins' house, as I had done with Big Boy at the Gohannases'.

They all liked my attitude, and it was out of their liking for me that I soon became accepted by them—as a mascot, I know now. They would talk about anything and everything with me standing right there hearing them, the same way people would talk freely in front of a pet canary. They would even talk about me, or about "niggers," as though I wasn't there, as if I wouldn't understand what the word meant. A hundred times a day, they used the word "nigger." I suppose that in their own minds, they meant no harm; in fact they probably meant well. It was the same with the cook, Lucille, and her husband, Duane. I remember one day when Mr. Swerlin, as nice as he was, came in from Lansing, where he had been through the Negro section, and said to Mrs. Swerlin right in front of me, "I just can't see how those niggers can be so happy and be so poor." He talked about how they lived in shacks, but had those big, shining cars out front.

And Mrs. Swerlin said, me standing right there, "Niggers are just that way. . . ." That scene always stayed with me.

It was the same with the other white people, most of them local politicians, when they would come visiting the Swerlins. One of their favorite parlor topics was "niggers." One of them was the judge who was in charge of me in Lansing. He was a close friend of the Swerlins. He would ask about me when he came, and they would call me in, and he would look me up and down, his expression approving, like he was examining a fine colt, or a pedigreed pup. I knew they must have told him how I acted and how I worked.

What I am trying to say is that it just never dawned upon them that I could understand, that I wasn't a pet, but a human being. They didn't give me credit for having the same sensitivity, intellect, and understanding that they would have been ready and willing to recognize in a white boy in my position. But it has historically been the case with white people, in their regard for black people, that even though we might be *with* them, we weren't considered *of* them. Even though they appeared to have opened the door, it was still closed. Thus they never did really see *me*.

This is the sort of kindly condescension which I try to clarify today, to these integration-hungry Negroes, about their "liberal" white friends, these so-called "good white people"—most of them anyway. I don't care how nice one is to you; the thing you must always remember is that almost never does he really see you as he sees himself, as he sees his own kind. He may stand with you through thin, but not thick; when the chips are down, you'll find that as fixed in him as his bone structure is his sometimes subconscious conviction that he's better than anybody black.

But I was no more than vaguely aware of anything like that in my detention-home years. I did my little chores around the house, and everything was fine. And each weekend, they didn't mind my catching a ride over to Lansing for the afternoon or evening. If I wasn't old enough, I sure was big enough by then, and nobody ever questioned my hanging out, even at night, in the streets of the Negro section.

I was growing up to be even bigger than Wilfred and Philbert, who had begun to meet girls at the school dances, and other places, and introduced me to a few. But the ones who seemed to like me, I didn't go for—and vice versa. I couldn't dance a lick, anyway, and I couldn't see squandering my few dimes on girls. So mostly I pleasured myself these Saturday nights by gawking around the Negro bars and restaurants. The jukeboxes were wailing Erskine Hawkins' "Tuxedo Junction," Slim and Slam's "Flatfoot Floogie," things like that. Sometimes, big bands from New York, out touring the one-night stands in the sticks, would play for big dances in Lansing. Everybody with legs would come out to see any performer who bore the magic name "New York." Which is how I first heard Lucky Thompson and Milt Jackson, both of whom I later got to know well in Harlem.

Many youngsters from the detention home, when their dates came up, went off to the reform school. But when mine came up—two or three times—it was always ignored. I saw new youngsters arrive and leave. I was glad and grateful. I knew it was Mrs. Swerlin's doing. I didn't want to leave.

She finally told me one day that I was going to be entered in Mason Junior High School. It was the only school in town. No ward of the detention home had ever gone to school there, at least while still a ward. So I entered their seventh grade. The only other Negroes there were some of the Lyons children, younger than I was, in the lower grades. The Lyonses and I, as it happened, were the town's only Negroes. They were, as Negroes, very much respected. Mr. Lyons was a smart, hardworking man, and Mrs. Lyons was a very good woman. She and my mother, I had heard my mother say, were two of the four West Indians in that whole section of Michigan.

Some of the white kids at school, I found, were even friendlier than some of those in Lansing had been. Though some, including the teachers, called me "nigger," it was easy to see that they didn't mean any more harm by it than the Swerlins. As the "nigger" of my class, I was in fact extremely popular—I suppose partly because I was kind of a novelty. I was in demand, I had top priority. But I also benefited from the special prestige of having the seal of approval from that Very Important Woman about the town of Mason, Mrs. Swerlin. Nobody in Mason would have dreamed of getting on the wrong side of her. It became hard for me to get through a school day without someone after me to join this or head up that—the debating society, the Junior High basketball team, or some other extracurricular activity. I never turned them down.

And I hadn't been in the school long when Mrs. Swerlin, knowing I could use spending money of my own, got me a job after school washing the dishes in a local restaurant. My boss there was the father of a white classmate whom I spent a lot of time with. His family lived over the restaurant. It was fine working there. Every Friday night when I got paid, I'd feel at least ten feet tall. I forget how much I made, but it seemed like a lot. It was the first time I'd ever had any money to speak of, all my own, in my whole life. As soon as I could afford it, I bought a green suit and some shoes, and at school I'd buy treats for the others in my class—at least as much as any of them did for me.

English and history were the subjects I liked most. My English teacher, I recall—a Mr. Ostrowski—was always giving advice about how to become something in life. The one thing I didn't like about history class was that the teacher, Mr. Williams, was a great one for "nigger" jokes. One day during my first week at school, I walked into the room and he started singing to the class, as a joke, " 'Way down yonder in the cotton field, some folks say that a nigger won't steal." Very funny. I liked history, but I never thereafter had much liking for Mr. Williams. Later, I remember, we came to the textbook section on Negro history. It was exactly one paragraph long. Mr. Williams laughed through it practically in a single breath, reading aloud how the Negroes had been slaves and then were freed, and how they were usually lazy and dumb and shiftless. He added, I remember, an anthropological footnote on his own, telling us between laughs how Negroes' feet were "so big that when they walk, they don't leave tracks, they leave a hole in the ground."

I'm sorry to say that the subject I most disliked was mathematics. I have thought about it. I think the reason was that mathematics leaves no room for argument. If you made a mistake, that was all there was to it.

Basketball was a big thing in my life, though. I was on the team; we traveled to neighboring towns such as Howell and Charlotte, and wherever I showed my face, the audiences in the gymnasiums "niggered" and "cooned" me to death. Or called me "Rastus." It didn't bother my teammates or my coach at all, and to tell the truth, it bothered me only vaguely. Mine was the same psychology that makes Negroes even today, though it bothers them down inside, keep letting the white man tell them how much "progress" they are making. They've heard it so much they've almost gotten brainwashed into believing it—or at least accepting it.

After the basketball games, there would usually be a school dance. Whenever our team walked into another school's gym for the dance, with me among them, I could feel the freeze. It would start to ease as they saw that I didn't try to mix, but stuck close to someone on our team, or kept to myself. I think I developed ways to do it without making it obvious. Even at our own school, I could sense it almost as a physical barrier, that despite all the beaming and smiling, the mascot wasn't supposed to dance with any of the white girls.

It was some kind of psychic message—not just from them, but also from within myself. I am proud to be able to say that much for myself, at least. I would just stand around and smile and talk and drink punch and eat sandwiches, and then I would make some excuse and get away early.

They were typical small-town school dances. Sometimes a little white band from Lansing would be brought in to play. But most often, the music was a phonograph set up on a table, with the volume turned up high, and the records scratchy, blaring things like Glenn Miller's "Moonlight Serenade"—his band was riding high then—or the Ink Spots, who were also very popular, singing "If I Didn't Care."

I used to spend a lot of time thinking about a peculiar thing. Many of these Mason white boys, like the ones at the Lansing school—especially if they knew me well, and if we hung out a lot together—would get me off in a corner somewhere and push me to proposition certain white girls, sometimes their own sisters. They would tell me that they'd already had the girls themselves—including their sisters—or that they were trying to and couldn't. Later on, I came to understand what was going on: If they could get the girls into the position of having broken the terrible taboo by slipping off with me somewhere, they would have that hammer over the girls' heads, to make them give in to them.

It seemed that the white boys felt that I, being a Negro, just naturally knew more about "romance," or sex, than they did—that I instinctively knew more about what to do and say with their own girls. I never did tell anybody that I really went for some of the white girls, and some of them went for me, too. They let me know in many ways. But anytime we found ourselves in any close conversations or potentially intimate situations, always there would come up between us some kind of a wall. The girls I really wanted to have were a couple of Negro girls whom Wilfred or Philbert had introduced me to in Lansing. But with these girls, somehow, I lacked the nerve.

From what I heard and saw on the Saturday nights I spent hanging around in the Negro district I knew that race-mixing went on in Lansing. But strangely enough, this didn't have any kind of effect on me. Every Negro in Lansing, I guess, knew how white men would drive along certain streets in the black neighborhoods and pick up Negro streetwalkers who patrolled the area. And, on the other hand, there was a bridge that separated the Negro and Polish neighborhoods, where white women would drive or walk across and pick up Negro men, who would hang around in certain places close to the bridge, waiting for them. Lansing's white women, even in those days, were famous for chasing Negro men. I didn't yet appreciate how most whites accord to the Negro this reputation for prodigious sexual prowess. There in Lansing, I never heard of any trouble about this mixing, from either side. I imagine that everyone simply took it for granted, as I did.

Anyway, from my experience as a little boy at the Lansing school, I had become fairly adept at avoiding the white-girl issue—at least for a couple of years yet.

Then, in the second semester of the seventh grade, I was elected class president. It surprised me even more than other people. But I can see now why the class might have done it. My grades were among the highest in the school. I was unique in my class, like a pink poodle. And I was proud; I'm not going to say I wasn't. In fact, by then, I didn't really have much feeling about being a Negro, because I was trying so hard, in every way I could, to be white. Which is why I am spending much of my life today telling the American black man that he's wasting his time straining to "integrate." I know from personal experience. I tried hard enough.

"Malcolm, we're just so *proud* of you!" Mrs. Swerlin exclaimed when she heard about my election. It was all over the restaurant where I worked. Even the state man, Maynard Allen, who still dropped by to see me once in a while, had a word of praise. He said he never saw anybody prove better exactly what "reform" meant. I really liked him—except for one thing: he now and then would drop something that hinted my mother had let us down somehow.

Fairly often, I would go and visit the Lyonses, and they acted as happy as though I was one of their children. And it was the same warm feeling when I went into Lansing to visit my brothers and sisters, and the Gohannases.

I remember one thing that marred this time for me: the movie "Gone with the Wind." When it played in Mason, I was the only Negro in the theater, and when Butterfly McQueen went into her act, I felt like crawling under the rug.

Every Saturday, just about, I would go into Lansing. I was going on fourteen, now. Wilfred and Hilda still lived out by themselves at the old family home. Hilda kept the house very clean. It was easier than my mother's plight, with eight of us always underfoot or running around. Wilfred worked wherever he could, and he still read every book he could get his hands on. Philbert was getting a reputation as one of the better amateur fighters in this part of the state; everyone really expected that he was going to become a professional.

Reginald and I, after my fighting fiasco, had finally gotten back on good terms. It made me feel great to visit him and Wesley over at Mrs. Williams'. I'd offhandedly give them each a couple of dollars to just stick in their pockets, to have something to spend. And little Yvonne and Robert were doing okay, too, over at the home of the West Indian lady, Mrs. McGuire. I'd give them about a quarter apiece; it made me feel good to see how they were coming along.

None of us talked much about our mother. And we never mentioned our father. I guess none of us knew what to say. We didn't want anybody else to mention our mother either, I think. From time to time, though, we would all go over to Kalamazoo to visit her. Most often we older ones went singly, for it was something you didn't want to have to experience with anyone else present, even your brother or sister.

During this period, the visit to my mother that I most remember was toward the end of that seventh-grade year, when our father's grown daughter by his first marriage, Ella, came from Boston to visit us. Wilfred and Hilda had exchanged some letters with Ella, and I, at Hilda's suggestion, had written to her from the Swerlins'. We were all excited and happy when her letter told us that she was coming to Lansing.

I think the major impact of Ella's arrival, at least upon me, was that she was the first really proud black woman I had ever seen in my life. She was plainly proud of her very dark skin. This was unheard of among Negroes in those days, especially in Lansing.

I hadn't been sure just what day she would come. And then one afternoon I got home from school and there she was. She hugged me, stood me away, looked me up and down. A commanding woman, maybe even bigger than Mrs. Swerlin. Ella wasn't just black, but like our father, she was jet black. The way she sat, moved, talked, did everything, bespoke somebody who did and got exactly what she wanted. This was the woman my father had boasted of so often for having brought so many of their family out of Georgia to Boston. She owned some property, he would say, and she was "in society." She had come North with nothing, and she had worked and saved and had invested in property that she built up in value, and then she started sending money to Georgia for another sister, brother, cousin, niece or nephew to come north to Boston. All that I had heard was reflected in Ella's appearance and bearing. I had never been so impressed with anybody. She was in her second marriage; her first husband had been a doctor.

Ella asked all kinds of questions about how I was doing; she had already heard from Wilfred and Hilda about my election as class president. She asked especially about my grades, and I ran and got my report cards. I was then one of the three highest in the class. Ella praised me. I asked her about her brother, Earl, and her sister, Mary. She had the exciting news that Earl was a singer with a band in Boston. He was singing under the name of Jimmy Carleton. Mary was also doing well.

Ella told me about other relatives from that branch of the family. A number of them I'd never heard of; she had helped them up from Georgia. They, in their turn, had helped up others. "We Littles have to stick together," Ella said. It thrilled me to hear her say that, and even more, the way she said it. I had become a mascot; our branch of the family was split to pieces; I had just about forgotten about being a Little in any family sense. She said that different members of the family were working in good jobs, and some even had small businesses going. Most of them were homeowners.

When Ella suggested that all of us Littles in Lansing accompany her on a visit to our mother, we all were grateful. We all felt that if anyone could do anything that could help our mother, that might help her get well and come back, it would be Ella. Anyway, all of us, for the first time together, went with Ella to Kalamazoo.

Our mother was smiling when they brought her out. She was extremely surprised when she saw Ella. They made a striking contrast, the thin near-white woman and the big black one hugging each other. I don't remember much about the rest of the visit, except that there was a lot of talking, and Ella had everything in hand, and we left with all of us feeling better than we ever had about the circumstances. I know that for the first time, I felt as though I had visited with someone who had some kind of physical illness that had just lingered on.

A few days later, after visiting the homes where each of us were staying, Ella left Lansing and returned to Boston. But before leaving, she told me to write to her regularly. And she had suggested that I might like to spend my summer holiday visiting her in Boston. I jumped at that chance.

That summer of 1940, in Lansing, I caught the Greyhound bus for Boston with my cardboard suitcase, and wearing my green suit. If someone had hung a sign, "HICK," around my neck, I couldn't have looked much more obvious. They didn't have the turnpikes then; the bus stopped at what seemed every corner and cowpatch. From my seat in—you guessed it—the back of the bus, I gawked out of the window at white man's America rolling past for what seemed a month, but must have been only a day and a half.

When we finally arrived, Ella met me at the terminal and took me home. The house was on Waumbeck Street in the Sugar Hill section of Roxbury, the Harlem of Boston. I met Ella's second husband, Frank, who was now a soldier; and her brother Earl, the singer who called himself Jimmy Carleton; and Mary, who was very different from her older sister. It's funny how I seemed to think of Mary as Ella's sister, instead of her being, just as Ella is, my own half-sister. It's probably because Ella and I always were much closer as basic types; we're dominant people, and Mary has always been mild and quiet, almost shy.

Ella was busily involved in dozens of things. She belonged to I don't know how many different clubs; she was a leading light of local so-called "black society." I saw and met a hundred black people there whose big-city talk and ways left my mouth hanging open.

I couldn't have feigned indifference if I had tried to. People talked casually about Chicago, Detroit, New York. I didn't know the world contained as many Negroes as I saw thronging downtown Roxbury at night, especially on Saturdays. Neon lights, nightclubs, poolhalls, bars, the cars they drove! Restaurants made the streets smell—rich, greasy, down-home black cooking! Jukeboxes blared Erskine Hawkins, Duke Ellington, Cootie Williams, dozens of others. If somebody had told me then that some day I'd know them all personally, I'd have found it hard to believe. The biggest bands, like these, played at the Roseland State Ballroom, on Boston's Massachusetts Avenue—one night for Negroes, the next night for whites.

I saw for the first time occasional black-white couples strolling around arm in arm. And on Sundays, when Ella, Mary, or somebody took me to church, I saw churches for black people such as I had never seen. They were many times finer than the white church I had attended back in Mason, Michigan. There, the white people just sat and worshiped with words; but the Boston Negroes, like all other Negroes I had ever seen at church, threw their souls and bodies wholly into worship.

Two or three times, I wrote letters to Wilfred intended for everybody back in Lansing. I said I'd try to describe it when I got back.

But I found I couldn't.

My restlessness with Mason—and for the first time in my life a restlessness with being around white people—began as soon as I got back home and entered eighth grade.

I continued to think constantly about all that I had seen in Boston, and about the way I had felt there. I know now that it was the sense of being a real part of a mass of my own kind, for the first time.

The white people—classmates, the Swerlins, the people at the restaurant where I worked—noticed the change. They said, "You're acting so strange. You don't seem like yourself, Malcolm. What's the matter?"

I kept close to the top of the class, though. The topmost scholastic standing, I remember, kept shifting between me, a girl named Audrey Slaugh, and a boy named Jimmy Cotton.

It went on that way, as I became increasingly restless and disturbed through the first semester. And then one day, just about when those of us who had passed were about to move up to 8-A, from which we would enter high school the next year, something happened which was to become the first major turning point of my life.

Somehow, I happened to be alone in the classroom with Mr. Ostrowski, my English teacher. He was a tall, rather reddish white man and he had a thick mustache. I had gotten some of my best marks under him, and he had always made me feel that he liked me. He was, as I have mentioned, a natural-born "advisor," about what you ought to read, to do, or think—about any and everything. We used to make unkind jokes about him: why was he teaching in Mason instead of somewhere else, getting for himself some of the "success in life" that he kept telling us how to get?

I know that he probably meant well in what he happened to advise me that day. I doubt that he meant any harm. It was just in his nature as an American white man. I was one of his top students, one of the school's top students—but all he could see for me was the kind of future "in your place" that almost all white people see for black people.

He told me, "Malcolm, you ought to be thinking about a career. Have you been giving it thought?"

The truth is, I hadn't. I never have figured out why I told him,

"Well, yes, sir, I've been thinking I'd like to be a lawyer." Lansing certainly had no Negro lawyers—or doctors either—in those days, to hold up an image I might have aspired to. All I really knew for certain was that a lawyer didn't wash dishes, as I was doing.

Mr. Ostrowski looked surprised, I remember, and leaned back in his chair and clasped his hands behind his head. He kind of half-smiled and said, "Malcolm, one of life's first needs is for us to be realistic. Don't misunderstand me, now. We all here like you, you know that. But you've got to be realistic about being a nigger. A lawyer—that's no realistic goal for a nigger. You need to think about something you *can* be. You're good with your hands—making things. Everybody admires your carpentry shop work. Why don't you plan on carpentry? People like you as a person—you'd get all kinds of work."

The more I thought afterwards about what he said, the more uneasy it made me. It just kept treading around in my mind.

What made it really begin to disturb me was Mr. Ostrowski's advice to others in my class—all of them white. Most of them had told him they were planning to become farmers. But those who wanted to strike out on their own, to try something new, he had encouraged. Some, mostly girls, wanted to be teachers. A few wanted other professions, such as one boy who wanted to become a county agent; another, a veterinarian; and one girl wanted to be a nurse. They all reported that Mr. Ostrowski had encouraged what they had wanted. Yet nearly none of them had earned marks equal to mine.

It was a surprising thing that I had never thought of it that way before, but I realized that whatever I wasn't, I *was* smarter than nearly all of those white kids. But apparently I was still not intelligent enough, in their eyes, to become whatever *I* wanted to be.

It was then that I began to change—inside.

I drew away from white people. I came to class, and I answered when called upon. It became a physical strain simply to sit in Mr. Ostrowski's class.

Where "nigger" had slipped off my back before, wherever I heard it now, I stopped and looked at whoever said it. And they looked surprised that I did.

I quit hearing so much "nigger" and "What's wrong?"—

which was the way I wanted it. Nobody, including the teachers, could decide what had come over me. I knew I was being discussed.

In a few more weeks, it was that way, too, at the restaurant where I worked washing dishes, and at the Swerlins'.

One day soon after, Mrs. Swerlin called me into the living room, and there was the state man, Maynard Allen. I knew from their faces that something was about to happen. She told me that none of them could understand why—after I had done so well in school, and on my job, and living with them, and after everyone in Mason had come to like me—I had lately begun to make them all feel that I wasn't happy there anymore.

She said she felt there was no need for me to stay at the detention home any longer, and that arrangements had been made for me to go and live with the Lyons family, who liked me so much.

She stood up and put out her hand. "I guess I've asked you a hundred times, Malcolm—do you want to tell me what's wrong?"

I shook her hand, and said, "Nothing, Mrs. Swerlin." Then I went and got my things, and came back down. At the living-room door I saw her wiping her eyes. I felt very bad. I thanked her and went out in front to Mr. Allen, who took me over to the Lyons'.

Mr. and Mrs. Lyons, and their children, during the two months I lived with them—while finishing eighth grade—also tried to get me to tell them what was wrong. But somehow I couldn't tell them, either.

I went every Saturday to see my brothers and sisters in Lansing, and almost every other day I wrote to Ella in Boston. Not saying why, I told Ella that I wanted to come there and live.

I don't know how she did it, but she arranged for official custody of me to be transferred from Michigan to Massachusetts, and the very week I finished the eighth grade, I again boarded the Greyhound bus for Boston.

I've thought about that time a lot since then. No physical move in my life has been more pivotal or profound in its repercussions.

If I had stayed on in Michigan, I would probably have married

one of those Negro girls I knew and liked in Lansing. I might
have become one of those state capitol building shoeshine boys,
or a Lansing Country Club waiter, or gotten one of the other
menial jobs which, in those days, among Lansing Negroes,
would have been considered "successful"—or even become a
carpenter.

Whatever I have done since then, I have driven myself to
become a success at it. I've often thought that if Mr. Ostrowski
had encouraged me to become a lawyer, I would today probably
be among some city's professional black bourgeoisie, sipping
cocktails and palming myself off as a community spokesman for
and leader of the suffering black masses, while my primary con-
cern would be to grab a few more crumbs from the groaning
board of the two-faced whites with whom they're begging to
"integrate."

All praise is due to Allah that I went to Boston when I did. If
I hadn't, I'd probably still be a brainwashed black Christian.

CHAPTER THREE

"HOMEBOY"

I looked like Li'l Abner. Mason, Michigan, was written all over me. My kinky, reddish hair was cut hick style, and I didn't even use grease in it. My green suit's coat sleeves stopped above my wrists, the pants legs showed three inches of socks. Just a shade lighter green than the suit was my narrow-collared, three-quarter length Lansing department store topcoat. My appearance was too much for even Ella. But she told me later she had seen countrified members of the Little family come up from Georgia in even worse shape than I was.

Ella had fixed up a nice little upstairs room for me. And she was truly a Georgia Negro woman when she got into the kitchen with her pots and pans. She was the kind of cook who would heap up your plate with such as ham hock, greens, black-eyed peas, fried fish, cabbage, sweet potatoes, grits and gravy, and cornbread. And the more you put away the better she felt. I worked out at Ella's kitchen table like there was no tomorrow.

Ella still seemed to be as big, black, outspoken and impressive a woman as she had been in Mason and Lansing. Only about two weeks before I arrived, she had split up with her second husband—the soldier, Frank, whom I had met there the previous summer; but she was taking it right in stride. I could see, though I didn't say, how any average man would find it almost impossible to live for very long with a woman whose every instinct was to run everything and everybody she had anything to do with—including me. About my second day there in Roxbury, Ella told me that she didn't want me to start hunting for a job right away, like most newcomer Negroes did. She said that she had told all those she'd brought North to take their time, to walk around, to travel the buses and the subway, and get the feel of Boston, before they tied themselves down working somewhere, because they would never again have the time to really see and get to know anything about the city they were living in. Ella said she'd help me find a job when it was time for me to go to work.

So I went gawking around the neighborhood—the Waumbeck and Humboldt Avenue Hill section of Roxbury, which is something like Harlem's Sugar Hill, where I'd later live. I saw those Roxbury Negroes acting and living differently from any black people I'd ever dreamed of in my life. This was the snooty-black neighborhood; they called themselves the "Four Hundred," and looked down their noses at the Negroes of the black ghetto, or so-called "town" section where Mary, my other half-sister, lived.

What I thought I was seeing there in Roxbury were high-class, educated, important Negroes, living well, working in big jobs and positions. Their quiet homes sat back in their mowed yards. These Negroes walked along the sidewalks looking haughty and dignified, on their way to work, to shop, to visit, to church. I know now, of course, that what I was really seeing was only a big-city version of those "successful" Negro bootblacks and janitors back in Lansing. The only difference was that the ones in Boston had been brainwashed even more thoroughly. They prided themselves on being incomparably more "cultured," "cultivated," "dignified," and better off than their black brethren down in the ghetto, which was no further away than you could throw a rock. Under the pitiful misapprehension that it would make them "better," these Hill Negroes were breaking their backs trying to imitate white people.

Any black family that had been around Boston long enough to own the home they lived in was considered among the Hill elite. It didn't make any difference that they had to rent out rooms to make ends meet. Then the native-born New Englanders among them looked down upon recently migrated Southern home-owners who lived next door, like Ella. And a big percentage of the Hill dwellers were in Ella's category—Southern strivers and scramblers, and West Indian Negroes, whom both the New Englanders and the Southerners called "Black Jews."

Usually it was the Southerners and the West Indians who not only managed to own the places where they lived, but also at least one other house which they rented as income property. The snooty New Englanders usually owned less than they.

In those days on the Hill, any who could claim "professional" status—teachers, preachers, practical nurses—also considered themselves superior. Foreign diplomats could have modeled their conduct on the way the Negro postmen, Pullman porters, and dining car waiters of Roxbury acted, striding around as if they were wearing top hats and cutaways.

I'd guess that eight out of ten of the Hill Negroes of Roxbury, despite the impressive-sounding job titles they affected, actually worked as menials and servants. "He's in banking," or "He's in securities." It sounded as though they were discussing a Rockefeller or a Mellon—and not some gray-headed, dignity-posturing bank janitor, or bond-house messenger. "I'm with an old family" was the euphemism used to dignify the professions of white folks' cooks and maids who talked so affectedly among their own kind in Roxbury that you couldn't even understand them. I don't know how many forty- and fifty-year-old errand boys went down the Hill dressed like ambassadors in black suits and white collars, to downtown jobs "in government," "in finance," or "in law." It has never ceased to amaze me how so many Negroes, then and now, could stand the indignity of that kind of self-delusion.

Soon I ranged out of Roxbury and began to explore Boston proper. Historic buildings everywhere I turned, and plaques and markers and statues for famous events and men. One statue in the Boston Commons astonished me: a Negro named Crispus Attucks, who had been the first man to fall in the Boston Massacre. I had never known anything like that.

I roamed everywhere. In one direction, I walked as far as Boston University. Another day, I took my first subway ride. When most of the people got off, I followed. It was Cambridge, and I circled all around in the Harvard University campus. Somewhere, I had already heard of Harvard—though I didn't know much more about it. Nobody that day could have told me I would give an address before the Harvard Law School Forum some twenty years later.

I also did a lot of exploring downtown. Why a city would

have *two* big railroad stations—North Station and South Station—I couldn't understand. At both of the stations, I stood around and watched people arrive and leave. And I did the same thing at the bus station where Ella had met me. My wanderings even led me down along the piers and docks where I read plaques telling about the old sailing ships that used to put into port there.

In a letter to Wilfred, Hilda, Philbert, and Reginald back in Lansing, I told them about all this, and about the winding, narrow, cobblestoned streets, and the houses that jammed up against each other. Downtown Boston, I wrote them, had the biggest stores I'd ever seen, and white people's restaurants and hotels. I made up my mind that I was going to see every movie that came to the fine, air-conditioned theaters.

On Massachusetts Avenue, next door to one of them, the Loew's State Theater, was the huge, exciting Roseland State Ballroom. Big posters out in front advertised the nationally famous bands, white and Negro, that had played there. "COMING NEXT WEEK," when I went by that first time, was Glenn Miller. I remember thinking how nearly the whole evening's music at Mason High School dances had been Glenn Miller's records. What wouldn't that crowd have given, I wondered, to be standing where Glenn Miller's band was actually going to play? I didn't know how familiar with Roseland I was going to become.

Ella began to grow concerned, because even when I had finally had enough sight-seeing, I didn't stick around very much on the Hill. She kept dropping hints that I ought to mingle with the "nice young people my age" who were to be seen in the Townsend Drugstore two blocks from her house, and a couple of other places. But even before I came to Boston, I had always felt and acted toward anyone my age as if they were in the "kid" class, like my younger brother Reginald. They had always looked up to me as if I were considerably older. On weekends back in Lansing where I'd go to get away from the white people in Mason, I'd hung around in the Negro part of town with Wilfred's and Philbert's set. Though all of them were several years older than me, I was bigger, and I actually looked older than most of them.

I didn't want to disappoint or upset Ella, but despite her advice, I began going down into the town ghetto section. That world of grocery stores, walk-up flats, cheap restaurants, poolrooms, bars, storefront churches, and pawnshops seemed to hold a natural lure for me.

Not only was this part of Roxbury much more exciting, but I felt more relaxed among Negroes who were being their natural selves and not putting on airs. Even though I did live on the Hill, my instincts were never—and still aren't—to feel myself better than any other Negro.

I spent the first month in town with my mouth hanging open. The sharp-dressed young "cats" who hung on the corners and in the poolrooms, bars and restaurants, and who obviously didn't work anywhere, completely entranced me. I couldn't get over marveling at how their hair was straight and shiny like white men's hair; Ella told me this was called a "conk." I had never tasted a sip of liquor, never even smoked a cigarette, and here I saw little black children, ten and twelve years old, shooting craps, playing cards, fighting, getting grown-ups to put a penny or a nickel on their number for them, things like that. And these children threw around swear words I'd never heard before, even, and slang expressions that were just as new to me, such as "stud" and "cat" and "chick" and "cool" and "hip." Every night as I lay in bed I turned these new words over in my mind. It was shocking to me that in town, especially after dark, you'd occasionally see a white girl and a Negro man strolling arm in arm along the sidewalk, and mixed couples drinking in the neon-lighted bars—not slipping off to some dark corner, as in Lansing. I wrote Wilfred and Philbert about that, too.

I wanted to find a job myself, to surprise Ella. One afternoon, something told me to go inside a poolroom whose window I was looking through. I had looked through that window many times. I wasn't yearning to play pool; in fact, I had never held a cue stick. But I was drawn by the sight of the cool-looking "cats" standing around inside, bending over the big, green, felt-topped tables, making bets and shooting the bright-colored balls into the holes. As I stared through the window this particular afternoon, something made me decide to venture inside and talk to a dark, stubby, conk-headed fellow who racked up balls for the pool-players, whom I'd heard called "Shorty." One day he had come outside and seen me standing there and said "Hi, Red," so that made me figure he was friendly.

As inconspicuously as I could, I slipped inside the door and around the side of the poolroom, avoiding people, and on to the back, where Shorty was filling an aluminum can with the powder that pool players dust on their hands. He looked up at me. Later on, Shorty would enjoy teasing me about how with that first glance he knew my whole story. "Man, that cat still *smelled* country!" he'd say, laughing. "Cat's legs was so long and his pants so short his knees showed—an' his head looked like a briar patch!"

But that afternoon Shorty didn't let it show in his face how "country" I appeared when I told him I'd appreciate it if he'd tell me how could somebody go about getting a job like his.

"If you mean racking up balls," said Shorty, "I don't know of no pool joints around here needing anybody. You mean you just want any slave you can find?" A "slave" meant work, a job.

He asked what kind of work I had done. I told him that I'd washed restaurant dishes in Mason, Michigan. He nearly dropped the powder can. "My homeboy! Man, gimme some skin! I'm from Lansing!"

I never told Shorty—and he never suspected—that he was about ten years older than I. He took us to be about the same age. At first I would have been embarrassed to tell him, later I just never bothered. Shorty had dropped out of first-year high school in Lansing, lived awhile with an uncle and aunt in Detroit, and had spent the last six years living with his cousin in Roxbury. But when I mentioned the names of Lansing people and places, he remembered many, and pretty soon we sounded as if we had been raised in the same block. I could sense Shorty's genuine gladness, and I don't have to say how lucky I felt to find a friend as hip as he obviously was.

"Man, this is a swinging town if you dig it," Shorty said. "You're my homeboy—I'm going to school you to the happenings." I stood there and grinned like a fool. "You got to go anywhere now? Well, stick around until I get off."

One thing I liked immediately about Shorty was his frankness. When I told him where I lived, he said what I already knew—that nobody in town could stand the Hill Negroes. But he thought a sister who gave me a "pad," not charging me rent, not even running me out to find "some slave," couldn't be all bad.

Shorty's slave in the poolroom, he said, was just to keep ends together while he learned his horn. A couple of years before, he'd hit the numbers and bought a saxophone. "Got it right in there in the closet now, for my lesson tonight." Shorty was taking lessons "with some other studs," and he intended one day to organize his own small band. "There's a lot of bread to be made gigging right around here in Roxbury," Shorty explained to me. "I don't dig joining some big band, one-nighting all over just to say I played with Count or Duke or somebody." I thought that was smart. I wished I had studied a horn; but I never had been exposed to one.

All afternoon, between trips up front to rack balls, Shorty talked to me out of the corner of his mouth: which hustlers—standing around, or playing at this or that table—sold "reefers," or had just come out of prison, or were "second-story men." Shorty told me that he played at least a dollar a day on the numbers. He said as soon as he hit a number, he would use the winnings to organize his band.

I was ashamed to have to admit that I had never played the numbers. "Well, you ain't never had nothing to play with," he said, excusing me, "but you start when you get a slave, and if you hit, you got a stake for something."

He pointed out some gamblers and some pimps. Some of them had white whores, he whispered. "I ain't going to lie—I dig them two-dollar white chicks," Shorty said. "There's a lot of that action around here, nights: you'll see it." I said I already had seen some. "You ever had one?" he asked.

My embarrassment at my inexperience showed. "Hell, man," he said, "don't be ashamed. I had a few before I left Lansing—them Polack chicks that used to come over the bridge. Here, they're mostly Italians and Irish. But it don't matter what kind, they're something else! Ain't no different nowhere—there's nothing they love better than a black stud."

Through the afternoon, Shorty introduced me to players and loungers. "My homeboy," he'd say, "he's looking for a slave if you hear anything." They all said they'd look out.

At seven o'clock, when the night ball-racker came on, Shorty told me he had to hurry to his saxophone lesson. But before he left, he held out to me the six or seven dollars he had collected that day in nickel and dime tips. "You got enough bread, home-boy?"

I was okay, I told him—I had two dollars. But Shorty made me take three more. "Little fattening for your pocket," he said. Before we went out, he opened his saxophone case and showed me the horn. It was gleaming brass against the green velvet, an alto sax. He said, "Keep cool, homeboy, and come back to-morrow. Some of the cats will turn you up a slave."

When I got home, Ella said there had been a telephone call from somebody named Shorty. He had left a message that over at the Roseland State Ballroom, the shoeshine boy was quitting that night, and Shorty had told him to hold the job for me.

"Malcolm, you haven't had any experience shining shoes," Ella said. Her expression and tone of voice told me she wasn't happy about my taking that job. I didn't particularly care, be-cause I was already speechless thinking about being somewhere close to the greatest bands in the world. I didn't even wait to eat any dinner.

The ballroom was all lighted when I got there. A man at the front door was letting in members of Benny Goodman's band. I told him I wanted to see the shoeshine boy, Freddie.

"You're going to be the new one?" he asked. I said I thought I was, and he laughed, "Well, maybe you'll hit the numbers and get a Cadillac, too." He told me that I'd find Freddie up-stairs in the men's room on the second floor.

But downstairs before I went up, I stepped over and snatched a glimpse inside the ballroom. I just couldn't believe the size of that waxed floor! At the far end, under the soft, rose-colored lights, was the bandstand with the Benny Goodman musicians moving around, laughing and talking, arranging their horns and stands.

A wiry, brown-skinned, conked fellow upstairs in the men's room greeted me. "You Shorty's homeboy?" I said I was, and he said he was Freddie. "Good old boy," he said. "He called me, he just heard I hit the big number, and he figured right I'd be quitting." I told Freddie what the man at the front door had said about a Cadillac. He laughed and said, "Burns them white cats up when you get yourself something. Yeah, I told them I was going to get me one—just to bug them."

Freddie then said for me to pay close attention, that he was going to be busy and for me to watch but not get in the way, and he'd try to get me ready to take over at the next dance, a couple of nights later.

As Freddie busied himself setting up the shoeshine stand, he told me, "Get here early . . . your shoeshine rags and brushes by this footstand . . . your polish bottles, paste wax, suede brushes over here . . . everything in place, you get rushed, you never need to waste motion. . . ."

While you shined shoes, I learned, you also kept watch on customers inside, leaving the urinals. You darted over and offered a small white hand towel. "A lot of cats who ain't planning to wash their hands, sometimes you can run up with a towel and shame them. Your towels are really your best hustle in here. Cost you a penny apiece to launder—you always get at least a nickel tip."

The shoeshine customers, and any from the inside rest room who took a towel, you whiskbroomed a couple of licks. "A nickel or a dime tip, just give 'em that," Freddie said. "But for two bits, Uncle Tom a little—white cats especially like that. I've had them to come back two, three times a dance."

From down below, the sound of the music had begun floating up. I guess I stood transfixed. "You never seen a big dance?" asked Freddie. "Run on awhile, and watch."

There were a few couples already dancing under the rose-colored lights. But even more exciting to me was the crowd thronging in. The most glamorous-looking white women I'd ever seen—young ones, old ones, white cats buying tickets at the window, sticking big wads of green bills back into their pockets, checking the women's coats, and taking their arms and squiring them inside.

Freddie had some early customers when I got back upstairs. Between the shoeshine stand and thrusting towels to them just as they approached the washbasin, Freddie seemed to be doing four things at once. "Here, you can take over the whiskbroom," he said, "just two or three licks—but let 'em feel it."

When things slowed a little, he said, "You ain't seen nothing tonight. You wait until you see a spooks' dance! Man, our people carry *on*!" Whenever he had a moment, he kept schooling me. "Shoelaces, this drawer here. You just starting out, I'm going to make these to you as a present. Buy them for a nickel a pair, tell cats they need laces if they do, and charge two bits.''

Every Benny Goodman record I'd ever heard in my life, it seemed, was filtering faintly into where we were. During another customer lull, Freddie let me slip back outside again to listen. Peggy Lee was at the mike singing. Beautiful! She had just joined the band and she was from North Dakota and had been singing with a group in Chicago when Mrs. Benny Goodman discovered her, we had heard some customers say. She finished the song and the crowd burst into applause. She was a big hit.

"It knocked me out, too, when I first broke in here," Freddie said, grinning, when I went back in there. "But, look, you ever shined any shoes?" He laughed when I said I hadn't, excepting my own. "Well, let's get to work. I never had neither." Freddie got on the stand and went to work on his own shoes. Brush, liquid polish, brush, paste wax, shine rag, lacquer sole dressing . . . step by step, Freddie showed me what to do.

"But you got to get a whole lot faster. You can't waste time!" Freddie showed me how fast on my own shoes. Then, because business was tapering off, he had time to give me a demonstration of how to make the shine rag pop like a firecracker. "Dig the action?" he asked. He did it in slow motion. I got down and tried it on his shoes. I had the principle of it. "Just got to do it faster," Freddie said. "It's a jive noise, that's all. Cats tip better, they figure you're knocking yourself out!"

By the end of the dance, Freddie had let me shine the shoes of three or four stray drunks he talked into having shines, and I had practiced picking up my speed on Freddie's shoes until they looked like mirrors. After we had helped the janitors to clean up the ballroom after the dance, throwing out all the paper and cigarette butts and empty liquor bottles, Freddie was nice enough to drive me all the way home to Ella's on the Hill in the secondhand maroon Buick he said he was going to trade in on his Cadillac. He talked to me all the way. "I guess it's all right if I tell you, pick up a couple of dozen packs of rubbers, two-bits apiece. You notice some of those cats that came up to me around the end of the dance? Well, when some have new chicks going right, they'll come asking you for rubbers. Charge a dollar, generally you'll get an extra tip.''

He looked across at me. "Some hustles you're too new for. Cats will ask you for liquor, some will want reefers. But you don't need to have nothing except rubbers—until you can dig who's a cop."

"You can make ten, twelve dollars a dance for yourself if you work everything right," Freddie said, before I got out of the car in front of Ella's. "The main thing you got to remember is that everything in the world is a hustle. So long, Red."

The next time I ran into Freddie I was downtown one night a few weeks later. He was parked in his pearl-gray Cadillac, sharp as a tack, "cooling it."

"Man, you sure schooled me!" I said, and he laughed; he knew what I meant. It hadn't taken me long on the job to find out that Freddie had done less shoeshining and towel-hustling than selling liquor and reefers, and putting white "Johns" in touch with Negro whores. I also learned that white girls always flocked to the Negro dances—some of them whores whose pimps brought them to mix business and pleasure, others who came with their black boy friends, and some who came in alone, for a little freelance lusting among a plentiful availability of enthusiastic Negro men.

At the white dances, of course, nothing black was allowed, and that's where the black whores' pimps soon showed a new shoeshine boy what he could pick up on the side by slipping a phone number or address to the white Johns who came around the end of the dance looking for "black chicks."

Most of Roseland's dances were for whites only, and they had white bands only. But the only white band ever to play there at a Negro dance, to my recollection, was Charlie Barnet's. The fact is that very few white bands could have satisfied the Negro dancers. But I know that Charlie Barnet's "Cherokee" and his "Redskin Rhumba" drove those Negroes wild. They'd jam-pack that ballroom, the black girls in way-out silk and satin dresses and shoes, their hair done in all kinds of styles, the men sharp in their zoot suits and crazy conks, and everybody grinning and greased and gassed.

Some of the bandsmen would come up to the men's room at about eight o'clock and get shoeshines before they went to work. Duke Ellington, Count Basie, Lionel Hampton, Cootie Williams, Jimmie Lunceford were just a few of those who sat in my chair. I would really make my shine rag sound like someone had set off Chinese firecrackers. Duke's great alto saxman, Johnny Hodges—he was Shorty's idol—still owes me for a shoeshine I gave him. He was in the chair one night, having a friendly argument with the drummer, Sonny Greer, who was standing there, when I tapped the bottom of his shoes to signal that I was finished. Hodges stepped down, reaching his hand in his pocket to pay me, but then snatched his hand out to gesture, and just forgot me, and walked away. I wouldn't have dared to bother the man who could do what he did with "Daydream" by asking him for fifteen cents.

I remember that I struck up a little shoeshine-stand conversation with Count Basie's great blues singer, Jimmie Rushing. (He's the one famous for "Sent For You Yesterday, Here You Come Today" and things like that.) Rushing's feet, I remember, were big and funny-shaped—not long like most big feet, but they were round and roly-poly like Rushing. Anyhow, he even introduced me to some of the other Basie cats, like Lester Young, Harry Edison, Buddy Tate, Don Byas, Dickie Wells, and Buck Clayton. They'd walk in the rest room later, by themselves. "Hi, Red." They'd be up there in my chair, and my shine rag was popping to the beat of all of their records, spinning in my head. Musicians never have had, anywhere, a greater shoeshine-boy fan than I was. I would write to Wilfred and Hilda and Philbert and Reginald back in Lansing, trying to describe it.

I never got any decent tips until the middle of the Negro dances, which is when the dancers started feeling good and getting generous. After the white dances, when I helped to clean out the ballroom, we would throw out perhaps a dozen empty liquor bottles. But after the Negro dances, we would have to throw out cartons full of empty fifth bottles—not rotgut, either, but the best brands, and especially Scotch.

During lulls up there in the men's room, sometimes I'd get in five minutes of watching the dancing. The white people danced as though somebody had trained them—left, one, two; right, three, four—the same steps and patterns over and over, as though somebody had wound them up. But those Negroes—nobody in the world could have choreographed the way they did whatever they felt—just grabbing partners, even the white chicks who came to the Negro dances. And my black brethren today may hate me for saying it, but a lot of black girls nearly got run over by some of those Negro males scrambling to get at those white women; you would have thought God had lowered some of his angels. Times have sure changed; if it happened today, those same black girls would go after those Negro men—and the white women, too.

Anyway, some couples were so abandoned—flinging high and wide, improvising steps and movements—that you couldn't believe it. I could feel the beat in my bones, even though I had never danced.

"Showtime!" people would start hollering about the last hour of the dance. Then a couple of dozen really wild couples would stay on the floor, the girls changing to low white sneakers. The band now would really be blasting, and all the other dancers would form a clapping, shouting circle to watch that wild competition as it began, covering only a quarter or so of the ballroom floor. The band, the spectators and the dancers would be making the Roseland Ballroom feel like a big, rocking ship. The spotlight would be turning, pink, yellow, green, and blue, picking up the couples lindy-hopping as if they had gone mad. *"Wail, man, wail!"* people would be shouting at the band; and it *would* be wailing, until first one and then another couple just ran out of strength and stumbled off toward the crowd, exhausted and soaked with sweat. Sometimes I would be down there standing inside the door jumping up and down in my gray jacket with the whiskbroom in the pocket, and the manager would have to come and shout at me that I had customers upstairs.

The first liquor I drank, my first cigarettes, even my first reefers, I can't specifically remember. But I know they were all mixed together with my first shooting craps, playing cards, and betting my dollar a day on the numbers, as I started hanging out at night with Shorty and his friends. Shorty's jokes about how country I had been made us all laugh. I still was country, I know now, but it all felt so great because I was accepted. All of us would be in somebody's place, usually one of the girls', and we'd be turning on, the reefers making everybody's head light, or the whisky aglow in our middles. Everybody understood that my head had to stay kinky awhile longer, to grow long enough for Shorty to conk it for me. One of these nights, I remarked that I had saved about half enough to get a zoot.

"Save?" Shorty couldn't believe it. "Homeboy, you never heard of credit?" He told me he'd call a neighborhood clothing store the first thing in the morning, and that I should be there early.

A salesman, a young Jew, met me when I came in. "You're Shorty's friend?" I said I was; it amazed me—all of Shorty's contacts. The salesman wrote my name on a form, and the Roseland as where I worked, and Ella's address as where I lived. Shorty's name was put down as recommending me. The salesman said, "Shorty's one of our best customers."

I was measured, and the young salesman picked off a rack a zoot suit that was just wild: sky-blue pants thirty inches in the knee and angle-narrowed down to twelve inches at the bottom, and a long coat that pinched my waist and flared out below my knees.

As a gift, the salesman said, the store would give me a narrow leather belt with my initial "L" on it. Then he said I ought to also buy a hat, and I did—blue, with a feather in the four-inch brim. Then the store gave me another present: a long, thick-linked, gold-plated chain that swung down lower than my coat hem. I was sold forever on credit.

When I modeled the zoot for Ella, she took a long look and said, "Well, I guess it had to happen." I took three of those twenty-five-cent sepia-toned, while-you-wait pictures of myself, posed the way "hipsters" wearing their zoots would "cool it"—hat dangled, knees drawn close together, feet wide apart, both index fingers jabbed toward the floor. The long coat and swinging chain and the Punjab pants were much more dramatic if you stood that way. One picture, I autographed and airmailed to my brothers and sisters in Lansing, to let them see how well I was doing. I gave another one to Ella, and the third to Shorty, who was really moved: I could tell by the way he said, "Thanks, homeboy." It was part of our "hip" code not to show that kind of affection.

Shorty soon decided that my hair was finally long enough to be conked. He had promised to school me in how to beat the barbershops' three- and four-dollar price by making up congolene, and then conking ourselves.

I took the little list of ingredients he had printed out for me, and went to a grocery store, where I got a can of Red Devil lye, two eggs, and two medium-sized white potatoes. Then at a drugstore near the poolroom, I asked for a large jar of Vaseline, a large bar of soap, a large-toothed comb and a fine-toothed comb, one of those rubber hoses with a metal spray-head, a rubber apron and a pair of gloves.

"Going to lay on that first conk?" the drugstore man asked me. I proudly told him, grinning, "Right!"

Shorty paid six dollars a week for a room in his cousin's shabby apartment. His cousin wasn't at home. "It's like the pad's mine, he spends so much time with his woman," Shorty said. "Now, you watch me—"

He peeled the potatoes and thin-sliced them into a quart-sized Mason fruit jar, then started stirring them with a wooden spoon as he gradually poured in a little over half the can of lye. "Never use a metal spoon; the lye will turn it black," he told me.

A jelly-like, starchy-looking glop resulted from the lye and potatoes, and Shorty broke in the two eggs, stirring real fast— his own conk and dark face bent down close. The congolene turned pale-yellowish. "Feel the jar," Shorty said. I cupped my hand against the outside, and snatched it away. "Damn right, it's hot, that's the lye," he said. "So you know it's going to burn when I comb it in—it burns *bad*. But the longer you can stand it, the straighter the hair."

He made me sit down, and he tied the string of the new rubber apron tightly around my neck, and combed up my bush of hair. Then, from the big Vaseline jar, he took a handful and massaged it hard all through my hair and into the scalp. He also thickly Vaselined my neck, ears and forehead. "When I get to washing out your head, be sure to tell me anywhere you feel any little stinging," Shorty warned me, washing his hands, then pulling on the rubber gloves, and tying on his own rubber apron. "You always got to remember that any congolene left in burns a sore into your head."

The congolene just felt warm when Shorty started combing it in. But then my head caught fire.

I gritted my teeth and tried to pull the sides of the kitchen table together. The comb felt as if it was raking my skin off.

My eyes watered, my nose was running. I couldn't stand it

any longer; I bolted to the washbasin. I was cursing Shorty with every name I could think of when he got the spray going and started soap-lathering my head.

He lathered and spray-rinsed, lathered and spray-rinsed, maybe ten or twelve times, each time gradually closing the hot-water faucet, until the rinse was cold, and that helped some.

"You feel any stinging spots?"

"No," I managed to say. My knees were trembling.

"Sit back down, then. I think we got it all out okay."

The flame came back as Shorty, with a thick towel, started drying my head, rubbing hard. *"Easy, man, easy!"* I kept shouting.

"The first time's always worst. You get used to it better before long. You took it real good, homeboy. You got a good conk."

When Shorty let me stand up and see in the mirror, my hair hung down in limp, damp strings. My scalp still flamed, but not as badly; I could bear it. He draped the towel around my shoulders, over my rubber apron, and began again Vaselining my hair.

I could feel him combing, straight back, first the big comb, then the fine-tooth one.

Then, he was using a razor, very delicately, on the back of my neck. Then, finally, shaping the sideburns.

My first view in the mirror blotted out the hurting. I'd seen some pretty conks, but when it's the first time, on your *own* head, the transformation, after the lifetime of kinks, is staggering.

The mirror reflected Shorty behind me. We both were grinning and sweating. And on top of my head was this thick, smooth sheen of shining red hair—real red—as straight as any white man's.

How ridiculous I was! Stupid enough to stand there simply lost in admiration of my hair now looking "white," reflected in the mirror in Shorty's room. I vowed that I'd never again be without a conk, and I never was for many years.

This was my first really big step toward self-degradation: when I endured all of that pain, literally burning my flesh to have it look like a white man's hair. I had joined that multitude of Negro men and women in America who are brainwashed into believing that the black people are "inferior"—and white people "superior"—that they will even violate and mutilate their God-created bodies to try to look "pretty" by white standards.

Look around today, in every small town and big city, from two-bit catfish and soda-pop joints into the "integrated" lobby of the Waldorf-Astoria, and you'll see conks on black men. And you'll see black women wearing these green and pink and purple and red and platinum-blonde wigs. They're all more ridiculous than a slapstick comedy. It makes you wonder if the Negro has completely lost his sense of identity, lost touch with himself.

You'll see the conk worn by many, many so-called "upper-class" Negroes, and, as much as I hate to say it about them, on all too many Negro entertainers. One of the reasons that I've especially admired some of them, like Lionel Hampton and Sidney Poitier, among others, is that they have kept their natural hair and fought to the top. I admire any Negro man who has never had himself conked, or who has had the sense to get rid of it—as I finally did.

I don't know which kind of self-defacing conk is the greater shame—the one you'll see on the heads of the black so-called "middle class" and "upper class," who ought to know better, or the one you'll see on the heads of the poorest, most downtrodden, ignorant black men. I mean the legal-minimum-wage ghetto-dwelling kind of Negro, as I was when I got my first one. It's generally among these poor fools that you'll see a black kerchief over the man's head, like Aunt Jemima; he's trying to make his conk last longer, between trips to the barbershop. Only for special occasions is this kerchief-protected conk exposed—to show off how "sharp" and "hip" its owner is. The ironic thing is that I have never heard any woman, white or black, express any admiration for a conk. Of course, any white woman with a black man isn't thinking about his hair. But I don't see how on earth a black woman with any race pride could walk down the street with any black man wearing a conk—the emblem of his shame that he is black.

To my own shame, when I say all of this I'm talking first of all about myself—because you can't show me any Negro who ever conked more faithfully than I did. I'm speaking from personal experience when I say of any black man who conks today, or any white-wigged black woman, that if they gave the brains in their heads just half as much attention as they do their hair, they would be a thousand times better off.

CHAPTER FOUR

LAURA

Shorty would take me to groovy, frantic scenes in different chicks' and cats' pads, where with the lights and juke down mellow, everybody blew gage and juiced back and jumped. I met chicks who were fine as May wine, and cats who were hip to all happenings.

That paragraph is deliberate, of course; it's just to display a bit more of the slang that was used by everyone I respected as "hip" in those days. And in no time at all, I was talking the slang like a lifelong hipster.

Like hundreds of thousands of country-bred Negroes who had come to the Northern black ghetto before me, and have come since, I'd also acquired all the other fashionable ghetto adornments—the zoot suits and conk that I have described, liquor, cigarettes, then reefers—all to erase my embarrassing background. But I still harbored one secret humiliation: I couldn't dance.

I can't remember when it was that I actually learned how—that is to say, I can't recall the specific night or nights. But dancing was the chief action at those "pad parties," so I've no doubt about how and why my initiation into lindy-hopping came about. With alcohol or marijuana lightening my head, and that wild music wailing away on those portable record players, it didn't take long to loosen up the dancing instincts in my African heritage. All I remember is that during some party around this time, when nearly everyone but me was up dancing, some girl grabbed me—they often would take the initiative and grab a

59

partner, for no girl at those parties ever would dream that anyone present couldn't dance—and there I was out on the floor.

I was up in the jostling crowd—and suddenly, unexpectedly, I got the idea. It was as though somebody had clicked on a light. My long-suppressed African instincts broke through, and loose.

Having spent so much time in Mason's white environment, I had always believed and feared that dancing involved a certain order or pattern of specific steps—as dancing *is* done by whites. But here among my own less inhibited people, I discovered it was simply letting your feet, hands and body spontaneously act out whatever impulses were stirred by the music.

From then on, hardly a party took place without me turning up—inviting myself, if I had to—and lindy-hopping my head off.

I'd always been fast at picking up new things. I made up for lost time now so fast that soon girls were asking me to dance with them. I worked my partners hard; that's why they liked me so much.

When I was at work, up in the Roseland men's room, I just couldn't keep still. My shine rag popped with the rhythm of those great bands rocking the ballroom. White customers on the shine stand, especially, would laugh to see my feet suddenly break loose on their own and cut a few steps. Whites are correct in thinking that black people are natural dancers. Even little kids are—except for those Negroes today who are so "integrated," as I had been, that their instincts are inhibited. You know those "dancing jibagoo" toys that you wind up? Well, I was like a live one—music just wound me up.

By the next dance for the Boston black folk—I remember that Lionel Hampton was coming in to play—I had given my notice to the Roseland's manager.

When I told Ella why I had quit, she laughed aloud: I told her I couldn't find time to shine shoes and dance, too. She was glad, because she had never liked the idea of my working at that no-prestige job. When I told Shorty, he said he'd known I'd soon outgrow it anyway.

Shorty could dance all right himself but, for his own reasons, he never cared about going to the big dances. He loved just the music-making end of it. He practiced his saxophone and listened to records. It astonished me that Shorty didn't care to go and hear the big bands play. He had his alto sax idol, Johnny Hodges, with Duke Ellington's band, but he said he thought too many young musicians were only carbon-copying the big-band names on the same instrument. Anyway, Shorty was really serious about nothing except his music, and about working for the day when he could start his own little group to gig around Boston.

The morning after I quit Roseland, I was down at the men's clothing store bright and early. The salesman checked and found that I'd missed only one weekly payment: I had "A-1" credit. I told him I'd just quit my job, but he said that didn't make any difference; I could miss paying them for a couple of weeks if I had to; he knew I'd get straight.

This time, I studied carefully everything in my size on the racks. And finally I picked out my second zoot. It was a shark-skin gray, with a big, long coat, and pants ballooning out at the knees and then tapering down to cuffs so narrow that I had to take off my shoes to get them on and off. With the salesman urging me on, I got another shirt, and a hat, and new shoes— the kind that were just coming into hipster style; dark orange colored, with paper-thin soles and knob style toes. It all added up to seventy or eighty dollars.

It was such a red-letter day that I even went and got my first barbershop conk. This time it didn't hurt so much, just as Shorty had predicted.

That night, I timed myself to hit Roseland as the thick of the crowd was coming in. In the throughing lobby, I saw some of the real Roxbury hipsters eyeing my zoot, and some fine women were giving me that look. I sauntered up to the men's room for a short drink from the pint in my inside coat-pocket. My replacement was there—a scared, narrow-faced, hungry-looking little brown-skinned fellow just in town from Kansas City. And when he recognized me, he couldn't keep down his admiration and wonder. I told him to "keep cool," that he'd soon catch on to the happenings. Everything felt right when I went into the ball-room.

Hamp's band was working, and that big, waxed floor was packed with people lindy-hopping like crazy. I grabbed some girl I'd never seen, and the next thing I knew we were out there lindying away and grinning at each other. It couldn't have been finer.

I'd been lindying previously only in cramped little apartment living rooms, and now I had room to maneuver. Once I really got myself warmed and loosened up, I was snatching partners from among the hundreds of unattached, free-lancing girls along the sidelines—almost every one of them could really dance—and I just about went wild! Hamp's band wailing. I was whirling girls so fast their skirts were snapping. Black girls, brownskins, high yellows, even a couple of the white girls there. Boosting them over my hips, my shoulders, into the air. Though I wasn't quite sixteen then, I was tall and rawboned and looked like twenty-one; I was also pretty strong for my age. Circling, tap-dancing, I was underneath them when they landed—doing the "flapping eagle," "the kangaroo" and the "split."

After that, I never missed a Roseland lindy-hop as long as I stayed in Boston.

The greatest lindy-dancing partner I had, everything consid-ered, was a girl named Laura. I met her at my next job. When I quit shoeshining, Ella was so happy that she went around ask-ing about a job for me—one she would approve. Just two blocks from her house, the Townsend Drug Store was about to replace its soda fountain clerk, a fellow who was leaving to go off to college.

When Ella told me, I didn't like it. She knew I couldn't stand those Hill characters. But speaking my mind right then would have made Ella mad. I didn't want that to happen, so I put on the white jacket and started serving up sodas, sundaes, splits, shakes and all the rest of that fountain stuff to those fancy-acting Negroes.

Every evening when I got off at eight and came home, Ella would keep saying, "I hope you'll meet some of these nice young people your age here in Roxbury." But those penny-ante squares who came in there putting on their millionaires' airs, the young ones and the old ones both, only annoyed me. People like the sleep-in maid for Beacon Hill white folks who used to come in with her "ooh, my deah" manners and order corn plas-ters in the Jew's drugstore for black folks. Or the hospital cafeteria-line serving woman sitting there on her day off with a cat fur around her neck, telling the proprietor she was a "dieti-tian"—both of them knowing she was lying. Even the young ones, my age, whom Ella was always talking about. The soda fountain was one of their hang-outs. They soon had me ready to quit, with their accents so phonied up that if you just heard them and didn't see them, you wouldn't even know they were Negroes. I couldn't wait for eight o'clock to get home to eat out of those soul-food pots of Ella's, then get dressed in my zoot and head for some of my friends' places in town, to lindy-hop and get high, or something, for relief from those Hill clowns.

Before long, I didn't see how I was going to be able to stick it out there eight hours a day; and I nearly didn't. I remember one night, I nearly quit because I had hit the numbers for ten cents—the first time I had ever hit—on one of the sideline bets that I'd made in the drugstore. (Yes, there were several runners on the Hill; even dignified Negroes played the numbers.) I won sixty dollars, and Shorty and I had a ball with it. I wished I had hit for the daily dollar that I played with my town man, paying him by the week. I would surely have quit the drugstore. I could have bought a car.

Anyway, Laura lived in a house that was catercorner across the street from the drugstore. After a while, as soon as I saw her coming in, I'd start making up a banana split. She was a real bug for them, and she came in late every afternoon—after school. I imagine I'd been shoving that ice cream dish under her nose for five or six weeks before somehow it began to sink in that she wasn't like the rest. She was certainly the only Hill girl that came in there and acted in any way friendly and natural.

She always had some book with her, and poring over it, she would make a thirty-minute job of that daily dish of banana split. I began to notice the books she read. They were pretty heavy school stuff—Latin, algebra, things like that. Watching her made me reflect that I hadn't read even a newspaper since leaving Mason.

Laura. I heard her name called by a few of the others who came in when she was there. But I could see they didn't know her too well; they said "hello"—that was about the extent of it. She kept to herself, and she never said more than "Thank you" to me. Nice voice. Soft. Quiet. Never another word. But no airs like the others, no black Bostonese. She was just herself.

I liked that. Before too long, I struck up a conversation. Just what subject I got off on I don't remember, but she readily opened up and began talking, and she was very friendly. I found out that she was a high school junior, an honor student. Her parents had split up when she was a baby, and she had been raised by her grandmother, an old lady on a pension, who was very strict and old-fashioned and religious. Laura had just one close friend, a girl who lived over in Cambridge, whom she had gone to school with. They talked on the telephone every day. Her grandmother scarcely ever let her go to the movies, let alone on dates.

But Laura really liked school. She said she wanted to go on to college. She was keen for algebra, and she planned to major in science. Laura never would have dreamed that she was a year older than I was. I gauged that indirectly. She looked up to me as though she felt I had a world of experience more than she did—which really was the truth. But sometimes, when she had gone, I felt let down, thinking how I had turned away from the books I used to like when I was back in Michigan.

I got to the point where I looked forward to her coming in every day after school. I stopped letting her pay, and gave her extra ice cream. And she wasn't hiding the fact that she liked me.

It wasn't long before she had stopped reading her books when she came in, and would just sit and eat and talk with me. And soon she began trying to get me to talk about myself. I was immediately sorry when I dropped that I had once thought about becoming a lawyer. She didn't want to let me rest about that. "Malcolm, there's no reason you can't pick up right where you are and become a lawyer." She had the idea that my sister Ella would help me as much as she could. And if Ella had ever thought that she could help any member of the Little family put up any kind of professional shingle—as a teacher, a foot-doctor, anything—why, you would have had to tie her down to keep her from taking in washing.

I never mentioned Laura to Shorty. I just knew she never would have understood him, or that crowd. And they wouldn't have understood her. She had never been touched, I'm certain she hadn't, or even had a drink, and she wouldn't even have known what a reefer was.

It was a great surprise to me when one afternoon Laura happened to let drop that she "just loved" lindy-hopping. I asked her how had she been able to go out dancing. She said she'd been introduced to lindy-hopping at a party given by the parents of some Negro friend just accepted by Harvard.

It was just about time to start closing down the soda fountain, and I said that Count Basie was playing the Roseland that weekend, and would she like to go?

Laura's eyes got wide. I thought I'd have to catch her, she was so excited. She said she'd never been there, she'd heard so much about it, she'd imagined what it was like, she'd just give anything—but her grandma would have a fit.

So I said maybe some other time.

But the afternoon before the dance, Laura came in full of excitement. She whispered that she'd never lied to her grandma before, but she had told her she had to attend some school function that evening. If I'd get her home early, she'd meet me—if I'd still take her.

I told her we'd have to go by for me to change clothes at the house. She hesitated, but said okay. Before we left, I telephoned Ella to say I'd be bringing a girl by on the way to the dance. Though I'd never before done anything like it, Ella covered up her surprise.

I laughed to myself a long time afterward about how Ella's mouth flew open when we showed up at the front door—me and a well-bred Hill girl. Laura, when I introduced her, was warm and sincere. And Ella, you would have thought she was closing in on her third husband.

While they sat and talked downstairs, I dressed upstairs in my room. I remember changing my mind about the wild sharkskin gray zoot I had planned to wear, and deciding instead to put on the first one I'd gotten, the blue zoot. I knew I should wear the most conservative thing I had.

They were like old friends when I came back down. Ella had even made tea. Ella's hawk-eye just about raked my zoot right off my back. But I'm sure she was grateful that I'd at least put on the blue one. Knowing Ella, I knew that she had already extracted Laura's entire life story—and all but had the wedding bells around my neck. I grinned all the way to the Roseland in the taxi, because I had showed Ella I could hang out with Hill girls if I wanted to.

Laura's eyes were so big. She said almost none of her acquaintances knew her grandmother, who never went anywhere but to church, so there wasn't much danger of it getting back to her. The only person she had told was her girl friend, who had shared her excitement.

Then, suddenly, we were in the Roseland's jostling lobby. And I was getting waves and smiles and greetings. They shouted "My man!" and "Hey, Red!" and I answered "Daddy-o."

She and I never before had danced together, but that certainly was no problem. Any two people who can lindy at all can lindy together. We just started out there on the floor among a lot of other couples.

It was maybe halfway in the number before I became aware of how she danced.

If you've ever lindy-hopped, you'll know what I'm talking about. With most girls, you kind of work opposite them, circling, side-stepping, leading. Whichever arm you lead with is half-bent out there, your hands are giving that little pull, that little push, touching her waist, her shoulders, her arms. She's in, out, turning, whirling, wherever you guide her. With poor partners, you feel their weight. They're slow and heavy. But with really good partners, all you need is just the push-pull suggestion. They guide nearly effortlessly, even off the floor and into the air, and your little solo maneuver is done on the floor before they land, when they join you, whirling, right in step.

I'd danced with plenty of good partners. But what I became suddenly aware of with Laura was that I'd never before felt so little weight! I'd nearly just *think* a maneuver, and she'd respond.

Anyway, as she danced up, down, under my arm, flinging out, while I felt her out and examined her style, I glimpsed her footwork. I can close my eyes right now and see it, like some blurring ballet—beautiful! And her lightness, like a shadow! My perfect partner, if somebody had asked me, would have been one who handled as lightly as Laura and who would have had the strength to last through a long, tough showtime. But I knew that Laura wouldn't begin to be that strong.

In Harlem, years later, a friend of mine called "Sammy The Pimp" taught me something I wish I had known then to look for in Laura's face. It was what Sammy declared was his infallible clue for determining the "unconscious, true personality" of women. Considering all the women he had picked out of crowds and turned into prostitutes, Sammy qualified as an expert. Anyway, he swore that if a woman, any woman, gets really carried away while dancing, what she truly is—at least potentially—will surface and show on her face.

I'm not suggesting that a lady-of-easy-virtue look danced to the surface in Laura—although life did deal her cruel blows, starting with her meeting me. All I am saying is that it may be that if I had been equipped with Sammy's ability, I might have spotted in Laura then some of the subsurface potential, destined to become real, that would have shocked her grandma.

A third of the way or so through the evening the main vocalizing and instrumental stylings would come—and then showtime, when only the greatest lindy-hoppers would stay on the floor, to try and eliminate each other. All the other dancers would form a big "U" with the band at the open end.

The girls who intended to compete would slip over to the sidelines and change from high heels into low white sneakers. In competition, they never could survive in heels. And always among them were four or five unattached girls who would run around trying to hook up with some guy they knew could really lindy.

Now Count Basie turned on the showtime blast, and the other dancers moved off the floor, shifting for good watching positions, and began their hollering for their favorites. "All right now, Red!" they shouted to me, "Go get 'em, Red." And then a free-lancing lindy-girl I'd danced with before, Mamie Bevels, a waitress and a wild dancer, ran up to me, with Laura standing right there. I wasn't sure what to do. But Laura started backing away toward the crowd, still looking at me.

The Count's band was wailing. I grabbed Mamie and we started to work. She was a big, rough, strong gal, and she lindied like a bucking horse. I remember the very night that she became known as one of the showtime favorites there at the Roseland. A band was screaming when she kicked off her shoes and got barefooted, and shouted, and shook herself as if she were in some African jungle frenzy, and then she let loose with some dancing, shouting with every step, until the guy that was out there with her nearly had to fight to control her. The crowd loved any way-out lindying style that made a colorful show like that. It was how Mamie had become known.

Anyway, I started driving her like a horse, the way she liked. When we came off the floor after the first number, we both were wringing wet with sweat, and people were shouting and pounding our backs.

I remember leaving early with Laura, to get her home in time. She was very quiet. And she didn't have much to say for the next week or so when she came into the drugstore. Even then, I had learned enough about women to know not to pressure them when they're thinking something out; they'll tell you when they're ready.

Every time I saw Ella, even brushing my teeth in the morning, she turned on the third degree. When was I seeing Laura again? Was I going to bring her by again? "What a nice girl she is!" Ella had picked her out for me.

But in that kind of way, I thought hardly anything about the girl. When it came to personal matters, my mind was strictly on getting "sharp" in my zoot as soon as I left work, and racing downtown to hang out with Shorty and the other guys—and with the girls they knew—a million miles away from the stuck-up Hill.

I wasn't even thinking about Laura when she came up to me in the drugstore and asked me to take her to the next Negro dance at the Roseland. Duke Ellington was going to play, and she was beside herself with excitement. I had no way to know what was going to happen.

She asked me to pick her up at her house this time. I didn't want any contact with the old grandma she had described, but I went. Grandma answered the door—an old-fashioned, wrinkled black woman, with fuzzy gray hair. She just opened the door enough for me to get in, not even saying as much as "Come in, dog." I've faced armed detectives and gangsters less hostile than she was.

I remember the musty living room, full of those old Christ pictures, prayers woven into tapestries, statuettes of the crucifixion, other religious objects on the mantel, shelves, table tops, walls, everywhere.

Since the old lady wasn't speaking to me, I didn't speak to her, either. I completely sympathize with her now, of course.

What could she have thought of me in my zoot and conk and orange shoes? She'd have done us all a favor if she had run screaming for the police. If something looking as I did then ever came knocking at my door today, asking to see one of my four daughters, I know I would explode.

When Laura rushed into the room, jerking on her coat, I could see that she was upset and angry and embarrassed. And in the taxi, she started crying. She had hated herself for lying before; she had decided to tell the truth about where she was going, and there had been a screaming battle with grandma. Laura had told the old lady that she was going to start going out when and where she wanted to, or she would quit school and get a job and move out on her own—and her grandma had pitched a fit. Laura just walked out.

When we got to the Roseland, we danced the early part of the evening with each other and with different partners. And finally the Duke kicked off showtime.

I knew, and Laura knew, that she couldn't match the veteran showtime girls, but she told me that she wanted to compete. And the next thing I knew, she was among those girls over on the sidelines changing into sneakers. I shook my head when a couple of the free-lancing girls ran up to me.

As always, the crowd clapped and shouted in time with the blasting band. "Go, Red, go!" Partly it was my reputation, and partly Laura's ballet style of dancing that helped to turn the spotlight—and the crowd's attention—to us. They never had seen the feather-lightness that she gave to lindying, a completely fresh style—and they were connoisseurs of styles. I turned up the steam, Laura's feet were flying; I had her in the air, down, sideways, around; backwards, up again, down, whirling. . . .

The spotlight was working mostly just us. I caught glimpses of the four or five other couples, the girls jungle-strong, animal-like, bucking and charging. But little Laura inspired me to drive to new heights. Her hair was all over her face, it was running sweat, and I couldn't believe her strength. The crowd was shouting and stomping. A new favorite was being discovered; there was a wall of noise around us. I felt her weakening, she was lindying like a fighter out on her feet, and we stumbled off to the sidelines. The band was still blasting. I had to half-carry her; she was gasping for air. Some of the men in the band applauded.

And even Duke Ellington half raised up from his piano stool and bowed.

If a showtime crowd liked your performance, when you came off you were mobbed, mauled, grasped, and pummeled like the team that's just taken the series. One bunch of the crowd swarmed Laura; they had her clear up off her feet. And I was being pounded on the back . . . when I caught this fine blonde's eyes. . . . This one I'd never seen among the white girls who came to the Roseland black dances. She was eyeing me levelly.

Now at that time, in Roxbury, in any black ghetto in America, to have a white woman who wasn't a known, common whore was—for the average black man, at least—a status symbol of the first order. And this one, standing there, eyeing me, was almost too fine to believe. Shoulder-length hair, well built, and her clothes had cost somebody plenty.

It's shameful to admit, but I had just about forgotten Laura when she got loose from the mob and rushed up, big-eyed—and stopped. I guess she saw what there was to see in that girl's face—and mine—as we moved out to dance.

I'm going to call her Sophia.

She didn't dance well, at least not by Negro standards. But who cared? I could feel the staring eyes of other couples around us. We talked. I told her she was a good dancer, and asked her where she'd learned. I was trying to find out why she was there. Most white women came to the black dances for reasons I knew, but you seldom saw her kind around there.

She had vague answers for everything. But in the space of that dance, we agreed that I would get Laura home early and rush back in a taxicab. And then she asked if I'd like to go for a drive later. I felt very lucky.

Laura was home and I was back at the Roseland in an hour flat. Sophia was waiting outside.

About five blocks down, she had a low convertible. She knew where she was going. Beyond Boston, she pulled off into a side road, and then off that into a deserted lane. And turned off everything but the radio.

For the next several months, Sophia would pick me up downtown, and I'd take her to dances, and to the bars around Roxbury. We drove all over. Sometimes it would be nearly daylight when she let me out in front of Ella's.

I paraded her. The Negro men loved her. And she just seemed to love all Negroes. Two or three nights a week, we would go out together. Sophia admitted that she also had dates with white fellows, "just for the looks of things," she said. She swore that a white man couldn't interest her.

I wondered for a long time, but I never did find out why she approached me so boldly that very first night. I always thought it was because of some earlier experience with another Negro, but I never asked, and she never said. Never ask a woman about other men. Either she'll tell you a lie, and you still won't know, or if she tells you the truth, you might not have wanted to hear it in the first place.

Anyway, she seemed entranced with me. I began to see less of Shorty. When I did see him and the gang, he would gibe, "Man, I had to comb the burrs out of my homeboy's head, and now he's got a Beacon Hill chick." But truly, because it was known that Shorty had "schooled" me, my having Sophia gave Shorty status. When I introduced her to him, she hugged him like a sister, and it just about finished Shorty off. His best had been white prostitutes and a few of those poor specimens that worked around in the mills and had "discovered" Negroes.

It was when I began to be seen around town with Sophia that I really began to mature into some real status in black downtown Roxbury. Up to then I had been just another among all of the conked and zooted youngsters. But now, with the best-looking white woman who ever walked in those bars and clubs, and with her giving me the money I spent, too, even the big, important black hustlers and "smart boys"—the club managers, name gamblers, numbers bankers, and others—were clapping me on the back, setting us up to drinks at special tables, and calling me "Red." Of course I knew their reason like I knew my own name: they wanted to steal my fine white woman away from me.

In the ghetto, as in suburbia, it's the same status struggle to stand out in some envied way from the rest. At sixteen, I didn't have the money to buy a Cadillac, but she had her own fine "rubber," as we called a car in those days. And I had her, which was even better.

* * *

Laura never again came to the drugstore as long as I continued to work there. The next time I saw her, she was a wreck of a woman, notorious around black Roxbury, in and out of jail. She had finished high school, but by then she was already going the wrong way. Defying her grandmother, she had started going out late and drinking liquor. This led to dope, and that to selling herself to men. Learning to hate the men who bought her, she also became a Lesbian. One of the shames I have carried for years is that I blame myself for all of this. To have treated her as I did for a white woman made the blow doubly heavy. The only excuse I can offer is that like so many of my black brothers today, I was just deaf, dumb, and blind.

In any case, it wasn't long after I met Sophia that Ella found out about it, and watching from the windows one early morning, saw me getting out of Sophia's car. Not surprisingly, Ella began treating me like a viper.

About then, Shorty's cousin finally moved in with the woman he was so crazy about, and Sophia financed me to take over half of the apartment with Shorty—and I quit the drugstore and soon found a new job.

I became a busboy at the Parker House in Boston. I wore a starched white jacket out in the dining room, where the waiters would put the customers' dirty plates and silver on big aluminum trays which I would take back to the kitchen's dishwashers.

A few weeks later, one Sunday morning, I ran in to work expecting to get fired, I was so late. But the whole kitchen crew was too excited and upset to notice: Japanese planes had just bombed a place called Pearl Harbor.

CHAPTER FIVE

HARLEMITE

"Get'cha goood haaaaam an' cheeeeese . . . sandwiches! Coffee! Candy! Cake! Ice Cream!" Rocking along the tracks every other day for four hours between Boston and New York in the coach aisles of the New York, New Haven & Hartford's "Yankee Clipper."

Old Man Rountree, an elderly Pullman porter and a friend of Ella's, had recommended the railroad job for me. He had told her the war was snatching away railroad men so fast that if I could pass for twenty-one, he could get me on.

Ella wanted to get me out of Boston and away from Sophia. She would have loved nothing better than to have seen me like one of those Negroes who were already thronging Roxbury in the Army's khaki and thick shoes—home on leave from boot camp. But my age of sixteen stopped that.

I went along with the railroad job for my own reasons. For a long time I'd wanted to visit New York City. Since I had been in Roxbury, I had heard a lot about "the Big Apple," as it was called by the well-traveled musicians, merchant mariners, salesmen, chauffeurs for white families, and various kinds of hustlers I ran into. Even as far back as Lansing, I had been hearing about how fabulous New York was, and especially Harlem. In fact, my father had described Harlem with pride, and showed us pictures of the huge parades by the Harlem followers of Marcus Garvey. And every time Joe Louis won a fight against a white opponent, big front-page pictures in the Negro newspapers such as the *Chicago Defender*, the *Pittsburgh Courier* and the *Afro-American* showed a sea of Harlem Negroes cheering and waving and the Brown Bomber waving back at them from the balcony of Harlem's Theresa Hotel. Everything I'd ever heard about New York City was exciting—things like Broadway's bright lights and the Savoy Ballroom and Apollo Theater in Harlem, where great bands played and famous songs and dance steps and Negro stars originated.

But you couldn't just pick up and go to visit New York from Lansing, or Boston, or anywhere else—not without money. So I'd never really given too much thought to getting to New York until the free way to travel there came in the form of Ella's talk with old man Rountree, who was a member of Ella's church.

What Ella didn't know, of course, was that I would continue to see Sophia. Sophia could get away only a few nights a week. She said, when I told her about the train job, that she'd get away every night I got back into Boston, and this would mean every other night, if I got the run I wanted. Sophia didn't want me to leave at all, but she believed I was draft age already, and thought the train job would keep me out of the Army.

Shorty thought it would be a great chance for me. He was worried sick himself about the draft call that he knew was soon to come. Like hundreds of the black ghetto's young men, he was taking some stuff that, it was said, would make your heart sound defective to the draft board's doctors.

Shorty felt about the war the same way I and most ghetto Negroes did: "Whitey owns everything. He wants us to go and bleed for him? Let him fight."

Anyway, at the railroad personnel hiring office down on Dover Street, a tired-acting old white clerk got down to the crucial point, when I came to sign up. "Age, Little?" When I told him "Twenty-one," he never lifted his eyes from his pencil. I knew I had the job.

I was promised the first available Boston-to-New York fourth-cook job. But for a while, I worked there in the Dover Street Yard, helping to load food requisitions onto the trains. Fourth cook, I knew, was just a glorified name for dishwasher, but it wouldn't be my first time, and just as long as I traveled where I wanted, it didn't make any difference to me. Temporarily though, they put me on "The Colonial" that ran to Washington, D.C.

The kitchen crew, headed by a West Indian chef named Duke

Vaughn, worked with almost unbelievable efficiency in the cramped quarters. Against the sound of the train clacking along, the waiters were jabbering the customers' orders, the cooks operated like machines, and five hundred miles of dirty pots and dishes and silverware rattled back to me. Then, on the overnight layover, I naturally went sightseeing in downtown Washington. I was astounded to find in the nation's capital, just a few blocks from Capitol Hill, thousands of Negroes living worse than any I'd ever seen in the poorest sections of Roxbury; in dirt-floor shacks along unspeakably filthy lanes with names like Pig Alley and Goat Alley. I had seen a lot, but never such a dense concentration of stumblebums, pushers, hookers, public crap-shooters, even little kids running around at midnight begging for pennies, half-naked and barefooted. Some of the railroad cooks and waiters had told me to be very careful, because muggings, knifings and robberies went on every night among these Negroes . . . just a few blocks from the White House.

But I saw other Negroes better off; they lived in blocks of rundown red brick houses. The old "Colonial" railroaders had told me about Washington having a lot of "middle-class" Negroes with Howard University degrees, who were working as laborers, janitors, porters, guards, taxi-drivers, and the like. For the Negro in Washington, mail-carrying was a prestige job.

After a few of the Washington runs, I snatched the chance when one day personnel said I could temporarily replace a sandwich man on the "Yankee Clipper" to New York. I was into my zoot suit before the first passenger got off.

The cooks took me up to Harlem in a cab. White New York passed by like a movie set, then abruptly, when we left Central Park at the upper end, at 110th Street, the people's complexion began to change.

Busy Seventh Avenue ran along in front of a place called Small's Paradise. The crew had told me before we left Boston that it was their favorite night spot in Harlem, and not to miss it. No Negro place of business had ever impressed me so much. Around the big, luxurious-looking, circular bar were thirty or forty Negroes, mostly men, drinking and talking.

I was hit first, I think, by their conservative clothes and manners. Wherever I'd seen as many as ten Boston Negroes—let alone Lansing Negroes—drinking, there had been a big noise.

But with all of these Harlemites drinking and talking, there was just a low murmur of sound. Customers came and went. The bartenders knew what most of them drank and automatically fixed it. A bottle was set on the bar before some.

Every Negro I'd ever known had made a point of flashing whatever money he had. But these Harlem Negroes quietly laid a bill on the bar. They drank. They nonchalantly nodded to the bartender to pour a drink for some friend, while the bartenders, smooth as any of the customers, kept making change from the money on the bar.

Their manners seemed natural; they were not putting on any airs. I was awed. Within the first five minutes in Small's, I had left Boston and Roxbury forever.

I didn't yet know that these weren't what you might call everyday or average Harlem Negroes. Later on, even later that night, I would find out that Harlem contained hundreds of thousands of my people who were just as loud and gaudy as Negroes anywhere else. But these were the cream of the older, more mature operators in Harlem. The day's "numbers" business was done. The night's gambling and other forms of hustling hadn't yet begun. The usual night-life crowd, who worked on regular jobs all day, were at home eating their dinners. The hustlers at this time were in the daily six o'clock congregation, having their favorite bars all over Harlem largely to themselves.

From Small's, I taxied over to the Apollo Theater. (I remember so well that Jay McShann's band was playing, because his vocalist was later my close friend, Walter Brown, the one who used to sing "Hooty Hooty Blues.") From there, on the other side of 125th Street, at Seventh Avenue, I saw the big, tall, gray Theresa Hotel. It was the finest in New York City where Negroes could then stay, years before the downtown hotels would accept the black man. (The Theresa is now best known as the place where Fidel Castro went during his U.N. visit, and achieved a psychological coup over the U.S. State Department when it confined him to Manhattan, never dreaming that he'd stay uptown in Harlem and make such an impression among the Negroes.)

The Braddock Hotel was just up 126th Street, near the Apollo's backstage entrance. I knew its bar was famous as a Negro celebrity hang-out. I walked in and saw, along that jam-packed bar, such famous stars as Dizzy Gillespie, Billy Eckstine, Billie Holiday, Ella Fitzgerald, and Dinah Washington.

As Dinah Washington was leaving with some friends, I overheard someone say she was on her way to the Savoy Ballroom where Lionel Hampton was appearing that night—she was then Hamp's vocalist. The ballroom made the Roseland in Boston look small and shabby by comparison. And the lindy-hopping there matched the size and elegance of the place. Hampton's hard-driving outfit kept a red-hot pace with his greats such as Arnett Cobb, Illinois Jacquet, Dexter Gordon, Alvin Hayse, Joe Newman, and George Jenkins. I went a couple of rounds on the floor with girls from the sidelines.

Probably a third of the sideline booths were filled with white people, mostly just watching the Negroes dance; but some of them danced together, and, as in Boston, a few white women were with Negroes. The people kept shouting for Hamp's "Flyin' Home," and finally he did it. (I could believe the story I'd heard in Boston about this number—that once in the Apollo, Hamp's "Flyin' Home" had made some reefer-smoking Negro in the second balcony believe he could fly, so he tried—and jumped—and broke his leg, an event later immortalized in song when Earl Hines wrote a hit tune called "Second Balcony Jump.") I had never seen such fever-heat dancing. After a couple of slow numbers cooled the place off, they brought on Dinah Washington. When she did her "Salty Papa Blues," those people just about tore the Savoy roof off. (Poor Dinah's funeral was held not long ago in Chicago. I read that over twenty thousand people viewed her body, and I should have been there myself. Poor Dinah! We became great friends, back in those days.)

But this night of my first visit was Kitchen Mechanics' Night at the Savoy, the traditional Thursday night off for domestics. I'd say there were twice as many women as men in there, not only kitchen workers and maids, but also war wives and defense-worker women, lonely and looking. Out in the street, when I left the ballroom, I heard a prostitute cursing bitterly that the professionals couldn't do any business because of the amateurs.

Up and down along and between Lenox and Seventh and Eighth avenues, Harlem was like some technicolor bazaar. Hundreds of Negro soldiers and sailors, gawking and young like me, passed by. Harlem by now was officially off limits to white servicemen. There had already been some muggings and robberies, and several white servicemen had been found murdered. The police were also trying to discourage white civilians from coming uptown, but those who wanted to still did. Every man without a woman on his arm was being "worked" by the prostitutes. "Baby, wanna have some fun?" The pimps would sidle up close, stage-whispering, "All kinds of women, Jack—want a white woman?" And the hustlers were merchandising: "Hundred-dollar ring, man, diamond; ninety-dollar watch, too—look at 'em. Take 'em both for twenty-five."

In another two years, I could have given them all lessons. But that night, I was mesmerized. This world was where I belonged. On that night I had started on my way to becoming a Harlemite. I was going to become one of the most depraved parasitical hustlers among New York's eight million people—four million of whom work, and the other four million of whom live off them.

I couldn't quite believe all that I'd heard and seen that night as I lugged my shoulder-strap sandwich box and that heavy five-gallon aluminum coffee pot up and down the aisles of the "Yankee Clipper" back to Boston. I wished that Ella and I had been on better terms so that I could try to describe to her how I felt. But I did talk to Shorty, urging him to at least go to see the Big Apple music world. Sophia listened to me, too. She told me that I'd never be satisfied anywhere but New York. She was so right. In one night, New York—Harlem—had just about narcotized me.

That sandwich man I'd replaced had little chance of getting his job back. I went bellowing up and down those train aisles. I sold sandwiches, coffee, candy, cake, and ice cream as fast as the railroad's commissary department could supply them. It didn't take me a week to learn that all you had to do was give white people a show and they'd buy anything you offered them. It was like popping your shoeshine rag. The dining car waiters and Pullman porters knew it too, and they faked their Uncle Tomming to get bigger tips. We were in that world of Negroes who are both servants and psychologists, aware that white people are so obsessed with their own importance that they will pay liberally, even dearly, for the impression of being catered to and entertained.

Every layover night in Harlem, I ran and explored new places. I first got a room at the Harlem YMCA, because it was less than a block from Small's Paradise. Then, I got a cheaper room at Mrs. Fisher's rooming house which was close to the YMCA. Most of the railroad men stayed at Mrs. Fisher's. I combed not only the bright-light areas, but Harlem's residential areas from best to worst, from Sugar Hill up near the Polo Grounds, where many famous celebrities lived, down to the slum blocks of old rat-trap apartment houses, just crawling with everything you could mention that was illegal and immoral. Dirt, garbage cans overflowing or kicked over; drunks, dope addicts, beggars. Sleazy bars, store-front churches with gospels being shouted inside, "bargain" stores, hockshops, undertaking parlors. Greasy "home-cooking" restaurants, beauty shops smoky inside from Negro women's hair getting fried, barbershops advertising conk experts. Cadillacs, secondhand and new, conspicuous among the cars on the streets.

All of it was Lansing's West Side or Roxbury's South End magnified a thousand times. Little basement dance halls with "For Rent" signs on them. People offering you little cards advertising "rent-raising parties." I went to one of these—thirty or forty Negroes sweating, eating, drinking, dancing, and gambling in a jammed, beat-up apartment, the record player going full blast, the fried chicken or chitlins with potato salad and collard greens for a dollar a plate, and cans of beer or shots of liquor for fifty cents. Negro and white canvassers sidled up alongside you, talking fast as they tried to get you to buy a copy of the *Daily Worker:* "This paper's trying to keep your rent controlled . . . Make that greedy landlord kill them rats in your apartment . . . This paper represents the only political party that ever ran a black man for the Vice Presidency of the United States . . . Just want you to read, won't take but a little of your time . . . Who do you think fought the hardest to help free those Scottsboro boys?" Things I overheard among Negroes when the salesmen were around let me know that the paper somehow was tied in with the Russians, but to my sterile mind in those early days, it didn't mean much; the radio broadcasts and the newspapers were then full of our-ally-Russia, a strong, muscular people, peasants, with their backs to the wall helping America to fight Hitler and Mussolini.

But New York was heaven to me. And Harlem was Seventh Heaven! I hung around in Small's and the Braddock bar so much that the bartenders began to pour a shot of bourbon, my favorite brand of it, when they saw me walk in the door. And the steady customers in both places, the hustlers in Small's and the entertainers in the Braddock, began to call me "Red," a natural enough nickname in view of my bright red conk. I now had my conk done in Boston at the shop of Abbott and Fogey; it was the best conk shop on the East Coast, according to the musical greats who had recommended it to me.

My friends now included musicians like Duke Ellington's great drummer, Sonny Greer, and that great personality with the violin, Ray Nance. He's the one who used to sing in that wild "scat" style: "Blip-blip-de-blop-de-blam-blam—" And people like Cootie Williams, and Eddie "Cleanhead" Vinson, who'd kid me about his conk—he had nothing up there but skin. He was hitting the heights then with his song, "Hey, Pretty Mama, Chunk Me In Your Big Brass Bed." I also knew Sy Oliver; he was married to a red-complexioned girl, and they lived up on Sugar Hill; Sy did a lot of arranging for Tommy Dorsey in those days. His most famous tune, I believe, was "Yes, Indeed!"

The regular "Yankee Clipper" sandwich man, when he came back, was put on another train. He complained about seniority, but my sales record made them placate him some other way. The waiters and cooks had begun to call me "Sandwich Red."

By that time, they had a laughing bet going that I wasn't going to last, sales or not, because I had so rapidly become such an uncouth, wild young Negro. Profanity had become my language. I'd even curse customers, especially servicemen; I couldn't stand them. I remember that once, when some passenger complaints had gotten me a warning, and I wanted to be careful, I was working down the aisle and a big, beefy, red-faced cracker soldier got up in front of me, so drunk he was weaving, and announced loud enough that everybody in the car heard him, "I'm going to fight you, nigger." I remember the tension. I laughed and told him, "Sure, I'll fight, but you've got too many clothes on." He had on a big Army overcoat. He took that off, and I kept laughing and said he still had on too many. I was able to keep that cracker stripping off clothes until he stood there drunk with nothing on from his pants up, and the whole car was laughing at him, and some other soldiers got him out of the way. I went on. I never would forget that—that I couldn't have whipped that white man as badly with a club as I had with my mind.

Many of the New Haven Line's cooks and waiters still in railroad service today will remember old Pappy Cousins. He was the "Yankee Clipper" steward, a white man, of course, from Maine. (Negroes had been in dining car service as much as thirty and forty years, but in those days there were no Negro stewards on the New Haven Line.) Anyway, Pappy Cousins loved whisky, and he liked everybody, even me. A lot of passenger complaints about me, Pappy had let slide. He'd ask some of the old Negroes working with me to try and calm me down.

"Man, you can't tell him nothing!" they'd exclaim. And they couldn't. At home in Roxbury, they would see me parading with Sophia, dressed in my wild zoot suits. Then I'd come to work, loud and wild and half-high on liquor or reefers, and I'd stay that way, jamming sandwiches at people until we got to New York. Off the train, I'd go through that Grand Central Station afternoon rush-hour crowd, and many white people simply stopped in their tracks to watch me pass. The drape and the cut of a zoot suit showed to the best advantage if you were tall—and I was over six feet. My conk was fire-red. I was really a clown, but my ignorance made me think I was "sharp." My knob-toed, orange-colored "kick-up" shoes were nothing but Florsheims, the ghetto's Cadillac of shoes in those days. (Some shoe companies made these ridiculous styles for sale only in the black ghettoes where ignorant Negroes like me would pay the big-name price for something that we associated with being rich.) And then, between Small's Paradise, the Braddock Hotel, and other places—as much as my twenty- or twenty-five-dollar pay would allow, I drank liquor, smoked marijuana, painted the Big Apple red with increasing numbers of friends, and finally in Mrs. Fisher's rooming house I got a few hours of sleep before the "Yankee Clipper" rolled again.

It was inevitable that I was going to be fired sooner or later. What finally finished me was an angry letter from a passenger. The conductors added their bit, telling how many verbal complaints they'd had, and how many warnings I'd been given.

But I didn't care, because in those wartime days such jobs as I could aspire to were going begging. When the New Haven Line paid me off, I decided it would be nice to make a trip to visit my brothers and sisters in Lansing. I had accumulated some railroad free-travel privileges.

None of them back in Michigan could believe it was me. Only my oldest brother, Wilfred, wasn't there; he was away at Wilberforce University in Ohio studying a trade. But Philbert and Hilda were working in Lansing. Reginald, the one who had always looked up to me, had gotten big enough to fake his age, and he was planning soon to enter the merchant marine. Yvonne, Wesley and Robert were in school.

My conk and whole costume were so wild that I might have been taken as a man from Mars. I caused a minor automobile collision; one driver stopped to gape at me, and the driver behind bumped into him. My appearance staggered the older boys I had once envied; I'd stick out my hand, saying "Skin me, daddy-o!" My stories about the Big Apple, my reefers keeping me sky-high—wherever I went, I was the life of the party. "My man! . . . Gimme some skin!"

The only thing that brought me down to earth was the visit to the state hospital in Kalamazoo. My mother sort of half-sensed who I was.

And I looked up Shorty's mother. I knew he'd be touched by my doing that. She was an old lady, and she was glad to hear from Shorty through me. I told her that Shorty was doing fine and one day was going to be a great leader of his own band. She asked me to tell Shorty that she wished he'd write her, and send her something.

And I dropped over to Mason to see Mrs. Swerlin, the woman at the detention home who had kept me those couple of years. Her mouth flew open when she came to the door. My sharkskin gray "Cab Calloway" zoot suit, the long, narrow, knob-toed shoes, and the four-inch-brimmed pearl-gray hat over my conked fire-red hair; it was just about too much for Mrs. Swerlin. She just managed to pull herself together enough to invite me in. Between the way I looked and my style of talk, I made her so nervous and uncomfortable that we were both glad when I left.

The night before I left, a dance was given in the Lincoln School gymnasium. (I've since learned that in a strange city, to find the Negroes without asking where, you just check in the phone book for a "Lincoln School." It's always located in the segregated black ghetto—at least it was, in those days.) I'd left Lansing unable to dance, but now I went around the gymnasium floor flinging little girls over my shoulders and hips, showing my most startling steps. Several times, the little band nearly stopped, and nearly everybody left the floor, watching with their eyes like saucers. That night, I even signed autographs— "Harlem Red"—and I left Lansing shocked and rocked.

Back in New York, stone broke and without any means of support, I realized that the railroad was all that I actually knew anything about. So I went over to the Seaboard Line's hiring office. The railroads needed men so badly that all I had to do was tell them I had worked on the New Haven, and two days later I was on the "Silver Meteor" to St. Petersburg and Miami. Renting pillows and keeping the coaches clean and the white passengers happy, I made about as much as I had with sandwiches.

I soon ran afoul of the Florida cracker who was assistant conductor. Back in New York, they told me to find another job. But that afternoon, when I walked into Small's Paradise, one of the bartenders, knowing how much I loved New York, called me aside and said that if I were willing to quit the railroad, I might be able to replace a day waiter who was about to go into the Army.

The owner of the bar was Ed Small. He and his brother Charlie were inseparable, and I guess Harlem didn't have two more popular and respected people. They knew I was a railroad man, which, for a waiter, was the best kind of recommendation. Charlie Small was the one I actually talked with in their office. I was afraid he'd want to wait to ask some of his old-timer railroad friends for their opinion. Charlie wouldn't have gone for anybody he heard was wild. But he decided on the basis of his own impression, having seen me in his place so many times, sitting quietly, almost in awe, observing the hustling set. I told him, when he asked, that I'd never been in trouble with the police— and up to then, that was the truth. Charlie told me their rules for employees: no lateness, no laziness, no stealing, no kind of hustling off any customers, especially men in uniform. And I was hired.

This was in 1942. I had just turned seventeen.

* * *

With Small's practically in the center of everything, waiting tables there was Seventh Heaven seven times over. Charlie Small had no need to caution me against being late; I was so anxious to be there, I'd arrive an hour early. I relieved the morning waiter. As far as he was concerned, mine was the slowest, most no-tips time of day, and sometimes he'd stick around most of that hour teaching me things, for he didn't want to see me fired.

Thanks to him, I learned very quickly dozens of little things that could really ingratiate a new waiter with the cooks and bartenders. Both of these, depending on how they liked the waiter, could make his job miserable or pleasant—and I meant to become indispensable. Inside of a week, I had succeeded with both. And the customers who had seen me among them around the bar, recognizing me now in the waiter's jacket, were pleased and surprised; and they couldn't have been more friendly. And I couldn't have been more solicitous.

"Another drink? . . . Right away, sir . . . Would you like dinner? . . . It's very good . . . Could I get you a menu, sir? . . . Well, maybe a sandwich?"

Not only the bartenders and cooks, who knew everything about everything, it seemed to me, but even the customers, also began to school me, in little conversations by the bar when I wasn't busy. Sometimes a customer would talk to me as he ate. Sometimes I'd have long talks—absorbing everything—with the real old-timers, who had been around Harlem since Negroes first came there.

That, in fact, was one of my biggest surprises: that Harlem hadn't always been a community of Negroes.

It first had been a Dutch settlement, I learned. Then began the massive waves of poor and half-starved and ragged immigrants from Europe, arriving with everything they owned in the world in bags and sacks on their backs. The Germans came first; the Dutch edged away from them, and Harlem became all German.

Then came the Irish, running from the potato famine. The Germans ran, looking down their noses at the Irish, who took over Harlem. Next, the Italians; same thing—the Irish ran from them. The Italians had Harlem when the Jews came down the gangplanks—and then the Italians left.

Today, all these same immigrants' descendants are running as hard as they can to escape the descendants of the Negroes who helped to unload the immigrant ships.

I was staggered when old-timer Harlemites told me that while this immigrant musical chairs game had been going on, Negroes had been in New York City since 1683, before any of them came, and had been ghettoed all over the city. They had first been in the Wall Street area; then they were pushed into Greenwich Village. The next shove was up to the Pennsylvania Station area. And then, the last stop before Harlem, the black ghetto was concentrated around 52nd Street, which is how 52nd Street got the Swing Street name and reputation that lasted long after the Negroes were gone.

Then, in 1910, a Negro real estate man somehow got two or three Negro families into one Jewish Harlem apartment house. The Jews flew from that house, then from that block, and more Negroes came in to fill their apartments. Then whole blocks of Jews ran, and still more Negroes came uptown, until in a short time, Harlem was like it still is today—virtually all black.

Then, early in the 1920's music and entertainment sprang up as an industry in Harlem, supported by downtown whites who poured uptown every night. It all started about the time a tough young New Orleans cornet man named Louis "Satchmo" Armstrong climbed off a train in New York wearing clodhopper policemen's shoes, and started playing with Fletcher Henderson. In 1925, Small's Paradise had opened with crowds all across Seventh Avenue; in 1926, the great Cotton Club, where Duke Ellington's band would play for five years; also in 1926 the Savoy Ballroom opened, a whole block front on Lenox Avenue, with a two-hundred-foot dance floor under spotlights before two bandstands and a disappearing rear stage.

Harlem's famous image spread until it swarmed nightly with white people from all over the world. The tourist buses came there. The Cotton Club catered to whites only, and hundreds of other clubs ranging on down to cellar speakeasies catered to white people's money. Some of the best-known were Connie's Inn, the Lenox Club, Barron's, The Nest Club, Jimmy's Chicken Shack, and Minton's. The Savoy, the Golden Gate, and the

Renaissance ballrooms battled for the crowds—the Savoy introduced such attractions as Thursday Kitchen Mechanics' Nights, bathing beauty contests, and a new car given away each Saturday night. They had bands from all across the country in the ballrooms and the Apollo and Lafayette theaters. They had colorful bandleaders like 'Fess Williams in his diamond-studded suit and top hat, and Cab Calloway in his white zoot suit to end all zoots, and his wide-brimmed white hat and string tie, setting Harlem afire with "Tiger Rag" and "St. James Infirmary" and "Minnie the Moocher."

Blacktown crawled with white people, with pimps, prostitutes, bootleggers, with hustlers of all kinds, with colorful characters, and with police and prohibition agents. Negroes danced like they never have anywhere before or since. I guess I must have heard twenty-five of the old-timers in Small's swear to me that they had been the first to dance in the Savoy the "Lindy Hop" which was born there in 1927, named for Lindbergh, who had just made his flight to Paris.

Even the little cellar places with only piano space had fabulous keyboard artists such as James P. Johnson and Jelly Roll Morton, and singers such as Ethel Waters. And at four A.M., when all the legitimate clubs had to close, from all over town the white and Negro musicians would come to some prearranged Harlem after-hours spot and have thirty- and forty-piece jam sessions that would last into the next day.

When it all ended with the stock market crash in 1929, Harlem had a world reputation as America's Casbah. Small's had been a part of all that. There, I heard the old-timers reminisce about all those great times.

Every day I listened raptly to customers who felt like talking, and it all added to my education. My ears soaked it up like sponges when one of them, in a rare burst of confidence, or a little beyond his usual number of drinks, would tell me inside things about the particular form of hustling that he pursued as a way of life. I was thus schooled well, by experts in such hustles as the numbers, pimping, con games of many kinds, peddling dope, and thievery of all sorts, including armed robbery.

CHAPTER SIX

DETROIT RED

Every day, I would gamble all of my tips—as high as fifteen and twenty dollars—on the numbers, and dream of what I would do when I hit.

I saw people on their long, wild spending sprees, after big hits. I don't mean just hustlers who always had some money. I mean ordinary working people, the kind that we otherwise almost never saw in a bar like Small's, who, with a good enough hit, had quit their jobs working somewhere downtown for the white man. Often they had bought a Cadillac, and sometimes for three and four days, they were setting up drinks and buying steaks for all their friends. I would have to pull two tables together into one, and they would be throwing me two- and three-dollar tips each time I came with my tray.

Hundreds of thousands of New York City Negroes, every day but Sunday, would play from a penny on up to large sums on three-digit numbers. A hit meant duplicating the last three figures of the Stock Exchange's printed daily total of U.S. domestic and foreign sales.

With the odds at six hundred to one, a penny hit won $6, a dollar won $600, and so on. On $15, the hit would mean $9,000. Famous hits like that had bought controlling interests in lots of Harlem's bars and restaurants, or even bought some of them outright. The chances of hitting were a thousand to one. Many players practiced what was called "combinating." For example six cents would put one penny on each of the six possible combinations of three digits. The number 840, combinated, would include 840, 804, 048, 084, 408, and 480.

Practically everyone played every day in the poverty-ridden black ghetto of Harlem. Every day, someone you knew was likely to hit and of course it was neighborhood news; if big enough a hit, neighborhood excitement. Hits generally were small; a nickel, dime, or a quarter. Most people tried to play a dollar a day, but split it up among different numbers and combinated.

Harlem's numbers industry hummed every morning and into the early afternoon, with the runners jotting down people's bets on slips of paper in apartment house hallways, bars, barbershops, stores, on the sidewalks. The cops looked on; no runner lasted long who didn't, out of his pocket, put in a free "figger" for his working area's foot cops, and it was generally known that the numbers bankers paid off at higher levels of the police department.

The daily small army of runners each got ten percent of the money they turned in, along with the bet slips, to their controllers. (And if you hit, you gave the runner a ten percent tip.) A controller might have as many as fifty runners working for him, and the controller got five percent of what he turned over to the banker, who paid off the hit, paid off the police, and got rich off the balance.

Some people played one number all year. Many had lists of the daily hit numbers going back for years; they figured reappearance odds, and used other systems. Others played their hunches: addresses, license numbers of passing cars, any numbers on letters, telegrams, laundry slips, numbers from anywhere. Dream books that cost a dollar would say what number nearly any dream suggested. Evangelists who on Sundays peddled Jesus, and mystics, would pray a lucky number for you, for a fee.

Recently, the last three numbers of the post office's new Zip Code for a postal district of Harlem hit, and one banker almost went broke. Let this very book circulate widely in the black ghettoes of the country, and—although I'm no longer a gambling person—I'd lay a small wager for your favorite charity that millions of dollars would be bet by my poor, foolish black brothers and sisters upon, say, whatever happens to be the number of this page, or whatever is the total of the whole book's pages.

Every day in Small's Paradise Bar was fascinating to me. And from a Harlem point of view, I couldn't have been in a more educational situation. Some of the ablest of New York's black hustlers took a liking to me, and knowing that I still was green by their terms, soon began in a paternal way to "straighten Red out."

Their methods would be indirect. A dark, businessman-looking West Indian often would sit at one of my tables. One day when I brought his beer, he said, "Red, hold still a minute." He went over me with one of those yellow tape measures, and jotted figures in his notebook. When I came to work the next afternoon, one of the bartenders handed me a package. In it was an expensive, dark blue suit, conservatively cut. The gift was thoughtful, and the message clear.

The bartenders let me know that this customer was one of the top executives of the fabulous Forty Thieves gang. That was the gang of organized boosters, who would deliver, to order, in one day, C.O.D., any kind of garment you desired. You would pay about one-third of the store's price.

I heard how they made mass hauls. A well-dressed member of the gang who wouldn't arouse suspicion by his manner would go into a selected store about closing time, hide somewhere, and get locked inside when the store closed. The police patrols would have been timed beforehand. After dark, he'd pack suits in bags, then turn off the burglar alarm, and use the telephone to call a waiting truck and crew. When the truck came, timed with the police patrols, it would be loaded and gone within a few minutes. I later got to know several members of the Forty Thieves.

Plainclothes detectives soon were quietly identified to me, by a nod, a wink. Knowing the law people in the area was elementary for the hustlers, and, like them, in time I would learn to sense the presence of any police types. In late 1942, each of the military services had their civilian-dress eyes and ears picking up anything of interest to them, such as hustles being used to avoid the draft, or who hadn't registered, or hustles that were being worked on servicemen.

Longshoremen, or fences for them, would come into the bars selling guns, cameras, perfumes, watches, and the like, stolen from the shipping docks. These Negroes got what white-longshoreman thievery left over. Merchant marine sailors often brought in foreign items, bargains, and the best marijuana cigarettes to be had were made of the *gunja* and *kisca* that merchant sailors smuggled in from Africa and Persia.

In the daytime, whites were given a guarded treatment. Whites who came at night got a better reception; the several Harlem nightclubs they patronized were geared to entertain and jive the night white crowd to get their money.

And with so many law agencies guarding the "morals" of servicemen, any of them that came in, and a lot did, were given what they asked for, and were spoken to if they spoke, and that was all, unless someone knew them as natives of Harlem.

What I was learning was the hustling society's first rule; that you never trusted anyone outside of your own closemouthed circle, and that you selected with time and care before you made any intimates even among these.

The bartenders would let me know which among the regular customers were mostly "fronts," and which really had something going; which were really in the underworld, with downtown police or political connections; which really handled some money, and which were making it from day to day; which were the real gamblers, and which had just hit a little luck; and which ones never to run afoul of in any way.

The latter were extremely well known about Harlem, and they were feared and respected. It was known that if upset, they would break open your head and think nothing of it. These were old-timers, not to be confused with the various hotheaded, wild, young hustlers out trying to make a name for themselves for being crazy with a pistol trigger or a knife. The old heads that I'm talking about were such as "Black Sammy," "Bub" Hewlett, "King" Padmore and "West Indian Archie." Most of these tough ones had worked as strongarm men for Dutch Schultz back when he muscled into the Harlem numbers industry after white gangsters had awakened to the fortunes being made in what they had previously considered "nigger pennies"; and the numbers game was referred to by the white racketeers as "nigger pool."

Those tough Negroes' heyday had been before the big 1931 Seabury Investigation that started Dutch Schultz on the way out, until his career ended with his 1934 assassination. I heard stories of how they had "persuaded" people with lead pipes, wet cement, baseball bats, brass knuckles, fists, feet, and blackjacks.

Nearly every one of them had done some time, and had come back on the scene, and since had worked as top runners for the biggest bankers who specialized in large bettors.

There seemed to be an understanding that these Negroes and the tough black cops never clashed; I guess both knew that someone would die. They had some bad black cops in Harlem, too. The Four Horsemen that worked Sugar Hill—I remember the worst one had freckles—there was a tough quartet. The biggest, blackest, worst cop of them all in Harlem was the West Indian, Brisbane. Negroes crossed the street to avoid him when he walked his 125th Street and Seventh Avenue beat. When I was in prison, someone brought me a story that Brisbane had been shot to death by a scared, nervous young kid who hadn't been up from the South long enough to realize how bad Brisbane was.

The world's most unlikely pimp was "Cadillac" Drake. He was shiny baldheaded, built like a football; he used to call his huge belly "the chippies' playground." Cadillac had a string of about a dozen of the stringiest, scrawniest, black and white street prostitutes in Harlem. Afternoons around the bar, the old-timers who knew Cadillac well enough would tease him about how women who looked like his made enough to feed themselves, let alone him. He'd roar with laughter right along with us; I can hear him now, "Bad-looking women work harder."

Just about the complete opposite of Cadillac was the young, smooth, independent-acting pimp, "Sammy the Pimp." He could, as I have mentioned, pick out potential prostitutes by watching their expressions in dance halls. Sammy and I became, in time, each other's closest friend. Sammy, who was from Kentucky, was a cool, collected expert in his business, and his business was women. Like Cadillac, he too had both black and white women out making his living, but Sammy's women—who would come into Small's sometimes, looking for him, to give him money, and have him buy them a drink—were about as beautiful as any prostitutes who operated anywhere, I'd imagine.

One of his white women, known as "Alabama Peach," a blonde, could put everybody in stitches with her drawl; even the several Negro women numbers controllers around Small's really liked her. What made a lot of Negroes around the bar laugh the hardest was the way she would take three syllables to say "nigger.'' But what she usually was saying was "Ah jes' lu-uv ni-uh-guhs—.'' Give her two drinks and she would tell her life story in a minute; how in whatever little Alabama town it was she came from, the first thing she remembered being conscious of was that she was supposed to "hate niggers.'' And then she started hearing older girls in grade school whispering the hush-hush that "niggers'' were such sexual giants and athletes, and she started growing up secretly wanting to try one. Finally, right in her own house, with her family away, she threatened a Negro man who worked for her father that if he didn't take her she would swear he tried rape. He had no choice, except that he quit working for them. And from then until she finished high school, she managed it several times with other Negroes—and she some-how came to New York, and went straight to Harlem. Later on, Sammy told me how he had happened to spot her in the Savoy, not even dancing with anybody, just standing on the side-lines, watching, and he could tell. And once she really *went* for Negroes, the more the better, Sammy said, and wouldn't have a white man. I have wondered what ever became of her.

There was a big, fat pimp we called "Dollarbill.'' He loved to flash his "Kansas City roll,'' probably fifty one-dollar bills folded with a twenty on the inside and a one-hundred dollar bill on the outside. We always wondered what Dollarbill would do if someone ever stole his hundred-dollar "cover.''

A man who, in his prime, could have stolen Dollarbill's whole roll, blindfolded, was threadbare, comic old "Fewclothes.'' Fewclothes had been one of the best pickpockets in Harlem, back when the white people swarmed up every night in the 1920's, but then during the Depression, he had contracted a bad case of arthritis in his hands. His finger joints were knotted and gnarled so that it made people uncomfortable to look at them. Rain, sleet, or snow, every afternoon, about six, Fewclothes would be at Small's, telling tall tales about the old days, and it was one of the day's rituals for one or another regular customer to ask the bartender to give him drinks, and me to feed him.

My heart goes out to all of us who in those afternoons at Small's enacted our scene with Fewclothes. I wish you could have seen him, pleasantly "high'' with drinks, take his seat with dignity—no begging, not on anybody's Welfare—and open his napkin, and study the day's menu that I gave him, and place his order. I'd tell the cooks it was Fewclothes and he'd get the best in the house. I'd go back and serve it as though he were a millionaire.

Many times since, I have thought about it, and what it really meant. In one sense, we were huddled in there, bonded together in seeking security and warmth and comfort from each other, and we didn't know it. All of us—who might have probed space, or cured cancer, or built industries—were, instead, black victims of the white man's American social system. In another sense, the tragedy of the once master pickpocket made him, for those brother old-timer hustlers, a "there but for the grace of God" symbol. To wolves who still were able to catch some rabbits, it had meaning that an old wolf who had lost his fangs was still eating.

Then there was the burglar, "Jumpsteady." In the ghettoes the white man has built for us, he has forced us not to aspire to greater things, but to view everyday living as *survival*—and in that kind of a community, survival is what is respected. In any average white neighborhood bar, you couldn't imagine a known cat-man thief regularly exposing himself, as one of the most popular people in there. But if Jumpsteady missed a few days running in Small's, we would begin inquiring for him.

Jumpsteady was called that because, it was said, when he worked in white residential areas downtown, he jumped from roof to roof and was so steady that he maneuvered along window ledges, leaning, balancing, edging with his toes. If he fell, he'd have been dead. He got into apartments through windows. It was said that he was so cool that he had stolen even with people in the next room. I later found out that Jumpsteady always keyed himself up high on dope when he worked. He taught me some things that I was to employ in later years when hard times would force me to have my own burglary ring.

I should stress that Small's wasn't any nest of criminals. I dwell upon the hustlers because it was their world that fascinated me. Actually, for the night-life crowd, Small's was one of Harlem's two or three most decorous nightspots. In fact, the New York City police department recommended Small's to white people who would ask for a "safe" place in Harlem.

The first room I got after I left the railroad (half of Harlem roomed) was in the 800 block of St. Nicholas Avenue. You could walk into one or another room in this house and get a hot fur coat, a good camera, fine perfume, a gun, anything from hot women to hot cars, even hot ice. I was one of the very few males in this rooming house. This was during the war, when you couldn't turn on the radio and not hear about Guadalcanal or North Africa. In several of the apartments the women tenants were prostitutes. The minority were in some other racket or hustle—boosters, numbers runners, or dope-peddlers—and I'd guess that everyone who lived in the house used dope of some kind. This shouldn't reflect too badly on that particular building, because almost everyone in Harlem needed some kind of hustle to survive, and needed to stay high in some way to forget what they had to *do* to survive.

It was in this house that I learned more about women than I ever did in any other single place. It was these working prostitutes who schooled me to things that every wife and every husband should know. Later on, it was chiefly the women who weren't prostitutes who taught me to be very distrustful of most women; there seemed to be a higher code of ethics and sisterliness among those prostitutes than among numerous ladies of the church who have more men for kicks than the prostitutes have for pay. And I am talking about both black and white. Many of the black ones in those wartime days were right in step with the white ones in having husbands fighting overseas while they were laying up with other men, even giving them their husbands' money. And many women just faked as mothers and wives, while playing the field as hard as prostitutes—with their husbands and children right there in New York.

I got my first schooling about the cesspool morals of the white man from the best possible source, from his own women. And then as I got deeper into my own life of evil, I saw the white man's morals with my own eyes. I even made my living helping to guide him to the sick things he wanted.

I was young, working in the bar, not bothering with these women. Probably I touched their kid-brother instincts, something like that. Some would drop into my room when they weren't busy, and we would smoke reefers and talk. It generally would be after their morning rush—but let me tell you about that rush.

Seeing the hallways and stairs busy any hour of the night with white and black men coming and going was no more than one would expect when one lived in a building out of which prostitutes were working. But what astonished me was the full-house crowd that rushed in between, say, six and seven-thirty in the morning, then rushed away, and by about nine, I would be the only man in the house.

It was husbands—who had left home in time to stop by this St. Nicholas Avenue house before they went on to work. Of course not the same ones every day, but always enough of them to make up the rush. And it included white men who had come in cabs all the way up from downtown.

Domineering, complaining, demanding wives who had just about psychologically castrated their husbands were responsible for the early rush. These wives were so disagreeable and had made their men so tense that they were robbed of the satisfaction of being men. To escape this tension and the chance of being ridiculed by his own wife, each of these men had gotten up early and come to a prostitute.

The prostitutes had to make it their business to be students of men. They said that after most men passed their virile twenties, they went to bed mainly to satisfy their egos, and because a lot of women don't understand it that way, they damage and wreck a man's ego. No matter how little virility a man has to offer, prostitutes make him feel for a time that he is the greatest man in the world. That's why these prostitutes had that morning rush of business. More wives could keep their husbands if they realized their greatest urge is *to be men*.

Those women would tell me anything. Funny little stories about the bedroom differences they saw between white and black men. The perversities! I thought I had heard the whole range of perversities until I later became a steerer taking white men to what they wanted. Everyone in the house laughed about the little Italian fellow whom they called the "Ten Dollar A Minute Man." He came without fail every noontime, from his little basement restaurant up near the Polo Grounds; the joke was he never lasted more than two minutes . . . but he always left twenty dollars.

Most men, the prostitutes felt, were too easy to push around. Every day these prostitutes heard their customers complaining that they never heard anything but griping from women who were being taken care of and given everything. The prostitutes said that most men needed to know what the pimps knew. A woman should occasionally be babied enough to show her the man had affection, but beyond that she should be treated firmly. These tough women said that it worked with *them*. All women, by their nature, are fragile and weak: they are attracted to the male in whom they see strength.

From time to time, Sophia would come over to see me from Boston. Even among Harlem Negroes, her looks gave me status. They were just like the Negroes everywhere else. That was why the white prostitutes made so much money. It didn't make any difference if you were in Lansing, Boston, or New York— what the white racist said, and still says, was right in those days! All you had to do was put a white girl anywhere close to the average black man, and he would respond. The black woman also made the white man's eyes light up—but he was slick enough to hide it.

Sophia would come in on a late afternoon train. She would come to Small's and I'd introduce her around until I got off from work. She was bothered about me living among the prostitutes until I introduced her to some of them, and they talked, and she thought they were great. They would tell her they were keeping me straight for her. We would go to the Braddock Hotel bar, where we would meet some of the musicians who now would greet me like an old friend, "Hey, Red—who have we got here?" They would make a big deal over her; I couldn't even think about buying a drink. No Negroes in the world were more white-woman-crazy in those days than most of those musicians. People in show business, of course, were less inhibited by social and racial taboos.

The white racist won't tell you that it also works in reverse. When it got late, Sophia and I would go to some of the after-hours places and speakeasies. When the downtown nightclubs had closed, most of these Harlem places crawled with white people. These whites were just mad for Negro "atmosphere," especially some of the places which had what you might call Negro *soul*. Sometimes Negroes would talk about how a lot of whites seemed unable to have enough of being close around us, and among us—in groups. Both white men and women, it seemed, would get almost mesmerized by Negroes.

I remember one really peculiar case of this—a white girl who never missed a single night in the Savoy Ballroom. She fascinated my friend Sammy; he had watched her several times. Dancing only with Negroes, she seemed to go nearly into a trance. If a white man asked her to dance, she would refuse. Then when the place was ready to close, early in the morning, she would let a Negro take her as far as the subway entrance. And that was it. She never would tell anyone her name, let alone reveal where she lived.

Now, I'll tell you another peculiar case that worked out differently, and which taught me something I have since learned in a thousand other ways. This was my best early lesson in how most white men's hearts and guts will turn over inside of them, whatever they may have you otherwise believe, whenever they see a Negro man on close terms with a white woman.

A few of the white men around Harlem, younger ones whom we called "hippies," acted more Negro than Negroes. This particular one talked more "hip" talk than we did. He would have fought anyone who suggested he felt any race difference. Musicians around the Braddock could hardly move without falling over him. Every time I saw him, it was "Daddy! Come on, let's get our heads tight!" Sammy couldn't stand him; he was underfoot wherever you went. He even wore a wild zoot suit, used a heavy grease in his hair to make it look like a conk, and he wore the knob-toed shoes, the long, swinging chain—everything. And he not only wouldn't be seen with any woman but a black one, but in fact he lived with *two* of them in the same little apartment. I never was sure how they worked that one out, but I had my idea.

About three or four o'clock one morning, we ran into this white boy, in Creole Bill's speakeasy. He was high—in that marijuana glow where the world relaxes. I introduced Sophia; I went away to say hello to someone else. When I returned, Sophia looked peculiar—but she wouldn't tell me until we left. He had asked her, "Why is a white girl like you throwing yourself away with a spade?"

Creole Bill—naturally you know he was from New Orleans—became another good friend of mine. After Small's closed, I'd bring fast-spending white people who still wanted some drinking action to Creole Bill's speakeasy. That was my earliest experience at steering. The speakeasy was only Creole Bill's apartment. I think a partition had been knocked out to make the living room larger. But the atmosphere, plus the food, made the place one of Harlem's soul spots.

A record player maintained the right, soft music. There was any kind of drink. And Bill sold plates of his spicy, delicious Creole dishes—gumbo, jambalaya. Bill's girl friend—a beautiful black girl—served the customers. Bill called her "Brown Sugar," and finally everyone else did. If a good number of customers were to be served at one time, Creole Bill would bring out some pots, Brown Sugar would bring the plates, and Bill would serve everyone big platefuls; and he'd heap a plate for himself and eat with us. It was a treat to watch him eat; he loved his food so; it *was* good. Bill could cook rice like the Chinese— I mean rice that stood every grain on its own, but I never knew the Chinese to do what Bill could with seafood and beans.

Bill made money enough in that apartment speakeasy to open up a Creole restaurant famous in Harlem. He was a great baseball fan. All over the walls were framed, autographed photographs of major league stars, and also some political and show business celebrities who would come there to eat, bringing friends. I wonder what's become of Creole Bill? His place is sold, and I haven't heard anything of him. I must remember to ask some of the Seventh Avenue old-timers, who would know.

Once, when I called Sophia in Boston, she said she couldn't get away until the following weekend. She had just married some well-to-do Boston white fellow. He was in the service, he had been home on leave, and he had just gone back. She didn't mean it to change a thing between us. I told her it made no difference. I had of course introduced Sophia to my friend Sammy, and we had gone out together some nights. And Sammy and I had thoroughly discussed the black man and white woman psychology. I had Sammy to thank that I was entirely prepared for Sophia's marriage.

Sammy said that white women were very practical; he had heard so many of them express how they felt. They knew that the black man had all the strikes against him, that the white man kept the black man down, under his heel, unable to get anywhere, really. The white woman wanted to be comfortable, she wanted to be looked upon with favor by her own kind, but also she wanted to have her pleasure. So some of them just married a white man for convenience and security, and kept right on going with a Negro. It wasn't that they were necessarily in love with the Negro, but they were in love with lust—particularly "taboo" lust.

A white man was not too unusual if he had a ten-, twenty-, thirty-, forty-, or fifty-thousand-dollar-a-year job. A Negro man who made even five thousand in the white man's world was unusual. The white woman with a Negro man would be with him for one of two reasons: either extremely insane love, or to satisfy her lust.

When I had been around Harlem long enough to show signs of permanence, inevitably I got a nickname that would identify me beyond any confusion with two other red-conked and well-known "Reds" who were around. I had met them both; in fact, later on I'd work with them both. One, "St. Louis Red," was a professional armed robber. When I was sent to prison, he was serving time for trying to stick up a dining car steward on a train between New York and Philadelphia. He was finally freed; now, I hear, he is in prison for a New York City jewel robbery.

The other was "Chicago Red." We became good buddies in a speakeasy where later on I was a waiter; Chicago Red was the funniest dishwasher on this earth. Now he's making his living being funny as a nationally known stage and nightclub comedian. I don't see any reason why old Chicago Red would mind me telling that he is Redd Foxx.

Anyway, before long, my nickname happened. Just when, I don't know—but people, knowing I was from Michigan, would ask me what city. Since most New Yorkers had never heard of Lansing, I would name Detroit. Gradually, I began to be called "Detroit Red"—and it stuck.

One afternoon in early 1943, before the regular six o'clock crowd had gathered, a black soldier sat drinking by himself at one of my tables. He must have been there an hour or more. He looked dumb and pitiful and just up from the Deep South. The fourth or fifth drink I served this soldier, wiping the table I bent over close and asked him if he wanted a woman.

I knew better. It wasn't only Small's Paradise law, it was the law of every tavern that wanted to stay in business—never get involved with anything that could be interpreted as "impairing the morals" of servicemen, or any kind of hustling off them. This had caused trouble for dozens of places: some had been put off limits by the military; some had lost their state or city licenses.

I played right into the hands of a military spy. He sure would like a woman. He acted so grateful. He even put on an extreme Southern accent. And I gave him the phone number of one of my best friends among the prostitutes where I lived.

But something felt wrong. I gave the fellow a half-hour to get there, and then I telephoned. I expected the answer I got—that no soldier had been there.

I didn't even bother to go back out to the bar. I just went straight to Charlie Small's office.

"I just did something, Charlie," I said. "I don't know why I did it—" and I told him.

Charlie looked at me. "I wish you hadn't done that, Red." We both knew what he meant.

When the West Indian plainclothes detective, Joe Baker, came in, I was waiting. I didn't even ask him any questions. When we got to the 135th Street precinct, it was busy with police in uniform, and MP's with soldiers in tow. I was recognized by some other detectives who, like Joe Baker, sometimes dropped in at Small's.

Two things were in my favor. I'd never given the police any trouble, and when that black spy soldier had tried to tip me, I had waved it away, telling him I was just doing him a favor. They must have agreed that Joe Baker should just scare me.

I didn't know enough to be aware that I wasn't taken to the desk and booked. Joe Baker took me back inside of the precinct building, into a small room. In the next room, we could hear somebody getting whipped. *Whop! Whop!* He'd cry out, "Please! Please don't beat my face, that's how I make my living!" I knew from that it was some pimp. *Whop! Whop!* "Please! Please!"

(Not much later, I heard that Joe Baker had gotten trapped over in New Jersey, shaking down a Negro pimp and his white prostitute. He was discharged from the New York City police force, the State of New Jersey convicted him, and he went off to do some time.)

More bitter than getting fired, I was barred from Small's. I could understand. Even if I wasn't actually what was called "hot," I was now going to be under surveillance—and the Small brothers had to protect their business.

Sammy proved to be my friend in need. He put the word on the wire for me to come over to his place. I had never been there. His place seemed to me a small palace; his women really kept him in style. While we talked about what kind of a hustle I should get into, Sammy gave me some of the best marijuana I'd ever used.

Various numbers controllers, Small's regulars, had offered me jobs as a runner. But that meant I would earn very little until I could build up a clientele. Pimping, as Sammy did, was out. I felt I had no abilities in that direction, and that I'd certainly starve to death trying to recruit prostitutes.

Peddling reefers, Sammy and I pretty soon agreed, was the best thing. It was a relatively uninvolved lone-wolf type of operation, and one in which I could make money immediately. For anyone with even a little brains, no experience was needed, especially if one had any knack at all with people.

Both Sammy and I knew some merchant seamen and others who could supply me with loose marijuana. And musicians, among whom I had so many good contacts, were the heaviest consistent market for reefers. And then, musicians also used the heavier narcotics, if I later wanted to graduate to them. That would be more risky, but also more money. Handling heroin and cocaine could earn one hundreds of dollars a day, but it required a lot of experience with the narcotics squad for one to be able to last long enough to make anything.

I had been around long enough either to know or to spot instinctively most regular detectives and cops, though not the narcotics people. And among the Small's veteran hustler regulars, I had a variety of potentially helpful contacts. This was important because just as Sammy could get me supplied with marijuana, a large facet of any hustler's success was knowing where he could get help when he needed it. The help could involve police and detectives—as well as higher ups. But I hadn't yet reached that stage. So Sammy staked me, about twenty dollars, I think it was.

Later that same night, I knocked at his door and gave him back his money and asked him if I could lend him some. I had gone straight from Sammy's to a supplier he had mentioned. I got just a small amount of marijuana, and I got some of the paper to roll up my own sticks. As they were only about the size of stick matches, I was able to make enough of them so that, after selling them to musicians I knew at the Braddock Hotel, I could pay back Sammy and have enough profit to be in business. And those musicians when they saw their buddy, and their fan, in business: "My man!" "Crazy, Red!"

In every band, at least half of the musicians smoked reefers. I'm not going to list names; I'd have to include some of those most prominent then in popular music, even a number of them around today. In one case, every man in one of the bands which is still famous was on marijuana. Or again, any number of musicians could tell you who I mean when I say that one of the most famous singers smoked his reefers through a chicken thigh-bone. He had smoked so many through the bone that he could just light a match before the empty bone, draw the heat through, and get what he called a "contact" high.

I kept turning over my profit, increasing my supplies, and I sold reefers like a wild man. I scarcely slept; I was wherever musicians congregated. A roll of money was in my pocket. Every day, I cleared at least fifty or sixty dollars. In those days (or for that matter these days), this was a fortune to a seventeen-year-old Negro. I felt, for the first time in my life, that great feeling of *free*! Suddenly, now, I was the peer of the other young hustlers I had admired.

It was at this time that I discovered the movies. Sometimes I made as many as five in one day, both downtown and in Harlem. I loved the tough guys, the action, Humphrey Bogart in "Casablanca," and I loved all of that dancing and carrying on in such films as "Stormy Weather" and "Cabin in the Sky." After leaving the movies, I'd make my connections for supplies, then roll my sticks, and, about dark, I'd start my rounds. I'd give a couple of extra sticks when someone bought ten, which was five dollars' worth. And I didn't sell and run, because my customers were my friends. Often I'd smoke along with them. None of them stayed any more high than I did.

Free now to do what I pleased, upon an impulse I went to Boston. Of course, I saw Ella. I gave her some money: it was just a token of appreciation, I told her, for helping me when I had come from Lansing. She wasn't the same old Ella; she still hadn't forgiven me for Laura. She never mentioned her, nor did I. But, even so, Ella acted better than she had when I had left for New York. We reviewed the family changes. Wilfred had proved so good at his trade they had asked him to stay on at Wilberforce as an instructor. And Ella had gotten a card from Reginald who had managed to get into the merchant marine.

From Shorty's apartment, I called Sophia. She met me at the apartment just about as Shorty went off to work. I would have liked to take her out to some of the Roxbury clubs, but Shorty had told us that, as in New York, the Boston cops used the war as an excuse to harass interracial couples, stopping them and grilling the Negro about his draft status. Of course Sophia's now being married made us more cautious, too.

When Sophia caught a cab home, I went to hear Shorty's band. Yes, he had a band now. He had succeeded in getting a 4-F classification, and I was pleased for him and happy to go. His band was—well, fair. But Shorty was making out well in Boston, playing in small clubs. Back in the apartment, we talked into the next day. "Homeboy, you're something else!" Shorty kept saying. I told him some of the wild things I'd done in Harlem, and about the friends I had. I told him the story of Sammy the Pimp.

In Sammy's native Paducah, Kentucky, he had gotten a girl pregnant. Her parents made it so hot that Sammy had come to Harlem, where he got a job as a restaurant waiter. When a woman came in to eat alone, and he found she really was alone, not married, or living with somebody, it generally was not hard for smooth Sammy to get invited to her apartment. He'd insist on going out to a nearby restaurant to bring back some dinner, and while he was out he would have her key duplicated. Then, when he knew she was away, Sammy would go in and clean out all her valuables. Sammy was then able to offer some little stake, to help her back on her feet. This could be the beginning of an emotional and financial dependency, which Sammy knew how to develop until she was his virtual slave.

Around Harlem, the narcotics squad detectives didn't take long to find out I was selling reefers, and occasionally one of them would follow me. Many a peddler was in jail because he had been caught with the evidence on his person; I figured a way to avoid that. The law specified that if the evidence wasn't actually in your possession, you couldn't be arrested. Hollowed-out shoe heels, fake hat-linings, these things were old stuff to the detectives.

I carried about fifty sticks in a small package inside my coat, under my armpit, keeping my arm flat against my side. Moving about, I kept my eyes open. If anybody looked suspicious, I'd quickly cross the street, or go through a door, or turn a corner, loosening my arm enough to let the package drop. At night, when I usually did my selling, any suspicious person wouldn't be likely to see the trick. If I decided I had been mistaken, I'd go back and get my sticks.

However, I lost many a stick this way. Sometimes, I knew I had frustrated a detective. And I kept out of the courts.

One morning, though, I came in and found signs that my room had been entered. I knew it had been detectives. I'd heard too many times how if they couldn't find any evidence, they would plant some, where you would never find it, then they'd come back in and "find" it. I didn't even have to think twice what to do. I packed my few belongings and never looked back. When I went to sleep again, it was in another room.

It was then that I began carrying a little .25 automatic. I got it, for some reefers, from an addict who I knew had stolen it somewhere. I carried it pressed under my belt right down the center of my back. Someone had told me that the cops never hit there in any routine patting-down. And unless I knew who I was with, I never allowed myself to get caught in any crush of people. The narcotics cops had been known to rush up and get their hands on you and plant evidence while "searching." I felt that as long as I kept on the go, and in the open, I had a good chance. I don't know now what my real thoughts were about carrying the pistol. But I imagine I felt that I wasn't going to get put away if somebody tried framing me in any situation that I could help.

I sold less than before because having to be so careful consumed so much time. Every now and then, on a hunch, I'd move to another room. I told nobody but Sammy where I slept.

Finally, it was on the wire that the Harlem narcotics squad had me on its special list.

Now, every other day or so, usually in some public place, they would flash the badge to search me. But I'd tell them at once, loud enough for others standing about to hear me, that I had nothing on me, and I didn't want to get anything planted on me. Then they wouldn't, because Harlem already thought little enough of the law, and they did have to be careful that some crowd of Negroes would not intervene roughly. Negroes were starting to get very tense in Harlem. One could almost smell trouble ready to break out—as it did very soon.

But it was really tough on me then. I was having to hide my sticks in various places near where I was selling. I'd put five sticks in an empty cigarette pack, and drop the empty-looking pack by a lamppost, or behind a garbage can, or a box. And I'd first tell customers to pay me, and then where to pick up.

But my regular customers didn't go for that. You couldn't expect a well-known musician to go grubbing behind a garbage can. So I began to pick up some of the street trade, the people you could see looked high. I collected a number of empty Red Cross bandage boxes and used them for drops. That worked pretty good.

But the middle-Harlem narcotics force found so many ways to harass me that I had to change my area. I moved down to lower Harlem, around 110th Street. There were many more reefer smokers around there, but these were a cheaper type, this was the worst of the ghetto, the poorest people, the ones who in every ghetto keep themselves narcotized to keep from having to face their miserable existence. I didn't last long down there, either. I lost too much of my product. After I sold to some of those reefer smokers who had the instincts of animals, they followed me and learned my pattern. They would dart out of a doorway, I'd drop my stuff, and they would be on it like a chicken on corn. When you become an animal, a vulture, in the ghetto, as I had become, you enter a world of animals and vultures. It becomes truly the survival of only the fittest.

Soon I found myself borrowing little stakes, from Sammy,

from some of the musicians. Enough to buy supplies, enough to keep high myself, enough sometimes to just eat.

Then Sammy gave me an idea.

"Red, you still got your old railroad identification?" I did have it. They hadn't taken it back. "Well, why don't you use it to make a few runs, until the heat cools?"

He was right.

I found that if you walked up and showed a railroad line's employee identification card, the conductor—even a real cracker, if you approached him right, not begging—would just wave you aboard. And when he came around he would punch you one of those little coach seat slips to ride wherever the train went.

The idea came to me that, this way, I could travel all over the East Coast selling reefers among my friends who were on tour with their bands.

I had the New Haven identification. I worked a couple of weeks for other railroads, to get their identification, and then I was set.

In New York, I rolled and packed a great quantity of sticks, and sealed them into jars. The identification card worked perfectly. If you persuaded the conductor you were a fellow employee who had to go home on some family business, he just did the favor for you without a second thought. Most whites don't give a Negro credit for having sense enough to fool them—or nerve enough.

I'd turn up in towns where my friends were playing. "Red!" I was an old friend from home. In the sticks, I was somebody from the Braddock Hotel. *"My man! Daddy-o!"* And I had Big Apple reefers. Nobody had ever heard of a traveling reefer peddler.

I followed no particular band. Each band's musicians knew the other bands' one-nighter touring schedules. When I ran out of supplies, I'd return to New York, and load up, then hit the road again. Auditoriums or gymnasiums all lighted up, the band's chartered bus outside, the dressed-up, excited, local dancers pouring in. At the door, I'd announce that I was some bandman's brother; in most cases they thought I was one of the musicians. Throughout the dance, I'd show the country folks some plain and fancy lindy-hopping. Sometimes, I'd stay overnight in a town. Sometimes I'd ride the band's bus to their next stop. Sometimes, back in New York, I would stay awhile. Things had cooled down. Word was around that I had left town, and the narcotics squad was satisfied with that. In some of the small towns, people thinking I was with the band even mobbed me for autographs. Once, in Buffalo, my suit was nearly torn off.

My brother Reginald was waiting for me one day when I pulled into New York. The day before, his merchant ship had put into port over in New Jersey. Thinking I still worked at Small's, Reginald had gone there, and the bartenders had directed him to Sammy, who put him up.

It felt good to see my brother. It was hard to believe that he was once the little kid who tagged after me. Reginald now was almost six feet tall, but still a few inches shorter than me. His complexion was darker than mine, but he had greenish eyes, and a white streak in his hair, which was otherwise dark reddish, something like mine.

I took Reginald everywhere, introducing him. Studying my brother, I liked him. He was a lot more self-possessed than I had been at sixteen.

I didn't have a room right at the time, but I had some money, so did Reginald, and we checked into the St. Nicholas Hotel on Sugar Hill. It has since been torn down.

Reginald and I talked all night about the Lansing years, about our family. I told him things about our father and mother that he couldn't remember. Then Reginald filled me in on our brothers and sisters. Wilfred was still a trade instructor at Wilberforce University. Hilda, still in Lansing, was talking of getting married; so was Philbert.

Reginald and I were the next two in line. And Yvonne, Wesley, and Robert were still in Lansing, in school.

Reginald and I laughed about Philbert, who, the last time I had seen him, had gotten deeply religious; he wore one of those round straw hats.

Reginald's ship was in for about a week getting some kind of repairs on its engines. I was pleased to see that Reginald, though he said little about it, admired my living by my wits. Reginald dressed a little too loudly, I thought. I got a reefer customer of mine to get him a more conservative overcoat and suit. I told

Reginald what I had learned: that in order to get something you had to look as though you already had something.

Before Reginald left, I urged him to leave the merchant marine and I would help him get started in Harlem. I must have felt that having my kid brother around me would be a good thing. Then there would be two people I could trust—Sammy was the other.

Reginald was cool. At his age, I would have been willing to run behind the train, to get to New York and to Harlem. But Reginald, when he left, said, "I'll think about it."

Not long after Reginald left, I dragged out the wildest zoot suit in New York. This was 1943. The Boston draft board had written me at Ella's, and when they had no results there, had notified the New York draft board, and, in care of Sammy, I received Uncle Sam's Greetings.

In those days only three things in the world scared me: jail, a job, and the Army. I had about ten days before I was to show up at the induction center. I went right to work. The Army Intelligence soldiers, those black spies in civilian clothes, hung around in Harlem with their ears open for the white man downtown. I knew exactly where to start dropping the word. I started noising around that I was frantic to join . . . the Japanese Army.

When I sensed that I had the ears of the spies, I would talk and act high and crazy. A lot of Harlem hustlers actually had reached that state—as I would later. It was inevitable when one had gone long enough on heavier and heavier narcotics, and under the steadily tightening vise of the hustling life. I'd snatch out and read my Greetings aloud, to make certain they heard who I was, and when I'd report downtown. (This was probably the only time my real name was ever heard in Harlem in those days.)

The day I went down there, I costumed like an actor. With my wild zoot suit I wore the yellow knob-toe shoes, and I frizzled my hair up into a reddish bush of conk.

I went in, skipping and tipping, and I thrust my tattered Greetings at that reception desk's white soldier—"Crazy-o, daddy-o, get me moving. I can't wait to get in that brown"—very likely that soldier hasn't recovered from me yet.

They had their wire on me from uptown, all right. But they still put me through the line. In that big starting room were forty or fifty other prospective inductees. The room had fallen vacuum-quiet, with me running my mouth a mile a minute, talking nothing but slang. I was going to fight on all fronts; I was going to be a general, man, before I got done—such talk as that.

Most of them were white, of course. The tender-looking ones appeared ready to run from me. Some others had that vinegary "worst kind of nigger" look. And a few were amused, seeing me as the "Harlem jigaboo" archetype.

Also amused were some of the room's ten or twelve Negroes. But the stony-faced rest of them looked as if they were ready to sign up to go off killing somebody—they would have liked to start with me.

The line moved along. Pretty soon, stripped to my shorts, I was making my eager-to-join comments in the medical examination rooms—and everybody in the white coats that I saw had 4-F in his eyes.

I stayed in the line longer than I expected, before they siphoned me off. One of the white coats accompanied me around a turning hallway: I knew we were on the way to a headshrinker—the Army psychiatrist.

The receptionist there was a Negro nurse. I remember she was in her early twenties, and not bad to look at. She was one of those Negro "firsts."

Negroes know what I'm talking about. Back then, the white man during the war was so pressed for personnel that he began letting some Negroes put down their buckets and mops and dust rags and use a pencil, or sit at some desk, or hold some twenty-five-cent title. You couldn't read the Negro press for the big pictures of smug black "firsts."

Somebody was inside with the psychiatrist. I didn't even have to put on any act for this black girl; she was already sick of me.

When, finally, a buzz came at her desk, she didn't send me, *she* went in. I knew what she was doing, she was going to make clear, in advance, what she thought of me. This is still one of the black man's big troubles today. So many of those so-called "upper-class" Negroes are so busy trying to impress on the white man that they are "different from those others" that they can't see they are only helping the white man to keep his low opinion of *all* Negroes.

And then, with her prestige in the clear, she came out and nodded to me to go in.

I must say this for that psychiatrist. He tried to be objective and professional in his manner. He sat there and doodled with his blue pencil on a tablet, listening to me spiel to him for three or four minutes before he got a word in.

His tack was quiet questions, to get at why I was so anxious. I didn't rush him; I circled and hedged, watching him closely, to let him think he was pulling what he wanted out of me. I kept jerking around, backward, as though somebody might be listening. I knew I was going to send him back to the books to figure what kind of a case I was.

Suddenly, I sprang up and peeped under both doors, the one I'd entered and another that probably was a closet. And then I bent and whispered fast in his ear. "Daddy-o, now you and me, we're from up North here, so don't you tell nobody. . . . I want to get sent down South. Organize them nigger soldiers, you dig? Steal us some guns, and kill us crackers!"

That psychiatrist's blue pencil dropped, and his professional manner fell off in all directions. He stared at me as if I were a snake's egg hatching, fumbling for his red pencil. I knew I had him. I was going back out past Miss First when he said, "That will be all."

A 4-F card came to me in the mail, and I never heard from the Army anymore, and never bothered to ask why I was rejected.

CHAPTER SEVEN

HUSTLER

I can't remember all the hustles I had during the next two years in Harlem, after the abrupt end of my riding the trains and peddling reefers to the touring bands.

Negro railroad men waited for their trains in their big locker room on the lower level of Grand Central Station. Big blackjack and poker games went on in there around the clock. Sometimes five hundred dollars would be on the table. One day, in a blackjack game, an old cook who was dealing the cards tried to be slick, and I had to drop my pistol in his face.

The next time I went into one of those games, intuition told me to stick my gun under my belt right down the middle of my back. Sure enough, someone had squealed. Two big, beefy-faced Irish cops came in. They frisked me—and they missed my gun where they hadn't expected one.

The cops told me never again to be caught in Grand Central Station unless I had a ticket to ride somewhere. And I knew that by the next day, every railroad's personnel office would have a blackball on me, so I never tried to get another railroad job.

There I was back in Harlem's streets among all the rest of the hustlers. I couldn't sell reefers; the dope squad detectives were too familiar with me. I was a true hustler—uneducated, unskilled at anything honorable, and I considered myself nervy and cunning enough to live by my wits, exploiting any prey that presented itself. I would risk just about anything.

Right now, in every big city ghetto, tens of thousands of yesterday's and today's school dropouts are keeping body and soul together by some form of hustling in the same way I did.

And they inevitably move into more and more, worse and worse, illegality and immorality. Full-time hustlers never can relax to appraise what they are doing and where they are bound. As is the case in any jungle, the hustler's every waking hour is lived with both the practical and the subconscious knowledge that if he ever relaxes, if he ever slows down, the other hungry, restless foxes, ferrets, wolves, and vultures out there with him won't hesitate to make him their prey.

During the next six to eight months, I pulled my first robberies and stick-ups. Only small ones. Always in other, nearby cities. And I got away. As the pros did, I too would key myself to pull these jobs by my first use of hard dope. I began with Sammy's recommendation—sniffing cocaine.

Normally now, for street wear, I might call it, I carried a hardly noticeable little flat, blue-steel .25 automatic. But for working, I carried a .32, a .38 or a .45. I saw how when the eyes stared at the big black hole, the faces fell slack and the mouths sagged open. And when I spoke, the people seemed to hear as though they were far away, and they would do whatever I asked.

Between jobs, staying high on narcotics kept me from getting nervous. Still, upon sudden impulses, just to play safe, I would abruptly move from one to another fifteen- to twenty-dollar-a-week room, always in my favorite 147th–150th Street area, just flanking Sugar Hill.

Once on a job with Sammy, we had a pretty close call. Someone must have seen us. We were making our getaway, running, when we heard the sirens. Instantly, we slowed to walking. As a police car screeched to a stop, we stepped out into the street, meeting it, hailing it to ask for directions. They must have thought we were about to give them some information. They just cursed us and raced on. Again, it didn't cross the white men's minds that a trick like that might be pulled on them by Negroes.

The suits that I wore, the finest, I bought hot for about thirty-five to fifty dollars. I made it my rule never to go after more than I needed to live on. Any experienced hustler will tell you that getting greedy is the quickest road to prison. I kept "cased" in my head vulnerable places and situations and I would perform the next job only when my bankroll in my pocket began to get too low.

Some weeks, I bet large amounts on the numbers. I still played with the same runner with whom I'd started in Small's Paradise. Playing my hunches, many a day I'd have up to forty dollars on two numbers, hoping for that fabulous six hundred-to-one pay-off. But I never did hit a big number full force. There's no telling what I would have done if ever I'd landed $10,000 or $12,000 at one time. Of course, once in a while I'd hit a small combination figure. Sometimes, flush like that, I'd telephone Sophia to come over from Boston for a couple of days.

I went to the movies a lot again. And I never missed my musician friends wherever they were playing, either in Harlem, downtown at the big theaters, or on 52nd Street.

Reginald and I got very close the next time his ship came back into New York. We discussed our family, and what a shame it was that our book-loving oldest brother Wilfred had never had the chance to go to some of those big universities where he would have gone far. And we exchanged thoughts we had never shared with anyone.

Reginald, in his quiet way, was a mad fan of musicians and music. When his ship sailed one morning without him, a principal reason was that I had thoroughly exposed him to the exciting musical world. We had wild times backstage with the musicians when they were playing the Roxy, or the Paramount. After selling reefers with the bands as they traveled, I was known to almost every popular Negro musician around New York in 1944–1945.

Reginald and I went to the Savoy Ballroom, the Apollo Theater, the Braddock Hotel bar, the nightclubs and speakeasies, wherever Negroes played music. The great Lady Day, Billie Holiday, hugged him and called him "baby brother." Reginald shared tens of thousands of Negroes' feelings that the living end of the big bands was Lionel Hampton's. I was very close to many of the men in Hamp's band; I introduced Reginald to them, and also to Hamp himself, and Hamp's wife and business manager, Gladys Hampton. One of this world's sweetest people is Hamp. Anyone who knows him will tell you that he'd often do the most generous things for people he barely knew. As much money as Hamp has made, and still makes, he would be broke today if his money and his business weren't handled by Gladys, who is one of the brainiest women I ever met. The Apollo Theater's owner, Frank Schiffman, could tell you. He generally signed bands to play for a set weekly amount, but I know that

once during those days Gladys Hampton instead arranged a deal
for Hamp's band to play for a cut of the gate. Then the usual
number of shows was doubled up—if I'm not mistaken, eight
shows a day, instead of the usual four—and Hamp's pulling
power cleaned up. Gladys Hampton used to talk to me a lot, and
she tried to give me good advice: "Calm down, Red." Gladys
saw how wild I was. She saw me headed toward a bad end.

One of the things I liked about Reginald was that when I left
him to go away "working," Reginald asked me no questions.
After he came to Harlem, I went on more jobs than usual. I
guess that what influenced me to get my first actual apartment
was my not wanting Reginald to be knocking around Harlem
without anywhere to call "home." That first apartment was
three rooms, for a hundred dollars a month, I think, in the front
basement of a house on 147th Street between Convent and St.
Nicholas Avenues. Living in the rear basement apartment, right
behind Reginald and me, was one of Harlem's most successful
narcotics dealers.

With the apartment as our headquarters, I gradually got
Reginald introduced around to Creole Bill's, and other Harlem
after-hours spots. About two o'clock every morning, as the
downtown white nightclubs closed, Reginald and I would stand
around in front of this or that Harlem after-hours place, and I'd
school him to what was happening.

Especially after the nightclubs downtown closed, the taxis and
black limousines would be driving uptown, bringing those white
people who never could get enough of Negro *soul*. The places
popular with these whites ranged all the way from the big locally
famous ones such as Jimmy's Chicken Shack, and Dickie Wells',
to the little here-tonight-gone-tomorrow-night private clubs, so-
called, where a dollar was collected at the door for "member-
ship."

Inside every after-hours spot, the smoke would hurt your eyes.
Four white people to every Negro would be in there drinking
whisky from coffee cups and eating fried chicken. The generally
flush-faced white men and their makeup-masked, glittery-eyed
women would be pounding each other's backs and uproariously
laughing and applauding the music. A lot of the whites, drunk,
would go staggering up to Negroes, the waiters, the owners, or
Negroes at tables, wringing their hands, even trying to hug them,

"You're just as good as I am—I want you to know that!" The most famous places drew both Negro and white celebrities who enjoyed each other. A jam-packed four-thirty A.M. crowd at Jimmy's Chicken Shack or Dickie Wells' might have such jam-session entertainment as Hazel Scott playing the piano for Billie Holiday singing the blues. Jimmy's Chicken Shack, incidentally, was where once, later on, I worked briefly as a waiter. That's where Redd Foxx was the dishwasher who kept the kitchen crew in stitches.

After a while, my brother Reginald had to have a hustle, and I gave much thought to what would be, for him, a good, safe hustle. After he'd learned his own way around, it would be up to him to take risks for himself—if he wanted to make more and quicker money.

The hustle I got Reginald into really was very simple. It utilized the psychology of the ghetto jungle. Downtown, he paid the two dollars, or whatever it was, for a regular city peddler's license. Then I took him to a manufacturers' outlet where we bought a supply of cheap imperfect "seconds"—shirts, underwear, cheap rings, watches, all kinds of quick-sale items.

Watching me work this hustle back in Harlem, Reginald quickly caught on to how to go into barbershops, beauty parlors, and bars acting very nervous as he let the customers peep into his small valise of "loot." With so many thieves around anxious to get rid of stolen good-quality merchandise cheaply, many Harlemites, purely because of this conditioning, jumped to pay hot prices for inferior goods whose sale was perfectly legitimate. It never took long to get rid of a valiseful for at least twice what it had cost. And if any cop stopped Reginald, he had in his pocket both the peddler's license and the manufacturers' outlet bills of sale. Reginald only had to be certain that none of the customers to whom he sold ever saw that he was legitimate.

I assumed that Reginald, like most of the Negroes I knew, would go for a white woman. I'd point out Negro-happy white women to him, and explain that a Negro with any brains could wrap these women around his fingers. But I have to say this for Reginald: he never liked white women. I remember the one time he met Sophia; he was so cool it upset Sophia, and it tickled me.

Reginald got himself a black woman. I'd guess she was pushing thirty; an "old settler," as we called them back in those days. She was a waitress in an exclusive restaurant downtown. She lavished on Reginald everything she had, she was so happy to get a young man. I mean she bought him clothes, cooked and washed for him, and everything, as though he were a baby.

That was just another example of why my respect for my younger brother kept increasing. Reginald showed, in often surprising ways, more sense than a lot of working hustlers twice his age. Reginald then was only sixteen, but, a six-footer, he looked and acted much older than his years.

All through the war, the Harlem racial picture never was too bright. Tension built to a pretty high pitch. Old-timers told me that Harlem had never been the same since the 1935 riot, when millions of dollars worth of damage was done by thousands of Negroes, infuriated chiefly by the white merchants in Harlem refusing to hire a Negro even as their stores raked in Harlem's money.

During World War II, Mayor LaGuardia officially closed the Savoy Ballroom. Harlem said the real reason was to stop Negroes from dancing with white women. Harlem said that no one dragged the white women in there. Adam Clayton Powell made it a big fight. He had successfully fought Consolidated Edison and the New York Telephone Company until they had hired Negroes. Then he had helped to battle the U.S. Navy and the U.S. Army about their segregating of uniformed Negroes. But Powell couldn't win this battle. City Hall kept the Savoy closed for a long time. It was just another one of the "liberal North" actions that didn't help Harlem to love the white man any.

Finally, rumor flashed that in the Braddock Hotel, white cops had shot a Negro soldier. I was walking down St. Nicholas Avenue; I saw all of these Negroes hollering and running north from 125th Street. Some of them were loaded down with armfuls of stuff. I remember it was the bandleader Fletcher Henderson's nephew "Shorty" Henderson who told me what had happened. Negroes were smashing store windows, and taking everything they could grab and carry—furniture, food, jewelry, clothes, whisky. Within an hour, every New York City cop seemed to be in Harlem. Mayor LaGuardia and the NAACP's then Secretary, the famed late Walter White, were in a red firecar, riding around pleading over a loudspeaker to all of those shouting, milling, angry Negroes to please go home and stay inside.

Just recently I ran into Shorty Henderson on Seventh Avenue. We were laughing about a fellow whom the riot had left with the nickname of "Left Feet." In a scramble in a women's shoe store, somehow he'd grabbed five shoes, all of them for left feet! And we laughed about the scared little Chinese whose restaurant didn't have a hand laid on it, because the rioters just about convulsed laughing when they saw the sign the Chinese had hastily stuck on his front door: "Me Colored Too."

After the riot, things got very tight in Harlem. It was terrible for the night-life people, and for those hustlers whose main income had been the white man's money. The 1935 riot had left only a relative trickle of the money which had poured into Harlem during the 1920's. And now this new riot ended even that trickle.

Today the white people who visit Harlem, and this mostly on weekend nights, are hardly more than a few dozen who do the twist, the frug, the Watusi, and all the rest of the current dance crazes in Small's Paradise, owned now by the great basketball champion "Wilt the Stilt" Chamberlain, who draws crowds with his big, clean, All-American-athlete image. Most white people today are physically afraid to come to Harlem—and it's for good reasons, too. Even for Negroes, Harlem night life is about finished. Most of the Negroes who have money to spend are spending it downtown somewhere in this hypocritical "integration," in places where previously the police would have been called to haul off any Negro insane enough to try and get in. The already Croesus-rich white man can't get another skyscraper hotel finished and opened before all these integration-mad Negroes, who themselves don't own a tool shed, are booking the swanky new hotel for "cotillions" and "conventions." Those rich whites could afford it when they used to throw away their money in Harlem. But Negroes can't afford to be taking their money downtown to the white man.

Sammy and I, on a robbery job, got a bad scare, a very close call.

Things had grown so tight in Harlem that some hustlers had been forced to go to work. Even some prostitutes had gotten jobs as domestics, and cleaning office buildings at night. The pimping was so poor, Sammy had gone on the job with me. We had selected one of those situations considered "impossible." But wherever people think that, the guards will unconsciously grow gradually more relaxed, until sometimes those can be the easiest jobs of all.

But right in the middle of the act, we had some bad luck. A bullet grazed Sammy. We just barely escaped.

Sammy fortunately wasn't really hurt. We split up, which was always wise to do.

Just before daybreak, I went to Sammy's apartment. His newest woman, one of those beautiful but hot-headed Spanish Negroes, was in there crying and carrying on over Sammy. She went for me, screaming and clawing; she knew I'd been in on it with him. I fended her off. Not able to figure out why Sammy didn't shut her up, I did . . . and from the corner of my eye, I saw Sammy going for his gun.

Sammy's reaction that way to my hitting his woman—close as he and I were—was the only weak spot I'd ever glimpsed. The woman screamed and dove for him. She knew as I did that when your best friend draws a gun on you, he usually has lost all control of his emotions, and he intends to shoot. She distracted Sammy long enough for me to bolt through the door. Sammy chased me, about a block.

We soon made up—on the surface. But things never are fully right again with anyone you have seen trying to kill you.

Intuition told us that we had better lay low for a good while. The worst thing was that we'd been seen. The police in that nearby town had surely circulated our general descriptions.

I just couldn't forget that incident over Sammy's woman. I came to rely more and more upon my brother Reginald as the only one in my world I could completely trust.

Reginald was lazy, I'd discovered that. He had quit his hustle altogether. But I didn't mind that, really, because one could be as lazy as he wanted, if he would only use his head, as Reginald was doing. He had left my apartment by now. He was living off his "old settler" woman—when he was in town. I had also taught Reginald how he could work a little while for a railroad, then use his identification card to travel for nothing—and Reginald loved to travel. Several times, he had gone visiting all around, among our brothers and sisters. They had now begun to scatter to different cities. In Boston, Reginald was closer to our sister Mary than to Ella, who had been my favorite. Both Reginald and Mary were quiet types, and Ella and I were extroverts. And Shorty in Boston had given my brother a royal time.

Because of my reputation, it was easy for me to get into the numbers racket. That was probably Harlem's only hustle which hadn't slumped in business. In return for a favor to some white mobster, my new boss and his wife had just been given a six-months numbers banking privilege for the Bronx railroad area called Motthaven Yards. The white mobsters had the numbers racket split into specific areas. A designated area would be assigned to someone for a specified period of time. My boss's wife had been Dutch Schultz's secretary in the 1930's, during the time when Schultz had strong-armed his way into control of the Harlem numbers business.

My job now was to ride a bus across the George Washington Bridge where a fellow was waiting for me to hand him a bag of numbers betting slips. We never spoke. I'd cross the street and catch the next bus back to Harlem. I never knew who that fellow was. I never knew who picked up the betting money for the slips that I handled. You didn't ask questions in the rackets.

My boss's wife and Gladys Hampton were the only two women I ever met in Harlem whose business ability I really respected. My boss's wife, when she had the time and the inclination to talk, would tell me many interesting things. She would talk to me about the Dutch Schultz days—about deals that she had known, about graft paid to officials—rookie cops and shyster lawyers right on up into the top levels of police and politics. She knew from personal experience how crime existed only to the degree that the law cooperated with it. She showed me how, in the country's entire social, political and economic structure, the criminal, the law, and the politicians were actually inseparable partners.

It was at this time that I changed from my old numbers man, the one I'd used since I first worked in Small's Paradise. He hated to lose a heavy player, but he readily understood why I would now want to play with a runner of my own outfit. That was how I began placing my bets with West Indian Archie. I've mentioned him before—one of Harlem's really *bad* Negroes;

one of those former Dutch Schultz strong-arm men around Harlem.

West Indian Archie had finished time in Sing Sing not long before I came to Harlem. But my boss's wife had hired him not just because she knew him from the old days. West Indian Archie had the kind of photographic memory that put him among the elite of numbers runners. He never wrote down your number; even in the case of combination plays, he would just nod. He was able to file all the numbers in his head, and write them down for the banker only when he turned in his money. This made him the ideal runner because cops could never catch him with any betting slips.

I've often reflected upon such black veteran numbers men as West Indian Archie. If they had lived in another kind of society, their exceptional mathematical talents might have been better used. But they were black.

Anyway, it was status just to be known as a client of West Indian Archie's, because he handled only sizable bettors. He also required integrity and sound credit: it wasn't necessary that you pay as you played; you could pay West Indian Archie by the week. He always carried a couple of thousand dollars on him, his own money. If a client came up to him and said he'd hit for some moderate amount, say a fifty-cent or one-dollar combination, West Indian Archie would peel off the three or six hundred dollars, and later get his money back from the banker.

Every weekend, I'd pay my bill—anywhere from fifty to even one hundred dollars, if I had really plunged on some hunch. And when, once or twice, I did hit, always just some combination, as I've described, West Indian Archie paid me off from his own roll.

The six months finally ended for my boss and his wife. They had done well. Their runners got nice tips, and promptly were snatched up by other bankers. I continued working for my boss and his wife in a gambling house they opened.

A Harlem madam I'd come to know—through having done a friend of hers a favor—introduced me to a special facet of the Harlem night world, something which the riot had only interrupted. It was the world where, behind locked doors, Negroes catered to monied white people's weird sexual tastes.

The whites I'd known loved to rub shoulders publicly with black folks in the after-hours clubs and speakeasies. These, on the other hand, were whites who did not want it known that they had been anywhere near Harlem. The riot had made these exclusive white customers nervous. Their slipping into and about Harlem hadn't been so noticeable when other whites were also around. But now they would be conspicuous; they also feared the recently aroused anger of Harlem Negroes. So the madam was safeguarding her growing operation by offering me a steerer's job.

During the war, it was extremely difficult to get a telephone. One day the madam told me to stay at my apartment the next morning. She talked to somebody. I don't know who it was, but before the next noon, I dialed the madam from my own telephone—unlisted.

This madam was a specialist in her field. If her own girls could not—or would not—accommodate a customer, she would send me to another place, usually an apartment somewhere else in Harlem, where the requested "specialty" was done.

My post for picking up the customers was right outside the Astor Hotel, that always-busy northwest corner of 45th Street and Broadway. Watching the moving traffic, I was soon able to spot the taxi, car, or limousine—even before it slowed down—with the anxious white faces peering out for the tall, reddish-brown-complexioned Negro wearing a dark suit, or raincoat, with a white flower in his lapel.

If they were in a private car, unless it was chauffeured I would take the wheel and drive where we were going. But if they were in a taxi, I would always tell the cabbie, "The Apollo Theater in Harlem, please," since among New York City taxis a certain percentage are driven by cops. We would get another cab—driven by a black man—and I'd give him the right address.

As soon as I got that party settled, I'd telephone the madam. She would generally have me rush by taxi right back downtown to be on the 45th Street and Broadway corner at a specified time. Appointments were strictly punctual; rarely was I on the corner as much as five minutes. And I knew how to keep moving about so as not to attract the attention of any vice squad plainclothesmen or uniformed cops.

With tips, which were often heavy, sometimes I would make

over a hundred dollars a night steering up to ten customers in a party—to see anything, to do anything, to have anything done to them, that they wanted. I hardly ever knew the identities of my customers, but the few I did recognize, or whose names I happened to hear, remind me now of the Profumo case in England. The English are not far ahead of rich and influential Americans when it comes to seeking rarities and oddities.

Rich men, middle-aged and beyond, men well past their prime: these weren't college boys, these were their Ivy League fathers. Even grandfathers, I guess. Society leaders. Big politicians. Tycoons. Important friends from out of town. City government big shots. All kinds of professional people. Star performing artists. Theatrical and Hollywood celebrities. And, of course, racketeers.

Harlem was their sin-den, their fleshpot. They stole off among taboo black people, and took off whatever antiseptic, important, dignified masks they wore in their white world. These were men who could afford to spend large amounts of money for two, three, or four hours indulging their strange appetites.

But in this black-white nether world, nobody judged the customers. Anything they could name, anything they could imagine, anything they could describe, they could do, or could have done to them, just as long as they paid.

In the Profumo case in England, Christine Keeler's friend testified that some of her customers wanted to be whipped. One of my main steers to one specialty address away from the madam's house was the apartment of a big, coal-black girl, strong as an ox, with muscles like a dockworker's. A funny thing, it generally was the oldest of these white men—in their sixties, I know, some maybe in their seventies—they couldn't seem to recover quickly enough from their last whipping so they could have me meet them again at 45th and Broadway to take them back to that apartment, to cringe on their knees and beg and cry out for mercy under that black girl's whip. Some of them would pay me extra to come and watch them being beaten. That girl greased her big Amazon body all over to look shinier and blacker. She used small, plaited whips, she would draw blood, and she was making herself a small fortune off those old white men.

I wouldn't tell all the things I've seen. I used to wonder, later on, when I was in prison, what a psychiatrist would make of it all. And so many of these men held responsible positions; they exercised guidance, influence, and authority over others.

In prison later, I'd think, too, about another thing. Just about all of those whites specifically expressed as their preference black, *black*, "the blacker the better!" The madam, having long since learned this, had in her house nothing but the blackest accommodating women she could find.

In all of my time in Harlem, I never saw a white prostitute touched by a white man. White girls were in some of the various Harlem specialty places. They would participate in customers' most frequent exhibition requests—a sleek, black Negro male having a white woman. Was this the white man wanting to witness his deepest sexual fear? A few times, I even had parties that included white women whom the men had brought with them to watch this. I never steered any white women other than in these instances, brought by their own men, or who had been put into contact with me by a white Lesbian whom I knew, who was another variety of specialty madam.

This Lesbian, a beautiful white woman, had a male Negro stable. Her vocabulary was all profanity. She supplied Negro males, on order, to well-to-do white women.

I'd seen this Lesbian and her blonde girl friend around Harlem, drinking and talking at bars, always with young Negroes. No one who didn't know would ever guess that the Lesbian was recruiting. But one night I gave her and her girl friend some reefers which they said were the best they'd ever smoked. They lived in a hotel downtown, and after that, now and then, they would call me, and I would bring them some reefers, and we'd talk.

She told me how she had accidentally gotten started in her specialty. As a Harlem habitué, she had known Harlem Negroes who liked white women. Her role developed from a pattern of talk she often heard from bored, well-to-do white women where she worked, in an East Side beauty salon. Hearing the women complain about sexually inadequate mates, she would tell what she'd "heard" about Negro men. Observing how excited some of the women seemed to become, she finally arranged some dates with some of the Harlem Negroes she knew at her own apartment.

Eventually, she rented three midtown apartments where a

woman customer could meet a Negro by appointment. Her customers recommended her service to their friends. She quit the beauty salon, set up a messenger service as an operating front, and ran all of her business by telephone.

She had also noticed the color preference. I never could substitute in an emergency, she would tell me with a laugh, because I was too light. She told me that nearly every white woman in her clientele would specify "a black one"; sometimes they would say "a *real* one," meaning black, no brown Negroes, no red Negroes.

The Lesbian thought up her messenger service idea because some of her trade wanted the Negroes to come to their homes, at times carefully arranged by telephone. These women lived in neighborhoods of swank brownstones and exclusive apartment houses, with doormen dressed like admirals. But white society never thinks about challenging any Negro in a servant role. Doormen would telephone up and hear "Oh, yes, send him right up, James"; service elevators would speed those neatly dressed Negro messenger boys right up—so that they could "deliver" what had been ordered by some of the most privileged white women in Manhattan.

The irony is that those white women had no more respect for those Negroes than white men have had for the Negro women they have been "using" since slavery times. And, in turn, Negroes have no respect for the whites they get into bed with. I know the way I felt about Sophia, who still came to New York whenever I called her.

The West Indian boy friend of the Profumo scandal's Christine Keeler, Lucky Gordon, and his friends must have felt the same way. After England's leaders had been with those white girls, those girls, for their satisfaction, went to Negroes, to smoke reefers and make fun of some of England's greatest peers as cuckolds and fools. I don't doubt that Lucky Gordon knows the identity of "the man in the mask" and much more. If Gordon told everything those white girls told him, he would give England a new scandal.

It's no different from what happens in some of America's topmost white circles. Twenty years ago, I saw them nightly, with my own eyes, I heard them with my own ears.

The hypocritical white man will talk about the Negro's "low

morals.'' But who has the world's lowest morals if not whites? And not only that, but the "upper-class" whites! Recently, details were published about a group of suburban New York City white housewives and mothers operating as a professional call-girl ring. In some cases, these wives were out prostituting with the agreement, even the cooperation, of husbands, some of whom even waited at home, attending the children. And the customers—to quote a major New York City morning newspaper: "Some 16 ledgers and books with names of 200 Johns, many important social, financial and political figures, were seized in the raid Friday night.''

I have also read recently about groups of young white couples who get together, the husbands throw their house keys into a hat, then, blindfolded, the husbands draw out a key and spend the night with the wife that the house key matches. I have never heard of anything like that being done by Negroes, even Negroes who live in the worst ghettoes and alleys and gutters.

Early one morning in Harlem, a tall, light Negro wearing a hat and with a woman's stocking drawn down over his face held up a Negro bartender and manager who were counting up the night's receipts. Like most bars in Harlem, Negroes fronted, and a Jew really owned the place. To get a license, one had to know somebody in the State Liquor Authority, and Jews working with Jews seemed to have the best S.L.A. contacts. The black manager hired some Negro hoodlums to go hunting for the hold-up man. And the man's description caused them to include me among their suspects. About daybreak that same morning, they kicked in the door of my apartment.

I told them I didn't know a thing about it, that I hadn't had a thing to do with whatever they were talking about. I told them I had been out on my hustle, steering, until maybe four in the morning, and then I had come straight to my apartment and gone to bed.

The strong-arm thugs were bluffing. They were trying to flush out the man who had done it. They still had other suspects to check out—that's all that saved me.

I put on my clothes and took a taxi and I woke up two people, the madam, then Sammy. I had some money, but the madam gave me some more, and I told Sammy I was going to see my brother Philbert in Michigan. I gave Sammy the address, so that he could let me know when things got straightened out.

This was the trip to Michigan in the wintertime when I put congolene on my head, then discovered that the bathroom sink's pipes were frozen. To keep the lye from burning up my scalp, I had to stick my head into the stool and flush and flush to rinse out the stuff.

A week passed in frigid Michigan before Sammy's telegram came. Another red Negro had confessed, which enabled me to live in Harlem again.

But I didn't go back into steering. I can't remember why I didn't. I imagine I must have felt like staying away from hustling for a while, going to some of the clubs at night, and narcotizing with my friends. Anyway, I just never went back to the madam's job.

It was at about this time, too, I remember, that I began to be sick. I had colds all the time. It got to be a steady irritation, always sniffling and wiping my nose, all day, all night. I stayed so high that I was in a dream world. Now, sometimes, I smoked opium with some white friends, actors who lived downtown. And I smoked more reefers than ever before. I didn't smoke the usual wooden-match-sized sticks of marijuana. I was so far gone by now that I smoked it almost by the ounce.

After awhile, I worked downtown for a Jew. He liked me because of something I had managed to do for him. He bought rundown restaurants and bars. Hymie was his name. He would remodel these places, then stage a big, gala reopening, with banners and a spotlight outside. The jam-packed, busy place with the big "Under New Management" sign in the window would attract speculators, usually other Jews who were around looking for something to invest money in. Sometimes even in the week of the new opening, Hymie would re-sell, at a good profit.

Hymie really liked me, and I liked him. He loved to talk. I loved to listen. Half his talk was about Jews and Negroes. Jews who had anglicized their names were Hymie's favorite hate. Spitting and curling his mouth in scorn, he would reel off names of people he said had done this. Some of them were famous names whom most people never thought of as Jews.

"Red, I'm a Jew and you're black," he would say. "These

Gentiles don't like either one of us. If the Jew wasn't smarter than the Gentile, he'd get treated worse than your people."

Hymie paid me good money while I was with him, sometimes two hundred and three hundred dollars a week. I would have done anything for Hymie. I did do all kinds of things. But my main job was transporting bootleg liquor that Hymie supplied, usually to those spruced-up bars which he had sold to someone.

Another fellow and I would drive out to Long Island where a big bootleg whisky outfit operated. We'd take with us cartons of empty bonded whisky bottles that were saved illegally by bars we supplied. We would buy five-gallon containers of bootleg, funnel it into the bottles, then deliver, according to Hymie's instructions, this or that many crates back to the bars.

Many people claiming they drank only such-and-such a brand couldn't tell their only brand from pure week-old Long Island bootleg. Most ordinary whisky drinkers are "brand" chumps like this. On the side, with Hymie's approval, I was myself at that time supplying some lesser quantities of bootleg to reputable Harlem bars, as well as to some of the few speakeasies still in Harlem.

But one weekend on Long Island, something happened involving the State Liquor Authority. One of New York State's biggest recent scandals has been the exposure of wholesale S.L.A. graft and corruption. In the bootleg racket I was involved in, someone high up must have been taken for a real pile. A rumor about some "inside" tipster spread among Hymie and the others. One day Hymie didn't show up where he had told me to meet him. I never heard from him again . . . but I did hear that he was put in the ocean and I knew he couldn't swim.

Up in the Bronx, a Negro held up some Italian racketeers in a floating crap game. I heard about it on the wire. Whoever did it, aside from being a fool, was said to be a "tall, light-skinned" Negro, masked with a woman's stocking. It has always made me wonder if that bar stickup had really been solved, or if the wrong man had confessed under beatings. But, anyway, the past suspicion of me helped to revive suspicion of me again.

Up in Fat Man's Bar on the hill overlooking the Polo Grounds, I had just gone into a telephone booth. Everyone in the bar—all over Harlem, in fact—was drinking up, excited about the news that Branch Rickey, the Brooklyn Dodgers' owner, had just signed Jackie Robinson to play in major league baseball, with the Dodgers' farm team in Montreal—which would place the time in the fall of 1945.

Earlier in the afternoon, I had collected from West Indian Archie for a fifty-cent combination bet; he had paid me three hundred dollars right out of his pocket. I was telephoning Jean Parks. Jean was one of the most beautiful women who ever lived in Harlem. She once sang with Sarah Vaughan in the Bluebonnets, a quartet that sang with Earl Hines. For a long time, Jean and I had enjoyed a standing, friendly deal that we'd go out and celebrate when either of us hit the numbers. Since my last hit, Jean had treated me twice, and we laughed on the phone, glad that now I'd treat her to a night out. We arranged to go to a 52nd Street nightclub to hear Billie Holiday, who had been on the road and was just back in New York.

As I hung up, I spotted the two lean, tough-looking *paisanos* gazing in at me cooped up in the booth.

I didn't need any intuition. And I had no gun. A cigarette case was the only thing in my pocket. I started easing my hand down into my pocket, to try bluffing . . . and one of them snatched open the door. They were dark olive, swarthy-featured Italians. I had my hand down into my pocket.

"Come on outside, we'll hold court," one said.

At that moment, a cop walked through the front door. The two thugs slipped out. I never in my life have been so glad to see a cop.

I was still shaking when I got to the apartment of my friend, Sammy the Pimp. He told me that not long before, West Indian Archie had been there looking for me.

Sometimes, recalling all of this, I don't know, to tell the truth, how I am alive to tell it today. They say God takes care of fools and babies. I've so often thought that Allah was watching over me. Through all of this time of my life, I really *was* dead—mentally dead. I just didn't know that I was.

Anyway, to kill time, Sammy and I sniffed some of his cocaine, until the time came to pick up Jean Parks, to go down and hear Lady Day. Sammy's having told me about West Indian Archie looking for me didn't mean a thing . . . not right then.

CHAPTER EIGHT

TRAPPED

There was the knocking at the door. Sammy, lying on his bed in pajamas and a bathrobe, called "Who?"

When West Indian Archie answered, Sammy slid the round, two-sided shaving mirror under the bed, with what little of the cocaine powder—or crystals, actually—was left, and I opened the door.

"Red—I want my money!"

A .32-20 is a funny kind of gun. It's bigger than a .32. But it's not as big as a .38. I had faced down some dangerous Negroes. But no one who wasn't ready to die messed with West Indian Archie.

I couldn't believe it. He truly scared me. I was so incredulous at what was happening that it was hard to form words with my brain and my mouth.

"Man—what's the beef?"

West Indian Archie said he'd thought I was trying something when I'd told him I'd hit, but he'd paid me the three hundred dollars until he could double-check his written betting slips; and, as he'd thought, I hadn't combinated the number I'd claimed, but another.

"Man, you're crazy!" I talked fast; I'd seen out of the corner of my eye Sammy's hand easing under his pillow where he kept his Army .45. "Archie, smart a man as you're supposed to be, you'd pay somebody who hadn't hit?"

The .32-20 moved, and Sammy froze. West Indian Archie told him, "I ought to shoot you through the ear." And he looked back at me. "You don't have my money?"

I must have shaken my head.

"I'll give you until twelve o'clock tomorrow."

And he put his hand behind him and pulled open the door. He backed out, and slammed it.

It was a classic hustler-code impasse. The money wasn't the problem. I still had about two hundred dollars of it. Had money been the issue, Sammy could have made up the difference; if it wasn't in his pocket, his women could quickly have raised it. West Indian Archie himself, for that matter, would have loaned me three hundred dollars if I'd ever asked him, as many thousands of dollars of mine as he'd gotten ten percent of. Once, in fact, when he'd heard I was broke, he had looked me up and handed me some money and grunted, "Stick this in your pocket."

The issue was the position which his action had put us both into. For a hustler in our sidewalk jungle world, "face" and "honor" were important. No hustler could have it known that he'd been "hyped," meaning outsmarted or made a fool of. And worse, a hustler could never afford to have it demonstrated that he could be bluffed, that he could be frightened by a threat, that he lacked nerve.

West Indian Archie knew that some young hustlers rose in stature in our world when they somehow hoodwinked older hustlers, then put it on the wire for everyone to hear. He believed I was trying that.

In turn, I knew he would be protecting his stature by broadcasting all over the wire his threat to me.

Because of this code, in my time in Harlem I'd personally known a dozen hustlers who, threatened, left town, disgraced.

Once the wire had it, any retreat by either of us was unthinkable. The wire would be awaiting the report of the showdown.

I'd also known of at least another dozen showdowns in which one took the Dead On Arrival ride to the morgue, and the other went to prison for manslaughter or the electric chair for murder.

Sammy let me hold his .32. My guns were at my apartment. I put the .32 in my pocket, with my hand on it, and walked out.

I couldn't stay out of sight. I had to show up at all of my usual haunts. I was glad that Reginald was out of town. He might have tried protecting me, and I didn't want him shot in the head by West Indian Archie.

I stood awhile on the corner, with my mind confused—the muddled thinking that's characteristic of the addict. Was West Indian Archie, I began to wonder, bluffing a hype on me? To make fun of me? Some old hustlers did love to hype younger ones. I knew he wouldn't do it as some would, just to pick up three hundred dollars. But everyone was so slick. In this Harlem jungle people would hype their brothers. Numbers runners often had hyped addicts who had hit, who were so drugged that, when challenged, they really couldn't be sure if they had played a certain number.

I began to wonder whether West Indian Archie might not be right. Had I really gotten my combination confused? I certainly knew the two numbers I'd played; I knew I'd told him to combinate only one of them. Had I gotten mixed up about which number?

Have you ever been so sure you did something that you never would have thought of it again—unless it was brought up again? Then you start trying to mentally confirm—and you're only about half-sure?

It was just about time for me to go and pick up Jean Parks, to go downtown to see Billie at the Onyx Club. So much was swirling in my head. I thought about telephoning her and calling it off, making some excuse. But I knew that running now was the worst thing I could do. So I went on and picked up Jean at her place. We took a taxi on down to 52nd Street. "*Billie Holiday*" and those big photo blow-ups of her were under the lights outside. Inside, the tables were jammed against the wall, tables about big enough to get two drinks and four elbows on; the Onyx was one of those very little places.

Billie, at the microphone, had just finished a number when she saw Jean and me. Her white gown glittered under the spotlight, her face had that coppery, Indianish look, and her hair was in that trademark ponytail. For her next number she did the one she knew I always liked so: "You Don't Know What Love Is"—"until you face each dawn with sleepless eyes . . . until you've lost a love you hate to lose—"

When her set was done, Billie came over to our table. She and Jean, who hadn't seen each other in a long time, hugged each other. Billie sensed something wrong with me. She knew that I was always high, but she knew me well enough to see that something else was wrong, and asked in her customary profane language what was the matter with me. And in my own foul vocabulary of those days, I pretended to be without a care, so she let it drop.

We had a picture taken by the club photographer that night. The three of us were sitting close together. That was the last time I ever saw Lady Day. She's dead; dope and heartbreak stopped that heart as big as a barn and that sound and style that no one successfully copies. Lady Day sang with the *soul* of Negroes from the centuries of sorrow and oppression. What a shame that proud, fine, black woman never lived where the true greatness of the black race was appreciated!

In the Onyx Club men's room, I sniffed the little packet of cocaine I had gotten from Sammy. Jean and I, riding back up to Harlem in a cab, decided to have another drink. She had no idea what was happening when she suggested one of my main hangouts, the bar of the La Marr-Cheri on the corner of 147th Street and St. Nicholas Avenue. I had my gun, and the cocaine courage, and I said okay. And by the time we'd had the drink, I was so high that I asked Jean to take a cab on home, and she did. I never have seen Jean again, either.

Like a fool, I didn't leave the bar. I stayed there, sitting, like a bigger fool, with my back to the door, thinking about West Indian Archie. Since that day, I have never sat with my back to a door—and I never will again. But it's a good thing I was then. I'm positive if I'd seen West Indian Archie come in, I'd have shot to kill.

The next thing I knew West Indian Archie was standing before me, cursing me, loud, his gun on me. He was really making his public point, floor-showing for the people. He called me foul names, threatened me.

Everyone, bartenders and customers, sat or stood as though carved, drinks in mid-air. The jukebox, in the rear, was going. I had never seen West Indian Archie high before. Not a whisky high, I could tell it was something else. I knew the hustlers' characteristic of keying up on dope to do a job.

I was thinking, "I'm going to kill Archie . . . I'm just going to wait until he turns around—to get the drop on him." I could feel my own .32 resting against my ribs where it was tucked under my belt, beneath my coat.

West Indian Archie, seeming to read my mind, quit cursing. And his words jarred me.

"You're thinking you're going to kill me first, Red. But I'm going to give you something to think about. I'm sixty. I'm an old man. I've been to Sing Sing. My life is over. You're a young man. Kill me, you're lost anyway. All you can do is go to prison."

I've since thought that West Indian Archie may have been trying to scare me into running, to save both his face and his life. It may be that's why he was high. No one knew that I hadn't killed anyone, but no one who knew me, including myself, would doubt that I'd kill.

I can't guess what might have happened. But under the code, if West Indian Archie had gone out of the door, after having humiliated me as he had, I'd have had to follow him out. We'd have shot it out in the street.

But some friends of West Indian Archie moved up alongside him, quietly calling his name, "Archie . . . Archie."

And he let them put their hands on him—and they drew him aside. I watched them move him past where I was sitting, glaring at me. They were working him back toward the rear.

Then, taking my time, I got down off the stool. I dropped a bill on the bar for the bartender. Without looking back, I went out.

I stood outside, in full view of the bar, with my hand in my pocket, for perhaps five minutes. When West Indian Archie didn't come out, I left.

It must have been five in the morning when, downtown, I woke up a white actor I knew who lived in the Howard Hotel on 45th Street, off Sixth Avenue.

I knew I had to stay high.

The amount of dope I put into myself within the next several hours sounds inconceivable. I got some opium from that fellow. I took a cab back up to my apartment and I smoked it. My gun was ready if I heard a mosquito cough.

My telephone rang. It was the white Lesbian who lived downtown. She wanted me to bring her and her girl friend fifty dollars worth of reefers.

I felt that if I had always done it, I had to do it now. Opium had me drowsy. I had a bottle of benzedrine tablets in my bathroom; I swallowed some of them to perk up. The two drugs working in me had my head going in opposite directions at the same time.

I knocked at the apartment right behind mine. The dealer let me have loose marijuana on credit. He saw I was so high that he even helped me roll it—a hundred sticks. And while we were rolling it, we both smoked some.

Now opium, benzedrine, reefers.

I stopped by Sammy's on the way downtown. His flashing-eyed Spanish Negro woman opened the door. Sammy had gotten weak for that woman. He had never let any other of his women hang around so much; now she was even answering his doorbell. Sammy was by this time very badly addicted. He seemed hardly to recognize me. Lying in bed, he reached under and again brought out that inevitable shaving mirror on which, for some reason, he always kept his cocaine crystals. He motioned for me to sniff some. I didn't refuse.

Going downtown to deliver the reefers, I felt sensations I cannot describe, in all those different grooves at the same time. The only word to describe it was a *timelessness*. A day might have seemed to me five minutes. Or a half-hour might have seemed a week.

I can't imagine how I looked when I got to the hotel. When the Lesbian and her girl friend saw me, they helped me to a bed; I fell across it and passed out.

That night, when they woke me up, it was half a day beyond West Indian Archie's deadline. Late, I went back uptown. It was on the wire. I could see people who knew me finding business elsewhere. I knew nobody wanted to be caught in a cross-fire.

But nothing happened. The next day, either. I just stayed high.

Some raw kid hustler in a bar, I had to bust in his mouth. He came back, pulling a blade; I would have shot him, but somebody grabbed him. They put him out, cursing that he was going to kill me.

Intuition told me to get rid of my gun. I gave a hustler the eye across the bar. I'd no more than slipped him the gun from my belt when a cop I'd seen about came in the other door. He had his hand on his gun butt. He knew what was all over the wire; he was certain I'd be armed. He came slowly over toward me, and I knew if I sneezed, he'd blast me down.

He said, "Take your hand out of your pocket, Red—*real* carefully."

I did. Once he saw me empty handed, we both could relax a little. He motioned for me to walk outside, ahead of him, and I did. His partner was waiting on the sidewalk, opposite their patrol car, double-parked with its radio going. With people stopping, looking, they patted me down there on the sidewalk.

"What are you looking for?" I asked them when they didn't find anything.

"Red, there's a report you're carrying a gun."

"I had one," I said. "But I threw it in the river."

The one who had come into the bar said, "I think I'd leave town if I were you, Red."

I went back into the bar. Saying that I had thrown my gun away had kept them from taking me to my apartment. Things I had there could have gotten me more time than ten guns, and could have gotten them a promotion.

Everything was building up, closing in on me. I was trapped in so many cross turns. West Indian Archie gunning for me. The Italians who thought I'd stuck up their crap game after me. The scared kid hustler I'd hit. The cops.

For four years, up to that point, I'd been lucky enough, or slick enough, to escape jail, or even getting arrested. Or any *serious* trouble. But I knew that any minute now something had to give.

Sammy had done something that I've often wished I could have thanked him for.

When I heard the car's horn, I was walking on St. Nicholas Avenue. But my ears were hearing a gun. I didn't dream the horn could possibly be for me.

"*Homeboy!*"

I jerked around; I came close to shooting.

Shorty—from Boston!

I'd scared him nearly to death.

"*Daddy-o!*"

I couldn't have been happier.

Inside the car, he told me Sammy had telephoned about how I was jammed up tight and told him he'd better come and get me. And Shorty did his band's date, then borrowed his piano man's car, and burned up the miles to New York.

I didn't put up any objections to leaving. Shorty stood watch outside my apartment. I brought out and stuffed into the car's trunk what little stuff I cared to hang on to. Then we hit the highway. Shorty had been without sleep for about thirty-six hours. He told me afterward that through just about the whole ride back, I talked out of my head.

CHAPTER NINE

CAUGHT

Ella couldn't believe how atheist, how uncouth I had become. I believed that a man should do anything that he was slick enough, or bad and bold enough, to do and that a woman was nothing but another commodity. Every word I spoke was hip or profane. I would bet that my working vocabulary wasn't two hundred words.

Even Shorty, whose apartment I now again shared, wasn't prepared for how I lived and thought—like a predatory animal. Sometimes I would catch him watching me.

At first, I slept a lot—even at night. I had slept mostly in the daytime during the preceding two years. When awake, I smoked reefers. Shorty had originally introduced me to marijuana, and my consumption of it now astounded him.

I didn't want to talk much, at first. When awake, I'd play records continuously. The reefers gave me a feeling of contentment. I would enjoy hours of floating, day dreaming, imaginary conversations with my New York musician friends.

Within two weeks, I'd had more sleep than during any two months when I had been in Harlem hustling day and night. When I finally went out in the Roxbury streets, it took me only a little while to locate a peddler of "snow"—cocaine. It was when I got back into that familiar snow feeling that I began to want to talk.

Cocaine produces, for those who sniff its powdery white crystals, an illusion of supreme well-being, and a soaring over-confidence in both physical and mental ability. You think you could whip the heavyweight champion, and that you are smarter than anybody. There was also that feeling of timelessness. And there were intervals of ability to recall and review things that had happened years back with an astonishing clarity.

Shorty's band played at spots around Boston three or four nights a week. After he left for work, Sophia would come over and I'd talk about my plans. She would be gone back to her husband by the time Shorty returned from work, and I'd bend his ear until daybreak.

Sophia's husband had gotten out of the military, and he was some sort of salesman. He was supposed to have a big deal going which soon would require his traveling a lot to the West Coast. I didn't ask questions, but Sophia often indicated they weren't doing too well. I know *I* had nothing to do with that. He never dreamed I existed. A white woman might blow up at her husband and scream and yell and call him every name she can think of, and say the most vicious things in an effort to hurt him, and talk about his mother and his grandmother, too, but one thing she never will tell him herself is that she is going with a black man. That's one automatic red murder flag to the white man, and his woman knows it.

Sophia always had given me money. Even when I had hundreds of dollars in my pocket, when she came to Harlem I would take everything she had short of her train fare back to Boston. It seems that some women love to be exploited. When they are not exploited, they exploit the man. Anyway, it was his money that she gave me, I guess, because she never had worked. But now my demands on her increased, and she came up with more; again, I don't know where she got it. Always, every now and then, I had given her a hard time, just to keep her in line. Every once in a while a woman seems to need, in fact *wants* this, too. But now, I would feel evil and slap her around worse than ever, some of the nights when Shorty was away. She would cry, curse me, and swear that she would never be back. But I knew she wasn't even thinking about not coming back.

Sophia's being around was one of Shorty's greatest pleasures about my homecoming. I have said it before, I never in my life have seen a black man that desired white women as sincerely as Shorty did. Since I had known him, he had had several. He had never been able to keep a white woman any length of time, though, because he was too good to them, and, as I have said, any woman, white or black, seems to get bored with that.

It happened that Shorty was between white women when one night Sophia brought to the house her seventeen-year-old sister. I never saw anything like the way that she and Shorty nearly jumped for each other. For him, she wasn't only a white girl, but a *young* white girl. For her, he wasn't only a Negro, but a Negro *musician*. In looks, she was a younger version of Sophia, who still turned heads. Sometimes I'd take the two girls to Negro places where Shorty played. Negroes showed thirty-two teeth apiece as soon as they saw the white girls. They would come over to your booth, or your table; they would stand there and drool. And Shorty was no better. He'd stand up there playing and watching that young girl waiting for him, and waving at him, and winking. As soon as the set was over, he'd practically run over people getting down to our table.

I didn't lindy-hop any more now, I wouldn't even have thought of it now, just as I wouldn't have been caught in a zoot suit now. All of my suits were conservative. A banker might have worn my shoes.

I met Laura again. We were really glad to see each other. She was a lot more like me now, a good-time girl. We talked and laughed. She looked a lot older than she really was. She had no one man, she free-lanced around. She had long since moved away from her grandmother. Laura told me she had finished school, but then she gave up the college idea. Laura was high whenever I saw her, now, too; we smoked some reefers together.

After about a month of "laying dead," as inactivity was called, I knew I had to get some kind of hustle going.

A hustler, broke, needs a stake. Some nights when Shorty was playing, I would take whatever Sophia had been able to get for me, and I'd try to run it up into something, playing stud poker at John Hughes' gambling house.

When I had lived in Roxbury before, John Hughes had been a big gambler who wouldn't have spoken to me. But during the war the Roxbury "wire" had carried a lot about things I was doing in Harlem, and now the New York name magic was on me. That was the feeling that hustlers everywhere else had: if you could hustle and make it in New York, they were well off to know you; it gave them prestige. Anyway, through the same flush war years, John Hughes had hustled profitably enough to be able to open a pretty good gambling house.

John, one night, was playing in a game I was in. After the first two cards were dealt around the table, I had an ace showing. I looked beneath it at my hole card; another ace—a pair, back-to-back.

My ace showing made it my turn to bet.

But I didn't rush. I sat there and studied.

Finally, I knocked my knuckles on the table, passing, leaving the betting to the next man. My action implied that beneath my ace was some "nothing" card that I didn't care to risk my money on.

The player sitting next to me took the bait. He bet pretty heavily. And the next man raised him. Possibly each of them had small pairs. Maybe they just wanted to scare me out before I drew another ace. Finally, the bet reached John, who had a queen showing; he raised everybody.

Now, there was no telling what John had. John truly was a clever gambler. He could gamble as well as anybody I had gambled with in New York.

So the bet came back to me. It was going to cost me a lot of money to call all the raises. Some of them obviously had good cards but I knew I had every one of them beat. But again I studied, and studied; I pretended perplexity. And finally I put in my money, calling the bets.

The same betting pattern went on, with each new card, right around to the last card. And when that last card went around, I hit another ace in sight. Three aces. And John hit another queen in sight.

He bet a pile. Now, everyone else studied a long time—and, one by one, all folded their hands. Except me. All I could do was put what I had left on the table.

If I'd had the money, I could have raised five hundred dollars or more, and he'd have had to call me. John couldn't have gone the rest of his life wondering if I had bluffed him out of a pot that big.

I showed my hole card ace; John had three queens. As I hauled in the pot, something over five hundred dollars—my first real stake in Boston—John got up from the table. He'd quit. He told his house man, "Anytime Red comes in here and wants anything, let him have it." He said, "I've never seen a young man play his hole card like he played."

John said "young man," being himself about fifty, I guess, although you can never be certain about a Negro's age. He thought, as most people would have, that I was about thirty. No one in Roxbury except my sisters Ella and Mary suspected my real age.

The story of that poker game helped my on-scene reputation among the other gamblers and hustlers around Roxbury. Another thing that happened in John's gambling house contributed: the incident that made it known that I carried not a gun, but some guns.

John had a standing rule that anyone who came into the place to gamble had to check his guns if he had any. I always checked two guns. Then, one night, when a gambler tried to pull something slick, I drew a third gun, from its shoulder holster. This added to the rest of my reputation the word that I was "trigger-happy" and "crazy."

Looking back, I think I really was at least slightly out of my mind. I viewed narcotics as most people regard food. I wore my guns as today I wear my neckties. Deep down, I actually believed that after living as fully as humanly possible, one should then die violently. I expected then, as I still expect today, to die at any time. But then, I think I deliberately invited death in many, sometimes insane, ways.

For instance, a merchant marine sailor who knew me and my reputation came into a bar carrying a package. He motioned me to follow him downstairs into the men's room. He unwrapped a stolen machine gun; he wanted to sell it. I said, "How do I know it works?" He loaded it with a cartridge clip, and told me that all I would have to do then was squeeze the trigger release. I took the gun, examined it, and the first thing he knew I had it jammed right up in his belly. I told him I would blow him wide open. He went backwards out of the rest room and up the stairs the way Bill "Bojangles" Robinson used to dance going backwards. He knew I was crazy enough to kill him. I was insane enough not to consider that he might just wait his chance to kill me. For perhaps a month I kept the machine gun at Shorty's before I was broke and sold it.

When Reginald came to Roxbury visiting, he was shocked at

what he'd found out upon returning to Harlem. I spent some time with him. He still was the kid brother whom I still felt more "family" toward than I felt now even for our sister Ella. Ella still liked me. I would go to see her once in a while. But Ella had never been able to reconcile herself to the way I had changed. She has since told me that she had a steady foreboding that I was on my way into big trouble. But I always had the feeling that Ella somehow admired my rebellion against the world, because she, who had so much more drive and guts than most men, often felt stymied by having been born female.

Had I been thinking only in terms of myself, maybe I would have chosen steady gambling as a hustle. There were enough chump gamblers that hung around John Hughes' for a good gambler to make a living off them; chumps that worked, usually. One would just have to never miss the games on their paydays. Besides, John Hughes had offered me a job dealing for games; I didn't want that.

But I had come around to thinking not only of myself. I wanted to get something going that could help Shorty, too. We had been talking; I really felt sorry for Shorty. The same old musician story. The so-called glamor of being a musician, earning just about enough money so that after he paid rent and bought his reefers and food and other routine things, he had nothing left. Plus debts. How could Shorty have anything? I'd spent years in Harlem and on the road around the most popular musicians, the "names," even, who really were making big money for musicians—and they had nothing.

For that matter, all the thousands of dollars I'd handled, and *I* had nothing. Just satisfying my cocaine habit alone cost me about twenty dollars a day. I guess another five dollars a day could have been added for reefers and plain tobacco cigarettes that I smoked; besides getting high on drugs, I chain-smoked as many as four packs a day. And, if you ask me today, I'll tell you that tobacco, in all its forms, is just as much an addiction as any narcotic.

When I opened the subject of a hustle with Shorty, I started by first bringing him to agree with my concept—of which he was a living proof—that only squares kept on believing they could ever get anything by slaving.

And when I mentioned what I had in mind—house burglary—

Shorty, who always had been so relatively conservative, really surprised me by how quickly he agreed. He didn't even know anything about burglarizing.

When I began to explain how it was done, Shorty wanted to bring in this friend of his, whom I had met, and liked, called Rudy.

Rudy's mother was Italian, his father was a Negro. He was born right there in Boston, a short, light fellow, a pretty boy type. Rudy worked regularly for an employment agency that sent him to wait on tables at exclusive parties. He had a side deal going, a hustle that took me right back to the old steering days in Harlem. Once a week, Rudy went to the home of this old, rich Boston blueblood, pillar-of-society aristocrat. He paid Rudy to undress them both, then pick up the old man like a baby, lay him on his bed, then stand over him and sprinkle him all over with *talcum powder*.

Rudy said the old man would actually reach his climax from that.

I told him and Shorty about some of the things I'd seen. Rudy said that as far as he knew, Boston had no organized specialty sex houses, just individual rich whites who had their private specialty desires catered to by Negroes who came to their homes camouflaged as chauffeurs, maids, waiters, or some other accepted image. Just as in New York, these were the rich, the highest society—the predominantly old men, past the age of ability to conduct any kind of ordinary sex, always hunting for new ways to be "sensitive."

Rudy, I remember, spoke of one old white man who paid a black couple to let him watch them have intercourse on his bed. Another was so "sensitive" that he paid to sit on a chair outside a room where a couple was—he got his satisfaction just from imagining what was going on inside.

A good burglary team includes, I knew, what is called a "finder." A finder is one who locates lucrative places to rob. Another principal need is someone able to "case" these places' physical layouts—to determine means of entry, the best getaway routes, and so forth. Rudy qualified on both counts. Being sent to work in rich homes, he wouldn't be suspected when he sized up their loot and cased the joint, just running around looking busy with a white coat on.

Rudy's reaction, when he was told what we had in mind, was something, I remember, like "Man, when do we start?"

But I wasn't rushing off half-cocked. I had learned from some of the pros, and from my own experience, how important it was to be careful and plan. Burglary, properly executed, though it had its dangers, offered the maximum chances of success with the minimum risk. If you did your job so that you never met any of your victims, it first lessened your chances of having to attack or perhaps kill someone. And if through some slip-up you were caught, later, by the police, there was never a positive eyewitness.

It is also important to select an area of burglary and stick to that. There are specific specialities among burglars. Some work apartments only, others houses only, others stores only, or warehouses; still others will go after only safes or strongboxes.

Within the residence burglary category, there are further specialty distinctions. There are the day burglars, the dinner- and theater-time burglars, the night burglars. I think that any city's police will tell you that very rarely do they find one type who will work at another time. For instance Jumpsteady, in Harlem, was a nighttime apartment specialist. It would have been hard to persuade Jumpsteady to work in the daytime if a millionaire had gone out for lunch and left his front door wide open.

I had one very practical reason never to work in the daytime, aside from my inclinations. With my high visibility, I'd have been sunk in the daytime. I could just hear people: "A reddish-brown Negro over six feet tall." One glance would be enough.

Setting up what I wanted to be the perfect operation, I thought about pulling the white girls into it for two reasons. One was that I realized we'd be too limited relying only upon places where Rudy worked as a waiter. He didn't get to work in too many places; it wouldn't be very long before we ran out of sources. And when other places had to be found and cased in the rich, white residential areas, Negroes hanging around would stick out like sore thumbs, but these white girls could get invited into the right places.

I disliked the idea of having too many people involved, all at the same time. But with Shorty and Sophia's sister so close now, and Sophia and me as though we had been together for fifty years, and Rudy as eager and cool as he was, nobody would be apt to spill, everybody would be under the same risk; we would be like a family unit.

I never doubted that Sophia would go along. Sophia would do anything I said. And her sister would do anything that Sophia said. They both went for it. Sophia's husband was away on one of his trips to the coast when I told her and her sister.

Most burglars, I knew, were caught not on the job, but trying to dispose of the loot. Finding the fence we used was a rare piece of luck. We agreed upon the plan for operations. The fence didn't work with us directly. He had a representative, an ex-con, who dealt with me, and no one else in my gang. Aside from his regular business, he owned around Boston several garages and small warehouses. The arrangement was that before a job, I would alert the representative, and give him a general idea of what we expected to get, and he'd tell me at which garage or warehouse we should make the drop. After we had made our drop, the representative would examine the stolen articles. He would remove all identifying marks from everything. Then he would call the fence, who would come and make a personal appraisal. The next day the representative would meet me at a prearranged place and would make the payment for what we had stolen—in cash.

One thing I remember. This fence always sent your money in crisp, brand-new bills. He was smart. Somehow that had a very definite psychological effect upon all of us, after we had pulled a job, walking around with that crisp green money in our pockets. He may have had other reasons.

We needed a base of operations—not in Roxbury. The girls rented an apartment in Harvard Square. Unlike Negroes, these white girls could go shopping for the locale and physical situation we wanted. It was on the ground floor, where, moving late at night, all of us could come and go without attracting notice.

In any organization, someone must be the boss. If it's even just one person, you've got to be the boss of yourself.

At our gang's first meeting in the apartment, we discussed how we were going to work. The girls would get into houses to case them by ringing bells and saying they were saleswomen, poll-takers, college girls making a survey, or anything else suitable. Once in the houses, they would get around as much as they could without attracting attention. Then, back, they would report what special valuables they had seen, and where. They would draw the layout for Shorty, Rudy, and me. We agreed that the girls would actually burglarize only in special cases where there would be some advantage. But generally the three men would go, two of us to do the job while the third kept watch in the getaway car, with the motor running.

Talking to them, laying down the plans, I had deliberately sat on a bed away from them. All of a sudden, I pulled out my gun, shook out all five bullets, and then let them see me put back only one bullet. I twirled the cylinder, and put the muzzle to my head.

"Now, I'm going to see how much guts all of you have," I said.

I grinned at them. All of their mouths had flapped open. I pulled the trigger—we all heard it *click*.

"I'm going to do it again, now."

They begged me to stop. I could see in Shorty's and Rudy's eyes some idea of rushing me.

We all heard the hammer *click* on another empty cylinder.

The women were in hysterics. Rudy and Shorty were begging, *"Man . . . Red . . . cut it out, man! . . . Freeze!"* I pulled the trigger once more.

"I'm doing this, showing you I'm not afraid to die," I told them. "Never cross a man not afraid to die . . . now, let's get to work!"

I never had one moment's trouble with any of them after that. Sophia acted awed, her sister all but called me "Mr. Red." Shorty and Rudy were never again quite the same with me. Neither of them ever mentioned it. They thought I was crazy. They were afraid of me.

We pulled the first job that night—the place of the old man who hired Rudy to sprinkle him with talcum powder. A cleaner job couldn't have been asked for. Everything went like clockwork. The fence was full of praise; he proved he meant it with his crisp, new money. The old man later told Rudy how a small army of detectives had been there—and they decided that the job had the earmarks of some gang which had been operating around Boston for about a year.

We quickly got it down to a science. The girls would scout and case in wealthy neighborhoods. The burglary would be pulled; sometimes it took no more than ten minutes. Shorty and I did most of the actual burglary. Rudy generally had the getaway car.

If the people weren't at home, we'd use a passkey on a common door lock. On a patent lock, we'd use a jimmy, as it's called, or a lockpick. Or, sometimes, we would enter by windows from a fire-escape, or a roof. Gullible women often took the girls all over their houses, just to hear them exclaiming over the finery. With the help of the girls' drawings and a fingerbeam searchlight, we went straight to the things we wanted.

Sometimes the victims were in their beds asleep. That may sound very daring. Actually, it was almost easy. The first thing we had to do when people were in the house was to wait, very still, and pick up the sounds of breathing. Snorers we loved; they made it real easy. In stockinged feet, we'd go right into the bedrooms. Moving swiftly, like shadows, we would lift clothes, watches, wallets, handbags, and jewelry boxes.

The Christmas season was Santa Claus for us; people had expensive presents lying all over their houses. And they had taken more cash than usual out of their banks. Sometimes, working earlier than we usually did, we even worked houses that we hadn't cased. If the shades were drawn full, and no lights were on, and there was no answer when one of the girls rang the bell, we would take the chance and go in.

I can give you a very good tip if you want to keep burglars out of your house. A light on for the burglar to see is the very best single means of protection. One of the ideal things is to leave a bathroom light on all night. The bathroom is one place where somebody could be, for any length of time, at any time of the night, and he would be likely to hear the slightest strange sound. The burglar, knowing this, won't try to enter. It's also the cheapest possible protection. The kilowatts are a lot cheaper than your valuables.

We became efficient. The fence sometimes relayed tips as to where we could find good loot. It was in this way that for one period, one of our best periods, I remember, we specialized in Oriental rugs. I have always suspected that the fence himself sold the rugs to the people we stole them from. But, anyway, you wouldn't imagine the value of those things. I remember one small one that brought us a thousand dollars. There's no telling what the fence got for it. Every burglar knew that fences robbed the burglars worse than the burglars had robbed the victims.

Our only close brush with the law came once when we were making our getaway, three of us in the front seat of the car, and the back seat loaded with stuff. Suddenly we saw a police car round the corner, coming toward us, and it went on past us. They were just cruising. But then in the rear-view mirror, we saw them make a U-turn, and we knew they were going to flash us to stop. They had spotted us, in passing, as Negroes, and they knew that Negroes had no business in the area at that hour.

It was a close situation. There was a lot of robbery going on; we weren't the only gang working, we knew, not by any means. But I knew that the white man is rare who will ever consider that a Negro can outsmart him. Before their light began flashing, I told Rudy to stop. I did what I'd done once before—got out and flagged them, walking toward them. When they stopped, I was at their car. I asked them, bumbling my words like a confused Negro, if they could tell me how to get to a Roxbury address. They told me, and we, and they, went on about our respective businesses.

We were going along fine. We'd make a good pile and then lay low awhile, living it up. Shorty still played with his band, Rudy never missed attending his sensitive old man, or the table-waiting at his exclusive parties, and the girls maintained their routine home schedules.

Sometimes, I still took the girls out to places where Shorty played, and to other places, spending money as though it were going out of style, the girls dressed in jewelry and furs they had selected from our hauls. No one knew our hustle, but it was clear that we were doing fine. And sometimes, the girls would come over and we'd meet them either at Shorty's in Roxbury or in our Harvard Square place, and just smoke reefers, and play music. It's a shame to tell on a man, but Shorty was so obsessed with the white girl that even if the lights were out, he would pull up the shade to be able to see that white flesh by the street lamp from outside.

Early evenings when we were laying low between jobs, I often went to a Massachusetts Avenue nightclub called the Savoy. And Sophia would telephone me there punctually. Even when we pulled jobs, I would leave from this club, then rush back there after the job. The reason was so that if it was ever necessary, people could testify that they had seen me at just about the time the job was pulled. Negroes being questioned by policemen would be very hard to pin down on any exact time.

Boston at this time had two Negro detectives. Ever since I had come back on the Roxbury scene, one of these detectives, a dark brown fellow named Turner, had never been able to stand me, and it was mutual. He talked about what he would do to me, and I had promptly put an answer back on the wire. I knew from the way he began to act that he had heard it. Everyone knew that I carried guns. And he did have sense enough to know that I wouldn't hesitate to use them—and on him, detective or not.

This early evening I was in this place when at the usual time, the phone in the booth rang. It rang just as this detective Turner happened to walk in through the front door. He saw me start to get up, he knew the call was for me, but stepped inside the booth, and answered.

I heard him saying, looking straight at me, "Hello, hello, hello—" And I knew that Sophia, taking no chances with the strange voice, had hung up.

"Wasn't that call for me?" I asked Turner.

He said that it was.

I said, "Well, why didn't you say so?"

He gave me a rude answer. I knew he wanted me to make a move, first. We both were being cagey. We both knew that we wanted to kill each other. Neither wanted to say the wrong thing. Turner didn't want to say anything that, repeated, would make him sound bad. I didn't want to say anything that could be interpreted as a threat to a cop.

But I remember exactly what I said to him anyway, purposely loud enough for some people at the bar to hear me. I said, "You know, Turner—you're trying to make history. Don't you know that if you play with me, you certainly will go down in history because you've got to kill me?"

Turner looked at me. Then he backed down. He walked on by me. I guess he wasn't ready to make history.

I had gotten to the point where I was walking on my own coffin.

It's a law of the rackets that every criminal expects to get caught. He tries to stave off the inevitable for as long as he can.

Drugs helped me push the thought to the back of my mind. They were the center of my life. I had gotten to the stage where every day I used enough drugs—reefers, cocaine, or both—so that I felt above any worries, any strains. If any worries did manage to push their way through to the surface of my consciousness, I could float them back where they came from until tomorrow, and then until the next day.

But where, always before, I had been able to smoke the reefers and to sniff the snow and rarely show it very much, by now it was not that easy.

One week when we weren't working—after a big haul—I was just staying high, and I was out nightclubbing. I came into this club, and from the bartender's face when he spoke, "Hello, Red," I knew that something was wrong. But I didn't ask him anything. I've always had this rule—never ask anybody in that kind of situation; they will tell you what they want you to know. But the bartender didn't get a chance to tell me, if he had meant to. When I sat down on a stool and ordered a drink, I saw them.

Sophia and her sister sat at a table inside, near the dance floor, with a white man.

I don't know how I ever made such a mistake as I next did. I could have talked to her later. I didn't know, or care, who the white fellow was. My cocaine told me to get up.

It wasn't Sophia's husband. It was his closest friend. They had served in the war together. With her husband out of town, he had asked Sophia and her sister out to dinner, and they went. But then, later, after dinner, driving around, he had suddenly suggested going over to the black ghetto.

Every Negro who lives in a city has seen the type a thousand times, the Northern cracker who will go to visit "niggertown," to be amused at "the coons."

The girls, so well known in the Negro places in Roxbury, had tried to change his mind, but he had insisted. So they had just held their breaths coming into this club where they had been a hundred times. They walked in stiff-eyeing the bartenders and waiters who caught their message and acted as though they never had seen them before. And they were sitting there with drinks before them, praying that no Negro who knew them would barge up to their table.

Then up I came. I know I called them "Baby." They were chalky-white, he was beet-red.

That same night, back at the Harvard Square place, I really got sick. It was less of a physical sickness than it was all of the last five years catching up. I was in my pajamas in bed, half asleep, when I heard someone knock.

I knew that something was wrong. We all had keys. No one ever knocked at the door. I rolled off and under the bed; I was so groggy it didn't cross my mind to grab for my gun on the dresser.

Under the bed, I heard the key turn, and I saw the shoes and pants cuffs walk in. I watched them walk around. I saw them stop. Every time they stopped, I knew what the eyes were looking at. And I knew, before he did, that he was going to get down and look under the bed. He did. It was Sophia's husband's friend. His face was about two feet from mine. It looked congealed.

"Ha, ha, ha, I fooled you, didn't I?" I said. It wasn't at all funny. I got out from under the bed, still fake-laughing. He didn't run, I'll say that for him. He stood back; he watched me as though I were a snake.

I didn't try to hide what he already knew. The girls had some things in the closets, and around; he had seen all of that. We even talked some. I told him the girls weren't there, and he left. What shook me the most was realizing that I had trapped myself under the bed without a gun. I really was slipping.

I had put a stolen watch into a jewelry shop to replace a broken crystal. It was about two days later, when I went to pick up the watch, that things fell apart.

As I have said, a gun was as much a part of my dress as a necktie. I had my gun in a shoulder holster, under my coat.

The loser of the watch, the person from whom it had been stolen by us, I later found, had described the repair that it needed. It was a very expensive watch, that's why I had kept it for myself. And all of the jewelers in Boston had been alerted.

The Jew waited until I had paid him before he laid the watch on the counter. He gave his signal—and this other fellow suddenly appeared, from the back, walking toward me.

One hand was in his pocket. I knew he was a cop.

He said, quietly, "Step into the back."

Just as I started back there, an innocent Negro walked into

the shop. I remember later hearing that he had just that day gotten out of the military. The detective, thinking he was with me, turned to him.

There I was, wearing my gun, and the detective talking to that Negro with his back to me. Today I believe that Allah was with me even then. I didn't try to shoot him. And that saved my life.

I remember that his name was Detective Slack.

I raised my arm, and motioned to him, "Here, take my gun."

I saw his face when he took it. He was shocked. Because of the sudden appearance of the other Negro, he had never thought about a gun. It really moved him that I hadn't tried to kill him.

Then, holding my gun in his hand, he signaled. And out from where they had been concealed walked two other detectives. They'd had me covered. One false move, I'd have been dead.

I was going to have a long time in prison to think about that.

If I hadn't been arrested right when I was, I could have been dead another way. Sophia's husband's friend had told her husband about me. And the husband had arrived that morning, and had gone to the apartment with a gun, looking for me. He was at the apartment just about when they took me to the precinct.

The detectives grilled me. They didn't beat me. They didn't even put a finger on me. And I knew it was because I hadn't tried to kill the detective.

They got my address from some papers they found on me. The girls soon were picked up. Shorty was pulled right off the bandstand that night. The girls also had implicated Rudy. To this day, I have always marveled at how Rudy, somehow, got the word, and I know he must have caught the first thing smoking out of Boston, and he got away. They never got him.

I have thought a thousand times, I guess, about how I so narrowly escaped death twice that day. That's why I believe that everything is written.

The cops found the apartment loaded with evidence—fur coats, some jewelry, other small stuff—plus the tools of our trade. A jimmy, a lockpick, glass cutters, screwdrivers, pencil-beam flashlights, false keys . . . and my small arsenal of guns.

The girls got low bail. They were still white—burglars or not. Their worst crime was their involvement with Negroes. But Shorty and I had bail set at $10,000 each, which they knew we were nowhere near able to raise.

The social workers worked on us. White women in league with Negroes was their main obsession. The girls weren't so-called "tramps," or "trash," they were well-to-do upper-middle-class whites. That bothered the social workers and the forces of the law more than anything else.

How, where, when, had I met them? Did we sleep together? Nobody wanted to know anything at all about the robberies. All they could see was that we had taken the white man's women.

I just looked at the social workers: "Now, what do *you* think?"

Even the court clerks and the bailiffs: "Nice white girls . . . goddam niggers—" It was the same even from our court-appointed lawyers as we sat down, under guard, at a table, as our hearing assembled. Before the judge entered, I said to one lawyer, "We seem to be getting sentenced because of those girls." He got red from the neck up and shuffled his papers: "You had no business with white girls!"

Later, when I had learned the full truth about the white man, I reflected many times that the average burglary sentence for a first offender, as we all were, was about two years. But we weren't going to get the average—not for *our* crime.

I want to say before I go on that I have never previously told anyone my sordid past in detail. I haven't done it now to sound as though I might be proud of how bad, how evil, I was.

But people are always speculating—why am I as I am? To understand that of any person, his whole life, from birth, must be reviewed. All of our experiences fuse into our personality. Everything that ever happened to us is an ingredient.

Today, when everything that I do has an urgency, I would not spend one hour in the preparation of a book which had the ambition to perhaps titillate some readers. But I am spending many hours because the full story is the best way that I know to have it seen, and understood, that I had sunk to the very bottom of the American white man's society when—soon now, in prison—I found Allah and the religion of Islam and it completely transformed my life.

CHAPTER TEN

SATAN

Shorty didn't know what the word "concurrently" meant.

Somehow, Lansing-to-Boston bus fare had been scraped up by Shorty's old mother. "Son, read the Book of Revelations and pray to God!" she had kept telling Shorty, visiting him, and once me, while we awaited our sentencing. Shorty had read the Bible's Revelation pages; he had actually gotten down on his knees, praying like some Negro Baptist deacon.

Then we were looking up at the judge in Middlesex County Court. (Our, I think, fourteen counts of crime were committed in that county.) Shorty's mother was sitting, sobbing with her head bowing up and down to her Jesus, over near Ella and Reginald. Shorty was the first of us called to stand up.

"Count one, eight to ten years—

"Count two, eight to ten years—

"Count three . . ."

And, finally, "The sentences to run concurrently."

Shorty, sweating so hard that his black face looked as though it had been greased, and not understanding the word "concurrently," had counted in his head to probably over a hundred years; he cried out, he began slumping. The bailiffs had to catch and support him.

In eight to ten seconds, Shorty had turned as atheist as I had been to start with.

I got ten years.

The girls got one to five years, in the Women's Reformatory at Framingham, Massachusetts.

154

This was in February, 1946. I wasn't quite twenty-one. I had not even started shaving.

They took Shorty and me, handcuffed together, to the Charlestown State Prison.

I can't remember any of my prison numbers. That seems surprising, even after the dozen years since I have been out of prison. Because your number in prison became part of you. You never heard your name, only your number. On all of your clothing, every item, was your number, stenciled. It grew stenciled on your brain.

Any person who claims to have deep feeling for other human beings should think a long, long time before he votes to have other men kept behind bars—caged. I am not saying there shouldn't be prisons, but there shouldn't be bars. Behind bars, a man never reforms. He will never forget. He never will get completely over the memory of the bars.

After he gets out, his mind tries to erase the experience, but he can't. I've talked with numerous former convicts. It has been very interesting to me to find that all of our minds had blotted away many details of years in prison. But in every case, he will tell you that he can't forget those bars.

As a "fish" (prison slang for a new inmate) at Charlestown, I was physically miserable and as evil-tempered as a snake, being suddenly without drugs. The cells didn't have running water. The prison had been built in 1805—in Napoleon's day—and was even styled after the Bastille. In the dirty, cramped cell, I could lie on my cot and touch both walls. The toilet was a covered pail; I don't care how strong you are, you can't stand having to smell a whole cell row of defecation.

The prison psychologist interviewed me and he got called every filthy name I could think of, and the prison chaplain got called worse. My first letter, I remember, was from my religious brother Philbert in Detroit, telling me his "holiness" church was going to pray for me. I scrawled him a reply I'm ashamed to think of today.

Ella was my first visitor. I remember seeing her catch herself, then try to smile at me, now in the faded dungarees stenciled with my number. Neither of us could find much to say, until I wished she hadn't come at all. The guards with guns watched about fifty convicts and visitors. I have heard scores of new prisoners swearing back in their cells that when free their first act would be to waylay those visiting-room guards. Hatred often focused on them.

I first got high in Charlestown on nutmeg. My cellmate was among at least a hundred nutmeg men who, for money or cigarettes, bought from kitchen-worker inmates penny matchboxes full of stolen nutmeg. I grabbed a box as though it were a pound of heavy drugs. Stirred into a glass of cold water, a penny matchbox full of nutmeg had the kick of three or four reefers.

With some money sent by Ella, I was finally able to buy stuff for better highs from guards in the prison. I got reefers, Nembutal, and benzedrine. Smuggling to prisoners was the guards' sideline; every prison's inmates know that's how guards make most of their living.

I served a total of seven years in prison. Now, when I try to separate that first year-plus that I spent at Charlestown, it runs all together in a memory of nutmeg and the other semi-drugs, of cursing guards, throwing things out of my cell, balking in the lines, dropping my tray in the dining hall, refusing to answer my number—claiming I forgot it—and things like that.

I preferred the solitary that this behavior brought me. I would pace for hours like a caged leopard, viciously cursing aloud to myself. And my favorite targets were the Bible and God. But there was a legal limit to how much time one could be kept in solitary. Eventually, the men in the cellblock had a name for me: "Satan." Because of my antireligious attitude.

The first man I met in prison who made any positive impression on me whatever was a fellow inmate, "Bimbi." I met him in 1947, at Charlestown. He was a light, kind of red-complexioned Negro, as I was; about my height, and he had freckles. Bimbi, an old-time burglar, had been in many prisons. In the license plate shop where our gang worked, he operated the machine that stamped out the numbers. I was along the conveyor belt where the numbers were painted.

Bimbi was the first Negro convict I'd known who didn't respond to "What'cha know, Daddy?" Often, after we had done our day's license plate quota, we would sit around, perhaps fifteen of us, and listen to Bimbi. Normally, white prisoners wouldn't think of listening to Negro prisoners' opinions on anything, but guards, even, would wander over close to hear Bimbi on any subject.

He would have a cluster of people riveted, often on odd subjects you never would think of. He would prove to us, dipping into the science of human behavior, that the only difference between us and outside people was that we had been caught. He liked to talk about historical events and figures. When he talked about the history of Concord, where I was to be transferred later, you would have thought he was hired by the Chamber of Commerce, and I wasn't the first inmate who had never heard of Thoreau until Bimbi expounded upon him. Bimbi was known as the library's best customer. What fascinated me with him most of all was that he was the first man I had ever seen command total respect . . . with his words.

Bimbi seldom said much to me; he was gruff to individuals, but I sensed he liked me. What made me seek his friendship was when I heard him discuss religion. I considered myself beyond atheism—I was Satan. But Bimbi put the atheist philosophy in a framework, so to speak. That ended my vicious cursing attacks. My approach sounded so weak alongside his, and he never used a foul word.

Out of the blue one day, Bimbi told me flatly, as was his way, that I had some brains, if I'd use them. I had wanted his friendship, not that kind of advice. I might have cursed another convict, but nobody cursed Bimbi. He told me I should take advantage of the prison correspondence courses and the library.

When I had finished the eighth grade back in Mason, Michigan, that was the last time I'd thought of studying anything that didn't have some hustle purpose. And the streets had erased everything I'd ever learned in school; I didn't know a verb from a house. My sister Hilda had written a suggestion that, if possible in prison, I should study English and penmanship; she had barely been able to read a couple of picture postcards I had sent her when I was selling reefers on the road.

So, feeling I had time on my hands, I did begin a correspondence course in English. When the mimeographed listings of available books passed from cell to cell, I would put my number next to titles that appealed to me which weren't already taken.

Through the correspondence exercises and lessons, some of the mechanics of grammar gradually began to come back to me.

After about a year, I guess, I could write a decent and legible letter. About then, too, influenced by having heard Bimbi often explain word derivations, I quietly started another correspondence course—in Latin.

Under Bimbi's tutelage, too, I had gotten myself some little cellblock swindles going. For packs of cigarettes, I beat just about anyone at dominoes. I always had several cartons of cigarettes in my cell; they were, in prison, nearly as valuable a medium of exchange as money. I booked cigarette and money bets on fights and ball games. I'll never forget the prison sensation created that day in April, 1947, when Jackie Robinson was brought up to play with the Brooklyn Dodgers. Jackie Robinson had, then, his most fanatic fan in me. When he played, my ear was glued to the radio, and no game ended without my refiguring his average up through his last turn at bat.

One day in 1948, after I had been transferred to Concord Prison, my brother Philbert, who was forever joining something, wrote me this time that he had discovered the "natural religion for the black man." He belonged now, he said, to something called "the Nation of Islam." He said I should "pray to Allah for deliverance." I wrote Philbert a letter which, although in improved English, was worse than my earlier reply to his news that I was being prayed for by his "holiness" church.

When a letter from Reginald arrived, I never dreamed of associating the two letters, although I knew that Reginald had been spending a lot of time with Wilfred, Hilda, and Philbert in Detroit. Reginald's letter was newsy, and also it contained this instruction: "Malcolm, don't eat any more pork, and don't smoke any more cigarettes. I'll show you how to get out of prison."

My automatic response was to think he had come upon some way I could work a hype on the penal authorities. I went to sleep—and woke up—trying to figure what kind of a hype it could be. Something psychological, such as my act with the New York draft board? Could I, after going without pork and smoking no cigarettes for a while, claim some physical trouble that could bring about my release?

"Get out of prison." The words hung in the air around me, I wanted out so badly.

I wanted, in the worst way, to consult with Bimbi about it. But something big, instinct said, you spilled to nobody.

Quitting cigarettes wasn't going to be too difficult. I had been conditioned by days in solitary without cigarettes. Whatever this chance was, I wasn't going to fluff it. After I read that letter, I finished the pack I then had open. I haven't smoked another cigarette to this day, since 1948.

It was about three or four days later when pork was served for the noon meal.

I wasn't even thinking about pork when I took my seat at the long table. Sit-grab-gobble-stand-file out; that was the Emily Post in prison eating. When the meat platter was passed to me, I didn't even know what the meat was; usually, you couldn't tell, anyway—but it was suddenly as though *don't eat any more pork* flashed on a screen before me.

I hesitated, with the platter in mid-air; then I passed it along to the inmate waiting next to me. He began serving himself; abruptly, he stopped. I remember him turning, looking surprised at me.

I said to him, "I don't eat pork."

The platter then kept on down the table.

It was the funniest thing, the reaction, and the way that it spread. In prison, where so little breaks the monotonous routine, the smallest thing causes a commotion of talk. It was being mentioned all over the cell block by night that Satan didn't eat pork.

It made me very proud, in some odd way. One of the universal images of the Negro, in prison and out, was that he couldn't do without pork. It made me feel good to see that my not eating it had especially startled the white convicts.

Later I would learn, when I had read and studied Islam a good deal, that, unconsciously, my first pre-Islamic submission had been manifested. I had experienced, for the first time, the Muslim teaching, "If you will take one step toward Allah—Allah will take two steps toward you."

My brothers and sisters in Detroit and Chicago had all become converted to what they were being taught was the "natural religion for the black man" of which Philbert had written to me. They all prayed for me to become converted while I was in prison. But after Philbert reported my vicious reply, they discussed what was the best thing to do. They had decided that Reginald, the latest convert, the one to whom I felt closest, would best know how to approach me, since he knew me so well in the street life.

Independently of all this, my sister Ella had been steadily working to get me transferred to the Norfolk, Massachusetts, Prison Colony, which was an experimental rehabilitation jail. In other prisons, convicts often said that if you had the right money, or connections, you could get transferred to this Colony whose penal policies sounded almost too good to be true. Somehow, Ella's efforts in my behalf were successful in late 1948, and I was transferred to Norfolk.

The Colony was, comparatively, a heaven, in many respects. It had flushing toilets; there were no bars, only walls—and within the walls, you had far more freedom. There was plenty of fresh air to breathe; it was not in a city.

There were twenty-four "house" units, fifty men living in each unit, if memory serves me correctly. This would mean that the Colony had a total of around 1200 inmates. Each "house" had three floors and, greatest blessing of all, each inmate had his own room.

About fifteen per cent of the inmates were Negroes, distributed about five to nine Negroes in each house.

Norfolk Prison Colony represented the most enlightened form of prison that I have ever heard of. In place of the atmosphere of malicious gossip, perversion, grafting, hateful guards, there was more relative "culture," as "culture" is interpreted in prisons. A high percentage of the Norfolk Prison Colony inmates went in for "intellectual" things, group discussions, debates, and such. Instructors for the educational rehabilitation programs came from Harvard, Boston University, and other educational institutions in the area. The visiting rules, far more lenient than other prisons', permitted visitors almost every day, and allowed them to stay two hours. You had your choice of sitting alongside your visitor, or facing each other.

Norfolk Prison Colony's library was one of its outstanding features. A millionaire named Parkhurst had willed his library there; he had probably been interested in the rehabilitation program. History and religions were his special interests. Thousands of his books were on the shelves, and in the back were boxes and crates full, for which there wasn't space on the shelves. At Norfolk, we could actually go into the library, with permission—walk up and down the shelves, pick books. There were hundreds of old volumes, some of them probably quite rare. I read aimlessly, until I learned to read selectively, with a purpose.

I hadn't heard from Reginald in a good while after I got to Norfolk Prison Colony. But I had come in there not smoking cigarettes, or eating pork when it was served. That caused a bit of eyebrow-raising. Then a letter from Reginald telling me when he was coming to see me. By the time he came, I was really keyed up to hear the hype he was going to explain.

Reginald knew how my street-hustler mind operated. That's why his approach was so effective.

He had always dressed well, and now, when he came to visit, was carefully groomed. I was aching with wanting the "no pork and cigarettes" riddle answered. But he talked about the family, what was happening in Detroit, Harlem the last time he was there. I have never pushed anyone to tell me anything before he is ready. The offhand way Reginald talked and acted made me know that something big was coming.

He said, finally, as though it had just happened to come into his mind, "Malcolm, if a man knew every imaginable thing that there is to know, who would he be?"

Back in Harlem, he had often liked to get at something through this kind of indirection. It had often irritated me, because my way had always been direct. I looked at him. "Well, he would have to be some kind of a god—"

Reginald said, "There's a *man* who knows everything."

I asked, "Who is that?"

"God is a man," Reginald said. "His real name is Allah."

Allah. That word came back to me from Philbert's letter; it was my first hint of any connection. But Reginald went on. He said that God had 360 degrees of knowledge. He said that 360 degrees represented "the sum total of knowledge."

To say I was confused is an understatement. I don't have to remind you of the background against which I sat hearing my brother Reginald talk like this. I just listened, knowing he was taking his time in putting me onto something. And if somebody is trying to put you onto something, you need to listen.

"The devil has only thirty-three degrees of knowledge— known as Masonry," Reginald said. I can so specifically remember the exact phrases since, later, I was going to teach them so many times to others. "The devil uses his Masonry to rule other people."

He told me that this God had come to America, and that he had made himself known to a man named Elijah—"a black man, just like us." This God had let Elijah know, Reginald said, that the devil's "time was up."

I didn't know what to think. I just listened.

"The devil is also a man," Reginald said.

"What do you mean?"

With a slight movement of his head, Reginald indicated some white inmates and their visitors talking, as we were, across the room.

"Them," he said. "The white man is the devil."

He told me that all whites knew they were devils—"especially Masons."

I never will forget: my mind was involuntarily flashing across the entire spectrum of white people I had ever known; and for some reason it stopped upon Hymie, the Jew, who had been so good to me.

Reginald, a couple of times, had gone out with me to that Long Island bootlegging operation to buy and bottle up the bootleg liquor for Hymie.

I said, "Without any exception?"

"Without any exception."

"What about Hymie?"

"What is it if I let you make five hundred dollars to let me make ten thousand?"

After Reginald left, I thought. I thought. Thought.

I couldn't make of it head, or tail, or middle.

The white people I had known marched before my mind's eye. From the start of my life. The state white people always in our house after the other whites I didn't know had killed my father . . . the white people who kept calling my mother "crazy" to her face and before me and my brothers and sisters, until she finally was taken off by white people to the Kalamazoo asylum . . . the white judge and others who had split up the children . . . the Swerlins, the other whites around Mason . . . white youngsters I was in school there with, and the teachers—the one who told me in the eighth grade to "be a carpenter" because thinking of being a lawyer was foolish for a Negro. . . .

My head swam with the parading faces of white people. The ones in Boston, in the white-only dances at the Roseland Ballroom where I shined their shoes . . . at the Parker House where I took their dirty plates back to the kitchen . . . the railroad crewmen and passengers . . . Sophia. . . .

The whites in New York City—the cops, the white criminals I'd dealt with . . . the whites who piled into the Negro speakeasies for a taste of Negro *soul* . . . the white women who wanted Negro men . . . the men I'd steered to the black "specialty sex" they wanted. . . .

The fence back in Boston, and his ex-con representative . . . Boston cops . . . Sophia's husband's friend, and her husband, whom I'd never seen, but knew so much about . . . Sophia's sister . . . the Jew jeweler who'd helped trap me . . . the social workers . . . the Middlesex County Court people . . . the judge who gave me ten years . . . the prisoners I'd known, the guards and the officials. . . .

A celebrity among the Norfolk Prison Colony inmates was a rich, older fellow, a paralytic, called John. He had killed his baby, one of those "mercy" killings. He was a proud, big-shot type, always reminding everyone that he was a 33rd-degree Mason, and what powers Masons had—that only Masons ever had been U.S. Presidents, that Masons in distress could secretly signal to judges and other Masons in powerful positions.

I kept thinking about what Reginald had said. I wanted to test it with John. He worked in a soft job in the prison's school. I went over there.

"John," I said, "how many degrees in a circle?"

He said, "Three hundred and sixty."

I drew a square. "How many degrees in that?" He said three hundred and sixty.

I asked him was three hundred and sixty degrees, then, the maximum of degrees in anything?

He said "Yes."

I said, "Well, why is it that Masons go only to thirty-three degrees?"

He had no satisfactory answer. But for me, the answer was

that Masonry, actually, is only thirty-three degrees of the religion of Islam, which is the full projection, forever denied to Masons, although they know it exists.

Reginald, when he came to visit me again in a few days, could gauge from my attitude the effect that his talking had had upon me. He seemed very pleased. Then, very seriously, he talked for two solid hours about "the devil white man" and "the brainwashed black man."

When Reginald left, he left me rocking with some of the first serious thoughts I had ever had in my life: that the white man was fast losing his power to oppress and exploit the dark world; that the dark world was starting to rise to rule the world again, as it had before; that the white man's world was on the way down, it was on the way out.

"You don't even know who you are," Reginald had said. "You don't even know, the white devil has hidden it from you, that you are of a race of people of ancient civilizations, and riches in gold and kings. You don't even know your true family name, you wouldn't recognize your true language if you heard it. You have been cut off by the devil white man from all true knowledge of your own kind. You have been a victim of the evil of the devil white man ever since he murdered and raped and stole you from your native land in the seeds of your forefathers. . . ."

I began to receive at least two letters every day from my brothers and sisters in Detroit. My oldest brother, Wilfred, wrote, and his first wife, Bertha, the mother of his two children (since her death, Wilfred has met and married his present wife, Ruth). Philbert wrote, and my sister Hilda. And Reginald visited, staying in Boston awhile before he went back to Detroit, where he had been the most recent of them to be converted. They were all Muslims, followers of a man they described to me as "The Honorable Elijah Muhammad," a small, gentle man, whom they sometimes referred to as "The Messenger of Allah." He was, they said, "a black man, like us." He had been born in America on a farm in Georgia. He had moved with his family to Detroit, and there had met a Mr. Wallace D. Fard who he claimed was "God in person." Mr. Wallace D. Fard had given to Elijah Muhammad Allah's message for the black people who were "the Lost-Found Nation of Islam here in this wilderness of North America."

All of them urged me to "accept the teachings of The Honorable Elijah Muhammad." Reginald explained that pork was not eaten by those who worshiped in the religion of Islam, and not smoking cigarettes was a rule of the followers of The Honorable Elijah Muhammad, because they did not take injurious things such as narcotics, tobacco, or liquor into their bodies. Over and over, I read, and heard, "The key to a Muslim is submission, the attunement of one toward Allah."

And what they termed "the true knowledge of the black man" that was possessed by the followers of The Honorable Elijah Muhammad was given shape for me in their lengthy letters, sometimes containing printed literature.

"The true knowledge," reconstructed much more briefly than I received it, was that history had been "whitened" in the white man's history books, and that the black man had been "brainwashed for hundreds of years." Original Man was black, in the continent called Africa where the human race had emerged on the planet Earth.

The black man, original man, built great empires and civilizations and cultures while the white man was still living on all fours in caves. "The devil white man," down through history, out of his devilish nature, had pillaged, murdered, raped, and exploited every race of man not white.

Human history's greatest crime was the traffic in black flesh when the devil white man went into Africa and murdered and kidnapped to bring to the West in chains, in slave ships, millions of black men, women, and children, who were worked and beaten and tortured as slaves.

The devil white man cut these black people off from all knowledge of their own kind, and cut them off from any knowledge of their own language, religion, and past culture, until the black man in America was the earth's only race of people who had absolutely no knowledge of his true identity.

In one generation, the black slave women in America had been raped by the slavemaster white man until there had begun to emerge a homemade, handmade, brainwashed race that was no longer even of its true color, that no longer even knew its true family names. The slavemaster forced his family name upon this rape-mixed race, which the slavemaster began to call "the Negro."

This "Negro" was taught of his native Africa that it was peopled by heathen, black savages, swinging like monkeys from trees. This "Negro" accepted this along with every other teaching of the slavemaster that was designed to make him accept and obey and worship the white man.

And where the religion of every other people on earth taught its believers of a God with whom they could identify, a God who at least looked like one of their own kind, the slavemaster injected his Christian religion into this "Negro." This "Negro" was taught to worship an alien God having the same blond hair, pale skin, and blue eyes as the slavemaster.

This religion taught the "Negro" that black was a curse. It taught him to hate everything black, including himself. It taught him that everything white was good, to be admired, respected, and loved. It brainwashed this "Negro" to think he was superior if his complexion showed more of the white pollution of the slavemaster. This white man's Christian religion further deceived and brainwashed this "Negro" to always turn the other cheek, and grin, and scrape, and bow, and be humble, and to sing, and to pray, and to take whatever was dished out by the devilish white man; and to look for his pie in the sky, and for his heaven in the hereafter, while right here on earth the slavemaster white man enjoyed *his* heaven.

Many a time, I have looked back, trying to assess, just for myself, my first reactions to all this. Every instinct of the ghetto jungle streets, every hustling fox and criminal wolf instinct in me, which would have scoffed at and rejected anything else, was struck numb. It was as though all of that life merely was back there, without any remaining effect, or influence. I remember how, some time later, reading the Bible in the Norfolk Prison Colony library, I came upon, then I read, over and over, how Paul on the road to Damascus, upon hearing the voice of Christ, was so smitten that he was knocked off his horse, in a daze. I do not now, and I did not then, liken myself to Paul. But I do understand his experience.

I have since learned—helping me to understand what then began to happen within me—that the truth can be quickly received, or received at all, only by the sinner who knows and admits that he is guilty of having sinned much. Stated another way: only guilt admitted accepts truth. The Bible again: the one people whom Jesus could not help were the Pharisees; they didn't feel they needed any help.

The very enormity of my previous life's guilt prepared me to accept the truth.

Not for weeks yet would I deal with the direct, personal application to myself, as a black man, of the truth. It still was like a blinding light.

Reginald left Boston and went back to Detroit. I would sit in my room and stare. At the dining-room table, I would hardly eat, only drink the water. I nearly starved. Fellow inmates, concerned, and guards, apprehensive, asked what was wrong with me. It was suggested that I visit the doctor, and I didn't. The doctor, advised, visited me. I don't know what his diagnosis was, probably that I was working on some act.

I was going through the hardest thing, also the greatest thing, for any human being to do; to accept that which is already within you, and around you.

I learned later that my brothers and sisters in Detroit put together the money for my sister Hilda to come and visit me. She told me that when The Honorable Elijah Muhammad was in Detroit, he would stay as a guest at my brother Wilfred's home, which was on McKay Street. Hilda kept urging me to write to Mr. Muhammad. He understood what it was to be in the white man's prison, she said, because he, himself, had not long before gotten out of the federal prison at Milan, Michigan, where he had served five years for evading the draft.

Hilda said that The Honorable Elijah Muhammad came to Detroit to reorganize his Temple Number One, which had become disorganized during his prison time; but he lived in Chicago, where he was organizing and building his Temple Number Two.

It was Hilda who said to me, "Would you like to hear how the white man came to this planet Earth?"

And she told me that key lesson of Mr. Elijah Muhammad's teachings, which I later learned was the demonology that every religion has, called "Yacub's History." Elijah Muhammad teaches his followers that, first, the moon separated from the earth. Then, the first humans, Original Man, were a black people. They founded the Holy City Mecca.

Among this black race were twenty-four wise scientists. One of the scientists, at odds with the rest, created the especially strong black tribe of Shabazz, from which America's Negroes, so-called, descend.

About sixty-six hundred years ago, when seventy per cent of the people were satisfied, and thirty per cent were dissatisfied, among the dissatisfied was born a "Mr. Yacub." He was born to create trouble, to break the peace, and to kill. His head was unusually large. When he was four years old, he began school. At the age of eighteen, Yacub had finished all of his nation's colleges and universities. He was known as "the big-head scientist." Among many other things, he had learned how to breed races scientifically.

This big-head scientist, Mr. Yacub, began preaching in the streets of Mecca, making such hosts of converts that the authorities, increasingly concerned, finally exiled him with 59,999 followers to the island of Patmos—described in the Bible as the island where John received the message contained in Revelations in the New Testament.

Though he was a black man, Mr. Yacub, embittered toward Allah now, decided, as revenge, to create upon the earth a devil race—a bleached-out, white race of people.

From his studies, the big-head scientist knew that black men contained two germs, black and brown. He knew that the brown germ stayed dormant as, being the lighter of the two germs, it was the weaker. Mr. Yacub, to upset the law of nature, conceived the idea of employing what we today know as the recessive genes structure, to separate from each other the two germs, black and brown, and then grafting the brown germ to progressively lighter, weaker stages. The humans resulting, he knew, would be, as they became lighter, and weaker, progressively also more susceptible to wickedness and evil. And in this way finally he would achieve the intended bleached-out white race of devils.

He knew that it would take him several total color-change stages to get from black to white. Mr. Yacub began his work by setting up a eugenics law on the island of Patmos.

Among Mr. Yacub's 59,999 all-black followers, every third

or so child that was born would show some trace of brown. As these became adult, only brown and brown, or black and brown, were permitted to marry. As their children were born, Mr. Yacub's law dictated that, if a black child, the attending nurse, or midwife, should stick a needle into its brain and give the body to cremators. The mothers were told it had been an "angel baby," which had gone to heaven, to prepare a place for her.

But a brown child's mother was told to take very good care of it.

Others, assistants, were trained by Mr. Yacub to continue his objective. Mr. Yacub, when he died on the island at the age of one hundred and fifty-two, had left laws, and rules, for them to follow. According to the teachings of Mr. Elijah Muhammad, Mr. Yacub, except in his mind, never saw the bleached-out devil race that his procedures and laws and rules created.

A two-hundred-year span was needed to eliminate on the island of Patmos all of the black people—until only brown people remained.

The next two hundred years were needed to create from the brown race the red race—with no more browns left on the island.

In another two hundred years, from the red race was created the yellow race.

Two hundred years later—the white race had at last been created.

On the island of Patmos was nothing but these blond, pale-skinned, cold-blue-eyed devils—savages, nude and shameless; hairy, like animals, they walked on all fours and they lived in trees.

Six hundred more years passed before this race of people returned to the mainland, among the natural black people.

Mr. Elijah Muhammad teaches his followers that within six months' time, through telling lies that set the black men fighting among each other, this devil race had turned what had been a peaceful heaven on earth into a hell torn by quarreling and fighting.

But finally the original black people recognized that their sudden troubles stemmed from this devil white race that Mr. Yacub had made. They rounded them up, put them in chains. With little aprons to cover their nakedness, this devil race was marched off across the Arabian desert to the caves of Europe.

The lambskin and the cable-tow used in Masonry today are symbolic of how the nakedness of the white man was covered when he was chained and driven across the hot sand.

Mr. Elijah Muhammad further teaches that the white devil race in Europe's caves was savage. The animals tried to kill him. He climbed trees outside his cave, made clubs, trying to protect his family from the wild beasts outside trying to get in.

When this devil race had spent two thousand years in the caves, Allah raised up Moses to civilize them, and bring them out of the caves. It was written that this devil white race would rule the world for six thousand years.

The Books of Moses are missing. That's why it is not known that he was in the caves.

When Moses arrived, the first of these devils to accept his teachings, the first he led out, were those we call today the Jews.

According to the teachings of this "Yacub's History," when the Bible says "Moses lifted up the serpent in the wilderness," that serpent is symbolic of the devil white race Moses lifted up out of the caves of Europe, teaching them civilization.

It was written that after Yacub's bleached white race had ruled the world for six thousand years—down to our time—the black original race would give birth to one whose wisdom, knowledge, and power would be infinite.

It was written that some of the original black people should be brought as slaves to North America—to learn to better understand, at first hand, the white devil's true nature, in modern times.

Elijah Muhammad teaches that the greatest and mightiest God who appeared on the earth was Master W. D. Fard. He came from the East to the West, appearing in North America at a time when the history and the prophecy that is written was coming to realization, as the non-white people all over the world began to rise, and as the devil white civilization, condemned by Allah, was, through its devilish nature, destroying itself.

Master W. D. Fard was half black and half white. He was made in this way to enable him to be accepted by the black people in America, and to lead them, while at the same time he was enabled to move undiscovered among the white people, so that he could understand and judge the enemy of the blacks.

Master W. D. Fard, in 1931, posing as a seller of silks, met, in Detroit, Michigan, Elijah Muhammad. Master W. D. Fard gave to Elijah Muhammad Allah's message, and Allah's divine guidance, to save the Lost-Found Nation of Islam, the so-called Negroes, here in "this wilderness of North America."

When my sister, Hilda, had finished telling me this "Yacub's History," she left. I don't know if I was able to open my mouth and say good-bye.

I was to learn later that Elijah Muhammad's tales, like this one of "Yacub," infuriated the Muslims of the East. While at Mecca, I reminded them that it was their fault, since they themselves hadn't done enough to make real Islam known in the West. Their silence left a vacuum into which any religious faker could step and mislead our people.

CHAPTER ELEVEN

SAVED

I did write to Elijah Muhammad. He lived in Chicago at that time, at 6116 South Michigan Avenue. At least twenty-five times I must have written that first one-page letter to him, over and over. I was trying to make it both legible and understandable. I practically couldn't read my handwriting myself; it shames even to remember it. My spelling and my grammar were as bad, if not worse. Anyway, as well as I could express it, I said I had been told about him by my brothers and sisters, and I apologized for my poor letter.

Mr. Muhammad sent me a typed reply. It had an all but electrical effect upon me to see the signature of the "Messenger of Allah." After he welcomed me into the "true knowledge," he gave me something to think about. The black prisoner, he said, symbolized white society's crime of keeping black men oppressed and deprived and ignorant, and unable to get decent jobs, turning them into criminals.

He told me to have courage. He even enclosed some money for me, a five-dollar bill. Mr. Muhammad sends money all over the country to prison inmates who write to him, probably to this day.

Regularly my family wrote to me, "Turn to Allah . . . pray to the East."

The hardest test I ever faced in my life was praying. You understand. My comprehending, my believing the teachings of Mr. Muhammad had only required my mind's saying to me, "That's right!" or "I never thought of that."

But bending my knees to pray—that *act*—well, that took me a week.

You know what my life had been. Picking a lock to rob someone's house was the only way my knees had ever been bent before.

I had to force myself to bend my knees. And waves of shame and embarrassment would force me back up.

For evil to bend its knees, admitting its guilt, to implore the forgiveness of God, is the hardest thing in the world. It's easy for me to see and to say that now. But then, when I was the personification of evil, I was going through it. Again, again, I would force myself back down into the praying-to-Allah posture. When finally I was able to make myself stay down—I didn't know what to say to Allah.

For the next years, I was the nearest thing to a hermit in the Norfolk Prison Colony. I never have been more busy in my life. I still marvel at how swiftly my previous life's thinking pattern slid away from me, like snow off a roof. It is as though someone else I knew of had lived by hustling and crime. I would be startled to catch myself thinking in a remote way of my earlier self as another person.

The things I felt, I was pitifully unable to express in the one-page letter that went every day to Mr. Elijah Muhammad. And I wrote at least one more daily letter, replying to one of my brothers and sisters. Every letter I received from them added something to my knowledge of the teachings of Mr. Muhammad. I would sit for long periods and study his photographs.

I've never been one for inaction. Everything I've ever felt strongly about, I've done something about. I guess that's why, unable to do anything else, I soon began writing to people I had known in the hustling world, such as Sammy the Pimp, John Hughes, the gambling-house owner, the thief Jumpsteady, and several dope peddlers. I wrote them all about Allah and Islam and Mr. Elijah Muhammad. I had no idea where most of them lived. I addressed their letters in care of the Harlem or Roxbury bars and clubs where I'd known them.

I never got a single reply. The average hustler and criminal was too uneducated to write a letter. I have known many slick, sharp-looking hustlers, who would have you think they had an interest in Wall Street; privately, they would get someone else to read a letter if they received one. Besides, neither would I have replied to anyone writing me something as wild as "the white man is the devil."

What certainly went on the Harlem and Roxbury wires was that Detroit Red was going crazy in stir, or else he was trying some hype to shake up the warden's office.

During the years that I stayed in the Norfolk Prison Colony, never did any official directly say anything to me about those letters, although, of course, they all passed through the prison censorship. I'm sure, however, they monitored what I wrote to add to the files which every state and federal prison keeps on the conversion of Negro inmates by the teachings of Mr. Elijah Muhammad.

But at that time, I felt that the real reason was that the white man knew that he was the devil.

Later on, I even wrote to the Mayor of Boston, to the Governor of Massachusetts, and to Harry S Truman. They never answered; they probably never even saw my letters. I hand-scratched to them how the white man's society was responsible for the black man's condition in this wilderness of North America.

It was because of my letters that I happened to stumble upon starting to acquire some kind of a homemade education.

I became increasingly frustrated at not being able to express what I wanted to convey in letters that I wrote, especially those to Mr. Elijah Muhammad. In the street, I had been the most articulate hustler out there—I had commanded attention when I said something. But now, trying to write simple English, I not only wasn't articulate, I wasn't even functional. How would I sound writing in slang, the way I would *say* it, something such as, "Look, daddy, let me pull your coat about a cat, Elijah Muhammad—"

Many who today hear me somewhere in person, or on television, or those who read something I've said, will think I went to school far beyond the eighth grade. This impression is due entirely to my prison studies.

It had really begun back in the Charlestown Prison, when Bimbi first made me feel envy of his stock of knowledge. Bimbi had always taken charge of any conversation he was in, and I had tried to emulate him. But every book I picked up had few sentences which didn't contain anywhere from one to nearly all of the words that might as well have been in Chinese. When I just skipped those words, of course, I really ended up with little idea of what the book said. So I had come to the Norfolk Prison Colony still going through only book-reading motions. Pretty soon, I would have quit even these motions, unless I had received the motivation that I did.

I saw that the best thing I could do was get hold of a dictionary—to study, to learn some words. I was lucky enough to reason also that I should try to improve my penmanship. It was sad. I couldn't even write in a straight line. It was both ideas together that moved me to request a dictionary along with some tablets and pencils from the Norfolk Prison Colony school.

I spent two days just riffling uncertainly through the dictionary's pages. I'd never realized so many words existed! I didn't know *which* words I needed to learn. Finally, just to start some kind of action, I began copying.

In my slow, painstaking, ragged handwriting, I copied into my tablet everything printed on that first page, down to the punctuation marks.

I believe it took me a day. Then, aloud, I read back, to myself, everything I'd written on the tablet. Over and over, aloud, to myself, I read my own handwriting.

I woke up the next morning, thinking about those words—immensely proud to realize that not only had I written so much at one time, but I'd written words that I never knew were in the world. Moreover, with a little effort, I also could remember what many of these words meant. I reviewed the words whose meanings I didn't remember. Funny thing, from the dictionary first page right now, that "aardvark" springs to my mind. The dictionary had a picture of it, a long-tailed, long-eared, burrowing African mammal, which lives off termites caught by sticking out its tongue as an anteater does for ants.

I was so fascinated that I went on—I copied the dictionary's next page. And the same experience came when I studied that. With every succeeding page, I also learned of people and places and events from history. Actually the dictionary is like a miniature encyclopedia. Finally the dictionary's A section had filled a whole tablet—and I went on into the B's. That was the way I started copying what eventually became the entire dictionary. It went a lot faster after so much practice helped me to pick up handwriting speed. Between what I wrote in my tablet, and writing letters, during the rest of my time in prison I would guess I wrote a million words.

I suppose it was inevitable that as my word-base broadened, I could for the first time pick up a book and read and now begin to understand what the book was saying. Anyone who has read a great deal can imagine the new world that opened. Let me tell you something: from then until I left that prison, in every free moment I had, if I was not reading in the library, I was reading on my bunk. You couldn't have gotten me out of books with a wedge. Between Mr. Muhammad's teachings, my correspondence, my visitors—usually Ella and Reginald—and my reading of books, months passed without my even thinking about being imprisoned. In fact, up to then, I never had been so truly free in my life.

The Norfolk Prison Colony's library was in the school building. A variety of classes was taught there by instructors who came from such places as Harvard and Boston universities. The weekly debates between inmate teams were also held in the school building. You would be astonished to know how worked up convict debaters and audiences would get over subjects like "Should Babies Be Fed Milk?"

Available on the prison library's shelves were books on just about every general subject. Much of the big private collection that Parkhurst had willed to the prison was still in crates and boxes in the back of the library—thousands of old books. Some of them looked ancient: covers faded, old-time parchment-looking binding. Parkhurst, I've mentioned, seemed to have been principally interested in history and religion. He had the money and the special interest to have a lot of books that you wouldn't have in general circulation. Any college library would have been lucky to get that collection.

As you can imagine, especially in a prison where there was heavy emphasis on rehabilitation, an inmate was smiled upon if he demonstrated an unusually intense interest in books. There was a sizable number of well-read inmates, especially the popular debaters. Some were said by many to be practically walking encyclopedias. They were almost celebrities. No university would ask any student to devour literature as I did when this new world opened to me, of being able to read and *understand*.

I read more in my room than in the library itself. An inmate who was known to read a lot could check out more than the permitted maximum number of books. I preferred reading in the total isolation of my own room.

When I had progressed to really serious reading, every night at about ten P.M. I would be outraged with the "lights out." It always seemed to catch me right in the middle of something engrossing.

Fortunately, right outside my door was a corridor light that cast a glow into my room. The glow was enough to read by, once my eyes adjusted to it. So when "lights out" came, I would sit on the floor where I could continue reading in that glow.

At one-hour intervals the night guards paced past every room. Each time I heard the approaching footsteps, I jumped into bed and feigned sleep. And as soon as the guard passed, I got back out of bed onto the floor area of that light-glow, where I would read for another fifty-eight minutes—until the guard approached again. That went on until three or four every morning. Three or four hours of sleep a night was enough for me. Often in the years in the streets I had slept less than that.

The teachings of Mr. Muhammad stressed how history had been "whitened"—when white men had written history books, the black man simply had been left out. Mr. Muhammad couldn't have said anything that would have struck me much harder. I had never forgotten how when my class, me and all of those whites, had studied seventh-grade United States history back in Mason, the history of the Negro had been covered in one paragraph, and the teacher had gotten a big laugh with his joke, "Negroes' feet are so big that when they walk, they leave a hole in the ground."

This is one reason why Mr. Muhammad's teachings spread so swiftly all over the United States, among *all* Negroes, whether or not they became followers of Mr. Muhammad. The teachings ring true—to every Negro. You can hardly show me a black adult in America—or a white one, for that matter—who knows from the history books anything like the truth about the black man's role. In my own case, once I heard of the "glorious history of the black man," I took special pains to hunt in the library for books that would inform me on details about black history.

I can remember accurately the very first set of books that really impressed me. I have since bought that set of books and have it at home for my children to read as they grow up. It's called *Wonders of the World*. It's full of pictures of archeological finds, statues that depict, usually, non-European people.

I found books like Will Durant's *Story of Civilization*. I read H. G. Wells' *Outline of History*. *Souls Of Black Folk* by W. E. B. Du Bois gave me a glimpse into the black people's history before they came to this country. Carter G. Woodson's *Negro History* opened my eyes about black empires before the black slave was brought to the United States, and the early Negro struggles for freedom.

J. A. Rogers' three volumes of *Sex and Race* told about race-mixing before Christ's time; about Aesop being a black man who told fables; about Egypt's Pharaohs; about the great Coptic Christian Empires; about Ethiopia, the earth's oldest continuous black civilization, as China is the oldest continuous civilization.

Mr. Muhammad's teaching about how the white man had been created led me to *Findings In Genetics* by Gregor Mendel. (The dictionary's G section was where I had learned what "genetics" meant.) I really studied this book by the Austrian monk. Reading it over and over, especially certain sections, helped me to understand that if you started with a black man, a white man could be produced; but starting with a white man, you never could produce a black man—because the white gene is recessive. And since no one disputes that there was but one Original Man, the conclusion is clear.

During the last year or so, in the *New York Times*, Arnold Toynbee used the word "bleached" in describing the white man. (His words were: "White (i.e. bleached) human beings of North European origin. . . .") Toynbee also referred to the European geographic area as only a peninsula of Asia. He said there is no such thing as Europe. And if you look at the globe, you will see for yourself that America is only an extension of Asia. (But at the same time Toynbee is among those who have helped to bleach history. He has written that Africa was the only continent that produced no history. He won't write that again. Every day now, the truth is coming to light.)

I never will forget how shocked I was when I began reading about slavery's total horror. It made such an impact upon me that it later became one of my favorite subjects when I became a minister of Mr. Muhammad's. The world's most monstrous crime, the sin and the blood on the white man's hands, are almost impossible to believe. Books like the one by Frederick Olmstead opened my eyes to the horrors suffered when the slave was landed in the United States. The European woman, Fannie Kimball, who had married a Southern white slaveowner, described how human beings were degraded. Of course I read _Uncle Tom's Cabin._ In fact, I believe that's the only novel I have ever read since I started serious reading.

Parkhurst's collection also contained some bound pamphlets of the Abolitionist Anti-Slavery Society of New England. I read descriptions of atrocities, saw those illustrations of black slave women tied up and flogged with whips; of black mothers watching their babies being dragged off, never to be seen by their mothers again; of dogs after slaves, and of the fugitive slave catchers, evil white men with whips and clubs and chains and guns. I read about the slave preacher Nat Turner, who put the fear of God into the white slavemaster. Nat Turner wasn't going around preaching pie-in-the-sky and "non-violent" freedom for the black man. There in Virginia one night in 1831, Nat and seven other slaves started out at his master's home and through the night they went from one plantation "big house" to the next, killing, until by the next morning 57 white people were dead and Nat had about 70 slaves following him. White people, terrified for their lives, fled from their homes, locked themselves up in public buildings, hid in the woods, and some even left the state. A small army of soldiers took two months to catch and hang Nat Turner. Somewhere I have read where Nat Turner's example is said to have inspired John Brown to invade Virginia and attack Harper's Ferry nearly thirty years later, with thirteen white men and five Negroes.

I read Herodotus, "the father of History," or, rather, I read about him. And I read the histories of various nations, which opened my eyes gradually, then wider and wider, to how the whole world's white men had indeed acted like devils, pillaging and raping and bleeding and draining the whole world's non-white people. I remember, for instance, books such as Will Durant's story of Oriental civilization, and Mahatma Gandhi's accounts of the struggle to drive the British out of India.

Book after book showed me how the white man had brought upon the world's black, brown, red, and yellow peoples every variety of the sufferings of exploitation. I saw how since the sixteenth century, the so-called "Christian trader" white man began to ply the seas in his lust for Asian and African empires, and plunder, and power. I read, I saw, how the white man never has gone among the non-white peoples bearing the Cross in the true manner and spirit of Christ's teachings—meek, humble, and Christ-like.

I perceived, as I read, how the collective white man had been actually nothing but a piratical opportunist who used Faustian machinations to make his own Christianity his initial wedge in criminal conquests. First, always "religiously," he branded "heathen" and "pagan" labels upon ancient non-white cultures and civilizations. The stage thus set, he then turned upon his non-white victims his weapons of war.

I read how, entering India—half a *billion* deeply religious brown people—the British white man, by 1759, through promises, trickery and manipulations, controlled much of India through Great Britain's East India Company. The parasitical British administration kept tentacling out to half of the sub-continent. In 1857, some of the desperate people of India finally mutinied—and, excepting the African slave trade, nowhere has history recorded any more unnecessary bestial and ruthless human carnage than the British suppression of the non-white Indian people.

Over 115 million African blacks—close to the 1930's population of the United States—were murdered or enslaved during the slave trade. And I read how when the slave market was glutted, the cannibalistic white powers of Europe next carved up, as their colonies, the richest areas of the black continent. And Europe's chancelleries for the next century played a chess game of naked exploitation and power from Cape Horn to Cairo.

Ten guards and the warden couldn't have torn me out of those books. Not even Elijah Muhammad could have been more elo-quent than those books were in providing indisputable proof that the collective white man had acted like a devil in virtually every contact he had with the world's collective non-white man. I listen today to the radio, and watch television, and read the headlines about the collective white man's fear and tension concerning China. When the white man professes ignorance about why the Chinese hate him so, my mind can't help flashing back to what I read, there in prison, about how the blood forebears of this same white man raped China at a time when China was trusting and helpless. Those original white "Christian traders" sent into China millions of pounds of opium. By 1839, so many of the Chinese were addicts that China's desperate government destroyed twenty thousand chests of opium. The first Opium War was promptly declared by the white man. Imagine! Declaring *war* upon someone who objects to being narcotized! The Chinese were severely beaten, with Chinese-invented gunpowder.

The Treaty of Nanking made China pay the British white man for the destroyed opium; forced open China's major ports to British trade; forced China to abandon Hong Kong; fixed China's import tariffs so low that cheap British articles soon flooded in, maiming China's industrial development.

After a second Opium War, the Tientsin Treaties legalized the ravaging opium trade, legalized a British-French-American control of China's customs. China tried delaying that Treaty's ratification; Peking was looted and burned.

"Kill the foreign white devils!" was the 1901 Chinese war cry in the Boxer Rebellion. Losing again, this time the Chinese were driven from Peking's choicest areas. The vicious, arrogant white man put up the famous signs, "Chinese and dogs not allowed."

Red China after World War II closed its doors to the Western white world. Massive Chinese agricultural, scientific, and industrial efforts are described in a book that *Life* magazine recently published. Some observers inside Red China have reported that the world never has known such a hate-white campaign as is now going on in this non-white country where, present birth-rates continuing, in fifty more years Chinese will be half the earth's population. And it seems that some Chinese chickens will soon come home to roost, with China's recent successful nuclear tests.

Let us face reality. We can see in the United Nations a new world order being shaped, along color lines—an alliance among the non-white nations. America's U.N. Ambassador Adlai Stevenson complained not long ago that in the United Nations "a skin game" was being played. He was right. He was facing reality. A "skin game" *is* being played. But Ambassador Stevenson sounded like Jesse James accusing the marshal of carrying a gun. Because who in the world's history ever has played a worse "skin game" than the white man?

Mr. Muhammad, to whom I was writing daily, had no idea of what a new world had opened up to me through my efforts to document his teachings in books.

When I discovered philosophy, I tried to touch all the landmarks of philosophical development. Gradually, I read most of the old philosophers, Occidental and Oriental. The Oriental philosophers were the ones I came to prefer; finally, my impression was that most Occidental philosophy had largely been borrowed from the Oriental thinkers. Socrates, for instance, traveled in Egypt. Some sources even say that Socrates was initiated into some of the Egyptian mysteries. Obviously Socrates got some of his wisdom among the East's wise men.

I have often reflected upon the new vistas that reading opened to me. I knew right there in prison that reading had changed forever the course of my life. As I see it today, the ability to read awoke inside me some long dormant craving to be mentally alive. I certainly wasn't seeking any degree, the way a college confers a status symbol upon its students. My homemade education gave me, with every additional book that I read, a little bit more sensitivity to the deafness, dumbness, and blindness that was afflicting the black race in America. Not long ago, an English writer telephoned me from London, asking questions. One was, "What's your alma mater?" I told him, "Books." You will never catch me with a free fifteen minutes in which I'm not studying something I feel might be able to help the black man.

Yesterday I spoke in London, and both ways on the plane across the Atlantic I was studying a document about how the United Nations proposes to insure the human rights of the oppressed minorities of the world. The American black man is the world's most shameful case of minority oppression. What makes the black man think of himself as only an internal United States issue is just a catch-phrase, two words, "civil rights." How is the black man going to get "civil rights" before first he wins his *human* rights? If the American black man will start thinking about his *human* rights, and then start thinking of himself as part of one of the world's great peoples, he will see he has a case for the United Nations.

I can't think of a better case! Four hundred years of black blood and sweat invested here in America, and the white man still has the black man begging for what every immigrant fresh off the ship can take for granted the minute he walks down the gangplank.

But I'm digressing. I told the Englishman that my alma mater was books, a good library. Every time I catch a plane, I have with me a book that I want to read—and that's a lot of books these days. If I weren't out here every day battling the white man, I could spend the rest of my life reading, just satisfying my curiosity—because you can hardly mention anything I'm not curious about. I don't think anybody ever got more out of going to prison than I did. In fact, prison enabled me to study far more intensively than I would have if my life had gone differently and I had attended some college. I imagine that one of the biggest troubles with colleges is there are too many distractions, too much panty-raiding, fraternities, and boola-boola and all of that. Where else but in a prison could I have attacked my ignorance by being able to study intensely sometimes as much as fifteen hours a day?

Schopenhauer, Kant, Nietzsche, naturally, I read all of those. I don't respect them; I am just trying to remember some of those whose theories I soaked up in those years. These three, it's said, laid the groundwork on which the Fascist and Nazi philosophy was built. I don't respect them because it seems to me that most of their time was spent arguing about things that are not really important. They remind me of so many of the Negro "intellectuals," so-called, with whom I have come in contact—they are always arguing about something useless.

Spinoza impressed me for a while when I found out that he was black. A black Spanish Jew. The Jews excommunicated him because he advocated a pantheistic doctrine, something like the "allness of God," or "God in everything." The Jews read their burial services for Spinoza, meaning that he was dead as far as they were concerned; his family was run out of Spain, they ended up in Holland, I think.

I'll tell you something. The whole stream of Western philosophy has now wound up in a cul-de-sac. The white man has perpetrated upon himself, as well as upon the black man, so gigantic a fraud that he has put himself into a crack. He did it through his elaborate, neurotic necessity to hide the black man's true role in history.

And today the white man is faced head on with what is happening on the Black Continent, Africa. Look at the artifacts being discovered there, that are proving over and over again, how the black man had great, fine, sensitive civilizations before the white man was out of the caves. Below the Sahara, in the places where most of America's Negroes' foreparents were kidnapped, there is being unearthed some of the finest craftsmanship, sculpture and other objects, that has ever been seen by modern man. Some of these things now are on view in such places as New York City's Metropolitan Museum of Art. Gold work of such fine tolerance and workmanship that it has no rival. Ancient objects produced by black hands . . . refined by those black hands with results that no human hand today can equal.

History has been so "whitened" by the white man that even the black professors have known little more than the most ignorant black man about the talents and rich civilizations and cultures of the black man of millenniums ago. I have lectured in Negro colleges and some of these brainwashed black Ph.D.'s, with their suspenders dragging the ground with degrees, have run to the white man's newspapers calling me a "black fanatic." Why, a lot of them are fifty years behind the times. If I were president of one of these black colleges, I'd hock the campus if I had to, to send a bunch of black students off digging in Africa for more, more and more proof of the black race's historical greatness. The white man now is in Africa digging and searching. An African elephant can't stumble without falling on some white man with a shovel. Practically every week, we read about some great new find from Africa's lost civilizations. All that's new is white science's attitude. The ancient civilizations of the black man have been buried on the Black Continent all the time.

Here is an example: a British anthropologist named Dr. Louis S. B. Leakey is displaying some fossil bones—a foot, part of a hand, some jaws, and skull fragments. On the basis of these, Dr. Leakey has said it's time to rewrite completely the history of man's origin.

This species of man lived 1,818,036 years before Christ. And these bones were found in Tanganyika. In the Black Continent.

It's a crime, the lie that has been told to generations of black men and white men both. Little innocent black children, born of parents who believed that their race had no history. Little black children seeing, before they could talk, that their parents considered themselves inferior. Innocent black children growing up, living out their lives, dying of old age—and all of their lives ashamed of being black. But the truth is pouring out of the bag now.

Two other areas of experience which have been extremely formative in my life since prison were first opened to me in the Norfolk Prison Colony. For one thing, I had my first experiences in opening the eyes of my brainwashed black brethren to some truths about the black race. And, the other: when I had read enough to know something, I began to enter the Prison Colony's weekly debating program—my baptism into public speaking.

I have to admit a sad, shameful fact. I had so loved being around the white man that in prison I really disliked how Negro convicts stuck together so much. But when Mr. Muhammad's teachings reversed my attitude toward my black brothers, in my guilt and shame I began to catch every chance I could to recruit for Mr. Muhammad.

You have to be careful, very careful, introducing the truth to the black man who has never previously heard the truth about himself, his own kind, and the white man. My brother Reginald had told me that all Muslims experienced this in their recruiting for Mr. Muhammad. The black brother is so brainwashed that he may even be repelled when he first hears the truth. Reginald advised that the truth had to be dropped only a little bit at a time. And you had to wait a while to let it sink in before advancing the next step.

I began first telling my black brother inmates about the glorious history of the black man—things they never had dreamed. I told them the horrible slavery-trade truths that they never knew.

I would watch their faces when I told them about that, because the white man had completely erased the slaves' past, a Negro in America can never know his true family name, or even what tribe he was descended from: the Mandingos, the Wolof, the Serer, the Fula, the Fanti, the Ashanti, or others. I told them that some slaves brought from Africa spoke Arabic, and were Islamic in their religion. A lot of these black convicts still wouldn't believe it unless they could see that a white man had said it. So, often, I would read to these brothers selected passages from white men's books. I'd explain to them that the real truth was known to some white men, the scholars; but there had been a conspiracy down through the generations to keep the truth from black men.

I would keep close watch on how each one reacted. I always had to be careful. I never knew when some brainwashed black imp, some dyed-in-the-wool Uncle Tom, would nod at me and then go running to tell the white man. When one was ripe—and I could tell—then away from the rest, I'd drop it on him, what Mr. Muhammad taught: "The white man is the devil."

That would shock many of them—until they started thinking about it.

This is probably as big a single worry as the American prison system has today—the way the Muslim teachings, circulated among all Negroes in the country, are converting new Muslims among black men in prison, and black men are in prison in far greater numbers than their proportion in the population.

The reason is that among all Negroes the black convict is the most perfectly preconditioned to hear the words, "the white man is the devil."

You tell that to any Negro. Except for those relatively few "integration"-mad so-called "intellectuals," and those black men who are otherwise fat, happy, and deaf, dumb, and blinded, with their crumbs from the white man's rich table, you have struck a nerve center in the American black man. He may take a day to react, a month, a year; he may never respond, openly; but of one thing you can be sure—when he thinks about his own life, he is going to see where, to him, personally, the white man sure has acted like a devil.

And, as I say, above all Negroes, the black prisoner. Here is a black man caged behind bars, probably for years, put there by the white man. Usually the convict comes from among those bottom-of-the-pile Negroes, the Negroes who through their entire lives have been kicked about, treated like children—Negroes who never have met one white man who didn't either take something from them or do something to them.

You let this caged-up black man start thinking, the same way I did when I first heard Elijah Muhammad's teachings: let him start thinking how, with better breaks when he was young and ambitious he might have been a lawyer, a doctor, a scientist, anything. You let this caged-up black man start realizing, as I did, how from the first landing of the first slave ship, the millions of black men in America have been like sheep in a den of wolves. That's why black prisoners become Muslims so fast when Elijah Muhammad's teachings filter into their cages by way of other Muslim convicts. "The white man is the devil" is a perfect echo of that black convict's lifelong experience.

I've told how debating was a weekly event there at the Norfolk Prison Colony. My reading had my mind like steam under pressure. Some way, I had to start telling the white man about himself to his face. I decided I could do this by putting my name down to debate.

Standing up and speaking before an audience was a thing that throughout my previous life never would have crossed my mind. Out there in the streets, hustling, pushing dope, and robbing, I could have had the dreams from a pound of hashish and I'd never have dreamed anything so wild as that one day I would speak in coliseums and arenas, at the greatest American universities, and on radio and television programs, not to mention speaking all over Egypt and Africa and in England.

But I will tell you that, right there, in the prison, debating, speaking to a crowd, was as exhilarating to me as the discovery of knowledge through reading had been. Standing up there, the faces looking up at me, things in my head coming out of my mouth, while my brain searched for the next best thing to follow what I was saying, and if I could sway them to my side by handling it right, then I had won the debate—once my feet got wet, I was gone on debating. Whichever side of the selected subject was assigned to me, I'd track down and study everything I could find on it. I'd put myself in my opponent's place and decide how I'd try to win if I had the other side; and then I'd figure a way to knock down those points. And if there was any way in the world, I'd work into my speech the devilishness of the white man.

"Compulsory Military Training—Or None?" That's one good chance I got unexpectedly, I remember. My opponent flailed the air about the Ethiopians throwing rocks and spears at Italian airplanes, "proving" that compulsory military training was needed. I said the Ethiopians' black flesh had been spattered against trees by bombs the Pope in Rome had blessed, and the Ethiopians would have thrown even their bare bodies at the airplanes because they had seen that they were fighting the devil incarnate.

They yelled "foul," that I'd made the subject a race issue. I said it wasn't race, it was a historical fact, that they ought to go and read Pierre van Paassen's *Days of Our Years*, and something not surprising to me, that book, right after the debate, disappeared from the prison library. It was right there in prison that I made up my mind to devote the rest of my life to telling the white man about himself—or die. In a debate about whether or not Homer had ever existed, I threw into those white faces the theory that Homer only symbolized how white Europeans kidnapped black Africans, then blinded them so that they could never get back to their own people. (Homer and Omar and *Moor*, you see, are related terms; it's like saying Peter, Pedro, and *petra*, all three of which mean rock.) These blinded Moors the Europeans taught to sing about the Europeans' glorious accomplishments. I made it clear that was the devilish white man's idea of kicks. Aesop's *Fables*—another case in point. "Aesop" was only the Greek name for an Ethiopian.

Another hot debate I remember I was in had to do with the identity of Shakespeare. No color was involved there; I just got intrigued over the Shakespearean dilemma. The King James translation of the Bible is considered the greatest piece of literature in English. Its language supposedly represents the ultimate in using the King's English. Well, Shakespeare's language and the Bible's language are one and the same. They say that from 1604 to 1611, King James got poets to translate, to write the Bible. Well, if Shakespeare existed, he was then the top poet around. But Shakespeare is nowhere reported connected with the Bible. If he existed, why didn't King James use him? And if he did use him, why is it one of the world's best kept secrets?

I know that many say that Francis Bacon was Shakespeare. If that is true, why would Bacon have kept it secret? Bacon wasn't royalty, when royalty sometimes used the *nom de plume* because it was "improper" for royalty to be artistic or theatrical. What would Bacon have had to lose? Bacon, in fact, would have had everything to gain.

In the prison debates I argued for the theory that King James himself was the real poet who used the *nom de plume* Shakespeare. King James was brilliant. He was the greatest king who ever sat on the British throne. Who else among royalty, in his time, would have had the giant talent to write Shakespeare's works? It was he who poetically "fixed" the Bible—which in itself and its present King James version has enslaved the world.

When my brother Reginald visited, I would talk to him about new evidence I found to document the Muslim teachings. In either volume 43 or 44 of The Harvard Classics, I read Milton's *Paradise Lost*. The devil, kicked out of Paradise, was trying to regain possession. He was using the forces of Europe, personified by the Popes, Charlemagne, Richard the Lionhearted, and other knights. I interpreted this to show that the Europeans were motivated and led by the devil, or the personification of the devil. So Milton and Mr. Elijah Muhammad were actually saying the same thing.

I couldn't believe it when Reginald began to speak ill of Elijah Muhammad. I can't specify the exact things he said. They were more in the nature of implications against Mr. Muhammad—the pitch of Reginald's voice, or the way that Reginald looked, rather than what he said.

It caught me totally unprepared. It threw me into a state of confusion. My blood brother, Reginald, in whom I had so much confidence, for whom I had so much respect, the one who had introduced me to the Nation of Islam. I couldn't believe it! And now Islam meant more to me than anything I ever had known in my life. Islam and Mr. Elijah Muhammad had changed my whole world.

Reginald, I learned, had been suspended from the Nation of Islam by Elijah Muhammad. He had not practiced moral restraint. After he had learned the truth, and had accepted the truth, and the Muslim laws, Reginald was still carrying on improper relations with the then secretary of the New York Temple. Some other Muslim who learned of it had made charges against Reginald to Mr. Muhammad in Chicago, and Mr. Muhammad had suspended Reginald.

When Reginald left, I was in torment. That night, finally, I wrote to Mr. Muhammad, trying to defend my brother, appealing for him. I told him what Reginald was to me, what my brother meant to me.

I put the letter into the box for the prison censor. Then all the rest of that night, I prayed to Allah. I don't think anyone ever prayed more sincerely to Allah. I prayed for some kind of relief from my confusion.

It was the next night, as I lay on my bed, I suddenly, with a start, became aware of a man sitting beside me in my chair. He had on a dark suit, I remember. I could see him as plainly as I see anyone I look at. He wasn't black, and he wasn't white. He was light-brown-skinned, an Asiatic cast of countenance, and he had oily black hair.

I looked right into his face.

I didn't get frightened. I knew I wasn't dreaming. I couldn't move, I didn't speak, and he didn't. I couldn't place him racially—other than that I knew he was a non-European. I had no idea whatsoever who he was. He just sat there. Then, suddenly as he had come, he was gone.

Soon, Mr. Muhammad sent me a reply about Reginald. He wrote, "If you once believed in the truth, and now you are beginning to doubt the truth, you didn't believe the truth in the first place. What could make you doubt the truth other than your own weak self?"

That struck me. Reginald was not leading the disciplined life of a Muslim. And I knew that Elijah Muhammad was right, and my blood brother was wrong. Because right is right, and wrong is wrong. Little did I then realize the day would come when Elijah Muhammad would be accused by his own sons as being guilty of the same acts of immorality that he judged Reginald and so many others for.

But at that time, all of the doubt and confusion in my mind was removed. All of the influence that my brother had wielded over me was broken. From that day on, as far as I am concerned, everything that my brother Reginald has done is wrong.

But Reginald kept visiting me. When he had been a Muslim, he had been immaculate in his attire. But now, he wore things like a T-shirt, shabby-looking trousers, and sneakers. I could see him on the way down. When he spoke, I heard him coldly. But I would listen. He was my blood brother.

Gradually, I saw the chastisement of Allah—what Christians would call "the curse"—come upon Reginald. Elijah Muhammad said that Allah was chastising Reginald—and that anyone who challenged Elijah Muhammad would be chastened by Allah. In Islam we were taught that as long as one didn't know the truth, he lived in darkness. But once the truth was accepted, and recognized, he lived in light, and whoever would then go against it would be punished by Allah.

Mr. Muhammad taught that the five-pointed star stands for justice, and also for the five senses of man. We were taught that Allah executes justice by working upon the five senses of those who rebel against His Messenger, or against His truth. We were taught that this was Allah's way of letting Muslims know His sufficiency to defend His Messenger against any and all opposition, as long as the Messenger himself didn't deviate from the path of truth. We were taught that Allah turned the minds of any defectors into a turmoil. I thought truly that it was Allah doing this to my brother.

One letter, I think from my brother Philbert, told me that Reginald was with them in Detroit. I heard no more about Reginald until one day, weeks later, Ella visited me; she told me that Reginald was at her home in Roxbury, sleeping. Ella said she had heard a knock, she had gone to the door, and there was Reginald, looking terrible. Ella said she had asked, "Where did you come from?" And Reginald had told her he came from Detroit. She said she asked him, "How did you get here?" And he had told her, "I walked."

I believed he *had* walked. I believed in Elijah Muhammad, and he had convinced us that Allah's chastisement upon Reginald's mind had taken away Reginald's ability to gauge distance and time. There is a dimension of time with which we are not familiar here in the West. Elijah Muhammad said that under Allah's chastisement, the five senses of a man can be so deranged by those whose mental powers are greater than his that in five minutes his hair can turn snow white. Or he will walk nine hundred miles as he might walk five blocks.

In prison, since I had become a Muslim, I had grown a beard. When Reginald visited me, he nervously moved about in his chair; he told me that each hair on my beard was a snake. Everywhere, he saw snakes.

He next began to believe that he was the "Messenger of Allah." Reginald went around in the streets of Roxbury, Ella reported to me, telling people that he had some divine power. He graduated from this to saying that he was Allah.

He finally began saying he was *greater* than Allah.

Authorities picked up Reginald, and he was put into an institution. They couldn't find what was wrong. They had no way to understand Allah's chastisement. Reginald was released. Then he was picked up again, and was put into another institution.

Reginald is in an institution now. I know where, but I won't say. I would not want to cause him any more trouble than he has already had.

I believe, today, that it was written, it was meant, for Reginald to be used for one purpose only: as a bait, as a minnow to reach into the ocean of blackness where I was, to save me.

I cannot understand it any other way.

After Elijah Muhammad himself was later accused as a very immoral man, I came to believe that it wasn't a divine chastisement upon Reginald, but the pain he felt when his own family totally rejected him for Elijah Muhammad, and this hurt made Reginald turn insanely upon Elijah Muhammad.

It's impossible to dream, or to see, or to have a vision of someone whom you never have seen before—and to see him exactly as he is. To see someone, and to see him exactly as he looks, is to have a pre-vision.

I would later come to believe that my pre-vision was of Master W. D. Fard, the Messiah, the one whom Elijah Muhammad said had appointed him—Elijah Muhammad—as His Last Messenger to the black people of North America.

My last year in prison was spent back in the Charlestown Prison. Even among the white inmates, the word had filtered around. Some of those brainwashed black convicts talked too much. And I know that the censors had reported on my mail. The Norfolk Prison Colony officials had become upset. They used as a reason for my transfer that I refused to take some kind of shots, an inoculation or something.

The only thing that worried me was that I hadn't much time left before I would be eligible for parole-board consideration. But I reasoned that they might look at my representing and spreading Islam in another way: instead of keeping me in they might want to get me out.

I had come to prison with 20/20 vision. But when I got sent back to Charlestown, I had read so much by the lights-out glow in my room at the Norfolk Prison Colony that I had astigmatism and the first pair of the eyeglasses that I have worn ever since.

I had less maneuverability back in the much stricter Charles-town Prison. But I found that a lot of Negroes attended a Bible class, and I went there.

Conducting the class was a tall, blond, blue-eyed (a perfect "devil") Harvard Seminary student. He lectured, and then he started in a question-and-answer session. I don't know which of us had read the Bible more, he or I, but I had to give him credit; he really was heavy on his religion. I puzzled and puzzled for a way to upset him, and to give those Negroes present something to think and talk about and circulate.

Finally, I put up my hand; he nodded. He had talked about Paul.

I stood up and asked, "What color was Paul?" And I kept talking, with pauses, "He had to be black . . . because he was a Hebrew . . . and the original Hebrews were black . . . weren't they?"

He had started flushing red. You know the way white people do. He said "Yes."

I wasn't through yet. "What color was Jesus . . . he was Hebrew, too . . . wasn't he?"

Both the Negro and the white convicts had sat bolt upright. I don't care how tough the convict, be he brainwashed black Christian, or a "devil" white Christian, neither of them is ready to hear anybody saying Jesus wasn't white. The instructor walked around. He shouldn't have felt bad. In all of the years since, I never have met any intelligent white man who would try to insist that Jesus was white. How could they? He said, "Jesus was brown."

I let him get away with that compromise.

Exactly as I had known it would, almost overnight the Charlestown convicts, black and white, began buzzing with the story. Wherever I went, I could feel the nodding. And anytime I got a chance to exchange words with a black brother in stripes, I'd say, "My man! You ever heard about somebody named Mr. Elijah Muhammad?"

CHAPTER TWELVE

SAVIOR

During the spring of nineteen fifty-two I joyously wrote Elijah Muhammad and my family that the Massachusetts State Parole Board had voted that I should be released. But still a few months were taken up with the red tape delay of paper work that went back and forth, arranging for my parole release in the custody of my oldest brother, Wilfred, in Detroit, who now managed a furniture store. Wilfred got the Jew who owned the store to sign a promise that upon release I would be given immediate employment.

By the prison system wire, I heard that Shorty also was up for parole. But Shorty was having trouble getting some reputable person to sign for him. (Later, I found out that in prison Shorty had studied musical composition. He had even progressed to writing some pieces; one of them I know he named "The Bastille Concerto.")

My going to Detroit instead of back to Harlem or Boston was influenced by my family's feeling expressed in their letters. Especially my sister Hilda had stressed to me that although I felt I understood Elijah Muhammad's teachings, I had much to learn, and I ought to come to Detroit and become a member of a temple of practicing Muslims.

It was in August when they gave me a lecture, a cheap L'il Abner suit, and a small amount of money, and I walked out of the gate. I never looked back, but that doesn't make me any different from a million inmates who have left a prison behind them.

The first stop I made was at a Turkish bath. I got some of that physical feeling of prison-taint steamed off me. Ella, with whom I stayed only overnight, had also agreed that it would be best for me to start again in Detroit. The police in a new city wouldn't have it in for me; that was Ella's consideration—not the Muslims, for whom Ella had no use. Both Hilda and Reginald had tried to work on Ella. But Ella, with her strong will, didn't go for it at all. She told me that she felt anyone could be whatever he wanted to be, Holy Roller, Seventh Day Adventist, or whatever it was, but she wasn't going to become any Muslim.

Hilda, the next morning, gave me some money to put in my pocket. Before I left, I went out and bought three things I remember well. I bought a better-looking pair of eyeglasses than the pair the prison had issued to me; and I bought a suitcase and a wrist watch.

I have thought, since, that without fully knowing it, I was preparing for what my life was about to become. Because those are three things I've used more than anything else. My eyeglasses correct the astigmatism that I got from all the reading in prison. I travel so much now that my wife keeps alternate suitcases packed so that, when necessary, I can just grab one. And you won't find anybody more time-conscious than I am. I live by my watch, keeping appointments. Even when I'm using my car, I drive by my watch, not my speedometer. Time is more important to me than distance.

I caught a bus to Detroit. The furniture store that my brother Wilfred managed was right in the black ghetto of Detroit; I'd better not name the store, if I'm going to tell the way they robbed Negroes. Wilfred introduced me to the Jews who owned the store. And, as agreed, I was put to work, as a salesman.

"Nothing Down" advertisements drew poor Negroes into that store like flypaper. It was a shame, the way they paid three and four times what the furniture had cost, because they could get credit from those Jews. It was the same kind of cheap, gaudy-looking junk that you can see in any of the black ghetto furniture stores today. Fabrics were stapled on the sofas. Imitation "leopard skin" bedspreads, "tiger skin" rugs, such stuff as that. I would see clumsy, work-hardened, calloused hands scrawling and scratching signatures on the contract, agreeing to highway-robbery interest rates in the fine print that never was read.

I was seeing in real life the same point made in a joke that during the 1964 Presidential campaign *Jet* magazine reported that Senator Barry Goldwater had told somewhere. It was that a white man, a Negro, and a Jew were given one wish each. The white man asked for securities; the Negro asked for a lot of money; the Jew asked for some imitation jewelry ''and that colored boy's address.''

In all my years in the streets, I'd been looking at the exploitation that for the first time I really saw and understood. Now I watched brothers entwining themselves in the economic clutches of the white man who went home every night with another bag of the money drained out of the ghetto. I saw that the money, instead of helping the black man, was going to help enrich these white merchants, who usually lived in an ''exclusive'' area where a black man had better not get caught unless he worked there for somebody white.

Wilfred invited me to share his home, and gratefully I accepted. The warmth of a home and a family was a healing change from the prison cage for me. It would deeply move almost any newly freed convict, I think. But especially this Muslim home's atmosphere sent me often to my knees to praise Allah. My family's letters while I was in prison had included a description of the Muslim home routine, but to truly appreciate it, one had to be a part of the routine. Each act, and the significance of that act, was gently, patiently explained to me by my brother Wilfred.

There was none of the morning confusion that exists in most homes. Wilfred, the father, the family protector and provider, was the first to rise. ''The father prepares the way for his family,'' he said. He, then I, performed the morning ablutions. Next came Wilfred's wife, Ruth, and then their children, so that orderliness prevailed in the use of the bathroom.

''In the name of Allah, I perform the ablution,'' the Muslim said aloud before washing first the right hand, then the left hand. The teeth were thoroughly brushed, followed by three rinsings of the mouth. The nostrils were also rinsed out thrice. A shower then completed the whole body's purification in readiness for prayer.

Each family member, even children upon meeting each other for that new day's first time, greeted softly and pleasantly, ''As-Salaam-Alaikum'' (the Arabic for ''Peace be unto you''). ''Wa-Alaikum-Salaam'' (''and unto you be peace'') was the other's reply. Over and over again, the Muslim said in his own mind, "Allahu-Akbar, Allahu-Akbar" ("Allah is the greatest").

The prayer rug was spread by Wilfred while the rest of the family purified themselves. It was explained to me that a Muslim family prayed with the sun near the horizon. If that time was missed, the prayer had to be deferred until the sun was beyond the horizon. "Muslims are not sun-worshipers. We pray facing the East to be in unity with the rest of our 725 million brothers and sisters in the entire Muslim world."

All the family, in robes, lined up facing East. In unison, we stepped from our slippers to stand on the prayer rug.

Today, I say with my family in the Arabic tongue the prayer which I first learned in English: "I perform the morning prayer to Allah, the Most High, Allah is the greatest. Glory to Thee Oh Allah, Thine is the praise, Blessed is Thy Name, and Exalted is Thy Majesty. I bear witness that nothing deserves to be served or worshiped besides Thee."

No solid food, only juice and coffee, was taken for our breakfasts. Wilfred and I went off to work. There, at noon and again at around three in the afternoon, unnoticed by others in the furniture store, we would rinse our hands, faces and mouths, and softly meditate.

Muslim children did likewise at school, and Muslim wives and mothers interrupted their chores to join the world's 725 million Muslims in communicating with God.

Wednesdays, Fridays, and Sundays were the meeting days of the relatively small Detroit Temple Number One. Near the temple, which actually was a storefront, were three hog-slaughtering pens. The squealing of hogs being slaughtered filtered into our Wednesday and Friday meetings. I'm describing the condition that we Muslims were in back in the early 1950's.

The address of Temple Number One was 1470 Frederick Street, I think. The first Temple to be formed, back in 1931, by Master W. D. Fard, was formed in Detroit, Michigan. I never had seen any Christian-believing Negroes conduct themselves like the Muslims, the individuals and the families alike. The men were quietly, tastefully dressed. The women wore ankle-length gowns, no makeup, and scarves covered their heads. The neat children were mannerly not only to adults but to other children as well.

I had never dreamed of anything like that atmosphere among black people who had learned to be proud they were black, who had learned to love other black people instead of being jealous and suspicious. I thrilled to how we Muslim men used both hands to grasp a black brother's both hands, voicing and smiling our happiness to meet him again. The Muslim sisters, both married and single, were given an honor and respect that I'd never seen black men give to their women, and it felt wonderful to me. The salutations which we all exchanged were warm, filled with mutual respect and dignity: "Brother" . . . "Sister" . . . "Ma'am" . . . "Sir." Even children speaking to other children used these terms. Beautiful!

Lemuel Hassan then was the Minister at Temple Number One. "As-Salaikum," he greeted us. "Wa-Salaikum," we returned. Minister Lemuel stood before us, near a blackboard. The blackboard had fixed upon it in permanent paint, on one side, the United States flag and under it the words "Slavery, Suffering and Death," then the word "Christianity" alongside the sign of the Cross. Beneath the Cross was a painting of a black man hanged from a tree. On the other side was painted what we were taught was the Muslim flag, the crescent and star on a red background with the words "Islam: Freedom, Justice, Equality," and beneath that "Which One Will Survive the War of Armageddon?"

For more than an hour, Minister Lemuel lectured about Elijah Muhammad's teachings. I sat raptly absorbing Minister Lemuel's every syllable and gesture. Frequently, he graphically illustrated points by chalking key words or phrases on the blackboard.

I thought it was outrageous that our small temple still had some empty seats. I complained to my brother Wilfred that there should be no empty seats, with the surrounding streets full of our brainwashed black brothers and sisters, drinking, cursing, fighting, dancing, carousing, and using dope—the very things that Mr. Muhammad taught were helping the black man to stay under the heel of the white man here in America.

From what I could gather, the recruitment attitude at the temple seemed to me to amount to a self-defeating waiting view

. . . an assumption that Allah would bring us more Muslims. I felt that Allah would be more inclined to help those who helped themselves. I had lived for years in ghetto streets; I knew the Negroes in those streets. Harlem or Detroit were no different. I said I disagreed, that I thought we should go out into the streets and get more Muslims into the fold. All of my life, as you know, I had been an activist, I had been impatient. My brother Wilfred counseled me to keep patience. And for me to be patient was made easier by the fact that I could anticipate soon seeing and perhaps meeting the man who was called "The Messenger," Elijah Muhammad himself.

Today, I have appointments with world-famous personages, including some heads of nations. But I looked forward to the Sunday before Labor Day in 1952 with an eagerness never since duplicated. Detroit Temple Number One Muslims were going in a motor caravan—I think about ten automobiles—to visit Chicago Temple Number Two, to hear Elijah Muhammad.

Not since childhood had I been so excited as when we drove in Wilfred's car. At great Muslim rallies since then I have seen, and heard, and felt ten thousand black people applauding and cheering. But on that Sunday afternoon when our two little temples assembled, perhaps only two hundred Muslims, the Chicagoans welcoming and greeting us Detroiters, I experienced tinglings up my spine as I've never had since.

I was totally unprepared for the Messenger Elijah Muhammad's physical impact upon my emotions. From the rear of Temple Number Two, he came toward the platform. The small, sensitive, gentle, brown face that I had studied in photographs, until I had dreamed about it, was fixed straight ahead as the Messenger strode, encircled by the marching, strapping Fruit of Islam guards. The Messenger, compared to them, seemed fragile, almost tiny. He and the Fruit of Islam were dressed in dark suits, white shirts, and bow ties. The Messenger wore a gold-embroidered fez.

I stared at the great man who had taken the time to write to me when I was a convict whom he knew nothing about. He was the man whom I had been told had spent years of his life in suffering and sacrifice to lead us, the black people, because he loved us so much. And then, hearing his voice, I sat leaning forward, riveted upon his words. (I try to reconstruct what Elijah

Muhammad said from having since heard him speak hundreds of times.)

"I have not stopped one day for the past twenty-one years. I have been standing, preaching to you throughout those past twenty-one years, while I was free, and even while I was in bondage. I spent three and one-half years in the federal penitentiary, and also over a year in the city jail for teaching this truth. I was also deprived of a father's love for his family for seven long years while I was running from hypocrites and other enemies of this word and revelation of God—which will give life to you, and put you on the same level with all other civilized and independent nations and peoples of this planet earth. . . ."

Elijah Muhammad spoke of how in this wilderness of North America, for centuries the "blue-eyed devil white man" had brainwashed the "so-called Negro." He told us how, as one result, the black man in America was "mentally, morally and spiritually dead." Elijah Muhammad spoke of how the black man was Original Man, who had been kidnapped from his homeland and stripped of his language, his culture, his family structure, his family name, until the black man in America did not even realize who he was.

He told us, and showed us, how his teachings of the true knowledge of ourselves would lift up the black man from the bottom of the white man's society and place the black man where he had begun, at the top of civilization.

Concluding, pausing for breath, he called my name.

It was like an electrical shock. Not looking at me directly, he asked me to stand.

He told them that I was just out of prison. He said how "strong" I had been while in prison. "Every day," he said, "for years, Brother Malcolm has written a letter from prison to me. And I have written to him as often as I could."

Standing there, feeling the eyes of the two hundred Muslims upon me, I heard him make a parable about me.

When God bragged about how faithful Job was, said Elijah Muhammad, the devil said only God's hedge around Job kept Job so faithful. "Remove that protective hedge," the devil told God, "and I will make Job curse you to your face."

The devil could claim that, hedged in prison, I had just used Islam, Mr. Muhammad said. But the devil would say that now, out of prison, I would return to my drinking, smoking, dope, and life of crime.

"Well, now, our good brother Malcolm's hedge is removed and we will see how he does," Mr. Muhammad said. "I believe that he is going to remain faithful."

And Allah blessed me to remain true, firm and strong in my faith in Islam, despite many severe trials to my faith. And even when events produced a crisis between Elijah Muhammad and me, I told him at the beginning of the crisis, with all the sincerity I had in me, that I still believed in him more strongly than he believed in himself.

Mr. Muhammad and I are not together today only because of envy and jealousy. I had more faith in Elijah Muhammad than I could ever have in any other man upon this earth.

You will remember my having said that, when I was in prison, Mr. Muhammad would be my brother Wilfred's house guest whenever he visited Detroit Temple Number One. Every Muslim said that never could you do as much for Mr. Muhammad as he would do for you in return. That Sunday, after the meeting, he invited our entire family group and Minister Lemuel Hassan to be his guests for dinner that evening, at his new home.

Mr. Muhammad said that his children and his followers had insisted that he move into this larger, better eighteen-room house in Chicago at 4847 Woodlawn Avenue. They had just moved in that week, I believe. When we arrived, Mr. Muhammad showed us where he had just been painting. I had to restrain my impulse to run and bring a chair for the Messenger of Allah. Instead, as I had heard he would do, he was worrying about my comfort.

We had hoped to hear his wisdom during the dinner, but instead he encouraged us to talk. I sat thinking of how our Detroit Temple more or less just sat and awaited Allah to bring converts—and, beyond that, of the millions of black people all over America, who never had heard of the teachings that could stir and wake and resurrect the black man . . . and there at Mr. Muhammad's table, I found my tongue. I have always been one to speak my mind.

During a conversational lull, I asked Mr. Muhammad how many Muslims were supposed to be in our Temple Number One in Detroit.

He said, "There are supposed to be thousands."

"Yes, sir," I said. "Sir, what is your opinion of the best way of getting thousands there?"

"Go after the young people," he said. "Once you get them, the older ones will follow through shame."

I made up my mind that we were going to follow that advice.

Back in Detroit, I talked with my brother Wilfred. I offered my services to our Temple's Minister, Lemuel Hassan. He shared my determination that we should apply Mr. Muhammad's formula in a recruitment drive. Beginning that day, every evening, straight from work at the furniture store, I went doing what we Muslims later came to call "fishing." I knew the thinking and the language of ghetto streets: "My man, let me pull your coat to something—"

My application had, of course, been made and during this time I received from Chicago my "X." The Muslim's "X" symbolized the true African family name that he never could know. For me, my "X" replaced the white slavemaster name of "Little" which some blue-eyed devil named Little had imposed upon my paternal forebears. The receipt of my "X" meant that forever after in the nation of Islam, I would be known as Malcolm X. Mr. Muhammad taught that we would keep this "X" until God Himself returned and gave us a Holy Name from His own mouth.

Recruit as I would in the Detroit ghetto bars, in the poolrooms, and on the corners, I found my poor, ignorant, brainwashed black brothers mostly too deaf, dumb, and blind, mentally, morally, and spiritually, to respond. It angered me that only now and then would one display even a little curiosity about the teachings that would resurrect the black man.

These few I would almost beg to visit Temple Number One at our next meeting. But then not half of those who agreed to come would actually show up.

Gradually, enough were made interested, though, that each month, a few more automobiles lengthened our caravans to Temple Two in Chicago. But even after seeing and hearing Elijah Muhammad in person, only a few of the interested visitors would apply by formal letter to Mr. Muhammad to be accepted for Nation of Islam membership.

With a few months of plugging away, however, our storefront Temple One about tripled its membership. And that so deeply pleased Mr. Muhammad that he paid us the honor of a personal visit.

Mr. Muhammad gave me warm praise when Minister Lemuel Hassan told how hard I had labored in the cause of Islam.

Our caravans grew. I remember with what pride we led twenty-five automobiles to Chicago. And each time we went, we were honored with dinner at the home of Elijah Muhammad. He was interested in my potential, I could tell from things he would say.

And I worshiped him.

In early 1953, I left the furniture store. I earned a little better weekly pay check working at the Gar Wood factory in Detroit, where big garbage truck bodies were made. I cleaned up behind the welders each time they finished another truck body.

Mr. Muhammad was saying at his dining table by this time that one of his worst needs was more young men willing to work as hard as they would have to in order to bear the responsibilities of his ministers. He was saying that the teachings should be spreading further than they had, and temples needed to be established in other cities.

It simply had never occurred to me that *I* might be a minister. I had never felt remotely qualified to directly represent Mr. Muhammad. If someone had asked me about becoming a minister, I would have been astonished, and told them I was happy and willing to serve Mr. Muhammad in the lowliest capacity.

I don't know if Mr. Muhammad suggested it or if our Temple One Minister Lemuel Hassan on his own decision encouraged me to address our assembled brothers and sisters. I know that I testified to what Mr. Muhammad's teachings had done for me: "If I told you the life I have lived, you would find it hard to believe me. . . . When I say something about the white man, I am not talking about someone I don't know. . . ."

Soon after that, Minister Lemuel Hassan urged me to address the brothers and sisters with an extemporaneous lecture. I was uncertain, and hesitant—but at least I had debated in prison, and I tried my best. (Of course, I can't remember exactly what I said, but I do know that in my beginning efforts my favorite subject was Christianity and the horrors of slavery, where I felt well-equipped from so much reading in prison.)

"My brothers and sisters, our white slavemaster's Christian

religion has taught us black people here in the wilderness of North America that we will sprout wings when we die and fly up into the sky where God will have for us a special place called heaven. This is white man's Christian religion used to *brainwash* us black people! We have *accepted* it! We have *embraced* it! We have *believed* it! We have *practiced* it! And while we are doing all of that, for himself, this blue-eyed devil has *twisted* his Christianity, to keep his *foot* on our backs . . . to keep our eyes fixed on the pie in the sky and heaven in the hereafter . . . while *he* enjoys *his* heaven right *here* . . . on *this earth* . . . in *this life*."

Today when thousands of Muslims and others have been audiences out before me, when audiences of millions have been beyond radio and television microphones, I'm sure I rarely feel as much electricity as was then generated in me by the upturned faces of those seventy-five or a hundred Muslims, plus other curious visitors, sitting there in our storefront temple with the squealing of pigs filtering in from the slaughterhouse just outside.

In the summer of 1953—all praise is due to Allah—I was named Detroit Temple Number One's Assistant Minister.

Every day after work, I walked, "fishing" for potential converts in the Detroit black ghetto. I saw the African features of my black brothers and sisters whom the devilish white man had brainwashed. I saw the hair as mine had been for years, conked by cooking it with lye until it lay limp, looking straight like the white man's hair. Time and again Mr. Muhammad's teachings were rebuffed and even ridiculed. . . . "Aw, man, get out of my face, you niggers are crazy!" My head would reel sometimes, with mingled anger and pity for my poor blind black brothers. I couldn't wait for the next time our Minister Lemuel Hassan would let me speak:

"We didn't land on Plymouth Rock, my brothers and sisters—Plymouth Rock landed on *us!*" . . . "Give *all* you can to help Messenger Elijah Muhammad's independence program for the black man! . . . This white man always has controlled us black people by keeping us running to him begging, 'Please, lawdy, please, Mr. White Man, boss, would you push me off another crumb down from your table that's sagging with riches. . . .'

". . . my *beautiful*, black brothers and sisters! And when we say 'black,' we mean everything not white, brothers and sisters! Because *look* at your skins! We're all black to the white man, but we're a thousand and one different colors. Turn around, *look* at each other! What shade of black African polluted by devil white man are you? You see me—well, in the streets they used to call me Detroit Red. Yes! Yes, that raping, red-headed devil was my *grandfather!* That close, yes! My *mother's* father! She didn't like to speak of it, can you blame her? She said she never laid eyes on him! She was *glad* for that! I'm *glad* for her! If I could drain away *his* blood that pollutes *my* body, and pollutes *my* complexion, I'd do it! Because I hate every drop of the rapist's blood that's in me!

"And it's not just me, it's *all* of us! During slavery, *think* of it, it was a *rare* one of our black grandmothers, our great-grandmothers and our great-great-grandmothers who escaped the white rapist slavemaster. That rapist slavemaster who emasculated the black man . . . with threats, with fear . . . until even today the black man lives with fear of the white man in his heart! Lives even today still under the heel of the white man!

"*Think* of it—think of that black slave man filled with fear and dread, hearing the screams of his wife, his mother, his daughter being *taken*—in the barn, the kitchen, in the bushes! *Think* of it, my dear brothers and sisters! *Think* of hearing wives, mothers, daughters, being *raped!* And you were too filled with *fear* of the rapist to do anything about it! And his vicious, animal attacks' offspring, this white man named things like 'mulatto' and 'quadroon' and 'octoroon' and all those other things that he has called us—you and me—when he is not calling us *'nigger'!*

"Turn around and look at each other, brothers and sisters, and *think* of this! You and me, polluted all these colors—and this devil has the arrogance and the gall to think we, his victims, should *love* him!"

I would become so choked up that sometimes I would walk in the streets until late into the night. Sometimes I would speak to no one for hours, thinking to myself about what the white man had done to our poor people here in America.

At the Gar Wood factory where I worked, one day the supervisor came, looking nervous. He said that a man in the office was waiting to see me.

The white man standing in there said, "I'm from the F.B.I." He flipped open—that way they do, to shock you—his little folded black leather case containing his identification. He told me to come with him. He didn't say for what, or why.

I went with him. They wanted to know, at their office, why hadn't I registered for the Korean War draft?

"I just got out of prison," I said. "I didn't know you took anybody with prison records."

They really believed I thought ex-convicts weren't supposed to register. They asked a lot of questions. I was glad they didn't ask if I intended to put on the white man's uniform, because I didn't. They just took it for granted that I would. They told me they weren't going to send me to jail for failing to register, that they were going to give me a break, but that I would have to register immediately.

So I went straight from there to the draft board. When they gave me a form to fill out, I wrote in the appropriate places that I was a Muslim, and that I was a conscientious objector.

I turned in the form. This middle-aged, bored-acting devil who scanned it looked out from under his eyes at me. He got up and went into another office, obviously to consult someone over him. After a while, he came out and motioned for me to go in there.

These three—I believe there were three, as I remember—older devils sat behind desks. They all wore that "troublesome nigger" expression. And I looked "white devil" right back into their eyes. They asked me on what basis did I claim to be a Muslim in my religion. I told them that the Messenger of Allah was Mr. Elijah Muhammad, and that all who followed Mr. Muhammad here in America were Muslims. I knew they had heard this before from some Temple One young brothers who had been there before me.

They asked if I knew what "conscientious objector" meant. I told them that when the white man asked me to go off somewhere and fight and maybe die to preserve the way the white man treated the black man in America, then my conscience made me object.

They told me that my case would be "pending." But I was put through the physical anyway, and they sent me a card with some kind of a classification. That was 1953, then I heard no more for seven years, when I received another classification card in the mail. In fact, I carry it in my wallet right now. Here: it's card number 20 219 25 1377, it's dated November 21, 1960. It says, "Class 5-A," whatever that means, and stamped on the card's back is "Michigan Local Board No. 19, Wayne County, 3604 South Wayne Road, Wayne, Michigan."

Every time I spoke at our Temple One, my voice would still be hoarse from the last time. My throat took a long time to get into condition.

"Do you know *why* the white man really hates you? It's because every time he sees your face, he sees a mirror of his crime—and his guilty conscience can't bear to face it!

"Every white man in America, when he looks into a black man's eyes, should fall to his knees and say 'I'm sorry, I'm sorry—my kind has committed history's greatest crime against your kind; will you give me the chance to atone?' But do you brothers and sisters expect any white man to do that? *No*, you *know* better! And why won't he do it? Because he *can't* do it. The white man has *created* a devil, to bring chaos upon this earth. . . ."

Somewhere about this time, I left the Gar Wood factory and I went to work for the Ford Motor Company, one of the Lincoln-Mercury Division assembly lines.

As a young minister, I would go to Chicago and see Mr. Elijah Muhammad every time I could get off. He encouraged me to come when I could. I was treated as if I had been one of the sons of Mr. Muhammad and his dark, good wife Sister Clara Muhammad. I saw their children only occasionally. Most of them in those years worked around Chicago in various jobs, laborers, driving taxis, and things such as that. Also living in the home was Mr. Muhammad's dear Mother Marie.

I would spend almost as much time with Mother Marie as I did with Mr. Muhammad. I loved to hear her reminiscences about her son Elijah's early life when they lived in Sandersville, Georgia, where he was born in 1897.

Mr. Muhammad would talk with me for hours. After eating good, healthful Muslim food, we would stay at the dinner table and talk. Or I would ride with him as he drove on his daily rounds between the few grocery stores that the Muslims then owned in Chicago. The stores were examples to help black people see what they could do for themselves by hiring their own kind and trading with their own kind and thus quit being exploited by the white man.

In the Muslim-owned combination grocery-drug store on Wentworth and 31st Street, Mr. Muhammad would sweep the floor or something like that. He would do such work himself as an example to his followers whom he taught that idleness and laziness were among the black man's greatest sins against himself. I would want to snatch the broom from Mr. Muhammad's hand, because I thought he was too valuable to be sweeping a floor. But he wouldn't let me do anything but stay with him and listen while he advised me on the best ways to spread his message.

The way we were with each other, it would make me think of Socrates on the steps of the Athens market place, spreading his wisdom to his students. Or how one of those students, Aristotle, had his students following behind him, walking through the Lyceum.

One day, I remember, a dirty glass of water was on a counter and Mr. Muhammad put a clean glass of water beside it. "You want to know how to spread my teachings?" he said, and he pointed to the glasses of water. "Don't condemn if you see a person has a dirty glass of water," he said, "just show them the clean glass of water that you have. When they inspect it, you won't have to say that yours is better."

Of all the things that Mr. Muhammad ever was to teach me, I don't know why, that still stands out in my mind. Although I haven't always practiced it. I love too much to battle. I'm inclined to tell somebody if his glass of water is dirty.

Mother Marie, when Mr. Muhammad was busy, would tell me about her son's boyhood and of his growing up in Georgia to young manhood.

Mother Marie's account of her son began when she was herself but seven years old. She told me that then she had a vision that one day she would be the mother of a very great man. She married a Baptist minister, Reverend Poole, who worked around Sandersville on the farms, and in the sawmills. Among their thirteen children, said Mother Marie, little Elijah was very different, almost from when he could walk and talk.

The small, frail boy usually settled his older brothers' and sisters' disputes, Mother Marie said. And young as he was, he became regarded by them as their leader. And Elijah, about the time he entered school, began displaying a strong race consciousness. After the fourth grade, because the family was so poor, Elijah had to quit school and begin full-time working. An older sister taught Elijah as much as she was able at night.

Mother Marie said that Elijah spent hours poring through the Bible, with tears shining in his eyes. (Mr. Muhammad told me himself later that as a boy he felt that the Bible's words were a locked door, that could be unlocked, if only he knew how, and he cried because of his frustrated anxiety to receive understanding.) Elijah grew up into a still-frail teenager who displayed a most uncommonly strong love for his race, and, Mother Marie said, instead of condemning Negroes' faults, young Elijah always would speak of reasons for those faults.

Mother Marie has since died. I believe that she had as large a funeral as Chicago has seen. Not only Muslims, but others knew of the deep bond that Messenger Elijah had with his mother.

"I am not ashamed to say how little learning I have had," Mr. Muhammad told me. "My going to school no further than the fourth grade proves that I can know nothing except the truth I have been taught by Allah. Allah taught me mathematics. He found me with a sluggish tongue, and taught me how to pronounce words."

Mr. Muhammad said that somehow, he never could stand how the Sandersville white farmers, the sawmill foremen, or other white employers would habitually and often curse Negro workers. He said he would politely ask any for whom he worked never to curse him. "I would ask them to just fire me if they didn't like my work, but just don't curse me." (Mr. Muhammad's ordinary conversation was the manner he used when making speeches. He was not "eloquent," as eloquence is usually meant, but whatever he uttered had an impact on me that trained orators did not begin to have.) He said that on the jobs he got, he worked so honestly that generally he was put in charge of the other Negroes.

After Mr. Muhammad and Sister Clara met and married and their first two children had been born, a white employer early in 1923 did curse Mr. Muhammad, then Elijah Poole. Elijah Poole, determined to avoid trouble, took his family to Detroit, arriving when he was twenty-five. Five more children would be born there in Detroit, and, finally, the last one in Chicago.

In Detroit in 1931, Mr. Muhammad met Master W. D. Fard.

The effects of the depression were bad everywhere, but in the black ghetto they were horrible, Mr. Muhammad told me. A small, light brown–skinned man knocked from door to door at the apartments of the poverty-stricken Negroes. The man offered for sale silks and other yard goods, and he identified himself as "a brother from the East."

This man began to tell Negroes how they came from a distant land, in the seeds of their forefathers.

He warned them against eating the "filthy pig" and other "wrong foods" that it was habitual for Negroes to eat.

Among the Negroes whom he found most receptive, he began holding little meetings in their poor homes. The man taught both the Quran and the Bible, and his students included Elijah Poole.

This man said his name was W. D. Fard. He said that he was born in the *Koreish* tribe of Muhammad ibn Abdullah, the Arabian prophet Himself. This peddler of silks and yard goods, Mr. W. D. Fard, knew the Bible better than any of the Christian-bred Negroes.

In the essence, Mr. W. D. Fard taught that God's true name was Allah, that His true religion was Islam, that the true name for that religion's people was Muslims.

Mr. W. D. Fard taught that the Negroes in America were directly descended from Muslims. He taught that Negroes in America were Lost Sheep, lost for four hundred years from the Nation of Islam, and that he, Mr. Fard, had come to redeem and return the Negro to his true religion.

No heaven was in the sky, Mr. Fard taught, and no hell was in the ground. Instead, both heaven and hell were conditions in which people lived right here on this planet Earth. Mr. Fard taught that the Negro in America had been for four hundred years in hell, and he, Mr. Fard, had come to return them to where heaven for them was—back home, among their own kind.

Master Fard taught that as hell was on earth, also on earth was the devil—the white race which was bred from black Original Man six thousand years before, purposely to create a hell on earth for the next six thousand years.

The black people, God's children, were Gods themselves,

Master Fard taught. And he taught that among them was one, also a human being like the others, who was the God of Gods: The Most, Most High, The Supreme Being, supreme in wisdom and power—and His proper name was Allah.

Among his handful of first converts in 1931 in Detroit, Master W. D. Fard taught that every religion says that near the Last Day, or near the End of Time, God would come, to resurrect the Lost Sheep, to separate them from their enemies, and restore them to their own people. Master Fard taught that Prophecy referred to this Finder and Savior of the Lost Sheep as The Son of Man, or God in Person, or The Lifegiver, The Redeemer, or The Messiah, who would come as lightning from the East and appear in the West.

He was the One to whom the Jews referred as The Messiah, the Christians as The Christ, and the Muslims as The Mahdi.

I would sit, galvanized, hearing what I then accepted from Mr. Muhammad's own mouth as being the true history of our religion, the true religion for the black man. Mr. Muhammad told me that one evening he had a revelation that Master W. D. Fard represented the fulfillment of the prophecy.

"I asked Him," said Mr. Muhammad, " 'Who are you, and what is your real name?' And He said, 'I am The One the world has been looking for to come for the past two thousand years.'

"I said to Him again," said Mr. Muhammad, " 'What is your *true* name?' And then He said, 'My name is Mahdi. I came to guide you into the right path.' "

Mr. Elijah Muhammad says that he sat listening with an open heart and an open mind—the way I was sitting listening to Mr. Muhammad. And Mr. Muhammad said he never doubted any word that the "Savior" taught him.

Starting to organize, Master W. D. Fard set up a class for training ministers to carry the teachings to America's black people. In giving names to these first ministers, Master Fard named Elijah Poole "Elijah Karriem."

Next, Master W. D. Fard established in 1931 in Detroit a University of Islam. It had adult classes which taught, among other things, mathematics, to help the poor Negroes quit being duped and deceived by the "tricknology" of "the blue-eyed devil white man."

Starting a school in the rough meant that it lacked qualified teachers, but a start had to be made somewhere. Mr. Elijah Karriem removed his own children from Detroit public schools, to start a nucleus of children in the University of Islam.

Mr. Muhammad told me that his older children's lack of formal education reflected their sacrifice to form the backbone for today's Universities of Islam in Detroit and Chicago which have better-qualified faculties.

Master W. D. Fard selected Elijah Karriem to be the Supreme Minister, over all other ministers, and among all of those others sprang up a bitter jealousy. All of them had better education than Elijah Karriem, and also they were more articulate than he was. They raged, even in his presence, "Why should we bow down to someone who appears less qualified?"

But Mr. Elijah Karriem was then in some way re-named "Elijah Muhammad," who as the Supreme Minister began to receive from Master W. D. Fard for the next three and a half years private teachings, during which time he says he "heard things never revealed to others."

During this period, Mr. Elijah Muhammad and Master W. D. Fard went to Chicago and established Temple Number Two. They also established in Milwaukee the beginnings of a Temple Number Three.

In 1934, Master W. D. Fard disappeared, without a trace.

Elijah Muhammad says that attempts were made upon his life, because the other ministers' jealousy had reached such a pitch. He says that these "hypocrites" forced him to flee to Chicago. Temple Number Two became his headquarters until the "hypocrites" pursued him there, forcing him to flee again. In Washington, D.C., he began Temple Number Four. Also while there, in the Congressional Library, he studied books which he says Master W. D. Fard had told him contained different pieces of the truth that devil white man had recorded, but which were not in books generally available to the public.

Saying that he was still pursued by the "hypocrites," Mr. Muhammad fled from city to city, never staying long in any. Whenever able, now and then, he slipped home to see his wife and his eight young children, who were fed by other poor Muslims who shared what little they had. Even Mr. Muhammad's original Chicago followers wouldn't know he was at home, for he says the "hypocrites" made serious efforts to kill him.

In 1942, Mr. Muhammad was arrested. He says Uncle Tom Negroes had tipped off the devil white man to his teachings, and he was charged by this devil white man with draft-dodging, although he was too old for military service. He was sentenced to five years in prison. In the Milan, Michigan, federal prison, Mr. Muhammad served three and a half years, then he was paroled. He had returned to his work in 1946, to remove the blinders from the eyes of the black man in the wilderness of North America.

I can hear myself now, at the lectern in our little Muslim Temple, passionately addressing my black brothers and sisters:

"This little, gentle, sweet man! The Honorable Elijah Muhammad who is at this very hour teaching our brothers and sisters over there in Chicago! Allah's Messenger—which makes him the most powerful black man in America! For you and me, he has sacrificed seven years on the run from filthy hypocrites, he spent another three and a half years in a prison cage! He was put there by the devil white man! That devil white man does not want the Honorable Elijah Muhammad stirring awake the sleeping giant of you and me, and all of our ignorant, brainwashed kind here in the white man's heaven and the black man's hell here in the wilderness of North America!

"I have sat at our Messenger's feet, hearing the truth from his own mouth! I have pledged on my knees to Allah to tell the white man about his crimes and the black man the true teachings of our Honorable Elijah Muhammad. I don't care if it costs my life. . . ."

This was my attitude. These were my uncompromising words, uttered anywhere, without hesitation or fear. I was his most faithful servant, and I know today that I did believe in him more firmly than he believed in himself.

In the years to come, I was going to have to face a psychological and spiritual crisis.

CHAPTER THIRTEEN

MINISTER MALCOLM X

I quit the Ford Motor Company's Lincoln-Mercury Division. It had become clear to me that Mr. Muhammad needed ministers to spread his teachings, to establish more temples among the twenty-two million black brothers who were brainwashed and sleeping in the cities of North America.

My decision came relatively quickly. I have always been an activist, and my personal chemistry perhaps made me reach more quickly than most ministers in the Nation of Islam that stage of dedication. But every minister in the Nation, in his own time, in his own way, in the privacy of his own soul, came to the conviction that it was written that all of his "before" life had been only conditioning and preparation to become a disciple of Mr. Muhammad's.

Everything that happens—Islam teaches—is written.

Mr. Muhammad invited me to visit his home in Chicago, as often as possible, while he trained me, for months.

Never in prison had I studied and absorbed so intensely as I did now under Mr. Muhammad's guidance. I was immersed in the worship rituals; in what he taught us were the true natures of men and women; the organizational and administrative procedures; the real meanings, and the interrelated meanings, and uses, of the Bible and the Quran.

I went to bed every night ever more awed. If not Allah, who else could have put such wisdom into that little humble lamb of a man from the Georgia fourth grade and sawmills and cotton patches. The "lamb of a man" analogy I drew for myself from the prophecy in the Book of Revelations of a symbolic lamb with a two-edged sword in its mouth. Mr. Muhammad's two-edged sword was his teachings, which cut back and forth to free the black man's mind from the white man.

My adoration of Mr. Muhammad grew, in the sense of the Latin root word *adorare*. It means much more than our "adoration" or "adore." It means that my worship of him was so awesome that he was the first man whom I had ever feared—not fear such as of a man with a gun, but the fear such as one has of the power of the sun.

Mr. Muhammad, when he felt me able, permitted me to go to Boston. Brother Lloyd X lived there. He invited people whom he had gotten interested in Islam to hear me in his living room.

I quote what I said when I was just starting out, and then later on in other places, as I can best remember the general pattern that I used, in successive phases, in those days. I know that then I always liked to start off with my favorite analogy of Mr. Muhammad.

"God has given Mr. Muhammad some sharp truth," I told them. "It is like a two-edged sword. It cuts into you. It causes you great pain, but if you can take the truth, it will cure you and save you from what otherwise would be certain death."

Then I wouldn't waste any time to start opening their eyes about the devil white man. "I know you don't realize the enormity, the horrors, of the so-called *Christian* white man's crime. . . .

"Not even in the *Bible* is there such a crime! God in His wrath struck down with *fire* the perpetrators of *lesser* crimes! *One hundred million* of us black people! Your grandparents! Mine! *Murdered* by this white man. To get fifteen million of us here to make us his slaves, on the way he murdered one hundred million! I wish it was possible for me to show you the sea bottom in those days—the black bodies, the blood, the bones broken by boots and clubs! The pregnant black women who were thrown overboard if they got too sick! Thrown overboard to the sharks that had learned that following these slave ships was the way to grow fat!

"Why, the white man's raping of the black race's woman began right on those slave ships! The blue-eyed devil could not even wait until he got them here! Why, brothers and sisters, civilized mankind has never known such an orgy of greed and lust and murder. . . .''

The dramatization of slavery never failed intensely to arouse Negroes hearing its horrors spelled out for the first time. It's unbelievable how many black men and women have let the white man fool them into holding an almost romantic idea of what slave days were like. And once I had them fired up with slavery, I would shift the scene to themselves.

"I want you, when you leave this room, to start to *see* all this whenever you see this devil white man. Oh, yes, he's a devil! I just want you to start watching him, in his places where he doesn't want you around; watch him reveling in his preciousness, and his exclusiveness, and his vanity, while he continues to subjugate you and me.

"Every time you see a white man, think about the devil you're seeing! Think of how it was on *your* slave foreparents' bloody, sweaty backs that he *built* this empire that's today the richest of all nations—where his evil and his greed cause him to be hated around the world!''

Every meeting, the people who had been there before returned, bringing friends. None of them ever had heard the wraps taken off the white man. I can't remember any black man ever in those living-room audiences in Brother Lloyd X's home at 5, Wellington Street who didn't stand up immediately when I asked after each lecture, "Will all stand who *believe* what you have heard?'' And each Sunday night, some of them stood, while I could see others not quite ready, when I asked, "How many of you want to *follow* The Honorable Elijah Muhammad?''

Enough had stood up after about three months that we were able to open a little temple. I remember with what pleasure we rented some folding chairs. I was beside myself with joy when I could report to Mr. Muhammad a new temple address.

It was when we got this little mosque that my sister Ella first began to come to hear me. She sat, staring, as though she couldn't believe it was me. Ella never moved, even when I had only asked all who believed what they had heard to stand up. She contributed when our collection was held. It didn't bother or challenge me at all about Ella. I never even thought about converting her, as toughminded and cautious about joining anything as I personally knew her to be. I wouldn't have expected anyone short of Allah Himself to have been able to convert Ella.

I would close the meeting as Mr. Muhammad had taught me: "In the name of Allah, the beneficent, the merciful, all praise is due to Allah, the Lord of all the worlds, the beneficent, merciful master of the day of judgment in which we now live—Thee alone do we serve, and Thee alone do we beseech for Thine aid. Guide us on the right path, the path of those upon whom Thou has bestowed favors—not of those upon whom Thy wrath is brought down, nor the path of those who go astray after they have heard Thy teaching. I bear witness that there is no God but Thee and The Honorable Elijah Muhammad is Thy Servant and Apostle." I believed he had been divinely sent to our people by Allah Himself.

I would raise my hand, for them to be dismissed: "Do nothing unto anyone that you would not like to have done unto yourself. Seek peace, and never be the aggressor—but if anyone attacks you, we do not teach you to turn the other cheek. May Allah bless you to be successful and victorious in all that you do."

Except for that one day when I had stayed with Ella on the way to Detroit after prison, I had not been in the old Roxbury streets for seven years. I went to have a reunion with Shorty.

Shorty, when I found him, acted uncertain. The wire had told him I was in town, and on some "religious kick." He didn't know if I was serious, or if I was another of the hustling preacher-pimps to be found in every black ghetto, the ones with some little storefront churches of mostly hardworking, older women, who kept their "pretty boy" young preacher dressed in "sharp" clothes and driving a fancy car. I quickly let Shorty know how serious I was with Islam, but then, talking the old street talk, I quickly put him at his ease, and we had a great reunion. We laughed until we cried at Shorty's dramatization of his reactions when he heard that judge keep saying "Count one, ten years . . . count two, ten years—" We talked about how having those white girls with us had gotten us ten years where we had seen in prison plenty of worse offenders with far less time to serve.

Shorty still had a little band, and he was doing fairly well. He was rightfully very proud that in prison he had studied music. I told him enough about Islam to see from his reactions that he didn't really want to hear it. In prison, he had misheard about our religion. He got me off the subject by making a joke. He said that he hadn't had enough pork chops and white women. I don't know if he has yet, or not. I know that he's married to a white woman now . . . and he's fat as a hog from eating hog.

I also saw John Hughes, the gambling-house owner, and some others I had known who were still around Roxbury. The wire about me had made them all uncomfortable, but my "What you know, Daddy?" approach at least enabled us to have some conversations. I never mentioned Islam to most of them. I knew, from what I had been when I was with them, how brainwashed they were.

As Temple Eleven's minister, I served only briefly, because as soon as I got it organized, by March 1954, I left it in charge of Minister Ulysses X, and the Messenger moved me on to Philadelphia.

The City of Brotherly Love black people reacted even faster to the truth about the white man than the Bostonians had. And Philadelphia's Temple Twelve was established by the end of May. It had taken a little under three months.

The next month, because of those Boston and Philadelphia successes, Mr. Muhammad appointed me to be the minister of Temple Seven—in vital New York City.

I can't start to describe for you my welter of emotions. For Mr. Muhammad's teachings really to resurrect American black people, Islam obviously had to grow, to grow very big. And nowhere in America was such a single temple potential available as in New York's five boroughs.

They contained over a million black people.

It was nine years since West Indian Archie and I had been stalking the streets, momentarily expecting to try and shoot each other down like dogs.

"*Red!*" . . . "My man!" . . . "Red, this *can't* be you—"

With my natural kinky red hair now close-cropped, in place of the old long-haired, lye-cooked conk they had always known on my head, I know I looked much different.

"Gim'me some *skin*, man! A drink here, bartender—what? You *quit!* Aw, man, come off it!"

It was so good seeing so many whom I had known so well. You can understand how that was. But it was West Indian Ar-

chie and Sammy the Pimp for whom I was primarily looking.
And the first nasty shock came quickly, about Sammy. He had
quit pimping, he had gotten pretty high up in the numbers busi-
ness, and was doing well. Sammy even had married. Some fast
young girl. But then shortly after his wedding one morning he
was found lying dead across his bed—they said with twenty-five
thousand dollars in his pockets. (People don't want to believe
the sums that even the minor underworld handles. Why, listen:
in March 1964, a Chicago nickel-and-dime bets Wheel of For-
tune man, Lawrence Wakefield, died, and over $760,000 in
cash was in his apartment, in sacks and bags . . . all taken from
poor Negroes . . . and we wonder why we stay so poor.)

Sick about Sammy, I queried from bar to bar among old-
timers for West Indian Archie. The wire hadn't reported him
dead, or living somewhere else, but none seemed to know where
he was. I heard the usual hustler fates of so many others. Bullets,
knives, prison, dope, diseases, insanity, alcoholism. I imagine
it was about in that order. And so many of the survivors whom
I knew as tough hyenas and wolves of the streets in the old days
now were so pitiful. They had known all the angles, but beneath
that surface they were poor, ignorant, untrained black men; life
had eased up on them and hyped them. I ran across close to
twenty-five of these old-timers I had known pretty well, who in
the space of nine years had been reduced to the ghetto's minor,
scavenger hustles to scratch up room rent and food money. Some
now worked downtown, messengers, janitors, things like that.
I was thankful to Allah that I had become a Muslim and escaped
their fate.

There was Cadillac Drake. He was a big jolly, cigar-smoking,
fat, black, gaudy-dressing pimp, a regular afternoon character
when I was waiting on tables in Small's Paradise. Well, I rec-
ognized him shuffling toward me on the street. He had gotten
hooked on heroin; I'd heard that. He was the dirtiest, sloppiest
bum you ever laid eyes on. I hurried past because we would
both have been embarrassed if he recognized me, the kid he
used to toss a dollar tip.

The wire worked to locate West Indian Archie for me. The
wire of the streets, when it wants to, is something like Western
Union with the F.B.I. for messengers. At one of my early ser-
vices at Temple Seven, an old scavenger hustler, to whom I

gave a few dollars, came up when services were dismissed. He told me that West Indian Archie was sick, living up in a rented room in the Bronx.

I took a taxi to the address. West Indian Archie opened the door. He stood there in rumpled pajamas and barefooted, squinting at me.

Have you ever seen someone who seemed a ghost of the person you remembered? It took him a few seconds to fix me in his memory. He claimed, hoarsely, "Red! I'm so glad to see you!"

I all but hugged the old man. He was sick in that weak way. I helped him back. He sat down on the edge of his bed. I sat in his one chair, and I told him how his forcing me out of Harlem had saved my life by turning me in the direction of Islam.

He said, "I always liked you, Red," and he said that he had never really wanted to kill me. I told him it had made me shudder many times to think how close we had come to killing each other. I told him I had sincerely thought I had hit that combinated six-way number for the three hundred dollars he had paid me. Archie said that he had later wondered if he had made some mistake, since I was so ready to die about it. And then we agreed that it wasn't worth even talking about, it didn't mean anything anymore. He kept saying, over and over, in between other things, that he was so glad to see me.

I went into a little of Mr. Muhammad's teaching with Archie. I told him how I had found out that all of us who had been in the streets were victims of the white man's society. I told Archie what I had thought in prison about him; that his brain, which could tape-record hundreds of number combinations a day, should have been put at the service of mathematics or science. "Red, that sure is something to think about," I can remember him saying.

But neither of us would say that it was not too late. I have the feeling that he knew, as I could see, that the end was closing in on Archie. I became too moved about what he had been and what he had now become to be able to stay much longer. I didn't have much money, and he didn't want to accept what little I was able to press on him. But I made him take it.

I keep having to remind myself that then, in June 1954, Temple Seven in New York City was a little storefront. Why, it's almost unbelievable that one bus couldn't have been filled with the Muslims in New York City! Even among our own black people in the Harlem ghetto, you could have said "Muslim" to a thousand, and maybe only one would not have asked you "What's that?" As for white people, except for that relative handful privy to certain police or prison files, not five hundred white people in all of America knew we existed.

I began firing Mr. Muhammad's teaching at the New York members and the few friends they managed to bring in. And with each meeting, my discomfort grew that in Harlem, choked with poor, ignorant black men suffering all of the evils that Islam could cure, every time I lectured my heart out and then asked those who wanted to follow Mr. Muhammad to stand, only two or three would. And, I have to admit, sometimes not that many.

I think I was all the angrier with my own ineffectiveness because I *knew* the streets. I had to get myself together and think out the problem. And the big trouble, obviously, was that we were only one among the many voices of black discontent on every busy Harlem corner. The different Nationalist groups, the "Buy Black!" forces, and others like that; dozens of their stepladder orators were trying to increase their followings. I had nothing against anyone trying to promote independence and unity among black men, but they still were making it tough for Mr. Muhammad's voice to be heard.

In my first effort to get over this hurdle, I had some little leaflets printed. There wasn't a much-traveled Harlem street corner that five or six good Muslim brothers and I missed. We would step up right in front of a walking black man or woman so that they had to accept our leaflet, and if they hesitated one second, they had to hear us saying some catch thing such as "Hear how the white man kidnapped and robbed and raped our black race—"

Next, we went to work "fishing" on those Harlem corners— on the fringes of the Nationalist meetings. The method today has many refinements, but then it consisted of working the always shifting edges of the audiences that others had managed to draw. At a Nationalist meeting, everyone who was listening was interested in the revolution of the black race. We began to get visible results almost immediately after we began thrusting handbills in people's hands, "Come to hear us, too, brother.

The Honorable Elijah Muhammad teaches us how to cure the black man's spiritual, mental, moral, economic, and political sicknesses—''

I saw the new faces of our Temple Seven meetings. And then we discovered the best ''fishing'' audience of all, by far the best-conditioned audience for Mr. Muhammad's teachings: the Christian churches.

Our Sunday services were held at two P.M. All over Harlem during the hour or so before that, Christian church services were dismissing. We by-passed the larger churches with their higher ratio of so-called ''middle-class'' Negroes who were so full of pretense and ''status'' that they wouldn't be caught in our little storefront.

We went ''fishing'' fast and furiously when those little evangelical storefront churches each let out their thirty to fifty people on the sidewalk. ''Come to hear us, brother, sister—'' ''You haven't heard anything until you have heard the teachings of The Honorable Elijah Muhammad—'' These congregations were usually Southern migrant people, usually older, who would go anywhere to hear what they called ''good preaching.'' These were the church congregations who were always putting out little signs announcing that inside they were selling fried chicken and chitlin dinners to raise some money. And three or four nights a week, they were in their storefront rehearsing for the next Sunday, I guess, shaking and rattling and rolling the gospels with their guitars and tambourines.

I don't know if you know it, but there's a whole circuit of commercial gospel entertainers who have come out of these little churches in the city ghettoes or from down South. People such as Sister Rosetta Tharpe, The Clara Ward Singers are examples, and there must be five hundred lesser lights of the same general order. Mahalia Jackson, the greatest of them all—she was a preacher's daughter in Louisiana. She came up there to Chicago where she worked cooking and scrubbing for white people and then in a factory while she sang in the Negro churches the gospel style that, when it caught on, made her the first Negro that Negroes ever made famous. She was selling hundreds of thousands of records among Negroes before white people ever knew who Mahalia Jackson was. Anyway, I know that somewhere I once read that Mahalia said that every time she can, she will slip unannounced into some little ghetto storefront church and sing with her people. She calls that "my filling station."

The black Christians we "fished" to our Temple were conditioned, I found, by the very shock I could give them about what had been happening to them while they worshiped a blond, blue-eyed God. I knew the temple that I could build if I could really get to those Christians. I tailored the teachings for them. I would start to speak and sometimes be so emotionally charged I had to explain myself:

"You see my tears, brothers and sisters. . . . Tears haven't been in my eyes since I was a young boy. But I cannot help this when I feel the responsibility I have to help you comprehend for the first time what this white man's religion that we call Christianity has *done* to us. . . .

"Brothers and sisters here for the first time, please don't let that shock you. I know you didn't expect this. Because almost none of us black people have thought that maybe we were making a mistake not wondering if there wasn't a special religion somewhere for us—a special religion for the black man.

"Well, there *is* such a religion. It's called Islam. Let me spell it for you, I-s-l-a-m! *Islam!* But I'm going to tell you about Islam a little later. First, we need to understand some things about this Christianity before we can understand why the *answer* for us is Islam.

"Brothers and sisters, the white man has brainwashed us black people to fasten our gaze upon a blond-haired, blue-eyed Jesus! We're worshiping a Jesus that doesn't even *look* like us! Oh, yes! Now just bear with me, listen to the teachings of the Messenger of Allah, The Honorable Elijah Muhammad. Now, just think of this. The blond-haired, blue-eyed white man has taught you and me to worship a *white* Jesus, and to shout and sing and pray to this God that's *his* God, the white man's God. The white man has taught us to shout and sing and pray until we *die*, to wait until *death*, for some dreamy heaven-in-the-hereafter, when we're *dead*, while this white man has his milk and honey in the streets paved with golden dollars right here on *this* earth!

"You don't want to believe what I am telling you, brothers and sisters? Well, I'll tell you what you do. You go out of here, you just take a good look around where you live. Look at not only how *you* live, but look at how anybody that you *know* lives—that way, you'll be sure that you're not just a bad-luck accident. And when you get through looking at where *you* live, then you take you a walk down across Central Park, and start to look at what this white God had brought to the white man. I mean, take yourself a look down there at how the white man is living!

"And don't stop there. In fact, you won't be able to stop for long—his doormen are going to tell you 'Move on!' But catch a subway and keep on downtown. Anywhere you may want to get off, *look* at the white man's apartments, businesses! Go right on down to the tip of Manhattan Island that this devilish white man stole from the trusting Indians for twenty-four dollars! Look at his City Hall, down there; look at his Wall Street! Look at yourself! Look at *his* God!''

I had learned early one important thing, and that was to always teach in terms that the people could understand. Also, where the Nationalists whom we had "fished" were almost all men, among the storefront Christians, a heavy preponderance were women, and I had the sense to offer something special for them. *"Beautiful* black woman! The Honorable Elijah Muhammad teaches us that the black man is going around saying he wants respect; well, the black man never will get anybody's respect until he first learns to respect his own women! The black man needs *today* to stand up and throw off the weaknesses imposed upon him by the slavemaster white man! The black man needs to start today to shelter and protect and *respect* his black women!''

One hundred percent would stand up without hesitation when I said, "How many *believe* what they have heard?" But still never more than an agonizing few would stand up when I invited, "Will those stand who want to *follow* The Honorable Elijah Muhammad?''

I knew that our strict moral code and discipline was what repelled them most. I fired at this point, at the reason for our code. "The white man *wants* black men to stay immoral, unclean and ignorant. As long as we stay in these conditions we will keep on begging him and he will control us. We never can win freedom and justice and equality until we are doing something for ourselves!''

The code, of course, had to be explained to any who were

tentatively interested in becoming Muslims. And the word got around in their little storefronts quickly, which is why they would come to hear me, yet wouldn't join Mr. Muhammad. Any fornication was absolutely forbidden in the Nation of Islam. Any eating of the filthy pork, or other injurious or unhealthful foods; any use of tobacco, alcohol, or narcotics. No Muslim who followed Elijah Muhammad could dance, gamble, date, attend movies, or sports, or take long vacations from work. Muslims slept no more than health required. Any domestic quarreling, any discourtesy, especially to women, was not allowed. No lying or stealing, and no insubordination to civil authority, except on the grounds of religious obligation.

Our moral laws were policed by our Fruit of Islam—able, dedicated, and trained Muslim men. Infractions resulted in suspension by Mr. Muhammad, or isolation for various periods, or even expulsion for the worst offenses "from the only group that really cares about you."

Temple Seven grew somewhat with each meeting. It just grew too slowly to suit me. During the weekdays, I traveled by bus and train. I taught each Wednesday at Philadelphia's Temple Twelve. I went to Springfield, Massachusetts, to try to start a new temple. A temple which Mr. Muhammad numbered Thirteen was established there with the help of Brother Osborne, who had first heard of Islam from me in prison. A lady visiting a Springfield meeting asked if I'd come to Hartford, where she lived; she specified the next Thursday and said she would assemble some friends. And I was right there.

Thursday is traditionally domestic servants' day off. This sister had in her housing project apartment about fifteen of the maids, cooks, chauffeurs and house men who worked for the Hartford-area white people. You've heard that saying, "No man is a hero to his valet." Well, those Negroes who waited on wealthy whites hand and foot opened their eyes quicker than most Negroes. And when they went "fishing" enough among more servants, and other black people in and around Hartford, Mr. Muhammad before long was able to assign a Hartford temple the number Fourteen. And every Thursday I scheduled my teaching there.

Mr. Muhammad, when I went to see him in Chicago, had to

chastise me on some point during nearly every visit. I just couldn't keep from showing in some manner that with his ministers equipped with the power of his message, I felt the Nation should go much faster. His patience and his wisdom in chastising me would always humble me from head to foot. He said, one time, that no true leader burdened his followers with a greater load than they could carry, and no true leader sets too fast a pace for his followers to keep up.

"Most people seeing a man in an old touring car going real slow think the man doesn't want to go fast," Mr. Muhammad said, "but the man knows that to drive any faster would destroy the old car. When he gets a fast car, then he will drive at a fast speed." And I remember him telling me another time, when I complained about an inefficient minister at one of his mosques, "I would rather have a mule I can depend upon than a race horse that I can't depend upon."

I knew that Mr. Muhammad *wanted* that fast car to drive. And I don't think you could pick the same number of faithful brothers and sisters from the Nation of Islam today and find "fishing" teams to beat the efforts of those who helped to bring growth to the Boston, Philadelphia, Springfield, Hartford, and New York temples. I'm, of course, just mentioning those that I knew most about because I was directly involved. This was through 1955. And 1955 was the year I made my first trip of any distance. It was to help open the temple that today is Number Fifteen—in Atlanta, Georgia.

Any Muslim who ever moved for personal reasons from one city to another was of course exhorted to plant seeds for Mr. Muhammad. Brother James X, one of our top Temple Twelve brothers, had interested enough black people in Atlanta so that when Mr. Muhammad was advised, he told me to go to Atlanta and hold a first meeting. I think I have had a hand in most of Mr. Muhammad's temples, but I'll never forget that opening in Atlanta.

A funeral parlor was the only place large enough that Brother James X could afford to rent. Everything that the Nation of Islam did in those days, from Mr. Muhammad on down, was strictly on a shoestring. When we all arrived, though, a Christian Negro's funeral was just dismissing, so we had to wait awhile, and we watched the mourners out.

"You saw them all crying over their physical dead," I told our group when we got inside. "But the Nation of Islam is rejoicing over you, our mentally dead. That may shock you, but, oh, yes, you just don't realize how our whole black race in America is mentally dead. We are here today with Mr. Elijah Muhammad's teachings which resurrect the black man from the dead. . . ."

And, speaking of funerals, I should mention that we never failed to get some new Muslims when non-Muslims, family and friends of a Muslim deceased, attended our short, moving ceremony that illustrated Mr. Muhammad's teaching, "Christians have their funerals for the living, ours are for our departed."

As the minister of several temples, conducting the Muslim ceremony had occasionally fallen to my lot. As Mr. Muhammad had taught me, I would start by reading over the casket of the departed brother or sister a prayer to Allah. Next I read a simple obituary record of his or her life. Then I usually read from Job; two passages, in the seventh and fourteenth chapters, where Job speaks of no life after death. Then another passage where David, when his son died, spoke also of no life after death.

To the audience before me, I explained why no tears were to be shed, and why we had no flowers, or singing, or organ-playing. "We shed tears for our brother, and gave him our music and our tears while he was alive. If he wasn't wept for and given our music and flowers then, well, now there is no need, because he is no longer aware. We now will give his family any money we might have spent."

Appointed Muslim Sisters quickly passed small trays from which everyone took a thin, round patty of peppermint candy. At my signal, the candy was put into mouths. "We will file by now for a last look at our brother. We won't cry—just as we don't cry over candy. Just as this sweet candy will dissolve, so will our brother's sweetness that we have enjoyed when he lived now dissolve into a sweetness in our memories."

I have had probably a couple of hundred Muslims tell me that it was attending one of our funerals for a departed brother or sister that first turned them toward Allah. But I was to learn later that Mr. Muhammad's teaching about death and the Muslim funeral service was in drastic contradiction to what Islam taught in the East.

We had grown, by 1956—well, sizable. Every temple had "fished" with enough success that there were far more Muslims, especially in the major cities of Detroit, Chicago, and New York than anyone would have guessed from the outside. In fact, as you know, in the really big cities, you can have a very big organization and, if it makes no public show, or noise, no one will necessarily be aware that it is around.

But more than just increasing in numbers, Mr. Muhammad's version of Islam now had been getting in some other types of black people. We began now getting those with some education, both academic, and vocations and trades, and even some with "positions" in the white world, and all of this was starting to bring us closer to the desired fast car for Mr. Muhammad to drive. We had, for instance, some civil servants, some nurses, clerical workers, salesmen from the department stores. And one of the best things was that some brothers of this type were developing into smart, fine, aggressive young ministers for Mr. Muhammad.

I went without a lot of sleep trying to merit his increasing evidences of trust and confidence in my efforts to help build our Nation of Islam. It was in 1956 that Mr. Muhammad was able to authorize Temple Seven to buy and assign for my use a new Chevrolet. (The car was the Nation's, not mine. I had nothing that was mine but my clothes, wrist watch, and suitcase. As in the case of all of the Nation's ministers, my living expenses were paid and I had some pocket money. Where once you couldn't have named anything I wouldn't have done for money, now money was the last thing to cross my mind.) Anyway, in letting me know about the car, Mr. Muhammad told me he knew how I loved to roam, planting seeds for new Muslims, or more temples, so he didn't want me to be tied down.

In five months, I put about 30,000 miles of "fishing" on that car before I had an accident. Late one night a brother and I were coming through Weathersfield, Connecticut, when I stopped for a red light and a car smashed into me from behind. I was just shook up, not hurt. That excited devil had a woman with him, hiding her face, so I knew she wasn't his wife. We were exchanging our identification (he lived in Meriden, Connecticut) when the police arrived, and their actions told me he was somebody important. I later found out he was one of Connecticut's most prominent politicians; I won't call his name. Anyway, Temple Seven settled on a lawyer's advice, and that money went down on an Oldsmobile, the make of car I've been driving ever since.

I had always been very careful to stay completely clear of any personal closeness with any of the Muslim sisters. My total commitment to Islam demanded having no other interests, especially, I felt, no women. In almost every temple at least one single sister had let out some broad hint that she thought I needed a wife. So I always made it clear that marriage had no interest for me whatsoever; I was too busy.

Every month, when I went to Chicago, I would find that some sister had written complaining to Mr. Muhammad that I talked so hard against women when I taught our special classes about the different natures of the two sexes. Now, Islam has very strict laws and teachings about women, the core of them being that the true nature of a man is to be strong, and a woman's true nature is to be weak, and while a man must at all times respect his woman, at the same time he needs to understand that he must control her if he expects to get her respect.

But in those days I had my own personal reasons. I wouldn't have considered it possible for me to love any woman. I'd had too much experience that women were only tricky, deceitful, untrustworthy flesh. I had seen too many men ruined, or at least tied down, or in some other way messed up by women. Women talked too much. To tell a woman not to talk too much was like telling Jesse James not to carry a gun, or telling a hen not to cackle. Can you imagine Jesse James without a gun, or a hen that didn't cackle? And for anyone in any kind of a leadership position, such as I was, the worst thing in the world that he could have was the wrong woman. Even Samson, the world's strongest man, was destroyed by the woman who slept in his arms. She was the one whose words hurt him.

I mean, I'd had *so* much experience. I had talked to too many prostitutes and mistresses. They knew more about a whole lot of husbands than the wives of those husbands did. The wives always filled their husbands' ears so full of wife complaints that it wasn't the wives, it was the prostitutes and mistresses who heard the husbands' innermost problems and secrets. They thought of him, and comforted him, and that included listening to him, and so he would tell them everything.

Anyway, it had been ten years since I thought anything about any mistress, I guess, and as a minister now, I was thinking even less about getting any wife. And Mr. Muhammad himself encouraged me to stay single.

Temple Seven sisters used to tell brothers, "You're just staying single because Brother Minister Malcolm never looks at anybody." No, I didn't make it any secret to any of those sisters, how I felt. And, yes, I did tell the brothers to be very, very careful.

This sister—well, in 1956, she joined Temple Seven. I just noticed her, not with the slightest interest, you understand. For about the next year, I just noticed her. You know, she never would have dreamed I was even thinking about her. In fact, probably you couldn't have convinced her I even knew her name. It was Sister Betty X. She was tall, brown-skinned—darker than I was. And she had brown eyes.

I knew she was a native of Detroit, and that she had been a student at Tuskegee Institute down in Alabama—an education major. She was in New York at one of the big hospitals' school of nursing. She lectured to the Muslim girls' and women's classes on hygiene and medical facts.

I ought to explain that each week night a different Muslim class, or event, is scheduled. Monday night, every temple's Fruit of Islam trains. People think this is just military drill, judo, karate, things like that—which *is* part of the F.O.I. training, but only one part. The F.O.I. spends a lot more time in lectures and discussions on men learning to be men. They deal with the responsibilities of a husband and father; what to expect of women; the rights of women which are not to be abrogated by the husband; the importance of the father-male image in the strong household; current events; why honesty, and chastity, are vital in a person, a home, a community, a nation, and a civilization; why one should bathe at least once each twenty-four hours; business principles; and things of that nature.

Then, Tuesday night in every Muslim temple is Unity Night, where the brothers and sisters enjoy each other's conversational company and refreshments, such as cookies and sweet and sour fruit punches. Wednesday nights, at eight P.M., is what is called

Student Enrollment, where Islam's basic issues are discussed; it is about the equivalent of catechism class in the Catholic religion.

Thursday nights there are the M.G.T. (Muslim Girls' Training) and the G.C.C. (General Civilization Class), where the women and girls of Islam are taught how to keep homes, how to rear children, how to care for husbands, how to cook, sew, how to act at home and abroad, and other things that are important to being a good Muslim sister and mother and wife.

Fridays are devoted to Civilization Night, when classes are held for brothers and sisters in the area of the domestic relations, emphasizing how both husbands and wives must understand and respect each other's true natures. Then Saturday night is for all Muslims a free night, when, usually, they visit at each other's homes. And, of course, on Sundays, every Muslim temple holds its services.

On the Thursday M.G.T. and G.C.C. nights, sometimes I would drop in on the classes, and maybe at Sister Betty X's classes—just as on other nights I might drop in on the different brothers' classes. At first I would just ask her things like how were the sisters learning—things like that, and she would say "Fine, Brother Minister." I'd say, "Thank you, Sister." Like that. And that would be all there was to it. And after a while, I would have very short conversations with her, just to be friendly.

One day I thought it would help the women's classes if I took her—just because she happened to be an instructor, to the Museum of Natural History. I wanted to show her some Museum displays having to do with the tree of evolution, that would help her in her lectures. I could show her proofs of Mr. Muhammad's teachings of such things as that the filthy pig is only a large rodent. The pig is a graft between a rat, a cat and a dog, Mr. Muhammad taught us. When I mentioned my idea to Sister Betty X, I made it very clear that it was just to help her lectures to the sisters. I had even convinced myself that this was the only reason.

Then by the time of the afternoon I said we would go, well, I telephoned her; I told her I had to cancel the trip, that something important had come up. She said, "Well, you sure waited long enough to tell me, Brother Minister, I was just ready to walk out of the door." So I told her, well, all right, come on then, I'd make it somehow. But I wasn't going to have much time.

While we were down there, offhandedly I asked her all kinds of things. I just wanted some idea of her thinking; you understand, I mean *how* she thought. I was halfway impressed by her intelligence and also her education. In those days she was one of the few whom we had attracted who had attended college.

Then, right after that, one of the older sisters confided to me a personal problem that Sister Betty X was having. I was really surprised that when she had had the chance, Sister Betty X had not mentioned anything to me about it. Every Muslim minister is always hearing the problems of young people whose parents have ostracized them for becoming Muslims. Well, when Sister Betty X told her foster parents, who were financing her education, that she was a Muslim, they gave her a choice: leave the Muslims, or they'd cut off her nursing school.

It was right near the end of her term—but she was hanging on to Islam. She began taking baby-sitting jobs for some of the doctors who lived on the grounds of the hospital where she was training.

In my position, I would never have made any move without thinking how it would affect the Nation of Islam organization as a whole.

I got to turning it over in my mind. What would happen if I just *should* happen, sometime, to think about getting married to somebody? For instance Sister Betty X—although it could be any sister in any temple, but Sister Betty X, for instance, would just happen to be the right height for somebody my height, and also the right age.

Mr. Elijah Muhammad taught us that a tall man married to a too-short woman, or vice-versa, they looked odd, not matched. And he taught that a wife's ideal age was half the man's age, plus seven. He taught that women are physiologically ahead of men. Mr. Muhammad taught that no marriage could succeed where the woman did not look up with respect to the man. And that the man had to have something above and beyond the wife in order for her to be able to look to him for psychological security.

I was so shocked at myself, when I realized *what* I was thinking, I quit going anywhere near Sister Betty X, or any where I knew she would be. If she came into our restaurant and I was there, I went out somewhere. I was glad I knew that she had no idea what I had been thinking about. My not talking to her wouldn't give her any reason to think anything, since there had never been one *personal* word spoken between us—even if she had *thought* anything.

I studied about if I just *should* happen to say something to her—what would her position be? Because she wasn't going to get any chance to embarrass me. I had heard too many women bragging, "I told that chump 'Get lost!' " I'd had too much experience of the kind to make a man very cautious.

I knew one good thing; she had few relatives. My feeling about in-laws was that they were outlaws. Right among the Temple Seven Muslims, I had seen more marriages destroyed by in-laws, usually anti-Muslim, than any other single thing I knew of.

I wasn't about to say any of that romance stuff that Hollywood and television had filled women's heads with. If I was going to do something, I was going to do it directly. And anything I was going to do, I was going to do *my* way. And because *I* wanted to do it. Not because I saw somebody do it. Or read about it in a book. Or saw it in a moving picture somewhere.

I told Mr. Muhammad, when I visited him in Chicago that month, that I was thinking about a very serious step. He smiled when he heard what it was.

I told him I was just thinking about it, that was all. Mr. Muhammad said that he'd like to meet this sister.

The Nation by this time was financially able to bear the expenses so that instructor sisters from different temples could be sent to Chicago to attend the Headquarters Temple Two women's classes, and, while there, to meet The Honorable Elijah Muhammad in person. Sister Betty X, of course, knew all about this, so there was no reason for her to think anything of it when it was arranged for her to go to Chicago. And like all visiting instructor sisters, she was the house guest of the Messenger and Sister Clara Muhammad.

Mr. Muhammad told me that he thought that Sister Betty X was a fine sister.

If you are thinking about doing a thing, you ought to make up your mind if you are going to do it, or not do it. One Sunday night, after the Temple Seven meeting, I drove my car out on the Garden State Parkway. I was on my way to visit my brother Wilfred, in Detroit. Wilfred, the year before, in 1957, had been made the minister of Detroit's Temple One. I hadn't seen him, or any of my family, in a good while.

It was about ten in the morning when I got inside Detroit. Getting gas at a filling station, I just went to their pay phone on a wall; I telephoned Sister Betty X. I had to get Information to get the number of the nurses' residence at this hospital. Most numbers I memorized, but I had always made it some point never to memorize her number. Somebody got her to the phone finally. She said, "Oh, hello, Brother Minister—" I just said it to her direct: "Look, do you want to get married?"

Naturally, she acted all surprised and shocked.

The more I have thought about it, to this day I believe she was only putting on an act. Because women know. They know.

She said, just like I knew she would, "Yes." Then I said, well, I didn't have a whole lot of time, she'd better catch a plane to Detroit.

So she grabbed a plane. I met her foster parents who lived in Detroit. They had made up by this time. They were very friendly, and happily surprised. At least, they acted that way.

Then I introduced Sister Betty X at my oldest brother Wilfred's house. I had already asked him where people could get married without a whole lot of mess and waiting. He told me in Indiana.

Early the next morning, I picked up Betty at her parents' home. We drove to the first town in Indiana. We found out that only a few days before, the state law had been changed, and now Indiana had a long waiting period.

This was the fourteenth of January, 1958; a Tuesday. We weren't far from Lansing, where my brother Philbert lived. I drove there. Philbert was at work when we stopped at his house and I introduced Betty X. She and Philbert's wife were talking when I found out on the phone that we could get married in one day, if we rushed.

We got the necessary blood tests, then the license. Where the certificate said "Religion," I wrote "Muslim." Then we went to the Justice of the Peace.

An old hunchbacked white man performed the wedding. And all of the witnesses were white. Where you are supposed to say all those "I do's," we did. They were all standing there, smiling and watching every move. The old devil said, "I pronounce you man and wife," and then, "Kiss your bride."

I got her out of there. All of that Hollywood stuff! Like these women wanting men to pick them up and carry them across thresholds and some of them weigh more than you do. I don't know how many marriage breakups are caused by these movie- and television-addicted women expecting some bouquets and kissing and hugging and being swept out like Cinderella for dinner and dancing—then getting mad when a poor, scraggly husband comes in tired and sweaty from working like a dog all day, looking for some food.

We had dinner there at Philbert's home in Lansing. "I've got a surprise for you," I told him when we came in. "You haven't got any surprise for me," he said. When he got home from work and heard I'd been there introducing a Muslim sister, he knew I was either married, or on the way to get married.

Betty's nursing school schedule called for her to fly right back to New York, and she could return in four days. She claims she didn't tell anybody in Temple Seven that we had married.

That Sunday, Mr. Muhammad was going to teach at Detroit's Temple One. I had an Assistant Minister in New York now; I telephoned him to take over for me. Saturday, Betty came back. The Messenger, after his teaching on Sunday, made the announcement. Even in Michigan, my steering clear of all sisters was so well known, they just couldn't believe it.

We drove right back to New York together. The news really shook everybody in Temple Seven. Some young brothers looked at me as though I had betrayed them. But everybody else was grinning like Cheshire cats. The sisters just about ate up Betty. I never will forget hearing one exclaim, "You got him!" That's like I was telling you, the *nature* of women. She'd *got* me. That's part of why I never have been able to shake it out of my mind that she knew something—all the time. Maybe she did get me!

Anyway, we lived for the next two and a half years in Queens, sharing a house of two small apartments with Brother John Ali and his wife of that time. He's now the National Secretary in Chicago.

Attallah, our oldest daughter, was born in November 1958.

She's named for Attilah the Hun (he sacked Rome). Shortly after Attallah came, we moved to our present seven-room house in an all-black section of Queens, Long Island.

Another girl, Qubilah (named after Qubilah Khan) was born on Christmas Day of 1960. Then, Ilyasah ("Ilyas" is Arabic for "Elijah") was born in July 1962. And in 1964 our fourth daughter, Amilah, arrived.

I guess by now I will say I love Betty. She's the only woman I ever even thought about loving. And she's one of the very few—four women—whom I have ever trusted. The thing is, Betty's a good Muslim woman and wife. You see, Islam is the only religion that gives both husband and wife a true understanding of what love is. The Western "love" concept, you take it apart, it really is lust. But love transcends just the physical. Love is disposition, behavior, attitude, thoughts, likes, dislikes—these things make a beautiful woman, a beautiful wife. This is the beauty that never fades. You find in your Western civilization that when a man's wife's physical beauty fails, she loses her attraction. But Islam teaches us to look into the woman, and teaches her to look into us.

Betty does this, so she understands me. I would even say I don't imagine many other women might put up with the way I am. Awakening this brainwashed black man and telling this arrogant, devilish white man the truth about himself, Betty understands, is a full-time job. If I have work to do when I am home, the little time I am at home, she lets me have the quiet I need to work in. I'm rarely at home more than half of any week; I have been away as much as five months. I never get much chance to take her anywhere, and I know she likes to be with her husband. She is used to my calling her from airports anywhere from Boston to San Francisco, or Miami to Seattle, or, here lately, cabling her from Cairo, Accra, or the Holy City of Mecca. Once on the long-distance telephone, Betty told me in beautiful phrasing the way she thinks. She said, "You are present when you are away."

Later that year, after Betty and I were married, I exhausted myself trying to be everywhere at once, trying to help the Nation to keep growing. Guest-teaching at the Temple in Boston, I ended, as always, "Who among you wish to *follow* The Honorable Elijah Muhammad?'' And then I saw, in utter astonishment, that among those who were standing was my sister—*Ella!* We have a saying that those who are the hardest to convince make the best Muslims. And for Ella it had taken five years.

I mentioned, you will remember, how in a big city, a sizable organization can remain practically unknown, unless something happens that brings it to the general public's attention. Well, certainly no one in the Nation of Islam had any anticipation of the kind of thing that would happen in Harlem one night.

Two white policemen, breaking up a street scuffle between some Negroes, ordered other Negro passers-by to ''Move on!'' Of these bystanders, two happened to be Muslim brother Johnson Hinton and another brother of Temple Seven. They didn't scatter and run the way the white cops wanted. Brother Hinton was attacked with nightsticks. His scalp was split open, and a police car came and he was taken to a nearby precinct.

The second brother telephoned our restaurant. And with some telephone calls, in less than half an hour about fifty of Temple Seven's men of the Fruit of Islam were standing in ranks-formation outside the police precinct house.

Other Negroes, curious, came running, and gathered in excitement behind the Muslims. The police, coming to the station house front door, and looking out of the windows, couldn't believe what they saw. I went in, as the minister of Temple Seven, and demanded to see our brother. The police first said he wasn't there. Then they admitted he was, but said I couldn't see him. I said that until he was seen, and we were sure he received proper medical attention, the Muslims would remain where they were.

They were nervous and scared of the gathering crowd outside. When I saw our Brother Hinton, it was all I could do to contain myself. He was only semi-conscious. Blood had bathed his head and face and shoulders. I hope I never again have to withstand seeing another case of sheer police brutality like that.

I told the lieutenant in charge, ''That man belongs in the hospital.'' They called an ambulance. When it came and Brother Hinton was taken to Harlem Hospital, we Muslims followed, in loose formations, for about fifteen blocks along Lenox Avenue, probably the busiest thoroughfare in Harlem. Negroes who never had seen anything like this were coming out of stores and restaurants and bars and enlarging the crowd following us.

The crowd was big, and angry, behind the Muslims in front of Harlem Hospital. Harlem's black people were long since sick and tired of police brutality. And they never had seen any organization of black men take a firm stand as we were.

A high police official came up to me, saying "Get those people out of there." I told him that our brothers were standing peacefully, disciplined perfectly, and harming no one. He told me those others, behind them, weren't disciplined. I politely told him those others were his problem.

When doctors assured us that Brother Hinton was receiving the best of care, I gave the order and the Muslims slipped away. The other Negroes' mood was ugly, but they dispersed also, when we left. We wouldn't learn until later that a steel plate would have to be put into Brother Hinton's skull. (After that operation, the Nation of Islam helped him to sue; a jury awarded him over $70,000, the largest police brutality judgment that New York City has ever paid.)

For New York City's millions of readers of the downtown papers, it was, at that time, another one of the periodic "Racial Unrest in Harlem" stories. It was not played up, because of what had happened. But the police department, to be sure, pulled out and carefully studied the files on the Nation of Islam, and appraised us with new eyes. Most important, in Harlem, the world's most heavily populated black ghetto, the *Amsterdam News* made the whole story headline news, and for the first time the black man, woman, and child in the streets were discussing "those Muslims."

CHAPTER FOURTEEN

BLACK MUSLIMS

In the spring of nineteen fifty-nine—some months before Brother Johnson Hinton's case had awakened the Harlem black ghetto to us—a Negro journalist, Louis Lomax, then living in New York, asked me one morning whether our Nation of Islam would cooperate in being filmed as a television documentary program for the Mike Wallace Show, which featured controversial subjects. I told Lomax that, naturally, anything like that would have to be referred to The Honorable Elijah Muhammad. And Lomax did fly to Chicago to consult Mr. Muhammad. After questioning Lomax, then cautioning him against some things he did not desire, Mr. Muhammad gave his consent.

Cameramen began filming Nation of Islam scenes around our mosques in New York, Chicago, and Washington, D.C. Sound recordings were made of Mr. Muhammad and some ministers, including me, teaching black audiences the truths about the brainwashed black man and the devil white man.

At Boston University around the same time, C. Eric Lincoln, a Negro scholar then working for his doctorate, had selected for his thesis subject the Nation of Islam. Lincoln's interest had been aroused the previous year when, teaching at Clark College in Atlanta, Georgia, he received from one of his Religion students a term paper whose introduction I can now quote from Lincoln's book. It was the plainspoken convictions of one of Atlanta's numerous young black collegians who often visited our local Temple Fifteen.

"The Christian religion is incompatible with the Negro's aspirations for dignity and equality in America," the student had

240

written. "It has hindered where it might have helped; it has been evasive when it was morally bound to be forthright; it has separated believers on the basis of color, although it has declared its mission to be a universal brotherhood under Jesus Christ. Christian love is the white man's love for himself and for his race. For the man who is not white, Islam is the hope for justice and equality in the world we must build tomorrow."

After some preliminary research showed Professor Lincoln what a subject he had hold of, he had been able to obtain several grants, and a publisher's encouragement to expand his thesis into a book.

On the wire of our relatively small Nation, these two big developments—a television show, and a book about us—naturally were big news. Every Muslim happily anticipated that now, through the white man's powerful communications media, our brainwashed black brothers and sisters across the United States, and devils, too, were going to see, hear, and read Mr. Muhammad's teachings which cut back and forth like a two-edged sword.

We had made our own very limited efforts to employ the power of print. First, some time back, I had made an appointment to see editor James Hicks of the *Amsterdam News*, published in Harlem. Editor Hicks said he felt every voice in the community deserved to be heard. Soon, each week's *Amsterdam News* carried a little column that I wrote. Then, Mr. Muhammad agreed to write a column for that valuable *Amsterdam News* space, and my column was transferred to another black newspaper, the Los Angeles *Herald Dispatch*.

But I kept wanting to start, somehow, our own newspaper, that would be filled with Nation of Islam news.

Mr. Muhammad in 1957 sent me to organize a Temple in Los Angeles. When I had done that, being in that city where the *Herald Dispatch* was, I went visiting and I worked in their office; they let me observe how a newspaper was put together. I've always been blessed in that if I can once watch something being done, generally I can catch onto how to do it myself. Quick "picking up" was probably the number one survival rule when I'd been out there in the streets as a hustler.

Back in New York, I bought a secondhand camera. I don't know how many rolls of film I shot until I could take usable pictures. Every chance I had, I wrote some little news about interesting Nation of Islam happenings. One day every month, I'd lock up in a room and assemble my material and pictures for a printer that I found. I named the newspaper *Muhammad Speaks* and Muslim brothers sold it on the ghetto sidewalks. Little did I dream that later on, when jealousy set in among the hierarchy, nothing about me would be printed in the paper I had founded.

Anyway, national publicity was in the offing for the Nation of Islam when Mr. Muhammad sent me on a three-week trip to Africa. Even as small as we then were, some of the African and Asian personages had sent Mr. Muhammad private word that they liked his efforts to awaken and lift up the American black people. Sometimes, the messages had been sent through me. As Mr. Muhammad's emissary, I went to Egypt, Arabia, to the Sudan, to Nigeria, and Ghana.

You will often hear today a lot of the Negro leaders complaining that what thrust the Muslims into international prominence was the white man's press, radio, television, and other media. I have no shred of argument with that. They are absolutely correct. Why, none of us in the Nation of Islam remotely anticipated what was about to happen.

In late 1959, the television program was aired. "The Hate That Hate Produced"—the title—was edited tightly into a kaleidoscope of "shocker" images . . . Mr. Muhammad, me, and others speaking . . . strong-looking, set-faced black men, our Fruit of Islam . . . white-scarved, white-gowned Muslim sisters of all ages . . . Muslims in our restaurants, and other businesses . . . Muslims and other black people entering and leaving our mosques. . . .

Every phrase was edited to increase the shock mood. As the producers intended, I think people sat just about limp when the program went off.

In a way, the public reaction was like what happened back in the 1930's when Orson Welles frightened America with a radio program describing, as though it was actually happening, an invasion by "men from Mars."

No one now jumped from any windows, but in New York City there was an instant avalanche of public reaction. It's my personal opinion that the "Hate . . . Hate . . ." title was pri-

BLACK MUSLIMS   243

marily responsible for the reaction. Hundreds of thousands of
New Yorkers, black and white, were exclaiming "Did you hear
it? Did you see it? Preaching *hate* of white people!"

Here was one of the white man's most characteristic behavior
patterns—where black men are concerned. He loves himself so
much that he is startled if he discovers that his victims don't
share his vainglorious self-opinion. In America for centuries it
had been just fine as long as the victimized, brutalized and ex-
ploited black people had been grinning and begging and "Yessa,
Massa" and Uncle Tomming. But now, things were different.
First came the white newspapers—feature writers and colum-
nists: "Alarming" . . . "hate-messengers" . . . "threat to the
good relations between the races" . . . "black segregationists"
. . . "black supremacists," and the like.

And the newspapers' ink wasn't dry before the big national
weekly news magazines started: "Hate-teachers" . . . "violence-
seekers" . . . "black racists" . . . "black fascists" . . . "anti-
Christian" . . . "possibly Communist-inspired. . . ."

It rolled out of the presses of the biggest devil in the history
of mankind. And then the aroused white man made his next
move.

Since slavery, the American white man has always kept some
handpicked Negroes who fared much better than the black
masses suffering and slaving out in the hot fields. The white
man had these "house" and "yard" Negroes for his special
servants. He threw them more crumbs from his rich table, he
even let them eat in his kitchen. He knew that he could always
count on them to keep "good massa" happy in his self-image
of being so "good" and "righteous." "Good massa" always
heard just what he wanted to hear from these "house" and
"yard" blacks. "You're such a good, *fine* massa!" Or, "Oh,
massa, those old black nigger fieldhands out there, they're happy
just like they are; why, massa, they're not intelligent enough for
you to try and do any better for them, massa—"

Well, slavery time's "house" and "yard" Negroes had be-
come more sophisticated, that was all. When now the white man
picked up his telephone and dialed his "house" and "yard"
Negroes—why, he didn't even need to instruct the trained black
puppets. They had seen the television program; had read the

newspapers. They were already composing their lines. They knew what to do.

I'm not going to call any names. But if you make a list of the biggest Negro "leaders," so-called, in 1960, then you've named the ones who began to attack us "field" Negroes who were sounding *insane*, talking that way about "good massa."

"By no means do these Muslims represent the Negro masses—" That was the first worry, to reassure "good massa" that he had no reason to be concerned about his fieldhands in the ghettoes. "An irresponsible hate cult" . . . "an unfortunate Negro image, just when the racial picture is improving—"

They were stumbling over each other to get quoted. "A deplorable reverse-racism" . . . "Ridiculous pretenders to the ancient Islamic doctrine" . . . "Heretic anti-Christianity—"

The telephone in our then small Temple Seven restaurant nearly jumped off the wall. I had a receiver against my ear five hours a day. I was listening, and jotting in my notebook, as press, radio, and television people called, all of them wanting the Muslim reaction to the quoted attacks of these black "leaders." Or I was on long-distance to Mr. Muhammad in Chicago, reading from my notebook and asking for Mr. Muhammad's instructions.

I couldn't understand how Mr. Muhammad could maintain his calm and patience, hearing the things I told him. I could scarcely contain myself.

My unlisted home telephone number somehow got out. My wife Betty put down the phone after taking one message, and it was ringing again. It seemed that wherever I went, telephones were ringing.

The calls naturally were directed to me, New York City being the major news-media headquarters, and I was the New York minister of Mr. Muhammad. Calls came, long-distance from San Francisco to Maine . . . from even London, Stockholm, Paris. I would see a Muslim brother at our restaurant, or Betty at home, trying to keep cool; they'd hand me the receiver, and I couldn't believe it, either. One funny thing—in all that hectic period, something quickly struck my notice: the Europeans never pressed the "hate" question. Only the American white man was so plagued and obsessed with being "hated." He was so guilty, it was clear to me, of hating Negroes.

"Mr. Malcolm X, why do you teach black supremacy, and hate?" A red flag waved for me, something chemical happened inside me, every time I heard that. When we Muslims had talked about "the devil white man" he had been relatively abstract, someone we Muslims rarely actually came into contact with, but now here was that devil-in-the-flesh on the phone—with all of his calculating, cold-eyed, self-righteous tricks and nerve and gall. The voices questioning me became to me as breathing, living devils.

And I tried to pour on pure fire in return. "The white man so guilty of white supremacy can't hide *his* guilt by trying to accuse The Honorable Elijah Muhammad of teaching black supremacy and hate! All Mr. Muhammad is doing is trying to uplift the black man's mentality and the black man's social and economic condition in this country.

"The guilty, two-faced white man can't decide *what* he wants. Our slave foreparents would have been put to death for advocating so-called 'integration' with the white man. Now when Mr. Muhammad speaks of 'separation,' the white man calls us 'hate-teachers' and 'fascists'!

"The white man doesn't *want* the blacks! He doesn't *want* the blacks that are a parasite upon him! He doesn't *want* this black man whose presence and condition in this country expose the white man to the world for what he is! So why do you attack Mr. Muhammad?"

I'd have *scathing* in my voice; I *felt* it.

"For the white man to ask the black man if he hates him is just like the rapist asking the *raped*, or the wolf asking the *sheep*, 'Do you hate me?' The white man is in no moral *position* to accuse anyone else of hate!

"Why, when all of my ancestors are snake-bitten, and I'm snake-bitten, and I warn my children to avoid snakes, what does that *snake* sound like accusing *me* of hate-teaching?"

"Mr. Malcolm X," those devils would ask, "why is your Fruit of Islam being trained in judo and karate?" An image of black men learning anything suggesting self-defense seemed to terrify the white man. I'd turn their question around: "Why does judo or karate suddenly get so ominous because black men study it? Across America, the Boy Scouts, the YMCA, even the YWCA, the CYP, PAL—they *all* teach judo! It's all right, it's fine—until *black men* teach it! Even little grammar school classes, little girls, are taught to defend themselves—"

"How many of you are in your organization, Mr. Malcolm X? Right Reverend Bishop T. Chickenwing says you have only a handful of members—"

"Whoever tells you how many Muslims there are doesn't know, and whoever does know will never tell you—"

The Bishop Chickenwings were also often quoted about our "anti-Christianity." I'd fire right back on that:

"Christianity is the white man's religion. The Holy Bible in the white man's hands and his interpretations of it have been the greatest single ideological weapon for enslaving millions of non-white human beings. Every country the white man has conquered with his guns, he has always paved the way, and salved his conscience, by carrying the Bible and interpreting it to call the people 'heathens' and 'pagans'; then he sends his guns, then his missionaries behind the guns to mop up—"

White reporters, anger in their voices, would call us "demagogues," and I would try to be ready after I had been asked the same question two or three times.

"Well, let's go back to the Greek, and maybe you will learn the first thing you need to know about the word 'demagogue.' 'Demagogue' means, actually, 'teacher of the people.' And let's examine some demagogues. The greatest of all Greeks, Socrates, was killed as a 'demagogue.' Jesus Christ died on the cross because the Pharisees of His day were upholding their law, not the spirit. The modern Pharisees are trying to heap destruction upon Mr. Muhammad, calling him a demagogue, a crackpot, and fanatic. What about Gandhi? The man that Churchill called 'a naked little fakir,' refusing food in a British jail? But then a quarter of a billion people, a whole subcontinent, rallied behind Gandhi—and they twisted the British lion's tail! What about Galileo, standing before his inquisitors, saying 'The earth *does* move!' What about Martin Luther, nailing on a door his thesis against the all-powerful Catholic church which called him 'heretic'? We, the followers of The Honorable Elijah Muhammad, are today in the ghettoes as once the sect of Christianity's followers were like termites in the catacombs and the grottoes—and they were preparing the grave of the mighty Roman Empire!"

I can remember those hot telephone sessions with those reporters as if it were yesterday. The reporters were angry. I was angry. When I'd reach into history, they'd try to pull me back to the present. They would quit interviewing, quit their work, trying to defend their personal white devil selves. They would unearth Lincoln and his freeing of the slaves. I'd tell them things Lincoln said in speeches, *against* the blacks. They would drag up the 1954 Supreme Court decision on school integration.

"That was one of the greatest magical feats ever performed in America," I'd tell them. "Do you mean to tell me that nine Supreme Court judges, who are past masters of legal phraseology, couldn't have worked their decision to make it stick as *law?* No! It was trickery and magic that told Negroes they were desegregated—Hooray! Hooray!—and at the same time it told whites 'Here are your loopholes.' "

The reporters would try their utmost to raise some "good" white man whom I couldn't refute as such. I'll never forget how one practically lost his voice. He asked me did I feel *any* white men had ever done anything for the black man in America. I told him, "Yes, I can think of two. Hitler, and Stalin. The black man in America couldn't get a decent factory job until Hitler put so much pressure on the white man. And then Stalin kept up the pressure—"

But I don't care what points I made in the interviews, it practically never got printed the way I said it. I was learning under fire how the press, when it wants to, can twist, and slant. If I had said "Mary had a little lamb," what probably would have appeared was "Malcolm X Lampoons Mary."

Even so, my bitterness was less against the white press than it was against those Negro "leaders" who kept attacking us. Mr. Muhammad said he wanted us to try our best not to publicly counterattack the black "leaders" because one of the white man's tricks was keeping the black race divided and fighting against each other. Mr. Muhammad said that this had traditionally kept the black people from achieving the unity which was the worst need of the black race in America.

But instead of abating, the black puppets continued ripping and tearing at Mr. Muhammad and the Nation of Islam—until it began to appear as though we were afraid to speak out against these "important" Negroes. That's when Mr. Muhammad's patience wore thin. And with his nod, I began returning their fire.

"Today's Uncle Tom doesn't wear a handkerchief on his head. This modern, twentieth-century Uncle Thomas now often wears a top hat. He's usually well-dressed and well-educated. He's often the personification of culture and refinement. The twentieth-century Uncle Thomas sometimes speaks with a Yale or Harvard accent. Sometimes he is known as Professor, Doctor, Judge, and Reverend, even Right Reverend Doctor. This twentieth-century Uncle Thomas is a *professional* Negro . . . by that I mean his profession is being a Negro for the white man."

Never before in America had these hand-picked so-called "leaders" been publicly blasted in this way. They reacted to the truth about themselves even more hotly than the devilish white man. Now their "institutional" indictments of us began. Instead of "leaders" speaking as themselves, for themselves, now their weighty name organizations attacked Mr. Muhammad.

"Black bodies with white heads!" I called them what they were. Every one of those "Negro progress" organizations had the same composition. Black "leaders" were out in the public eye—to be seen by the Negroes for whom they were supposed to be fighting the white man. But obscurely, behind the scenes, was a white boss—a president, or board chairman, or some other title, pulling the real strings.

It was hot, hot copy, both in the white and the black press. *Life*, *Look*, *Newsweek* and *Time* reported us. Some newspaper chains began to run not one story, but a series of three, four, or five "exposures" of the Nation of Islam. The *Reader's Digest* with its worldwide circulation of twenty-four million copies in thirteen languages carried an article titled "Mr. Muhammad Speaks," by the writer to whom I am telling this book; and that led off other major monthly magazines' coverage of us.

Before very long, radio and television people began asking me to defend our Nation of Islam in panel discussions and debates. I was to be confronted by hand-picked scholars, both whites and some of those Ph.D. "house" and "yard" Negroes who had been attacking us. Every day, I was more incensed with the general misrepresentation and distortion of Mr. Muhammad's teachings; I truly think that not once did it cross my mind that previously I never had been *inside* a radio or television station—

let alone faced a microphone to audiences of millions of people. Prison debating had been my only experience speaking to anyone but Muslims.

From the old hustling days I knew that there were tricks to everything. In the prison debating, I had learned tricks to upset my opponents, to catch them where they didn't expect to be caught. I knew there were bound to be tricks I didn't know anything about arguing on the air.

I knew that if I closely studied what the others did, I could learn things in a hurry to help me to defend Mr. Muhammad and his teachings.

I'd walk into those studios. The devils and black Ph.D. puppets would be acting so friendly and "integrated" with each other—laughing and calling each other by first names, and all that; it was such a big lie it made me sick in my stomach. They would even be trying to act friendly toward me—we all knowing they had asked me there to try and beat out my brains. They would offer me coffee. I would tell them "No, thanks," to please just tell me where was I supposed to sit. Sometimes the microphone sat on the table before you, at other times a smaller, cylindrical microphone was hung on a cord around your neck. From the start, I liked those microphones better; I didn't have to keep constantly aware of my distance from a microphone on the table.

The program hosts would start with some kind of dice-loading, non-religious introduction for me. It would be something like "—and we have with us today the fiery, angry chief Malcolm X of the New York Muslims. . . ." I made up my own introduction. At home, or driving my car, I practiced until I could interrupt a radio or television host and introduce myself.

"I represent Mr. Elijah Muhammad, the spiritual head of the fastest-growing group of Muslims in the Western Hemisphere. We who follow him know that he has been divinely taught and sent to us by God Himself. We believe that the miserable plight of America's twenty million black people is the fulfillment of divine prophecy. We also believe the presence today in America of The Honorable Elijah Muhammad, his teachings among the so-called Negroes, and his naked warning to America concerning her treatment of these so-called Negroes, is all the fulfillment of divine prophecy. I am privileged to be the minister of our

Temple Number Seven here in New York City which is a part of the Nation of Islam, under the divine leadership of The Honorable Elijah Muhammad—''

I would look around at those devils and their trained black parrots staring at me, while I was catching my breath—and I had set my tone.

They would outdo each other, leaping in on me, hammering at Mr. Muhammad, at me, and at the Nation of Islam. Those ''integration''-mad Negroes—you know what they jumped on. *Why* couldn't Muslims *see* that ''integration'' was the answer to American Negroes' problems? I'd try to rip that to pieces.

''No *sane* black man really wants integration! No *sane* white man really wants integration! No sane black man really believes that the white man ever will give the black man anything more than token integration. No! The Honorable Elijah Muhammad teaches that for the black man in America the only solution is complete *separation* from the white man!''

Anyone who has ever heard me on radio or television programs knows that my technique is non-stop, until what I want to get said is said. I was developing the technique then.

''The Honorable Elijah Muhammad teaches us that since Western society is deteriorating, it has become overrun with immorality, and God is going to judge it, and destroy it. And the only way the black people caught up in this society can be saved is not to *integrate* into this corrupt society, but to *separate* from it, to a land of our *own*, where we can reform ourselves, lift up our moral standards, and try to be godly. The Western world's most learned diplomats have failed to solve this grave race problem. Her learned legal experts have failed. Her sociologists have failed. Her civil leaders have failed. Her fraternal leaders have failed. Since all of these have *failed* to solve this race problem, it is time for us to sit down and *reason!* I am certain that we will be forced to agree that it takes *God Himself* to solve this grave racial dilemma.''

Every time I mentioned ''separation,'' some of them would cry that we Muslims were standing for the same thing that white racists and demagogues stood for. I would explain the difference. ''No! We reject *segregation* even more militantly than you say you do! We want *separation*, which is not the same! The Honorable Elijah Muhammad teaches us that *segregation* is when your life and liberty are controlled, regulated, *by someone else*. To *segregate* means to control. Segregation is that which is forced upon inferiors by superiors. But *separation* is that which is done voluntarily, by two equals—for the good of both! The Honorable Elijah Muhammad teaches us that as long as our people here in America are dependent upon the white man, we will always be begging him for jobs, food, clothing, and housing. And he will always control our lives, regulate our lives, and have the power to segregate us. The Negro here in America has been treated like a child. A child stays within the mother until the time of birth! When the time of birth arrives, the child must be separated, or it will *destroy* its mother and itself. The mother can't carry that child after its time. The child cries for and needs its own world!''

Anyone who has listened to me will have to agree that I believed in Elijah Muhammad and represented him one hundred per cent. I never tried to take any credit for myself.

I was never in one of those panel discussions without some of them just waiting their chance to accuse me of ''inciting Negroes to violence.'' I didn't even have to do any special studying to prepare for that one.

''The greatest miracle Christianity has achieved in America is that the black man in white Christian hands has not grown violent. It *is* a miracle that 22 million black people have not *risen up* against their oppressors—in which they would have been justified by all moral criteria, and even by the democratic tradition! It is a miracle that a nation of black people has so fervently continued to believe in a turn-the-other-cheek and heaven-for-you-after-you-die philosophy! It *is a miracle* that the American black people have remained a peaceful people, while catching all the centuries of hell that they have caught, here in white man's heaven! The *miracle* is that the white man's puppet Negro 'leaders,' his preachers and the educated Negroes laden with degrees, and others who have been allowed to wax fat off their black poor brothers, have been able to hold the black masses quiet until now.''

I guarantee you one thing—every time I was mixed up in those studios with those brainwashed, ''integration''-mad black puppets, and those tricky devils trying to rip and tear me down, as long as the little red light glowed "on the air," I tried to represent Elijah Muhammad and the Nation of Islam to the utmost.

Dr. C. Eric Lincoln's book was published amid widening controversy about us Muslims, at just about the time we were starting to put on our first big mass rallies.

Just as the television "Hate That Hate Produced" title had projected that "hate-teaching" image of us, now Dr. Lincoln's book was titled *The Black Muslims in America*. The press snatched at that name. "Black Muslims" was in all the book reviews, which quoted from the book only what was critical of us, and generally praised Dr. Lincoln's writing.

The public mind fixed on "Black Muslims." From Mr. Muhammad on down, the name "Black Muslims" distressed everyone in the Nation of Islam. I tried for at least two years to kill off that "*Black* Muslims." Every newspaper and magazine writer and microphone I got close to: "*No!* We are black *people* here in America. Our *religion* is Islam. We are properly called 'Muslims'!" But that "Black Muslims" name never got dislodged.

Our mass rallies, from their very beginning, were astounding successes. Where once Detroit's struggling little Temple One proudly sent a ten-automobile caravan to Chicago to hear Mr. Muhammad, now, from East Coast Temples—the older Temples as well as the new ones that all of the massive publicity had helped us to bring into being—as many as 150, 200 and even as many as 300 big, chartered buses rolled the highways to wherever Mr. Muhammad was going to speak. On each bus, two Fruit of Islam men were in charge. Big three-by-nine-foot painted canvas banners hung on the buses' sides, to be read by the highway traffic and thousands of people at home and on the sidewalks of the towns the buses passed through.

Hundreds more Muslims and curious Negroes drove their own cars. And Mr. Muhammad with his personal jet plane from Chicago. From the airport to the rally hall, Mr. Muhammad's motorcade had a siren-screaming police escort. Law agencies once had scoffed at our Nation as "black crackpots"; now they took special pains to safeguard against some "white crackpots" causing any "incidents" or "accidents."

America had never seen such fantastic all-black meetings! To hear Elijah Muhammad, up to ten thousand and more black people poured from public and private transportation to overflow the big halls we rented, such as the St. Nicholas Arena in New York City, Chicago's Coliseum, and Washington, D.C.'s Uline Arena.

The white man was barred from attendance—the first time the American black man had ever dreamed of such a thing. And that brought us new attacks from the white man and his black puppets. "Black segregationists . . . racists!" Accusing *us* of segregation! Across America, whites barring blacks was standard.

Many hundreds arrived too late for us to seat them. We always had to wire up outside loudspeakers. An electric atmosphere excited the great, shifting masses of black people. The long lines, three and four abreast, funneling to the meeting hall, were kept in strict order by Fruit of Islam men communicating by walkie-talkie. In anterooms just inside the halls, more Fruit of Islam men and white-gowned, veiled mature Muslim sisters thoroughly searched every man, woman, and child seeking to enter. Any alcohol and tobacco had to be checked, and any objects which could possibly be used to attempt to harm Mr. Muhammad. He always seemed deathly afraid that some one would harm him, and he insisted that everyone be searched to forestall this. Today I understand better, why.

The hundreds of Fruit of Islam men represented contingents which had arrived early that morning, from their Temples in the nearest cities. Some were detailed as ushers, who seated the people by designated sections. The balconies and the rear half of the main floor were filled with black people of the general public. Ahead of them were the all-Muslim seating sections— the white-garbed beautiful black sisters, and the dark-suited, white-shirted brothers. A special section near the front was for black so-called "dignitaries." Many of these had been invited. Among them were our black puppet and parrot attackers, the intellectuals and professional Negroes over whom Mr. Muhammad grieved so much, for these were the educated ones who should have been foremost in leading their poor black brothers out of the maze of misery and want. We wanted them to miss not a single syllable of the truths from Mr. Muhammad in person.

The front two or three press rows were filled with the black reporters and cameramen representing the Negro press, or those who had been hired by the white man's newspapers, magazines, radio, and television. America's black writers should hold a banquet for Mr. Muhammad. Writing about the Nation of Islam was the path to success for most of the black writers who now are recognized.

Up on the speaker's platform, we ministers and other officials of the Nation, entering from backstage, found ourselves chairs in the five or six rows behind the big chair reserved for Mr. Muhammad. Some of the ministers had come hundreds of miles to be present. We would be turning about in our chairs, beaming with smiles, wringing each other's hands, and exchanging "As-Salaam-Alaikum" and "Wa-Alaikum-Salaam" in our genuine deep rejoicing to see each other again.

Always, meeting us older hands in Mr. Muhammad's service for the first time, there were several new ministers of small new Temples. My brothers Wilfred and Philbert were respectively now the ministers of the Detroit and Lansing Temples. Minister Jeremiah X headed Atlanta's Temple. Minister John X had Los Angeles' Temple. The Messenger's son, Minister Wallace Muhammad, had the Philadelphia Temple. Minister Woodrow X had the Atlantic City Temple. Some of our ministers had unusual backgrounds. The Washington, D.C., Temple Minister Lucius X was previously a Seventh Day Adventist and a 32nd degree Mason. Minister George X of the Camden, New Jersey, Temple was a pathologist. Minister David X was previously the minister of a Richmond, Virginia, Christian church; he and enough of his congregation had become Muslims so that the congregation split and the majority turned the church into our Richmond Temple. The Boston Temple's outstanding young Minister Louis X, previously a well-known and rising popular singer called "The Charmer," had written our Nation's popular first song, titled "White Man's Heaven is Black Man's Hell." Minister Louis X had also authored our first play, "Orgena" ("A Negro" spelled backwards); its theme was the all-black trial of a symbolic white man for his world crimes against non-whites; found guilty, sentenced to death, he was dragged off shouting about all he had done "for the nigra people."

Younger even than our talented Louis X were some newer ministers, Minister Thomas J. X of the Hartford Temple being one example, and another the Buffalo Temple's Minister Robert J. X.

I had either originally established or organized for Mr. Muhammad most of the represented temples. Greeting each of these Temples' brother ministers would bring back into my mind images of "fishing" for converts along the streets and from door-to-door wherever the black people were congregated. I remembered the countless meetings in living rooms where maybe seven would be a crowd; the gradually building, building—on up to renting folding chairs for dingy little storefronts which Muslims scrubbed to spotlessness.

We together on a huge hall's speaking platform, and that vast audience before us, miraculously manifested, as far as I was concerned, the incomprehensible power of Allah. For the first time, I truly understood something Mr. Muhammad had told me: he claimed that when he was going through the sacrificial trials of fleeing the black hypocrites from city to city, Allah had often sent him visions of great audiences who would one day hear the teachings; and Mr. Muhammad said the visions also buoyed him when he was locked up for years in the white man's prison.

The great audience's restless whisperings would cease. . . .

At the microphone would be the Nation's National Secretary John Ali, or the Boston Temple Minister Louis X. They enlivened the all-black atmosphere, speaking of the new world open to the black man through the Nation of Islam. Sister Tynetta Dynear would speak beautifully of the Muslim women's powerful, vital contributions, of the Muslim women's roles in our Nation's efforts to raise the physical, mental, moral, social, and political condition of America's black people.

Next, I would come to the microphone, specifically to condition the audience to hear Mr. Muhammad, who had flown from Chicago to teach us all in person.

I would raise up my hand, *"As-Salaikum-Salaam—"*

"Wa-Alaikum-Salaam!" It was a roared response from the great audience's Muslim seating section.

There was a general pattern that I would follow on these occasions:

"My black brothers and sisters—of all religious beliefs, or of no religious beliefs—we all have in common the greatest binding tie we could have . . . we all are *black* people!

"I'm not going to take all day telling you some of the greatnesses of The Honorable Elijah Muhammad. I'm just going to tell you now his *greatest* greatness! He is the *first*, the *only* black leader to identify, to you and me, *who* is our enemy!

"The Honorable Elijah Muhammad is the first black leader among us with the *courage* to tell us—out here in public— something which when you begin to think of it back in your homes, you will realize we black people have been *living* with, we have been *seeing*, we have been *suffering*, all of our lives!

"Our *enemy* is the *white man!*

"And why is Mr. Muhammad's teaching us this such a great thing? Because when you know *who* your enemy is, he can no longer keep you divided, and fighting, one brother against the other! Because when you *recognize* who your enemy is, he can no longer use trickery, promises, lies, hypocrisy, and his evil acts to keep you deaf, dumb, and blinded!

"When you recognize *who* your enemy is, he can no longer brainwash you, he can no longer pull wool over your eyes so that you never stop to see that you are living in pure *hell* on this earth, while *he* lives in pure *heaven* right on this same earth!— This enemy who tells you that you are both supposed to be worshiping the same white Christian God that—you are told— stands for the *same* things for *all* men!

"Oh, *yes*, that devil is our enemy. I'll *prove* it! Pick up any daily newspaper! Read the false charges leveled against our beloved religious leader. It only points up the fact that the Caucasian race never wants any black man who is not their puppet or parrot to speak for our people. This Caucasian devil slave-master does not want or trust us to leave him—yet when we stay here among him, he continues to keep us at the very *lowest level* of his society!

"The white man has always *loved* it when he could keep us black men tucked away somewhere, always out of sight, around the corner! The white man has always *loved* the kind of black leaders whom he could ask, 'Well, how's things with your people up there?' But because Mr. Elijah Muhammad takes an uncompromising stand with the white man, the white man *hates* him! When you hear the *white man* hate him, you, too, because you don't understand Biblical prophecy, wrongly label Mr. Muhammad—as a racist, a hate-teacher, or of being anti-white and teaching black supremacy—''

The audience suddenly would begin a rustling of turning. . . .

Mr. Muhammad would be rapidly moving along up a center aisle from the rear—as once he had entered our humble little mosques—this man whom we regarded as Islam's gentle, meek, brown-skinned Lamb. Stalwart, striding, close-cropped, handpicked Fruit of Islam guards were a circle surrounding him. He carried his Holy Bible, his holy Quran. The small, dark pillbox atop his head was gold-embroidered with Islam's flag, the sun, moon, and stars. The Muslims were crying out their adoration and their welcome. ''Little Lamb!'' ''As-Salaikum-Salaam!'' ''Praise be to Allah!''

Tears would be in more eyes than mine. He had rescued me when I was a convict; Mr. Muhammad had trained me in his home, as if I was his son. I think that my life's peaks of emotion, until recently, at least, were when, suddenly, the Fruit of Islam guards would stop stiffly at attention, and the platform's several steps would be mounted alone by Mr. Muhammad, and his ministers, including me, sprang around him, embracing him, wringing both his hands. . . .

I would turn right back to the microphone, not to keep waiting those world's biggest black audiences who had come to hear him.

''My black brothers and sisters—*no* one will know *who* we are . . . until *we* know who we are! We never will be able to *go* anywhere until we know *where* we are! The Honorable Elijah Muhammad is giving us a true identity, and a true position—the first time they have ever been *known* to the American black man!

''You can be around this man and never *dream* from his actions the power and the authority he has—'' (Behind me, believe me when I tell you, I could *feel* Mr. Muhammad's *power*.)

''He does not *display*, and *parade*, his *power*! But no other black leader in America has followers who will lay down their lives if he says so! And I don't mean all of this non-violent, begging-the-white-man kind of dying . . . all of this sitting-in, sliding-in, wading-in, eating-in, diving-in, and all the rest—

''My black brothers and sisters, you have come from your homes to hear—now you are *going* to hear—America's *wisest* black man! America's *boldest* black man! America's most *fearless* black man! This wilderness of North America's most *powerful* black man!''

Mr. Muhammad would come quickly to the stand, looking out over the vacuum-quiet audience, his gentle-looking face set, for just a fleeting moment. Then, ''As-Salaikum-Salaam—''

''WA-ALAIKUM-SALAAM!''

The Muslims roared it, as they settled to listen. From experience, they knew that for the next two hours Mr. Muhammad would wield his two-edged sword of truth. In fact, every Muslim worried that he overtaxed himself in the length of his speeches, considering his bronchial asthmatic condition.

''I don't have a degree like many of you out there before me have. But history don't care anything about your degrees.

''The white man, he has filled you with a fear of him from ever since you were little black babies. So over you is the greatest enemy a man can have—and that is fear. I know some of you are afraid to listen to the truth—you have been raised on fear and lies. But I am going to preach to you the truth until you are free of that fear. . . .

''Your slavemaster, he brought you over here, and of your past everything was destroyed. Today, you do not know your true language. What tribe are you from? You would not recognize your tribe's name if you heard it. You don't know nothing about your true culture. You don't even know your family's real name. You are wearing a *white man's* name! The white slavemaster, who *hates* you!

''You are a people who think you know all about the Bible, and all about Christianity. You even are foolish enough to believe that nothing is *right* but Christianity!

''You are the planet Earth's only group of people ignorant of yourself, ignorant of your own kind, of your true history, ignorant of your enemy! You know nothing at *all* but what your white slavemaster has chosen to tell you. And he has told you only that which will benefit himself, and his own kind. He has taught you, for *his* benefit, that you are a neutral, shiftless, helpless so-called 'Negro.'

''I say *'so-called'* because you are *not* a *'Negro.'* There is no such thing as a race of *'Negroes.'* You are members of the Asiatic nation, from the tribe of *Shabazz!* 'Negro' is a false label forced on you by your slavemaster! He has been pushing things onto you and me and our kind ever since he brought the first slave shipload of us black people here—''

When Mr. Muhammad paused, the Muslims before him cried out, "Little Lamb!" . . . "All praise is due to Allah!" . . . "*Teach*, Messenger!" He would continue.

"The *ignorance* we of the black race here in America have, and the *self-hatred* we have, they are fine examples of what the white slavemaster has seen fit to teach to us. Do we show the plain common sense, like every other people on this planet Earth, to unite among ourselves? No! We are humbling ourselves, sitting-in, and begging-in, trying to *unite* with the slavemaster! I don't seem able to imagine any more ridiculous sight. A thousand ways every day, the white man is telling you 'You can't live here, you can't enter here, you can't eat here, drink here, walk here, work here, you can't ride here, you can't play here, you can't study here.' Haven't we yet seen enough to see that he has no plan to *unite* with you?

"You have tilled his fields! Cooked his food! Washed his clothes! You have cared for his wife and children when he was away. In many cases, you have even suckled him at your *breast!* You have been far and away better Christians than this slavemaster who *taught* you his Christianity!

"You have sweated blood to help him build a country so rich that he can today afford to give away millions—even to his *enemies!* And when those enemies have gotten enough from him to then be able to attack him, you have been his brave soldiers, *dying* for him. And you have been always his most faithful servant during the so-called 'peaceful' times—

"And, *still*, this Christian American white man has not got it in him to find the human *decency*, and enough sense of *justice*, to recognize us, and accept us, the black people who have done so much for him, as fellow human beings!"

"YAH, Man!" . . . "*Um-huh!*" "*Teach*, Messenger!" . . . "*Yah!*" . . . "*Tell 'em!*" . . . "You *right!*" . . . "Take your *time* up there, little Messenger!" . . . "Oh, *yes!*"

Others besides the Muslims would be shouting now. We Muslims were less extroverted than Christian Negroes. It would sound now like an old-fashioned camp meeting.

"So let us, the black people, *separate* ourselves from this white man slavemaster, who despises us so much! You are out here begging him for some so-called *'integration!'* But what is this slavemaster white, *rapist*, going about saying! He is saying *he* won't integrate because black blood will *mongrelize* his race! *He* says that—and look at *us!* Turn around in your seats and look at each other! This slavemaster white man already has *'integrated'* us until you can hardly find among us today any more than a very few who are the black color of our foreparents!''

"God-a-mighty, the man's right!" . . . "*Teach*, Messenger—" "*Hear* him! *Hear* him!"

"He has left such a little black in us," Mr. Muhammad would go on, "that now he despises us so bad—meaning he despises *himself*, for what he has *done* to us—that he tells us that *legally* if we have got *one drop* of black blood in us, that means you are all-black as far as his laws are concerned! Well, if that's all we've got left, we want to *reclaim* that one drop!''

Mr. Muhammad's frail strength could be seen to be waning. But he would teach on:

"So let us *separate* from this white man, and for the same reason *he* says—in time to save ourselves from any more *'integration!'*

"Why *shouldn't* this white man who likes to think and call himself so good, and so generous, this white man who finances even his enemies—why *shouldn't* he subsidize a separate state, a separate territory, for we black people who have been such faithful slaves and servants? A separate territory on which we can lift *ourselves* out of these white man's *slums* for us, and his *breadlines* for us. And even for *those* he is complaining that we cost him too much! We can do something for *ourselves!* We never have done what we *could*—because we have been brainwashed so well by the slavemaster white man that we must come to him, begging him, for everything we want, and need—''

After perhaps ninety minutes, behind Mr. Muhammad, every minister would have to restrain himself from bolting up to his side, to urge him that it was enough. He would be pressing his hands tightly against the edges of the speaker's stand, to support himself.

"We black people don't *know* what we can do. You never can know what *anything* can do—until it is set *free*, to act by itself! If you have a cat in your house that you pamper and pet, you have to free that cat, set it on its *own*, in the woods, before you can see that the cat had it *in* him to shelter and feed itself!

"We, the black people here in America, we never have been *free* to find *out* what we really can *do!* We have knowledge and experience to pool to do for ourselves! All of our lives we have farmed—we can grow our own food. We can set up factories to manufacture our own necessities! We can build other kinds of businesses, to establish trade, and commerce—and become independent, as other civilized people are—

"We can *throw off* our brainwashing, and our self-hate, and live as *brothers* together . . .

". . . some land of our *own!* . . . Something for *ourselves!* . . . leave this white slavemaster to *himself.* . . . "

Mr. Muhammad always stopped abruptly when he was unable to speak any longer.

The standing ovation, a solid wall of sound, would go on unabating.

Standing up there, flailing my arms, finally I could quiet the audiences as Fruit of Islam ushers began to pass along the seating rows the large, waxed paper buckets we used to take up the collection. I would speak.

"You *know*, from what you have just heard, that no white money finances The Honorable Elijah Muhammad and his program—to 'advise' him and 'contain' him! Mr. Muhammad's program, and his followers, are not 'integrated.' Mr. Muhammad's program and organization are *all*-black!

"We are the *only* black organization that *only* black people support! These so-called 'Negro progress' organizations—Why, they insult your intelligence, claiming they are fighting in your behalf, to get you the equal rights you are asking for . . . claiming they are *fighting* the white man who refuses to give you your rights. Why, the white man *supports* those organizations! If you belong, you pay your two, or three, or five dollars a year—but *who* gives those organizations those two, and three, and five *thousand* dollar donations? The *white* man! He *feeds* those organizations! So he controls those organizations! He *advises* them—so he *contains* them! Use your common sense—aren't you going to advise and control and contain anyone that you support, like your child?

"The white man would love to support Mr. Elijah Muhammad. Because if Mr. Muhammad had to rely on his support, he could *advise* Mr. Muhammad. My black brothers and sisters, it is *only* because *your* money, *black* money, supports Mr. Muhammad, that he can hold these all-black meetings from city to city, telling us black men the *truth!* That's why we are asking for your all-black *support!*''

Nearly all bills—and far from all one-dollar bills, either, filled the waxed buckets. The buckets were swiftly emptied, then refilled, as the Fruit of Islam ushers covered the entire audience.

The audience atmosphere was almost as if the people had gone limp. The collections always covered the rally expenses, and anything beyond that helped to continue building the Nation of Islam.

After several big rallies, Mr. Muhammad directed that we would admit the white press. Fruit of Islam men thoroughly searched them, as everyone else was searched—their notebooks, their cameras, camera cases, and whatever else they carried. Later, Mr. Muhammad said that *any* whites who wanted to hear the truth could attend our public rallies, until a small separate section for whites was filled.

Most whites who came were students and scholars. I would watch their congealed and reddened faces staring up at Mr. Muhammad. ''The white man *knows* that his acts have been those of a devil!'' I would watch also the faces of the professional black men, the so-called intellectuals who attacked us. They possessed the academic know-how, they possessed the technical and the scientific skills that could help to lead their mass of poor, black brothers out of our condition. But all these intellectual and professional black men could seem to think of was humbling themselves, and begging, trying to ''integrate'' with the so-called ''liberal'' white man who was telling them, ''In time . . . everything's going to work out one day . . . just wait and have patience.'' These intellectual and professional Negroes couldn't use what they knew for the benefit of their own black kind simply because even among themselves they were disunited. United among themselves, united with their own kind, they could have benefited black people all over the world!

I would watch the faces of those intellectual and professional Negroes growing grave, and set—as the truth hit home to them. We were watched. Our telephones were tapped. Still right today, on my home telephone, if I said, "I'm going to bomb the Empire State Building," I guarantee you in five minutes it would be surrounded. When I was speaking publicly sometimes I'd guess which were F.B.I. faces in the audience, or other types of agents. Both the police and the F.B.I. intently and persistently visited and questioned us. "I do not fear them," Mr. Muhammad said. "I have all that I need—the truth."

Many a night, I drifted off to sleep, filled with wonder at how the two-edged-sword teachings so hurt, confused, concerned, and upset the government full of men trained highly in all of the modern sciences. I felt that it never could have been unless The Most Learned One, Allah Himself, had given the little fourth-grade-trained Messenger something.

Black agents were sent to infiltrate us. But the white man's "secret" spy often proved, first of all, a black man. I can't say *all* of them, of course, there's no way to know—but some of them, after joining us, and hearing, seeing and *feeling* the truth for every black man, revealed their roles to us. Some resigned from the white man's agencies and came to work in the Nation of Islam. A few kept their jobs to counterspy, telling us the white man's statements and plans about our Nation. This was how we learned that after wanting to know what happened within our Temples, the white law agencies' second major concern was the thing that I believe still ranks today as a big worry among America's penologists: the steadily increasing rate at which black convicts embrace Islam.

Generally, while still in prison, our convict-converts preconditioned themselves to meet our Nation's moral laws. As it had happened with me, when they left prison, they entered a Temple fully qualified to become registered Muslims. In fact, convict-converts usually were better prepared than were numerous prospective Muslims who never had been inside a prison.

We were not nearly so easy to enter as a Christian church. One did not merely declare himself a follower of Mr. Muhammad, then continue leading the same old, sinful, immoral life. The Muslim first had to change his physical and moral self to meet our strict rules. To remain a Muslim he had to maintain those rules.

Few temple meetings were held, for instance, without the

minister looking down upon some freshly shaved bald domes of new Muslim brothers in the audience. They had just banished from their lives forever that phony, lye-conked, metallic-looking hair, or "the process," as some call it these days. It grieves me that I don't care where you go, you see this symbol of ignorance and self-hate on so many Negroes' heads. I know it's bound to hurt the feelings of some of my good conked non-Muslim friends—but if you study closely any conked or "processed" Negro, you usually find he is an ignorant Negro. Whatever "show" or "front" he affects, his hair lye-cooked to be "white-looking" fairly shouts to everyone who looks at his head, "I'm ashamed to be a Negro." He will discover, just as I did, that he will be much-improved mentally whenever he discovers enough black self-pride to have that mess clipped off, and then wear the natural hair that God gives black men to wear.

No Muslim smokes—that was another of our rules. Some prospective Muslims found it more difficult to quit tobacco than others found quitting the dope habit. But black men and women quit more easily when we got them to consider seriously how the white man's government cared less about the public's health than about continuing the tobacco industry's *billions* in tax revenue. "What does a serviceman pay for a carton of cigarettes?" a prospective Muslim convert would be asked. It helped him to see that every regularly priced carton he bought meant that the white man's government took around two dollars of a black man's hard-earned money for taxes, not for tobacco.

You may have read somewhere—a lot has been written concerning it—about the Nation of Islam's phenomenal record of dope-addiction cures of longtime junkies. In fact, the *New York Times* carried a story about how some of the social agencies have asked representatives of the Muslim program for clinical suggestions.

The Muslim program began with recognizing that color and addiction have a distinct connection. It is no accident that in the entire Western Hemisphere, the greatest localized concentration of addicts is in *Harlem*.

Our cure program's first major ingredient was the painfully patient work of Muslims who previously were junkies themselves.

In the ghetto's dope jungle, the Muslim ex-junkies would fish out addicts who knew them back in those days. Then with an agonizing patience that might span anywhere from a few months to a year, our ex-junkie Muslims would conduct the addicts through the Muslim six-point therapeutic process.

The addict first was brought to admit to himself that he was an addict. Secondly, he was taught *why* he used narcotics. Third, he was shown that there was a *way* to stop addiction. Fourth, the addict's shattered self-image, and ego, were built up until the addict realized that he had, *within*, the self-power to end his addiction. Fifth, the addict voluntarily underwent a cold turkey break with drugs. Sixth, finally cured, now an ex-addict completes the cycle by "fishing" up other addicts whom he knows, and supervising their salvaging.

This sixth stage always instantly eliminated what so often defeats the average social agencies—the characteristic addict's hostility and suspicion. The addict who is "fished" up knew personally that the Muslim approaching him very recently had the same fifteen to thirty dollar a day habit. The Muslim may be this addict's buddy; they had plied the same dope jungle. They even may have been thieves together. The addict had *seen* the Muslim drifting off to sleep leaning against a building, or stepping as high over a matchstick as if it were a dog. And the Muslim, approaching the addict, uses the same old junkie jungle language.

Like the alcoholic, the junkie can never start to cure himself until he recognizes and accepts his true condition. The Muslim sticks like a leech, drumming at his old junkie buddy, "You're hooked, man!" It might take months before the addict comes to grips with this. The curative program is never really underway until this happens.

The next cure-phase is the addict's realization of *why* he takes dope. Still working on his man, right in the old jungle locale, in dives that you wouldn't believe existed, the Muslim often collects audiences of a dozen junkies. They listen only because they know the clean-cut proud Muslim had earlier been like them.

Every addict takes junk to escape something, the Muslim explains. He explains that most black junkies really are trying to narcotize themselves against being a black man in the white man's America. But, actually, the Muslim says, the black man taking dope is only helping the white man to "prove" that the black man is nothing.

The Muslim talks confidentially, and straight. "Daddy, you know I know how you feel. Wasn't I right out here with you? Scratching like a monkey, smelling all bad, living mad, hungry, stealing and running and hiding from Whitey. Man, what's a black man buying Whitey's dope for but to make Whitey richer—killing yourself!"

The Muslim can tell when his quarry is ready to be shown that the way for him to quit dope is through joining the Nation of Islam. The addict is brought into the local Muslim restaurant, he may occasionally be exposed to some other social situations—among proud, clean Muslims who show each other mutual affection and respect instead of the familiar hostility of the ghetto streets. For the first time in years, the addict hears himself called, genuinely, "Brother," "Sir", and "Mr." No one cares about his past. His addiction may casually be mentioned, but if so, it is spoken of as merely an especially tough challenge that he must face. Everyone whom this addict meets is confident that he will kick his habit.

As the addict's new image of himself builds, inevitably he begins thinking that he can break the habit. For the first time he is feeling the effects of black self-pride.

That's a powerful combination for a man who has been existing in the mud of society. In fact, once he is motivated no one can change more completely than the man who has been at the bottom. I call myself the best example of that.

Finally, vitally, this addict will decide for himself that he wants to go on cold turkey. This means to endure the physical agonies of abruptly quitting dope.

When this time comes, ex-addict Muslims will arrange to spend the necessary days in around-the-clock shifts, attending the addict who intends to purge himself, on the way to becoming a Muslim.

When the addict's withdrawal sets in, and he is screaming, cursing, and begging, "Just one shot, man!" the Muslims are right there talking junkie jargon to him. "Baby, knock that monkey off your back! Kick that habit! Kick Whitey off your back!" The addict, writhing in pain, his nose and eyes running, is pouring sweat from head to foot. He's trying to knock his head against the wall, flailing his arms, trying to fight his attendants, he is vomiting, suffering diarrhea. "Don't hold nothing back! Let Whitey go, baby! You're going to stand tall, man! I can see you now in the Fruit of Islam!"

When the awful ordeal is ended, when the grip of dope is broken, the Muslims comfort the weak ex-addict, feeding him soups and broths, to get him on his feet again. He will never forget these brothers who stood by him during this time. He will never forget that it was the Nation of Islam's program which rescued him from the special hell of dope. And that black brother (or the sister, whom Muslim sisters attend) rarely ever will return to the use of narcotics. Instead, the ex-addict when he is proud, clean, renewed, can scarcely wait to hit the same junkie jungle he was in, to "fish" out some buddy and salvage *him!*

If some white man, or "approved" black man, created a narcotics cure program as successful as the one conducted under the aegis of the Muslims, why, there would be government subsidy, and praise and spotlights, and headlines. But we were attacked instead. Why shouldn't the Muslims be subsidized to save millions of dollars a year for the government and the cities? I don't know what addicts' crimes cost nationally, but it is said to be *billions* a year in New York City. An estimated $12 million a year is lost to thieves in Harlem alone.

An addict doesn't work to supply his habit, which may cost anywhere from ten to fifty dollars a day. How could he earn that much? No! The addict steals, he hustles in other ways; he preys upon other human beings like a hawk or a vulture—as I did. Very likely, he is a school drop-out, the same as I was, an Army reject, psychologically unsuited to a job even if he was offered one, the same as I was.

Women addicts "boost" (shoplift), or they prostitute themselves. Muslim sisters talk hard to black prostitutes who are struggling to quit using dope in order to qualify morally to become registered Muslims. "You are helping the white man to regard your body as a garbage can—"

Numerous "exposés" of the Nation of Islam have implied that Mr. Muhammad's followers were chiefly ex-cons and junkies. In the early years, yes, the converts from society's lowest levels were a sizable part of the Nation's broad base of membership. Always Mr. Muhammad instructed us, "Go after the black man in the mud." Often, he said, those converted made the best Muslims.

But gradually we recruited other black people—the "good Christians" whom we "fished" from their churches. Then, an increase began in the membership percentage of educated and trained Negroes. For each rally attracted to the local temple a few more of that particular city's so-called "middle-class" Negroes, the type who previously had scoffed at us "Black Muslims" as "demagogues," and "hate-teachers," "black racists" and all the rest of the names. The Muslim truths—listened to, thought about—reaped for us a growing quota of young black men and women. For those with training and talents, the Nation of Islam had plenty of positions where those abilities were needed.

There were some registered Muslims who would never reveal their membership, except to other Muslims, because of their positions in the white man's world. There were, I know, a few, who because of their positions were known only to their ministers and to Mr. Elijah Muhammad.

In 1961, our Nation flourished. Our newspaper *Muhammad Speaks'* full back page carried an architect's drawing of a $20 million Islamic Center proposed to be built in Chicago. Every Muslim was making personal financial contribution toward the Center. It would include a beautiful mosque, school, library, and hospital, and a museum documenting the black man's glorious history.

Mr. Muhammad visited the Muslim countries, and upon his return he directed that we would begin calling our temples "mosques."

There was a sharp climb now, too, in the number of Muslim-owned small businesses. Our businesses sought to demonstrate to the black people what black people could do for themselves—if they would only unify, trade with each other—exclusively where possible—and hire each other, and in so doing, keep black money within the black communities, just as other minorities did.

Recordings of Mr. Muhammad's speeches were now regularly being broadcast across America over small radio stations. In Detroit and Chicago, school-age Muslim children attended our two Universities of Islam—through high school in Chicago, and through junior high in Detroit. Starting from kindergarten, they learned of the black man's glorious history and from the third grade they studied the black man's original language, Arabic.

Mr. Muhammad's eight children now were all deeply involved in key capacities in the Nation of Islam. I took a deep personal pride in having had something to do with that—at least in some cases, years before. When Mr. Muhammad had sent me out in his service as a minister, I began to feel it was a shame that his children worked as some of them then did for the white man, in factories, construction work, driving taxis, things like that. I felt that I should work for Mr. Muhammad's family as sincerely as I worked for him. I urged Mr. Muhammad to let me put on a special drive within our few small mosques, to raise funds which would enable those of his children working for the white man to be instead employed within our Nation. Mr. Muhammad agreed, the special fund drive did prove successful, and his children gradually did begin working for the Nation. Emanuel, the oldest, today runs the dry-cleaning plant. Sister Ethel (Muhammad) Sharrieff is the Muslim Sisters' Supreme Instructor. (Her husband, Raymond Sharrieff, is Supreme Captain of the Fruit of Islam.) Sister Lottie Muhammad supervises the two Universities of Islam. Nathaniel Muhammad assists Emanuel in the dry-cleaning plant. Herbert Muhammad now publishes *Muhammad Speaks*, the Nation's newspaper that I began. Elijah Muhammad, Jr., is the Fruit of Islam Assistant Supreme Captain. Wallace Muhammad was the Philadelphia Mosque Minister, until finally he was suspended from the Nation along with me—for reasons I will go into. The youngest child, Akbar Muhammad, the family student, attends the University of Cairo at El-Azhar. Akbar also has broken with his father.

I believe that it was too strenuous a marathon of long speeches that Mr. Muhammad made at our big rallies which, abruptly, badly aggravated his long-bothersome bronchial asthmatic condition.

Just in conversation, Mr. Muhammad would suddenly begin coughing, and the coughing tempo would increase until it racked his slight body.

Mr. Muhammad almost doubled up sometimes. Soon, he had to take to his bed. As hard as he tried not to, as deeply as it grieved him, he had to cancel several long-scheduled appearances at big-city rallies. Thousands were disappointed to have to hear me instead, or other poor substitutes for Mr. Muhammad in person.

Members of the Nation were deeply concerned. Doctors recommended a dry climate. The Nation bought Mr. Muhammad a home in Phoenix, Arizona. One of the first times I visited Mr. Muhammad there, I stepped off a plane into flashing and whirring cameras until I wondered who was behind me. Then I saw the cameramen's guns; they were from the Arizona Intelligence Division.

The wire of our Nation of Islam brought all Muslims the joyful news that the Arizona climate did vastly relieve the Messenger's suffering. Since then he has spent most of each year in Phoenix.

Despite the fact that Mr. Muhammad, convalescing, could no longer work the daily long hours he had previously worked in Chicago, he was now more than ever burdened with heavy decision-making and administrative duties. In every respect, the Nation was expanded both internally and externally. Mr. Muhammad simply could no longer allot as much time as previously to considering and deciding which public-speaking, radio, and television requests he felt I should accept—as well as to some organizational matters which I had always brought to him for advice or decision.

Mr. Muhammad evidenced the depth of his trust in me. In those areas I've described, he told me to make the decisions myself. He said that my guideline should be whatever I felt was wise—whatever was in the general good interests of our Nation of Islam.

"Brother Malcolm, I want you to become well known," Mr. Muhammad told me one day. "Because if you are well known, it will make *me* better known," he went on.

"But, Brother Malcolm, there is something you need to know. You will grow to be hated when you become well known. Because usually people get jealous of public figures."

Nothing that Mr. Muhammad ever said to me was more prophetic.

CHAPTER FIFTEEN

ICARUS

The more places I represented Mr. Muhammad on television and radio, and at colleges and elsewhere, the more letters came from people who had heard me. I'd say that ninety-five per cent of the letters were from white people.

Only a few of the letters fell into the "Dear Nigger X" category, or the death-threats. Most of my mail exposed to me the white man's two major dreads. The first one was his own private belief that God wrathfully is going to destroy this civilization. And the white man's second most pervading dread was his image of the black man entering the body of the white woman.

An amazing percentage of the white letter-writers agreed entirely with Mr. Muhammad's analysis of the problem—but not with his solution. One odd ambivalence was how some letters, otherwise all but championing Mr. Muhammad, would recoil at the expression "white devils." I tried to explain this in subsequent speeches:

"Unless we call one white man, by name, a 'devil,' we are not speaking of any *individual* white man. We are speaking of the *collective* white man's *historical* record. We are speaking of the collective white man's cruelties, and evils, and greeds, that have seen him *act* like a devil toward the non-white man. Any intelligent, honest, objective person cannot fail to realize that this white man's slave trade, and his subsequent devilish actions are directly *responsible* for not only the *presence* of this black man in America, but also for the *condition* in which we find this black man here. You cannot find *one* black man, I do

271

not care who he is, who has not been personally damaged in some way by the devilish acts of the collective white man!''

Nearly every day, some attack on the ''Black Muslims'' would appear in some newspapers. Increasingly, a focal target was something that I had said, ''Malcolm X'' as a ''demagogue.'' I would grow furious reading any harsh attack upon Mr. Muhammad. I didn't care what they said about me.

Those social workers and sociologists—they tried to take me apart. Especially the black ones, for some reason. Of course, I knew the reason: the white man signed their paychecks. If I wasn't ''polarizing the community,'' according to this bunch, I had ''erroneously appraised the racial picture.'' Or in some statement, I had ''over-generalized.'' Or when I had made some absolutely true point, ''Malcolm X conveniently manipulated. . . . ''

Once, one of my Mosque Seven Muslim brothers who worked with teenagers in a well-known Harlem community center showed me a confidential report. Some black senior social worker had been given a month off to investigate the ''Black Muslims'' in the Harlem area. Every paragraph sent me back to the dictionary—I guess that's why I've never forgotten one line about me. Listen to this: ''The dynamic interstices of the Harlem sub-culture have been oversimplified and distorted by Malcolm X to meet his own needs.''

Which of us, I wonder, knew more about that Harlem ghetto ''sub-culture''? I, who had hustled for years in those streets, or that black snob status-symbol-educated social worker?

But that's not important. What's important, to my way of thinking about it, is that among America's 22 million black people so relatively few have been lucky enough to attend a college—and here was one of those who had been lucky. Here was, to my way of thinking, one of those ''educated'' Negroes who never had understood the true intent, or purpose, or application of education. Here was one of those stagnant educations, never used except for parading a lot of big words.

Do you realize this is one of the major reasons why America's white man has so easily contained and oppressed America's black man? Because until just lately, among the few educated Negroes scarcely any applied their education, as I am forced to say the white man does—in searching and creative thinking, to further themselves and their own kind in this competitive, materialistic, dog-eat-dog white man's world. For generations, the so-called "educated" Negroes have "led" their black brothers by echoing the white man's thinking—which naturally has been to the exploitive white man's advantage.

The white man—give him his due—has an extraordinary intelligence, an extraordinary cleverness. His world is full of proof of it. You can't name a thing the white man can't make. You can hardly name a scientific problem he can't solve. Here he is now solving the problems of sending men exploring into outer space—and returning them safely to earth.

But in the arena of dealing with human beings, the white man's working intelligence is hobbled. His intelligence will fail him altogether if the humans happen to be non-white. The white man's emotions superseded his intelligence. He will commit against non-whites the most incredible spontaneous emotional acts, so psyche-deep is his "white superiority" complex.

Where was the A-bomb dropped . . . "to save American lives"? Can the white man be so naive as to think the clear import of this *ever* will be lost upon the non-white two-thirds of the earth's population?

Before that bomb was dropped—right over here in the United States, what about the one hundred thousand loyal naturalized and native-born Japanese-American citizens who were herded into camps, behind barbed wire? But how many German-born naturalized Americans were herded behind barbed wire? They were *white!*

Historically, the non-white complexion has evoked and exposed the "devil" in the very nature of the white man.

What else but a controlling emotional "devil" so blinded American white intelligence that it couldn't foresee that millions of black slaves, "freed," then permitted even limited education, would one day rise up as a terrifying monster within white America's midst?

The white man's brains that today explore space should have told the slavemaster that any slave, if he is educated, will no longer fear his master. History shows that an educated slave always begins to ask, and next demand, equality with his master.

Today, in many ways the black man sees the collective white

man in America better than that white man can see himself. And the 22 million blacks realize increasingly that physically, politically, economically, and even to some degree socially, the aroused black man can create a turmoil in white America's vitals—not to mention America's international image.

I had not intended to stray off. I had been telling how in 1963, I was trying to cope with the white newspaper, radio, and television reporters who were determined to defeat Mr. Muhammad's teachings.

I developed a mental image of reporters as human ferrets— steadily sniffing, darting, probing for some way to trick me, somehow to corner me in our interview exchanges.

Let some civil rights "leader" make some statement, displeasing to the white public power structure, and the reporters, in an effort to whip him back into line, would try to use me. I'll give an example. I'd get a question like this: "Mr. Malcolm X, you've often gone on record as disapproving of the sit-ins and similar Negro protest actions—what is your opinion of the Montgomery boycott that Dr. King is leading?"

Now my feeling was that although the civil rights "leaders" kept attacking us Muslims, still they were black people, still they were our own kind, and I would be most foolish to let the white man maneuver me against the civil rights movement.

When I was asked about the Montgomery boycott, I'd carefully review what led up to it. Mrs. Rosa Parks was riding home on a bus and at some bus stop the white cracker bus driver ordered Mrs. Parks to get up and give her seat to some white passenger who had just got on the bus. I'd say, "Now, just *imagine* that! This good, hard-working, Christian-believing black woman, she's paid her money, she's in her seat. Just because she's *black*, she's asked to get up! I mean, sometimes even for *me* it's hard to believe the white man's arrogance!"

Or I might say, "No one will ever know exactly what emotional ingredient made this relatively trivial incident a fuse for those Montgomery Negroes. There had been *centuries* of the worst kind of outrages against Southern black people—lynchings, rapings, shootings, beatings! But you know history has been triggered by trivial-seeming incidents. Once a little nobody Indian lawyer was put off a train, and fed up with injustice, he twisted a knot in the British Lion's tail. *His* name was Mahatma Gandhi!''

Or I might copy a trick I had seen lawyers use, both in life and on television. It was a way that lawyers would slip in before a jury something otherwise inadmissable. (Sometimes I think I really might have made it as a lawyer, as I once told that eighth-grade teacher in Mason, Michigan, I wanted to be, when he advised me to become a carpenter.) I would slide right over the reporter's question to drop into his lap a logical-extension hot potato for him.

"Well, sir, I see the same boycott reasoning for Negroes asked to join the Army, Navy, and Air Force. Why should we go off to die somewhere to preserve a so-called 'democracy' that gives a white immigrant of one day more than it gives the black man with four hundred years of slaving and serving in this country?''

Whites would prefer fifty local boycotts to having 22 million Negroes start thinking about what I had just said. I don't have to tell you that it never got printed the way I said it. It would be turned inside out if it got printed at all. And I could detect when the white reporters had gotten their heads together; they quit asking me certain questions.

If I had developed a good point, though, I'd bait a hook to get it said when I went on radio or television. I'd seem to slip and mention some recent so-called civil rights "advance." You know, where some giant industry had hired ten showpiece Negroes; some restaurant chain had begun making more money by serving Negroes; some Southern university had enrolled a black freshman without bayonets—like that. When I "slipped," the program host would leap on that bait: "Ahhh! Indeed, Mr. Malcolm X—you can't deny *that's* an advance for your race!''

I'd jerk the pole then. "I can't turn around without hearing about some 'civil rights advance'! White people seem to think the black man ought to be shouting 'hallelujah'! Four hundred years the white man has had his foot-long knife in the black man's back—and now the white man starts to *wiggle* the knife out, maybe six inches! The black man's supposed to be *grateful*? Why, if the white man jerked the knife *out*, it's still going to leave a *scar!*''

Similarly, just let some mayor or some city council somewhere boast of having "no Negro problem." That would get off the newsroom teletypes and it would soon be jammed right in my face. I'd say they didn't need to tell me where this was, because I knew that all it meant was that relatively very few Negroes were living there. That's true the world over, you know. Take "democratic" England—when 100,000 black West Indians got there, England stopped the black migration. Finland welcomed a Negro U.S. Ambassador. Well, let enough Negroes follow him to Finland! Or in Russia, when Khrushchev was in power, he threatened to cancel the visas of black African students whose anti-discrimination demonstration said to the world, "Russia, too. . . ."

The Deep South white press generally blacked me out. But they front-paged what I felt about Northern white and black Freedom Riders going *South* to "demonstrate." I called it "ridiculous"; their own Northern ghettoes, right at home, had enough rats and roaches to kill to keep all of the Freedom Riders busy. I said that ultra-liberal New York had more integration problems than Mississippi. If the Northern Freedom Riders wanted more to do, they could work on the roots of such ghetto evils as the little children out in the streets at midnight, with apartment keys on strings around their necks to let themselves in, and their mothers and fathers drunk, drug addicts, thieves, prostitutes. Or the Northern Freedom Riders could light some fires under Northern city halls, unions, and major industries to give more jobs to Negroes to remove so many of them from the relief and welfare rolls, which created laziness, and which deteriorated the ghettoes into steadily worse places for humans to live. It was all—it *is* all—the absolute truth; but what did I want to *say* it for? Snakes couldn't have turned on me faster than the liberal.

Yes, I will pull off that liberal's halo that he spends such efforts cultivating! The North's liberals have been for so long pointing accusing fingers at the South and getting away with it that they have fits when they are exposed as the world's worst hypocrites.

I believe my own life *mirrors* this hypocrisy. I know nothing about the South. I am a creation of the Northern white man and of his hypocritical attitude toward the Negro.

The white Southerner was always given his due by Mr. Muhammad. The white Southerner, you can say one thing—he is honest. He bares his teeth to the black man; he tells the black man, to his face, that Southern whites never will accept phony "integration." The Southern white goes further, to tell the black man that he means to fight him every inch of the way—against even the so-called "tokenism." The advantage of this is the Southern black man never has been under any illusions about the opposition he is dealing with.

You can say for many Southern white people that, individually, they have been paternalistically helpful to many individual Negroes. But the Northern white man, he grins with his teeth, and his mouth has always been full of tricks and lies of "equality" and "integration." When one day all over America, a black hand touched the white man's shoulder, and the white man turned, and there stood the Negro saying "Me, too . . ." why, that Northern liberal shrank from that black man with as much guilt and dread as any Southern white man.

Actually, America's most dangerous and threatening black man is the one who has been kept sealed up by the Northerner in the black ghettoes—the Northern white power structure's system to keep talking democracy while keeping the black man out of sight somewhere, around the corner.

The word "integration" was invented by a Northern liberal. The word has no real meaning. I ask you: in the racial sense in which it's used so much today, whatever "integration" is supposed to mean, can it precisely be defined? The truth is that "integration" is an *image*, it's a foxy Northern liberal's smokescreen that confuses the true wants of the American black man. Here in these fifty racist and neo-racist states of North America, this word "integration" has millions of white people confused, and angry, believing wrongly that the black masses want to live mixed up with the white man. That is the case only with the relative handful of these "integration"-mad Negroes.

I'm talking about these "token-integrated" Negroes who flee from their poor, downtrodden black brothers—from their own self-hate, which is what they're really trying to escape. I'm talking about these Negroes you will see who can't get enough of nuzzling up to the white man. These "chosen few" Negroes are more white-minded, more anti-black, than even the white man is.

Human rights! Respect as *human beings!* That's what America's black masses want. That's the true problem. The black masses want not to be shrunk from as though they are plague-ridden. They want not to be walled up in slums, in the ghettoes, like animals. They want to live in an open, free society where they can walk with their heads up, like men, and women!

Few white people realize that many black people today dislike and avoid spending any more time than they must around white people. This "integration" image, as it is popularly interpreted, has millions of vain, self-exalted white people convinced that black people want to sleep in bed with them—and that's a lie! Or you can't *tell* the average white man that the Negro man's prime desire isn't to have a white woman—another lie! Like a black brother recently observed to me, "Look, you ever smell one of them *wet?*"

The black masses prefer the company of their own kind. Why, even these fancy, bourgeois Negroes—when they get back home from the fancy "integrated" cocktail parties, what do they do but kick off their shoes and talk about those white liberals they just left as if the liberals were dogs. And the white liberals probably do the very same thing. I can't be sure about the whites, I am never around them in private—but the bourgeois Negroes know I'm not lying.

I'm telling it like it *is!* You *never* have to worry about me biting my tongue if something I know as truth is on my mind. Raw, naked truth exchanged between the black man and the white man is what a whole lot more of is needed in this country—to clear the air of the racial mirages, clichés, and lies that this country's very atmosphere has been filled with for four hundred years.

In many communities, especially small communities, white people have created a benevolent image of themselves as having had so much "good-will toward our Negroes," every time any "local Negro" begins suddenly letting the local whites know the truth—that the black people are sick of being hind-tit, second-class, disfranchised, that's when you hear, uttered so sadly, "Unfortunately now because of this, our whites of good-will are starting to turn against the Negroes. . . . It's so regrettable

. . . progress *was* being made . . . but now our communications between the races have broken down!''

What are they talking about? There never was any *communication*. Until after World War II, there wasn't a single community in the entire United States where the white man heard from any local Negro "leaders" the truth of what Negroes felt about the conditions that the white community imposed upon Negroes.

You need some proof? Well, then, why was it that when Negroes did start revolting across America, virtually all of white America was caught up in surprise and even shock? I would hate to be general of an army as badly informed as the American white man has been about the Negro in this country.

This is the situation which permitted Negro combustion to slowly build up to the revolution-point, without the white man realizing it. All over America, the local Negro "leader," in order to survive as a "leader," kept reassuring the local white man, in effect, "Everything's all right, everything's right in hand, boss!" When the "leader" wanted a little something for his people: "Er, boss, some of the people talking about we sure need a better school, boss." And if the local Negroes hadn't been causing any "trouble," the "benevolent" white man might nod and give them a school, or some jobs.

The white men belonging to the power structures in thousands of communities across America know that I'm right! They know that I am describing what has been the true pattern of "communications" between the "local whites of good-will" and the local Negroes. It has been a pattern created by domineering, ego-ridden whites. Its characteristic design permitted the white man to feel "noble" about throwing crumbs to the black man, instead of feeling guilty about the local community's system of cruelly exploiting Negroes.

But I want to tell you something. This pattern, this "system" that the white man created, of teaching Negroes to hide the truth from him behind a façade of grinning, "yessir-bossing," foot-shuffling and head-scratching—that system has done the American white man more harm than an invading army would do to him.

Why do I say this? Because all this has steadily helped this American white man to build up, deep in his psyche, absolute conviction that he *is* "superior." In how many, many communities have, thus, white men who didn't finish high school regarded condescendingly university-educated local Negro "leaders," principals of schools, teachers, doctors, other professionals?

The white man's system has been imposed upon non-white peoples all over the world. This is exactly the reason why wherever people who are anything but white live in this world today, the white man's governments are finding themselves in deeper and deeper trouble and peril.

Let's just face truth. Facts! Whether or not the white man of the world is able to face truth, and facts, about the true reasons for his troubles—that's what essentially will determine whether or not *he* will now survive.

Today we are seeing this revolution of the non-white peoples, who just a few years ago would have frozen in horror if the mighty white nations so much as lifted an eyebrow. What it is, simply, is that black and brown and red and yellow peoples have, after hundreds of years of exploitation and imposed "inferiority" and general misuse, become, finally, do-or-die sick and tired of the white man's heel on their necks.

How can the white American government figure on selling "democracy" and "brotherhood" to non-white peoples—if they read and hear every day what's going on right here in America, and see the better-than-a-thousand-words photographs of the American white man denying "democracy" and "brotherhood" even to America's native-born non-whites? The world's non-whites know how this Negro here has loved the American white man, and slaved for him, tended to him, nursed him. This Negro has jumped into uniform and gone off and died when this America was attacked by enemies both white and non-white. Such a faithful, loyal non-white as *this*—and *still* America bombs him, and sets dogs on him, and turns fire hoses on him, and jails him by the thousands, and beats him bloody, and inflicts upon him all manner of other crimes.

Of course these things, known and refreshed every day for the rest of the world's non-whites, are a vital factor in these burnings of ambassadors' limousines, these stonings, defilings, and wreckings of embassies and legations, these shouts of

"White man, go home!" these attacks on white Christian missionaries, and these bombings and tearing down of flags.

Is it clear why I have said that the American white man's malignant superiority complex has done him more harm than an invading army?

The American black man should be focusing his every effort toward building his *own* businesses, and decent homes for himself. As other ethnic groups have done, let the black people, wherever possible, however possible, patronize their own kind, hire their own kind, and start in those ways to build up the black race's ability to do for itself. That's the only way the American black man is ever going to get respect. One thing the white man never can give the black man is self-respect! The black man never can become independent and recognized as a human being who is truly equal with other human beings until he has what they have, and until he is doing for himself what others are doing for themselves.

The black man in the ghettoes, for instance, has to start self-correcting his own material, moral, and spiritual defects and evils. The black man needs to start his own program to get rid of drunkenness, drug addiction, prostitution. The black man in America has to lift up his own sense of values.

Only a few thousands of Negroes, relatively a very tiny number, are taking any part in "integration." Here, again, it is those few bourgeois Negroes, rushing to throw away their little money in the white man's luxury hotels, his swanky nightclubs, and big, fine, exclusive restaurants. The white people patronizing those places can afford it. But these Negroes you see in those places can't afford it, certainly most of them can't. Why, what does some Negro one installment payment away from disaster look like somewhere downtown out to dine, grinning at some headwaiter who has more money than the Negro? Those bourgeois Negroes out draping big tablecloth-sized napkins over their knees and ordering quail under glass and stewed snails—why, Negroes don't even *like* snails! What they're doing is proving they're integrated.

If you want to get right down to the real outcome of this so-called "integration," what you've got to arrive at is intermarriage.

I'm right *with* the Southern white man who believes that you can't have so-called "integration," at least not for long, without intermarriage increasing. And what good is this for anyone? Let's again face reality. In a world as color-hostile as this, man or woman, black or white, what do they want with a mate of the other race?

Certainly white people have served enough notice of their hostility to any blacks in their families and neighborhoods. And the way most Negroes feel today, a mixed couple probably finds that black families, black communities, are even more hostile than the white ones. So what's bound to face "integrated" marriages, except being unwelcomed, unwanted, "misfits" in whichever world they try to live in? What we arrive at is that "integration," socially, is no good for either side. "Integration," ultimately, would destroy the white race . . . and destroy the black race.

The white man's "integrating" with black women has already changed the complexion and characteristics of the black race in America. What's been proved by the "blacks" whose complexions are "whiter" than many "white" people? I'm told that there are in America today between two and five million "white Negroes," who are "passing" in white society. Imagine their torture! Living in constant fear that some black person they've known might meet and expose them. Imagine every day living a lie. *Imagine* hearing their own white husbands, their own white wives, even their own white children, talking about "those Negroes."

I would doubt if anyone in America has heard Negroes more bitter against the white man than some of those I have heard. But I will tell you that, without any question, the *most* bitter anti-white diatribes that I have ever heard have come from "passing" Negroes, living as whites, among whites, exposed every day to what white people say among themselves regarding Negroes—things that a recognized Negro never would hear. Why, if there was a racial showdown, these Negroes "passing" within white circles would become the black side's most valuable "spy" and ally.

Europe's "brown babies," now young men and women who are starting to marry, and produce families of their own . . .

have their experiences throughout their lives, scarred as racial freaks, proved anything positive for "integration"?

"Integration" is called "assimilation" if white ethnic groups alone are involved: it's fought against tooth and nail by those who want their heritage preserved. Look at how the Irish threw the English out of Ireland. The Irish knew the English would engulf them. Look at the French-Canadians, fanatically fighting to keep their identity.

In fact, history's most tragic result of a mixed, therefore diluted and weakened, ethnic identity has been experienced by a white ethnic group—the Jew in Germany.

He had made greater contributions to Germany than Germans themselves had. Jews had won over half of Germany's Nobel Prizes. Every culture in Germany was led by the Jew; he published the greatest newspaper. Jews were the greatest artists, the greatest poets, composers, stage directors. But those Jews made a fatal mistake—assimilating.

From World War I to Hitler's rise, the Jews in Germany had been increasingly intermarrying. Many changed their names and many took other religions. Their own Jewish religion, their own rich Jewish ethnic and cultural roots, they anesthetized, and cut off . . . until they began thinking of themselves as "Germans."

And the next thing they knew, there was Hitler, rising to power from the beer halls—with his emotional "Aryan master race" theory. And right at hand for a scapegoat was the self-weakened, self-deluded "German" Jew.

Most mysterious is how did those Jews—with all of their brilliant minds, with all of their power in every aspect of Germany's affairs—how did those Jews stand almost as if mesmerized, watching something which did not spring upon them overnight, but which was gradually developed—a monstrous plan for their own *murder*.

Their self-brainwashing had been so complete that not long after, in the gas chambers, a lot of them were still gasping, "It *can't* be true!"

If Hitler *had* conquered the world, as he meant to—that is a shuddery thought for every Jew alive today.

The Jew never will forget that lesson. Jewish intelligence eyes watch every neo-Nazi organization. Right after the war, the Jews' Haganah mediating body stepped up the longtime nego-

tiations with the British. But this time, the Stern gang was shoot-
ing the British. And this time the British acquiesced and helped
them to wrest Palestine away from the Arabs, the rightful own-
ers, and then the Jews set up Israel, their own country—the one
thing that every race of man in the world respects, and under-
stands.

Not long ago, the black man in America was fed a dose of
another form of the weakening, lulling and deluding effects of
so-called "integration." It was that "Farce on Washington," I
call it.

The idea of a mass of blacks marching on Washington was
originally the brainchild of the Brotherhood of Sleeping Car
Porters' A. Philip Randolph. For twenty or more years the March
on Washington idea had floated around among Negroes. And,
spontaneously, suddenly now, that idea caught on.

Overalled rural Southern Negroes, small town Negroes,
Northern ghetto Negroes, even thousands of previously Uncle
Tom Negroes began talking "March!"

Nothing since Joe Louis had so coalesced the masses of Ne-
groes. Groups of Negroes were talking of getting to Washington
any way they could—in rickety old cars, on buses, hitch-hiking—
walking, even, if they had to. They envisioned thousands of
black brothers converging together upon Washington—to lie
down in the streets, on airport runways, on government lawns—
demanding of the Congress and the White House some concrete
civil rights action.

This was a national bitterness; militant, unorganized, and
leaderless. Predominantly, it was young Negroes, defiant of
whatever might be the consequences, sick and tired of the black
man's neck under the white man's heel.

The white man had plenty of good reasons for nervous worry.
The right spark—some unpredictable emotional chemistry—
could set off a black uprising. The government knew that thou-
sands of milling, angry blacks not only could completely disrupt
Washington—but they could erupt in Washington.

The White House speedily invited in the major civil rights
Negro "leaders." They were asked to stop the planned March.
They truthfully said they hadn't begun it, they had no control

over it—the idea was national, spontaneous, unorganized, and leaderless. In other words, it was a black powder keg.

Any student of how "integration" can weaken the black man's movement was about to observe a master lesson.

The White House, with a fanfare of international publicity, "approved," "endorsed," and "welcomed" a March on Washington. The big civil rights organizations right at this time had been publicly squabbling about donations. The *New York Times* had broken the story. The N.A.A.C.P. had charged that other agencies' demonstrations, highly publicized, had attracted a major part of the civil rights donations—while the N.A.A.C.P. got left holding the bag, supplying costly bail and legal talent for the other organizations' jailed demonstrators.

It was like a movie. The next scene was the "big six" civil rights Negro "leaders" meeting in New York City with the white head of a big philanthropic agency. They were told that their money-wrangling in public was damaging their image. And a reported $800,000 was donated to a United Civil Rights Leadership council that was quickly organized by the "big six."

Now, what had instantly achieved black unity? The white man's money. What string was attached to the money? Advice. Not only was there this donation, but another comparable sum was promised, for sometime later on, after the March . . . obviously if all went well.

The original "angry" March on Washington was now about to be entirely changed.

Massive international publicity projected the "big six" as March on Washington leaders. It was news to those angry grassroots Negroes steadily adding steam to their March plans. They probably assumed that now those famous "leaders" were endorsing and joining them.

Invited next to join the March were four famous white public figures: one Catholic, one Jew, one Protestant, and one labor boss.

The massive publicity now gently hinted that the "big ten" would "supervise" the March on Washington's "mood," and its "direction."

The four white figures began nodding. The word spread fast among so-called "liberal" Catholics, Jews, Protestants, and laborites: it was "democratic" to join this black March.

And suddenly, the previously March-nervous whites began announcing *they* were going.

It was as if electrical current shot through the ranks of bourgeois Negroes—the very so-called "middle-class" and "upper-class" who had earlier been deploring the March on Washington talk by grass-roots Negroes.

But white people, now, were going to march.

Why, some downtrodden, jobless, hungry Negro might have gotten trampled. Those "integration"-mad Negroes practically ran over each other trying to find out where to sign up. The "angry blacks" March suddenly had been made chic. Suddenly it had a Kentucky Derby image. For the status-seeker, it was a status symbol. "Were you *there?*" You can hear that right today.

It had become an outing, a picnic.

The morning of the March, any rickety carloads of angry, dusty, sweating small-town Negroes would have gotten lost among the chartered jet planes, railroad cars, and air-conditioned buses. What originally was planned to be an angry riptide, one English newspaper aptly described now as "the gentle flood."

Talk about "integrated"! It was like salt and pepper. And, by now, there wasn't a single logistics aspect uncontrolled.

The marchers had been instructed to bring no signs—signs were provided. They had been told to sing one song: "We Shall Overcome." They had been told *how* to arrive, *when, where* to arrive, *where* to assemble, when to *start* marching, the *route* to march. First-aid stations were strategically located—even where to *faint!*

Yes, I was there. I observed that circus. Who ever heard of angry revolutionists all harmonizing "We Shall Overcome . . . Suum Day . . ." while tripping and swaying along arm-in-arm with the very people they were supposed to be angrily revolting against? Who ever heard of angry revolutionists swinging their bare feet together with their oppressor in lily-pad park pools, with gospels and guitars and "I Have A Dream" speeches?

And the black masses in America were—and still are—having a nightmare.

These "angry revolutionists" even followed their final instructions: to leave early. With all of those thousands upon thousands of "angry revolutionists," so few stayed over that the next morning the Washington hotel association reported a costly loss in empty rooms.

Hollywood couldn't have topped it.

In a subsequent press poll, not one Congressman or Senator with a previous record of opposition to civil rights said he had changed his views. What did anyone expect? How was a one-day "integrated" picnic going to counter-influence these representatives of prejudice rooted deep in the psyche of the American white man for four hundred years?

The very fact that millions, black and white, believed in this monumental farce is another example of how much this country goes in for the surface glossing over, the escape ruse, surfaces, instead of truly dealing with its deep-rooted problems.

What that March on Washington did do was lull Negroes for a while. But inevitably, the black masses started realizing they had been smoothly hoaxed again by the white man. And, inevitably, the black man's anger rekindled, deeper than ever, and there began bursting out in different cities, in the "long, hot summer" of 1964, unprecedented racial crises.

About a month before the "Farce on Washington," the *New York Times* reported me, according to its poll conducted on college and university campuses, as "the second most sought after" speaker at colleges and universities. The only speaker ahead of me was Senator Barry Goldwater.

I believe that what had generated such college popularity for me was Dr. Lincoln's book, *The Black Muslims in America*. It had been made required reading in numerous college courses. Then a long, candid interview with me was carried by *Playboy* magazine, whose circulation on college campuses is the biggest of any magazine's. And many students, having studied first the book and then the *Playboy* interview, wanted to hear in person this so-called "fiery Black Muslim."

When the *New York Times* poll was published, I had spoken at well over fifty colleges and universities, like Brown, Harvard, Yale, Columbia and Rutgers, in the Ivy League, and others throughout the country. Right now, I have invitations from Cornell, Princeton and probably a dozen others, as soon as my time and their available dates can be scheduled together. Among Negro institutions, I had then been to Atlanta University and Clark

College down in Atlanta, to Howard University in Washington, D.C., and to a number of others with small student bodies.

Except for all-black audiences, I liked the college audiences best. The college sessions sometimes ran two to four hours—they often ran overtime. Challenges, queries, and criticisms were fired at me by the usually objective and always alive and searching minds of undergraduate and graduate students, and their faculties. The college sessions never failed to be exhilarating. They never failed in helping me to further my own education. I never experienced one college session that didn't show me ways to improve upon my presentation and defense of Mr. Muhammad's teachings. Sometimes in a panel or debate appearance, I'd find a jam-packed audience to hear me, alone, facing six or eight student and faculty scholars—heads of departments such as sociology, psychology, philosophy, history, and religion, and each of them coming at me in his specialty.

At the outset, always I'd confront such panels with something such as: "Gentlemen, I finished the eighth grade in Mason, Michigan. My high school was the black ghetto of Roxbury, Massachusetts. My college was in the streets of Harlem, and my master's was taken in prison. Mr. Muhammad has taught me that I never need fear any man's intellect who tries to defend or to justify the white man's criminal record against the non-white man—especially the white man and the black man here in North America."

It was like being on a battlefield—with intellectual and philosophical bullets. It was an exciting battling with ideas. I got so I could feel my audiences' temperaments. I've talked with other public speakers; they agree that this ability is native to any person who has the "mass appeal" gift, who can get through to and move people. It's a psychic radar. As a doctor, with his finger against a pulse, is able to feel the heart rate, when I am up there speaking, I can *feel* the reaction to what I am saying.

I think I could be speaking blindfolded and after five minutes, I could tell you if sitting out there before me was an all-black or an all-white audience. Black audiences and white audiences feel distinguishably different. Black audiences feel warmer, there is almost a musical rhythm, for me, even in their silent response.

Question-and-answer periods are another area where, by now, again blindfolded, I can often tell you the ethnic source of a question. The most easily recognizable of these to me are a Jew in any audience situation, and a bourgeois Negro in "integrated" audiences.

My clue to the Jew's question and challenges is that among all other ethnic groups, his expressed thinking, his expressed concerns, are the most subjective. And the Jew is usually hypersensitive. I mean, you can't even say "Jew" without him accusing you of anti-Semitism. I don't care what a Jew is professionally, doctor, merchant, housewife, student, or whatever—first he, or she, thinks Jew.

Now, of course I can understand the Jew's hypersensitivity. For two thousand years, religious and personal prejudices against Jews have been vented and exercised, as strong as white prejudices against the non-white. But I know that America's five and a half million Jews (two million of them are concentrated in New York) look at it very practically, whether they know it or not: that all of the bigotry and hatred focused upon the black man keeps off the Jew a lot of heat that would be on him otherwise.

For an example of what I am talking about—in every black ghetto, Jews own the major businesses. Every night the owners of those businesses go home with that black community's money, which helps the ghetto to stay poor. But I doubt that I have ever uttered this absolute truth before an audience without being hotly challenged, and accused by a Jew of anti-Semitism. Why? I will bet that I have told five hundred such challengers that Jews as a group would never watch some other minority systematically siphoning out their community's resources without doing something about it. I have told them that if I tell the simple truth, it doesn't mean that I am anti-Semitic; it means merely that I am anti-exploitation.

The white liberal may be a little taken aback to know that from all-Negro audiences I never have had one challenge, never one question that defended the white man. That has been true even when a lot of those "black bourgeoisie" and "integration"-mad Negroes were among the blacks. All Negroes, among themselves, admit the white man's criminal record. They may not know as many details as I do, but they know the general picture.

But, let me tell you something significant: This very same

bourgeois Negro who, among Negroes, would never make a fool of himself in trying to defend the white man—watch that same Negro in a mixed black and white audience, knowing he's overheard by his beloved "Mr. Charlie." Why, you should hear those Negroes attack me, trying to justify, or forgive the white man's crimes! These Negroes are people who bring me nearest to breaking one of my principal rules, which is never to let myself become over-emotional and angry. Why, sometimes I've felt I ought to jump down off that stand and get *physical* with some of those brainwashed white man's tools, parrots, puppets. At the colleges, I've developed some stock put-downs for them: "You must be a law student, aren't you?" They have to say either yes, or no. And I say, "I thought you were. You defend this criminal white man harder than he defends his guilty self!"

One particular university's "token-integrated" black Ph.D. associate professor I never will forget; he got me so mad I couldn't see straight. As badly as our 22 millions of educationally deprived black people need the help of any brains he has, there he was looking like some fly in the buttermilk among white "colleagues"—and he was trying to *eat me up!* He was ranting about what a "divisive demagogue" and what a "reverse racist" I was. I was racking my head, to spear that fool; finally I held up my hand, and he stopped. "Do you know what white racists call black Ph.D's?" He said something like, "I believe that I happen not to be aware of that"—you know, one of these ultra-proper-talking Negroes. And I laid the word down on him, loud: *"Nigger!"*

Speaking in these colleges and universities was good for the Nation of Islam, I would report to Mr. Muhammad, because the devilish white man's best minds were developed and influenced in the colleges and universities. But for some reason that I could never understand until much later, Mr. Muhammad never really wanted me to speak at these colleges and universities.

I was to learn later, from Mr. Muhammad's own sons, that he was envious because he felt unequipped to speak at colleges himself. But nevertheless, in Mr. Muhammad's behalf at this time, I was finding these highly intelligent audiences amazingly open-minded and objective in their receptions of the raw, naked truths that I would tell them: .

"Time and time again, the black, the brown, the red, and the yellow races have witnessed and suffered the white man's small ability to understand the simple notes of the spirit. The white man seems tone deaf to the total orchestration of humanity. Every day, his newspapers' front pages show us the world that he has created.

"God's wrathful judgment is close upon this white man stumbling and groping blindly in wickedness and evil and spiritual darkness.

"Look—remaining today are only two giant white nations, America and Russia, each of them with mistrustful, nervous satellites. America is propping up most of the remaining white world. The French, the Belgians, the Dutch, the Portuguese, the Spanish and other white nations have weakened steadily as non-white Asians and Africans have recovered their lands.

"America is subsidizing what is left of the prestige and strength of the once mighty Britain. The sun has set forever on that monocled, pith-helmeted resident colonialist, sipping tea with his delicate lady in the non-white colonies being systematically robbed of every valuable resource. Britain's superfluous royalty and nobility now exist by charging tourists to inspect the once baronial castles, and by selling memoirs, perfumes, autographs, titles, and even themselves.

"The whole world knows that the white man cannot survive another war. If either of the two giant white nations pushes the button, white civilization will die!

"And we see again that not ideologies, but race, and color, is what binds human beings. Is it accidental that as Red Chinese visit African and Asian countries, Russia and America draw steadily closer to each other?

"The collective white man's history has left the non-white peoples no alternative, either, but to draw closer to each other. Characteristically, as always, the devilish white man lacks the moral strength and courage to cast off his arrogance. He wants, today, to 'buy' friends among the non-whites. He tries, characteristically, to cover up his past record. He does not possess the humility to admit his guilt, to try and atone for his crimes. The white man has perverted the simple message of love that the Prophet Jesus lived and taught when He walked upon this earth."

Audiences seemed surprised when I spoke about Jesus. I would explain that we Muslims believe in the Prophet Jesus. He was one of the three most important Prophets of the religion of Islam, the others being Muhammad and Moses. In Jerusalem there are Muslim shrines built to the Prophet Jesus. I would explain that it was our belief that Christianity did not perform what Christ taught. I never failed to cite that even Billy Graham, challenged in Africa, had himself made the distinction, "I believe in Christ, not Christianity."

I never will forget one little blonde co-ed after I had spoken at her New England college. She must have caught the next plane behind that one I took to New York. She found the Muslim restaurant in Harlem. I just happened to be there when she came in. Her clothes, her carriage, her accent, all showed Deep South white breeding and money. At that college, I told how the antebellum white slavemaster even devilishly manipulated his own woman. He convinced her that she was "too pure" for his base "animal instincts." With this "noble" ruse, he conned his own wife to look away from his obvious preference for the "animal" black woman. So the "delicate mistress" sat and watched the plantation's little mongrel-complexioned children, sired obviously by her father, her husband, her brothers, her sons. I said at that college that the guilt of American whites included their knowledge that in hating Negroes, they were hating, they were rejecting, they were denying, their own blood.

Anyway, I'd never seen anyone I ever spoke before more affected than this little white college girl. She demanded, right up in my face, "Don't you believe there are any *good* white people?" I didn't want to hurt her feelings. I told her, "People's *deeds* I believe in, Miss—not their words."

"What can I *do?*" she exclaimed. I told her, "Nothing." She burst out crying, and ran out and up Lenox Avenue and caught a taxi.

Mr. Muhammad—each time I'd go to see him in Chicago, or in Phoenix—would warm me with his expressions of his approval and confidence in me.

He left me in charge of the Nation of Islam's affairs when he made an Omra pilgrimage to the Holy City Mecca.

I believed so strongly in Mr. Muhammad that I would have hurled myself between him and an assassin.

A chance event brought crashing home to me that there was something—one thing—greater than my reverence for Mr. Muhammad.

It was the awesomeness of my reason to revere him.

I was the invited speaker at the Harvard Law School Forum. I happened to glance through a window. Abruptly, I realized that I was looking in the direction of the apartment house that was my old burglary gang's hideout.

It rocked me like a tidal wave. Scenes from my once depraved life lashed through my mind. *Living* like an animal; *thinking* like an animal!

Awareness came surging up in me—how deeply the religion of Islam had reached down into the mud to lift me up, to save me from being what I inevitably would have been: a dead criminal in a grave, or, if still alive, a flint-hard, bitter, thirty-seven-year-old convict in some penitentiary, or insane asylum. Or, at best, I would have been an old, fading Detroit Red, hustling, stealing enough for food and narcotics, and myself being stalked as prey by cruelly ambitious younger hustlers such as Detroit Red had been.

But Allah had blessed me to learn about the religion of Islam, which had enabled me to lift myself up from the muck and the mire of this rotting world.

And there I stood, the invited speaker, at Harvard.

A story that I had read in prison when I was reading a lot of Greek mythology flicked into my head.

The boy Icarus. Do you remember the story?

Icarus' father made some wings that he fastened with wax. "Never fly but so high with these wings," the father said. But soaring around, this way, that way, Icarus' flying pleased him so that he began thinking he was flying on his own merit. Higher, he flew—higher—until the heat of the sun melted the wax holding those wings. And down came Icarus—tumbling.

Standing there by that Harvard window, I silently vowed to Allah that I never would forget that any wings I wore had been put on by the religion of Islam. That fact I never have forgotten . . . not for one second.

CHAPTER SIXTEEN

OUT

In nineteen sixty-one, Mr. Muhammad's condition grew suddenly worse.

As he talked with me when I visited him, when he talked with anyone, he would unpredictably begin coughing harder, and harder, until his body was wracked and jerking in agonies that were painful to watch, and Mr. Muhammad would have to take to his bed.

We among Mr. Muhammad's officials, and his family, kept the situation to ourselves, while we could. Few other Muslims became aware of Mr. Muhammad's condition until there were last-minute cancellations of long-advertised personal appearances at some big Muslim rallies. Muslims knew that only something really serious would ever have stopped the Messenger from keeping his promise to be with them at their rallies. Their questions had to be answered, and the news of our leader's illness swiftly spread through the Nation of Islam.

Anyone not a Muslim could not conceive what the possible loss of Mr. Muhammad would have meant among his followers. To us, the Nation of Islam was Mr. Muhammad. What bonded us into the best organization black Americans ever had was every Muslim's devout regard for Mr. Muhammad as black America's moral, mental, and spiritual reformer.

Stated another way, we Muslims regarded ourselves as moral and mental and spiritual examples for other black Americans, because we followed the personal example of Mr. Muhammad. Black communities discussed with respect how Muslims were suspended if they lied, gambled, cheated, or smoked. For moral

294

crimes, such as fornication or adultery, Mr. Muhammad personally would mete out sentences of from one to five years of "isolation," if not complete expulsion from the Nation. And Mr. Muhammad would punish his officials more readily than the newest convert in a mosque. He said that any defecting official betrayed both himself and his position as a leader and example for other Muslims. For every Muslim, in his rejection of immoral temptation, the beacon was Mr. Muhammad. All Muslims felt as one that without his light, we would all be in darkness.

As I have related, doctors recommended a dry climate to ease Mr. Muhammad's condition. Quickly we found up for sale in Phoenix the home of the saxophone player, Louis Jordan. The Nation's treasury purchased the home, and Mr. Muhammad soon moved there.

Only by being two people could I have worked harder in the service of the Nation of Islam. I had every gratification that I wanted. I had helped bring about the progress and national impact such that none could call us liars when we called Mr. Muhammad the most powerful black man in America. I had helped Mr. Muhammad and his other ministers to revolutionize the American black man's thinking, opening his eyes until he would never again look in the same fearful, worshipful way at the white man. I had participated in spreading the truths that had done so much to help the American black man rid himself of the mirage that the white race was made up of "superior" beings. I had been a part of the tapping of something in the black secret soul.

If I harbored any personal disappointment whatsoever, it was that privately I was convinced that our Nation of Islam could be an even greater force in the American black man's overall struggle—if we engaged in more *action*. By that, I mean I thought privately that we should have amended, or relaxed, our general non-engagement policy. I felt that, wherever black people committed themselves, in the Little Rocks and the Birminghams and other places, militantly disciplined Muslims should also be there—for all the world to see, and respect, and discuss.

It could be heard increasingly in the Negro communities: "Those Muslims *talk* tough, but they never *do* anything, unless somebody bothers Muslims." I moved around among outsiders more than most other Muslim officials. I felt the very real potentiality that, considering the mercurial moods of the black masses, this labeling of Muslims as "talk only" could see us, powerful as we were, one day suddenly separated from the Negroes' front-line struggle.

But beyond that single personal concern, I couldn't have asked Allah to bless my efforts any more than he had. Islam in New York City was growing faster than anywhere in America. From the one tiny mosque to which Mr. Muhammad had originally sent me, I had now built three of the Nation's most powerful and aggressive mosques—Harlem's Seven-A in Manhattan, Corona's Seven-B in Queens, and Mosque Seven-C in Brooklyn. And on a national basis, I had either directly established, or I had helped to establish, most of the one hundred or more mosques in the fifty states. I was crisscrossing North America sometimes as often as four times a week. Often, what sleep I got was caught in the jet planes. I was maintaining a marathon schedule of press, radio, television, and public-speaking commitments. The only way that I could keep up with my job for Mr. Muhammad was by flying with the wings that he had given me.

As far back as 1961, when Mr. Muhammad's illness took that turn for the worse, I had heard chance negative remarks concerning me. I had heard veiled implications. I had noticed other little evidences of the envy and of the jealousy which Mr. Muhammad had prophesied. For example, it was being said that "Minister Malcolm is trying to take over the Nation," it was being said that I was "taking credit" for Mr. Muhammad's teaching, it was being said that I was trying to "build an empire" for myself. It was being said that I loved playing "coast-to-coast Mr. Big Shot."

When I heard these things, actually, they didn't anger me. They helped me to re-steel my inner resolve that such lies would never become true of me. I would always remember that Mr. Muhammad had prophesied this envy and jealousy. This would help me to ignore it, because I knew that *he* would understand if *he* ever should hear such talk.

A frequent rumor among non-Muslims was "Malcolm X is making a pile of money." All Muslims at least knew better than that. *Me* making money? The F.B.I. and the C.I.A. and the

I.R.S. all combined can't turn up a thing I got, beyond a car to drive and a seven-room house to live in. (And by now the Nation of Islam is jealously and greedily trying to take away even that house.) I had *access* to money. Yes! Elijah Muhammad would authorize for me any amount that I asked for. But he knew, as every Muslim official knew, that every nickel and dime I ever got was used to promote the Nation of Islam.

My attitude toward money generated the only domestic quarrel that I have ever had with my beloved wife Betty. As our children increased in number, so did Betty's hints to me that I should put away *something* for our family. But I refused, and finally we had this argument. I put my foot down. I knew I had in Betty a wife who would sacrifice her life for me if such an occasion ever presented itself to her, but still I told her that too many organizations had been destroyed by leaders who tried to benefit personally, often goaded into it by their wives. We nearly broke up over this argument. I finally convinced Betty that if anything ever happened to me, the Nation of Islam would take care of her for the rest of her life, and of our children until they were grown. I could never have been a bigger fool!

In every radio or television appearance, in every newspaper interview, I always made it crystal clear that I was Mr. Muhammad's *representative*. Anyone who ever heard me make a public speech during this time knows that at least once a minute I said, "The Honorable Elijah Muhammad teaches—" I would refuse to talk with any person who ever tried any so-called "joke" about my constant reference to Mr. Muhammad. Whenever anyone said, or wrote, "Malcolm X, the number two Black Muslim—" I would recoil. I have called up reporters and radio and television newscasters long-distance and asked them never to use that phrasing again, explaining to them: "*All* Muslims are number two—after Mr. Muhammad."

My briefcase was stocked with Mr. Muhammad's photographs. I gave them to photographers who snapped my picture. I would telephone editors asking them, "Please use Mr. Muhammad's picture instead of mine." When, to my joy, Mr. Muhammad agreed to grant interviews to white writers, I rarely spoke to a white writer, or a black one either, whom I didn't urge to visit Mr. Muhammad in person in Chicago—"Get the truth from the Messenger in person''—and a number of them did go there and meet and interview him.

Both white people and Negroes—even including Muslims—would make me uncomfortable, always giving me so much credit for the steady progress that the Nation of Islam was making. ''All praise is due to Allah,'' I told everybody. ''Anything creditable that I do is due to Mr. Elijah Muhammad.''

I believe that no man in the Nation of Islam could have gained the international prominence I gained with the wings Mr. Muhammad had put on me—plus having the freedom that he granted me to take liberties and do things on my own—and still have remained as faithful and as selfless a servant to him as I was.

I would say that it was in 1962 when I began to notice that less and less about me appeared in our Nation's *Muhammad Speaks*. I learned that Mr. Muhammad's son, Herbert, now the paper's publisher, had instructed that as little as possible be printed about me. In fact, there was more in the Muslim paper about integrationist Negro ''leaders'' than there was about me. I could read more about myself in the European, Asian, and African press.

I am not griping about publicity for myself. I already had received more publicity than many world personages. But I resented the fact that the Muslims' own newspaper denied them news of important things being done in their behalf, simply because it happened that I had done the things. I was conducting rallies, trying to propagate Mr. Muhammad's teachings, and because of jealousy and narrow-mindedness finally I got no coverage at all—for by now an order had been given to completely black me out of the newspaper. For instance, I spoke to eight thousand students at the University of California, and the press there gave big coverage to what I said of the power and program of Mr. Muhammad. But when I got to Chicago, expecting at least a favorable response and some coverage, I met only a chilly reaction. The same thing happened when, in Harlem, I staged a rally that drew seven thousand people. At that time, Chicago headquarters was even discouraging me from staging large rallies. But the next week, I held another Harlem rally that was even bigger and more successful than the first one—and obviously this only increased the envy of the Chicago headquarters.

But I would put these things out of my mind, as they occurred.

At least, as much as I humanly could, I put them out of my mind. I am not trying to make myself seem right and noble. I am telling the truth. I *loved* the Nation, and Mr. Muhammad. I *lived for* the Nation, and for Mr. Muhammad.

It made other Muslim officials jealous because my picture was often in the daily press. They wouldn't remember that my picture was there because of my fervor in championing Mr. Muhammad. They wouldn't simply reason that as vulnerable as the Nation of Islam was to distorted rumors and outright lies, we needed nothing so little as to have our public spokesman constantly denying the rumors. Common sense would have told any official that certainly Mr. Muhammad couldn't be running all over the country as his own spokesman. And whoever he appointed as his spokesman couldn't avoid a lot of press focus.

Whenever I caught any resentful feelings hanging on in my mind, I would be ashamed of myself, considering it a sign of weakness in myself. I knew that at least Mr. Muhammad knew that my life was totally dedicated to representing him.

But during 1963, I couldn't help being very hypersensitive to my critics in high posts within our Nation. I quit selecting certain of my New York brothers and giving them money to go and lay groundwork for new mosques in other cities—because slighting remarks were being made about "Malcolm's ministers." In a time in America when it was of arch importance for a militant black voice to reach mass audiences, *Life* magazine wanted to do a personal story of me, and I refused. I refused again when a cover story was offered by *Newsweek*. I refused again when I could have been a guest on the top-rated "Meet the Press" television program. Each refusal was a general loss for the black man, and, for the Nation of Islam, each refusal was a specific loss—and each refusal was made because of Chicago's attitude. There was jealousy because I had been requested to make these featured appearances.

When a high-powered-rifle slug tore through the back of the N.A.A.C.P. Field Secretary Medgar Evers in Mississippi, I wanted to say the blunt truths that needed to be said. When a bomb was exploded in a Negro Christian church in Birmingham, Alabama, snuffing out the lives of those four beautiful little black girls, I made comments—but not what should have been said about the climate of hate that the American white man was generating and nourishing. The more hate was permitted to lash out when there were ways it could have been checked, the more bold the hate became—until at last it was flaring out at even the white man's own kind, including his own leaders. In Dallas, Texas, for instance, the then Vice President and Mrs. Johnson were vulgarly insulted. And the U.S. Ambassador to the United Nations, Adlai Stevenson, was spat upon and hit on the head by a white woman picket.

Mr. Muhammad made me the Nation's first National Minister. At a late 1963 rally in Philadelphia, Mr. Muhammad, embracing me, said to that audience before us, "This is my most faithful, hard-working minister. He will follow me until he dies."

He had never paid such a compliment to any Muslim. No praise from any other earthly person could have meant more to me.

But this would be Mr. Muhammad's and my last public appearance together.

Not long before, I had been on the Jerry Williams radio program in Boston, when someone handed me an item hot off the Associated Press machine. I read that a chapter of the Louisiana Citizens Council had just offered a $10,000 reward for my death.

But the threat of death was much closer to me than somewhere in Louisiana.

What I am telling you is the truth. When I discovered who else wanted me dead, I am telling you—it nearly sent me to Bellevue.

In my twelve years as a Muslim minister, I had always taught so strongly on the moral issues that many Muslims accused me of being "anti-woman." The very keel of my teaching, and my most bone-deep personal belief, was that Elijah Muhammad in every aspect of his existence was a symbol of moral, mental, and spiritual reform among the American black people. For twelve years, I had taught that within the entire Nation of Islam; my own transformation was the best example I knew of Mr. Muhammad's power to reform black men's lives. From the time I entered prison until I married, about twelve years later, because of Mr. Muhammad's influence upon me, I had never touched a woman.

But around 1963, if anyone had noticed, I spoke less and less of religion. I taught social doctrine to Muslims, and current events, and politics. I stayed wholly off the subject of morality.

And the reason for this was that my faith had been shaken in a way that I can never fully describe. For I had discovered Muslims had been betrayed by Elijah Muhammad himself.

I want to make this as brief as I can, only enough so that my position and my reactions will be understood. As to whether or not I should reveal this, there's no longer any need for any question in my mind—for now the public knows. To make it concise, I will quote from one wire service story as it appeared in newspapers, and was reported over radio and television, across the United States:

"Los Angeles, July 3 (UPI)—Elijah Muhammad, 67-year-old leader of the Black Muslim movement, today faced paternity suits from two former secretaries who charged he fathered their four children. . . . Both women are in their twenties. . . . Miss Rosary and Miss Williams charged they had intimacies with Elijah Muhammad from 1957 until this year. Miss Rosary alleged he fathered her two children and said she was expecting a third child by him . . . the other plaintiff said he was the father of her daughter. . . ."

As far back as 1955, I had heard hints. But believe me when I tell you this: for me even to consider believing anything as insane-sounding as any slightest implication of any immoral behavior of Mr. Muhammad—why, the very idea made me shake with fear.

And so my mind simply refused to accept anything so grotesque as adultery mentioned in the same breath with Mr. Muhammad's name.

Adultery! Why, any Muslim guilty of adultery was summarily ousted in disgrace. One of the Nation's most closely kept scandals was that a succession of the personal secretaries of Mr. Muhammad had become pregnant. They were brought before Muslim courts and charged with adultery and they confessed. Humiliated before the general body, they received sentences of from one to five years of "isolation." That meant they were to have no contact whatsoever with any other Muslims.

I don't think I could say anything which better testifies to my depth of faith in Mr. Muhammad than that I totally and absolutely rejected my own intelligence. I simply refused to believe.

I didn't want Allah to "burn my brain" as I felt the brain of my brother Reginald had been burned for harboring evil thoughts about Mr. Elijah Muhammad. The last time I had seen Reginald, one day he walked into the Mosque Seven restaurant. I saw him coming in the door. I went and met him. I looked into my own brother's eyes; I told him he wasn't welcome among Muslims, and he turned around and left, and I haven't seen him since. I did that to my own blood brother because, years before, Mr. Muhammad had sentenced Reginald to "isolation" from all other Muslims—and I considered that I was a Muslim before I was Reginald's brother.

No one in the world could have convinced me that Mr. Muhammad would betray the reverence bestowed upon him by all of the mosques full of poor, trusting Muslims nickeling and diming up to faithfully support the Nation of Islam—when many of these faithful were scarcely able to pay their own rents.

But by late 1962, I learned reliably that numerous Muslims were leaving Mosque Two in Chicago. The ugly rumor was spreading swiftly—even among non-Muslim Negroes. When I thought how the press constantly sought ways to discredit the Nation of Islam, I trembled to think of such a thing reaching the ears of some newspaper reporter, either black or white.

I actually began to have nightmares . . . I saw *headlines*.

I was burdened with a leaden fear as I kept speaking engagements all over America. Any time a reporter came anywhere near me, I could *hear* him ask, "Is it true, Mr. Malcolm X, this report we hear, that . . . " And what was I going to say?

There was never any specific moment when I admitted the situation to myself. In the way that the human mind can do, somehow I slid over admitting to myself the ugly fact, even as I began dealing with it.

Both in New York and Chicago, non-Muslims whom I knew began to tell me indirectly they had heard—or they would ask me if I had heard. I would act as if I had no idea whatever of what they were talking about—and I was grateful when they chose not to spell out what they knew. I went around knowing that I looked to them like a total fool. I felt like a total fool, out there every day preaching, and apparently not knowing what was going on right under my nose, in my own organization, involving the very man I was praising so. To look like a fool unearthed emotions I hadn't felt since my Harlem hustler days. The worst thing in the hustler's world was to be a dupe.

I will give you an example. Backstage at the Apollo Theater in Harlem one day, the comedian Dick Gregory looked at me. "Man," he said, "Muhammad's nothing but a . . ."—I can't say the word he used. *Bam!* Just like that. My Muslim instincts said to attack Dick—but, instead, I felt weak and hollow. I think Dick sensed how upset I was and he let me get him off the subject. I knew Dick, a Chicagoan, was wise in the ways of the streets, and blunt-spoken. I wanted to plead with him not to say to anyone else what he had said to me—but I couldn't; it would have been my own admission.

I can't describe the torments I went through.

Always before, in any extremity, I had caught the first plane to Mr. Elijah Muhammad. He had virtually raised me from the dead. Everything I was that was creditable, he had made me. I felt that no matter what, I could not let him down.

There was no one I could turn to with this problem, except Mr. Muhammad himself. Ultimately that had to be the case. But first I went to Chicago to see Mr. Muhammad's second youngest son, Wallace Muhammad. I felt that Wallace was Mr. Muhammad's most strongly spiritual son, the son with the most objective outlook. Always, Wallace and I had shared an exceptional closeness and trust.

And Wallace knew, when he saw me, why I had come to see him. "I know," he said. I said I thought we should rally to help his father. Wallace said he didn't feel that his father would welcome any efforts to help him. I told myself that Wallace must be crazy.

Next, I broke the rule that no Muslim is supposed to have any contact with another Muslim in the "isolated" state. I looked up, and I talked with three of the former secretaries to Mr. Muhammad. From their own mouths, I heard their stories of who had fathered their children. And from their own mouths I heard that Elijah Muhammad had told them I was the best, the greatest minister he ever had, but that someday I would leave him, turn against him—so I was "dangerous." I learned from these former secretaries of Mr. Muhammad that while he was praising me to my face, he was tearing me apart behind my back.

That deeply hurt me.

Every day, I was meeting the microphones, cameras, press reporters, and other commitments, including the Muslims of my own Mosque Seven. I felt almost out of my mind.

Finally, the thing crystallized for me. As long as I did nothing, I felt it was the same as being disloyal. I felt that as long as I sat down, I was not helping Mr. Muhammad—when somebody needed to be standing up.

So one night I wrote to Mr. Muhammad about the poison being spread about him. He telephoned me in New York. He said that when he saw me he would discuss it.

I desperately wanted to find some way—some kind of a bridge—over which I was certain the Nation of Islam could be saved from self-destruction. I had faith in the Nation: we weren't some group of Christian Negroes, jumping and shouting and full of sins.

I thought of one bridge that could be used if and when the shattering disclosure should become public. Loyal Muslims could be taught that a man's accomplishments in his life outweigh his personal, human weaknesses. Wallace Muhammad helped me to review the Quran and the Bible for documentation. David's adultery with Bathsheba weighed less on history's scales, for instance, than the positive fact of David's killing Goliath. Thinking of Lot, we think not of incest, but of his saving the people from the destruction of Sodom and Gomorrah. Or, our image of Noah isn't of his getting drunk—but of his building the ark and teaching people to save themselves from the flood. We think of Moses leading the Hebrews from bondage, not of Moses' adultery with the Ethiopian women. In all of the cases I reviewed, the positive outweighed the negative.

I began teaching in New York Mosque Seven that a man's accomplishments in his life outweighed his personal, human weaknesses. I taught that a person's good deeds outweigh his bad deeds. I never mentioned the previously familiar subjects of adultery and fornication, and I never mentioned immoral evils.

By some miracle, the adultery talk which was so widespread in Chicago seemed to only leak a little in Boston, Detroit, and New York. Apparently, it hadn't reached other mosques around the country at all. In Chicago, increasing numbers of Muslims were leaving Mosque Two, I heard, and many non-Muslims who had been sympathetic to the Nation were now outspokenly anti-Muslim. In February 1963, I officiated at the University of Islam graduation exercises; when I introduced various members of the Muhammad family, I could feel the cold chill toward them from the Muslims in the audience.

Elijah Muhammad had me fly to Phoenix to see him in April, 1963.

We embraced, as always—and almost immediately he took me outside, where we began to walk by his swimming pool.

He was The Messenger of Allah. When I was a foul, vicious convict, so evil that other convicts had called me Satan, this man had rescued me. He was the man who had trained me, who had treated me as if I were his own flesh and blood. He was the man who had given me wings—to go places, to do things I otherwise never would have dreamed of. We walked, with me caught up in a whirlwind of emotions.

"Well, son," Mr. Muhammad said, "what is on your mind?"

Plainly, frankly, pulling no punches, I told Mr. Muhammad what was being said. And without waiting for any response from him, I said that with his son Wallace's help I had found in the Quran and the Bible that which might be taught to Muslims—if it became necessary—as the fulfillment of prophecy.

"Son, I'm not surprised," Elijah Muhammad said. "You always have had such a good understanding of prophecy, and of spiritual things. You recognize that's what all of this is— prophecy. You have the kind of understanding that only an old man has.

"I'm David," he said. "When you read about how David took another man's wife, I'm that David. You read about Noah, who got drunk—that's me. You read about Lot, who went and laid up with his own daughters. I have to fulfill all of those things."

I remembered that when an epidemic is about to hit somewhere, that community's people are inoculated against exposure with some of the same germs that are anticipated—and this prepares them to resist the oncoming virus.

I decided I had better prepare six other East Coast Muslim officials whom I selected.

I told them. And then I told them why I had told them—that I felt they should not be caught by surprise and shock if it became their job to teach the Muslims in their mosques the "ful-fillment of prophecy." I found then that some had already heard it; one of them, Minister Louis X of Boston, as much as seven months before. They had been living with the dilemma them-selves.

I never dreamed that the Chicago Muslim officials were going to make it appear that I was throwing gasoline on the fire instead of water. I never dreamed that they were going to try to make it appear that instead of inoculating against an epidemic, I had started it.

The stage in Chicago even then was being set for Muslims to shift their focus off the epidemic—and onto me.

Hating me was going to become the cause for people of shat-tered faith to rally around.

Non-Muslim Negroes who knew me well, and even some of the white reporters with whom I had some regular contact, were telling me, almost wherever I went, "Malcolm X, you're look-ing tired. You need a rest."

They didn't know a fraction of it. Since I had been a Muslim, this was the first time any white people really got to me in a personal way. I could tell that some of them were really honest and sincere. One of these, whose name I won't call—he might lose his job—said, "Malcolm X, the whites need your voice worse than the Negroes." I remember so well his saying this because it prefaced the first time since I became a Muslim that I had ever talked with any white man at any length about any-thing except the Nation of Islam and the American black man's struggle today.

I can't remember how, or why, he somehow happened to mention the Dead Sea Scrolls. I came back with something like, "Yes, those scrolls are going to take Jesus off the stained-glass windows and the frescoes where he has been lily-white, and put Him back into the true mainstream of history where Jesus ac-tually was non-white." The reporter was surprised, and I went on that the Dead Sea Scrolls were going to reaffirm that Jesus was a member of that brotherhood of Egyptian seers called the Essene—a fact already known from Philo, the famous Egyptian historian of Jesus' time. And the reporter and I got off on about two good hours of talking in the areas of archaeology, history, and religion. It was *so* pleasant. I almost forgot the heavy worries on my mind—for that brief respite. I remember we wound up agreeing that by the year 2000, every schoolchild will be taught the true color of great men of antiquity.

I've said that I expected headlines momentarily. I hadn't expected the kind which came.

No one needs to be reminded of who got assassinated in Dallas, Texas, on November 22, 1963.

Within hours after the assassination—I am telling nothing but the truth—every Muslim minister received from Mr. Elijah Muhammad a directive—in fact, *two* directives. Every minister was ordered to make no remarks at all concerning the assassination. Mr. Muhammad instructed that if pressed for comment, we should say: "No comment."

During that three-day period where there was no other news to be heard except relating to the murdered President, Mr. Muhammad had a previously scheduled speaking engagement in New York at the Manhattan Center. He cancelled his coming to speak, and as we were unable to get back the money already paid for the rental of the center, Mr. Muhammad told me to speak in his stead. And so I spoke.

Many times since then, I've looked at the speech notes I used that day, which had been prepared at least a week before the assassination. The title of my speech was "God's Judgment of White America." It was on the theme, familiar to me, of "as you sow, so shall you reap," or how the hypocritical American white man was reaping what he had sowed.

The question-and-answer period opened, I suppose inevitably, with someone asking me, "What do you think about President Kennedy's assassination? What is your opinion?"

Without a second thought, I said what I honestly felt—that it was, as I saw it, a case of "the chickens coming home to roost." I said that the hate in white men had not stopped with the killing of defenseless black people, but that hate, allowed to spread unchecked, finally had struck down this country's Chief of State. I said it was the same thing as had happened with Medgar Evers, with Patrice Lumumba, with Madame Nhu's husband.

The headlines and the news broadcasts promptly had it: *"Black Muslims' Malcolm X: 'Chickens Come Home to Roost.'"*

It makes me feel weary to think of it all now. All over America, all over the world, some of the world's most important personages were saying in various ways, and in far stronger ways than I did, that America's climate of hate had been responsible for the President's death. But when Malcolm X said the same thing, it was ominous.

My regular monthly visit to Mr. Muhammad was due the next day. Somehow, on the plane, I expected something. I've always had this strong intuition.

Mr. Muhammad and I embraced each other in greeting. I sensed some ingredient missing from his usual amiability. And I was suddenly tense—to me also very significant. For years, I had prided myself that Mr. Muhammad and I were so close that I knew how he felt by how I felt. If he was nervous, I was nervous. If I was relaxed, then I knew he was relaxed. Now, I felt the *tension*. . . .

First we talked of other things, sitting in his living room. Then he asked me, "Did you see the papers this morning?"

I said, "Yes, sir, I did."

"That was a very bad statement," he said. "The country loved this man. The whole country is in mourning. That was very ill-timed. A statement like that can make it hard on Muslims in general."

And then, as if Mr. Muhammad's voice came from afar, I heard his words: "I'll have to silence you for the next ninety days—so that the Muslims everywhere can be disassociated from the blunder."

I was numb.

But I was a follower of Mr. Muhammad. Many times I had said to my own assistants that anyone in a position to discipline others must be able to take disciplining himself.

I told Mr. Muhammad, "Sir, I agree with you, and I submit, one hundred per cent."

I flew back to New York psychologically preparing myself to tell my Mosque Seven assistants that I had been suspended—or "silenced."

But to my astonishment, upon arrival I learned that my assistants already had been informed.

What astonished me even more—a telegram had been sent to every New York City newspaper and radio and television station. It was the most quick and thorough publicity job that I had ever seen the Chicago officials initiate.

Every telephone where I could possibly be reached was ringing. London. Paris. A.P., U.P.I. Every television and radio network, and all of the newspapers were calling. I told them all, "I disobeyed Mr. Muhammad. I submit completely to his wisdom. Yes, I expect to be speaking again after ninety days."

"Malcolm X Silenced!" It was headlines.

My first worry was that if a scandal broke for the Nation of Islam within the next ninety days, I would be gagged when I could be the most experienced Muslim in dealing with the news media that would make the most of any scandal within the Nation.

I learned next that my "silencing" was even more thorough than I had thought. I was not only forbidden to talk with the press, I was not even to teach in my own Mosque Seven.

Next, an announcement was made throughout the Nation of Islam that I would be reinstated within ninety days, *"if he submits."*

This made me suspicious—for the first time. I had completely submitted. But, deliberately, Muslims were being given the impression that I had rebelled.

I hadn't hustled in the streets for years for nothing. I knew when I was being set up.

Three days later, the first word came to me that a Mosque Seven official who had been one of my most immediate assistants was telling certain Mosque Seven brothers: "If you knew what the Minister did, you'd go out and kill him yourself."

And then I knew. As any official in the Nation of Islam would instantly have known, any death-talk for me could have been approved of—if not actually initiated—by only one man.

My head felt like it was bleeding inside. I felt like my brain was damaged. I went to see Dr. Leona A. Turner, who has been my family doctor for years, who practices in East Elmhurst, Long Island. I asked her to give me a brain examination.

She did examine me. She said I was under great strain—and I needed rest.

Cassius Clay and I are not together today. But always I must be grateful to him that at just this time, when he was in Miami training to fight Sonny Liston, Cassius invited me, Betty, and the children to come there as his guests—as a sixth wedding anniversary present to Betty and me.

I had met Cassius Clay in Detroit in 1962. He and his brother Rudolph came into the Student's Luncheonette next door to the Detroit Mosque where Elijah Muhammad was about to speak at a big rally. Every Muslim present was impressed by the bearing and the obvious genuineness of the striking, handsome pair of prizefighter brothers. Cassius came up and pumped my hand, introducing himself as he later presented himself to the world, "I'm Cassius Clay." He acted as if I was supposed to know who he was. So I acted as though I did. Up to that moment, though, I had never even heard of him. Ours were two entirely different worlds. In fact, Elijah Muhammad instructed us Muslims against all forms of sports.

As Elijah Muhammad spoke, the two Clay brothers practically led the applause, further impressing everyone with their sincerity—since a Muslim rally was about the world's last place to seek fight fans.

Thereafter, now and then I heard how Cassius showed up in Muslim mosques and restaurants in various cities. And if I happened to be speaking anywhere within reasonable distance of wherever Cassius was, he would be present. I liked him. Some contagious quality about him made him one of the very few people I ever invited to my home. Betty liked him. Our children were crazy about him. Cassius was simply a likeable, friendly, clean-cut, down-to-earth youngster. I noticed how alert he was even in little details. I suspected that there was a plan in his public clowning. I suspected, and he confirmed to me, that he was doing everything possible to con and "psyche" Sonny Liston into coming into the ring angry, poorly trained, and overconfident, expecting another of his vaunted one-round knockouts. Not only was Cassius receptive to advice, he solicited it. Primarily, I impressed upon him to what a great extent a public figure's success depends upon how alert and knowledgeable he is to the true natures and to the true motives of all of the people who flock around him. I warned him about the "foxes," his expression for the aggressive, cute young females who flocked after him; I told Cassius that instead of "foxes," they really were wolves.

This was Betty's first vacation since we had married. And our three girls romped and played with the heavyweight contender.

I don't know what I might have done if I had stayed in New York during that crucial time—besieged by insistently ringing telephones, and by the press, and by all of the other people so anxious to gloat, to speculate and to "commiserate."

I was in a state of emotional shock. I was like someone who for twelve years had had an inseparable, beautiful marriage—and then suddenly one morning at breakfast the marriage partner had thrust across the table some divorce papers.

I felt as though something in *nature* had failed, like the sun, or the stars. It was that incredible a phenomenon to me—something too stupendous to conceive. I am not sparing myself. Around Cassius Clay's fight camp, around the Hampton House Motel where my family was staying, I talked with my own wife, and with other people, and actually I was only mouthing words that really meant nothing to me. Whatever I was saying at any time was being handled by a small corner of my mind. The rest of my mind was filled with a parade of a thousand and one different scenes from the past twelve years . . . scenes in the Muslim mosques . . . scenes with Mr. Muhammad . . . scenes with Mr. Muhammad's family . . . scenes with Muslims, individually, as my audiences, and at our social gatherings . . . and scenes with the white man in audiences, and the press.

I walked, I talked, I functioned. At the Cassius Clay fight camp, I told the various sportswriters repeatedly what I gradually had come to know within myself was a lie—that I would be reinstated within ninety days. But I could not yet let myself psychologically face what I knew: that already the Nation of Islam and I were physically divorced. Do you understand what I mean? A judge's signature on a piece of paper can grant to a couple a physical divorce—but for either of them, or maybe for both of them, if they have been a very close marriage team, to actually become *psychologically* divorced from each other might take years.

But in the physical divorce, I could not evade the obvious strategy and plotting coming out of Chicago to eliminate me from the Nation of Islam . . . if not from this world. And I felt that I perceived the anatomy of the plotting.

Any Muslim would have known that my "chickens coming

home to roost'' statement had been only an excuse to put into action the plan for getting me out. And step one had been already taken: the Muslims were given the impression that I had rebelled against Mr. Muhammad. I could now anticipate step two: I would remain ''suspended'' (and later I would be ''isolated'') indefinitely. Step three would be either to provoke some Muslim ignorant of the truth to take it upon himself to kill me as a ''religious duty''—or to ''isolate'' me so that I would gradually disappear from the public scene.

The only person who knew was my wife. I never would have dreamed that I would ever depend so much upon any woman for strength as I now leaned upon Betty. There was no exchange between us; Betty said nothing, being the caliber of wife that she is, with the depth of understanding that she has—but I could feel the envelopment of her comfort. I knew that she was as faithful a servant of Allah as I was, and I knew that whatever happened, she was with me.

The death talk was not my fear. Every second of my twelve years with Mr. Muhammad, I had been ready to lay down my life for him. The thing to me worse than death was the betrayal. I could conceive death. I couldn't conceive betrayal—not of the loyalty which I had given to the Nation of Islam, and to Mr. Muhammad. During the previous twelve years, if Mr. Muhammad had committed any civil crime punishable by death, I would have said and tried to prove that I did it—to save him—and I would have gone to the electric chair, as Mr. Muhammad's servant.

There as Cassius Clay's guest in Miami, I tried desperately to push my mind off my troubles and onto the Nation's troubles. I still struggled to persuade myself that Mr. Muhammad had been fulfilling prophecy. Because I actually had believed that if Mr. Muhammad was not God, then he surely stood next to God.

What began to break my faith was that, try as I might, I couldn't hide, I couldn't evade, that Mr. Muhammad, instead of facing what he had done before his followers, as a human weakness or as fulfillment of prophecy—which I sincerely believe that Muslims would have understood, or at least they would have accepted—Mr. Muhammad had, instead, been willing to hide, to cover up what he had done.

That was my major blow.

That was how I first began to realize that I had believed in Mr. Muhammad more than he believed in himself.

And that was how, after twelve years of never thinking for as much as five minutes about myself, I became able finally to muster the nerve, and the strength, to start facing the facts, to think for myself.

Briefly I left Florida to return Betty and the children to our Long Island home. I learned that the Chicago Muslim officials were further displeased with me because of the newspaper reports of me in the Cassius Clay camp. They felt that Cassius hadn't a prayer of a chance to win. They felt the Nation would be embarrassed through my linking the Muslim image with him. (I don't know if the champion today cares to remember that most newspapers in America were represented at the pre-fight camp—except *Muhammad Speaks*. Even though Cassius was a Muslim brother, the Muslim newspaper didn't consider his fight worth covering.)

I flew back to Miami feeling that it was Allah's intent for me to help Cassius prove Islam's superiority before the world—through proving that mind can win over brawn. I don't have to remind you of how people everywhere scoffed at Cassius Clay's chances of beating Liston.

This time, I brought from New York with me some photographs of Floyd Patterson and Sonny Liston in their fight camps, with white priests as their "spiritual advisors." Cassius Clay, being a Muslim, didn't need to be told how white Christianity had dealt with the American black man. "This fight is the *truth*," I told Cassius. "It's the Cross and the Crescent fighting in a prize ring—for the first time. It's a modern Crusades—a Christian and a Muslim facing each other with television to beam it off Telstar for the whole world to see what happens!" I told Cassius, "Do you think Allah has brought about all this intending for you to leave the ring as anything but the champion?" (You may remember that at the weighing-in, Cassius was yelling such things as "It is prophesied for me to be successful! I cannot be beaten!")

Sonny Liston's handlers and advisors had him fighting harder to "integrate" than he was training to meet Cassius. Liston finally had managed to rent a big, fine house over in a rich, wall-to-wall white section. To give you an idea, the owner of the neighboring house was the New York Yankees baseball club owner, Dan Topping. In the early evenings, when Cassius and I would sometimes walk where the black people lived, those Negroes' mouths would hang open in surprise that he was among them instead of whites as most black champions preferred. Again and again, Cassius startled those Negroes, telling them, ''You're my own kind. I get my strength from being around my own black people.''

What Sonny Liston was about to meet, in fact, was one of the most awesome frights that ever can confront any person—one who worships Allah, and who is completely without fear.

Among over eight thousand other seat holders in Miami's big Convention Hall, I received Seat Number Seven. Seven has always been my favorite number. It has followed me throughout my life. I took this to be Allah's message confirming to me that Cassius Clay was going to win. Along with Cassius, I really was more worried about how his brother Rudolph was going to do, fighting his first pro fight in the preliminaries.

While Rudolph was winning a four-round decision over a Florida Negro named ''Chip'' Johnson, Cassius stood at the rear of the auditorium watching calmly, dressed in a black tuxedo. After all of his months of antics, after the weighing-in act that Cassius had put on, this calmness should have tipped off some of the sportswriters who were predicting Clay's slaughter.

Then Cassius disappeared, dressing to meet Liston. As we had agreed, I joined him in a silent prayer for Allah's blessings. Finally, he and Liston were in their corners in the ring. I folded my arms and tried to appear the coolest man in the place, because a television camera can show you looking like a fool yelling at a prizefight.

Except for whatever chemical it was that got into Cassius' eyes and blinded him temporarily in the fourth and fifth rounds, the fight went according to his plan. He evaded Liston's powerful punches. The third round automatically began the tiring of the aging Liston, who was overconfidently trained to go only two rounds. Then, desperate, Liston lost. The secret of one of fight history's greatest upsets was that months before that night, Clay had out-thought Liston.

There probably never has been as quiet a new-champion party. The boyish king of the ring came over to my motel. He ate ice cream, drank milk, talked with football star Jimmy Brown and other friends, and some reporters. Sleepy, Cassius took a quick nap on my bed, then he went back home.

We had breakfast together the next morning, just before the press conference when Cassius calmly made the announcement which burst into international headlines that he was a "Black Muslim."

But let me tell you something about that. Cassius never announced himself a member of any "Black Muslims." The press reporters made that out of what he told them, which was this: "I believe in the religion of Islam, which means I believe there is no God but Allah, and Muhammad is His Apostle. This is the same religion that is believed in by over seven hundred million dark-skinned peoples throughout Africa and Asia."

Nothing in all of the furor which followed was more ridiculous than Floyd Patterson announcing that as a Catholic, he wanted to fight Cassius Clay—to save the heavyweight crown from being held by a Muslim. It was such a sad case of a brainwashed black Christian ready to do battle for the white man—who wants no part of him. Not three weeks later, the newspapers reported that in Yonkers, New York, Patterson was offering to sell his $140,000 house for a $20,000 loss. He had "integrated" into a neighborhood of whites who had made his life miserable. None were friendly. Their children called his children "niggers." One neighbor trained his dog to deface Patterson's property. Another erected a fence to hide the Negroes from sight. "I tried, it just didn't work," Patterson told the press.

The first direct order for my death was issued through a Mosque Seven official who previously had been a close assistant. Another previously close assistant of mine was assigned to do the job. He was a brother with a knowledge of demolition; he was asked to wire my car to explode when I turned the ignition key. But this brother, it happened, had seen too much of my total loyalty to the Nation to carry out his order. Instead, he came to me. I thanked him for my life. I told him what was really going on in Chicago. He was stunned almost beyond belief.

This brother was close to others in the Mosque Seven circle who might subsequently be called upon to eliminate me. He said he would take it upon himself to enlighten each of them enough so that they wouldn't allow themselves to be used.

This first direct death-order was how, finally, I began to arrive at my psychological divorce from the Nation of Islam.

I began to see, wherever I went—on the streets, in business places, on elevators, sidewalks, in passing cars—the faces of Muslims whom I knew, and I knew that any of them might be waiting the opportunity to try and put a bullet into me.

I was racking my brain. What was I going to do? My life was inseparably committed to the American black man's struggle. I was generally regarded as a "leader." For years, I had attacked so many so-called "black leaders" for their shortcomings. Now, I had to honestly ask myself what I could offer, how I was genuinely qualified to help the black people win their struggle for human rights. I had enough experience to know that in order to be a good organizer of anything which you expect to succeed—including yourself—you must almost mathematically analyze cold facts.

I had, as one asset, I knew, an international image. No amount of money could have bought that. I knew that if I said something newsworthy, people would read or hear of it, maybe even around the world, depending upon what it was. More immediately, in New York City, where I would naturally base any operation, I had a large, direct personal following of non-Muslims. This had been building up steadily ever since I had led Muslims in the dramatic protest to the police when our brother Hinton was beaten up. Hundreds of Harlem Negroes had seen, and hundreds of thousands of them had later heard how we had shown that almost anything could be accomplished by black men who would face the white man without fear. All of Harlem had seen how from then on, the police gave Muslims respect. (This was during the time that the Deputy Chief Inspector at the 28th Precinct had said of me, "No one man should have that much power.")

Over the ensuing years, I'd had various kinds of evidence that a high percentage of New York City's black people responded to what I said, including a great many who would not publicly say so. For instance, time and again when I spoke at street rallies, I would draw ten and twelve times as many people as most other so-called "Negro leaders." I knew that in any society, a true leader is one who earns and deserves the following he enjoys. True followers are bestowed by themselves, out of their own volition and emotions. I knew that the great lack of most of the big-named "Negro leaders" was their lack of any true rapport with the ghetto Negroes. How could they have rapport when they spent most of their time "integrating" with white people? I knew that the ghetto people knew that I never left the ghetto in spirit, and I never left it physically any more than I had to. I had a ghetto instinct; for instance, I could feel if tension was beyond normal in a ghetto audience. And I could speak and understand the ghetto's language. There was an example of this that always flew to my mind every time I heard some of the "big name" Negro "leaders" declaring they "spoke for" the ghetto black people.

After a Harlem street rally, one of these downtown "leaders" and I were talking when we were approached by a Harlem hustler. To my knowledge I'd never seen this hustler before; he said to me, approximately: "Hey, baby! I dig you holding this all-originals scene at the track . . . I'm going to lay a vine under the Jew's balls for a dime—got to give you a play . . . Got the shorts out here trying to scuffle up on some bread . . . Well, my man, I'll get on, got to go peck a little, and cop me some z's—" And the hustler went on up Seventh Avenue.

I would never have given it another thought, except that this downtown "leader" was standing, staring after that hustler, looking as if he'd just heard Sanskrit. He asked me what had been said, and I told him. The hustler had said he was aware that the Muslims were holding an all-black bazaar at Rockland Palace, which is primarily a dancehall. The hustler intended to pawn a suit for ten dollars to attend and patronize the bazaar. He had very little money but he was trying hard to make some. He was going to eat, then he would get some sleep.

The point I am making is that, as a "leader," I could talk over the ABC, CBS, or NBC microphones, at Harvard or at Tuskegee; I could talk with the so-called "middle class" Negro and with the ghetto blacks (whom all the other leaders just talked *about*). And because I had been a hustler, I knew better than all whites knew, and better than nearly all of the black "leaders" knew, that actually the most dangerous black man in America was the ghetto hustler.

Why do I say this? The hustler, out there in the ghetto jungles, has less respect for the white power structure than any other Negro in North America. The ghetto hustler is internally restrained by nothing. He has no religion, no concept of morality, no civic responsibility, no fear—nothing. To survive, he is out there constantly preying upon others, probing for any human weakness like a ferret. The ghetto hustler is forever frustrated, restless, and anxious for some "action." Whatever he undertakes, he commits himself to it fully, absolutely.

What makes the ghetto hustler yet more dangerous is his "glamor" image to the school-dropout youth in the ghetto. These ghetto teen-agers see the hell caught by their parents struggling to get somewhere, or see that they have given up struggling in the prejudiced, intolerant white man's world. The ghetto teen-agers make up their own minds they would rather be like the hustlers whom they see dressed "sharp" and flashing money and displaying no respect for anybody or anything. So the ghetto youth become attracted to the hustler worlds of dope, thievery, prostitution, and general crime and immorality.

It scared me the first time I really saw the danger of these ghetto teen-agers if they are ever sparked to violence. One sweltering summer afternoon, I attended a Harlem street rally which contained a lot of these teen-agers in the crowd. I had been invited by some "responsible" Negro leaders who normally never spoke to me; I knew they had just used my name to help them draw a crowd. The more I thought about it on the way there, the hotter I got. And when I got on the stand, I just told that crowd in the street that I wasn't really wanted up there, that my name had been used—and I walked off the speaker's stand.

Well, what did I want to do that for? Why, those young, teen-age Negroes got upset, and started milling around and yelling, upsetting the older Negroes in the crowd. The first thing you know traffic was blocked in four directions by a crowd whose mood quickly grew so ugly that I really got apprehensive. I got up on top of a car and began waving my arms and yelling at them to quiet down. They did quiet, and then I asked them to disperse—and they did.

This was when it began being said that I was America's only Negro who "could stop a race riot—or start one." I don't know if I could do either one. But I know one thing: it had taught me in a very few minutes to have a whole lot of respect for the human combustion that is packed among the hustlers and their young admirers who live in the ghettoes where the Northern white man has sealed-off the Negro—away from whites—for a hundred years.

The "long hot summer" of 1964 in Harlem, in Rochester, and in other cities, has given an idea of what could happen—and that's all, only an idea. For all of those riots were kept contained within where the Negroes lived. You let any of these bitter, seething ghettoes all over America receive the right igniting incident, and become really inflamed, and explode, and burst out of their boundaries into where whites live! In New York City, you let enraged blacks pour out of Harlem across Central Park and fan down the tunnels of Madison and Fifth and Lexington and Park Avenues. Or, take Chicago's South Side, an older, even worse slum—you let those Negroes swarm downtown. You let Washington, D.C.'s festering blacks head down Pennsylvania Avenue. Detroit has already seen a peaceful massing of more than a *hundred thousand* blacks—think about that. You name the city. Black social dynamite is in Cleveland, Philadelphia, San Francisco, Los Angeles . . . the black man's anger is there, fermenting.

I've strayed off onto some of the incidents and situations which have taught me to respect the danger in the ghettoes. I had been trying to explain how I honestly evaluated my own qualifications to be worthy of presenting myself as an independent "leader" among black men.

In the end, I reasoned that the decision already had been made for me. The ghetto masses already had entrusted me with an image of leadership among them. I knew the ghetto instinctively extends that trust only to one who had demonstrated that he would never sell them out to the white man. I not only had no such intention—to sell out was not even in my nature.

I felt a challenge to plan, and build, an organization that could help to cure the black man in North America of the sickness which has kept him under the white man's heel.

The black man in North America was mentally sick in his cooperative, sheeplike acceptance of the white man's culture.

The black man in North America was spiritually sick because for centuries he had accepted the white man's Christianity—

which asked the black so-called Christian to expect no true Brotherhood of Man, but to endure the cruelties of the white so-called Christians. Christianity had made black men fuzzy, nebulous, confused in their thinking. It had taught the black man to think if he had no shoes, and was hungry, "we gonna get shoes and milk and honey and fish fries in Heaven."

The black man in North America was economically sick and that was evident in one simple fact: as a consumer, he got less than his share, and as a producer gave *least*. The black American today shows us the perfect parasite image—the black tick under the delusion that he is progressing because he rides on the udder of the fat, three-stomached cow that is white America. For instance, annually, the black man spends over $3 billion for automobiles, but America contains hardly any franchised black automobile dealers. For instance, forty per cent of the expensive imported Scotch whisky consumed in America goes down the throats of the status-sick black man; but the only black-owned distilleries are in bathtubs, or in the woods somewhere. Or for instance—a scandalous shame—in New York City, with over a million Negroes, there aren't twenty black-owned businesses employing over ten people. It's because black men don't own and control their own community's retail establishments that they can't stabilize their own community.

The black man in North America was sickest of all politically. He let the white man divide him into such foolishness as considering himself a black "Democrat," a black "Republican," a black "Conservative," or a black "Liberal" . . . when a ten-million black vote bloc could be the deciding balance of power in American politics, because the white man's vote is almost always evenly divided. The polls are one place where every black man could fight the black man's cause with dignity, and with the power and the tools that the white man understands, and respects, and fears, and cooperates with. Listen, let me tell you something! If a black bloc committee told Washington's worst "nigger-hater," "We represent ten million votes," why, that "nigger-hater" would leap up: "Well, how *are* you? Come on *in* here!" Why, if the Mississippi black man voted in a bloc, Eastland would pretend to be more liberal than Jacob Javits—or Eastland would not survive in his office. Why else is it that racist politicians fight to keep black men from the polls?

Whenever any group can vote in a bloc, and decide the outcome of elections, and it *fails* to do this, then that group is politically sick. Immigrants once made Tammany Hall the most powerful single force in American politics. In 1880, New York City's first Irish Catholic Mayor was elected and by 1960 America had its first Irish Catholic President. America's black man, voting as a bloc, could wield an even more powerful force.

U.S. politics is ruled by special-interest blocs and lobbies. What group has a more urgent special interest, what group needs a bloc, a lobby, more than the black man? Labor owns one of Washington's largest non-government buildings—situated where they can literally watch the White House—and no political move is made that doesn't involve how Labor feels about it. A lobby got Big Oil its depletion allowance. The farmer, through his lobby, is the most government-subsidized special-interest group in America today, because a million farmers vote, not as Democrats, or Republicans, liberals, conservatives, but as farmers.

Doctors have the best lobby in Washington. Their special-interest influence successfully fights the Medicare program that's wanted, and needed, by millions of other people. Why, there's a Beet Growers' Lobby! A Wheat Lobby! A Cattle Lobby! A China Lobby! Little countries no one ever heard of have their Washington lobbies, representing their special interests.

The government has departments to deal with the special-interest groups that make themselves heard and felt. A Department of Agriculture cares for the farmers' needs. There is a Department of Health, Education and Welfare. There is a Department of the Interior—in which the Indians are included. Is the farmer, the doctor, the Indian, the greatest problem in America today? No—it is the black man! There ought to be a Pentagon-sized Washington department dealing with every segment of the black man's problems.

Twenty-two million black men! They have given America four hundred years of toil; they have bled and died in every battle since the Revolution; they were in America before the Pilgrims, and long before the mass immigrations—and they are still today at the bottom of everything!

Why, twenty-two million black people should tomorrow give a dollar apiece to build a skyscraper lobby building in Washington, D.C. Every morning, every legislator should receive a communication about what the black man in America expects and wants and needs. The demanding voice of the black lobby should be in the ears of every legislator who votes on any issue.

The cornerstones of this country's operation are economic and political strength and power. The black man doesn't have the economic strength—and it will take time for him to build it. But right now the American black man has the political strength and power to change his destiny overnight.

It was a big order—the organization I was creating in my mind, one which would help to challenge the American black man to gain his human rights, and to cure his mental, spiritual, economic, and political sicknesses. But if you ever intend to do anything worthwhile, you have to start with a worthwhile plan.

Substantially, as I saw it, the organization I hoped to build would differ from the Nation of Islam in that it would embrace all faiths of black men, and it would carry into practice what the Nation of Islam had only preached.

Rumors were swirling, particularly in East Coast cities—what was I going to do? Well, the first thing I was going to have to do was to attract far more willing heads and hands than my own. Each day, more militant, action brothers who had been with me in Mosque Seven announced their break from the Nation of Islam to come with me. And each day, I learned, in one or another way, of more support from non-Muslim Negroes, including a surprising lot of the "middle" and "upper class" black bourgeoisie, who were sick of the status-symbol charade. There was a growing clamor: "When are you going to call a meeting, to get organized?"

To hold a first meeting, I arranged to rent the Carver Ballroom of the Hotel Theresa, which is at the corner of 125th Street and Seventh Avenue, which might be called one of Harlem's fuse-box locations.

The *Amsterdam News* reported the planned meeting and many readers inferred that we were establishing our beginning mosque in the Theresa. Telegrams and letters and telephone calls came to the hotel for me, from across the country. Their general tone was that this was a move that people had waited for. People I'd never heard of expressed confidence in me in moving ways.

Numerous people said that the Nation of Islam's stringent moral restrictions had repelled them—and they wanted to join me.

A doctor who owned a small hospital telephoned long-distance to join. Many others sent contributions—even before our policies had been publicly stated. Muslims wrote from other cities that they would join me, their remarks being generally along the lines that "Islam is too inactive" . . . "The Nation is moving too slow."

Astonishing numbers of white people called, and wrote, offering contributions, or asking could *they* join? The answer was, no, they couldn't join; our membership was all black—but if their consciences dictated, they could financially help our constructive approach to America's race problems.

Speaking-engagement requests came in—twenty-two of them in one particular Monday morning's mail. It was startling to me that an unusual number of the requests came from groups of white Christian ministers.

I called a press conference. The microphones stuck up before me. The flashbulbs popped. The reporters, men and women, white and black, representing media that reached around the world, sat looking at me with their pencils and open notebooks.

I made the announcement: "I am going to organize and head a new mosque in New York City known as the Muslim Mosque, Inc. This will give us a religious base, and the spiritual force necessary to rid our people of the vices that destroy the moral fiber of our community.

"Muslim Mosque, Inc. will have its temporary headquarters in the Hotel Theresa in Harlem. It will be the working base for an action program designed to eliminate the political oppression, the economic exploitation, and the social degradation suffered daily by twenty-two million Afro-Americans."

Then the reporters began firing questions at me.

It was not all as simple as it may sound. I went few places without constant awareness that any number of my former brothers felt they would make heroes of themselves in the Nation of Islam if they killed me. I knew how Elijah Muhammad's followers thought; I had taught so many of them to think. I knew that no one would kill you quicker than a Muslim if he felt that's what Allah wanted him to do.

There was one further major preparation that I knew I needed. I'd had it in my mind for a long time—as a servant of Allah. But it would require money that I didn't have.

I took a plane to Boston. I was turning again to my sister Ella. Though at times I'd made Ella angry at me, beneath it all, since I had first come to her as a teen-aged hick from Michigan, Ella had never once really wavered from my corner.

"Ella," I said, "I want to make the pilgrimage to Mecca."

Ella said, "How much do you need?"

CHAPTER SEVENTEEN

MECCA

The pilgrimage to Mecca, known as Hajj, is a religious obliga-
tion that every orthodox Muslim fulfills, if humanly able, at least
once in his or her lifetime.

The Holy Quran says it, "Pilgrimage to the Ka'ba is a duty
men owe to God; those who are able, make the journey."

Allah said: "And proclaim the pilgrimage among men; they
will come to you on foot and upon each lean camel, they will
come from every deep ravine."

At one or another college or university, usually in the informal
gatherings after I had spoken, perhaps a dozen generally white-
complexioned people would come up to me, identifying them-
selves as Arabian, Middle Eastern or North African Muslims
who happened to be visiting, studying, or living in the United
States. They had said to me that, my white-indicting statements
notwithstanding, they felt that I was sincere in considering my-
self a Muslim—and they felt if I was exposed to what they al-
ways called "true Islam," I would "understand it, and embrace
it." Automatically, as a follower of Elijah Muhammad, I had
bridled whenever this was said.

But in the privacy of my own thoughts after several of these
experiences, I did question myself: if one was sincere in pro-
fessing a religion, why should he balk at broadening his
knowledge of that religion?

Once in a conversation I broached this with Wallace Muham-
mad, Elijah Muhammad's son. He said that yes, certainly, a
Muslim should seek to learn all that he could about Islam. I had
always had a high opinion of Wallace Muhammad's opinion.

Those orthodox Muslims whom I had met, one after another, had urged me to meet and talk with a Dr. Mahmoud Youssef Shawarbi. He was described to me as an eminent, learned Muslim, a University of Cairo graduate, a University of London Ph.D., a lecturer on Islam, a United Nations advisor and the author of many books. He was a full professor of the University of Cairo, on leave from there to be in New York as the Director of the Federation of Islamic Associations in the United States and Canada. Several times, driving in that part of town, I had resisted the impulse to drop in at the F.I.A. building, a brownstone at 1 Riverside Drive. Then one day Dr. Shawarbi and I were introduced by a newspaperman.

He was cordial. He said he had followed me in the press; I said I had been told of him, and we talked for fifteen or twenty minutes. We both had to leave to make appointments we had, when he dropped on me something whose logic never would get out of my head. He said, "No man has believed perfectly until he wishes for his brother what he wishes for himself."

Then, there was my sister Ella herself. I couldn't get over what she had done. I've said before, this is a *strong*, big, black, Georgia-born woman. Her domineering ways had gotten her put out of the Nation of Islam's Boston Mosque Eleven; they took her back, then she left on her own. Ella had started studying under Boston orthodox Muslims, then she founded a school where Arabic was taught! *She* couldn't speak it, she hired teachers who did. That's Ella! She deals in real estate, and *she* was saving up to make the pilgrimage. Nearly all night, we talked in her living room. She told me there was no question about it; it was more important that I go. I thought about Ella the whole flight back to New York. A *strong* woman. She had broken the spirits of three husbands, more driving and dynamic than all of them combined. She had played a very significant role in my life. No other woman ever was strong enough to point me in directions; I pointed women in directions. I had brought Ella into Islam, and now she was financing me to Mecca.

Allah always gives you signs, when you are with Him, that He is with you.

When I applied for a visa to Mecca at the Saudi Arabian Consulate, the Saudi Ambassador told me that no Muslim converted in America could have a visa for the Hajj pilgrimage without the signed approval of Dr. Mahmoud Shawarbi. But that was only the beginning of the sign from Allah. When I telephoned Dr. Shawarbi, he registered astonishment. "I was just going to get in touch with you," he said, "by all means come right over."

When I got to his office, Dr. Shawarbi handed me the signed letter approving me to make the Hajj in Mecca, and then a book. It was *The Eternal Message of Muhammad* by Abd-Al-Rahman Azzam.

The author had just sent the copy of the book to be given to me, Dr. Shawarbi said, and he explained that this author was an Egyptian-born Saudi citizen, an international statesman, and one of the closest advisors of Prince Faisal, the ruler of Arabia. "He has followed you in the press very closely." It was hard for me to believe.

Dr. Shawarbi gave me the telephone number of his son, Muhammad Shawarbi, a student in Cairo, and also the number of the author's son, Omar Azzam, who lived in Jedda, "your last stop before Mecca. Call them both, by all means."

I left New York quietly (little realizing that I was going to return noisily). Few people were told I was leaving at all. I didn't want some State Department or other roadblocks put in my path at the last minute. Only my wife, Betty, and my three girls and a few close associates came with me to Kennedy International Airport. When the Lufthansa Airlines jet had taken off, my two seatrow mates and I introduced ourselves. Another sign! Both were Muslims, one was bound for Cairo, as I was, and the other was bound for Jedda, where I would be in a few days.

All the way to Frankfurt, Germany, my seatmates and I talked, or I read the book I had been given. When we landed in Frankfurt, the brother bound for Jedda said his warm good-bye to me and the Cairo-bound brother. We had a few hours' layover before we would take another plane to Cairo. We decided to go sightseeing in Frankfurt.

In the men's room there at the airport, I met the first American abroad who recognized me, a white student from Rhode Island. He kept eyeing me, then he came over. "Are you X?" I laughed and said I was, I hadn't ever heard it that way. He exclaimed, "You can't be! Boy, I know no one will believe me when I tell them this!" He was attending school, he said, in France.

The brother Muslim and I both were struck by the cordial

hospitality of the people in Frankfurt. We went into a lot of shops and stores, looking more than intending to buy anything. We'd walk in, any store, every store, and it would be Hello! People who never saw you before, and knew you were strangers. And the same cordiality when we left, without buying anything. In America, you walk in a store and spend a hundred dollars, and leave, and you're still a stranger. Both you and the clerks act as though you're doing each other a favor. Europeans act more human, or humane, whichever the right word is. My brother Muslim, who could speak enough German to get by, would explain that we were Muslims, and I saw something I had already experienced when I was looked upon as a Muslim and not as a Negro, right in America. People seeing you as a Muslim saw you as a human being and they had a different look, different talk, everything. In one Frankfurt store—a little shop, actually—the storekeeper leaned over his counter to us and waved his hand, indicating the German people passing by: "This way one day, that way another day—" My Muslim brother explained to me that what he meant was that the Germans would rise again.

Back at the Frankfurt airport, we took a United Arab Airlines plane on to Cairo. Throngs of people, obviously Muslims from everywhere, bound on the pilgrimage, were hugging and embracing. They were of all complexions, the whole atmosphere was of warmth and friendliness. The feeling hit me that there really wasn't any color problem here. The effect was as though I had just stepped out of a prison.

I had told my brother Muslim friend that I wanted to be a tourist in Cairo for a couple of days before continuing to Jedda. He gave me his number and asked me to call him, as he wanted to put me with a party of his friends, who could speak English, and would be going on the pilgrimage, and would be happy to look out for me.

So I spent two happy days sightseeing in Cairo. I was impressed by the modern schools, housing developments for the masses, and the highways and the industrialization that I saw. I had read and heard that President Nasser's administration had built up one of the most highly industrialized countries on the African continent. I believe what most surprised me was that in Cairo, automobiles were being manufactured, and also buses.

I had a good visit with Dr. Shawarbi's son, Muhammad Shawarbi, a nineteen-year-old, who was studying economics and political science at Cairo University. He told me that his father's dream was to build a University of Islam in the United States.

The friendly people I met were astounded when they learned I was a Muslim—from America! They included an Egyptian scientist and his wife, also on their way to Mecca for the Hajj, who insisted I go with them to dinner in a restaurant in Heliopolis, a suburb of Cairo. They were an extremely well-informed and intelligent couple. Egypt's rising industrialization was one of the reasons why the Western powers were so anti-Egypt, it was showing other African countries what they should do, the scientist said. His wife asked me, "Why are people in the world starving when America has so much surplus food? What do they do, dump it in the ocean?" I told her, "Yes, but they put some of it in the holds of surplus ships, and in subsidized granaries and refrigerated space and let it stay there, with a small army of caretakers, until it's unfit to eat. Then another army of disposal people get rid of it to make space for the next surplus batch." She looked at me in something like disbelief. Probably she thought I was kidding. But the American taxpayer knows it's the truth. I didn't go on to tell her that right in the United States, there are hungry people.

I telephoned my Muslim friend, as he had asked, and the Hajj party of his friends was waiting for me. I made it eight of us, and they included a judge and an official of the Ministry of Education. They spoke English beautifully, and accepted me like a brother. I considered it another of Allah's signs, that wherever I turned, someone was there to help me, to guide me.

The literal meaning of Hajj in Arabic is to set out toward a definite objective. In Islamic law, it means to set out for Ka'ba, the Sacred House, and to fulfill the pilgrimage rites. The Cairo airport was where scores of Hajj groups were becoming *Muhrim*, pilgrims, upon entering the state of Ihram, the assumption of a spiritual and physical state of consecration. Upon advice, I arranged to leave in Cairo all of my luggage and four cameras, one a movie camera. I had bought in Cairo a small valise, just big enough to carry one suit, shirt, a pair of underwear sets and a pair of shoes into Arabia. Driving to the airport with our Hajj group, I began to get nervous, knowing that from there in, it was going to be watching others who knew what they were doing, and trying to do what they did.

Entering the state of Ihram, we took off our clothes and put on two white towels. One, the *Izar*, was folded around the loins. The other, the *Rida*, was thrown over the neck and shoulders, leaving the right shoulder and arm bare. A pair of simple sandals, the *na'l*, left the ankle-bones bare. Over the *Izar* waist-wrapper, a money belt was worn, and a bag, something like a woman's big handbag, with a long strap, was for carrying the passport and other valuable papers, such as the letter I had from Dr. Shawarbi.

Every one of the thousands at the airport, about to leave for Jedda, was dressed this way. You could be a king or a peasant and no one would know. Some powerful personages, who were discreetly pointed out to me, had on the same thing I had on. Once thus dressed, we all had begun intermittently calling out *"Labbayka! Labbayka!"* (Here I come, O Lord!) The airport sounded with the din of *Muhrim* expressing their intention to perform the journey of the Hajj.

Planeloads of pilgrims were taking off every few minutes, but the airport was jammed with more, and their friends and relatives waiting to see them off. Those not going were asking others to pray for them at Mecca. We were on our plane, in the air, when I learned for the first time that with the crush, there was not supposed to have been space for me, but strings had been pulled, and someone had been put off because they didn't want to disappoint an American Muslim. I felt mingled emotions of regret that I had inconvenienced and discomfited whoever was bumped off the plane for me, and, with that, an utter humility and gratefulness that I had been paid such an honor and respect.

Packed in the plane were white, black, brown, red, and yellow people, blue eyes and blond hair, and my kinky red hair— all together, brothers! All honoring the same God Allah, all in turn giving equal honor to each other.

From some in our group, the word was spreading from seat to seat that I was a Muslim from America. Faces turned, smiling toward me in greeting. A box lunch was passed out and as we ate that, the word that a Muslim from America was aboard got up into the cockpit.

The captain of the plane came back to meet me. He was an Egyptian, his complexion was darker than mine; he could have walked in Harlem and no one would have given him a second glance. He was delighted to meet an American Muslim. When he invited me to visit the cockpit, I jumped at the chance.

The co-pilot was darker than he was. I can't tell you the feeling it gave me. I had never seen a black man flying a jet. That instrument panel: no one ever could know what all of those dials meant! Both of the pilots were smiling at me, treating me with the same honor and respect I had received ever since I left America. I stood there looking through the glass at the sky ahead of us. In America, I had ridden in more planes than probably any other Negro, and I never had been invited up into the cockpit. And there I was, with two Muslim seatmates, one from Egypt, the other from Arabia, all of us bound for Mecca, with me up in the pilots' cabin. Brother, I *knew* Allah was with me.

I got back to my seat. All of the way, about an hour's flight, we pilgrims were loudly crying out, *"Labbayka! Labbayka!"* The plane landed at Jedda. It's a seaport town on the Red Sea, the arrival or disembarkation point for all pilgrims who come to Arabia to go to Mecca. Mecca is about forty miles to the east, inland.

The Jedda airport seemed even more crowded than Cairo's had been. Our party became another shuffling unit in the shifting mass with every race on earth represented. Each party was making its way toward the long line waiting to go through Customs. Before reaching Customs, each Hajj party was assigned a *Mutawaf*, who would be responsible for transferring that party from Jedda to Mecca. Some pilgrims cried *"Labbayka!"* Others, sometimes large groups, were chanting in unison a prayer that I will translate, "I submit to no one but Thee, O Allah, I submit to no one but Thee. I submit to Thee because Thou hast no partner. All praise and blessings come from Thee, and Thou art alone in Thy kingdom." The essence of the prayer is the Oneness of God.

Only officials were not wearing the *Ihram* garb, or the white skull caps, long, white, nightshirt-looking gown and the little slippers of the *Mutawaf*, those who guided each pilgrim party, and their helpers. In Arabic, an *mmmm* sound before a verb makes a verbal noun, so "*Mu*tawaf" meant "the one who guides" the pilgrims on the "*Tawaf,*" which is the circumambulation of the Ka'ba in Mecca.

I was nervous, shuffling in the center of our group in the line waiting to have our passports inspected. I had an apprehensive feeling. Look what I'm handing them. I'm in the Muslim world, right at The Fountain. I'm handing them the American passport which signifies the exact opposite of what Islam stands for.

The judge in our group sensed my strain. He patted my shoulder. Love, humility, and true brotherhood was almost a physical feeling wherever I turned. Then our group reached the clerks who examined each passport and suitcase carefully and nodded to the pilgrim to move on.

I was so nervous that when I turned the key in my bag, and it didn't work, I broke open the bag, fearing that they might think I had something in the bag that I shouldn't have. Then the clerk saw that I was handing him an American passport. He held it, he looked at me and said something in Arabic. My friends around me began speaking rapid Arabic, gesturing and pointing, trying to intercede for me. The judge asked me in English for my letter from Dr. Shawarbi, and he thrust it at the clerk, who read it. He gave the letter back, protesting—I could tell that. An argument was going on, *about* me. I felt like a stupid fool, unable to say a word, I couldn't even understand what was being said. But, finally, sadly, the judge turned to me.

I had to go before the *Mahgama Sharia*, he explained. It was the Muslim high court which examined all possibly nonauthentic converts to the Islamic religion seeking to enter Mecca. It was absolute that no non-Muslim could enter Mecca.

My friends were going to have to go on to Mecca without me. They seemed stricken with concern for me. And *I* was stricken. I found the words to tell them, "Don't worry, I'll be fine. Allah guides me." They said they would pray hourly in my behalf. The white-garbed *Mutawaf* was urging them on, to keep schedule in the airport's human crush. With all of us waving, I watched them go.

It was then about three in the morning, a Friday morning. I never had been in such a jammed mass of people, but I never had felt more alone, and helpless, since I was a baby. Worse, Friday in the Muslim world is a rough counterpart of Sunday in the Christian world. On Friday, all the members of a Muslim community gather, to pray together. The event is called *yaum al-jumu'a*—"the day of gathering." It meant that no courts were held on Friday. I would have to wait until Saturday, at least.

An official beckoned a young Arab *Mutawaf's* aide. In bro-

ken English, the official explained that I would be taken to a
place right at the airport. My passport was kept at Customs. I
wanted to object, because it is a traveler's first law never to get
separated from his passport, but I didn't. In my wrapped towels
and sandals, I followed the aide in his skull cap, long white
gown, and slippers. I guess we were quite a sight. People pass-
ing us were speaking all kinds of languages. I couldn't speak
anybody's language. I was in bad shape.

Right outside the airport was a mosque, and above the airport
was a huge, dormitory-like building, four tiers high. It was semi-
dark, not long before dawn, and planes were regularly taking
off and landing, their landing lights sweeping the runways, or
their wing and tail lights blinking in the sky. Pilgrims from
Ghana, Indonesia, Japan, and Russia, to mention some, were
moving to and from the dormitory where I was being taken. I
don't believe that motion picture cameras ever have filmed a
human spectacle more colorful than my eyes took in. We reached
the dormitory and began climbing, up to the fourth, top, tier,
passing members of every race on earth. Chinese, Indone-
sians, Afghanistanians. Many, not yet changed into the *Ihram*
garb, still wore their national dress. It was like pages out of
the *National Geographic* magazine.

My guide, on the fourth tier, gestured me into a compartment
that contained about fifteen people. Most lay curled up on their
rugs asleep. I could tell that some were women, covered head
and foot. An old Russian Muslim and his wife were not asleep.
They stared frankly at me. Two Egyptian Muslims and a Persian
roused and also stared as my guide moved us over into a corner.
With gestures, he indicated that he would demonstrate to me the
proper prayer ritual postures. Imagine, being a Muslim minister,
a leader in Elijah Muhammad's Nation of Islam, and not know-
ing the prayer ritual.

I tried to do what he did. I knew I wasn't doing it right. I could
feel the other Muslims' eyes on me. Western ankles won't do what
Muslim ankles have done for a lifetime. Asians squat when they
sit, Westerners sit upright in chairs. When my guide was down in
a posture, I tried everything I could to get down as he was, but
there I was, sticking up. After about an hour, my guide left, in-
dicating that he would return later.

I never even thought about sleeping. Watched by the Muslims,

I kept practicing prayer posture. I refused to let myself think how ridiculous I must have looked to them. After a while, though, I learned a little trick that would let me get down closer to the floor. But after two or three days, my ankle was going to swell.

As the sleeping Muslims woke up, when dawn had broken, they almost instantly became aware of me, and we watched each other while they went about their business. I began to see what an important role the rug played in the overall cultural life of the Muslims. Each individual had a small prayer rug, and each man and wife, or large group, had a larger communal rug. These Muslims prayed on their rugs there in the compartment. Then they spread a tablecloth over the rug and ate, so the rug became the dining room. Removing the dishes and cloth, they sat on the rug—a living room. Then they curl up and sleep on the rug—a bedroom. In that compartment, before I was to leave it, it dawned on me for the first time why the fence had paid such a high price for Oriental rugs when I had been a burglar in Boston. It was because so much intricate care was taken to weave fine rugs in countries where rugs were so culturally versatile. Later, in Mecca, I would see yet another use of the rug. When any kind of dispute arose, someone who was respected highly and who was not involved would sit on a rug with the disputers around him, which made the rug a courtroom. In other instances it was a classroom.

One of the Egyptian Muslims, particularly, kept watching me out of the corner of his eye. I smiled at him. He got up and came over to me. "Hel-lo—" he said. It sounded like the Gettysburg Address. I beamed at him, "Hello!" I asked his name. "Name? Name?" He was trying hard, but he didn't get it. We tried some words on each other. I'd guess his English vocabulary spanned maybe twenty words. Just enough to frustrate me. I was trying to get him to comprehend anything. "Sky." I'd point. He'd smile. "Sky," I'd say again, gesturing for him to repeat it after me. He would. "Airplane . . . rug . . . foot . . . sandal . . . eyes. . . ." Like that. Then an amazing thing happened. I was so glad I had some communication with a human being, I was just saying whatever came to mind. I said "Muhammad Ali Clay—" All of the Muslims listening lighted up like a Christmas tree. "You? You?" My friend was pointing at me. I shook my head, "No, no. Muhammad Ali Clay my friend—*friend!*" They half understood me. Some of them didn't understand, and that's how it began to get around that I was Cassius Clay, world heavyweight champion. I was later to learn that apparently every man, woman and child in the Muslim world had heard how Sonny Liston (who in the Muslim world had the image of a man-eating ogre) had been beaten in Goliath-David fashion by Cassius Clay, who then had told the world that his name was Muhammad Ali and his religion was Islam and Allah had given him his victory.

Establishing the rapport was the best thing that could have happened in the compartment. My being an American Muslim changed the attitudes from merely watching me to wanting to look out for me. Now, the others began smiling steadily. They came closer, they were frankly looking me up and down. Inspecting me. Very friendly. I was like a man from Mars.

The *Mutawaf's* aide returned, indicating that I should go with him. He pointed from our tier down at the mosque and I knew that he had come to take me to make the morning prayer, *El Sobh*, always before sunrise. I followed him down, and we passed pilgrims by the thousands, babbling languages, everything but English. I was angry with myself for not having taken the time to learn more of the orthodox prayer rituals before leaving America. In Elijah Muhammad's Nation of Islam, we hadn't prayed in Arabic. About a dozen or more years before, when I was in prison, a member of the orthodox Muslim movement in Boston, named Abdul Hameed, had visited me and had later sent me prayers in Arabic. At that time, I had learned those prayers phonetically. But I hadn't used them since.

I made up my mind to let the guide do everything first and I would watch him. It wasn't hard to get him to do things first. He wanted to anyway. Just outside the mosque there was a long trough with rows of faucets. Ablutions had to precede praying. I knew that. Even watching the *Mutawaf's* helper, I didn't get it right. There's an exact way that an orthodox Muslim washes, and the exact way is very important.

I followed him into the mosque, just a step behind, watching. He did his prostration, his head to the ground. I did mine. *"Bi-smi-llahi-r-Rahmain-r-Rahim—"* ("In the name of Allah, the Beneficent, the Merciful—") All Muslim prayers began that way. After that, I may not have been mumbling the right thing, but I was mumbling.

I don't mean to have any of this sound joking. It was far from a joke with me. No one who happened to be watching could tell that I wasn't saying what the others said.

After that Sunrise Prayer, my guide accompanied me back up to the fourth tier. By sign language, he said he would return within three hours, then he left.

Our tier gave an excellent daylight view of the whole airport area. I stood at the railing, watching. Planes were landing and taking off like clockwork. Thousands upon thousands of people from all over the world made colorful patterns of movement. I saw groups leaving for Mecca, in buses, trucks, cars. I saw some setting out to walk the forty miles. I wished that I could start walking. At least, I knew how to do that.

I was afraid to think what might lie ahead. Would I be rejected as a Mecca pilgrim? I wondered what the test would consist of, and when I would face the Muslim high court.

The Persian Muslim in our compartment came up to me at the rail. He greeted me, hesitantly, "Amer . . . American?" He indicated that he wanted me to come and have breakfast with him and his wife, on their rug. I knew that it was an immense offer he was making. You don't have tea with a Muslim's wife. I didn't want to impose, I don't know if the Persian understood or not when I shook my head and smiled, meaning "No, thanks." He brought me some tea and cookies, anyway. Until then, I hadn't even thought about eating.

Others made gestures. They would just come up and smile and nod at me. My first friend, the one who had spoken a little English, was gone. I didn't know it, but he was spreading the word of an American Muslim on the fourth tier. Traffic had begun to pick up, going past our compartment. Muslims in the *Ihram* garb, or still in their national dress, walked slowly past, smiling. It would go on for as long as I was there to be seen. But I hadn't yet learned that I was the attraction.

I have always been restless, and curious. The *Mutawaf's* aide didn't return in the three hours he had said, and that made me nervous. I feared that he had given up on me as beyond help. By then, too, I was really getting hungry. All of the Muslims in the compartment had offered me food, and I had refused. The trouble was, I have to admit it, at that point I didn't know if I could go for their manner of eating. Everything was in one pot on the dining-room rug, and I saw them just fall right in, using their hands.

I kept standing at the tier railing observing the courtyard below, and I decided to explore a bit on my own. I went down to the first tier. I thought, then, that maybe I shouldn't get too far, someone might come for me. So I went back up to our compartment. In about forty-five minutes, I went back down. I went farther this time, feeling my way. I saw a little restaurant in the courtyard. I went straight in there. It was jammed, and babbling with languages. Using gestures, I bought a whole roasted chicken and something like thick potato chips. I got back out in the courtyard and I tore up that chicken, using my hands. Muslims were doing the same thing all around me. I saw men at least seventy years old bringing both legs up under them, until they made a human knot of themselves, eating with as much aplomb and satisfaction as though they had been in a fine restaurant with waiters all over the place. All ate as One, and slept as One. Everything about the pilgrimage atmosphere accented the Oneness of Man under One God.

I made, during the day, several trips up to the compartment and back out in the courtyard, each time exploring a little further than before. Once, I nodded at two black men standing together. I nearly shouted when one spoke to me in British-accented English. Before their party approached, ready to leave for Mecca, we were able to talk enough to exchange that I was American and they were Ethiopians. I was heartsick. I had found two English-speaking Muslims at last—and they were leaving. The Ethiopians had both been schooled in Cairo, and they were living in Ryadh, the political capital of Arabia. I was later going to learn to my surprise that in Ethiopia, with eighteen million people, ten million are Muslims. Most people think Ethiopia is Christian. But only its government is Christian. The West has always helped to keep the Christian government in power.

I had just said my Sunset Prayer, *El Maghrib*; I was lying on my cot in the fourth-tier compartment, feeling blue and alone, when out of the darkness came a sudden light!

It was actually a sudden thought. On one of my venturings in the yard full of activity below, I had noticed four men, officials, seated at a table with a telephone. Now, I thought about seeing them there, and with *telephone*, my mind flashed to the connection that Dr. Shawarbi in New York had given me, the telephone number of the son of the author of the book which had been given to me. Omar Azzam lived right there in Jedda!

In a matter of a few minutes, I was downstairs and rushing to where I had seen the four officials. One of them spoke functional English. I excitedly showed him the letter from Dr. Shawarbi. He read it. Then he read it aloud to the other three officials. "A Muslim from America!" I could almost see it capture their imaginations and curiosity. They were very impressed. I asked the English-speaking one if he would please do me the favor of telephoning Dr. Omar Azzam at the number I had. He was glad to do it. He got someone on the phone and conversed in Arabic.

Dr. Omar Azzam came straight to the airport. With the four officials beaming, he wrung my hand in welcome, a young, tall, powerfully built man. I'd say he was six foot three. He had an extremely polished manner. In America, he would have been called a white man, but—it struck me, hard and instantly—from the way he acted, I had no *feeling* of him being a white man. "Why didn't you call before?" he demanded of me. He showed some identification to the four officials, and he used their phone. Speaking in Arabic, he was talking with some airport officials. "Come!" he said.

In something less than half an hour, he had gotten me released, my suitcase and passport had been retrieved from Customs, and we were in Dr. Azzam's car, driving through the city of Jedda, with me dressed in the *Ihram* two towels and sandals. I was speechless at the man's attitude, and at my own physical feeling of no difference between us as human beings. I had heard for years of Muslim hospitality, but one couldn't quite imagine such warmth. I asked questions. Dr. Azzam was a Swiss-trained engineer. His field was city planning. The Saudi Arabian government had borrowed him from the United Nations to direct all of the reconstruction work being done on Arabian holy places. And Dr. Azzam's sister was the wife of Prince Faisal's son. I was in a car with the brother-in-law of the son of the ruler of Arabia. Nor was that all that Allah had done. "My father will be so happy to meet you," said Dr. Azzam. The author who had sent me the book!

I asked questions about his father. Abd-Al-Rahman Azzam was known as Azzam Pasha, or Lord Azzam, until the Egyptian revolution, when President Nasser eliminated all "Lord" and "Noble" titles. "He should be at my home when we get there," Dr. Azzam said. "He spends much time in New York with his United Nations work, and he has followed you with great interest."

I was speechless.

It was early in the morning when we reached Dr. Azzam's home. His father was there, his father's brother, a chemist, and another friend—all up that early, waiting. Each of them embraced me as though I were a long-lost child. I had never seen these men before in my life, and they treated me so good! I am going to tell you that I had never been so honored in my life, nor had I ever received such true hospitality.

A servant brought tea and coffee, and disappeared. I was urged to make myself comfortable. No women were anywhere in view. In Arabia, you could easily think there were no females.

Dr. Abd-Al-Rahman Azzam dominated the conversation. Why hadn't I called before? They couldn't understand why I hadn't. Was I comfortable? They seemed embarrassed that I had spent the time at the airport; that I had been delayed in getting to Mecca. No matter how I protested that I felt no inconvenience, that I was fine, they would not hear it. "You must rest," Dr. Azzam said. He went to use the telephone.

I didn't know what this distinguished man was doing. I had no dream. When I was told that I would be brought back for dinner that evening, and that, meanwhile, I should get back in the car, how could I have realized that I was about to see the epitome of Muslim hospitality?

Abd-Al-Rahman Azzam, when at home, lived in a suite at the Jedda Palace Hotel. Because I had come to them with a letter from a friend, he was going to stay at his son's home, and let me use his suite, until I could get on to Mecca.

When I found out, there was no use protesting: I was in the suite; young Dr. Azzam was gone; there was no one to protest to. The three-room suite had a bathroom that was as big as a double at the New York Hilton. It was suite number 214. There was even a porch outside, affording a beautiful view of the ancient Red Sea city.

There had never before been in my emotions such an impulse to pray—and I did, prostrating myself on the living-room rug.

Nothing in either of my two careers as a black man in America had served to give me any idealistic tendencies. My instincts automatically examined the reasons, the motives, of anyone who did anything they didn't have to do for me. Always in my life, if it was any white person, I could see a selfish motive.

But there in that hotel that morning, a telephone call and a few hours away from the cot on the fourth-floor tier of the dormitory, was one of the few times I had been so awed that I was totally without resistance. That white man—at least he would have been considered "white" in America—related to Arabia's ruler, to whom he was a close advisor, truly an international man, with nothing in the world to gain, had given up his suite to me, for my transient comfort. He had *nothing* to gain. He didn't need me. He had everything. In fact, he had more to lose than gain. He had followed the American press about me. If he did that, he knew there was only stigma attached to me. I was supposed to have horns. I was a "racist." I was "anti-white"— and he from all appearances was white. I was supposed to be a criminal; not only that, but everyone was even accusing me of using his religion of Islam as a cloak for my criminal practices and philosophies. Even if he had had some motive to use me, he knew that I was separated from Elijah Muhammad and the Nation of Islam, my "power base," according to the press in America. The only organization that I had was just a few weeks old. I had no job. I had no money. Just to get over there, I had had to borrow money from my sister.

That morning was when I first began to reappraise the "white man." It was when I first began to perceive that "white man," as commonly used, means complexion only secondarily; primarily it described attitudes and actions. In America, "white man" meant specific attitudes and actions toward the black man, and toward all other non-white men. But in the Muslim world, I had seen that men with white complexions were more genuinely brotherly than anyone else had ever been.

That morning was the start of a radical alteration in my whole outlook about "white" men.

I should quote from my notebook here. I wrote this about noon, in the hotel: "My excitement, sitting here, waiting to go before the Hajj Committee, is indescribable. My window faces to the sea westward. The streets are filled with the incoming pilgrims from all over the world. The prayers are to Allah and verses from the Quran are on the lips of everyone. Never have I seen such a beautiful sight, nor witnessed such a scene, nor felt such an atmosphere. Although I am excited, I feel safe and secure, thousands of miles from the totally different life that I have known. Imagine that twenty-four hours ago, I was in the fourth-floor room over the airport, surrounded by people with whom I could not communicate, feeling uncertain about the future, and very lonely, and then *one* phone call, following Dr. Shawarbi's instructions. I have met one of the most powerful men in the Muslim world. I will soon sleep in his bed at the Jedda Palace. I know that I am surrounded by friends whose sincerity and religious zeal I can feel. I must pray again to thank Allah for this blessing, and I must pray again that my wife and children back in America will always be blessed for their sacrifices, too.''

I did pray, two more prayers, as I had told my notebook. Then I slept for about four hours, until the telephone rang. It was young Dr. Azzam. In another hour, he would pick me up to return me there for dinner. I tumbled words over one another, trying to express some of the thanks I felt for all of their actions. He cut me off. ''Ma sha'a-llah''—which means, ''It is as Allah has pleased.''

I seized the opportunity to run down into the lobby, to see it again before Dr. Azzam arrived. When I opened my door, just across the hall from me a man in some ceremonial dress, who obviously lived there, was also headed downstairs, surrounded by attendants. I followed them down, then through the lobby. Outside, a small caravan of automobiles was waiting. My neighbor appeared through the Jedda Palace Hotel's front entrance and people rushed and crowded him, kissing his hand. I found out who he was: the Grand Mufti of Jerusalem. Later, in the hotel, I would have the opportunity to talk with him for about a half-hour. He was a cordial man of great dignity. He was well up on world affairs, and even the latest events in America.

I will never forget the dinner at the Azzam home. I quote my notebook again: ''I couldn't say in my mind that these were 'white' men. Why, the men acted as if they were brothers of mine, the elder Dr. Azzam as if he were my father. His fatherly, scholarly speech. I *felt* like he was my father. He was, you could tell, a highly skilled diplomat, with a broad range of mind. His knowledge was so worldly. He was as current on world affairs as some people are to what's going on in their living room.

"The more we talked, the more his vast reservoir of knowledge and its variety seemed unlimited. He spoke of the racial lineage of the descendants of Muhammad the Prophet, and he showed how they were both black and white. He also pointed out how color, the complexities of color, and the problems of color which exist in the Muslim world, exist only where, and to the extent that, that area of the Muslim world has been influenced by the West. He said that if one encountered any differences based on attitude toward color, this directly reflected the degree of Western influence."

I learned during dinner that while I was at the hotel, the Hajj Committee Court had been notified about my case, and that in the morning I should be there. And I was.

The judge was Sheikh Muhammad Harkon. The Court was empty except for me and a sister from India, formerly a Protestant, who had converted to Islam, and was, like me, trying to make the Hajj. She was brown-skinned, with a small face that was mostly covered. Judge Harkon was a kind, impressive man. We talked. He asked me some questions, having to do with my sincerity. I answered him as truly as I could. He not only recognized me as a true Muslim, but he gave me two books, one in English, the other in Arabic. He recorded my name in the Holy Register of true Muslims, and we were ready to part. He told me, "I hope you will become a great preacher of Islam in America." I said that I shared that hope, and I would try to fulfill it.

The Azzam family were very elated that I was qualified and accepted to go to Mecca. I had lunch at the Jedda Palace. Then I slept again for several hours, until the telephone awakened me.

It was Muhammad Abdul Azziz Maged, the Deputy Chief of Protocol for Prince Faisal. "A special car will be waiting to take you to Mecca, right after your dinner," he told me. He advised me to eat heartily, as the Hajj rituals require plenty of strength.

I was beyond astonishment by then.

Two young Arabs accompanied me to Mecca. A well-lighted, modern turnpike highway made the trip easy. Guards at intervals along the way took one look at the car, and the driver made a sign, and we were passed through, never even having to slow down. I was, all at once, thrilled, important, humble, and thankful.

Mecca, when we entered, seemed as ancient as time itself. Our car slowed through the winding streets, lined by shops on both sides and with buses, cars, and trucks, and tens of thousands of pilgrims from all over the earth were everywhere.

The car halted briefly at a place where a *Mutawaf* was waiting for me. He wore the white skullcap and long nightshirt garb that I had seen at the airport. He was a short, dark-skinned Arab, named Muhammad. He spoke no English whatever.

We parked near the Great Mosque. We performed our ablutions and entered. Pilgrims seemed to be on top of each other, there were so many, lying, sitting, sleeping, praying, walking.

My vocabulary cannot describe the new mosque that was being built around the Ka'ba. I was thrilled to realize that it was only one of the tremendous rebuilding tasks under the direction of young Dr. Azzam, who had just been my host. The Great Mosque of Mecca, when it is finished, will surpass the architectural beauty of India's Taj Mahal.

Carrying my sandals, I followed the *Mutawaf*. Then I saw the Ka'ba, a huge black stone house in the middle of the Great Mosque. It was being circumambulated by thousands upon thousands of praying pilgrims, both sexes, and every size, shape, color, and race in the world. I knew the prayer to be uttered when the pilgrim's eyes first perceive the Ka'ba. Translated, it is "O God, You are peace, and peace derives from You. So greet us, O Lord, with peace." Upon entering the Mosque, the pilgrim should try to kiss the Ka'ba if possible, but if the crowds prevent him getting that close, he touches it, and if the crowds prevent that, he raises his hand and cries out "Takbir!" ("God is great!") I could not get within yards. "Takbir!"

My feeling there in the House of God was a numbness. My *Mutawaf* led me in the crowd of praying, chanting pilgrims, moving seven times around the Ka'ba. Some were bent and wizened with age; it was a sight that stamped itself on the brain. I saw incapacitated pilgrims being carried by others. Faces were enraptured in their faith. The seventh time around, I prayed two *Rak'a*, prostrating myself, my head on the floor. The first prostration, I prayed the Quran verse "Say He is God, the one and only''; the second prostration: "Say O you who are unbelievers, I worship not that which you worship. . . ."

As I prostrated, the *Mutawaf* fended pilgrims off to keep me from being trampled.

The *Mutawaf* and I next drank water from the well of Zem Zem. Then we ran between the two hills, Safa and Marwa, where Hajar wandered over the same earth searching for water for her child Ishmael.

Three separate times, after that, I visited the Great Mosque and circumambulated the Ka'ba. The next day we set out after sunrise toward Mount Arafat, thousands of us, crying in unison: "Labbayka! Labbayka!" and "Allah Akbar!" Mecca is surrounded by the crudest-looking mountains I have ever seen; they seem to be made of the slag from a blast furnace. No vegetation is on them at all. Arriving about noon, we prayed and chanted from noon until sunset, and the *asr* (afternoon) and *Maghrib* (sunset) special prayers were performed.

Finally, we lifted our hands in prayer and thanksgiving, repeating Allah's words: "There is no God but Allah. He has no partner. His are authority and praise. Good emanates from Him, and He has power over all things."

Standing on Mount Arafat had concluded the essential rites of being a pilgrim to Mecca. No one who missed it could consider himself a pilgrim.

The *Ihram* had ended. We cast the traditional seven stones at the devil. Some had their hair and beards cut. I decided that I was going to let my beard remain. I wondered what my wife Betty, and our little daughters, were going to say when they saw me with a beard, when I got back to New York. New York seemed a million miles away. I hadn't seen a newspaper that I could read since I left New York. I had no idea what was happening there. A Negro rifle club that had been in existence for over twelve years in Harlem had been "discovered" by the police; it was being trumpeted that I was "behind it." Elijah Muhammad's Nation of Islam had a lawsuit going against me, to force me and my family to vacate the house in which we lived on Long Island.

The major press, radio, and television media in America had representatives in Cairo hunting all over, trying to locate me, to interview me about the furor in New York that I had allegedly caused—when I knew nothing about any of it.

I only knew what I had left in America, and how it contrasted with what I had found in the Muslim world. About twenty of us Muslims who had finished the Hajj were sitting in a huge tent on Mount Arafat. As a Muslim from America, I was the center of attention. They asked me what about the Hajj had impressed me the most. One of the several who spoke English asked; they translated my answers for the others. My answer to that question was not the one they expected, but it drove home my point.

I said, "The *brotherhood!* The people of all races, colors, from all over the world coming together as *one!* It has proved to me the power of the One God."

It may have been out of taste, but that gave me an opportunity, and I used it, to preach them a quick little sermon on America's racism, and its evils.

I could tell the impact of this upon them. They had been aware that the plight of the black man in America was "bad," but they had not been aware that it was inhuman, that it was a psychological castration. These people from elsewhere around the world were shocked. As Muslims, they had a very tender heart for all unfortunates, and very sensitive feelings for truth and justice. And in everything I said to them, as long as we talked, they were aware of the yardstick that I was using to measure everything—that to me the earth's most explosive and pernicious evil is racism, the inability of God's creatures to live as One, especially in the Western world.

I have reflected since that the letter I finally sat down to compose had been subconsciously shaping itself in my mind.

The *color-blindness* of the Muslim world's religious society and the *color-blindness* of the Muslim world's human society: these two influences had each day been making a greater impact, and an increasing persuasion against my previous way of thinking.

The first letter was, of course, to my wife, Betty. I never had a moment's question that Betty, after initial amazement, would change her thinking to join mine. I had known a thousand reassurances that Betty's faith in me was total. I knew that she would see what I had seen—that in the land of Muhammad and the land of Abraham, I had been blessed by Allah with a new insight into the true religion of Islam, and a better understanding of America's entire racial dilemma.

After the letter to my wife, I wrote next essentially the same letter to my sister Ella. And I knew where Ella would stand. She had been saving to make the pilgrimage to Mecca herself.

I wrote to Dr. Shawarbi, whose belief in my sincerity had enabled me to get a passport to Mecca.

All through the night, I copied similar long letters for others who were very close to me. Among them was Elijah Muhammad's son Wallace Muhammad, who had expressed to me his conviction that the only possible salvation for the Nation of Islam would be its accepting and projecting a better understanding of Orthodox Islam.

And I wrote to my loyal assistants at my newly formed Muslim Mosque, Inc. in Harlem, with a note appended, asking that my letter be duplicated and distributed to the press.

I knew that when my letter became public knowledge back in America, many would be astounded—loved ones, friends, and enemies alike. And no less astounded would be millions whom I did not know—who had gained during my twelve years with Elijah Muhammad a "hate" image of Malcolm X.

Even I was myself astounded. But there was precedent in my life for this letter. My whole life had been a chronology of—*changes*.

Here is what I wrote . . . from my heart:

"Never have I witnessed such sincere hospitality and the overwhelming spirit of true brotherhood as is practiced by people of all colors and races here in this Ancient Holy Land, the home of Abraham, Muhammad, and all the other prophets of the Holy Scriptures. For the past week, I have been utterly speechless and spellbound by the graciousness I see displayed all around me by people *of all colors*.

"I have been blessed to visit the Holy City of Mecca. I have made my seven circuits around the Ka'ba, led by a young *Mutawaf* named Muhammad. I drank water from the well of Zem Zem. I ran seven times back and forth between the hills of Mt. Al-Safa and Al-Marwah. I have prayed in the ancient city of Mina, and I have prayed on Mt. Arafat.

"There were tens of thousands of pilgrims, from all over the world. They were of all colors, from blue-eyed blonds to black-skinned Africans. But we were all participating in the same ritual, displaying a spirit of unity and brotherhood that my experiences in America had led me to believe never could exist between the white and the non-white.

"America needs to understand Islam, because this is the one religion that erases from its society the race problem. Throughout my travels in the Muslim world, I have met, talked to, and even eaten with people who in America would have been considered 'white'—but the 'white' attitude was removed from their minds by the religion of Islam. I have never before seen *sincere* and *true* brotherhood practiced by all colors together, irrespective of their color.

"You may be shocked by these words coming from me. But on this pilgrimage, what I have seen, and experienced, has forced me to *re-arrange* much of my thought-patterns previously held, and to *toss aside* some of my previous conclusions. This was not too difficult for me. Despite my firm convictions, I have been always a man who tries to face facts, and to accept the reality of life as new experience and new knowledge unfolds it. I have always kept an open mind, which is necessary to the flexibility that must go hand in hand with every form of intelligent search for truth.

"During the past eleven days here in the Muslim world, I have eaten from the same plate, drunk from the same glass, and slept in the same bed (or on the same rug)—while praying to the *same God*—with fellow Muslims, whose eyes were the bluest of blue, whose hair was the blondest of blond, and whose skin was the whitest of white. And in the *words* and in the *actions* and in the *deeds* of the 'white' Muslims, I felt the same sincerity that I felt among the black African Muslims of Nigeria, Sudan, and Ghana.

"We were *truly* all the same (brothers)—because their belief in one God had removed the 'white' from their *minds*, the 'white' from their *behavior*, and the 'white' from their *attitude*.

"I could see from this, that perhaps if white Americans could accept the Oneness of God, then perhaps, too, they could accept *in reality* the Oneness of Man—and cease to measure, and hinder, and harm others in terms of their 'differences' in color.

"With racism plaguing America like an incurable cancer, the so-called 'Christian' white American heart should be more receptive to a proven solution to such a destructive problem. Perhaps it could be in time to save America from imminent disaster—the same destruction brought upon Germany by racism that eventually destroyed the Germans themselves.

"Each hour here in the Holy Land enables me to have greater spiritual insights into what is happening in America between black and white. The American Negro never can be blamed for his racial animosities—he is only reacting to four hundred years of the conscious racism of the American whites. But as racism leads America up the suicide path, I do believe, from the experiences that I have had with them, that the whites of the younger generation, in the colleges and universities, will see the handwriting on the wall and many of them will turn to the *spiritual* path of *truth*—the *only* way left to America to ward off the disaster that racism inevitably must lead to.

"Never have I been so highly honored. Never have I been made to feel more humble and unworthy. Who would believe the blessings that have been heaped upon an *American Negro?* A few nights ago, a man who would be called in America a 'white' man, a United Nations diplomat, an ambassador, a companion of kings, gave me *his* hotel suite, *his* bed. By this man, His Excellency Prince Faisal, who rules this Holy Land, was made aware of my presence here in Jedda. The very next morning, Prince Faisal's son, in person, informed me that by the will and decree of his esteemed father, I was to be a State Guest.

"The Deputy Chief of Protocol himself took me before the Hajj Court. His Holiness Sheikh Muhammad Harkon himself okayed my visit to Mecca. His Holiness gave me two books on Islam, with his personal seal and autograph, and he told me that he prayed that I would be a successful preacher of Islam in America. A car, a driver, and a guide, have been placed at my disposal, making it possible for me to travel about this Holy Land almost at will. The government provides air-conditioned quarters and servants in each city that I visit. Never would I have even thought of dreaming that I would ever be a recipient of such honors—honors that in America would be bestowed upon a King—not a Negro.

"All praise is due to Allah, the Lord of all the Worlds.

"Sincerely,

"El-Hajj Malik El-Shabazz
"(Malcolm X)"

CHAPTER EIGHTEEN

EL-HAJJ MALIK EL-SHABAZZ

Prince Faisal, the absolute ruler of Arabia, had made me a guest of the State. Among the courtesies and privileges which this brought to me, especially—shamelessly—I relished the chauffeured car which toured me around in Mecca with the chauffeur-guide pointing out sights of particular significance. Some of the Holy City looked as ancient as time itself. Other parts of it resembled a modern Miami suburb. I cannot describe with what feelings I actually pressed my hands against the earth where the great Prophets had trod four thousand years before.

"The Muslim from America" excited everywhere the most intense curiosity and interest. I was mistaken time and again for Cassius Clay. A local newspaper had printed a photograph of Cassius and me together at the United Nations. Through my chauffeur-guide-interpreter I was asked scores of questions about Cassius. Even children knew of him, and loved him there in the Muslim world. By popular demand, the cinemas throughout Africa and Asia had shown his fight. At that moment in young Cassius' career, he had captured the imagination and the support of the entire dark world.

My car took me to participate in special prayers at Mt. Arafat, and at Mina. The roads offered the wildest drives that I had ever known: nightmare traffic, brakes squealing, skidding cars, and horns blowing. (I believe that all of the driving in the Holy Land is done in the name of Allah.) I had begun to learn the prayers in Arabic; now, my biggest prayer difficulty was physical. The unaccustomed prayer posture had caused my big toe to swell, and it pained me.

But the Muslim world's customs no longer seemed strange to me. My hands now readily plucked up food from a common dish shared with brother Muslims; I was drinking without hesitation from the same glass as others; I was washing from the same little pitcher of water; and sleeping with eight or ten others on a mat in the open. I remember one night at Muzdalifa with nothing but the sky overhead I lay awake amid sleeping Muslim brothers and I learned that pilgrims from every land—every color, and class, and rank; high officials and the beggar alike—all snored in the same language.

I'll bet that in the parts of the Holy Land that I visited a million bottles of soft drinks were consumed—and ten million cigarettes must have been smoked. Particularly the Arab Muslims smoked constantly, even on the Hajj pilgrimage itself. The smoking evil wasn't invented in Prophet Muhammad's days—if it had been, I believe he would have banned it.

It was the largest Hajj in history, I was later told. Kasem Gulek, of the Turkish Parliament, beaming with pride, informed me that from Turkey alone over six hundred buses—over fifty thousand Muslims—had made the pilgrimage. I told him that I dreamed to see the day when shiploads and planeloads of American Muslims would come to Mecca for the Hajj.

There was a color pattern in the huge crowds. Once I happened to notice this, I closely observed it thereafter. Being from America made me intensely sensitive to matters of color. I saw that people who looked alike drew together and most of the time stayed together. This was entirely voluntary; there being no other reason for it. But Africans were with Africans. Pakistanis were with Pakistanis. And so on. I tucked it into my mind that when I returned home I would tell Americans this observation; that where true brotherhood existed among all colors, where no one felt segregated, where there was no "superiority" complex, no "inferiority" complex—then voluntarily, naturally, people of the same kind felt drawn together by that which they had in common.

It is my intention that by the time of my next Hajj pilgrimage, I will have at least a working vocabulary of Arabic. In my ignorant, crippled condition in the Holy Land, I had been lucky to have met patient friends who enabled me to talk by interpreting for me. Never before in my life had I felt so deaf and dumb as during the times when no interpreter was with me to tell me what was being said around me, or about me, or even *to* me, by other Muslims—before they learned that "the Muslim from America" knew only a few prayers in Arabic and, beyond that, he could only nod and smile.

Behind my nods and smiles, though, I was doing some American-type thinking and reflection. I saw that Islam's conversions around the world could double and triple if the colorfulness and the true spiritualness of the Hajj pilgrimage were properly advertised and communicated to the outside world. I saw that the Arabs are poor at understanding the psychology of non-Arabs and the importance of public relations. The Arabs said *"insha Allah"* ("God willing")—then they waited for converts. Even by this means, Islam was on the march, but I knew that with improved public relations methods the number of new converts turning to Allah could be turned into millions.

Constantly, wherever I went, I was asked questions about America's racial discrimination. Even with my background, I was astonished at the degree to which the major single image of America seemed to be discrimination.

In a hundred different conversations in the Holy Land with Muslims high and low, and from around the world—and, later, when I got to Black Africa—I don't have to tell you never once did I bite my tongue or miss a single opportunity to tell the truth about the crimes, the evils and the indignities that are suffered by the black man in America. Through my interpreter, I lost no opportunity to advertise the American black man's real plight. I preached it on the mountain at Arafat, I preached it in the busy lobby of the Jedda Palace Hotel. I would point at one after another—to bring it closer to home; "You . . . you . . . you— because of your dark skin, in America you, too, would be called 'Negro.' You could be bombed and shot and cattle-prodded and fire-hosed and beaten because of your complexions."

As some of the poorest pilgrims heard me preach, so did some of the Holy World's most important personages. I talked at length with the blue-eyed, blond-haired Hussein Amini, Grand Mufti of Jerusalem. We were introduced on Mt. Arafat by Kasem Gulick of the Turkish Parliament. Both were learned men; both were especially well-read on America. Kasem Gulick asked me why I had broken with Elijah Muhammad. I said that I preferred not to elaborate upon our differences, in the interests of preserving the American black man's unity. They both understood and accepted that.

I talked with the Mayor of Mecca, Sheikh Abdullah Eraif, who when he was a journalist had criticized the methods of the Mecca municipality—and Prince Faisal made him the Mayor, to see if he could do any better. Everyone generally acknowledged that Sheikh Eraif was doing fine. A filmed feature "The Muslim From America" was made by Ahmed Horyallah and his partner Essid Muhammad of Tunis' television station. In America once, in Chicago, Ahmed Horyallah had interviewed Elijah Muhammad.

The lobby of the Jedda Palace Hotel offered me frequent sizable informal audiences of important men from many different countries who were curious to hear the "American Muslim." I met many Africans who had either spent some time in America, or who had heard other Africans' testimony about America's treatment of the black man. I remember how before one large audience, one cabinet minister from Black Africa (he knew more about world-wide current events than anyone else I've ever met) told of his occasionally traveling in the United States, North and South, deliberately not wearing his national dress. Just recalling the indignities he had met as a black man seemed to expose some raw nerve in this highly educated, dignified official. His eyes blazed in his passionate anger, his hands hacked the air: "Why is the American black man so complacent about being trampled upon? Why doesn't the American black man *fight* to be a human being?"

A Sudanese high official hugged me, "You champion the American black people!" An Indian official wept in his compassion "for my brothers in your land." I reflected many, many times to myself upon how the American Negro has been entirely brainwashed from ever seeing or thinking of himself, as he should, as a part of the non-white peoples of the world. The American Negro has no conception of the hundreds of millions of other non-whites' concern for him: he has no conception of their feeling of brotherhood for and with him.

It was there in the Holy Land, and later in Africa, that I formed a conviction which I have had ever since—that a topmost requisite for any Negro leader in America ought to be extensive traveling in the non-white lands on this earth, and the travel should include many conferences with the ranking men of those lands. I guarantee that any honest, open-minded Negro leader would return home with more effective thinking about alternative avenues to solutions of the American black man's problem. Above all, the Negro leaders would find that many non-white officials of the highest standing, especially Africans, would tell them—privately—that they would be glad to throw their weight behind the Negro cause, in the United Nations, and in other ways. But these officials understandably feel that the Negro in America is so confused and divided that he doesn't himself know what his cause is. Again, it was mainly Africans who variously expressed to me that no one would wish to be embarrassed trying to help a brother who shows no evidence that he wants that help—and who seems to refuse to cooperate in his own interests.

The American black "leader's" most critical problem is lack of imagination! His thinking, his strategies, if any, are always limited, at least basically, to only that which is either advised, or approved by the white man. And the first thing the American power structure doesn't want any Negroes to start is thinking *internationally*.

I think the single worst mistake of the American black organizations, and their leaders, is that they have failed to establish direct brotherhood lines of communication between the independent nations of Africa and the American black people. Why, every day, the black African heads of state should be receiving direct accounts of the latest developments in the American black man's struggles—instead of the U.S. State Department's releases to Africans which always imply that the American black man's struggle is being "solved."

Two American authors, best-sellers in the Holy Land, had helped to spread and intensify the concern for the American black man. James Baldwin's books, translated, had made a tremendous impact, as had the book *Black Like Me*, by John Griffin. If you're unfamiliar with that book, it tells how the white man Griffin blackened his skin and spent two months traveling as a Negro about America; then Griffin wrote of the experiences that he met. "A frightening experience!" I heard exclaimed many times by people in the Holy World who had read the popular book. But I never heard it without opening their thinking further: "Well, if it was a frightening experience for him as nothing but a make-believe Negro for sixty days—then you think about what *real* Negroes in America have gone through for four hundred years."

One honor that came to me, I had prayed for: His Eminence, Prince Faisal, invited me to a personal audience with him.

As I entered the room, tall, handsome Prince Faisal came from behind his desk. I never will forget the reflection I had at that instant, that here was one of the world's most important men, and yet with his dignity one saw clearly his sincere humility. He indicated for me a chair opposite from his. Our interpreter was the Deputy Chief of Protocol, Muhammad Abdul Azziz Maged, an Egyptian-born Arab, who looked like a Harlem Negro.

Prince Faisal impatiently gestured when I began stumbling for words trying to express my gratitude for the great honor he had paid me in making me a guest of the State. It was only Muslim hospitality to another Muslim, he explained, and I was an unusual Muslim from America. He asked me to understand above all that whatever he had done had been his pleasure, with no other motives whatever.

A gliding servant served a choice of two kinds of tea as Prince Faisal talked. His son, Muhammad Faisal, had "met" me on American television while attending a Northern California university. Prince Faisal had read Egyptian writers' articles about the American "Black Muslims." "If what these writers say is true, the Black Muslims have the wrong Islam," he said. I explained my role of the previous twelve years, of helping to organize and to build the Nation of Islam. I said that my purpose for making the Hajj was to get an understanding of true Islam. "That is good," Prince Faisal said, pointing out that there was an abundance of English-translation literature about Islam—so that there was no excuse for ignorance, and no reason for sincere people to allow themselves to be misled.

The last of April, 1964, I flew to Beirut, the seaport capital of Lebanon. A part of me, I left behind in the Holy City of Mecca. And, in turn, I took away with me—forever—a part of Mecca.

I was on my way, now, to Nigeria, then Ghana. But some

friends I had made in the Holy Land had urged and insisted that I make some stops en route and I had agreed. For example, it had been arranged that I would first stop and address the faculty and the students at the American University of Beirut.

In Beirut's Palm Beach Hotel, I luxuriated in my first long sleep since I had left America. Then, I went walking—fresh from weeks in the Holy Land: immediately my attention was struck by the mannerisms and attire of the Lebanese women. In the Holy Land, there had been the very modest, very feminine Arabian women—and there was this sudden contrast of the half-French, half-Arab Lebanese women who projected in their dress and street manners more liberty, more boldness. I saw clearly the obvious European influence upon the Lebanese culture. It showed me how any country's moral strength, or its moral weakness, is quickly measurable by the street attire and attitude of its women—especially its young women. Wherever the spiritual values have been submerged, if not destroyed, by an emphasis upon the material things, invariably, the women reflect it. Witness the women, both young and old, in America—where scarcely any moral values are left. There seems in most countries to be either one extreme or the other. Truly a paradise could exist wherever material progress and spiritual values could be properly balanced.

I spoke at the University of Beirut the truth of the American black man's condition. I've previously made the comment that any experienced public speaker can feel his audience's reactions. As I spoke, I felt the subjective and defensive reactions of the American white students present—but gradually their hostilities lessened as I continued to present the unassailable facts. But the students of African heritage—well, I'll *never* get over how the African displays his emotions.

Later, with astonishment, I heard that the American press carried stories that my Beirut speech caused a "riot." What kind of a riot? I don't know how any reporter, in good conscience, could have cabled that across the ocean. The Beirut *Daily Star* front-page report of my speech mentioned no "riot"—because there was none. When I was done, the African students all but besieged me for autographs; some of them even hugged me. Never have even American Negro audiences accepted me as I have been accepted time and again by the less inhibited, more down-to-earth Africans.

From Beirut, I flew back to Cairo, and there I took a train to Alexandria, Egypt. I kept my camera busy during each brief stopover. Finally I was on a plane to Nigeria.

During the six-hour flight, when I was not talking with the pilot (who had been a 1960 Olympics swimmer), I sat with a passionately political African. He almost shouted in his fervor. "When people are in a stagnant state, and are being brought out of it, there is no *time* for voting!" His central theme was that no new African nation, trying to decolonize itself, needed any political system that would permit division and bickering. "The people don't know what the vote means! It is the job of the enlightened leaders to raise the people's intellect."

In Lagos, I was greeted by Professor Essien-Udom of the Ibadan University. We were both happy to see each other. We had met in the United States as he had researched the Nation of Islam for his book, *Black Nationalism*. At his home, that evening, a dinner was held in my honor, attended by other professors and professional people. As we ate, a young doctor asked me if I knew that New York City's press was highly upset about a recent killing in Harlem of a white woman—for which, according to the press, many were blaming me at least indirectly. An elderly white couple who owned a Harlem clothing store had been attacked by several young Negroes, and the wife was stabbed to death. Some of these young Negroes, apprehended by the police, had described themselves as belonging to an organization they called "Blood Brothers." These youths, allegedly, had said or implied that they were affiliated with "Black Muslims" who had split away from the Nation of Islam to join up with me.

I told the dinner guests that it was my first word of any of it, but that I was not surprised when violence happened in any of America's ghettoes where black men had been living packed like animals and treated like lepers. I said that the charge against me was typical white man scapegoat-seeking—that whenever something white men disliked happened in the black community, typically white public attention was directed not at the cause, but at a selected scapegoat.

As for the "Blood Brothers," I said I considered all Negroes to be my blood brothers. I said that the white man's efforts to make my name poison actually succeeded only in making millions of black people regard me like Joe Louis.

Speaking in the Ibadan University's Trenchard Hall, I urged that Africa's independent nations needed to see the necessity of helping to bring the Afro-American's case before the United Nations. I said that just as the American Jew is in political, economic, and cultural harmony with world Jewry, I was convinced that it was time for all Afro-Americans to join the world's Pan-Africanists. I said that physically we Afro-Americans might remain in America, fighting for our Constitutional rights, but that philosophically and culturally we Afro-Americans badly needed to "return" to Africa—and to develop a working unity in the framework of Pan-Africanism.

Young Africans asked me politically sharper questions than one hears from most American adults. Then an astonishing thing happened when one old West Indian stood and began attacking me—for attacking America. "Shut up! Shut up!" students yelled, booing, and hissing. The old West Indian tried to express defiance of them, and in a sudden rush a group of students sprang up and were after him. He barely escaped ahead of them. I never saw anything like it. Screaming at him, they ran him off the campus. (Later, I found out that the old West Indian was married to a white woman, and he was trying to get a job in some white-influenced agency which had put him up to challenge me. Then, I understood his problem.)

This wasn't the last time I'd see the Africans' almost fanatic expression of their political emotions.

Afterward, in the Students' Union, I was plied with questions, and I was made an honorary member of the Nigerian Muslim Students' Society. Right here in my wallet is my card: "Alhadji Malcolm X. Registration No. M-138." With the membership, I was given a new name: "Omowale." It means, in the Yoruba language, "the son who has come home." I meant it when I told them I had never received a more treasured honor.

Six hundred members of the Peace Corps were in Nigeria, I learned. Some white Peace Corps members who talked with me were openly embarrassed at the guilt of their race in America. Among the twenty Negro Peace Corpsmen I talked with, a very impressive fellow to me was Larry Jackson, a Morgan State

College graduate from Fort Lauderdale, Florida, who had joined the Peace Corps in 1962.

I made Nigerian radio and television program appearances. When I remember seeing black men operating their *own* communications agencies, a thrill still runs up my spine. The reporters who interviewed me included an American Negro from *Newsweek* magazine—his name was Williams. Traveling through Africa, he had recently interviewed Prime Minister Nkrumah.

Talking with me privately, one group of Nigerian officials told me how skillfully the U.S. Information Agency sought to spread among Africans the impression that American Negroes were steadily advancing, and that the race problem soon would be solved. One high official told me, "Our informed leaders and many, many others know otherwise." He said that behind the "diplomatic front" of every African U.N. official was recognition of the white man's gigantic duplicity and conspiracy to keep the world's peoples of African heritage separated—both physically and ideologically—from each other.

"In your land, how many black people think about it that South and Central and North America contain over *eighty million* people of African descent?" he asked me.

"The world's course will change the day the African-heritage peoples come together as brothers!"

I never had heard that kind of global black thinking from any black man in America.

From Lagos, Nigeria, I flew on to Accra, Ghana.

I think that nowhere is the black continent's wealth and the natural beauty of its people richer than in Ghana, which is so proudly the very fountainhead of Pan-Africanism.

I stepped off the plane into a jarring note. A red-faced American white man recognized me; he had the nerve to come up grabbing my hand and telling me in a molasses drawl that he was from Alabama, and then he invited me to his home for dinner!

My hotel's dining room, when I went to breakfast, was full of more of those whites—discussing Africa's untapped wealth as though the African waiters had no ears. It nearly ruined my meal, thinking how in America they sicked police dogs on black people, and threw bombs in black churches, while blocking the doors of their white churches—and now, once again in the land where their forefathers had stolen blacks and thrown them into slavery, was that white man.

Right there at my Ghanaian breakfast table was where I made up my mind that as long as I was in Africa, every time I opened my mouth, I was going to make things hot for that white man, grinning through his teeth wanting to exploit Africa again—it had been her human wealth the last time, now he wanted Africa's mineral wealth.

And I knew that my reacting as I did presented no conflict with the convictions of brotherhood which I had gained in the Holy Land. The Muslims of "white" complexions who had changed my opinions were men who had showed me that they practiced genuine brotherhood. And I knew that any American white man with a genuine brotherhood for a black man was hard to find, no matter how much he grinned.

The author Julian Mayfield seemed to be the leader of Ghana's little colony of Afro-American expatriates. When I telephoned Mayfield, in what seemed no time at all I was sitting in his home surrounded by about forty black American expatriates; they had been waiting for my arrival. There were business and professional people, such as the militant former Brooklynites Dr. and Mrs. Robert E. Lee, both of them dentists, who had given up their United States' citizenship. Such others as Alice Windom, Maya Angelou Make, Victoria Garvin, and Leslie Lacy had even formed a "Malcolm X Committee" to guide me through a whirlwind calendar of appearances and social events.

In my briefcase here are some of the African press stories which had appeared when it was learned that I was en route:

"Malcolm X's name is almost as familiar to Ghanaians as the Southern dogs, fire hoses, cattle prods, people sticks, and the ugly, hate-contorted white faces. . . ."

"Malcolm X's decision to enter the mainstream of the struggle heralds a hopeful sign on the sickeningly dismal scene of brutalized, non-violent, passive resistance. . . ."

"An extremely important fact is that Malcolm X is the first Afro-American leader of national standing to make an independent trip to Africa since Dr. Du Bois came to Ghana. This may be the beginning of a new phase in our struggle. Let's make sure we don't give it less thought than the State Department is doubtless giving it right now.''

And another: "Malcolm X is one of our most significant and miltant leaders. We are in a battle. Efforts will be made to malign and discredit him. . . .''

I simply couldn't believe this kind of reception five thousand miles from America! The officials of the press had even arranged to pay my hotel expenses, and they would hear no objection that I made. They included T. D. Baffoe, the Editor-in-Chief of the *Ghanaian Times*; G. T. Anim, the Managing Director of the Ghana News Agency; Kofi Batsa, the Editor of *Spark* and the Secretary-General of the Pan-African Union of Journalists; and Mr. Cameron Duodu; and others. I could only thank them all. Then, during the beautiful dinner which had been prepared by Julian Mayfield's pretty Puerto Rican wife, Ana Livia (she was in charge of Accra's district health program), I was plied with questions by the eagerly interested black expatriates from America who had returned to Mother Africa.

I can only wish that every American black man could have shared my ears, my eyes, and my emotions throughout the round of engagements which had been made for me in Ghana. And my point in saying this is not the reception that I personally received as an individual of whom they had heard, but it was the reception tendered to me as the symbol of the militant American black man, as I had the honor to be regarded.

At a jam-packed press club conference, I believe the very first question was why had I split with Elijah Muhammad and the Nation of Islam. The Africans had heard such rumors as that Elijah Muhammad had built a palace in Arizona. I straightened out that falsehood, and I avoided any criticism. I said that our disagreement had been in terms of political direction and involvement in the extra-religious struggle for human rights. I said I respected the Nation of Islam for its having been a psychologically revitalizing movement and a source of moral and social reform, and that Elijah Muhammad's influence upon the American black man had been basic.

I stressed to the assembled press the need for mutual communication and support between the Africans and Afro-Americans whose struggles were interlocked. I remember that in the press conference, I used the word "Negro," and I was firmly corrected. "The word is not favored here, Mr. Malcolm X. The term Afro-American has greater meaning, and dignity." I sincerely apologized. I don't think that I said "Negro" again as long as I was in Africa. I said that the 22 million Afro-Americans in the United States could become for Africa a great positive force—while, in turn, the African nations could and should exert positive force at diplomatic levels against America's racial discrimination. I said, "All of Africa unites in opposition to South Africa's apartheid, and to the oppression in the Portuguese territories. But you waste your time if you don't realize that Verwoerd and Salazar, and Britain and France, never could last a day if it were not for United States support. So until you expose the man in Washington, D.C., you haven't accomplished anything."

I knew that the State Department's G. Mennen Williams was officially visiting in Africa. I said, "Take my word for it—you be suspicious of all these American officials who come to Africa grinning in your faces when they don't grin in ours back home." I told them that my own father was murdered by whites in the state of Michigan where G. Mennen Williams once was the Governor.

I was honored at the Ghana Club, by more press representatives and dignitaries. I was the guest at the home of the late black American author Richard Wright's daughter, beautiful, slender, soft-voiced Julia, whose young French husband publishes a Ghanaian paper. Later, in Paris, I was to meet Richard Wright's widow, Ellen, and a younger daughter, Rachel.

I talked with Ambassadors, at their embassies. The Algerian Ambassador impressed me as a man who was dedicated totally to militancy, and to world revolution, as the way to solve the problems of the world's oppressed masses. His perspective was attuned not just to Algerians, but to include the Afro-Americans and all others anywhere who were oppressed. The Chinese Ambassador, Mr. Huang Ha, a most perceptive, and also most militant man, focused upon the efforts of the West to divide Africans from the peoples of African heritage elsewhere. The Nigerian Ambassador was deeply concerned about the Afro-Americans' plight in America. He had personal knowledge of their suffering, having lived and studied in Washington, D.C. Similarly, the most sympathetic Mali Ambassador had been in New York at the United Nations. I breakfasted with Dr. Makonnen of British Guiana. We discussed the need for the type of Pan-African unity that would also include the Afro-Americans. And I had a talk in depth about Afro-American problems with Nana Nketsia, the Ghanaian Minister of Culture.

Once when I returned to my hotel, a New York City call was waiting for me from Mal Goode of the American Broadcasting Company. Over the telephone Mal Goode asked me questions that I answered for his beeping tape recorder, about the "Blood Brothers" in Harlem, the rifle clubs for Negroes, and other subjects with which I was being kept identified in the American press.

In the University of Ghana's Great Hall, I addressed the largest audience that I would in Africa—mostly Africans, but also numerous whites. Before this audience, I tried my best to demolish the false image of American race relations that I knew was spread by the U.S. Information Agency. I tried to impress upon them all the true picture of the Afro-American's plight at the hands of the white man. I worked on those whites there in the audience:

"I've never *seen* so many whites so nice to so many blacks as you white people here in Africa. In America, Afro-Americans are struggling for integration. They should come here—to Africa—and see how you grin at Africans. You've really got integration here. But can you tell the Africans that in America you grin at the black people? No, you can't! And you don't honestly like these Africans any better, either—but what you *do* like is the *minerals* Africa has under her soil. . . ."

Those whites out in the audience turned pink and red. They knew I was telling the truth. "I'm not anti-American, and I didn't come here to *condemn* America—I want to make that very clear!" I told them. "I came here to tell the truth—and if the *truth* condemns America, then she stands condemned!"

One evening I met most of the officials in Ghana—all of those with whom I had previously talked, and more—at a party that was given for me by the Honorable Kofi Baako, the Ghanaian Minister of Defense, and the Leader of the National Assembly. I was told that this was the first time such an honor was accorded to a foreigner since Dr. W. E. B. Du Bois had come to Ghana. There was music, dancing, and fine Ghanaian food. Several persons at the party were laughing among themselves, saying that at an earlier party that day, U.S. Ambassador Mahomey was knocking himself out being exceptionally friendly and jovial. Some thought that he was making a strong effort to counteract the truth about America that I was telling every chance I got.

Then an invitation came to me which exceeded my wildest dream. I would never have imagined that I would actually have an opportunity to address the members of the Ghanaian Parliament!

I made my remarks brief—but I made them strong: "How can you condemn Portugal and South Africa while our black people in America are being bitten by dogs and beaten with clubs?" I said I felt certain that the only reason black Africans—our black brothers—could be so silent about what happened in America was that they had been misinformed by the American government's propaganda agencies.

At the end of my talk, I heard "Yes! We support the Afro-American . . . morally, physically, materially if necessary!"

In Ghana—or in all of black Africa—my highest single honor was an audience at the Castle with Osagyefo Dr. Kwame Nkrumah.

Before seeing him, I was searched most thoroughly. I respected the type of security the Ghanaians erect around their leader. It gave me that much more respect for independent black men. Then, as I entered Dr. Nkrumah's long office, he came out from behind his desk at the far end. Dr. Nkrumah wore ordinary dress, his hand was extended and a smile was on his sensitive face. I pumped his hand. We sat on a couch and talked. I knew that he was particularly well-informed on the Afro-American's plight, as for years he had lived and studied in America. We discussed the unity of Africans and peoples of African descent. We agreed that Pan-Africanism was the key also to the problems of those of African heritage. I could feel the warm, likeable and very down-to-earth qualities of Dr. Nkrumah. My time with him was up all too soon. I promised faithfully that when I returned to the United States, I would relay to Afro-Americans his personal warm regards.

That afternoon, thirty-nine miles away in Winneba, I spoke at the Kwame Nkrumah Ideological Institute—where two hundred students were being trained to carry forward Ghana's intellectual revolution, and here again occurred one of those astounding demonstrations of the young African's political fervor. After I had spoken, during the question-and-answer period, some young Afro-American stood up, whom none there seemed to know. "I am an American Negro," he announced himself. Vaguely, he defended the American white man. The African students booed and harassed him. Then instantly when the meeting was over, they cornered this fellow with verbal abuse, "Are you an agent of Rockefeller?" . . . "Stop corrupting our children!" (The fellow had turned out to be a local secondary school teacher, placed in the job by an American agency.) . . . "Come to this Institute for some orientation!" Temporarily, a teacher rescued the fellow—but then the students rushed him and drove him away, shouting, "Stooge!" . . . "C.I.A." . . . "American agent!"

Chinese Ambassador and Mrs. Huang Hua gave a state dinner in my honor. The guests included the Cuban and the Algerian ambassadors, and also it was here that I met Mrs. W. E. B. Du Bois. After the excellent dinner, three films were shown. One, a color film, depicted the People's Republic of China in celebration of its Fourteenth Anniversary. Prominently shown in this film was the militant former North Carolina Afro-American Robert Williams, who has since taken refuge in Cuba after his advocacy that the American black people should take up arms to defend and protect themselves. The second film focused upon the Chinese people's support for the Afro-American struggle. Chairman Mao Tse-tung was shown delivering his statement of that support, and the film offered sickening moments of graphic white brutality—police and civilian—to Afro-Americans who were demonstrating in various U.S. cities, seeking civil rights. And the final film was a dramatic presentation of the Algerian Revolution.

The "Malcolm X Committee" rushed me from the Chinese Embassy dinner to where a soiree in my honor had already begun at the Press Club. It was my first sight of Ghanaians dancing the high-life. A high and merry time was being had by everyone, and I was pressed to make a short speech. I stressed again the need for unity between Africans and Afro-Americans. I cried out of my heart, "Now, dance! Sing! But as you do—remember

Mandela, remember Sobokwe! Remember Lumumba in his grave! Remember South Africans now in jail!''

I said, ''You wonder why *I* don't dance? Because I want you to remember twenty-two million Afro-Americans in the U.S.!''

But I sure felt like dancing! The Ghanaians performed the high-life as if possessed. One pretty African girl sang ''Blue Moon'' like Sarah Vaughan. Sometimes the band sounded like Milt Jackson, sometimes like Charlie Parker.

The next morning, a Saturday, I heard that Cassius Clay and his entourage had arrived. There was a huge reception for him at the airport. I thought that if Cassius and I happened to meet, it would likely prove embarrassing for Cassius, since he had elected to remain with Elijah Muhammad's version of Islam. I would not have been embarrassed, but I knew that Cassius would have been forbidden to associate with me. I knew that Cassius knew I had been with him, and for him, and believed in him, when those who later embraced him felt that he had no chance. I decided to avoid Cassius so as not to put him on the spot.

A luncheon was given for me that afternoon by the Nigerian High Commissioner, His Excellency Alhadji Isa Wali, a short, bespectacled, extremely warm and friendly man who had lived in Washington, D.C. for two years. After lunch, His Excellency spoke to the guests of his American encounters with discrimination, and of friendships he had made with Afro-Americans, and he reaffirmed the bonds between Africans and Afro-Americans.

His Excellency held up before the luncheon guests a large and handsome issue of an American magazine, *Horizon*; it was opened to an article about the Nation of Islam, written by Dr. Morroe Berger of Princeton University. One full page was a photograph of me; the opposite full page was a beautiful color illustration of a black royal Nigerian Muslim, stalwart and handsome, of hundreds of years ago.

''When I look at these photographs, I know these two people are one,'' said His Excellency. ''The only difference is in their attire—and one was born in America and the other in Africa.

''So to let everyone know that I believe we are brothers, I am going to give to Alhadji Malcolm X a robe like that worn by the Nigerian in this photo.''

I was overwhelmed by the splendor of the beautiful blue robe and the orange turban which His Excellency then presented to me. I bent over so that he, a short man, could properly arrange the turban on my head. His Excellency Alhadji Isa Wali also presented me with a two-volume translation of the Holy Quran.

After this unforgettable luncheon, Mrs. Shirley Graham Du Bois drove me to her home, so that I could see and photograph the home where her famed late husband, Dr. W. E. B. Du Bois, had spent his last days. Mrs. Du Bois, a writer, was the Director of Ghanaian television, which was planned for educational purposes. When Dr. Du Bois had come to Ghana, she told me, Dr. Nkrumah had set up the aging great militant Afro-American scholar like a king, giving to Dr. Du Bois everything he could wish for. Mrs. Du Bois told me that when Dr. Du Bois was failing fast, Dr. Nkrumah had visited, and the two men had said good-bye, both knowing that one's death was near—and Dr. Nkrumah had gone away in tears.

My final Ghanaian social event was a beautiful party in my honor given by His Excellency Mr. Armando Entralgo Gonzalez, the Cuban Ambassador to Ghana. The next morning—it was Sunday—the "Malcolm X Committee" was waiting at my hotel, to accompany me to the airport. As we left the hotel, we met Cassius Clay with some of his entourage, returning from his morning walk. Cassius momentarily seemed uncertain—then he spoke, something almost monosyllabic, like "How are you?" It flashed through my mind how close we had been before the fight that had changed the course of his life. I replied that I was fine—something like that—and that I hoped he was, which I sincerely meant. Later on, I sent Cassius a message by wire, saying that I hoped that he would realize how much he was loved by Muslims wherever they were; and that he would not let anyone use him and maneuver him into saying and doing things to tarnish his image.

The "Malcolm X Committee" and I were exchanging good-byes at the Accra airport when a small motorcade of *five Ambassadors* arrived—to see me off!

I no longer had any words.

In the plane, bound for Monrovia, Liberia, to spend a day, I knew that after what I had experienced in the Holy Land, the second most indelible memory I would carry back to America would be the Africa seething with serious awareness of itself, and of Africa's wealth, and of her power, and of her destined role in the world.

From Monrovia, I flew to Dakar, Senegal. The Senegalese in the airport, hearing about the Muslim from America, stood in line to shake my hand, and I signed many autographs. "Our people can't speak Arabic, but we have Islam in our hearts," said one Senegalese. I told them that exactly described their fellow Afro-American Muslims.

From Dakar, I flew to Morocco, where I spent a day sightseeing. I visited the famous Casbah, the ghetto which had resulted when the ruling white French wouldn't let the darkskinned natives into certain areas of Casablanca. Thousands upon thousands of the subjugated natives were crowded into the ghetto, in the same way that Harlem, in New York City, became America's Casbah.

It was Tuesday, May 19, 1964—my thirty-ninth birthday— when I arrived in Algiers. A lot of water had gone under the bridge in those years. In some ways, I had had more experiences than a dozen men. The taxi driver, while taking me to the Hotel Aletti, described the atrocities the French had committed, and personal measures that he had taken to get even. I walked around Algiers, hearing rank-and-file expressions of hatred for America for supporting the oppressors of the Algerians. They were true revolutionists, not afraid of death. They had, for so long, faced death.

The Pan American jet which took me home—it was Flight 115—landed at New York's Kennedy Air Terminal on May 21, at 4:25 in the afternoon. We passengers filed off the plane and toward Customs. When I saw the crowd of fifty or sixty reporters and photographers, I honestly wondered what celebrity I had been on the plane with.

But I was the "villain" they had come to meet.

In Harlem especially, and also in some other U.S. cities, the 1964 long, hot summer's predicted explosions had begun. Article after article in the white man's press had cast me as a symbol—if not a causative agent—of the "revolt" and of the "violence" of the American black man, wherever it had sprung up.

In the biggest press conference that I had ever experienced

anywhere, the camera bulbs flashed, and the reporters fired questions.

"Mr. Malcolm X, what about those 'Blood Brothers,' reportedly affiliated with your organization, reportedly trained for violence, who have killed innocent white people?" . . . "Mr. Malcolm X, what about your comment that Negroes should form rifle clubs? . . ."

I answered the questions. I knew I was back in America again, hearing the subjective, scapegoat-seeking questions of the white man. New York white youth were killing victims; that was a "sociological" problem. But when black youth killed somebody, the power structure was looking to hang somebody. When black men had been lynched or otherwise murdered in cold blood, it was always said, "Things will get better." When whites had rifles in their homes, the Constitution gave them the right to protect their home and themselves. But when black people even spoke of having rifles in their homes, that was "ominous."

I slipped in on the reporters something they hadn't been expecting. I said that the American black man needed to quit thinking what the white man had taught him—which was that the black man had no alternative except to beg for his so-called "civil rights." I said that the American black man needed to recognize that he had a strong, airtight case to take the United States before the United Nations on a formal accusation of "denial of human rights"—and that if Angola and South Africa were precedent cases, then there would be no easy way that the U.S. could escape being censured, right on its own home ground.

Just as I had known, the press wanted to get me off that subject. I was asked about my "Letter From Mecca"—I was all set with a speech regarding that:

"I hope that once and for all my Hajj to the Holy City of Mecca has established our Muslim Mosque's authentic religious affiliation with the 750 million Muslims of the orthodox Islamic World. And I *know* once and for all that the Black Africans look upon America's 22 million blacks as long-lost *brothers!* They *love* us! They *study* our struggle for freedom! They were so *happy* to hear how we are awakening from our long sleep—after so-called 'Christian' white America had taught us to be *ashamed* of our African brothers and homeland!

"Yes—I wrote a letter from Mecca. You're asking me 'Didn't

you say that now you accept white men as brothers?' Well, my answer is that in the Muslim World, I saw, I felt, and I wrote home how my thinking was broadened! Just as I wrote, I shared true, brotherly love with many white-complexioned Muslims who never gave a single thought to the race, or to the complexion, of another Muslim.

"My pilgrimage broadened my scope. It blessed me with a new insight. In two weeks in the Holy Land, I saw what I never had seen in thirty-nine years here in America. I saw all *races*, all *colors*,—blue-eyed blonds to black-skinned Africans—in *true* brotherhood! In unity! Living as one! Worshiping as one! No segregationists—no liberals; they would not have known how to interpret the meaning of those words.

"In the past, yes, I have made sweeping indictments of *all* white people. I never will be guilty of that again—as I know now that some white people *are* truly sincere, that some truly are capable of being brotherly toward a black man. The true Islam has shown me that a blanket indictment of all white people is as wrong as when whites make blanket indictments against blacks.

"Yes, I have been convinced that *some* American whites do want to help cure the rampant racism which is on the path to *destroying* this country!

"It was in the Holy World that my attitude was changed, by what I experienced there, and by what I witnessed there, in terms of brotherhood—not just brotherhood toward me, but brotherhood between all men, of all nationalities and complexions, who were there. And now that I am back in America, my attitude here concerning white people has to be governed by what my black brothers and I experience here, and what we witness here—in terms of brotherhood. The *problem* here in America is that we meet such a small minority of individual so-called 'good,' or 'brotherly' white people. Here in the United States, notwithstanding those few 'good' white people, it is the *collective* 150 million white people whom the *collective* 22 million black people have to deal with!

"Why, here in America, the seeds of racism are so deeply rooted in the white people collectively, their belief that they are 'superior' in some way is so deeply rooted, that these things are in the national white subconsciousness. Many whites are even actually unaware of their own racism, until they face some test, and then their racism emerges in one form or another.

"Listen! The white man's racism toward the black man here in America is what has got him in such trouble all over this world, with other non-white peoples. The white man can't separate himself from the stigma that he automatically feels about anyone, no matter who, who is not his color. And the non-white peoples of the world are sick of the condescending white man! That's why you've got all of this trouble in places like Viet Nam. Or right here in the Western Hemisphere—probably 100 million people of African descent are divided against each other, taught by the white man to hate and to mistrust each other. In the West Indies, Cuba, Brazil, Venezuela, all of South America, Central America! All of those lands are full of people with African blood! On the African continent, even, the white man has maneuvered to divide the black African from the brown Arab, to divide the so-called 'Christian African' from the Muslim African. Can you imagine what can happen, what would certainly happen, if all of these African-heritage peoples ever *realize* their blood bonds, if they ever realize they all have a common goal—if they ever *unite?*"

The press was glad to get rid of me that day. I believe that the black brothers whom I had just recently left in Africa would have felt that I did the subject justice. Nearly through the night, my telephone at home kept ringing. My black brothers and sisters around New York and in some other cities were calling to congratulate me on what they had heard on the radio and television news broadcasts, and people, mostly white, were wanting to know if I would speak here or there.

The next day I was in my car driving along the freeway when at a red light another car pulled alongside. A white woman was driving and on the passenger's side, next to me, was a white man. *"Malcolm X!"* he called out—and when I looked, he stuck his hand out of his car, across at me, grinning. "Do you mind shaking hands with a white man?" Imagine that! Just as the traffic light turned green, I told him, "I don't mind shaking hands with human beings. Are you one?"

CHAPTER NINETEEN

1965

I must be honest. Negroes—Afro-Americans—showed no incli-
nation to rush to the United Nations and demand justice for
themselves here in America. I really had known in advance that
they wouldn't. The American white man has so thoroughly
brainwashed the black man to see himself as only a domestic
"civil rights" problem that it will probably take longer than I
live before the Negro sees that the struggle of the American
black man is international.

And I had known, too, that Negroes would not rush to follow
me into the orthodox Islam which had given me the insight and
perspective to see that the black men and white men truly could
be brothers. America's Negroes—especially older Negroes—are
too indelibly soaked in Christianity's double standard of op-
pression.

So, in the "public invited" meetings which I began holding
each Sunday afternoon or evening in Harlem's well-known Au-
dubon Ballroom, as I addressed predominantly non-Muslim Ne-
gro audiences, I did not immediately attempt to press the Islamic
religion, but instead to embrace all who sat before me:

"—not Muslim, nor Christian, Catholic, nor Protestant . . .
Baptist nor Methodist, Democrat nor Republican, Mason nor
Elk! I mean the black people of America—and the black people
all over this earth! Because it is as this collective mass of black
people that we have been deprived not only of our civil rights,
but even of our human rights, the right to human dignity. . . ."

On the streets, after my speeches, in the faces and the voices
of the people I met—even those who would pump my hands and

want my autograph—I would feel the wait-and-see attitude. I would feel—and I understood—their uncertainty about where I stood. Since the Civil War's "freedom," the black man has gone down so many fruitless paths. His leaders, very largely, had failed him. The religion of Christianity had failed him. The black man was scarred, he was cautious, he was apprehensive.

I understood it better now than I had before. In the Holy World, away from America's race problem, was the first time I ever had been able to think clearly about the basic divisions of white people in America, and how their attitudes and their motives related to, and affected Negroes. In my thirty-nine years on this earth, the Holy City of Mecca had been the first time I had ever stood before the Creator of All and felt like a complete human being.

In that peace of the Holy World—in fact, the very night I have mentioned when I lay awake surrounded by snoring brother pilgrims—my mind took me back to personal memories I would have thought were gone forever . . . as far back, even, as when I was just a little boy, eight or nine years old. Out behind our house, out in the country from Lansing, Michigan, there was an old, grassy "Hector's Hill," we called it—which may still be there. I remembered there in the Holy World how I used to lie on the top of Hector's Hill, and look up at the sky, at the clouds moving over me, and daydream, all kinds of things. And then, in a funny contrast of recollections, I remembered how years later, when I was in prison, I used to lie on my cell bunk—this would be especially when I was in solitary: what we convicts called "The Hole"—and I would picture myself talking to large crowds. I don't have any idea why such previsions came to me. But they did. To tell that to anyone then would have sounded crazy. Even I didn't have, myself, the slightest inkling. . . .

In Mecca, too, I had played back for myself the twelve years I had spent with Elijah Muhammad as if it were a motion picture. I guess it would be impossible for anyone ever to realize fully how complete was my belief in Elijah Muhammad. I believed in him not only as a leader in the ordinary *human* sense, but also I believed in him as a *divine* leader. I believed he had no human weaknesses or faults, and that, therefore, he could make no mistakes and that he could do no wrong. There on a Holy World hilltop, I realized how very dangerous it is for people to hold any human being in such esteem, especially to consider anyone some sort of "divinely guided" and "protected" person.

My thinking had been opened up wide in Mecca. In the long letters I wrote to friends, I tried to convey to them my new insights into the American black man's struggle and his problems, as well as the depths of my search for truth and justice.

"I've had enough of someone else's propaganda," I had written to these friends. "I'm for truth, no matter who tells it. I'm for justice, no matter who it is for or against. I'm a human being first and foremost, and as such I'm for whoever and whatever benefits humanity *as a whole*."

Largely, the American white man's press refused to convey that I was now attempting to teach Negroes a new direction. With the 1964 "long, hot summer" steadily producing new incidents, I was constantly accused of "stirring up Negroes." Every time I had another radio or television microphone at my mouth, when I was asked about "stirring up Negroes" or "inciting violence," I'd get hot.

"It takes no one to stir up the sociological dynamite that stems from the unemployment, bad housing, and inferior education already in the ghettoes. This explosively criminal condition has existed for so long, it needs no fuse; it fuses itself; it spontaneously combusts from within itself. . . ."

They called me "the angriest Negro in America." I wouldn't deny that charge. I spoke exactly as I felt. "I *believe* in anger. The Bible says there is a *time* for anger." They called me "a teacher, a fomentor of violence." I would say point blank, "That is a lie. I'm not for wanton violence, I'm for justice. I feel that if white people were attacked by Negroes—if the forces of law prove unable, or inadequate, or reluctant to protect those whites from those Negroes—then those white people should protect and defend themselves from those Negroes, using arms if necessary. And I feel that when the law fails to protect Negroes from whites' attack, then those Negroes should use arms, if necessary, to defend themselves."

"Malcolm X Advocates Armed Negroes!"

What was wrong with that? I'll tell you what was wrong. I was a black man talking about physical defense against the white man. The white man can lynch and burn and bomb and beat

Negroes—that's all right: "Have patience" . . . "The customs are entrenched" . . . "Things are getting better."

Well, I believe it's a crime for anyone who is being brutalized to continue to accept that brutality without doing something to defend himself. If that's how "Christian" philosophy is interpreted, if that's what Gandhian philosophy teaches, well, then, I will call them criminal philosophies.

I tried in every speech I made to clarify my new position regarding white people—"I don't speak against the sincere, well-meaning, good white people. I have learned that there *are* some. I have learned that not all white people are racists. I am speaking against and my fight is against the white *racists*. I firmly believe that Negroes have the right to fight against these racists, by any means that are necessary."

But the white reporters kept wanting me linked with that word "violence." I doubt if I had one interview without having to deal with that accusation.

"I *am* for violence if non-violence means we continue postponing a solution to the American black man's problem—just to *avoid* violence. I don't go for non-violence if it also means a delayed solution. To me a delayed solution is a non-solution. Or I'll say it another way. If it must take violence to get the black man his human rights in this country, I'm *for* violence exactly as you know the Irish, the Poles, or Jews would be if they were flagrantly discriminated against. I am just as they would be in that case, and they would be for violence—no matter what the consequences, no matter who was hurt by the violence."

White society *hates* to hear anybody, especially a black man, talk about the crime the white man has perpetrated on the black man. I have always understood that's why I have been so frequently called "a revolutionist." It sounds as if *I* have done some crime! Well, it may be the American black man does need to become involved in a *real* revolution. The word for "revolution" in German is *Umwälzung*. What it means is a complete overturn—a complete change. The overthrow of King Farouk in Egypt and the succession of President Nasser is an example of a true revolution. It means the destroying of an old system, and its replacement with a new system. Another example is the Algerian revolution, led by Ben Bella; they threw out the French who had been there over 100 years. So how does anybody sound talking about the Negro in America waging some "revolution"? Yes, he is condemning a system—but he's not trying to overturn the system, or to destroy it. The Negro's so-called "revolt" is merely an asking to be *accepted* into the existing system! A *true* Negro revolt might entail, for instance, fighting for separate black states within this country—which several groups and individuals have advocated, long before Elijah Muhammad came along.

When the white man came into this country, he certainly wasn't demonstrating any "non-violence." In fact, the very man whose name symbolizes non-violence here today has stated:

"Our nation was born in genocide when it embraced the doctrine that the original American, the Indian, was an inferior race. Even before there were large numbers of Negroes on our shores, the scar of racial hatred had already disfigured colonial society. From the sixteenth century forward, blood flowed in battles over racial supremacy. We are perhaps the only nation which tried as a matter of national policy to wipe out its indigenous population. Moreover, we elevated that tragic experience into a noble crusade. Indeed, even today we have not permitted ourselves to reject or to feel remorse for this shameful episode. Our literature, our films, our drama, our folklore all exalt it. Our children are still taught to respect the violence which reduced a red-skinned people of an earlier culture into a few fragmented groups herded into impoverished reservations."

"Peaceful coexistence!" That's another one the white man has always been quick to cry. Fine! But what have been the deeds of the white man? During his entire advance through history, he has been waving the banner of Christianity . . . and carrying in his other hand the sword and the flintlock.

You can go right back to the very beginning of Christianity. Catholicism, the genesis of Christianity as we know it to be presently constituted, with its hierarchy, was conceived in Africa—by those whom the Christian church calls "The Desert Fathers." The Christian church became infected with racism when it entered white Europe. The Christian church returned to Africa under the banner of the Cross—conquering, killing, exploiting, pillaging, raping, bullying, beating—and teaching white supremacy. This is how the white man thrust himself into the position of leadership of the world—through the use of naked physical power. And he was totally inadequate spiritually. Mankind's history has proved from one era to another that the true criterion of leadership is spiritual. Men are attracted by spirit. By power, men are *forced*. Love is engendered by spirit. By power, anxieties are created.

I am in agreement one hundred per cent with those racists who say that no government laws ever can *force* brotherhood. The only true world solution today is governments guided by true religion—of the spirit. Here in race-torn America, I am convinced that the Islam religion is desperately needed, particularly by the American black man. The black man needs to reflect that he has been America's most fervent Christian—and where has it gotten him? In fact, in the white man's hands, in the white man's interpretation . . . where has Christianity brought this *world* ?

It has brought the non-white two-thirds of the human population to rebellion. Two-thirds of the human population today is telling the one-third minority white man, "Get out!" And the white man is leaving. And as he leaves, we see the non-white peoples returning in a rush to their original religions, which had been labeled "pagan" by the conquering white man. Only one religion—Islam—had the power to stand and fight the white man's Christianity for a *thousand years!* Only Islam could keep white Christianity at bay.

The Africans are returning to Islam and other indigenous religions. The Asians are returning to being Hindus, Buddhists and Muslims.

As the Christian Crusade once went East, now the Islamic Crusade is going West. With the East—Asia—closed to Christianity, with Africa rapidly being converted to Islam, with Europe rapidly becoming un-Christian, generally today it is accepted that the "Christian" civilization of America—which is propping up the white race around the world—is Christianity's remaining strongest bastion.

Well, if *this* is so—if the so-called "Christianity" now being practiced in America displays the best that world Christianity has left to offer—no one in his right mind should need any much greater proof that very close at hand is the *end* of Christianity.

Are you aware that some Protestant theologians, in their writings, are using the phrase "post-Christian era"—and they mean *now?*

And what is the greatest single reason for this Christian church's failure? It is its failure to combat racism. It is the old "You sow, you reap" story. The Christian church sowed racism—blasphemously; now it reaps racism.

Sunday mornings in this year of grace 1965, imagine the "Christian conscience" of congregations guarded by deacons barring the door to black would-be worshipers, telling them "You can't enter *this* House of God!"

Tell me, if you can, a sadder irony than that St. Augustine, Florida—a city named for the black African saint who saved Catholicism from heresy—was recently the scene of bloody race riots.

I believe that God now is giving the world's so-called "Christian" white society its last opportunity to repent and atone for the crimes of exploiting and enslaving the world's non-white peoples. It is exactly as when God gave Pharaoh a chance to repent. But Pharaoh persisted in his refusal to give justice to those whom he oppressed. And, we know, God finally destroyed Pharaoh.

Is white America really sorry for her crimes against the black people? Does white America have the capacity to repent—and to atone? Does the capacity to repent, to atone, exist in a majority, in one-half, in even one-third of American white society?

Many black men, the victims—in fact most black men—would like to be able to forgive, to forget, the crimes.

But most American white people seem not to have it in them to make any serious atonement—to do justice to the black man.

Indeed, how *can* white society atone for enslaving, for raping, for unmanning, for otherwise brutalizing *millions* of human beings, for centuries? What atonement would the God of Justice demand for the robbery of the black people's labor, their lives, their true identities, their culture, their history—and even their human dignity?

A desegregated cup of coffee, a theater, public toilets—the whole range of hypocritical "integration"—these are not atonement.

After a while in America, I returned abroad—and this time, I spent eighteen weeks in the Middle East and Africa.

The world leaders with whom I had private audiences this time included President Gamal Abdel Nasser, of Egypt; President Julius K. Nyerere, of Tanzania; President Nnamoi Azikiwe, of Nigeria; Osagyefo Dr. Kwame Nkrumah, of Ghana; President Sekou Touré, of Guinea; President Jomo Kenyatta, of Kenya; and Prime Minister Dr. Milton Obote, of Uganda.

I also met with religious leaders—African, Arab, Asian, Muslim, and non-Muslim. And in all of these countries, I talked with Afro-Americans and whites of many professions and backgrounds.

An American white ambassador in one African country was Africa's most respected American ambassador: I'm glad to say that this was told to me by one ranking African leader. We talked for an entire afternoon. Based on what I had heard of him, I had to believe him when he told me that as long as he was on the African continent, he never thought in terms of race, that he dealt with human beings, never noticing their color. He said he was more aware of language differences than of color differences. He said that only when he returned to America would he become aware of color differences.

I told him, "What you are telling me is that it isn't the American white *man* who is a racist, but it's the American political, economic, and social *atmosphere* that automatically nourishes a racist psychology in the white man." He agreed.

We both agreed that American society makes it next to impossible for humans to meet in America and not be conscious of their color differences. And we both agreed that if racism could be removed, America could offer a society where rich and poor could truly live like human beings.

That discussion with the ambassador gave me a new insight—one which I like: that the white man is *not* inherently evil, but America's racist society influences him to act evilly. The society has produced and nourishes a psychology which brings out the lowest, most base part of human beings.

I had a totally different kind of talk with another white man I met in Africa—who, to me, personified exactly what the ambassador and I had discussed. Throughout my trip, I was of course aware that I was under constant surveillance. The agent was a particularly obvious and obnoxious one; I am not sure for what agency, as he never identified it, or I would say it. Anyway, this one finally got under my skin when I found I couldn't seem to eat a meal in the hotel without seeing him somewhere around watching me. You would have thought I was John Dillinger or somebody.

I just got up from my breakfast one morning and walked over to where he was and I told him I knew he was following me, and if he wanted to know anything, why didn't he ask me. He started to give me one of those too-lofty-to-descend-to-you attitudes. I told him then right to his face he was a fool, that he didn't know me, or what I stood for, so that made him one of those people who let somebody else do their thinking; and that no matter what job a man had, at least he ought to be able to think for himself. That stung him; he let me have it.

I was, to hear him tell it, anti-American, un-American, seditious, subversive, and probably Communist. I told him that what he said only proved how little he understood about me. I told him that the only thing the F.B.I, the C.I.A., or anybody else could ever find me guilty of, was being open-minded. I said I was seeking for the truth, and I was trying to weigh—objectively—everything on its own merit. I said what I was against was strait-jacketed thinking, and strait-jacketed societies. I said I respected every man's right to believe whatever his intelligence tells him is intellectually sound, and I expect everyone else to respect my right to believe likewise.

This super-sleuth then got off on my "Black Muslim" religious beliefs. I asked him hadn't his headquarters bothered to brief him—that my attitudes and beliefs were changed? I told him that the Islam I believed in now was the Islam which was taught in Mecca—that there was no God but Allah, and that Muhammad ibn Abdullah who lived in the Holy City of Mecca fourteen hundred years ago was the Last Messenger of Allah.

Almost from the first I had been guessing about something; and I took a chance—and I really shook up that "super-sleuth." From the consistent subjectivity in just about everything he asked and said, I had deduced something, and I told him, "You know, I think you're a Jew with an Anglicized name." His involuntary expression told me I'd hit the button. He asked me how I knew. I told him I'd had so much experience with how Jews would attack me that I usually could identify them. I told him all I held against the Jew was that so many Jews actually were hypocrites in their claim to be friends of the American black man, and it burned me up to be so often called "anti-Semitic" when I spoke things I knew to be the absolute truth about Jews. I told him that, yes, I gave the Jew credit for being among all other whites the most active, and the most vocal, financier, "leader" and "liberal" in the Negro civil rights movement. But I said at the same time I knew that the Jew played these roles for a very careful strategic reason: the more prejudice in America could be focused upon the Negro, then the more the white Gentiles' prejudice would keep diverted off the Jew. I said that to me, one proof that all the civil rights posturing of so many Jews wasn't sincere was that so often in the North the quickest segregationists were Jews themselves. Look at practically everything the black man is trying to "integrate" into for instance; if Jews are not the actual owners, or are not in controlling positions, then they have major stockholdings or they are otherwise in powerful leverage positions—and do they really sincerely exert these influences? No!

And an even clearer proof for me of how Jews truly regard Negroes, I said, was what invariably happened wherever a Negro moved into any white residential neighborhood that was thickly Jewish. Who would always lead the whites' exodus? The Jews! Generally in these situations, some whites stay put—you just notice who they are: they're Irish Catholics, they're Italians; they're rarely ever any Jews. And, ironically, the Jews themselves often still have trouble being "accepted."

Saying this, I know I'll hear "anti-Semitic" from every direction again. Oh, yes! But truth is truth.

Politics dominated the American scene while I was traveling abroad this time. In Cairo and again in Accra, the American press wire services reached me with trans-Atlantic calls, asking whom did I favor, Johnson—or Goldwater?

I said I felt that as far as the American black man was concerned they were both just about the same. I felt that it was for the black man only a question of Johnson, the fox, or Goldwater, the wolf.

"Conservatism" in America's politics means "Let's keep the niggers in their place." And "liberalism" means "Let's keep the *knee*-grows in their place—but tell them we'll treat them a little better; let's fool them more, with more promises." With these choices, I felt that the American black man only needed to choose which one to be eaten by, the "liberal" fox or the "conservative" wolf—because both of them would eat him.

I didn't go for Goldwater any more than for Johnson—except that in a wolf's den, I'd always known exactly where I stood; I'd watch the dangerous wolf closer than I would the smooth, sly fox. The wolf's very growling would keep me alert and fighting him to survive, whereas I *might* be lulled and fooled by the tricky fox. I'll give you an illustration of the fox. When the assassination in Dallas made Johnson President, who was the first person he called for? It was for his best friend, "Dicky"— Richard Russell of Georgia. Civil rights was "a moral issue," Johnson was declaring to everybody—while his best friend was the Southern racist who *led* the civil rights opposition. How would some sheriff sound, declaring himself so against bank robbery—and Jesse James his best friend?

Goldwater as a man, I respected for speaking out his true convictions—something rarely done in politics today. He wasn't whispering to racists and smiling at integrationists. I felt Goldwater wouldn't have risked his unpopular stand without conviction. He flatly told black men he wasn't for them—and there is this to consider: always, the black people have advanced further when they have seen they had to rise up against a system that they clearly saw was outright against them. Under the steady lullabies sung by foxy liberals, the Northern Negro became a beggar. But the Southern Negro, facing the honestly snarling white man, rose up to battle that white man for his freedom— long before it happened in the North.

Anyway, I didn't feel that Goldwater was any better for black men than Johnson, or vice-versa. I wasn't in the United States at election time, but if I had been, I wouldn't have put myself in the position of voting for either candidate for the Presidency, or of recommending to any black man to do so. It has turned out that it's Johnson in the White House—and black votes were a major factor in his winning as decisively as he wanted to. If it had been Goldwater, all I am saying is that the black people would at least have known they were dealing with an honestly growling wolf, rather than a fox who could have them half-digested before they even knew what was happening.

I kept having all kinds of troubles trying to develop the kind of Black Nationalist organization I wanted to build for the American Negro. Why Black Nationalism? Well, in the competitive American society, how can there ever be any white-black solidarity before there is first some black solidarity? If you will remember, in my childhood I had been exposed to the Black Nationalist teachings of Marcus Garvey—which, in fact, I had been told had led to my father's murder. Even when I was a follower of Elijah Muhammad, I had been strongly aware of how the Black Nationalist political, economic and social philosophies had the ability to instill within black men the racial dignity, the incentive, and the confidence that the black race needs today to get up off its knees, and to get on its feet, and get rid of its scars, and to take a stand for itself.

One of the major troubles that I was having in building the organization that I wanted—an all-black organization whose ultimate objective was to help create a society in which there could exist honest white-black brotherhood—was that my earlier public image, my old so-called "Black Muslim" image, kept blocking me. I was trying to gradually reshape that image. I was trying to turn a corner, into a new regard by the public, especially Negroes; I was no less angry than I had been, but at the same time the true brotherhood I had seen in the Holy World had influenced me to recognize that anger can blind human vision.

Every free moment I could find, I did a lot of talking to key people whom I knew around Harlem, and I made a lot of speeches, saying: "True Islam taught me that it takes *all* of the religious, political, economic, psychological, and racial ingredients, or characteristics, to make the Human Family and the Human Society complete.

"Since I learned the *truth* in Mecca, my dearest friends have come to include *all* kinds—some Christians, Jews, Buddhists, Hindus, agnostics, and even atheists! I have friends who are called capitalists, Socialists, and Communists! Some of my friends are moderates, conservatives, extremists—some are even Uncle Toms! My friends today are black, brown, red, yellow, and *white!*"

I said to Harlem street audiences that only when mankind would submit to the One God who created all—only then would mankind even approach the "peace" of which so much *talk* could be heard . . . but toward which so little *action* was seen.

I said that on the American racial level, we had to approach the black man's struggle against the white man's racism as a human problem, that we had to forget hypocritical politics and propaganda. I said that both races, as human beings, had the obligation, the responsibility, of helping to correct America's human problem. The well-meaning white people, I said, had to combat, actively and directly, the racism in other white people. And the black people had to build within themselves much greater awareness that along with equal rights there had to be the bearing of equal responsibilities.

I knew, better than most Negroes, how many white people truly wanted to see American racial problems solved. I knew that many whites were as frustrated as Negroes. I'll bet I got fifty letters some days from white people. The white people in meeting audiences would throng around me, asking me, after I had addressed them somewhere, "What *can* a sincere white person do?"

When I say that here now, it makes me think about that little co-ed I told you about, the one who flew from her New England college down to New York and came up to me in the Nation of Islam's restaurant in Harlem, and I told her that there was "nothing" she could do. I regret that I told her that. I wish that now I knew her name, or where I could telephone her, or write to her, and tell her what I tell white people now when they present themselves as being sincere, and ask me, one way or another, the same thing that she asked.

The first thing I tell them is that at least where my own particular Black Nationalist organization, the Organization of Afro-American Unity, is concerned, they can't *join* us. I have these very deep feelings that white people who want to join black organizations are really just taking the escapist way to salve their consciences. By visibly hovering near us, they are "proving" that they are "with us." But the hard truth is this *isn't* helping to solve America's racist problem. The Negroes aren't the racists. Where the really sincere white people have got to do their "proving" of themselves is not among the black *victims*, but out on the battle lines of where America's racism really *is*—and that's in their own home communities; America's racism is among their own fellow whites. That's where the sincere whites who really mean to accomplish something have got to work.

Aside from that, I mean nothing against any sincere whites when I say that as members of black organizations, generally whites' very presence subtly renders the black organization automatically less effective. Even the best white members will slow down the Negroes' discovery of what they need to do, and particularly of what they can do—for themselves, working by themselves, among their own kind, in their own communities.

I sure don't want to hurt anybody's feelings, but in fact I'll even go so far as to say that I never really trust the kind of white people who are always so anxious to hang around Negroes, or to hang around in Negro communities. I don't trust the kind of whites who love having Negroes always hanging around them. I don't know—this feeling may be a throwback to the years when I was hustling in Harlem and all of those red-faced, drunk whites in the afterhours clubs were always grabbing hold of some Negroes and talking about "I just want you to know you're just as good as I am—" And then they got back in their taxicabs and black limousines and went back downtown to the places where they lived and worked, where no blacks except servants had better get caught. But, anyway, I know that every time that whites join a black organization, you watch, pretty soon the blacks will be leaning on the whites to support it, and before you know it a black may be up front with a title, but the whites, because of their money, are the real controllers.

I tell sincere white people, "Work in conjunction with us—each of us working among our own kind." Let sincere white individuals find all other white people they can who feel as they do—and let them form their own all-white groups, to work trying to convert other white people who are thinking and acting so racist. Let sincere whites go and teach non-violence to white people!

We will completely respect our white co-workers. They will deserve every credit. We will give them every credit. We will meanwhile be working among our own kind, in our own black communities—showing and teaching black men in ways that only other black men can—that the black man has got to help himself. Working separately, the sincere white people and sincere black people actually will be working together.

In our mutual sincerity we might be able to show a road to the salvation of America's very soul. It can only be salvaged if human rights and dignity, in full, are extended to black men. Only such real, meaningful actions as those which are sincerely motivated from a deep sense of humanism and moral responsibility can get at the basic causes that produce the racial explosions in America today. Otherwise, the racial explosions are only going to grow worse. Certainly nothing is ever going to be solved by throwing upon me and other so-called black "extremists" and "demagogues" the blame for the racism that is in America.

Sometimes, I have dared to dream to myself that one day, history may even say that my voice—which disturbed the white man's smugness, and his arrogance, and his complacency—that my voice helped to save America from a grave, possibly even a fatal catastrophe.

The goal has always been the same, with the approaches to it as different as mine and Dr. Martin Luther King's non-violent marching, that dramatizes the brutality and the evil of the white man against defenseless blacks. And in the racial climate of this country today, it is anybody's guess which of the "extremes" in approach to the black man's problems might *personally* meet a fatal catastrophe first—"non-violent" Dr. King, or so-called "violent" me.

Anything I do today, I regard as urgent. No man is given but so much time to accomplish whatever is his life's work. My life in particular never has stayed fixed in one position for very long. You have seen how throughout my life, I have often known unexpected drastic changes.

I am only facing the facts when I know that any moment of any day, or any night, could bring me death. This is particularly true since the last trip that I made abroad. I have seen the nature of things that are happening, and I have heard things from sources which are reliable.

To speculate about dying doesn't disturb me as it might some people. I never have felt that I would live to become an old man. Even before I was a Muslim—when I was a hustler in the ghetto jungle, and then a criminal in prison, it always stayed on my mind that I would die a violent death. In fact, it runs in my family. My father and most of his brothers died by violence—my father because of what he believed in. To come right down to it, if I take the kind of things in which I believe, then add to that the kind of temperament that I have, plus the one hundred per cent dedication I have to whatever I believe in—these are ingredients which make it just about impossible for me to die of old age.

I have given to this book so much of whatever time I have because I feel, and I hope, that if I honestly and fully tell my life's account, read objectively it might prove to be a testimony of some social value.

I think that an objective reader may see how in the society to which I was exposed as a black youth here in America, for me to wind up in a prison was really just about inevitable. It happens to so many thousands of black youth.

I think that an objective reader may see how when I heard "The white man is the devil," when I played back what had been my own experiences, it was inevitable that I would respond positively; then the next twelve years of my life were devoted and dedicated to propagating that phrase among the black people.

I think, I hope, that the objective reader, in following my life—the life of only one ghetto-created Negro—may gain a better picture and understanding than he has previously had of the black ghettoes which are shaping the lives and the thinking of almost all of the 22 million Negroes who live in America.

Thicker each year in these ghettoes is the kind of teen-ager that I was—with the wrong kinds of heroes, and the wrong kinds of influences. I am not saying that all of them become the kind of parasite that I was. Fortunately, by far most do not. But still, the small fraction who do add up to an annual total of more and more costly, dangerous youthful criminals. The F.B.I. not long ago released a report of a shocking rise in crime each successive year since the end of World War II—ten to twelve per cent each year. The report did not say so in so many words, but I am saying that the majority of that crime increase is annually spawned in the black ghettoes which the American racist society permits to exist. In the 1964 "long, hot summer" riots in major cities across the United States, the socially disinherited black ghetto youth were always at the forefront.

In this year, 1965, I am certain that more—and worse—riots are going to erupt, in yet more cities, in spite of the conscience-salving Civil Rights Bill. The reason is that the *cause* of these riots, the racist malignancy in America, has been too long un-attended.

I believe that it would be almost impossible to find anywhere in America a black man who has lived further down in the mud of human society than I have; or a black man who has been any more ignorant than I have been; or a black man who has suffered more anguish during his life than I have. But it is only after the deepest darkness that the greatest joy can come; it is only after slavery and prison that the sweetest appreciation of freedom can come.

For the freedom of my 22 million black brothers and sisters here in America, I do believe that I have fought the best that I knew how, and the best that I could, with the shortcomings that I have had. I know that my shortcomings are many.

My greatest lack has been, I believe, that I don't have the kind of academic education I wish I had been able to get—to have been a lawyer, perhaps. I do believe that I might have made a good lawyer. I have always loved verbal battle, and challenge. You can believe me that if I had the time right now, I would not be one bit ashamed to go back into any New York City public school and start where I left off at the ninth grade, and go on through a degree. Because I don't begin to be academically equipped for so many of the interests that I have. For instance, I love languages. I wish I were an accomplished linguist. I don't know anything more frustrating than to be around people talking something you can't understand. Especially when they are people who look just like you. In Africa, I heard original mother tongues, such as Hausa, and Swahili, being spoken, and there I was standing like some little boy, waiting for someone to tell me what had been said; I never will forget how ignorant I felt.

Aside from the basic African dialects, I would try to learn Chinese, because it looks as if Chinese will be the most powerful political language of the future. And already I have begun studying Arabic, which I think is going to be the most powerful spiritual language of the future.

I would just like to *study*. I mean ranging study, because I have a wide-open mind. I'm interested in almost any subject you can mention. I know this is the reason I have come to really like, as individuals, some of the hosts of radio or television panel programs I have been on, and to respect their minds—because even if they have been almost steadily in disagreement with me on the race issue, they still have kept their minds open and objective about the truths of things happening in this world. Irv Kupcinet in Chicago, and Barry Farber, Barry Gray and Mike Wallace in New York—people like them. They also let me see that they respected my mind—in a way I know they never realized. The way I knew was that often they would invite my opinion on subjects off the race issue. Sometimes, after the programs, we would sit around and talk about all kinds of things, current events and other things, for an hour or more. You see, most whites, even when they credit a Negro with some intelligence, will still feel that all he can talk about is the race issue; most whites never feel that Negroes can contribute anything to other areas of thought, and ideas. You just notice how rarely you will ever hear whites asking any Negroes what they think about the problem of world health, or the space race to land men on the moon.

Every morning when I wake up, now, I regard it as having another borrowed day. In any city, wherever I go, making speeches, holding meetings of my organization, or attending to other business, black men are watching every move I make, awaiting their chance to kill me. I have said publicly many times that I know that they have their orders. Anyone who chooses not to believe what I am saying doesn't know the Muslims in the Nation of Islam.

But I am also blessed with faithful followers who are, I believe, as dedicated to me as I once was to Mr. Elijah Muhammad. Those who would hunt a man need to remember that a jungle also contains those who hunt the hunters.

I know, too, that I could suddenly die at the hands of some white racists. Or I could die at the hands of some Negro hired by the white man. Or it could be some brainwashed Negro acting on his own idea that by eliminating me he would be helping out the white man, because I talk about the white man the way I do.

Anyway, now, each day I live as if I am already dead, and I

tell you what I would like for you to do. When I *am* dead—I say it that way because from the things I *know*, I do not expect to live long enough to read this book in its finished form—I want you to just watch and see if I'm not right in what I say: that the white man, in his press, is going to identify me with "hate."

He will make use of me dead, as he has made use of me alive, as a convenient symbol of "hatred"—and that will help him to escape facing the truth that all I have been doing is holding up a mirror to reflect, to show, the history of unspeakable crimes that his race has committed against my race.

You watch. I will be labeled as, at best, an "irresponsible" black man. I have always felt about this accusation that the black "leader" whom white men consider to be "responsible" is invariably the black "leader" who never gets any results. You only get action as a black man if you are regarded by the white man as "irresponsible." In fact, this much I had learned when I was just a little boy. And since I have been some kind of a "leader" of black people here in the racist society of America, I have been more reassured each time the white man resisted me, or attacked me harder—because each time made me more certain that I was on the right track in the American black man's best interests. The racist white man's opposition automatically made me know that I did offer the black man something worthwhile.

Yes, I have cherished my "demagogue" role. I know that societies often have killed the people who have helped to change those societies. And if I can die having brought any light, having exposed any meaningful truth that will help to destroy the racist cancer that is malignant in the body of America—then, all of the credit is due to Allah. Only the mistakes have been mine.

ALEX HALEY

EPILOGUE

During nineteen fifty-nine, when the public was becoming aware of the Muslims after the New York telecast "The Hate That Hate Produced," I was in San Francisco, about to retire after twenty years in the U.S. Coast Guard. A friend returned from a visit to her Detroit home and told me of a startling "black man's" religion, "The Nation of Islam," to which, to her surprise, her entire family was converted. I listened with incredulity to how a "mad scientist Mr. Yacub" had genetically "grafted" the white race from an original black people. The organization's leader was described as "The Honorable Elijah Muhammad" and a "Minister Malcolm X" was apparently chief of staff.

When I entered a civilian writing career in New York City, I collected, around Harlem, a good deal of provocative material and then proposed an article about the cult to the *Reader's Digest*. Visiting the Muslim restaurant in Harlem, I asked how I could meet Minister Malcolm X, who was pointed out talking in a telephone booth right behind me. Soon he came out, a gangling, tall, reddish-brownskinned fellow, at that time thirty-five years old; when my purpose was made known, he bristled, his eyes skewering me from behind the horn-rimmed glasses. "You're another one of the white man's tools sent to spy!" he accused me sharply. I said I had a legitimate writing assignment and showed him my letter from the magazine stating that an objective article was wanted, one that would balance what the Muslims said of themselves and what their attackers said about them. Malcolm X snorted that no white man's promise was worth the paper it was on; he would need time to decide if he

390

would cooperate or not. Meanwhile, he suggested that I could attend some of the Harlem Temple Number 7 meetings ("temples" have since been renamed "mosques") which were open to non-Muslim Negroes.

Around the Muslim's restaurant, I met some of the converts, all of them neatly dressed and almost embarrassingly polite. Their manners and miens reflected the Spartan personal discipline the organization demanded, and none of them would utter anything but Nation of Islam clichés. Even excellent weather was viewed as a blessing from Allah, with corollary credit due to "The Honorable Elijah Muhammad."

Finally, Minister Malcolm X told me that he would not take personal responsibility. He said that I should talk about an article with Mr. Muhammad personally. I expressed willingness, an appointment was made, and I flew to Chicago. The slightly built, shy-acting, soft-voiced Mr. Muhammad invited me to dinner with his immediate family in his mansion. I was aware that I was being carefully sized up while he talked primarily of F.B.I. and Internal Revenue Service close surveillance of his organization, and of a rumored forthcoming Congressional probe. "But I have no fear of any of them; I have all that I need—the truth," Mr. Muhammad said. The subject of my writing an article somehow never got raised, but Malcolm X proved far more cooperative when I returned.

He would sit with me at a white-topped table in the Muslim restaurant and answer guardedly any questions I asked between constant interruptions by calls from the New York press in the telephone booth. When I asked if I could see Muslim activities in some other cities, he arranged with other ministers for me to attend meetings at temples in Detroit, Washington, and Philadelphia.

My article entitled "Mr. Muhammad Speaks" appeared in early 1960, and it was the first featured magazine notice of the phenomenon. A letter quickly came from Mr. Muhammad appreciating that the article kept my promise to be objective, and Malcolm X telephoned similar compliments. About this time, Dr. C. Eric Lincoln's book *The Black Muslims in America* was published and the Black Muslims became a subject of growing interest. During 1961 and 1962, the *Saturday Evening Post* teamed me with a white writer, Al Balk, to do an article; next I did a personal interview of Malcolm X for *Playboy* magazine, which had promised to print verbatim whatever response he made to my questions. During that interview of several days' duration, Malcolm X repeatedly exclaimed, after particularly blistering anti-Christian or anti-white statements: "You know that devil's not going to print that!" He was very much taken aback when *Playboy* kept its word.

Malcolm X began to warm up to me somewhat. He was most aware of the national periodicals' power, and he had come to regard me, if still suspiciously, as one avenue of access. Occasionally now he began to telephone me advising me of some radio, television, or personal speaking appearance he was about to make, or he would invite me to attend some Black Muslim bazaar or other public affair.

I was in this stage of relationship with the Malcolm X who often described himself on the air as "the angriest black man in America" when in early 1963 my agent brought me together with a publisher whom the *Playboy* interview had given the idea of the autobiography of Malcolm X. I was asked if I felt I could get the now nationally known firebrand to consent to telling the intimate details of his entire life. I said I didn't know, but I would ask him. The editor asked me if I could sketch the likely highlights of such a book, and as I commenced talking, I realized how little I knew about the man personally, despite all my interviews. I said that the question had made me aware of how careful Malcolm X had always been to play himself down and to play up his leader Elijah Muhammad.

All that I knew, really, I said, was that I had heard Malcolm X refer in passing to his life of crime and prison before he became a Black Muslim; that several times he had told me: "You wouldn't believe my past," and that I had heard others say that at one time he had peddled dope and women and committed armed robberies.

I knew that Malcolm X had an almost fanatical obsession about time. "I have less patience with someone who doesn't wear a watch than with anyone else, for this type is not time-conscious," he had once told me. "In all our deeds, the proper value and respect for time determines success or failure." I knew how the Black Muslim membership was said to increase wherever Malcolm X lectured, and I knew his pride that Negro prisoners in most prisons were discovering the Muslim religion as he had when he was a convict. I knew he professed to eat only what a Black Muslim (preferably his wife Betty) had cooked and he drank innumerable cups of coffee which he lightened with cream, commenting wryly, "Coffee is the only thing I like integrated." Over our luncheon table, I told the editor and my agent how Malcolm X could unsettle non-Muslims—as, for instance, once when he offered to drive me to a subway, I began to light a cigarette and he drily observed, "That would make you the first person ever to smoke in this automobile."

Malcolm X gave me a startled look when I asked him if he would tell his life story for publication. It was one of the few times I have ever seen him uncertain. "I will have to give a book a lot of thought," he finally said. Two days later, he telephoned me to meet him again at the Black Muslim restaurant. He said, "I'll agree. I think my life story may help people to appreciate better how Mr. Muhammad salvages black people. But I don't want my motives for this misinterpreted by anybody—the Nation of Islam must get every penny that might come to me." Of course, Mr. Muhammad's agreement would be necessary, and I would have to ask Mr. Muhammad myself.

So I flew again to see Mr. Muhammad, but this time to Phoenix, Arizona, where the Nation of Islam had bought him the house in the hot, dry climate that relieved his severe bronchial condition. He and I talked alone this time. He told me how his organization had come far with largely uneducated Muslims and that truly giant strides for the black man could be made if his organization were aided by some of the talents which were available in the black race. He said, "And one of our worst needs is writers"—but he did not press me to answer. He suddenly began coughing, and rapidly grew worse and worse until I rose from my seat and went to him, alarmed, but he waved me away, gasping that he would be all right. Between gasps, he told me he felt that "Allah approves" the book. He said, "Malcolm is one of my most outstanding ministers." After arranging for his chauffeur to return me to the Phoenix airport, Mr. Muhammad quickly bade me good-bye and rushed from the room coughing.

Back East, Malcolm X carefully read and then signed the publication contract, and he withdrew from his wallet a piece of paper filled with his sprawling longhand. "This is this book's dedication," he said. I read: "This book I dedicate to The Honorable Elijah Muhammad, who found me here in America in the muck and mire of the filthiest civilization and society on this earth, and pulled me out, cleaned me up, and stood me on my feet, and made me the man that I am today."

The contract provided that all monies accruing to Malcolm X "shall be made payable by the agent to 'Muhammad's Mosque No. 2,' " but Malcolm X felt this was insufficient. He dictated to me a letter to type for his signature, which I did: "Any and all monies representing my contracted share of the financial returns should be made payable by the literary agent to Muhammad's Mosque No. 2. These payments should be mailed to the following address: Mr. Raymond Sharrieff, 4847 Woodlawn Avenue, Chicago 15, Illinois."

Another letter was dictated, this one an agreement between him and me: "Nothing can be in this book's manuscript that I didn't say, and nothing can be left out that I want in it."

In turn, I asked Malcolm X to sign for me a personal pledge that however busy he was, he would give me a priority quota of his time for the planned 100,000-word "as told to" book which would detail his entire life. And months later, in a time of strain between us, I asked for—and he gave—his permission that at the end of the book I could write comments of my own about him which would not be subject to his review.

Malcolm X promptly did begin to pay me two- and three-hour visits, parking his blue Oldsmobile outside the working studio I then had in Greenwich Village. He always arrived around nine or ten at night carrying his flat tan leather briefcase which along with his scholarly look gave him a resemblance to a hard-working lawyer. Inevitably, he was tired after his long busy day, and sometimes he was clearly exhausted.

We got off to a very poor start. To use a word he liked, I think both of us were a bit "spooky." Sitting right there and staring at me was the fiery Malcolm X who could be as acid toward Negroes who angered him as he was against whites in general. On television, in press conferences, and at Muslim rallies, I had heard him bitterly attack other Negro writers as "Uncle Toms," "yard Negroes," "black men in white clothes." And there I sat staring at him, proposing to spend a year plumbing his innermost secrets when he had developed a near phobia for secrecy during his years of crime and his years in the Muslim hierarchy. My twenty years in military service and my Christian religious persuasion didn't help, either; he often jeered publicly at these affiliations for Negroes. And although he now would indirectly urge me to write for national magazines about the Muslims, he had told me several times, in various ways, that "you blacks with professional abilities of any kind will one of these days wake up and find out that you must unite under the leadership of The Honorable Elijah Muhammad for your own salvation." Malcolm X was also convinced that the F.B.I. had "bugged" my studio; he probably suspected that it may even have been done with my cooperation. For the first several weeks, he never entered the room where we worked without exclaiming, "Testing, testing—one, two, three. . . ."

Tense incidents occurred. One night a white friend was in the studio when Malcolm X arrived a little earlier than anticipated, and they passed each other in the corridor. Malcolm X's manner during all of that session suggested that his worst doubts had been confirmed. Another time when Malcolm X sat haranguing me about the glories of the Muslim organization, he was gesturing with his passport in his hand; he saw that I was trying to read its perforated number and suddenly he thrust the passport toward me, his neck flushed reddish: "Get the number straight, but it won't be anything the white devil doesn't already know. He issued me the passport."

For perhaps a month I was afraid we weren't going to get any book. Malcolm X was still stiffly addressing me as "Sir!" and my notebook contained almost nothing but Black Muslim philosophy, praise of Mr. Muhammad, and the "evils" of "the white devil." He would bristle when I tried to urge him that the proposed book was *his* life. I was thinking that I might have to advise the publisher that I simply couldn't seem to get through to my subject when the first note of hope occurred. I had noticed that while Malcolm X was talking, he often simultaneously scribbled with his red-ink ball-point pen on any handy paper. Sometimes it was the margin of a newspaper he brought in, sometimes it was on index cards that he carried in the back of a small, red-backed appointment book. I began leaving two white paper napkins by him every time I served him more coffee, and the ruse worked when he sometimes scribbled on the napkins, which I retrieved when he left. Some examples are these:

"Here lies a YM, killed by a BM, fighting for the WM, who killed all the RM." (Decoding that wasn't difficult, knowing Malcolm X. "YM" was for yellow man, "BM" for black man, "WM" for white man, and "RM" was for red man.)

"Nothing ever happened without cause. Cause BM condition WM won't face. WM obsessed with hiding his guilt."

"If Christianity had asserted itself in Germany, six million Jews would have lived."

"WM so quick to tell BM 'Look what I have done for you!' No! Look what you have done *to* us!"

"BM dealing with WM who put our eyes out, now he condemns us because we cannot see."

"Only persons really changed history those who changed men's thinking about themselves. Hitler as well as Jesus, Stalin as well as Buddha . . . Hon. Elijah Muhammad. . . ."

It was through a clue from one of the scribblings that finally I cast a bait that Malcolm X took. "Woman who cries all the time is only because she knows she can get away with it," he had scribbled. I somehow raised the subject of women. Suddenly, between sips of coffee and further scribbling and doodling, he vented his criticisms and skepticisms of women. "You never can fully trust any woman," he said. "I've got the only one I ever met whom I would trust seventy-five per cent. I've told her that," he said. "I've told her like I tell you I've seen too many men destroyed by their wives, or their women.

"I don't *completely* trust anyone," he went on, "not even myself. I have seen too many men destroy themselves. Other people I trust from not at all to highly, like The Honorable Elijah Muhammad." Malcolm X looked squarely at me. "You I trust about twenty-five per cent."

Trying to keep Malcolm X talking, I mined the woman theme for all it was worth. Triumphantly, he exclaimed, "Do you know why Benedict Arnold turned traitor—a woman!" He said, "Whatever else a woman is, I don't care who the woman is, it starts with her being vain. I'll prove it, something you can do anytime you want, and I know what I'm talking about, I've done it. You think of the hardest-looking, meanest-acting woman you know, one of those women who never smiles. Well, every day you see that woman you look her right in the eyes and tell her 'I think you're beautiful,' and you watch what happens. The first day she may curse you out, the second day, too—but you watch, you keep on, after a while one day she's going to start smiling just as soon as you come in sight.''

When Malcolm X left that night, I retrieved napkin scribblings that further documented how he could be talking about one thing and thinking of something else:

''Negroes have too much righteousness. WM says, 'I want this piece of land, how do I get those couple of thousand BM on it off?' ''

''I have wife who understands, or even if she doesn't she at least pretends.''

''BM struggle never gets open support from abroad it needs unless BM first forms own united front.''

''Sit down, talk with people with brains I respect, all of us want same thing, do some brainstorming.''

''Would be shocking to reveal names of the BM leaders who have secretly met with THEM.'' (The capitalized letters stood for The Honorable Elijah Muhammad.)

Then one night, Malcolm X arrived nearly out on his feet from fatigue. For two hours, he paced the floor delivering a tirade against Negro leaders who were attacking Elijah Muhammad and himself. I don't know what gave me the inspiration to say once when he paused for breath, ''I wonder if you'd tell me something about your mother?''

Abruptly he quit pacing, and the look he shot at me made me sense that somehow the chance question had hit him. When I look back at it now, I believe I must have caught him so physically weak that his defenses were vulnerable.

Slowly, Malcolm X began to talk, now walking in a tight circle. ''She was always standing over the stove, trying to stretch whatever we had to eat. We stayed so hungry that we were dizzy. I remember the color of dresses she used to wear—they were a kind of faded-out gray. . . .'' And he kept on talking until dawn, so tired that the big feet would often almost stumble in their pacing. From this stream-of-consciousness reminiscing I finally got out of him the foundation for this book's beginning chapters, ''Nightmare'' and ''Mascot.'' After that night, he never again hesitated to tell me even the most intimate details of his personal life, over the next two years. His talking about his mother triggered something.

Malcolm X's mood ranged from somber to grim as he recalled his childhood. I remember his making a great point of how he learned what had been a cardinal awareness of his ever since: "It's the hinge that squeaks that gets the grease." When his narration reached his moving to Boston to live with his half-sister Ella, Malcolm X began to laugh about how "square" he had been in the ghetto streets. "Why, I'm telling you things I haven't thought about since then!" he would exclaim. Then it was during recalling the early Harlem days that Malcolm X really got carried away. One night, suddenly, wildly, he jumped up from his chair and, incredibly, the fearsome black demagogue was scat-singing and popping his fingers, "re-bop-de-bop-blap-blam—" and then grabbing a vertical pipe with one hand (as the girl partner) he went jubilantly lindy-hopping around, his coattail and the long legs and the big feet flying as they had in those Harlem days. And then almost as suddenly, Malcolm X caught himself and sat back down, and for the rest of that session he was decidedly grumpy. Later on in the Harlem narrative, he grew somber again. "The only thing I considered wrong was what I got caught doing wrong. I had a jungle mind, I was living in a jungle, and everything I did was done by instinct to survive." But he stressed that he had no regrets about his crimes, "because it was all a result of what happens to thousands upon thousands of black men in the white man's Christian world."

His enjoyment resumed when the narrative entered his prison days. "Let me tell you how I'd get those white devil convicts and the guards, too, to do anything I wanted. I'd whisper to them, 'If you don't, I'll start a rumor that you're really a light Negro just passing as white.' That shows you what the white devil thinks about the black man. He'd rather die than be thought a Negro!" He told me about the reading he had been able to do in prison: "I didn't know what I was doing, but just by instinct I liked the books with intellectual vitamins." And another time: "In the hectic pace of the world today, there is no time for meditation, or for deep thought. A prisoner has time that he can put to good use. I'd put prison second to college as the best place for a man to go if he needs to do some thinking. If he's *motivated*, in prison he can change his life.''

Yet another time, Malcolm X reflected, ''Once a man has been to prison, he never looks at himself or at other people the same again. The 'squares' out here whose boat has been in smooth waters all the time turn up their noses at an ex-con. But an ex-con can keep his head up when the 'squares' sink.''

He scribbled that night (I kept both my notebooks and the paper napkins dated): ''This WM created and dropped A-bomb on non-whites; WM now calls 'Red' and lives in fear of other WM he knows may bomb us.''

Also: ''Learn wisdom from the pupil of the eye that looks upon all things and yet to self is blind. Persian poet.''

At intervals, Malcolm X would make a great point of stressing to me, ''Now, I don't want anything in this book to make it sound that I think I'm somebody important.'' I would assure him that I would try not to, and that in any event he would be checking the manuscript page by page, and ultimately the galley proofs. At other times, he would end an attack upon the white man and, watching me take the notes, exclaim. ''That devil's not going to print that, I don't care what he says!'' I would point out that the publishers had made a binding contract and had paid a sizable sum in advance. Malcolm X would say, ''You trust them, and I don't. You studied what he wanted you to learn about him in schools, I studied him in the streets and in prison, where you see the truth.''

Experiences which Malcolm X had had during a day could flavor his interview mood. The most wistful, tender anecdotes generally were told on days when some incident had touched him. Once, for instance, he told me that he had learned that a Harlem couple, not Black Muslims, had named their newborn son ''Malcolm'' after him. ''What do you know about *that?*'' he kept exclaiming. And that was the night he went back to his own boyhood again and this time recalled how he used to lie on his back on Hector's Hill and think. That night, too: ''I'll never forget the day they elected me the class president. A girl named Audrey Slaugh, whose father owned a car repair shop, nominated me. And a boy named James Cotton seconded the nomination. The teacher asked me to leave the room while the class voted. When I returned I was the class president. I couldn't believe it.''

Any interesting book which Malcolm X had read could get him going about his love of books. "People don't realize how a man's whole life can be changed by *one* book." He came back again and again to the books that he had studied when in prison. "Did you ever read *The Loom of Language?*" he asked me and I said I hadn't. "You should. Philology, it's a tough science— all about how words can be recognized, no matter where you find them. Now, you take 'Caesar,' it's Latin, in Latin it's pronounced like 'Kaiser,' with a hard C. But we anglicize it by pronouncing a soft C. The Russians say 'Czar' and mean the same thing. Another Russian dialect says 'Tsar.' Jakob Grimm was one of the foremost philologists, I studied his 'Grimm's Law' in prison—all about consonants. Philology is related to the science of etymology, dealing in root words. I dabbled in both of them.''

When I turn that page in my notebook, the next bears a note that Malcolm X had telephoned me saying "I'm going to be out of town for a few days." I assumed that as had frequently been the case before, he had speaking engagements or other Muslim business to attend somewhere and I was glad for the respite in which to get my notes separated under the chapter headings they would fit. But when Malcolm X returned this time, he reported triumphantly, "I have something to tell you that will surprise you. Ever since we discussed my mother, I've been thinking about her. I realized that I had blocked her out of my mind—it was just unpleasant to think about her having been twenty-some years in that mental hospital." He said, "I don't want to take the credit. It was really my sister Yvonne who thought it might be possible to get her out. Yvonne got my brothers Wilfred, Wesley and Philbert together, and I went out there, too. It was Philbert who really handled it.

"It made me face something about myself," Malcolm X said. "My mind had closed about our mother. I simply didn't feel the problem could be solved, so I had shut it out. I had built up subconscious defenses. The white man does this. He shuts out of his mind, and he builds up subconscious defenses against anything he doesn't want to face up to. I've just become aware how closed my mind was now that I've opened it up again.

That's one of the characteristics I don't like about myself. If I meet a problem I feel I can't solve, I shut it out. I make believe that it doesn't exist. But it exists."

It was my turn to be deeply touched. Not long afterward, he was again away for a few days. When he returned this time, he said that at his brother Philbert's home, "we had dinner with our mother for the first time in all those years!" He said, "She's sixty-six, and her memory is better than mine and she looks young and healthy. She has more of her teeth than those who were instrumental in sending her to the institution."

When something had angered Malcolm X during the day, his face would be flushed redder when he visited me, and he generally would spend much of the session lashing out bitterly. When some Muslims were shot by Los Angeles policemen, one of them being killed, Malcolm X, upon his return from a trip he made there, was fairly apoplectic for a week. It had been in this mood that he had made, in Los Angeles, the statement which caused him to be heavily censured by members of both races. "I've just heard some good news!"—referring to a plane crash at Orly Field in Paris in which thirty-odd white Americans, mostly from Atlanta, Georgia, had been killed instantly. (Malcolm X never publicly recanted this statement, to my knowledge, but much later he said to me simply, "That's one of the things I wish I had never said.")

Anytime the name of the present Federal Judge Thurgood Marshall was raised, Malcolm X still practically spat fire in memory of what the judge had said years before when he was the N.A.A.C.P. chief attorney: "The Muslims are run by a bunch of thugs organized from prisons and jails and financed, I am sure, by some Arab group." The only time that I have ever heard Malcolm X use what might be construed as a curse word, it was a "hell" used in response to a statement that Dr. Martin Luther King made that Malcolm X's talk brought "misery upon Negroes." Malcolm X exploded to me, "How in the hell can my talk do this? It's always a Negro responsible, not what the white man does!" The "extremist" or "demagogue" accusation invariably would burn Malcolm X. "Yes, I'm an extremist. The black race here in North America is in extremely bad condition. You show me a black man who isn't an extremist and I'll show you one who needs psychiatric attention!"

Once when he said, "Aristotle shocked people. Charles Darwin outraged people. Aldous Huxley scandalized millions!" Malcolm X immediately followed the statement with "Don't print that, people would think I'm trying to link myself with them." Another time, when something provoked him to exclaim, "These Uncle Toms make me think about how the Prophet Jesus was criticized in his own country!" Malcolm X promptly got up and silently took my notebook, tore out that page and crumpled it and put it into his pocket, and he was considerably subdued during the remainder of that session.

I remember one time we talked and he showed me a newspaper clipping reporting where a Negro baby had been bitten by a rat. Malcolm X said, "Now, just read that, just think of that a minute! Suppose it was *your* child! Where's that slumlord—on some beach in Miami!" He continued fuming throughout our interview. I did not go with him when later that day he addressed a Negro audience in Harlem and an incident occurred which Helen Dudar reported in the *New York Post*.

"Malcolm speaking in Harlem stared down at one of the white reporters present, the only whites admitted to the meeting, and went on, 'Now, there's a reporter who hasn't taken a note in half an hour, but as soon as I start talking about the Jews, he's busy taking notes to prove that I'm anti-Semitic.'

"Behind the reporter, a male voice spoke up, 'Kill the bastard, kill them all.' The young man, in his unease, smiled nervously and Malcolm jeered, 'Look at him laugh. He's really not laughing, he's just laughing with his teeth.' An ugly tension curled the edges of the atmosphere. Then Malcolm went on: 'The white man doesn't know how to laugh. He just shows his teeth. But *we* know how to laugh. We laugh deep down, from the bottom up.' The audience laughed, deep down, from the bottom up and, as suddenly as Malcolm had stirred it, so, skillfully and swiftly, he deflected it. It had been at once a masterful and shabby performance."

I later heard somewhere, or read, that Malcolm X telephoned an apology to the reporter. But this was the kind of evidence which caused many close observers of the Malcolm X phenomenon to declare in absolute seriousness that he was the only

Negro in America who could either start a race riot—or stop one. When I once quoted this to him, tacitly inviting his comment, he told me tartly, "I don't know if I could start one. I don't know if I'd want to stop one." It was the kind of statement he relished making.

Over the months, I had gradually come to establish something of a telephone acquaintance with Malcolm X's wife, whom I addressed as "Sister Betty," as I had heard the Muslims do. I admired how she ran a home, with, then, three small daughters, and still managed to take all of the calls which came for Malcolm X, surely as many calls as would provide a job for an average switchboard operator. Sometimes when he was with me, he would telephone home and spend as much as five minutes rapidly jotting on a pad the various messages which had been left for him.

Sister Betty, generally friendly enough on the phone with me, sometimes would exclaim in spontaneous indignation, "The man never gets any *sleep!*" Malcolm X rarely put in less than an 18-hour workday. Often when he had left my studio at four A.M. and a 40-minute drive lay between him and home in East Elmhurst, Long Island, he had asked me to telephone him there at nine A.M. Usually this would be when he wanted me to accompany him somewhere, and he was going to tell me, after reviewing his commitments, when and where he wanted me to meet him. (There were times when I didn't get an awful lot of sleep, myself.) He was always accompanied, either by some of his Muslim colleagues like James 67X (the 67th man named "James" who had joined Harlem's Mosque Number 7), or Charles 37X, or by me, but he never asked me to be with him when they were. I went with him to college and university lectures, to radio and television stations for his broadcasts, and to public appearances in a variety of situations and locations.

If we were driving somewhere, motorists along the highway would wave to Malcolm X, the faces of both whites and Negroes spontaneously aglow with the wonderment that I had seen evoked by other "celebrities." No few airline hostesses had come to know him, because he flew so much; they smiled prettily at him, he was in turn the essence of courtly gentlemanliness, and inevitably the word spread and soon an unusual flow of bathroom traffic would develop, passing where he sat. Whenever we arrived at our destination, it became familiar to hear "There's Malcolm X!" *"Where?"* "The tall one." Passers-by of both races stared at him. A few of both races, more Negroes than whites, would speak or nod to him in greeting. A high percentage of white people were visibly uncomfortable in his presence, especially within the confines of small areas, such as in elevators. "I'm the only black man they've ever been close to who they know speaks the *truth* to them," Malcolm X once explained to me. "It's their guilt that upsets them, not me." He said another time, "The white man is afraid of truth. The truth takes the white man's breath and drains his strength—you just watch his face get red anytime you tell him a little truth."

There was something about this man when he was in a room with people. He commanded the room, whoever else was present. Even out of doors; once I remember in Harlem he sat on a speaker's stand between Congressman Adam Clayton Powell and the former Manhattan Borough President Hulan Jack, and when the street rally was over the crowd focus was chiefly on Malcolm X. I remember another time that we had gone by railway from New York City to Philadelphia where he appeared in the Philadelphia Convention Hall on the radio station WCAU program of Ed Harvey. "You are the man who has said 'All Negroes are angry and I am the angriest of all'; is that correct?" asked Harvey, on the air, introducing Malcolm X, and as Malcolm X said crisply, "That quote is correct!" the gathering crowd of bystanders stared at him, riveted.

We had ridden to Philadelphia in reserved parlor car seats. "I can't get caught on a coach, I could get into trouble on a coach," Malcolm X had said. Walking to board the parlor car, we had passed a dining car toward which he jerked his head, "I used to work on that thing." Riding to our destination, he conversationally told me that the F.B.I. had tried to bribe him for information about Elijah Muhammad; that he wanted me to be sure and read a new book, *Crisis in Black and White* by Charles Silberman—"one of the very few white writers I know with the courage to tell his kind the truth"; and he asked me to make a note to please telephone the *New York Post*'s feature writer Helen Dudar and tell her he thought very highly of her recent series—he did not want to commend her directly.

After the Ed Harvey Show was concluded, we took the train to return to New York City. The parlor car, packed with businessmen behind their newspapers, commuting homeward after their workdays, was electric with Malcolm X's presence. After the white-jacketed Negro porter had made several trips up and down the aisle, he was in the middle of another trip when Malcolm X *sotto-voced* in my ear, "He used to work with me, I forget his name, we worked right on this very train together. He knows it's me. He's trying to make up his mind what to do." The porter went on past us, poker-faced. But when he came through again, Malcolm X suddenly leaned forward from his seat, smiling at the porter. "Why, sure, I know who you are!" the porter suddenly said, loudly. "You washed dishes right on this train! I was just telling some of the fellows you were in my car here. We all follow you!"

The tension on the car could have been cut with a knife. Then, soon, the porter returned to Malcolm X, his voice expansive. "One of our guests would like to meet you." Now a young, clean-cut white man rose and came up, his hand extended, and Malcolm X rose and shook the proffered hand firmly. Newspapers dropped just below eye-level the length of the car. The young white man explained distinctly, loudly, that he had been in the Orient for a while, and now was studying at Columbia. "I don't agree with everything you say," he told Malcolm X, "but I have to admire your presentation."

Malcolm's voice in reply was cordiality itself. "I don't think you could search America, sir, and find two men who agree on everything." Subsequently, to another white man, an older businessman, who came up and shook hands, he said evenly, "Sir, I know how you feel. It's a hard thing to speak out against me when you are agreeing with so much that I say." And we rode on into New York under, now, a general open gazing.

In Washington, D.C., Malcolm X slashed at the government's reluctance to take positive steps in the Negro's behalf. I gather that even the White House took notice, for not long afterward I left off interviewing Malcolm X for a few days and went to the White House to do a *Playboy* interview of the then White House Press Secretary Pierre Salinger, who grimaced spontaneously when I said I was writing the life story of Malcolm X. Another time I left Malcolm X to interview the U.S.

Nazi Party Commander George Lincoln Rockwell, who frankly stated that he admired the courage of Malcolm X, and he felt that the two of them should speak together across the United States, and they could thus begin a real solution to the race problem—one of voluntary separation of the white and black races, with Negroes returning to Africa. I reported this to Malcolm X, who snorted, "He must think I'm nuts! What am *I* going to look like going speaking with a *devil!*" Yet another time, I went off to Atlanta and interviewed for *Playboy* Dr. Martin Luther King. He was privately intrigued to hear little-known things about Malcolm X that I told him; for publication, he discussed him with reserve, and he did say that he would sometime like to have an opportunity to talk with him. Hearing this, Malcolm X said drily, "You think I ought to send him a telegram with my telephone number?" (But from other things that Malcolm X said to me at various times, I deduced that he actually had a reluctant admiration for Dr. King.)

Malcolm X and I reached the point, ultimately, where we shared a mutual camaraderie that, although it was never verbally expressed, was a warm one. He was for me unquestionably one of the most engaging personalities I had ever met, and for his part, I gathered, I was someone he had learned he could express himself to, with candor, without the likelihood of hearing it repeated, and like any person who lived amid tension, he enjoyed being around someone, another man, with whom he could psychically relax. When I made trips now, he always asked me to telephone him when I would be returning to New York, and generally, if he could squeeze it into his schedule, he met me at the airport. I would see him coming along with his long, gangling strides, and wearing the wide, toothy, good-natured grin, and as he drove me into New York City he would bring me up to date on things of interest that had happened since I left. I remember one incident within the airport that showed me how Malcolm X never lost his racial perspective. Waiting for my baggage, we witnessed a touching family reunion scene as part of which several cherubic little children romped and played, exclaiming in another language. "By tomorrow night, they'll know how to say their first English word—*nigger*," observed Malcolm X.

When Malcolm X made long trips, such as to San Francisco

or Los Angeles, I did not go along, but frequently, usually very late at night, he would telephone me, and ask how the book was coming along, and he might set up the time for our next interview upon his return. One call that I never will forget came at close to four A.M., waking me; he must have just gotten up in Los Angeles. His voice said, "Alex Haley?" I said, sleepily, "Yes? Oh, *hey*, Malcolm!" His voice said, "I trust you seventy per cent"—and then he hung up. I lay a short time thinking about him and I went back to sleep feeling warmed by that call, as I still am warmed to remember it. Neither of us ever mentioned it.

Malcolm X's growing respect for individual whites seemed to be reserved for those who ignored on a personal basis the things he said about whites and who jousted with him as a *man*. He, moreover, was convinced that he could tell a lot about any person by listening. "There's an art to listening well," he told me. "I listen closely to the sound of a man's voice when he's speaking. I can hear sincerity." The newspaper person whom he ultimately came to admire probably more than any other was the *New York Times'* M. S. Handler. (I was very happy when I learned that Handler had agreed to write this book's Introduction; I know that Malcolm X would have liked that.) The first time I ever heard Malcolm X speak of Handler, whom he had recently met, he began, "I was talking with this devil—" and abruptly he cut himself off in obvious embarrassment. "It's a reporter named Handler, from the *Times*—" he resumed. Malcolm X's respect for the man steadily increased, and Handler, for his part, was an influence upon the inner Malcolm X. "He's the most genuinely unprejudiced white man I ever met," Malcolm X said to me, speaking of Handler months later. "I have asked him things and tested him. I have listened to him talk, closely."

I saw Malcolm X too many times exhilarated in after-lecture give-and-take with predominantly white student bodies at colleges and universities to ever believe that he nurtured at his core any blanket white-hatred. "The young whites, and blacks, too, are the only hope that America has," he said to me once. "The rest of us have always been living in a lie."

Several Negroes come to mind now who I know, in one way or another, had vastly impressed Malcolm X. (Some others come to mind whom I know he has vastly abhorred, but these I will not mention.) Particularly high in his esteem, I know, was the great photographer, usually associated with *Life* magazine, Gordon Parks. It was Malcolm X's direct influence with Elijah Muhammad which got Parks permitted to enter and photograph for publication in *Life* the highly secret self-defense training program of the Black Muslim Fruit of Islam, making Parks, as far as I know, the only non-Muslim who ever has witnessed this, except for policemen and other agency representatives who had feigned "joining" the Black Muslims to infiltrate them. "His success among the white man never has made him lose touch with black reality," Malcolm X said of Parks once.

Another person toward whom Malcolm X felt similarly was the actor Ossie Davis. Once in the middle of one of our interviews, when we had been talking about something else, Malcolm X suddenly asked me, "Do you know Ossie Davis?" I said I didn't. He said, "I ought to introduce you sometime, that's one of the finest black men." In Malcolm X's long dealings with the staff of the Harlem weekly newspaper *Amsterdam News*, he had come to admire Executive Editor James Hicks and the star feature writer James Booker. He said that Hicks had "an open mind, and he never panics for the white man." He thought that Booker was an outstanding reporter; he also was highly impressed with Mrs. Booker when he met her.

It was he who introduced me to two of my friends today, Dr. C. Eric Lincoln who was at the time writing the book *The Black Muslims in America*, and Louis Lomax who was then writing various articles about the Muslims. Malcolm X deeply respected the care and depth which Dr. Lincoln was putting into his research. Lomax, he admired for his ferreting ear and eye for hot news. "If I see that rascal Lomax running somewhere, I'll grab my hat and get behind him," Malcolm X said once, "because I know he's onto something." Author James Baldwin Malcolm X also admired. "He's so brilliant he confuses the white man with words on paper." And another time, "He's upset the white man more than anybody except The Honorable Elijah Muhammad."

Malcolm X had very little good to say of Negro ministers, very possibly because most of them had attacked the Black Muslims. Excepting reluctant admiration of Dr. Martin Luther

King, I heard him speak well of only one other, The Reverend Eugene L. Callender of Harlem's large Presbyterian Church of the Master. "He's a preacher, but he's a fighter for the black man," said Malcolm X. I later learned that somewhere the direct, forthright Reverend Callender had privately cornered Malcolm X and had read him the riot act about his general attacks upon the Negro clergy. Malcolm X also admired The Reverend Adam Clayton Powell, in his Congressman political role: "I'd think about retiring if the black man had ten like him in Washington." He had similar feelings about the N.A.A.C.P. lawyer, now a New York State Assemblyman, Percy Sutton, and later Sutton was retained as his personal attorney. Among Negro educators, of whom Malcolm X met many in his college and university lecturing, I never heard him speak well of any but one, Dr. Kenneth B. Clark. "There's a black man with brains gone to bed," Malcolm X told me once, briefly lapsing into his old vernacular. He had very distinct reservations about Negro professional intelligentsia as a category. They were the source from which most of the Black Muslims' attackers came. It was for this reason that some of his most bristling counter-attacks against "these so-called educated Uncle Thomases, Ph.D." were flung out at his audiences at Negro institutions of higher learning.

Where I witnessed the Malcolm X who was happiest and most at ease among members of our own race was when sometimes I chanced to accompany him on what he liked to call "my little daily rounds" around the streets of Harlem, among the Negroes that he said the "so-called black leaders" spoke of "as black masses statistics." On these tours, Malcolm X generally avoided the arterial 125th Street in Harlem; he plied the side streets, especially in those areas which were thickest with what he described as "the black man down in the gutter where I came from," the poverty-ridden with a high incidence of dope addicts and winos.

Malcolm X here indeed was a hero. Striding along the sidewalks, he bathed all whom he met in the boyish grin, and his conversation with any who came up was quiet and pleasant. "It's just what the white devil wants you to do, brother," he might tell a wino, "he wants you to get drunk so he will have an excuse to put a club up beside your head." Or I remember once he halted at a stoop to greet several older women: "Sisters, let me ask you something," he said conversationally, "have you ever known *one* white man who either didn't do something to you, or take something from you?" One among that audience exclaimed after a moment, "I sure *ain't!*" whereupon all of them joined in laughter and we walked on with Malcolm X waving back to cries of "He's *right!*"

I remember that once in the early evening we rounded a corner to hear a man, shabbily dressed, haranguing a small crowd around his speaking platform of an upturned oblong wooden box with an American flag alongside. "I don't respect or believe in this damn flag, it's there because I can't hold a public meeting without it unless I want the white man to put me in jail. And that's what I'm up here to talk about—these crackers getting rich off the blood and bones of your and my people!" Said Malcolm X, grinning, "He's *working!*"

Malcolm X rarely exchanged any words with those Negro men with shiny, "processed" hair without giving them a nudge. Very genially: "Ahhhh, brother, the white devil has taught you to hate yourself so much that you put hot lye in your hair to make it look more like his hair."

I remember another stoopful of women alongside the door of a small grocery store where I had gone for something, leaving Malcolm X talking across the street. As I came out of the store, one woman was excitedly describing for the rest a Malcolm X lecture she had heard in Mosque Number 7 one Sunday. "Oooooh, he *burnt* that white man, burnt him *up*, chile . . . chile, he told us we descendin' from black kings an' queens—Lawd, I didn't know it!" Another woman asked, "You believe that?" and the first vehemently responded, "Yes, I *do!*"

And I remember a lone, almost ragged guitarist huddled on a side street playing and singing just for himself when he glanced up and instantly recognized the oncoming, striding figure. "Huh-*ho!*" the guitarist exclaimed, and jumping up, he snapped into a mock salute. "My *man!*"

Malcolm X loved it. And they loved him. There was no question about it: whether he was standing tall beside a street lamp chatting with winos, or whether he was firing his radio and television broadsides to unseen millions of people, or whether he was titillating small audiences of sophisticated whites with his small-talk such as, "My hobby is stirring up Negroes, that's spelled *knee*-grows the way you liberals pronounce it"—the man had charisma, and he had *power*. And I was not the only one who at various times marveled at how he could continue to receive such an awesome amount of international personal publicity and still season liberally practically everything he said, both in public and privately, with credit and hosannas to "The Honorable Elijah Muhammad." Often I made side notes to myself about this. I kept, in effect, a double-entry set of notebooks. Once, noting me switching from one to the other, Malcolm X curiously asked me what for? I told him some reason, but not that one notebook was things he said for his book and the other was for my various personal observations about him; very likely he would have become self-conscious. "You must have written a million words by now," said Malcolm X. "Probably," I said. "This white man's crazy," he mused. "I'll prove it to you. Do you think I'd publicize somebody knocking me like I do him?"

"Look, tell me the truth," Malcolm X said to me one evening, "you travel around. Have you heard anything?"

Truthfully, I told him I didn't know what he had reference to. He dropped it and talked of something else.

From Malcolm X himself, I had seen, or heard, a few unusual things which had caused me some little private wonder and speculation, and then, with nothing to hang them onto, I had dismissed them. One day in his car, we had stopped for the red light at an intersection; another car with a white man driving had stopped alongside, and when this white man saw Malcolm X, he instantly called across to him, "I don't blame your people for turning to you. If I were a Negro I'd follow you, too. Keep up the fight!" Malcolm X said to the man very sincerely, "I wish I could have a white chapter of the people I meet like you." The light changed, and as both cars drove on, Malcolm X quickly said to me, firmly, "Not only don't write that, never repeat it. Mr. Muhammad would have a fit." The significant thing about the incident, I later reflected, was that it was the first time I had ever heard him speak of Elijah Muhammad with anything less than reverence.

About the same time, one of the scribblings of Malcolm X's that I had retrieved had read, enigmatically, "My life has always been one of changes." Another time, this was in September,

1963, Malcolm X had been highly upset about something during an entire session, and when I read the *Amsterdam News* for that week, I guessed that he had been upset about an item in Jimmy Booker's column that Booker had heard that Elijah Muhammad and Malcolm X were feuding. (Booker was later to reveal that after his column was written, he had gone on vacation, and on his return he learned that Malcolm X "stormed into the *Amsterdam News* with three followers . . . 'I want to see Jimmy Booker. I don't like what he wrote. There is no fight between me and Elijah Muhammad. I believe in Mr. Muhammad and will lay down my life for him.' ")

Also, now and then, when I chanced to meet a few other key Muslims, mainly when I was with Malcolm X, but when he was not immediately present, I thought I detected either in subtle phrasing, or in manner, something less than total admiration of their famous colleague—and then I would tell myself I had misinterpreted. And during these days, Dr. C. Eric Lincoln and I would talk on the phone fairly often. We rarely would fail to mention how it seemed almost certain that seeds of trouble lay in the fact that however much Malcolm X praised Elijah Muhammad, it was upon dramatic, articulate Malcolm X that the communications media and hence the general public focused the great bulk of their attention. I never dreamed, though, what Malcolm X was actually going through. He never breathed a word, at least not to me, until the actual rift became public.

When Malcolm X left me at around two A.M. on that occasion, he asked me to call him at nine A.M. The telephone in the home in East Elmhurst rang considerably longer than usual, and Sister Betty, when she answered, sounded strained, choked up. When Malcolm X came on, he, too, sounded different. He asked me, "Have you heard the radio or seen the newspapers?" I said I hadn't. He said, "Well, do!" and that he would call me later.

I went and got the papers. I read with astonishment that Malcolm X had been suspended by Elijah Muhammad—the stated reason being the "chickens coming home to roost" remark that Malcolm X recently had made as a comment upon the assassination of President Kennedy.

Malcolm X did telephone, after about an hour, and I met him at the Black Muslims' newspaper office in Harlem, a couple of blocks further up Lenox Avenue from their mosque and restaurant. He was seated behind his light-brown metal desk and his brown hat lay before him on the green blotter. He wore a dark suit with a vest, a white shirt, the inevitable leaping-sailfish clip held his narrow tie, and the big feet in the shined black shoes pushed the swivel chair pendulously back and forth as he talked into the telephone.

"I'm always hurt over any act of disobedience on my part concerning Mr. Muhammad. . . . Yes, sir—anything The Honorable Elijah Muhammad does is all right with me. I believe absolutely in his wisdom and authority." The telephone would ring again instantly every time he put it down. "Mr. Peter Goldman! I haven't heard your voice in a good while! Well, sir, I just should have kept my big mouth shut." To the *New York Times*: "Sir? Yes—he suspended me from making public appearances for the time being, which I fully understand. I say the same thing to you that I have told others, I'm in complete submission to Mr. Muhammad's judgment, because I have always found his judgment to be based on sound thinking." To C.B.S.: "I think that anybody who is in a position to discipline others should first learn to accept discipline himself."

He brought it off, the image of contriteness, the best he could—throughout the harshly trying next several weeks. But the back of his neck was reddish every time I saw him. He did not yet put into words his obvious fury at the public humiliation. We did very little interviewing now, he was so busy on telephones elsewhere; but it did not matter too much because by now I had the bulk of the needed life story material in hand. When he did find some time to visit me, he was very preoccupied, and I could *feel* him rankling with anger and with inactivity, but he tried hard to hide it.

He scribbled one night, "You have not converted a man because you have silenced him. John Viscount Morley." And the same night, almost illegibly, "I was going downhill until he picked me up, but the more I think of it, we picked each other up."

When I did not see him for several days, a letter came. "I have cancelled all public appearances and speaking engagements for a number of weeks. So within that period it should be possible to finish this book. With the fast pace of newly developing incidents today, it is easy for something that is done or said tomorrow to be outdated even by sunset on the same day. Malcolm X.''

I pressed to get the first chapter, ''Nightmare,'' into a shape that he could review. When it was ready in a readable rough draft, I telephoned him. He came as quickly as he could drive from his home—which made me see how grinding an ordeal it was to him to just be sitting at home, inactive, and knowing his temperament, my sympathies went out to Sister Betty.

He pored over the manuscript pages, raptly the first time, then drawing out his red-ink ball-point pen he read through the chapter again, with the pen occasionally stabbing at something. ''You can't bless Allah!'' he exclaimed, changing ''bless'' to ''praise.'' In a place that referred to himself and his brothers and sisters, he scratched red through ''we kids.'' ''Kids are *goats!*'' he exclaimed sharply.

Soon, Malcolm X and his family flew to Miami. Cassius Clay had extended the invitation as a sixth wedding anniversary present to Malcolm X and Sister Betty, and they had accepted most gratefully. It was Sister Betty's first vacation in the six years of the taut regimen as a Black Muslim wife, and it was for Malcolm X both a saving of face and something to *do.*

Very soon after his arrival, he telegraphed me his phone number at a motel. I called him and he told me, ''I just want to tell you something. I'm not a betting man anymore, but if you are, you bet on Cassius to beat Liston, and you will win.'' I laughed and said he was prejudiced. He said, ''Remember what I told you when the fight's over.'' I received later a picture postcard, the picture in vivid colors being of a chimpanzee at the Monkey Jungle in Miami. Malcolm X had written on the reverse side, ''One hundred years after the Civil War, and these *chimpanzees* get more recognition, respect and freedom in America than our people do. Bro. Malcolm X.'' Another time, an envelope came, and inside it was a clipping of an Irv Kupcinet column in the Chicago *Sun-Times.* Malcolm X's red pen had encircled an item which read, ''Insiders are predicting a split in the Black Muslims. Malcolm X, ousted as No. 2 man in the organization, may form a splinter group to oppose Elijah Muhammad.'' Alongside the item, Malcolm X had scribbled ''Imagine this!!!''

The night of the phenomenal upset, when Clay *did* beat Liston, Malcolm X telephoned me, and sounds of excitement were in the background. The victory party was in his motel suite, Malcolm X told me. He described what was happening, mentioned some of those who were present, and that the new heavyweight king was "in the next room, my bedroom here" taking a nap. After reminding me of the fight prediction he had made, Malcolm X said that I should look forward now to Clay's "quick development into a major world figure. I don't know if you really realize the world significance that this is the first *Muslim* champion."

It was the following morning when Cassius Clay gave the press interview which resulted in national headlines that he was actually a "Black Muslim," and soon after, the newspapers were carrying pictures of Malcolm X introducing the heavyweight champion to various African diplomats in the lobbies of the United Nations headquarters in New York City. Malcolm X toured Clay about in Harlem, and in other places, functioning, he said, as Clay's "friend and religious advisor."

I had now moved upstate to finish my work on the book, and we talked on the telephone every three or four days. He said things suggesting that he might never be returned to his former Black Muslim post, and he now began to say things quietly critical of Elijah Muhammad. *Playboy* magazine asked me to do an interview for them with the new champion Cassius Clay, and when I confidently asked Malcolm X to arrange for me the needed introduction to Clay, Malcolm X hesitantly said, "I think you had better ask somebody else to do that." I was highly surprised at the reply, but I had learned never to press him for information. And then, very soon after, I received a letter. "Dear Alex Haley: A quick note. Would you prepare a properly worded letter that would enable me to change the reading of the contract so that all remaining proceeds now would go to the Muslim Mosque, Inc., or in the case of my death then to go directly to my wife, Mrs. Betty X Little? The sooner this letter or contract is changed, the more easily I will rest." Under the signature of Malcolm X, there was a P.S.: "How is it possible to write one's autobiography in a world so fast-changing as this?"

Soon I read in the various newspapers that rumors were being heard of threats on Malcolm X's life. Then there was an article in the *Amsterdam News*: The caption was "Malcolm X Tells Of Death Threat," and the story reported that he had said that former close associates of his in the New York mosque had sent out "a special squad" to "try to kill me in cold blood. Thanks to Allah, I learned of the plot from the very same brothers who had been sent out to murder me. These brothers had heard me represent and defend Mr. Muhammad for too long for them to swallow the lies about me without first asking me some questions for their own clarification."

I telephoned Malcolm X, and expressed my personal concern for him. His voice sounded weary. He said that his "uppermost interest" was that any money which might come due him in the future would go directly to his new organization, or to his wife, as the letter he had signed and mailed had specified. He told me, "I know I've got to get a will made for myself, I never did because I never have had anything to will to anybody, but if I don't have one and something happened to me, there could be a mess." I expressed concern for him, and he told me that he had a loaded rifle in his home, and "I can take care of myself."

The "Muslim Mosque, Inc." to which Malcolm X had referred was a new organization which he had formed, which at that time consisted of perhaps forty or fifty Muslims who had left the leadership of Elijah Muhammad.

Through a close associate of Cassius Clay, whom Malcolm X had finally suggested to me, my interview appointment was arranged with the heavyweight champion, and I flew down to New York City to do the interview for *Playboy*. Malcolm X was "away briefly," Sister Betty said on the phone—and she spoke brusquely. I talked with one Black Muslim lady whom I had known before she had joined, and who had been an admirer of Malcolm X. She had elected to remain in the original fold, "but I'll tell you, brother, what a lot in the mosque are saying, you know, it's like if you divorced your husband, you'd still like to see him once in a while." During my interviews with Cassius Clay in his three-room suite at Harlem's Theresa Hotel, inevitably the questions got around to Clay's Muslim membership, then to a query about what had happened to his formerly very close relationship with Malcolm X. Evenly, Clay said, "You just don't buck Mr. Muhammad and get away with it. I don't want to talk about him no more."

Elijah Muhammad at his headquarters in Chicago grew "emotionally affected" whenever the name of Malcolm X had to be raised in his presence, one of the Muslims in Clay's entourage told me. Mr. Muhammad reportedly had said, "Brother Malcolm got to be a *big* man. I made him big. I was about to make him a *great* man." The faithful Black Muslims predicted that soon Malcolm X would be turned upon by the defectors from Mosque Number 7 who had joined him: "They will feel betrayed." Said others, "A great chastisement of Allah will fall upon a hypocrite." Mr. Muhammad reportedly had said at another time, "Malcolm is destroying himself," and that he had no wish whatever to see Malcolm X die, that he "would rather see him live and suffer his treachery."

The general feeling among Harlemites, non-Muslims, with whom I talked was that Malcolm X had been powerful and influential enough a minister that eventually he would split the mosque membership into two hostile camps, and that in New York City at least, Elijah Muhammad's unquestioned rule would be ended.

Malcolm X returned. He said that he had been in Boston and Philadelphia. He spent ample time with me, now during the day, in Room 1936 in the Hotel Americana. His old total ease was no longer with him. As if it was the most natural thing in the world to do, at sudden intervals he would stride to the door; pulling it open, he would look up and down the corridor, then shut the door again. "If I'm alive when this book comes out, it will be a miracle," he said by way of explanation. "I'm not saying it distressingly—" He leaned forward and touched the buff gold bedspread. "I'm saying it like I say that's a bedspread."

For the first time he talked with me in some detail about what had happened. He said that his statement about President Kennedy's assassination was not why he had been ousted from the Muslims. "It wasn't the reason at all. Nobody said anything when I made stronger statements before." The real reason, he said, was "jealousy in Chicago, and I had objected to the immorality of the man who professed to be more moral than anybody."

Malcolm X said that he had increased the Nation of Islam membership from about 400 when he had joined to around 40,000. "I don't think there were more than 400 in the country when I joined, I really don't. They were mostly older people, and many of them couldn't even pronounce Mr. Muhammad's name, and he stayed mostly in the background.''

Malcolm X worked hard not to show it, but he was upset. "There is nothing more frightful than ignorance in action. Goethe," he scribbled one day. He hinted about Cassius Clay a couple of times, and when I responded only with anecdotes about my interview with Clay, he finally asked what Clay had said of him. I dug out the index card on which the question was typed in advance and Clay's response was beneath in longhand. Malcolm X stared at the card, then out of the window, and he got up and walked around; one of the few times I ever heard his voice betray his hurt was when he said, "I felt like a blood big-brother to him." He paused. "I'm not against him now. He's a fine young man. Smart. He's just let himself be used, led astray."

And at another time there in the hotel room he came the nearest to tears that I ever saw him, and also the only time I ever heard him use, for his race, one word. He had been talking about how hard he had worked building up the Muslim organization in the early days when he was first moved to New York City, when abruptly he exclaimed hoarsely, "We had the *best* organization the black man's ever had—*niggers* ruined it!"

A few days later, however, he wrote in one of his memo books this, which he let me read, "Children have a lesson adults should learn, to not be ashamed of failing, but to get up and try again. Most of us adults are so afraid, so cautious, so 'safe,' and therefore so shrinking and rigid and afraid that it is why so many humans fail. Most middle-aged adults have resigned themselves to failure.''

Telephone calls came frequently for Malcolm X when he was in the room with me, or he would make calls; he would talk in a covert, guarded manner, clearly not wishing me to be able to follow the discussion. I took to going into the bathroom at these times, and closing the door, emerging when the murmuring of his voice had stopped—hoping that made him more comfortable. Later, he would tell me that he was hearing from some Muslims who were still ostensibly Elijah Muhammad's followers. "I'm a marked man," he said one day, after such a call. "I've had highly placed people tell me to be very careful every move I make." He thought about it. "Just as long as my family doesn't get hurt, I'm not frightened for myself." I have the impression that Malcolm X heard in advance that the Muslim organization was going to sue to make him vacate the home he and his family lived in.

I had become worried that Malcolm X, bitter, would want to go back through the chapters in which he had told of his Black Muslim days and re-edit them in some way. The day before I left New York City to return upstate, I raised my concern to Malcolm X. "I have thought about that," he said. "There are a lot of things I could say that passed through my mind at times even then, things I saw and heard, but I threw them out of my mind. I'm going to let it stand the way I've told it. I want the book to be the way it was."

Then—March 26, 1964—a note came from Malcolm X: "There is a chance that I may make a quick trip to several very important countries in Africa, including a pilgrimage to the Muslim Holy Cities of Mecca and Medina, beginning about April 13th. Keep this to yourself."

While abroad, Malcolm X wrote letters and postcards to almost everyone he knew well. His letters now were signed "El-Hajj Malik El-Shabazz."

Then, in mid-May, Sister Betty telephoned me, her voice jubilant: Malcolm X was returning. I flew to New York City. On May 21, the phone rang in my hotel room and Sister Betty said, "Just a minute, please—," then the deep voice said, "How are you?"

"Well! El-Hajj Malik El-Shabazz! How are *you?*"

He said, "Just a little bit tired." He had arrived on a Pan-American Airlines flight at 4:30. He was going to have a press conference at seven P.M. at the Hotel Theresa. "I'll pick you up at 6:30 at 135th and Lenox, on the uptown side—all right?"

When the blue Oldsmobile stopped, and I got in, El-Hajj Malcolm, broadly beaming, wore a seersucker suit, the red hair needed a barber's attention, and he had grown a beard. Also in the car was Sister Betty. It was the first time we had ever seen each other after more than a year of talking several times a week on the telephone. We smiled at each other. She wore dark glasses, a blue maternity suit, and she was pregnant with what would be her fourth child.

There must have been fifty still and television photographers and reporters jockeying for position, up front, and the rest of the Skyline Ballroom was filling with Negro followers of Malcolm X, or his well-wishers, and the curious. The room lit up with flickering and flooding lights as he came in the door squiring Sister Betty, holding her arm tenderly, and she was smiling broadly in her pride that this man was her man. I recognized the *Times'* M. S. Handler and introduced myself; we warmly shook hands and commandeered a little two-chair table. The reporters in a thick semicircle before Malcolm X seated on the podium fired questions at him, and he gave the impression that all of his twelve years' oratorical practice had prepared him for this new image.

"Do we correctly understand that you now do not think that all whites are evil?"

"*True*, sir! My trip to Mecca has opened my eyes. I no longer subscribe to racism. I have adjusted my thinking to the point where I believe that whites are human beings"—a significant pause—"as long as this is borne out by their humane attitude toward Negroes."

They picked at his "racist" image. "I'm *not* a racist. I'm not condemning whites for being whites, but for their deeds. I condemn what whites collectively have done to our people collectively."

He almost continually flashed about the room the ingratiating boyish smile. He would pick at the new reddish beard. They asked him about that, did he plan to keep it? He said he hadn't decided yet, he would have to see if he could get used to it or not. Was he maneuvering to now join the major civil rights leaders whom he had previously bitterly attacked? He answered that one sideways: "I'll explain it this way, sir. If some men are in a car, driving with a destination in mind, and you know they are going the wrong way, but they are convinced they are going the right way, then you get into the car with them, and ride with them, talking—and finally when they see they are on the wrong road, not getting where they were intending, then you tell them, and they will listen to you *then*, what road to take." He had never been in better form, weighing, parrying, answering the questions.

The *Times'* Handler, beside me, was taking notes and muttering under his breath, "Incredible! Incredible!" I was thinking the same thing. I was thinking, some of the time, that if a pebble were dropped from the window behind Malcolm X, it would have struck on a sidewalk eight floors below where years before he had skulked, selling dope.

As I resumed writing upstate, periodic notes came from Malcolm X. "I hope the book is proceeding rapidly, for events concerning my life happen so swiftly, much of what has already been written can easily be outdated from month to month. In life, nothing is permanent; not even life itself (smile). So I would advise you to rush it on out as fast as possible." Another note, special delivery, had a tone of irritation with me: he had received from the publisher a letter which indicated that he had received a $2500 check when the book contract was signed, "and therefore I will be expected to pay *personal* income tax on this. As you know, it was my repeated specification that this entire transaction was to be made at that time directly with and to the Mosque. In fact, I have never seen that check to this very day."

The matter was straightened out, and I sent Malcolm X some rough chapters to read. I was appalled when they were soon returned, red-inked in many places where he had told of his almost father-and-son relationship with Elijah Muhammad. Telephoning Malcolm X, I reminded him of his previous decision, and I stressed that if those chapters contained such telegraphing to readers of what would lie ahead, then the book would automatically be robbed of some of its building suspense and drama. Malcolm X said, gruffly, "Whose book is this?" I told him "yours, of course," and that I only made the objection in my position as a writer. He said that he would have to think about it. I was heart-sick at the prospect that he might want to re-edit the entire book into a polemic against Elijah Muhammad. But late that night, Malcolm X telephoned. "I'm sorry. You're right. I was upset about something. Forget what I wanted changed, let what you already had stand." I never again gave him chapters to review unless I was with him. Several times I would covertly watch him frown and wince as he read, but he never again asked for any change in what he had originally said. And the only thing that he ever indicated that he wished had been different in his life came when he was reading the chapter "Laura." He said, "That was a smart girl, a *good* girl. She tried her best to make something out of me, and look what I started her into—dope and prostitution. I wrecked that girl.''

Malcolm X was busy, busy, busy; he could not visit my hotel room often, and when he did, it shortly would get the feeling of Grand Central Station. It seemed that when the telephone was not ringing for him, he was calling someone else, consulting the jotted numbers in his ever-ready memorandum book. Now he had begun to talk a great deal with various people from the Middle East or Africa who were in New York. Some of these came to see him at the hotel room. At first, I would sit by the window engrossed in reading while they talked by the room's door in low tones. He was very apologetic when this occurred, and I told him I felt no sensitivity about it; then, afterwards, I would generally step out into the hallway, or perhaps take the elevator down to the lobby, then watch the elevators until I saw the visitor leave. One day, I remember, the phone had rung steadily with such callers as C.B.S., A.B.C., N.B.C., every New York City paper, the London *Daily Express*, and numerous individuals—he and I had gotten no work at all accomplished; then a television camera crew arrived and filled the room to tape an interview with Malcolm X by A.B.C.'s commentator Bill Beutel. As the crew was setting up its floodlights on tripods, a Dayton, Ohio, radio station called, wishing to interview Malcolm X by telephone. He asked me to ask them to call him the following day at his sister Ella's home in Boston. Then the Ghana Ministry of Information called. I turned with a note to Malcolm X to whom the commentator Beutel had just said, ''I won't take much of your time, I just have a few probably stupid questions.'' Glancing at my note, Malcolm X said to Beutel, ''Only the unasked question is stupid,'' and then to me, ''Tell them I'll call them back, please.'' Then just as the television cameras began rolling, with Beutel and Malcolm X talking, the telephone rang again and it was *Life* magazine reporter Marc Crawford to whom I whispered what was happening. Crawford, undaunted, asked if the open receiver could be placed where he could hear the interview, and I complied, relieved that it was one way to let the interview proceed without interruption.

The manuscript copy which Malcolm X was given to review was in better shape now, and he pored through page by page, intently, and now and then his head would raise with some comment. "You know," he said once, "why I have been able to have some effect is because I make a study of the weaknesses of this country and because the more the white man yelps, the more I know I have struck a nerve." Another time, he put down upon the bed the manuscript he was reading, and he got up from his chair and walked back and forth, stroking his chin, then he looked at me. "You know this place here in this chapter where I told you how I put the pistol up to my head and kept pulling the trigger and scared them so when I was starting the burglary ring—well," he paused, "I don't know if I ought to tell you this or not, but I want to tell the truth." He eyed me, speculatively. "I palmed the bullet." We laughed together. I said, "Okay, give that page here, I'll fix it." Then he considered, "No, leave it that way. Too many people would be so quick to say that's what I'm doing today, bluffing."

Again when reading about the period when he had discovered the prison library, Malcolm X's head jerked up. "Boy! I never will forget that old aardvark!" The next evening, he came into the room and told me that he had been to the Museum of Natural History and learned something about the aardvark. "Now, aardvark actually means 'earth hog.' That's a good example of root words, as I was telling you. When you study the science of philology, you learn the laws governing how a consonant can lose its shape, but it keeps its identity from language to language." What astonished me here was that I knew that on that day, Malcolm X's schedule had been crushing, involving both a television and radio appearance and a live speech, yet he had gone to find out something about the aardvark.

Before long, Malcolm X called a press conference, and announced, "My new Organization of Afro-American Unity is a non-religious and non-sectarian group organized to unite Afro-Americans for a constructive program toward attainment of human rights." The new OAAU's tone appeared to be one of militant black nationalism. He said to the questions of various reporters in subsequent interviews that the OAAU would seek to convert the Negro population from non-violence to active self-defense against white supremacists across America. On the subject of politics he offered an enigma, "Whether you use bullets or ballots, you've got to aim well; don't strike at the puppet, strike at the puppeteer.'' Did he envision any special area of activity? "I'm going to join in the fight wherever Negroes ask for my help.'' What about alliance with other Negro organizations? He said that he would consider forming some united front with certain selected Negro leaders. He conceded under questioning that the N.A.A.C.P. was "doing some good.'' Could any whites join his OAAU? "If John Brown were alive, maybe him.'' And he answered his critics with such statements as that he would send "armed guerrillas'' into Mississippi. "I am dead serious. We will send them not only to Mississippi, but to any place where black people's lives are threatened by white bigots. As far as I am concerned, Mississippi is anywhere south of the Canadian border.'' At another time, when Evelyn Cunningham of the *Pittsburgh Courier* asked Malcolm X in a kidding way, "Say something startling for my column,'' he told her, "Anyone who wants to follow me and my movement has got to be ready to go to jail, to the hospital, and to the cemetery before he can be truly free.'' Evelyn Cunningham, printing the item, commented, "He smiled and chuckled, but he was in dead earnest.''

His fourth child, yet another daughter, was born and he and Sister Betty named the baby Gamilah Lumumbah. A young waitress named Helen Lanier, at Harlem's Twenty Two Club where Malcolm X now often asked people to meet him, gave him a layette for the new baby. He was very deeply touched by the gesture. "Why, I hardly know that girl!''

He was clearly irked when a *New York Times* poll among New York City Negroes reflected that three-fourths had named Dr. Martin Luther King as "doing the best work for Negroes,'' and another one-fifth had voted for the N.A.A.C.P.'s Roy Wilkins, while only six per cent had voted for Malcolm X. "Brother,'' he said to me, "do you realize that some of history's greatest leaders never were recognized until they were safely in the ground!''

One morning in mid-summer 1964, Malcolm X telephoned me and said that he would be leaving "within the next two or three days'' for a planned six weeks abroad. I heard from him first in Cairo, about as the predicted "long, hot summer'' began in earnest, with riots and other uprisings of Negroes occurring in surburban Philadelphia, in Rochester, in Brooklyn, in Harlem, and other cities. The *New York Times* reported that a meeting of Negro intellectuals had agreed that Dr. Martin Luther King could secure the allegiance of the middle and upper classes of Negroes, but Malcolm X alone could secure the allegiance of Negroes at the bottom. "The Negroes respect Dr. King and Malcolm X because they sense in these men absolute integrity and know they will never sell them out. Malcolm X cannot be corrupted and the Negroes know this and therefore respect him. They also know that he comes from the lower depths, as they do, and regard him as one of their own. Malcolm X is going to play a formidable role, because the racial struggle has now shifted to the urban North . . . if Dr. King is convinced that he has sacrificed ten years of brilliant leadership, he will be forced to revise his concepts. There is only one direction in which he can move, and that is in the direction of Malcolm X." I sent a clipping of that story to Malcolm X in Cairo.

In Washington, D.C. and New York City, at least, powerful civic, private, and governmental agencies and individuals were keenly interested in what Malcolm X was saying abroad, and were speculating upon what would he say, and possibly do, when he returned to America. In upstate New York, I received a telephone call from a close friend who said he had been asked to ask me if I would come to New York City on an appointed day to meet with "a very high government official" who was interested in Malcolm X. I did fly down to the city. My friend accompanied me to the offices of a large private foundation well known for its activities and donations in the civil-rights area. I met the foundation's president and he introduced me to the Justice Department Civil Rights Section head, Burke Marshall. Marshall was chiefly interested in Malcolm X's finances, particularly how his extensive traveling since his Black Muslim ouster had been paid for. I told him that to the best of my knowledge the several payments from the publisher had financed Malcolm X, along with fees he received for some speeches, and possible donations that his organization received, and that Malcolm X had told me of borrowing money from his Sister Ella for the current trip, and that recently the *Saturday Evening Post* had bought the condensation rights of the book for a substantial sum that was soon to be received. Marshall listened quietly, intently, and asked a few questions concerning other aspects of

Malcolm X's life, then thanked me. I wrote to Malcolm X in Cairo that night about the interview. He never mentioned it.

The *Saturday Evening Post* flew photographer John Launois to Cairo to locate Malcolm X and photograph him in color. The magazine's September 12 issue appeared, and I sent a copy by airmail to Malcolm X. Within a few days, I received a stinging note, expressing his anger at the magazine's editorial regarding his life story. (The editorial's opening sentence read, "If Malcolm X were not a Negro, his autobiography would be little more than a journal of abnormal psychology, the story of a burglar, dope pusher, addict and jailbird—with a family history of insanity—who acquires messianic delusions and sets forth to preach an upside-down religion of 'brotherly' hatred.") I wrote to Malcolm X that he could not fairly hold me responsible for what the magazine had written in a separate editorial opinion. He wrote an apology, "but the greatest care must be exercised in the future."

His return from Africa was even more auspicious than when he had returned from the Hajj pilgrimage to Mecca. A large group of Negroes, his followers and well-wishers, kept gathering in the Overseas Arrival Building at Kennedy Airport. When I entered, white men with cameras were positioned on the second level, taking pictures of all the Negroes who entered, and almost as obvious were Negro plain-clothesmen moving about. Malcolm's greeters had draped across the glass overlooking the U.S. Customs Inspection line some large cloth banners on which were painted in bold letters, "Welcome Home, Malcolm."

He came in sight, stepping into one of the Customs Inspection lines; he heard the cheering and he looked up, smiling his pleasure.

Malcolm X wanted to "huddle" with me to fill me in on details from his trip that he wanted in the book. He said that he was giving me only the highlights, because he felt that his carefully kept diary might be turned into another book. We had intensive sessions in my hotel room, where he read what he selected from the diary, and I took notes. "What I want to stress is that I was trying to internationalize our problem," he said to me, "to make the Africans feel their *kinship* with us Afro-Americans. I made them *think* about it, that they are our blood brothers, and we all came from the same foreparents. That's why the Africans loved me, the same way the Asians loved me because I was religious.''

Within a few days, he had no more time to see me. He would call and apologize; he was beset by a host of problems, some of which he mentioned, and some of which I heard from other people. Most immediately, there was discontent within his organization, the OAAU. His having stayed away almost three times as long as he had said he would be gone had sorely tested the morale of even his key members, and there was a general feeling that his interest was insufficient to expect his followers' interest to stay high. I heard from one member that "a growing disillusion'' could be sensed throughout the organization.

In Harlem at large, in the bars and restaurants, on the street corners and stoops, there could be heard more blunt criticism of Malcolm X than ever before in his career. There were, variously expressed, two primary complaints. One was that actually Malcolm X only talked, but other civil-rights organizations were *doing*. "All he's *ever* done was talk, CORE and SNCC and some of them people of Dr. King's are out getting beat over the head.'' The second major complaint was that Malcolm X was himself too confused to be seriously followed any longer. "He doesn't know *what* he believes in. No sooner do you hear one thing than he's switched to something else.'' The two complaints were not helping the old firebrand Malcolm X image any, nor were they generating the local public interest that was badly needed by his small, young OAAU.

A court had made it clear that Malcolm X and his family would have to vacate the Elmhurst house for its return to the adjudged legal owners, Elijah Muhammad's Nation of Islam. And other immediate problems which Malcolm X faced included finances. Among his other expenses, a wife and four daughters had to be supported, along with at least one full-time OAAU official. Upon his return from Africa, our agent for the book had delivered to me for Malcolm X a check for a sizable sum; soon afterward Malcolm X told me, laughing wryly, "It's *evaporated*. I don't know where!''

Malcolm X plunged into a welter of activities. He wrote and telephoned dozens of acceptances to invitations to speak, predominantly at colleges and universities—both to expound his philosophies and to earn the $150–$300 honorariums above traveling expenses. When he was in New York City, he spent all the time he could in his OAAU's sparsely furnished office on the mezzanine floor of the Hotel Theresa, trying to do something about the OAAU's knotty problems. "I'm not exposing our size in numbers," he evaded the query of one reporter. "You know, the strongest part of a tree is the root, and if you expose the root, the tree dies. Why, we have many 'invisible' members, of all types. Unlike other leaders, I've practiced the flexibility to put myself into contact with every kind of Negro in the country."

Even at mealtimes, at his favorite Twenty Two Club, or elsewhere in Harlem, he could scarcely eat for the people who came up asking for appointments to discuss with him topics ranging from personal problems to his opinions on international issues. It seemed not in him to say "No" to such requests. And aides of his, volunteering their time, as often as not had to wait lengthy periods to get his ear for matters important to the OAAU, or to himself; often, even then, he most uncharacteristically showed an impatience with their questions or their suggestions, and they chafed visibly. And at least once weekly, generally on Sunday evenings, he would address as many Negroes as word of mouth and mimeographed advertising could draw to hear him in Harlem's Audubon Ballroom on West 166th Street between Broadway and St. Nicholas Avenue, near New York City's famous Columbia-Presbyterian Medical Center.

Malcolm X for some reason suddenly began to deliver a spate of attacks against Elijah Muhammad, making more bitter accusations of "religious fakery" and "immorality" than he ever had. Very possibly, Malcolm X had grown increasingly incensed by the imminence of the court's deadline for him to have to move his wife and four little daughters from the comfortable home in which they had lived for years in Elmhurst. And Sister Betty was again pregnant. "A home is really the only thing I've ever provided Betty since we've been married," he had told me, discussing the court's order, "and they want to take that away. Man, I can't keep on putting her through changes, all she's put up with—man, I've *got* to love this woman!"

A rash of death threats were anonymously telephoned to the police, to various newspapers, to the OAAU office, and to the family's home in Elmhurst. When he went to court again, fighting to keep the house, he was guarded by a phalanx of eight OAAU men, twenty uniformed policemen, and twelve plain-clothes detectives. The court's decision was that the order to vacate would not be altered. When Malcolm X reached home in Long Island, one of his followers, telephoning him there, got, instead, a telephone company operator who said that the OL 1-6320 number was "disconnected." A carload of his OAAU followers, racing to Long Island, found Malcolm X and his family perfectly safe. Inquiry of the telephone company revealed that a "Mrs. Small" had called and requested that the service for that number be disconnected, "for vacation." The OAAU followers drove back to Harlem. There was an ensuing confrontation between them and followers of Elijah Muhammad in front of the Black Muslim restaurant at 116th Street and Lenox Avenue. The incident wound up with policemen who rushed to the scene finding two guns in the OAAU car, and the six OAAU men were arrested.

Malcolm X had a date to speak in Boston, but he was too busy to go, and he sent an OAAU assistant who spoke instead. The car returning him to the Boston Airport was blocked at the East Boston Tunnel by another car. Reportedly, men with knives rushed out of the blockade car, but the Malcolm X forces showed a shotgun, and the attackers dispersed.

Malcolm X steadily accused the Black Muslims as the source of the various attacks and threats. "There is no group in the United States more able to carry out this threat than the Black Muslims," he said. "I know, because I taught them myself." Asked why he had attacked the Black Muslims and Elijah Muhammad when things had seemed to be cooled down, he said, "I would not have revealed any of this if they had left me alone." He let himself be photographed in his home holding an automatic carbine rifle with a full double clip of ammunition that he said he kept ready for action against any possible assassination efforts. "I have taught my wife to use it, and instructed her to fire on anyone, white, black, or yellow, who tries to force his way inside."

I went to New York City in December for Malcolm X's reading of final additions to the manuscript, to include the latest developments. He was further than I had ever seen him from his old assured self, it seemed to me. He kept saying that the press was making light of his statements about the threats on his life. "They act like I'm jiving!" He brought up again the *Saturday Evening Post* editorial. "You can't trust the publishing people, I don't care what they tell you." The agent for the book sent to my hotel a contract dealing with foreign publication rights which needed Malcolm X's and my signature. I signed it as he observed and handed the pen to him. He looked suspiciously at the contract, and said, "I had better show this thing to my lawyer," and put the contract in his inside coat pocket. Driving in Harlem about an hour later, he suddenly stopped the car across the street from the 135th Street Y.M.C.A. Building. Withdrawing the contract, he signed it, and thrust it to me. "I'll trust you," he said, and drove on.

With Christmas approaching, upon an impulse I bought for Malcolm X's two oldest daughters two large dolls, with painted brown complexions, the kind of dolls that would "walk" when held by the left hand. When Malcolm X next came to my room in the Hotel Wellington, I said, "I've gotten something for you to take to Attallah and Qubilah for Christmas gifts," and I "walked" out the dolls. Amazement, then a wide grin spread over his face. "Well, what do you know about that? Well, how about that!" He bent to examine the dolls. His expression showed how touched he was. "You know," he said after a while, "this isn't something I'm proud to say, but I don't think I've ever bought one gift for my children. Everything they play with, either Betty got it for them, or somebody gave it to them, never me. That's not good, I know it. I've always been too *busy*."

In early January, I flew from upstate New York to Kennedy Airport where I telephoned Malcolm X at home and told him that I was waiting for another plane to Kansas City to witness the swearing-in of my younger brother George who had recently been elected a Kansas State Senator. "Tell your brother for me to remember us in the alley," Malcolm X said. "Tell him that he and all of the other moderate Negroes who are getting somewhere need to always remember that it was us extremists who made it possible." He said that when I was ready to leave Kansas, to telephone him saying when I would arrive back in New

York, and if he could we could get together. I did this, and he met me at Kennedy Airport. He had only a little while, he was so pressed, he said; he had to leave that afternoon himself for a speaking engagement which had come up. So I made reservations for the next flight back upstate, then we went outside and sat and talked in his car in a parking lot. He talked about the pressures on him everywhere he turned, and about the frustrations, among them that no one wanted to accept anything relating to him except "my old 'hate' and 'violence' image." He said "the so-called moderate" civil rights organizations avoided him as "too militant" and the "so-called militants" avoided him as "too moderate." "They won't let me turn the corner!" he once exclaimed, "I'm caught in a trap!"

In a happier area, we talked about the coming baby. We laughed about the four girls in a row already. "This one will be the boy," he said. He beamed, "If not, the *next* one!" When I said it was close to time for my plane to leave, he said he had to be getting on, too. I said, "Give my best to Sister Betty," he said that he would, we shook hands and I got outside and stood as he backed the blue Oldsmobile from its parking space. I called out "See you!" and we waved as he started driving away. There was no way to know that it was the last time I would see him alive.

On January 19, Malcolm X appeared on the Pierre Berton television show in Canada and said, in response to a question about integration and intermarriage:

"I believe in recognizing every human being as a human being—neither white, black, brown, or red; and when you are dealing with humanity as a family there's no question of integration or intermarriage. It's just one human being marrying another human being or one human being living around and with another human being. I may say, though, that I don't think it should ever be put upon a black man, I don't think the burden to defend any position should ever be put upon the black man, because it is the white man collectively who has shown that he is hostile toward integration and toward intermarriage and toward these other strides toward oneness. So as a black man and especially as a black American, any stand that I formerly took, I don't think that I would have to defend it because it's still a reaction to the society, and it's a reaction that was produced by the society; and I think that it is the society that produced this that should be attacked, not the reaction that develops among the people who are the victims of that negative society."

From this, it would be fair to say that one month before his death, Malcolm had revised his views on intermarriage to the point where he regarded it as simply a personal matter.

On the 28th of January, Malcolm X was on TWA's Flight No. 9 from New York that landed at about three P.M. in Los Angeles. A special police intelligence squad saw Malcolm X greeted by two close friends, Edward Bradley and Allen Jamal, who drove him to the Statler-Hilton Hotel where Malcolm X checked into Room 1129. Said Bradley, "As we entered the lobby, six men came in right after us. I recognized them as Black Muslims." When Malcolm X returned downstairs to the lobby, he "practically bumped into the Muslim entourage. The Muslims were stunned. Malcolm's face froze, but he never broke his gait. Then, we knew we were facing trouble." Malcolm X's friends drove him to pick up "two former secretaries of Elijah Muhammad, who (had) filed paternity suits against him," and they went to the office of the colorful Los Angeles attorney Gladys Root. Mrs. Root said that Malcolm X made accusations about Elijah Muhammad's conduct with various former secretaries.

After dinner, Malcolm X's two friends drove him back to the hotel. "Black Muslims were all over the place," Bradley related. "Some were in cars and others stood around near the hotel. They had the hotel completely surrounded. Malcolm sized up the situation and jumped out of the car. He warned me to watch out and ran into the lobby. He went to his room and remained there for the rest of his stay in Los Angeles."

The car in which Malcolm X left the hotel, bound for the airport, was followed, said Bradley. "Hardly had we got on the Freeway when we saw two carloads of Black Muslims following us. The cars started to pull alongside. Malcolm picked up my walking cane and stuck it out of a back window as if it were a rifle. The two cars fell behind. We picked up speed, pulled off the airport ramp, and roared up to the front of the terminal. The police were waiting and Malcolm was escorted to the plane through an underground passageway. Then I saw Malcolm to the plane.''

Chicago police were waiting when the plane landed at O'Hare Airport that night at eight o'clock. Driven to the Bristol Hotel, Malcolm X checked in, and the adjoining suite was taken by members of the police force who would keep him under steady guard for the next three days in Chicago. Malcolm X testified at the office of the Attorney General of the State of Illinois which had been investigating the Nation of Islam. Another day he appeared on the television program of Irv Kupcinet; he described attempts that had been made to kill him. He said he had on his desk a letter naming the persons assigned to kill him. When police returned Malcolm X to his hotel ''at least 15 grim-faced Negroes (were) loitering nearby.'' Whispered Malcolm X to Detective Sergeant Edward McClellan, ''Those are all Black Muslims. At least two of them I recognize as being from New York. Elijah seems to know every move I make.'' Later, in his room, he told the detective, ''It's only going to be a matter of time before they catch up with me. I know too much about the Muslims. But their threats are not going to stop me from what I am determined to do.'' After that night spent in the hotel, Malcolm X was police-escorted back to O'Hare where he caught a plane to New York City's Kennedy Airport.

Right away, he was served with a court order of eviction from the Elmhurst home. He telephoned me upstate. His voice was strained. He told me that he had filed an appeal to the court order, that on the next day he was going to Alabama, and thence to England and France for scheduled speeches, and soon after returning he would go to Jackson, Mississippi, to address the Mississippi Freedom Democratic Party, on February 19. Then he said—the first time he had ever voiced to me such an admission—''Haley, my nerves are shot, my brain's tired.'' He said that upon his return from Mississippi, he would like to come and spend two or three days in the town where I was, and read the book's manuscript again. ''You say it's a quiet town. Just a couple of days of peace and quiet, that's what I need.'' I said that he knew he was welcome, but there was no need for him to tax himself reading through the long book again, as it had only a few very minor editing changes since he had only recently read it. ''I just want to read it one more time,'' he said, ''because

I don't expect to read it in finished form." So we made a tentative agreement that the day after his projected return from Mississippi, he would fly upstate to visit for a weekend with me. The projected date was the Saturday and Sunday of February 20–21.

Jet magazine reported Malcolm X's trip to Selma, Alabama, on the invitation of two members of the Student Nonviolent Coordinating Committee. Dr. Martin Luther King was in a Selma jail when Malcolm X's arrival sent officials of Dr. King's Southern Christian Leadership Conference "into a tailspin." Quickly, the SCLC's Executive Director Reverend Andrew Young and Reverend James Bevel met with Malcolm X, urging him not to incite any incidents and cautioning him that his presence could cause violence. "He listened with a smile," said Miss Faye Bellamy, secretary of the SNCC, who accompanied Malcolm X to a Negro church where he would address a mass meeting. "Remember this: nobody puts words in my mouth," he told Miss Bellamy. He told her that "in about two weeks" he planned to start Southern recruiting for his Harlem-based OAAU. At the church where he would speak, Malcolm X was seated on the platform next to Mrs. Martin Luther King, to whom he leaned and whispered that he was "trying to help," she told *Jet*. "He said he wanted to present an alternative; that it might be easier for whites to accept Martin's proposals after hearing him (Malcolm X). I didn't understand him at first," said Mrs. King. "He seemed rather anxious to let Martin know he was not causing trouble or making it difficult, but that he was trying to make it easier. . . . Later, in the hallway, he reiterated this. He seemed sincere. . . ."

Addressing the mass meeting Malcolm X reportedly shouted: "I don't advocate violence, but if a man steps on my toes, I'll step on his." . . . "Whites better be glad Martin Luther King is rallying the people because other forces are waiting to take over if he fails."

Returned to New York City, Malcolm X soon flew to France. He was scheduled to speak before a Congress of African Students. But he was formally advised that he would not be permitted to speak and, moreover, that he could consider himself officially barred forever from France as "an undesirable person." He was asked to leave—and he did, fuming with indignation. He flew on to London, and reporters of the British Broadcasting Corporation took him on an interviewing tour in Smethwick, a town near Birmingham with a large colored population. Numerous residents raised a storm of criticism that the B.B.C. was a party to a "fanning of racism" in the already tension-filled community. On this visit, he spoke also at the London School of Economics.

Malcolm X returned to New York City on Saturday, February 13th. He was asleep with his family when at about a quarter of three the following Sunday morning, a terrifying blast awakened them. Sister Betty would tell me later that Malcolm X, barking commands and snatching up screaming, frightened children, got the family safely out of the back door into the yard. Someone had thrown flaming Molotov cocktail gasoline bombs through the front picture window. It took the fire department an hour to extinguish the flames. Half the house was destroyed. Malcolm X had no fire insurance.

Pregnant, distraught Sister Betty and the four little daughters went to the home of close friends. Malcolm X steeled himself to catch a plane as scheduled that morning to speak in Detroit. He wore an open-necked sweater shirt under his suit. Immediately afterward, he flew back to New York. Monday morning, amid a flurry of emergency re-housing plans for his family, Malcolm X was outraged when he learned that Elijah Muhammad's New York Mosque Number 7 Minister James X had told the press that Malcolm X himself had fire-bombed the home "to get publicity."

Monday night, Malcolm X spoke to an audience in the familiar Audubon Ballroom. If he had possessed the steel nerves not to become rattled in public before, now he was: "I've reached the end of my rope!" he shouted to the audience of five hundred. "I wouldn't care for myself if they would not harm my family!" He declared flatly, "My house was bombed by the *Muslims!*" And he hinted at revenge. "There are hunters; there are also those who hunt the hunters!"

Tuesday, February 16th, Malcolm X telephoned me. He spoke very briefly, saying that the complications following the bombing of his home had thrown his plans so awry that he would be unable to visit me upstate on the weekend as he had said he would. He said he had also had to cancel his planned trip to

Jackson, Mississippi, which he was going to try and make later. He said he had to hurry to an appointment, and hung up. I would read later where also on that day, he told a close associate, "I have been marked for death in the next five days. I have the names of five Black Muslims who have been chosen to kill me. I will announce them at the meeting." And Malcolm X told a friend that he was going to apply to the Police Department for a permit to carry a pistol. "I don't know whether they will let me have one or not, as I served time in prison."

On Thursday he told a reporter, in an interview which did not appear until after his death: "I'm man enough to tell you that I can't put my finger on exactly what my philosophy is now, but I'm flexible."

The blackboard in the OAAU office counseled members and visitors that "Bro. Malcolm Speaks Thurs. Feb. 18, WINS Station, 10:30 P.M." Earlier Thursday, Malcolm X discussed locating another home with a real estate dealer. On Friday, he had an appointment with Gordon Parks, the *Life* magazine photographer-author whom he had long admired and respected. "He appeared calm and somewhat resplendent with his goatee and astrakhan hat," Parks would report later in *Life*. "Much of the old hostility and bitterness seemed to have left him, but the fire and confidence were still there." Malcolm X, speaking of the old Mosque Number 7 days, said, "That was a bad scene, brother. The sickness and madness of those days—I'm glad to be free of them. It's a time for martyrs now. And if I'm to be one, it will be in the cause of brotherhood. That's the only thing that can save this country. I've learned it the hard way—but I've learned it. . . ."

Parks asked Malcolm X if it was really true that killers were after him. "It's as true as we are standing here," Malcolm X said. "They've tried it twice in the last two weeks." Parks asked him about police protection, and Malcolm X laughed, "Brother, nobody can protect you from a Muslim but a Muslim—or someone trained in Muslim tactics. I know. I invented many of those tactics."

Recalling the incident of the young white college girl who had come to the Black Muslim restaurant and asked "What can I *do?*" and he told her "Nothing," and she left in tears, Malcolm X told Gordon Parks, "Well, I've lived to regret that incident. In many parts of the African continent I saw white students helping black people. Something like this kills a lot of argument. I did many things as a Muslim that I'm sorry for now. I was a zombie then—like all Muslims—I was hypnotized, pointed in a certain direction and told to march. Well, I guess a man's entitled to make a fool of himself if he's ready to pay the cost. It cost me twelve years.''

Saturday morning, he drove Sister Betty to see a real estate man. The house that the man then showed them that Malcolm X particularly liked, in a predominantly Jewish neighborhood also on Long Island, required a $3000 down payment. Sister Betty indicated her approval, too, and Malcolm X told the real estate man he thought they would take it. Driving Sister Betty back to the friends' home where she was staying with the children, they estimated that it would cost them about another $1000 to make the move. He stayed until mid-afternoon with Sister Betty at the friends' home, talking. He told her that he realized that she had been under protracted great strain, and that he was sorry about it. When he got his hat to leave, to drive into Manhattan, standing in the hallway, he told Sister Betty, ''We'll all be together. I want my family with me. Families shouldn't be separated. I'll never make another long trip without you. We'll get somebody to keep the children. I'll never leave you so long again.''

''I couldn't help but just break out grinning,'' Sister Betty would later tell me.

She figured that he must have stopped at a nearby drugstore to use the telephone booth when I later told her that Malcolm X had telephoned me upstate at about 3:30 that afternoon.

For the first time in nearly two years, I did not recognize immediately that the voice on the other end of the phone belonged to Malcolm X. He sounded as if he had a heavy, deep cold. He told me that in the middle of the night he and some friends had helped a moving company's men take out of the other house all of the family's furniture and other belongings salvageable after the fire-bombing—before a sheriff's eviction party would set the things out on the sidewalk. ''Betty and I have been looking at a house we want to buy''—he tried a chuckle—''you know nobody's going to *rent*, not to *me*, these days!'' He said, ''All I've got is about $150,'' and that he needed a $3000 down-payment plus $1000 moving costs; he asked if I thought the publisher would advance him $4000 against the projected profits from the book. I said that when our agent's offices opened on Monday morning, I would telephone and I knew that he would query the publisher to see if it couldn't be arranged, then Monday night I would call him back and let him know.

He said that he and Sister Betty had decided that although they were going to pay for the house, to avoid possible trouble they had gotten the agreement of his sister Ella who lived in Boston to let the house be bought in her name. He said that he still owed $1500 to his sister Ella which she had loaned him to make one trip abroad. Eventually they would change the house's title into Sister Betty's name, he said, or maybe into the name of their oldest daughter, Attallah.

He digressed on the dangers he faced. "But, you know, I'm going to tell you something, brother—the more I keep thinking about this thing, the things that have been happening lately, I'm not all that sure it's the Muslims. I know what they can do, and what they can't, and they can't do some of the stuff recently going on. Now, I'm going to tell you, the more I keep thinking about what happened to me in France, I think I'm going to quit saying it's the Muslims."

Then—it seemed to me such an odd, abrupt change of subject: "You know, I'm glad I've been the first to establish official ties between Afro-Americans and our blood brothers in Africa." And saying good-bye, he hung up.

After that telephone call, Malcolm X drove on into Manhattan and to the New York Hilton Hotel between 53rd and 54th Streets at Rockefeller Center. He checked the blue Oldsmobile into the hotel garage and then, in the lobby, he checked himself in and was assigned a twelfth-floor room, to which a bellman accompanied him.

Soon some Negro men entered the giant hotel's busy lobby. They began asking various bellmen what room Malcolm X was in. The bellmen, of course, never would answer that question concerning any guest—and considering that it was Malcolm X whom practically everyone who read New York City newspapers knew was receiving constant death threats, the bellmen quickly notified the hotel's security chief. From then until Malcolm X checked out the next day, extra security vigilance was continuously maintained on the twelfth floor. During that time, Malcolm X left the room only once, to have dinner in the hotel's lobby-level, dimly lit Bourbon Room.

Sunday morning at nine o'clock, Sister Betty in Long Island was surprised when her husband telephoned her and asked if she felt it would be too much trouble for her to get all of the four children dressed and bring them to the two o'clock meeting that afternoon at the Audubon Ballroom in Harlem. She said, "Of course it won't!" On Saturday he had told her that she couldn't come to the meeting. He said to her, "You know what happened an hour ago? Exactly at eight o'clock, the phone woke me up. Some man said, 'Wake up, brother' and hung up." Malcolm X said good-bye to Sister Betty.

And four hours later, Malcolm X left his room and took an elevator down to the lobby, where he checked out. He got his car and in the clear, warm midday of Sunday, February 21, he drove uptown to the Audubon Ballroom.

The Audubon Ballroom, between Broadway and St. Nicholas Avenue, on the south side of West 166th Street, is a two-story building frequently rented for dances, organization functions, and other affairs. A dark, slender, pretty young lady, occupationally a receptionist and avocationally a hardworking OAAU assistant to Malcolm X, has since told me that she arrived early, about 1:30 P.M., having some preliminary work to do. Entering, she saw that the usual 400 wooden chairs had been set up, with aisles on either side, but no center aisle; the young lady (she wishes to be nameless) noticed that several people were already seated in the front rows, but she gave it no thought since some always came early, liking to get seats up close to the stage, to savor to the fullest the dramatic orator Malcolm X. On the stage, behind the speaker's stand, were eight straight brown chairs arranged in a row and behind it was the stage's painted backdrop, a mural of a restful country scene. The young lady's responsibilities for this day had included making arrangements and subsequent confirmations with the scheduled co-speaker, the Reverend Milton Galamison, the militant Brooklyn Presbyterian who in 1964 had led the two one-day Negro boycotts in New York City public schools, protesting "racial imbalance." She had similarly made arrangements with some other prominent Negroes who were due to appeal to the audience for their maximum possible contributions to aid the work of Malcolm X and his organization.

The people who entered the ballroom were not searched at the door. In recent weeks, Malcolm X had become irritable about this, saying "It makes people uncomfortable" and that it reminded him of Elijah Muhammad. "If I can't be safe among my own kind, where can I be?" he had once said testily. For this day, also, he had ordered the press—as such—barred, white or black. He was angry at what he interpreted as "slanted" press treatment recently; he felt especially that the newspapers had not taken seriously his statements of the personal danger he was in. United Press International reporter Stanley Scott, a Negro, had been admitted, he later said, when a Malcolm lieutenant decided, "As a Negro, you will be allowed to enter as a citizen if you like, but you must remove your press badge." The same criterion had applied to WMCA newsman Hugh Simpson. Both he and Scott came early enough so that they obtained seats up near the stage.

Malcolm X entered the ballroom at shortly before two o'clock, trudging heavily instead of with his usual lithe strides, his young lady assistant has told me. By this time several other of his assistants were filtering in and out of the small anteroom alongside the stage. He sat down sideways on a chair, his long legs folded around its bottom, and he leaned one elbow on a kind of counter before a rather rickety make-up mirror that entertainers used when dances were held in the ballroom. He wore a dark suit, white shirt and narrow dark tie. He said to a little group of his assistants that he wasn't going to talk about his personal troubles, "I don't want that to be the reason for anyone to come to hear me." He stood up and paced about the little room. He said he was going to state that he had been hasty to accuse the Black Muslims of bombing his home. "Things have happened since that are bigger than what they can do. I know what they can do. Things have gone beyond that."

Those in the anteroom could hear the sounds of the enlarging audience outside taking seats. "The way I feel, I ought not to go out there at all today," Malcolm X said. "In fact, I'm going to ease some of this tension by telling the black man not to fight himself—that's all a part of the white man's big maneuver, to keep us fighting among ourselves, against each other. I'm not fighting anyone, that's not what we're here for.'' He kept glancing at his wrist watch, anticipating the arrival of Reverend Galamison. ''Whenever you make any appointment with a minister,'' he said to his young lady assistant, ''you have to call them two or three hours before time, because they will change their mind. This is typical of ministers.''

''I felt bad, I felt that it was my fault,'' the young lady told me. ''It was time for the meeting to start, too.'' She turned to Malcolm X's stalwart assistant Benjamin X, known as a highly able speaker himself. ''Brother, will you speak?'' she asked— then, turning to Malcolm X, ''Is it all right if he speaks? And maybe he could introduce you.'' Malcolm X abruptly whirled on her, and barked, ''You know you shouldn't ask me right in front of him!'' Then, collecting himself quickly, he said ''Okay.'' Brother Benjamin X asked how long he should speak. Malcolm X said, glancing again at his wrist watch, ''Make it half an hour.'' And Brother Benjamin X went through the door leading onto the stage. They heard him expertly exhorting the audience about what is needed today by ''the black man here in these United States.''

The Reverend Galamison and other notables due hadn't arrived by three o'clock. ''Brother Malcolm looked so disappointed,'' the young lady says. ''He said to me 'I don't think any of them are coming, either.' I felt so terrible for him. It did seem as if no one cared. I told him 'Oh, don't worry, they're just late, they'll be here.' '' (It was also reported by another source that Galamison, unable to come to the meeting, did telephone earlier, and that Malcolm X was told of this before he went out to speak.)

Then Brother Benjamin X's half-hour was up, and the young lady and Malcolm X, alone back there in the anteroom, could hear him entering the introduction: ''And now, without further remarks, I present to you one who is willing to put himself on the line for you, a man who would give his life for you—I want you to hear, listen, to understand—one who is a *trojan* for the black man!''

Applause rose from the audience; at the anteroom door, Malcolm X turned and looked back at his young lady assistant.

"You'll have to forgive me for raising my voice to you—I'm just about at my wit's end."

"Oh, don't *mention* it!" she said quickly, "I understand."

His voice sounded far away, "I wonder if anybody *really* understands—" And he walked out onto the stage, into the applause, smiling and nodding at Brother Benjamin X who passed him en route to the anteroom.

The young lady had picked up some paperwork she had to do when Benjamin X came in, perspiring. She patted his hand, saying, "That was good!" Through the anteroom door, just ajar, she and Benjamin X heard the applause diminishing, then the familiar ringing greeting, "*Asalaikum*, brothers and sisters!"

"Asalaikum salaam!" some in the audience responded.

About eight rows of seats from the front, then, a disturbance occurred. In a sudden scuffling, a man's voice was raised angrily, "Take your hand out of my pocket!" The entire audience was swiveling to look. "Hold it! Hold it! Don't get excited," Malcolm X said crisply, "Let's cool it, brothers—"

With his own attention distracted, it is possible that he never saw the gunmen. One woman who was seated near the front says, "The commotion back there diverted me just for an instant, then I turned back to look at Malcolm X just in time to see at least three men in the front row stand and take aim and start firing simultaneously. It looked like a firing squad." Numerous persons later said they saw two men rushing toward the stage, one with a shotgun, the other with two revolvers. Said U.P.I. reporter Stanley Scott: "Shots rang out. Men, women and children ran for cover. They stretched out on the floor and ducked under tables." Radio Station WMCA reporter Hugh Simpson said, "Then I heard this muffled sound, I saw Malcolm hit with his hands still raised, then he fell back over the chairs behind him. Everybody was shouting. I saw one man firing a gun from under his coat behind me as I hit it [the floor], too. He was firing like he was in some Western, running backward toward the door and firing at the same time."

The young lady who was in the backstage anteroom told me, "It sounded like an army had taken over. Somehow, I knew. I wouldn't go and look. I wanted to remember him as he was."

Malcolm X's hand flew to his chest as the first of sixteen

shotgun pellets or revolver slugs hit him. Then the other hand flew up. The middle finger of the left hand was bullet-shattered, and blood gushed from his goatee. He clutched his chest. His big body suddenly fell back stiffly, knocking over two chairs; his head struck the stage floor with a thud.

In the bedlam of shouting, screaming, running people, some ran toward the stage. Among them Sister Betty scrambled up from where she had thrown her body over her children, who were shrieking; she ran crying hysterically, "My husband! They're killing my husband!" An unidentified photographer snapped shots of Malcolm X prone on the stage floor with people bent over him snatching apart his bloody shirt, loosening his tie, trying to give him mouth-to-mouth artificial respiration, first a woman, then a man. Said the woman, who identified herself only as a registered nurse, "I don't know how I got up on the stage, but I threw myself down on who I thought was Malcolm— but it wasn't. I was willing to die for the man, I would have taken the bullets myself; then I saw Malcolm, and the firing had stopped, and I tried to give him artificial respiration." Then Sister Betty came through the people, herself a nurse, and people recognizing her moved back; she fell on her knees looking down on his bare, bullet-pocked chest, sobbing, "They killed him!"

Patrolman Thomas Hoy, 22, was stationed outside the Audubon Ballroom entrance. "I heard the shooting and the place exploded." He rushed inside, he saw Malcolm X lying on the stage, and then some people chasing a man. Patrolman Hoy "grabbed the suspect."

Louis Michaux, the owner of the Nationalist Memorial Bookstore at 125th Street and Seventh Avenue in Harlem, said, "I was arriving late at the meeting where Malcolm X had invited me, I met a large number of people rushing out."

Sergeant Alvin Aronoff and Patrolman Louis Angelos happened to be cruising by in their radio car when they heard shots. "When we got there," said Aronoff, "the crowds were pushing out and screaming 'Malcolm's been shot!' and 'Get 'im, get 'im, don't let him go!' " The two policemen grabbed by the arms a Negro who was being kicked as he tried to escape. Firing a warning shot into the air, the policemen pushed the man into their police car, not wanting the angry crowd to close in, and drove him quickly to the police station.

Someone had run up to the Columbia-Presbyterian Hospital's Vanderbilt Clinic emergency entrance at 167th Street and grabbed a poles-and-canvas stretcher and brought it back to the Audubon Ballroom stage. Malcolm X was put on the stretcher and an unidentified photographer got a macabre picture of him, with his mouth open and his teeth bared, as men rushed him up to the hospital clinic emergency entrance. A hospital spokesman said later that it was about 3:15 P.M. when Malcolm X reached a third-floor operating room. He was "either dead, or in a death-appearing state," said the spokesman.

A team of surgeons cut through his chest to attempt to massage the heart. The effort was abandoned at 3:30 P.M.

Reporters who had descended upon the hospital office fired questions at the spokesman, who kept saying brusquely, "I don't know." Then he took the elevator upstairs to the emergency operating room. A small crowd of friends and Sister Betty had also pushed into the hospital office when the hospital spokesman returned. Collecting himself, he made an announcement: "The gentleman you know as Malcolm X is dead. He died from gunshot wounds. He was apparently dead before he got here. He was shot in the chest several times, and once in the cheek."

The group filed out of the hospital office. The Negro men were visibly fighting their emotions; one kept smashing his fist into the other cupped palm. Among the women, many were openly crying.

Moments after the news flashed throughout Harlem (and throughout the entire world), a crowd began to gather outside the Hotel Theresa where Malcolm X's OAAU had its headquarters. They learned over transistor radios that the man whom the two policemen had taken from the murder scene initially identified himself as Thomas Hagan, 22 (he was later identified as Talmadge Hayer), in whose right trousers pocket the policemen had found a .45 caliber cartridge clip containing four unused cartridges, and then at Jewish Memorial Hospital doctors had reported that Hayer had been shot in the left thigh, his forehead was bruised and his body was beaten. "If we hadn't gotten him away, they would have kicked him to death," Sergeant Aronoff had said, and Hayer had been taken to the Bellevue Hospital Prison Ward.

By five P.M., the crowd in front of the Theresa Hotel had been quietly, carefully dispersed, and the Black Muslim Mosque Number 7 and its restaurant around the corner, at 116th Street and Lenox Avenue, had been ordered closed as a precautionary measure, on the orders of the local 28th Precinct's Captain Lloyd Sealy, New York City's first Negro to command a precinct. When reporters telephoned the Black Muslim restaurant, a man's voice stated, "No one is available to make any statement." When the OAAU office in the Theresa Hotel was tried, the telephone kept ringing, unanswered. Precinct Captain Sealy soon appeared, walking by himself along 125th Street, swinging his nightstick and conversing with people he met.

At the 28th Precinct station house on West 123rd Street, the forty policemen who were to have gone off duty at four P.M. had been told they must remain on duty, and two full busloads of the highly trained New York City Police Tactical Patrol Force had arrived at the precinct. Various high police officials made press statements. A Tactical Patrol Force Captain, Harry Kaiser, said no unusual occurrences had been noted, and he anticipated no trouble. Deputy Police Commissioner Walter Arm said that "hundreds" of extra policemen would be put into the Harlem area, including some members of the Bureau of Special Services. An Assistant Chief Inspector, Harry Taylor, speculated that the assassins had not rushed from the ballroom among the crowd, but had kept running past the stage and escaped on 165th Street. In the early evening, the police department's Chief of Detectives Philip J. Walsh quit a vacation he was on to join the hunt for the killers, and he said he looked forward to "a long-drawn-out investigation." Police and reporters at the shooting scene had pictures taken of the stage, with white chalk marks now circling five bullet holes in the speaker's stand; there were other holes in the stage's mural backdrop, indicating slugs or shotgun pellets which had either missed Malcolm X or passed through him. Police declined to discuss a rumor sweeping Harlem that they had some motion pictures which had been taken in the Audubon Ballroom as the murder took place. Another rumor that gained swift momentum was that when Sister Betty had leaned over her husband's body, she had removed from his coat pocket a paper on which he had written the names of those he had supposedly learned were assigned to execute him.

Deputy Police Commissioner Walter Arm stressed that the

department had made efforts to protect Malcolm X. Twenty different times the department had offered protection to Malcolm X or to some of his assistants, and the protection was refused, said Commissioner Arm, and seventeen times uniformed police guards had been offered for the OAAU meetings at the Audubon Ballroom, the most recent time being "last Sunday." Asked about the pistol permit that Malcolm X had said publicly he planned to request, Commissioner Arm said that as far as he knew, Malcolm X had never actually filed a request.

A number of questions have been raised. The "suspect" arrested by Patrolman Hoy as he was being chased from the meeting has, at present writing, not been identified publicly. Deputy Police Commissioner Walter Arm's statement that Malcolm X refused police protection conflicts directly with the statements of many of his associates that during the week preceding his assassination Malcolm X complained repeatedly that the police would not take his requests for protection seriously. Finally, although police sources said that a special detail of twenty men had been assigned to the meeting and that it had even been attended by agents of the Bureau of Special Services, these men were nowhere in evidence during or after the assassination, and Talmadge Hayer, rescued from the crowd and arrested as a suspect immediately after the assassination, was picked up by two patrolmen in a squad car cruising by.

On long-distance telephones, reporters reached the Chicago mansion headquarters of Elijah Muhammad. He would not come to the telephone, but a spokesman of his said that Muhammad "has no comment today, but he might have something to say tomorrow." No statement could be obtained either from Malcolm X's oldest brother, Wilfred X, the Black Muslim minister of Mosque Number 1 in Detroit. At his home, a woman told reporters that Minister Wilfred X was not there, that he had not gone to New York, and she didn't believe he had any plans to do so. (Minister Wilfred X, reached later, said that he anticipated attending the Black Muslim convention in Chicago on the following Sunday, and regarding his brother, "My brother is dead and there is nothing we can do to bring him back.")

As dark fell, many Negro men and women assembled before Louis Michaux's bookstore, where most of Harlem's Black Nationalist public activity centered. A small group of OAAU members opened their Hotel Theresa headquarters and sat in the room and would not make any statements to reporters.

The New York *Daily News* came onto the newsstands with its cover page devoted to "Malcolm X Murdered" over the photograph of him being borne away on the stretcher, and a sub-caption, "Gunned Down at Rally." In Long Island, where she had been taken just after her father's murder, six-year-old Attallah carefully wrote a letter to him, "Dear Daddy, I love you so. O dear, O dear, I wish you wasn't dead."

The body—still listed as "John Doe" because it had not yet been formally identified—had been moved late Sunday to the New York City Medical Examiner's office at 520 First Avenue. The autopsy confirmed that shotgun pellet wounds in the heart had killed Malcolm X. Chief Medical Examiner Dr. Milton Helpern said that death followed the first sawed-off shotgun blast which caused thirteen wounds in the heart and chest, and he said that .38 and .45 caliber bullet wounds in the thighs and legs evidenced that Malcolm X had been shot at after he had fallen.

Monday morning the official identification was made at the Medical Examiner's office by Sister Betty, who was accompanied by Percy Sutton, Malcolm X's Boston half-sister Mrs. Ella Collins, and Joseph E. Hall, General Manager of the large Unity Funeral Home in Harlem. Leaving the Medical Examiner's office at about noon to go and complete funeral arrangements, Sister Betty told reporters, "No one believed what he said. They never took him seriously, even after the bombing of our home they said he did it himself!"

At the Unity Funeral Home on the east side of Eighth Avenue between 126th and 127th Streets, Sister Betty chose a six-foot-nine-inch bronze casket lined with egg-shell velvet. At her request, the funeral would be delayed until the following Saturday, five days away. The funeral home's manager Hall announced to the press that the body would be dressed in a business suit, and it would be put on view under a glass shield from Tuesday through Friday, then the Saturday services would be at a Harlem church.

Soon posted on the funeral home's directory was "El-Hajj Malik El-Shabazz." In Brooklyn, orthodox Moslem Sheik Al-Hajh Daoud Ahmed Faisal of the Islamic Mission of America said that the delayed funeral services violated a Moslem practice that the sun should not set twice on a believer's body, that the Koran prescribed burial inside twenty-four hours if possible, and Moslems believed that when a body grows cold the soul leaves it and when the body is put into the earth it comes alive again.

In Chicago, where policemen were watching all bus depots, railways, terminals, O'Hare Airport and highway entrances, Elijah Muhammad, under heavy guard in his three-story mansion, said, "Malcolm died according to his preaching. He seems to have taken weapons as his god. Therefore, we couldn't tolerate a man like that. He preached war. We preach peace. We are permitted to fight if we are attacked—that's the Scripture, the Koran, and the Bible, too. But we will never be the aggressor. I don't have the right to be frightened, because I was chosen by Allah. If Allah gives me up to the hands of the wicked, I am satisfied. My life is in the hands of Allah." The grounds outside the mansion were patrolled by both Chicago police and Fruit of Islam bodyguards. More of both patrolled before the University of Islam high school, and the offices of the newspaper *Muhammad Speaks*.

Malcolm X's lawyer, Assemblyman Percy Sutton, said that the police now had the names of those whom Malcolm X had said planned to kill him. All over Harlem, reporters were interviewing people, and microphones were being put before the mouths of the man-in-the-street. At police precinct station houses, people being questioned were leaving by side entrances. Said Assistant Chief Inspector Joseph Coyle, in charge of Manhattan North detectives, ". . . . a well-planned conspiracy. We're doing a screening process of the four hundred people who were in the hall at the time." Fifty detectives were on the case, he said, and he had been in touch with police in other cities.

Harlem was mostly asleep when around the Black Muslim Mosque Number 7, on the top floor of a four-story building at 116th Street and Lenox Avenue, an explosive sound at 2:15 A.M. ripped the night. Firemen were instantly summoned by the four policemen who had been guarding the sidewalk entrance to the mosque. Within a few minutes flames burst through the building's roof and leaped thirty feet into the air. For the next seven hours firemen would pour water into the building. On an adjacent roof they found an empty five-gallon gasoline can, a brown, gasoline-stained shopping bag, and oily rags. South-bound IRT subway service was re-routed for a while, also three bus lines. At the spectacular five-alarm fire's height, a wall of the building collapsed; it smashed two fire engines at the curb and injured five firemen, one seriously, and also a pedestrian who had been across the street buying a newspaper. By day-break, when the fire was declared "under control," the Black Muslim mosque and the Gethsemane Church of God in Christ on the floor beneath it were gutted, and seven street-level stores, including the Black Muslim restaurant, were "total losses." Fire Department sources said that replacing the ruined equip-ment would cost "around $50,000." Joseph X of the Black Muslims, who once had been the immediate assistant of Mal-colm X, said that Elijah Muhammad's followers had two alter-native mosques to meet in, one in Brooklyn and the other in Queens, Long Island. Both these mosques were under continu-ous police guard.

Across the nation in San Francisco on Tuesday afternoon two policemen discovered a fire beginning in the San Francisco Black Muslim Mosque, and quickly extinguished it. Kerosene had been splashed on the sidewalk and door and set afire.

The body of El-Hajj Malik El-Shabazz originally had been scheduled to go on public view at 2:30 P.M. Tuesday. Crowds stood in line behind police barricades waiting to be admitted and the policemen wherever one looked included numerous patrol cars and even sharpshooters on the roofs around the Unity Fu-neral Home. But the telephoned bomb-threats which had begun shortly after noon made necessary two evacuations of the funeral home for bomb-squad searches, which proved futile. A search was conducted even in the 43rd Street offices of the *New York Times* after a man telephoned complaining of an editorial about Malcolm X and said, "Your plant will be destroyed at four o'clock."

At the funeral home in Harlem, policemen inspected all pack-ages and floral pieces being delivered, as well as the large hand-bags of women mourners. It was 6:15 P.M. when a cordon of policemen arrived flanking Sister Betty and four close relatives and friends who entered the funeral home in a glare of flash-bulbs. "She's a black Jacqueline Kennedy," observed a white reporter. "She has class, she knows what to do and when, she handles herself beautifully."

It was 7:10 P.M. when the family party emerged and left. After ten minutes, the first of the waiting public was admitted. Between then and an hour before midnight, two thousand people, including scores of whites, had filed past the open coffin in which the body lay dressed in a dark business suit, a white shirt and dark tie, with a small, oblong brass plate above it inscribed, *"El-Hajj Malik El-Shabazz—May 19, 1925—Feb. 21, 1965."*

Malcolm X followers had been canvassing with growing anxiety for a Harlem church that would accept the Saturday funeral. Officials of several churches had refused, including a spokesman for the community's largest church, Abyssinian Baptist, of which Congressman-Reverend Adam Clayton Powell is the pastor; others which turned down requests, according to the *Amsterdam News*, included the Williams C.M.E. Church and The Refuge Temple of The Church of Our Lord Jesus Christ. Then the funeral was accepted by Bishop Alvin A. Childs for the Faith Temple, Church of God in Christ located at 147th Street and Amsterdam Avenue. The Faith Temple, a former movie theater which had been converted fifteen years previously, could seat a thousand in its auditorium and another seven hundred in its basement. Bishop Childs, who in 1964 had been elected as Harlem's "locality mayor," told the press that it was "as a humanitarian gesture" that he made his church available, and of Malcolm X, he said, ". . . a militant and vocal person. I did not agree with all of his philosophy, but this did not affect our friendship." Shortly after the news became known, Bishop Childs and his wife began to receive the first of a succession of bomb threats telephoned both to the church and to their home.

Prominent Negro figures were being quoted by the various press media. The famed psychologist Dr. Kenneth B. Clark told *Jet* magazine, "I had a deep respect for this man. I believe that he was sincerely groping to find a place in the fight for Civil Rights, on a level where he would be respected and understood fully. I looked forward to his growth along those lines. It doesn't matter so much about his past. It is tragic that he was cut down at the point when he seemed on the verge of achieving the position of respectability he sought." A *New York Times* correspondent in a London press conference quoted the author and dramatist James Baldwin, who thought the death of Malcolm X was "a major setback for the Negro movement." Pointing at white reporters, Baldwin accused, "You did it . . . whoever did it was formed in the crucible of the Western world, of the American Republic!" European "rape" of Africa began racial problems and was therefore the beginning of the end for Malcolm X, Baldwin said.

The bookstore owner in Harlem, Louis Michaux, a major voice in the community, told the *Amsterdam News*, "It's things like the murder of Malcolm X that drive the masses closer together. He died in the same manner that Patrice Lumumba met his death in the Congo. . . . We must unite, not fight."

"Malcolm X caused many young Negroes to take a new vision of themselves," said Bayard Rustin, a main figure in organizing the March on Washington in 1963. A "third party" was suspected of killing Malcolm X by CORE's National Director James Farmer, who said, "Malcolm's murder was calculated to produce more violence and murder and vengeance killings." A few days later, asked for his opinion of a rumor circulating about that a "Red Chinese" plot brought about the murder, Farmer said, "I would not say it is impossible."

"For the Negroes in America, the death of Malcolm X is the most portentous event since the deportation of Marcus Garvey in the 1920's," said Dr. C. Eric Lincoln, author of *The Black Muslims in America*, who talked to the press at Brown University in Providence, R.I., where he was a visiting professor and research fellow. "I doubt there are 'international implications' in the slaying. The answer is closer to home. The answer is in the local struggle among contending rivals for leadership of the black masses, which are potentially the most volatile sub-group in America." Said Roy Wilkins, Executive Secretary of the National Association for the Advancement of Colored People, "Master spell-binder that he was, Malcolm X in death cast a spell more far-flung and more disturbing than any he cast in life."

The New York City police investigators who were pursuing the case were unhappy that Malcolm's followers had "not come forward" to aid the investigation. At police request, the press printed a telephone number, SW 5-8117, for "strictly confidential'' information that anyone might offer concerning the slaying. The police had picked up and were holding Reuben Francis, described as a Malcolm X ''bodyguard,'' who was believed to be the person who had shot the suspected assassin Talmadge Hayer during the melee the previous Sunday at the Audubon Ballroom. Hayer remained in the Bellevue Prison Ward, awaiting surgery.

As thousands continued viewing the body of the slain Malcolm X amid intermittent new bomb-threats telephoned to the funeral home, and to the Faith Temple where his funeral was scheduled for Saturday, a new organization, the Federation of Independent Political Action, threatened to picket all Harlem business establishments which would not close from Thursday afternoon until Monday morning ''in tribute to Malcolm X.'' The FIPA's spokesman was Jesse Gray, the well-known rent-strike leader; Harlem pedestrians began to be handed printed sheets reading, in part, ''If the stores refuse to close, they identify with our enemy—therefore we must close them—pass them by. Those that shop along 125th Street during the hours that the stores are to be closed identify with the murderous stooge that allowed the power structure to use his hands to kill Brother Malcolm.'' At a late evening FIPA rally before Louis Michaux's bookstore, Jesse Gray declared that in 1965 a Negro should run for Mayor of New York ''in the name of Malcolm,'' and speculated that such a candidate should receive 100,000 votes. Shortly after the FIPA rally, merchants and other members of the Uptown Chamber of Commerce met and swiftly passed a resolution urging all Harlem stores to remain open and ''continue to serve their customers,'' and recommendation was made that full pay be given to any store employees who might wish to attend Malcolm X's funeral on Saturday morning. Then one after another, Harlem leaders sharply criticized the FIPA proposal as ''irresponsible.'' Finally, nearly all of the Harlem stores kept their doors open for business. The FIPA got together about twenty pickets who patrolled for a while before Harlem's largest store, Blumstein's; leading the pickets were two white men carrying signs reading ''All Stores Should Close. Honor Malcolm X.''

The weather had turned very cold. Icicles hung from the collapsed roof of the fire-ruined building that had housed Black

Muslim Mosque Number 7. The *Amsterdam News*, its offices barely a block down Eighth Avenue from the funeral home where Malcolm X's body lay, editorialized, "Steady, Eddie!" saying that orderly tributes to Malcolm X would "confound his critics, who would like nothing better than to see black people rioting over his remains."

The fear of serious mass rioting set off by some unpredictable spark hung steadily in the air. An increasing number of Harlem leaders declared that the principal reason for this was the downtown white press media, sensationalizing what was going on in a calm, dignified community. Finally the Harlem Ministers' Interfaith Association would issue a formal accusation: "The screaming headlines of many of our newspapers make it seem as if all of Harlem was an armed camp, ready to explode at any moment. The vast majority of the citizens of the Harlem community is not involved in the unfortunate acts of violence that have been grossly overplayed by the press. Many times the slanting of the news is able to bring about an atmosphere through which a few depraved and reckless individuals can take advantage."

"Malcolm X Died Broke"—that headline in Harlem's *Amsterdam News* came as a shock to many in the community. Few had reflected that Malcolm X, upon becoming a Black Muslim minister, had signed an oath of poverty, so that for twelve years he never acquired anything in his own name. (Somewhere I have read that Malcolm X in his Black Muslim days received about $175 weekly to cover his living and other expenses exclusive of travel.) "He left his four daughters and pregnant wife with no insurance of any kind, no savings, and no income," the *Amsterdam News* story said (and it might have added that he never drew up a will; he had made a February 26th appointment with his lawyer—five days after his death). Within the week, two groups had organized and were asking Harlemites for contributions to help Sister Betty raise and educate the children (since organized as the Malcolm X Daughters' Fund at Harlem's Freedom National Bank, 275 West 125th Street).

In Boston, Malcolm X's half-sister, Mrs. Ella Mae Collins, told a news conference that she would choose the leaders of the OAAU to succeed Malcolm X. Mrs. Collins operated the Sarah A. Little School of Preparatory Arts where, she said, children were taught Arabic, Swahili, French, and Spanish. In 1959, she, too, had broken away from Elijah Muhammad's Black Muslims, to which she had originally been converted by Malcolm X.

Far from Harlem, in lands where Malcolm X had traveled, the press had given the murder a coverage that had highly irritated the Director of the United States Information Agency, Carl T. Rowan, himself a Negro. In Washington, addressing the American Foreign Service Association, Rowan said that when he first heard of the murder, he knew it would be grossly misconstrued in some countries where people were unaware what Malcolm X represented, and he said the USIA had worked hard to inform the African press of the facts about Malcolm X and his preachments, but still there had been "a host of African reaction based on misinformation and misrepresentation."

Said USIA Director Rowan, "Mind you, here was a Negro who preached segregation and race hatred, killed by another Negro, presumably from another organization that preaches segregation and race hatred, and neither of them representative of more than a tiny minority of the Negro population of America—" Rowan held up some foreign newspapers. "All this about an ex-convict, ex-dope peddler who became a racial fanatic," continued Rowan. "I can only conclude that we Americans know less about what goes on in the minds of other peoples than we thought, or the need to inform is even greater than we in USIA thought it to be."

The *Daily Times* of Lagos, in Nigeria, had said: "Like all mortals, Malcolm X was not without his faults . . . but that he was a dedicated and consistent disciple of the movement for the emancipation of his brethren, no one can doubt . . . Malcolm X has fought and died for what he believed to be right. He will have a place in the palace of martyrs." The *Ghanaian Times*, Accra, called Malcolm X "the militant and most popular of Afro-American anti-segregationist leaders" and it added his name to "a host of Africans and Americans" ranging from John Brown to Patrice Lumumba "who were martyred in freedom's cause." Also in Accra, the *Daily Graphic*: "The assassination of Malcolm X will go down in history as the greatest blow the American integrationist movement has suffered since the shocking assassinations of Medgar Evers and John F. Kennedy."

The Pakistan *Hurriyet of Karachi* said: "A great Negro leader"; the *Pakistan Times* said, "His death is a definite setback to the Negro movement for emancipation." The Peking, China *People's Daily* said the killing happened "because Malcolm X . . . fought for the emancipation of the 23,000,000 American Negroes." According to correspondents' reports, the first Algerian headline said "the Ku Klux Klan" assassinated Malcolm X; the pro-Communist *Alger Republican*'s editorial on the slaying accused "American Fascism," and the *Times'* Algerian correspondent said Algerians showed "signs" of raising Malcolm X to martyrdom. The U.S. Consulate in Georgetown, British Guiana, was marched on by pickets accusing "American imperialists." Another Peking, China paper, *Jenmin Jihpao*, said that the death showed that "in dealing with imperialist oppressors, violence must be met with violence." *Pravda* in Moscow carried only brief stories and no editorial comment, the *New York Times* Moscow correspondent said, and another in Poland said there was no noticeable reaction of any kind, and that "few Poles had heard of Malcolm or were interested in the racial issue." Reportedly, the murder was only routinely reported with little special interest by the press in Cairo, Beirut, New Delhi, and Saigon. In Paris and Western Europe, the story was "essentially a one-day sensation," with the West German press handling it "as if it were in the Chicago gangster tradition." The *New York Times* said: "The London newspapers have probably played the story harder and longer than most, giving continuing emphasis to the police work on the murder. The *London Times* and the *London Daily Telegraph* both carried editorial comments, but neither treated Malcolm X as a major figure." Also reported by the *New York Times* London correspondent was that "a London group calling itself the Council of African Organizations had violently attacked the United States over the murder. This group is made up of students and other unofficial African representatives here. A press release described Malcolm as a 'leader in the struggle against American imperialism, oppression and racialism.' It said, 'the butchers of Patrice Lumumba are the very same monsters who have murdered Malcolm X in cold blood.' "

Friday morning New York City press headlines concerning Malcolm X's slaying were devoted to the police department's apprehension of a second slaying suspect. He was a stocky, round-faced, twenty-six-year-old karate expert named Norman 3X Butler, allegedly a Black Muslim, and a week later, this was followed by the arrest of Thomas 15X Johnson, also allegedly a Black Muslim. Both men had been earlier indicted in the January, 1965, shooting of Benjamin Brown, a New York City Correction Officer and a Black Muslim defector. Both men were indicted, along with Hayer, for the murder of Malcolm X on March 10.

With the news announcement of Butler's arrest, and his at least tentative identification as a member of Elijah Muhammad's organization, tension reached a new high among all who had any role in the feud. The Black Muslim National Convention was scheduled to begin that Friday in Chicago, to last for three days. Early Friday morning in New York at the Kennedy Airport dozens of policemen spent forty minutes searching a plane belonging to Capital Airlines, which back in December 1964 had accepted a Mosque Number 7 charter flight to Chicago and return, at a fee of $5,175.54 which the mosque had subsequently paid in increments.

Altogether, about three thousand Black Muslims from their mosques in most sizable cities were in Chicago for their annual "Saviour's Day" convention, regarded by them as similar to the holiday of Christmas. In the order of arrival, each group from the different mosques and cities assembled outside the big sports coliseum south of Chicago's business district, the brothers of all ages dressed in neat, dark suits and white shirts and the sisters garbed in flowing silk gowns and headdresses—and every individual was filtered through an intense security check that Chicago police sources said was unprecedented in Chicago except for a visiting President.

Searched even more closely were the relatively few non-Muslim Negroes who came to be spectators, and the press representatives both white and black. "Take off your hat, show some respect!" snapped a Black Muslim guard at a white reporter. As each person was "cleared" a Fruit of Islam man ushered him or her to a specific seat in the drafty interior of the 7500-seat coliseum. (Later, Muslim sources would blame the half-full house upon "the white man's dividing of Negroes," but observers who recalled the packed coliseum in 1964 said that bombing fears kept away many non-Muslim Negroes.) The audience sat lightly murmuring under the two huge hanging banners proclaiming "Welcome Elijah Muhammad—We Are Glad To Have You With Us" and "We Must Have Some Of This Land" (referring to Elijah Muhammad's demand that "one or more states" be turned over to the "23 million so-called Negroes" in America as partial reparation for "over a century of our free blood and sweat as slaves which helped to develop this wealthy nation where still today you show us you do not wish or intend to accept us as equals"). In front of the wide, raised speaker's platform were two nearly life-sized photographic blowups of Elijah Muhammad. Standing between the stage and the audience were Fruit of Islam guards. Others were prowling the aisles, scanning rows of faces, with intermittent peremptory demands for identification, "What mosque, brother?" Still more Fruit of Islam men were inspecting the coliseum's vacant balcony, backstage, downstairs, and rafters and roof.

The ghost of Malcolm X was in the coliseum. First, in a high drama for the Muslims, Elijah Muhammad's son, Wallace Delaney Muhammad, who once had sided with Malcolm X, faced the audience and begged forgiveness for his defection. Next, two brothers of Malcolm X, Wilfred and Philbert, both of them Black Muslim ministers, urged unity with Elijah Muhammad. Said Minister Wilfred X of the Detroit mosque, "We would be ignorant to get confused and go to arguing and fighting among ourselves and forget who the real enemy is." Said Minister Philbert X, of the Lansing mosque, "Malcolm was my own blood brother, next to me. . . . I was shocked. No man wants to see his own brother destroyed. But I knew that he was traveling on a very reckless and dangerous road. I made attempts to change his course. When he was living, I tried to keep him living; now that he is dead, there is nothing I can do." Indicating the seated Elijah Muhammad, Minister Philbert X declared, "Where he leads me, I will follow"—and then he introduced the Black Muslim leader to make his address.

Only the head of Elijah Muhammad was visible above the grim-faced Fruit of Islam men in a living wall, Cassius Clay among them. Crescents, stars, moons and suns were in gold-thread embroidery on the small fez that Elijah Muhammad wore. He said in his speech: "For a long time, Malcolm stood here where I stand. In those days, Malcolm was safe, Malcolm was loved. God, Himself, protected Malcolm. . . . For more than a year, Malcolm was given his freedom. He went everywhere—Asia, Europe, Africa, even to Mecca, trying to make enemies for me. He came back preaching that we should not hate the enemy. . . . He came here a few weeks ago to blast away his hate and mud-slinging; everything he could think of to disgrace me. . . . We didn't want to kill Malcolm and didn't try to kill him. They know I didn't harm Malcolm. They know I loved him. His foolish teaching brought him to his own end. . . ."

Both physically and emotionally worked up, often Elijah Muhammad would begin coughing. "Take it easy! Take your time!" his audience pleaded with him. "He had no right to reject me!" Elijah Muhammad declared. "He was a star, who went astray! . . . They knew I didn't harm Malcolm, but he tried to make war against me." He said that Malcolm X would have been given "the most glorious of burials" if he had stayed with the Black Muslims and had died a natural death; "instead, we stand beside the grave of a hypocrite! . . . *Malcolm!* Who was he leading? Who was he teaching? He has no truth! We didn't want to kill Malcolm! His foolish teaching would bring him to his own end! I am not going to let the crackpots destroy the good things Allah sent to you and me!"

Elijah Muhammad drove his frail energy to speak for about an hour and a half. He challenged any would-be assassins: "If you seek to snuff out the life of Elijah Muhammad, you are inviting your own doom! The Holy Quran tells us not to pick a fight but to defend ourselves. We will fight!" It was mid-afternoon when Elijah Muhammad turned back to his seat with some three thousand Black Muslim men, women, and children shouting "Yes, *sir!* . . . So sweet! . . . All praise to Muhammad!"

In the Unity Funeral Home in the Harlem community of New York City in the mid-afternoon, the public's viewing of the body of Malcolm X was interrupted by the arrival of a party of about a dozen people whose central figure was a white-turbaned, dark-robed elderly man whose white beard fell to his chest and who carried a forked stick. When reporters rushed to attempt interviews, another man in the party waved them away, saying, "A silent tongue does not betray its owner." The man was Sheik

Ahmed Hassoun, a Sudanese, a member of the Sunni Moslems, who had taught in Mecca for 35 years when he had met Malcolm X there, and then had soon come to the United States to serve as Malcolm X's spiritual advisor and to teach at the Muslim Mosque, Inc.

Sheik Hassoun prepared the body for burial in accordance with Moslem ritual. Removing the Western clothing in which the body had been on display, Sheik Hassoun washed the body with special holy oil. Then he draped the body in the traditional seven white linen shrouds, called the *kafan*. Only the face with its reddish moustache and goatee was left exposed. The mourners who had come with Sheik Hassoun filed to the bier and he read passages from the Koran. Then he turned to a funeral home representative: "Now the body is ready for burial." Soon, the sheik and his retinue left, and the viewing by the public resumed. When the word spread, numbers of persons who had come before returned for another wait in the long, slowly moving line, wanting to see the Moslem burial dress.

It was late during this Friday afternoon that I got into the quietly moving line, thinking about the Malcolm X with whom I had worked closely for about two years. Blue-uniformed policemen stood at intervals watching us shuffle along within the wooden gray-painted police barricades. Just across the street several men were looking at the line from behind a large side window of the "Lone Star Barber Shop, Eddie Johns, Prop., William Ashe, Mgr." Among the policemen were a few press representatives talking to each other to pass the time. Then we were inside the softly lit, hushed, cool, large chapel. Standing at either end of the long, handsome bronze coffin were two big, dark policemen, mostly looking straight ahead, but moving their lips when some viewer tarried. Within minutes I had reached the coffin. Under the glass lid, I glimpsed the delicate white shrouding over the chest and up like a hood about the face on which I tried to concentrate for as long as I could. All that I could think was that it was he, all right—Malcolm X. "Move on"—the policeman's voice was soft. Malcolm looked to me— just waxy and *dead*. The policeman's hand was gesturing at his waist level. I thought, *"Well—good-bye."* I moved on.

Twenty-two thousand people had viewed the body when the line was stopped that night for good, at eleven P.M. Quietly, between midnight and dawn, a dozen police cars flanked a hearse that went the twenty-odd blocks farther uptown to the Faith Temple. The bronze coffin was wheeled inside and placed upon a platform draped in thick dark red velvet, in front of the altar, and the coffin's lid was reopened. As the hearse pulled away, policemen stood at posts of vigil both inside and outside Faith Temple. It was crispy cold outside.

About six A.M., people began forming a line on the east side of Amsterdam Avenue. By nine A.M., an estimated six thousand persons thronged the nearby blocks, behind police barriers, and faces were in every window of the apartment buildings across the street; some stood shivering on fire escapes. From 145th Street to 149th Street, policemen had blocked off all automobile traffic except for their own cars, the newspapers' cars, and the equipment trucks for radio and television on-the-spot coverage. There were hundreds of policemen, some on the rooftops in the immediate area. Combing the crowd's edges were reporters with microphones and notebooks. "He was fascinating, a remarkably fascinating man, that's why I'm here," a white girl in her mid-twenties told a *New York Times* man; and a Negro woman, "I'm paying my respects to the greatest black man in this century. He's a black man. Don't say colored." Another woman, noticing steel helmets inside a television network car, laughed to the driver, "You getting ready for next summer?"

When the Faith Temple doors were opened at 9:20, a corps of OAAU members entered. Within the next quarter-hour, twenty of the men had ushered in six hundred seat-holders. Fifty press reporters, photographers and television cameramen clustered beneath religious murals to the rear of the altar, and some stood on chairs to see better. A Negro engineer monitored recording equipment between the altar and the coffin which was guarded by eight uniformed Negro policemen and two uniformed Negro policewomen. One Negro plain-clothes policeman sat on either side of heavily veiled Sister Betty in the second row. The raised lid of the coffin hid the Faith Temple's brass tithe box and candelabra; the head of the Islamic Mission of America, in Brooklyn, Sheik Al-Haj Daoud Ahmed Faisal, had counseled that any hint of Christianity in the services would make the deceased a *kafir*, an unbeliever. (The sheik had also dissented with the days of public exhibition of the body: "Death is a private matter between Allah and the deceased.")

Before the services began, OAAU ushers brought in one floral wreath—a two-by-five arrangement of the Islamic Star and Crescent in white carnations against a background of red carnations.

First, the actor Ossie Davis and his wife, actress Ruby Dee, read the notes, telegrams and cables of condolence. They came from every major civil-rights organization; from individual figures such as Dr. Martin Luther King; from organizations and governments abroad, such as The Africa-Pakistan-West-Indian Society of the London School of Economics, the Pan-African Congress of Southern Africa, the Nigerian Ambassador from Lagos, the President of the Republic of Ghana, Dr. Kwame Nkrumah: "The death of Malcolm X shall not have been in vain."

Next, Omar Osman stood, a representative of the Islam Center of Switzerland and the United States: "We knew Brother Malcolm as a blood brother, particularly after his pilgrimage to Mecca last year. The highest thing that a Moslem can aspire to is to die on the battlefield and not die at his bedside—" He paused briefly to wait out the applause from among the mourners. "Those who die on the battlefield are not dead, but are alive!" The applause was louder, and cries rose, "Right! Right!" Omar Osman then critically commented upon the remarks which USIA Director Carl Rowan had made in Washington, D.C., about the foreign press reaction to the death of the deceased. From the audience then hisses rose.

Again, the actor Ossie Davis stood. His deep voice delivered the eulogy to Malcolm X which was going to cause Davis subsequently to be hailed more than ever among Negroes in Harlem:

"Here—at this final hour, in this quiet place, Harlem has come to bid farewell to one of its brightest hopes—extinguished now, and gone from us forever. . . .

"Many will ask what Harlem finds to honor in this stormy, controversial and bold young captain—and we will smile. . . . They will say that he is of hate—a fanatic, a racist—who can only bring evil to the cause for which you struggle!

"And we will answer and say unto them: Did you ever talk to Brother Malcolm? Did you ever touch him, or have him smile at you? Did you ever really listen to him? Did he ever do a mean thing? Was he ever himself associated with violence or any public disturbance? For if you did you would know him. And if you knew him you would know why we must honor him: Malcolm was our manhood, our living, black manhood! This was his meaning to his people. And, in honoring him, we honor the best in ourselves. . . . And we will know him then for what he was and is—a Prince—our own black shining Prince!—who didn't hesitate to die, because he loved us so.''

Brief speeches were made by others. Then, the family, the OAAU members and other Muslims present stood and filed by the coffin to view the body for the last time. Finally, the two plain-clothes policemen ushered Sister Betty to have her last sight of her husband. She leaned over, kissing the glass over him; she broke into tears. Until then almost no crying had been heard in the services, but now Sister Betty's sobs were taken up by other women.

The services had lasted a little over an hour when the three minutes of prayers said for every Muslim who is dead were recited by Alhajj Heshaam Jaaber, of Elizabeth, New Jersey. At the phrase "Allahu Akbar"—"God is most great"—all Muslims in the audience placed their opened hands at the sides of their faces.

An official cortege, with the hearse, of three family cars, eighteen mourners' cars, twelve police cars and six press cars—followed by about fifty other cars—briskly drove the eighteen miles out of Manhattan and along the New York Thruway, then off its Exit 7 to reach the Ferncliff Cemetery in Ardsley, N.Y. All along the route, Negroes placed their hats or hands over their hearts, paying their final respects. At each bridge crossing in Manhattan County, police cars stood watch; the Westchester County police had stationed individual patrolmen at intervals en route to the cemetery.

Over the coffin, final Moslem prayers were said by Sheik Alhajj Heshaam Jaaber. The coffin was lowered into the grave, the head facing the east, in keeping with Islamic tradition. Among the mourners, the Moslems knelt beside the grave to pray with their foreheads pressed to the earth, in the Eastern manner. When the family left the gravesite, followers of Malcolm X would not let the coffin be covered by the white gravediggers who had stood a little distance away, waiting. Instead, seven OAAU men began dropping bare handfuls of earth down on the coffin; then they were given shovels and they carried dirt to fill the grave, and then mound it.

The night fell over the earthly remains of El-Hajj Malik El-Shabazz, who had been called Malcolm X; who had been called Malcolm Little; who had been called "Big Red" and "Satan" and "Homeboy" and other names—who had been buried as a Moslem. "According to the Koran," the *New York Times* reported, "the bodies of the dead remain in their graves until the Last Day, the Day of Judgment. On this day of cataclysm the heavens are rent and the mountains ground to dust, the graves open and men are called to account by Allah.

"The blessed—the godfearing, the humble, the charitable, those who have suffered and been persecuted for Allah's sake or fought in religious wars for Islam—are summoned to the Garden of Paradise.

"There, according to the teaching of Mohammed, the Prophet, they live forever by flowing streams, reclining on silken cushions, and enjoying the company of dark-eyed maidens and wives of perfect purity.

"The damned—the covetous, the evildoer, the follower of gods other than Allah—are sent to Eternal Fire, where they are fed boiling water and molten brass. 'The death from which ye flee will truly overtake you,' the Koran says. 'Then will ye be sent back to the Knower of things secret and open, and He will tell you the truth of the things that ye did.' "

After signing the contract for this book, Malcolm X looked at me hard. "A writer is what I want, not an interpreter." I tried to be a dispassionate chronicler. But he was the most electric personality I have ever met, and I still can't quite conceive him dead. It still feels to me as if he has just gone into some next chapter, to be written by historians.

New York, 1965

OSSIE DAVIS

ON MALCOLM X

Mr. Davis wrote the following in response to a magazine editor's question: Why did you eulogize Malcolm X?

You are not the only person curious to know why I would eulogize a man like Malcolm X. Many who know and respect me have written letters. Of these letters I am proudest of those from a sixth-grade class of young white boys and girls who asked me to explain. I appreciate your giving me this chance to do so.

You may anticipate my defense somewhat by considering the following fact: no Negro has yet asked me that question. (My pastor in Grace Baptist Church where I teach Sunday School preached a sermon about Malcolm in which he called him a "giant in a sick world.") Every one of the many letters I got from my own people lauded Malcolm as a man, and commended me for having spoken at his funeral.

At the same time—and this is important—most of them took special pains to disagree with much or all of what Malcolm said and what he stood for. That is, with one singing exception, they all, every last, black, glory-hugging one of them, knew that Malcolm—whatever else he was or was not—*Malcolm was a man!*

White folks do not need anybody to remind them that they are men. We do! This was his one incontrovertible benefit to his people.

Protocol and common sense require that Negroes stand back and let the white man speak up for us, defend us, and lead us from behind the scene in our fight. This is the essence of Negro politics. But Malcolm said to hell with that! Get up off your knees and fight your own battles. That's the way to win back your self-respect. That's the way to make the white man respect

464

you. And if he won't let you live like a man, he certainly can't keep you from dying like one!

Malcolm, as you can see, was refreshing excitement; he scared hell out of the rest of us, bred as we are to caution, to hypocrisy in the presence of white folks, to the smile that never fades. Malcolm knew that every white man in America profits directly or indirectly from his position vis-à-vis Negroes, profits from racism even though he does not practice it or believe in it.

He also knew that every Negro who did not challenge on the spot every instance of racism, overt or covert, committed against him and his people, who chose instead to swallow his spit and go on smiling, was an Uncle Tom and a traitor, without balls or guts, or any other commonly accepted aspects of manhood!

Now, we knew all these things as well as Malcolm did, but we also knew what happened to people who stick their necks out and say them. And if all the lies we tell ourselves by way of extenuation were put into print, it would constitute one of the great chapters in the history of man's justifiable cowardice in the face of other men.

But Malcolm kept snatching our lies away. He kept shouting the painful truth we whites and blacks did not want to hear from all the housetops. And he wouldn't stop for love nor money.

You can imagine what a howling, shocking nuisance this man was to both Negroes and whites. Once Malcolm fastened on you, you could not escape. He was one of the most fascinating and charming men I have ever met, and never hesitated to take his attractiveness and beat you to death with it. Yet his irritation, though painful to us, was most salutary. He would make you angry as hell, but he would also make you proud. It was impossible to remain defensive and apologetic about being a Negro in his presence. He wouldn't let you. And you always left his presence with the sneaky suspicion that maybe, after all, you *were* a man!

But in explaining Malcolm, let me take care not to explain him away. He had been a criminal, an addict, a pimp, and a prisoner; a racist, and a hater, he had really believed the white man was a devil. But all this had changed. Two days before his death, in commenting to Gordon Parks about his past life he said: "That was a mad scene. The sickness and madness of those days! I'm glad to be free of them."

And Malcolm was free. No one who knew him before and

after his trip to Mecca could doubt that he had completely abandoned racism, separatism, and hatred. But he had not abandoned his shock-effect statements, his bristling agitation for immediate freedom in this country not only for blacks, but for everybody.

And most of all, in the area of race relations, he still delighted in twisting the white man's tail, and in making Uncle Toms, compromisers, and accommodationists—I deliberately include myself—thoroughly ashamed of the urbane and smiling hypocrisy we practice merely to exist in a world whose values we both envy and despise.

But even had Malcolm not changed, he would still have been a relevant figure on the American scene, standing in relation as he does, to the "responsible" civil rights leaders, just about where John Brown stood in relation to the "responsible" abolitionists in the fight against slavery. Almost all disagreed with Brown's mad and fanatical tactics which led him foolishly to attack a Federal arsenal at Harpers Ferry, to lose two sons there, and later to be hanged for treason.

Yet, today the world, and especially the Negro people, proclaim Brown not a traitor, but a hero and a martyr in a noble cause. So in future, I will not be surprised if men come to see that Malcolm X was, within his own limitations, and in his own inimitable style, also a martyr in that cause.

But there is much controversy still about this most controversial American, and I am content to wait for history to make the final decision.

But in personal judgment, there is no appeal from instinct. I knew the man personally, and however much I disagreed with him, I never doubted that Malcolm X, even when he was wrong, was always that rarest thing in the world among us Negroes: a true man.

And if, to protect my relations with the many good white folks who make it possible for me to earn a fairly good living in the entertainment industry, I was too chicken, too cautious, to admit that fact when he was alive, I thought at least that now, when all the white folks are safe from him at last, I could be honest with myself enough to lift my hat for one final salute to that brave, black, ironic gallantry, which was his style and hallmark, that shocking *zing* of fire-and-be-damned-to-you, so absolutely absent in every other Negro man I know, which brought him, too soon, to his death.

(You thought—paused for kissing!)
Ash-tops too felonious
    Intercepted? Rather
Say—they well-nigh made euphonious
    Discord, helped to gather   *140*
Phrase, by phrase, turn patches
    Into simulated
Unity which botching matches—
    Scraps redintegrated.

He. Sweet, are you suggestive   *145*
    Of an old suspicion
Which has always found me restive
    To its admonition
When it ventured whisper
    "Fool, the strifes and struggles   *150*
Of your trembler—blusher—lisper
    Were so many juggles,
Tricks tried—oh, so often!—
    Which once more do duty,
Find again a heart to soften,   *155*
    Soul to snare with beauty."

Birth-blush of the briar-rose,
    Mist-bloom of the hedge-sloe,
Someone gains the prize: admire rose
    Would he, when noon's wedge—slow—   *160*
Sure, has pushed, expanded
    Rathe pink to raw redness?
Would he covet sloe when sanded
    By road-dust to deadness?
So—restore their value!   *165*
    Ply a water-sprinkle!
Then guess sloe is fingered, shall you?
    Find in rose a wrinkle?

Here what played Aquarius?°
    Distance—ash-tops aiding,   *170*

69 **Aquarius** constellation "water carrier," associated with rainy
weather.

Reconciled scraps else contrarious,
    Brightened stuff fast fading.
Distance—call your shyness:
    Was the fair one peevish?
175 Coyness softened out of slyness.
    Was she cunning, thievish,
All-but-proved impostor?
    Bear but one day's exile,
Ugly traits were wholly lost or
180   Screened by fancies flexile—

Ash-tops these, you take me?
    Fancies' interference
Changed . . .
       But since I sleep, don't wake me!
    What if all's appearance?
185 Is not outside seeming
    Real as substance inside?
Both are facts, so leave me dreaming:
    If who loses wins I'd
Ever lose—conjecture,
190   From one phrase trilled deftly,
All the piece. So, end your lecture
    Let who lied be left lie!